A
Garland Series

VICTORIAN FICTION

NOVELS OF FAITH AND DOUBT

A collection of 121 novels
in 92 volumes, selected by
Professor Robert Lee Wolff,
Harvard University,
with a separate introductory volume
written by him
especially for this series.

FATHER CLEMENT

Grace Kennedy

FATHER OSWALD

Anonymous

Garland Publishing, Inc., New York & London

1976

Library of Congress Cataloging in Publication Data

Kennedy, Grace, 1782-1825.
Father Clement.

(Victorian fiction : Novels of faith and doubt ; no. 1)
Reprint of the 1923 ed. of Father Clement published by W. Oliphant, Edinburgh, and of the 1842 ed. of Father Oswald published by C. Dolman, London.
1. English fiction--19th century. I. Father Oswald. 1976. II. Title: Father Clement. III. Series.
PZ1.K297Fat3 [PR1304] 823'.03 75-445
ISBN 0-8240-1525-8

Printed in the United States of America

FATHER CLEMENT

Bibliographical note:

this facsimile has been made from a copy in the British Museum (4413.f.36.1)

FATHER CLEMENT;

A ROMAN CATHOLIC STORY.

BY THE AUTHOR OF "THE DECISION," &c.

" La carita e paziente, e benefica; la carita non e astiosa, non e insolente, non si gonfia. Non e ambiziosa, non cerca il proprio interesse, non si muove a ira, non pensa male.—A tutto s'accodoma, tutto crede, tutto spera, tutto sopporta."

Martini's Trans. from the Vulgate.—1 Cor. xiii. 4, 5, 7.

EDINBURGH:
PUBLISHED BY WILLIAM OLIPHANT, 22, SOUTH BRIDGE STREET; AND SOLD BY M. OGLE, AND CHALMERS & COLLINS, GLASGOW; J. FINLAY, NEWCASTLE; BEILBY & KNOTTS, BIRMINGHAM; J. HATCHARD & SON, T. HAMILTON, J. NISBET, OGLE, DUNCAN & CO., B. J. HOLDSWORTH, F. WESTLEY, AND KNIGHT & LACEY, LONDON.

1823.

FATHER CLEMENT.

CHAPTER I.

Il commandamento mio e questo, che vi amiate l'un l'altro—
Martini's Trans.—John xv. 12.

———Fruit and wine had been set on the table—the last old grey-haired domestic had left the room—the broad-backed spaniel no longer watched for food from the fair hands which now ministered to his privileged old age, but had waddled to seek repose on a spot where the sun shone bright on the carpet—and cheerful family chat, and careless merriment went round—while Sir Herbert Montague, the father of the circle, sat almost in silence, leaning back in his chair, half listening and smiling—half absent to what was passing—or at times addressing an observation to the old chaplain, who sat next him, and with whom he seemed to be on the most intimately friendly footing. At last, one piece of intelligence he mentioned attracted the attention of the whole party.

"Young Clarenham is returned," said Sir Herbert, "and I rejoice he is so, for his poor mother's sake."

"Young Clarenham returned!" repeated the younger Montague, who sat next his father; "well, I wonder what sort of a fellow he is now. He used to be too grave and studious for me. He will probably still suit your taste best, Ernest," addressing his elder brother.

"I fear he will not suit any of us," replied Ernest, gravely. "Did you see him, Sir?" addressing his father.

"I did. I met him on his way to the Castle, just as I returned from my ride before dinner, and should have passed him as a stranger, had he not stopped his horse and named me. I soon recollected him when he spoke and smiled. He is a pleasing-looking youth, though much altered."

"What a meeting for his mother!" observed Lady Montague, her eyes filling with tears. "An only son, whom she has not seen for five years!"

"Was he alone?" asked Adeline, Sir Herbert's eldest daughter.

"No; he was accompanied by a young man of foreign appearance, whom he, however, introduced to me by an English name, Mr Dormer."

"Young!" repeated Adeline; "It could not then be Father Clement."

"Father Clement: And who may he be, Adeline?" asked Sir Herbert, looking inquisitively at his daughter.

She blushed,—"Maria Clarenham informed me, Sir, that the Father who has superintended her brother's education ever since he went abroad, and who also travelled with him for the last year, accompanies him home, and is to remain as chaplain at the Castle. Poor old Father Dennis has been appointed, by his order, to another situation."

"Call no man on earth, in that sense, Father, Miss Adeline," said Dr Lowther the chaplain, gravely. "These are words of Scripture."

Adeline blushed again; and, smiling affectionately to her old monitor, "Well, my dear Dr Lowther, old Mr Elliston is going away a few weeks hence. He only remains to perform, or offer up—or what shall I call it—some more masses for the soul of old Mr Clarenham."

"How sad!" exclaimed Lady Montague. "And what a change for Mrs Clarenham!—Her son's society to charm away her thoughts from those gloomy ceremonies! I met her this morning, returning from a visit of charity to poor old Alice Dawson. She seemed very unfit for any fatigue—but, the less so, the more meritorious, according to her spiritual guides. I would not have put myself in her way for the world, as she has not chosen to see me since Mr Clarenham's death, and I attempted to avoid doing so by turning into a briery little path which led into the road; but she saw my intention, and immediately hastened towards me, looking,—Oh so thin and pale! I could not help bursting into tears when she approached: She was overcome also, and could only press my hand and hurry on. I just stood and wept where she left me, thinking how little consolation she could receive from that religion which aggravated instead of lessening sorrow, by teaching that, when we close the eyes of those we love most on this side the grave, it is only that they may leave suffering here to enter into greater."

"The idea is softened to the minds of really pious Roman Catholics," said Ernest, "by the belief that the effect of that suffering is altogether purifying, and guided by a Father's love: and also by the belief that it is possible for friends on this side the grave to mitigate and shorten it."

"Nay, Ernest, if your charity goes so far as to defend the doctrine of purgatory," said Rowley, his younger brother, laughing, "I shall soon expect to see you on the road back to Rome."

"I am not defending the doctrine, Rowley. I know it is contrary to Scripture, and was never heard of in the Christian church till it had become full of corruptions: but I think we Protestants are too apt to consider the Romish faith as destitute of those resources on which a sensible and feeling mind can repose. We regard it as, on the part of the priest, a system of hypocrisy and fraud—and, on that of the people, of gloomy and absurd delusion. I only wish to be candid."

"I like no such candour," said Sir Herbert, in a voice of vexation.

Ernest seemed hurt. "My dear Sir, I have learnt that candour from the advice you have so often and so kindly given us all, never to judge of any subject till we knew something about it. After having, in some degree, got acquainted with the gross errors of the system, I have only attempted to discover what could be its attractions—"

"Attractions!" repeated Sir Herbert, fidgetting in his chair.

"My dear Sir," said Dr Lowther mildly, "All hearts are naturally formed alike. We never become truly devoted to any thing but through our affections. Your son has examined this subject as a philosopher."

"Well, well," interrupted Sir Herbert impatiently, "I am sure no one pities the poor souls more than I do. I wish not to say aught against them. That lad Clarenham, however, does not look as if there was any thing very attractive in his religion, though I hear he is a perfect bigot already. He is a pale, melancholy-looking youth, with a smile that makes him look sadder instead of merrier: and his companion ten times worse—a tall, gaunt spectre, with the same sad smile."

Adeline and Rowley laughed. "What an engaging picture you have drawn, Sir!" said Rowley.

"I hope none of my family will find any *realities* engaging at the Castle," replied Sir Herbert sternly, and glancing both towards Ernest and Adeline.

"Miss Adeline," said Dr Lowther, with an arch smile on his cheerful old countenance, "*You* will be able to tell me whether this new confessor is of the society of Jesuits?"

"He is," replied Adeline, looking timidly at

her father, "and is eminent, Maria tells me, for his sanctity."

Dr Lowther's countenance was, in his turn, immediately overcast, and he sighed deeply. Sir Herbert, on his part, seemed rather to enjoy the effect this intelligence had on his old friend. He said nothing, however, but rose from table, and smilingly addressed Lady Montague,—"The evening is fine, my dear: What would you think of leaving this Popish party with Dr Lowther, and going out with me on the lawn?"

Lady Montague immediately consented; and, soon after, Dr Lowther and the young party also separated.

At the period at which our story commences, though all religions were professedly tolerated in Britain, yet the principles on which that toleration was granted were not so well known, or so generally approved of as they now are, particularly with regard to Roman Catholics. By every denomination of Protestants they were regarded with suspicion; and even the most truly religious and benevolent of their opponents regarded it as a sin, in many instances, to permit the observances of their church; which they considered so idolatrous as to call on the strong arm of power to suppress them as offensive to Heaven. At this time the Roman Catholics barely enjoyed what could be called toleration; for, though no longer subjected to punishment for refusing to join in forms which were forbidden by their church, and allowed, unmolested, to attend their own private chapels, yet, nevertheless, many severe laws continued in force against them, and placed them on an entirely different footing, in almost every respect, from their fellow subjects. In this state of things they naturally associated, almost exclusively, with each other. The families of Clarenham and Montague were, however, relatives; and for this cause kept up a certain degree of intercourse. Lady Montague and Mrs Clarenham were first cousins—Mrs Clarenham the daughter of a Roman Catholic gentleman, of old family—Lady Montague the daughter of his sister. When very young, that sister had married a Protestant—soon adopted his faith—and carefully educated her family in the same profession. Mrs Clarenham had by her father been with equal care nurtured in the Romish faith. Lady Montague's father had, in his opinions regarding external forms, leant to puritanism; and, in his younger days, had, on several occasions, been both fined and imprisoned for non-conformity to the Church of England: and though, after the Revolution, he had joined that church, because he considered it somewhat less likely than formerly that its higher clergy would be permitted to meddle in the earthly government of the country, and might therefore be expected to devote themselves to the spiritual improvement of the people, still Lady Montague had been nurtured in the opinion that the church to which she belonged, though pure in its articles of faith, still required further reformation in its forms and ritual; and that, though its clergy might be preferable to an uneducated ministry dependent on the caprice of their flocks, still they too much resembled, in their domination over their brethren, and their great earthly riches, that corrupt church from which they had in other matters withdrawn: she, therefore, was easily reconciled to Sir Herbert Montague's slight difference of opinions. Sir Herbert was a Presbyterian. His family had been long settled in the north of England. He had constantly resided there—had been educated by a clergyman of the Church of Scotland—forced by the persecution of the times to leave his country and his flock, and was closely connected with many Presbyterian families in Scotland. Sir Herbert had, from these circumstances, long regarded Episcopacy as almost as antichristian as Popery. A great change had, however, taken place in his views a few years before our story begins. The Church of Scotland had then become settled and prosperous, but she did not extend her influence beyond the Tweed; and though there was a Presbyterian place of worship near Illerton Hall, yet the superintendence and instruction of the parish necessarily devolved on a clergyman of the Church of England. The clergyman who had filled that situation for the last few years, had convinced Sir Herbert that a minister of that church could really be zealous, steady, and laborious, in fulfilling the duties of his parish;

and, gradually and imperceptibly, the Rector of Illerton became a friend and favourite at the hall; and what was most surprising of all, particularly so with Dr Lowther, the Presbyterian chaplain. One point of union between these two Protestant clergymen, was their constant dread of the influence of Mr Elliston, the Roman Catholic chaplain, at Hallern Castle, commonly known by the name of Father Dennis. This priest was equally indefatigable in making proselytes, and ingenious in evading the laws which were in force against the encroachments of his church: and the only means by which the two Protestant clergymen found they could meet his efforts, was by exerting equal zeal on their parts. In this contest the families at the Castle and the Hall took a deep interest; because each was devoted to religion, and believed the other in dangerous error. Lady Montague had been married only a few months before Mrs Clarenham; and when the two cousins found themselves settled so near each other, while at a distance from their other relations, they met with feelings of sisterly kindness, and continued to feel the same affectionate and confiding regard during the many years they had remained in close neighbourhood. During those years they had passed through many similar joys and sorrows. They had both become the mothers of lovely and engaging childdren; and they had each mourned over several of their graves. They had sympathized deeply in each other's sorrows; but they had done so apart: for it was in times of sorrow only that they did not wish to meet. In such times religion was the refuge and consolation of both, and on that subject alone they could in few points agree. They had each, in their younger and more sanguine days, attempted the conversion of the other, but each had failed; and the feelings of coldness and alienation, which had followed those unsuccessful attempts, had been so painful, that, for several years, disputed points had been tacitly avoided on both sides and, excepting in hours of sorrow, the two cousins met as tried and affectionate friends. Sir Herbert and Mr Clarenham had however felt less suited to each other, during those years of intercourse between their families, and never sought to meet, excepting when absolutely obliged to do so as neighbours and relations; and both gentlemen dreaded the effects of close intimacy amongst their children, though neither, on his lady's account, chose to prevent it. The young people, however, were early aware, that, by their respective fathers at least, their intercourse was suffered on the score of relationship, but not approved of. Mr Clarenham had constantly said to his children,—" Bring the young Montagues as much as you will to the Castle, I shall be always glad to see them; but do not on any account—no, not for an instant—go to the Hall without my permission:" and that permission was always so unwillingly and so ungraciously given that it was a penance to ask it. Sir Herbert, on his part, expressed, on all occasions, similar wishes:—" What, on earth, my dears, can you find to attract you to that old Popish Castle? Cannot you bring your young cousins to the Hall, where you may be as merry and happy as you please, instead of going where that Jesuit priest will be watching every opportunity to infuse some of his Popish poison into your young minds. You must love and associate with your young relations, but do try to bring them to visit you." These difficulties, though they had not rendered the intercourse of the young people less agreeable or interesting, had made it less frequent; and, during the absence of young Clarenham, it had, on the part of the young men, ceased almost entirely. The young Montagues had also been absent;—Ernest to obtain that finish to his education which it was then, as it is now, thought could only be acquired by travelling; and his younger brother at college, in the hope, on his father's part, that he might acquire a taste for study, instead of what seemed much more congenial to his nature,—an eager propensity to hunt or shoot, or do any thing that required the use of his body rather than his mind. Adeline, and little Maude, Mrs Clarenham's name-child, had continued to visit at the Castle, and that more frequently since the death of Mr Clarenham; Sir Herbert making little objection:—"As to be sure, it could not be expected that the Clarenham girls, poor things, would leave their mother."

CHAPTER II.

"Dissegli Jesu: Io sono via, verita, e vita: nessuno va al Padre, se non per me."
Martini's Trans.—John xiv. 6.

"No doubt some of you will think it proper to pay a visit at the Castle, this forenoon," said Sir Herbert to his family, as they were separating to leave the breakfast room, on the morning after our story begins.

"I thought of doing so," said Ernest.

"Well, my boy, do go. I would myself accompany you, to welcome the poor lad back to his home and country, but am afraid his mother might think it right to see me; and somehow I would rather not meet with her yet. Say what you like from me to Clarenham, and invite him to come and see us."

"And Mr Dormer, Sir, whom he introduced

to you—shall I include him in the invitation?" asked Ernest, smiling.

"If he is a friend of Clarenham's, certainly; but if you discover him to be the new confessor, on no account whatever. You know old Elliston never crossed my hall door; why should a young successor be treated with more respect?"

"I thought, Sir, you had regretted having shown old Mr Elliston such marked incivility?"

"Then you thought wrong," replied Sir Herbert, shortly; "I never regretted any such thing."

"I beg your pardon, Sir; I had misunderstood you."

"You may have heard me say, Ernest, that, to do the man justice, he deserved no blame for having zealously acted up to his own principles. I have said so, because such thoughts do at times, as it were, flash upon my mind; and I am too apt to say what I think, without waiting to consider. I know not whether it is so or not, however; for the man has lived in the midst of light; and if he has continued zealous in promoting darkness, perhaps I am not justifiable in saying he deserves no blame; but that is not my affair. I do, however, for our own sakes, regret some uncharitable acts of zeal with which we have been chargeable against him; and, before the man goes away, I shall compel myself to ask his forgiveness. You could never hear me regret, however, Ernest, that I had not given a Jesuit priest access to my house."

Ernest said no more; and, an hour or two after, Adeline and Maude accompanied him across the lawn—then through a wooded walk which led to the top of the hill, where was the boundary which separated the grounds belonging to the Hall from the domains of Hallern Castle. From this hill, Ernest and his companions, for a time, viewed the beautiful scenery of the latter, as it lay before them.

"What makes one feel so sad," said little Maude at last, "when one looks at that old Castle? I am sure I have often been very merry within its walls; yet I could almost weep now, when I look at its grey towers rising from amongst those trees with their young gay foliage;—and that old window of the chapel does look so gloomy! Perhaps it is because papa said Basil Clarenham looked so sad; and poor Mrs Clarenham looks so sad now—I think there is something sad about all the Clarenhams, excepting Maria perhaps—she is merry enough; but Catherine—Oh! how sad to think that in one year she is to leave her mamma, Maria, Basil—all of us, to be shut up for ever in a nunnery! But I believe you have not seen Catherine since you returned home, Ernest; and she was abroad when you went away."

"I have not seen her for a long while," replied Ernest—"not since she was a child; and then she was about as sad as you, Maude, now are."

Maude laughed. "Ah! you will see a change then, Mr Incredulous," turning playfully away from him, but only walking a few steps homewards, and, when joined by Adeline, slyly returning on tiptoe to follow her grave, thoughtful brother, in order to ornament his back with a long streamer of clinging wild flowers. Ernest caught a glimpse of her as she approached, and turned round just in time to receive her, and catching the garland, wound it round and round, and pressed it to her, and then making a run, vaulted over a fence into the Hallern grounds, and looked back to laugh at the little sentimentalist disentangling herself from the weeds.

It was not because Ernest felt differently from little Maude when she discovered that there was something sad about all the Clarenhams, but the looks and language in which the light-hearted child expressed the very feelings which he himself at that moment painfully experienced, which, for an instant, struck him forcibly with a sense of the ridiculous; and, as he again pursued his way to the grey, old Castle of the Clarenhams, the same feelings resumed their influence.

It has been remarked that religious young men are generally melancholy. The truth of this, as a general remark, may certainly be disputed, but in Ernest's case it was just. He was grave and melancholy, and religion was the leading subject of his thoughts. He had from early childhood been taught to regard it as "The one thing needful;" and, according to the method of instruction followed in those days by the divines of the church to which he belonged, he had also been early led to the study of those deep and mysterious doctrines which are more particularly taught by the Calvinistic reformed churches; and which, as they lead directly to the contemplation of the character and ways of God himself, the source of all other being and action, are calculated to absorb all the powers of a reflecting young mind; or at least subordinate them all to this mighty and infinite subject. Still, however, that system of religion which, in its first principles, habituates the mind to regard all it contemplates as connected with the governing will of God, however powerful it may be, must necessarily lead to melancholy, while we observe and feel so much evil, and ignorance, and sorrow, within us and around us. Nothing is more certain than this, —That the more we study the divine character, as it is revealed to us in the Bible, the more impossible is it for us to believe that it is not altogether holy and altogether lovely: and the question,—" Why are evil, and grief, and sorrow, permitted to exist? accompanied as it is by a feeling of apprehension respecting the perfection of that goodness, which, at the same time, we cannot endure to doubt, may be, and is with many for a time, the source of the deepest melancholy. It had been so with Ernest: and now, though he could in general rest with peace in the belief that his difficulties, in reconciling the visible administration of Providence with the perfection of the divine character, arose from his incapacity to judge of the vast plans of an infinite mind,—still every object which excited melancholy feelings led his thoughts directly to the first cause and source of all things. As he approached Hallern Castle, every object excited those feelings. All around him wore the appearance of desolate neglect. The groves of fine old trees, scattered over the park, were become thickets, from the briers and underwood which had been suffered to grow in tangled masses amongst them. The turf was roughened everywhere with weeds, rushes, and mole-hills; and no living thing was to be seen, excepting at times a startled hare bounding from the thicket where it had been disturbed by Ernest's passing footstep, to seek shelter in one more distant; or a few deer timidly watching him from a distant part of the park. All this desolate state of things had been occasioned by the last Mr Clarenham's adherence to what, in Ernest's opinion, was a bad government and a false religion: and how perplexing, in the search after truth, is the fact, that men suffer to the last in defence of error; and how unavoidable, how unanswerable are the questions—"What is truth? What is error?" Often, before, had these questions presented themselves to Ernest's mind; and the only answer on which he could rest, became more and more satisfactory every time they recurred—"There is but one source of truth in the world—that is the Bible. The more deeply we drink at that source, the more does error and darkness on all subjects vanish before us. And thus far we may at least see without a cloud,—that the system which would debar the mind from free access to this only source of light, must be a system of which the end is not the promotion of the knowledge of truth.

So reasoned Ernest as he approached the Castle. The sun now shone bright upon its old towers and battlements: still, in his eyes, it looked dark and melancholy: and not the less so from the contrast produced by the bright heraldic colours of an escutcheon placed upon its front to mark the death of its late master. Ernest stopt to contemplate this emblazoned record of the antiquity and honours of the Clarenhams, whose fortunes were now so comparatively fallen; and even with him, valueless as his religion taught him such honours were, their contemplation, contrasted with the present state of things, added to the powerful interest he already felt. He had been observed, and a servant in deep mourning appeared to await his approach. Ernest hastened up the few broad steps to the wide landing-place, where the man stood; and, on inquiring for Mr Clarenham, was shown into an apartment, which appeared, from the books and ladies' works which lay on the table, to have been recently occupied by the family.

"My young master and the ladies are in the Chapel, Sir," said the servant; "but my Master will be with you immediately."

"Perhaps I have come at an unseasonable hour," said Ernest; "I do not wish Mr Clarenham to be disturbed, if he is engaged in religious duties."

"Oh no, Sir; my master is only seeing some new pictures put up in the chapel;" and the man crossed himself, with a look towards Ernest, which seemed to say—"let me show the heretic gentleman how devout I am." He then left the room, and Ernest took up one of the books which lay on the table. It was a Roman Catholic book of devotion; and, on looking over a page or two, he found it so altogether unlike those familiar to Protestants, that he was perusing it with considerable interest when young Clarenham entered.

The cousins had not met for five years, and the consciousness, on both sides, of difference in opinion on the two subjects considered at that time as the very tests of character, religion and politics, joined in both to natural reserve, threw a kind of restraint over their manners to each other, which, however, each made an evident effort to overcome: and, after a few rather formal attempts at conversation, Ernest said more easily:—

"I had got interested in this book the few

minutes I was here before you came. Who is it written by?"

Clarenham looked anxiously at the book.—"Oh, it is one of Francis Xavier's," appearing relieved. "I believe those of our communion are not singular in admiring his writings."

"I am entirely unacquainted with them," replied Ernest, as I indeed am with all your devotional writings. I have been supplied by Dr Lowther with some of the controversial writings of the Romish Church," glancing towards Clarenham a look that expressed his own recollection of their boyish days, on naming Dr Lowther; "but these are never attractive."

"Allow me to send that small volume for your perusal," said Clarenham, reddening. "If you find it interest you, either Father Clement, Mr Dormer I mean, or I, can furnish you with all the writings of the author."

Ernest immediately accepted of the offer:—"And may I venture, when I have read it, to express my opinion of it?" asked he.

"Certainly. How can you ask such a question?" replied Clarenham, again reddening.

"I have been led to believe that the members of your communion carefully avoid free discussion on the subject of religion."

Clarenham was thoughtful for a few moments, then answered frankly—"I see, Montague, that the subject has not lost its interest to you —neither has it to me, I assure you. I trust, however, that I am now better prepared to meet you than I was before we parted as boys. Yet I may avow that subjects which must afterwards make part of our confessions are naturally avoided by us. You know our spiritual fathers examine us very narrowly respecting our intercourse with——" he hesitated.

"Heretics," said Ernest, smiling.

Clarenham also smiled, then said—"I am quite willing to discuss any subject with you; only I think it but fair to warn you that you will have another person to combat also: for I have no concealments from Father Clement; and in these matters I feel happy in having a director so able."

"May I ask you one question?"

"Certainly."

"Were Father Clement to lead you into an error,—say one so dangerous as to involve the safety of your soul, would his soul suffer in your soul's stead?"

"You suppose an impossibility. I am a member of the true church. Should a priest of that church wilfully mislead me, he has committed mortal sin, but mine has been merely a sin of ignorance, which cannot endanger the soul of a Catholic. It is one of the proofs that the Catholic Church is the only true one, that she boldly undertakes to answer for the safety of those souls who enter into her communion.—No Protestant Church ventures so far."

"Heaven forbid they should," replied Ernest with great seriousness. "Protestants are taught that *they* only are of the one true church who believe in and obey Jesus Christ: and are exhorted by their pastors to examine whether they are so, not by the creed of one or other communions of those who profess themselves Christians, but by the infallible word of God."

"But the interpretation of that word," said Clarenham, "must belong to the church. Private judgment must err in a matter so difficult."

"Why then is it said of the Jews of Berea, to whom one of the apostles himself preached,

'These were more noble than those of Thessalonica, in that they received the word with all readiness of mind, and *searched the Scriptures daily*, whether those things were so; therefore many of them believed.'* Do not these words point out the duty of the teacher, and of the hearer, and the result to be expected when both are fulfilled?"

"I do not recollect ever having seen that passage," replied Clarenham.

Ernest marked the place from whence he had taken the passage on a bit of paper, and presenting it to Clarenham: "May I request of you to ask Mr Dormer's explanation of that passage?"

"Assuredly,—but now I must deliver my mother's message to you. She understands you are an admirer of good paintings, and desired me to say—that if you would enter a Catholic chapel, it would give her pleasure to show you some which are now there."

"To see paintings I can have no objection to enter the chapel," replied Ernest. "Indeed, I shall perhaps ask your permission to be pre-

* Acts xvii. 11.

sent on some other occasion. Would you admit me on Easter-day, I think you call it, if it is not past?"

"It is not. It falls very late this year," answered Clarenham, putting his arm kindly within Ernest's, as they together proceeded to the chapel, "and I invite you to be present whenever you choose. Before you go, I will make you acquainted with the entrance to a small private gallery, which is never occupied now, and from whence you may witness the service without yourself being observed. All my cousins are equally welcome to do so. Indeed I wish to convince you that we have no secrets—nothing but what we consider the service of God in its purest form in our chapels."

A low covered way led from the castle to the chapel. This was coarsely paved, as was also the little court surrounding the chapel; and there was nothing to lead any one to expect, from its exterior, more than a common rude little place of worship. So the persecutions, some years previous to this period, had taught the Roman Catholics to avoid those temptations to pillage which might have followed a more open display of the rich ornaments with which they adorned their chapels. After passing over this rough court, however, and through a short low-roofed passage into the chapel, an inner door appeared, on opening which, every object assumed a totally different character. The apartment into which this door led seemed only to be an outer court to the more sacred place of worship. It was, however, exquisitely ornamented. It was lighted by a large Gothic window, the painted glass of which threw a glow, resembling that of the setting sun, upon the beautifully sculptured arches which formed the roof, and upon the many paintings on the walls. The apartment was paved with marble, and everywhere ornamented with sculpture and mouldings of the finest workmanship. Ernest paused an instant. In his boyish days he had been strictly prohibited from entering this chapel—of late he had not visited at the castle, and never till now had been within the receptacle of all that was held most sacred by the Clarenhams. He now looked around and above him with evident feelings of admiration.

"How beautiful!" exclaimed he, pointing to the sculptured roof.

Clarenham appeared much gratified. "Surely," said he gently, "we do not err in bestowing whatever we can command that is most perfect in ornamenting the temple of God."

"Perhaps not," replied Ernest, "but those living stones which alone compose the true temple of God, must be sculptured by a divine power to make that temple a fit abode for him. What are our most perfect sculptures or ornaments to him who looks only on the heart?"

"But," answered Clarenham, "we thus prove our devotion of heart to him."

"Does he who sees the inmost recesses of our hearts require that we should sculpture their feelings on stone to convince him of their sincerity? Ah no!—the proofs of love to him which he requires are of another nature. Is there not a secret, or, I believe, in your church, an avowed expectation that men may thus add to their own merits in his sight?"

"And is not love to God the first and greatest of all merits?" asked Clarenham.

"It is the first principle of holiness in a regenerated soul," replied Ernest; "but, my dear Clarenham, what you have mentioned as a proof of love to God, is nowhere described or inculcated as such by Christ or his apostles, and may very easily be performed by those in whom there is not a feeling of any thing but a slavish dread and an ignorant hope that such services may propitiate an offended God."

"You have adopted the doctrines of the mystics, I perceive," said Clarenham, smiling. "I have found them, too, attractive; but you know the church has condemned them. I must not be tempted to listen to you."

"I am not conscious of having adopted their doctrines," replied Ernest; "indeed I know very little about them, and am not aware of having adopted any doctrine not clearly declared in the Bible. What have I said to lead you to suppose me a mystic?"

"I do not know that you have exactly expressed any of their doctrines," replied Clifford, advancing towards the door of the chapel; "but what you have said leads directly to their opinions." He seemed anxious to avoid saying more and, approaching the delicately sculptured door of the chapel, and softly opening it, withdrew his arm from Ernest's, and slowly and reverently made the sign of the cross. Ernest looked at Clarenham, as he did so, with feelings of affectionate interest. The expression of his countenance, and of every gesture, was so full of humility and sincerity, that he could not, for a moment, doubt that they proceeded from true devotion of heart to the Being he worshipped, whatever errors might mingle with that worship. Ernest's attention, however, was soon diverted from his companion to the group within. Mrs Clarenham immediately approached to meet him. She wore the deepest weeds, which made the almost unearthly paleness of her countenance the more striking. She was at first nearly overcome, but struggled to recover herself, and in a few moments succeeded; and, holding out her hand to Ernest—

"I am very glad to see you once more, cousin," said she kindly; then looking alternately at her son and at him,—"Basil is more changed than you are, Ernest. Italy has robbed him of his looks of health. I hope our English air, however, may restore them to him." Mrs

Clarenham then turned to her daughters:— "You and Maria have not, I believe, met lately. Catherine, do you remember your cousin?"

Maria frankly and affectionately received her old play-mate. Not so Catherine. On turning from Maria's cordial reception, to her, she drew back, and, casting her eyes on the ground, curtsied coldly and distantly. Ernest reddened, and his looks were instantly as coid as her own. His nature was not one to recover quickly from a repulse where he had felt only kindness, and his bow to Mr Dormer, who was next introduced to him, was cold and stiff. Dormer, however, had nothing in his appearance to excite coldness, but the contrary. To Ernest's distant and formal bow, he returned one of polished and respectful courtesy, and then turned again to join old Mr Elliston, who was busily arranging a painting so as to have the light thrown advantageously upon it. With Dormer's assistance he soon succeeded in placing it in the most favourable situation. Both priests then retired a few steps, and reverently knelt for a moment before the painting. Clarenham glanced towards Ernest, reddened, but followed the example of his spiritual guides, while Catherine made an extravagant display of reverential gestures. When Ernest looked towards Mrs Clarenham, she was standing mildly contemplating the picture; and on Maria's lively countenance he thought he perceived an expression of ridicule mingling with her assumed looks of gravity.

Mrs Clarenham turned to Ernest. "Is it not very fine?" asked she in a low tone of voice, as if the venerated subject of the painting had himself been present.

"I believe it is very well painted," replied Ernest; "but the subject is so little agreeable that I cannot admire it much."

"It is a St. Francis!" said Mrs Clarenham, with surprise;—"but you perhaps do not know his history. It was fasting, and mortification, and penance, which reduced him to that emaciated state."

Ernest smiled, and replied gently, "You know, my dear Mrs Clarenham, we Protestants see no religion in such self-inflictions, consequently they excite no feelings of respect or sympathy in us."

"Do Protestants, who appeal to Scripture in support of all their doctrines, see *there* no injunction to fast?" demanded Dormer, in rather an authoritative tone of voice, and looking at Ernest with an expression of mingled dignity and displeasure.

"They see there no *injunction* whatever about fasting," replied Ernest: "and the fasting which is commended in the New Testament *forbids* any such display of its effects as that"—pointing to the emaciated painting. Our Lord himself says, 'When ye fast, be not as the hypocrites, of a sad countenance, for they disfigure their faces that they may appear unto men to fast. Verily, I say unto you, they have their reward. But thou, when thou fastest, anoint thy head and wash thy face, that thou appear not unto men to fast, but unto thy Father which is in secret; and thy Father which seeth in secret shall reward thee openly.'"

Dormer listened with fixed attention, as Ernest gravely and emphatically repeated the words of Christ.

"You have described the purest and most holy mode of fasting," replied he, his countenance and manner resuming an expression of polished mildness. "And do not suppose, Mr Montague, that I mean to question in how far those of your communion thus fast; but allow me to say, that our Catholic and Apostolic Church has shown her heavenly wisdom in the care she has taken that none of her children shall neglect the performance of this holy duty: and those who have, as that saint did, (pointing to the picture,) far exceeded the injunctions of his church, in fasts, and other mortifications, have attained to that angelical degree of purity which makes them glorious models for us, and which has, according to the decision of the church, given them such favour with God as to encourage us to trust in the efficacy of their intercessions for us."

"All—all absolutely contrary to Scripture," replied Ernest, with deep seriousness of voice and manner. "Those open, known, stated, prescribed fasts, meritorious in proportion to the degree in which they disfigure, and emaciate, and make useless the human frame, and the neglect of which subjects the person to punishment from his church, is in direct contradiction to that private act of devotion and humiliation, known only to God and the soul, which is commended by the Lord and Head of the true Church: and the belief that the intercession of the spirits of men can avail us any thing, besides the many absurdities it involves, is in absolute opposition to the plainest declarations of Scripture. St Paul says,"—

"You understand Latin, Mr Montague," interrupted old Elliston. "Be so good as quote from Scripture in that language."

Ernest looked at Clarenham and smiled. He reddened—Dormer also reddened. "Father Dennis is right," said he, "we do not allow the correctness of your translation."

"I do not speak Latin in the presence of ladies," said Ernest, turning away from the priests; "but," addressing Clarenham, "you will find the passage I meant to quote in St Paul's Epistle to Timothy;* and it must surely be found most correctly given,—not in Latin, but in the original Greek."

Clarenham promised to examine the passage; and Ernest perceiving that he had, by his re-

* 1st Epistle to Timothy, chap. ii. v. 5.

marks, produced a degree of restraint in the manners of every one, now regarded in silence the different paintings which were busily displayed by old Elliston, only remarking the excellences of the different masters by whom they were *done.* The priests and Catherine still seemed prepared to feel delight, and to express their feelings by gestures of—what Ernest thought—adoration, on the appearance of every new subject of the many legends of their church. Each painting was viewed with so much interest and tediousness, that Ernest had time also to examine the chapel, the extreme richness and beauty of which astonished him. His Protestant feelings, however, led him to look with dissatisfaction on almost every object which surrounded him: and he felt indignant as he regarded the busy, bustling, old Elliston, and the polished, and he could not help confessing to himself, singularly interesting-looking Dormer, whose influence had thus drawn upon the ebbing fortunes of the half-ruined house of Clarenham, to support a system, which, if not one of idolatry, was at least completely addressed to the senses; and which, in his opinion, only served to place a barrier between the soul and God. The painted windows of the chapel,—the sculptured roof and pillars,—the masterly paintings,—the beautiful marble pavement,—and, above all, the altar, were of the most exquisite order. The steps up to the altar,—the whole space around it,—the altar itself, most delicately sculptured, were all of marble of the purest white. A large crucifix, of the same material, and beautiful workmanship, stood on the altar, amidst the various articles used in the Roman Catholic worship,—some of which were of wrought gold, others covered with jewels.

"That is surely foreign sculpture," said Ernest to Maria, on finding himself near her, and pointing to the altar.

"It is," replied she; "It was brought from Rome."

"It is quite beautiful," remarked Ernest.

"It is thought so," answered Maria with indifference.

Catherine approached, and put her arm within that of her sister. "Come a little this way,

Maria," said she; "St Catherine is divine when seen in this light."

Maria seemed teased, but went with her. She did not, however, join in the marks of reverence paid by Catherine to the picture of this saint, whose legend was known to Ernest, and regarded by him, as it is by all Protestants who know it, most blasphemous and disgusting. Maria soon returned, and again stood by Ernest.

"The altar-piece has been removed to make way for another," said she: "You will assist us, cousin, to choose between two paintings which Father Clement and my brother have brought home. They are considered equally appropriate. Do, Father Dennis," continued she, turning coaxingly to the old priest, "let us now choose for the altar. We can see all those saints at another time."

"I did not expect to hear my dear daughter speak so lightly of the saints," said Elliston, affectionately.

"It was not of the saints, Father; it was only of their pictures," replied Maria; "and, indeed, Father, I should not have spoken of the old paintings which are to be removed from the chapel, with any disrespect; but these new ones, though they mean to represent the same persons, are so utterly unlike the others, that they seem a company of entire strangers—"

"Pardon me, Miss Clarenham," interrupted Dormer, "if I say that such levity, on such a subject, and in such a place, is not common amongst the true members of our church."

"Fie, Maria," said Mrs Clarenham; "you allow your spirits to get the better of your good sense very unseasonably."

Catherine crossed herself, and Maria blushed deeply and remained silent. Mr Elliston, however, did not seem pleased to hear his lively young friend chidden, and immediately required Dormer's assistance to bring forward a large painting, and place it in a proper light. They then retired a few steps, and both reverently made the sign of the cross. The painting was a crucifixion by one of the first masters, and most forcibly and movingly represented—so much so, that Ernest could almost have joined Maria and her mother in the posture of adoration they immediately assumed: Without, however, thus far yielding to sympathy of feeling, he was so evidently moved, that Clarenham, who had narrowly observed him all the time he had been examining the pictures, now approached, and said in a low tone of voice,—

"Surely such representations are calculated to move our feelings and excite our devotion, and cannot, therefore, be wrong."

Ernest sighed deeply to relieve his breast from the oppression that the contemplation of the painting had gathered there.

"I could almost agree with you, Clarenham," replied he, in the same tone of voice; "but when I look at those," waving his hand towards the other paintings, "I perceive the wisdom of God in having so positively prohibited all such representations."

"But if rightly used?—"

"Nothing can be rightly used that is so plainly forbidden."

"Forbidden!" repeated Maria Clarenham; "Does the Bible forbid their use?"

"Protestants say so," answered old Elliston, quickly; then turning to Mrs Clarenham,

"Madam, it surprises me to hear the authority of the church held as nothing in the very sanctuary of the Clarenhams. Have they indeed suffered so much for her in vain?"

Mrs Clarenham looked alarmed; but Maria answered quickly, "Surely two Catholic priests, and four members of the true church, may find means to answer convincingly the erroneous opinions of one—heretic,"—hesitating, and looking at Ernest for forgiveness as she pronounced the word.

He smiled. "The opinions of the heretic, Miss Clarenham, were they merely his own, would have little chance of success in such a contest; but the words of God find so powerful an advocate for their truth in the human soul, that one—I shall not say heretic," again smiling;—"but one Christian, availing himself of them, need not shrink from combating an host of adversaries, who, in opposition to those words, only appeal to human authority."

"I am not surprised that Protestants should regard the authority of *their* church as human," observed old Elliston quickly: "It is the character of the true church, that her authority is divine."

"Protestant clergy claim no authority," replied Ernest, "for which they have not the plainest grounds in Scripture, and can support, not by human power, but by appealing to those Scriptures in the hands of all their people: Their authority is thus, to all who believe the Bible, plainly evinced to be given them by the Divine and only head of the true church, Jesus Christ. That authority which cannot be thus supported, and which shrinks from such examination, I call human, merely human. And I need not tell Mr Elliston, that Protestants consider the authority of the Romish priesthood of the last description. But forgive me, Madam," added Ernest, turning to Mrs Clarenham; "I have been unintentionally led into this conversation."

"We ought rather to ask your forgiveness, cousin," replied Mrs Clarenham. "You are our guest; and such subjects cannot be agreeable to you, and were introduced by us."

"Unless,—as we must all allow has just been

the case,"—observed Dormer, with his usual mild politeness, "the consciousness of having apparently had the best side of the argument could make them so. I hope Mr Montague will, however, on some future occasion, give Father Dennis or I an opportunity to attempt doing away the unfavourable opinions he entertains of the Catholic clergy."

Ernest modestly assented, while Dormer's very respectful address excited the thought,—"This artful Jesuit priest means to blind me by addressing himself to my vanity."

The party still continued in the chapel; and Catherine's devotion to one or two more paintings which were displayed, particularly to one of the Virgin Mary, continued unabated in ardour. Ernest's attention, however, though he could not altogether withdraw it from this young enthusiast, as he considered her, was yet greatly more engaged by Dormer. He found, with all his prejudices, that there was something strangely prepossessing about this priest—this Jesuit. He acknowledged to himself, that, had he wished to find a model for the exterior of a Christian minister, he could at once have fixed on Dormer; and nothing but the appellation, *Father* Clement, and the recollection that he was a Roman Catholic and a Jesuit, would have prevented Ernest from at once yielding to the interest he inspired, and seeking that place in his regard which his manner bespoke him prepared to give. Ernest, however, as a duty, resisted those kindly feelings. Still his eyes followed Dormer, and he listened with interest to all he said. There was, too, in the devotional gestures used by Dormer, something altogether different from those of Catherine and the elder priest. He seemed to look beyond what was visible, while they appeared completely engrossed with the present representation. To Ernest he seemed an interesting visionary, and they pitiable idolators. Dormer did not appear more than thirty,—tall, thin, and pale; his forehead high and finely formed. His hair and eyes very dark: his countenance marked, and full of expression; but its leading character, mild, grave, chastened, and lowly. His manners, though unusually polished, partook remarkably of the same character. The only time since Ernest had entered the chapel, and observed him, in which he had for a moment appeared otherwise, was that in which he had defended the fasts enjoined by his church; and, as Ernest now regarded him, he thought it likely that he had felt warmly on that point, from its being one of the duties which he practised with extreme strictness.

Ernest at last took leave of his interesting cousins, and their equally interesting chaplain. Mrs Clarenham very kindly invited him to return, and also expressed a wish to see Lady Montague. Maria cordially shook hands with her cousin, and intrusted him with a note she had written with a pencil to her friend Adeline. To Catherine he bowed stiffly; but she was, or pretended to be, too deeply engaged to observe his departure. Old Elliston nodded as he would have done to a school-boy, and Dormer stood apparently mildly waiting to return any courtesy which might be bestowed upon him. Ernest bowed respectfully, and then Dormer still more so. Clarenham left the chapel with his young friend, and conducted him to the small gallery he had mentioned, again warmly inviting him to be present at the services in the chapel on any occasion in which he could find himself sufficiently interested to be so. The young friends then walked together across the park, and separated with mutual assurances of their intentions to meet soon again.

CHAPTER III.

—"E quand' ebbi visto, e udito mi prostrai a' piedi dell' Angelo, che tali cose mostravami, per adorarlo. E dissemi: guardati da far cio: adora Dio." *Martini's Trans.*—Rev. xxii. 8.

"Do come, and walk with me, Adeline," said Ernest to his sister, on the evening of the day on which he had visited the Clarenhams. "The air is balm—every thing is lovely; and I have a thousand questions to ask you." Adeline most willingly consented, and was soon ready to accompany him. Hours were much earlier in those days; and, though only the middle of April, Ernest and his sister had a long evening before them, ere they must return to family worship and supper; the last, at that time substantial meal, occurring about the same hour at which families of similar rank now meet at dinner.

The air was indeed balm, and all around was the loveliness of spring; but Adeline and her brother soon forgot all else in the earnestness with which they talked of the Clarenhams.

"Tell me," said Ernest, "something about that affected girl, Catherine. I am certain there is as much affectation as enthusiasm in her character."

"Do not ask me about her," replied Adeline; "she has treated me with so much contempt and rudeness that I cannot be just to her."

Ernest laughed. "Then we are equally in her good graces. Is it because we are Protestants she thus scorns us?"

"Entirely. Maria tries to persuade me that it is a matter of conscience with her; and that I ought to forgive it in one who is so soon to give up the world, and who dreads having her affections in the smallest degree drawn back to it by any one, particularly by those of a different faith."

"Poor thing!" said Ernest compassionately.

"O do not waste your pity on her!" returned Adeline; "she regards herself as quite superior to us all. You would be provoked if you heard how she lectures and reproves Maria:

and, after all, I think Maria more under the influence of true religion than she is."

"And how does Maria receive those reproofs and lectures?"

"Most amiably. She has been in the habit of regarding Catherine as far superior in sanctity to herself. She believes also that she has a call from heaven, so devoted is she already to the life to which she is destined, and therefore listens to her with deference. But I shall tell you some of those saintly deeds which raise her so highly in her own opinion and that of her family."

"And how do you happen to know them?"

"Maria tells me. She does so in the hope, I believe, of converting me; and, in return, I tell her my opinions, always supporting them by passages from Scripture, to which Maria listens with extreme interest: and I think, though she may not avow it to herself, that these passages have already succeeded in at least weakening her belief in the efficacy of some of those superstitious rites taught by Popish priests."

"In the efficacy of paying reverence to the pictures of saints, I am sure, from what I saw this morning, she has no faith," observed Ernest. "Yet she was ignorant of its being prohibited in the Bible."

"I have not yet ventured to tell her that it is," answered Adeline. "I dreaded that had I shown her the ten commandments, as they are really written in the Bible, and told her that her priests absolutely dared to suppress one altogether—dividing another into two, in order to blind their people,—and all this to support the system of image worship, she would not have credited me, and would have felt herself obliged to mention the circumstance to Mr Elliston at her next confession, who would probably have found means to prevent our having any further intercourse."

"You have acted very prudently, dear Adeline; much more so than I. This forenoon, and in their chapel, before both priests, I told Clarenham that it was so." Ernest then told his sister what had passed.

"I rejoice to hear it," replied Adeline. "I am glad Maria heard you, and expressed her surprise before Mr Elliston. I have often told her that Scripture forbid many things enjoined by her priests: and that I did not tell her half the wicked things done by the Romish clergy to support their authority, because she would not believe me. I say such things laughing, but they make an impression."

"But does she admit the correctness of the English translation of the Bible?"

"She says not; but I think I have convinced her judgment that it is impossible it should be incorrect, considering that it is the very leading principle of Protestantism to lay open the Bible to every one, and to invite, and inculcate, and intreat its examination, while it is the leading principle of Popery to shut it out of the sight of all but the clergy. Maria has been carefully instructed regarding the many different opinions among Protestants; but she knows also that there is quite as much learning amongst those different sects as in her own communion, therefore is too sensible not to perceive that the learned men belonging to these sects would proclaim it to the world did those differing from them venture to corrupt the translation. But we have forgot Catherine."

"No, indeed," replied Ernest, laughing, "I shall not soon forget her."

"You bear much malice for one offence," said Adeline; "but listen, and I am sure you will feel pity also. You know the poor girl retires in less than a year to her convent to take the veil. It is usual, I believe, for those in her situation to spend this last year with their friends cheerfully, and partaking of their innocent amusements and pleasures. Not so Catherine. Her's is to be a term of the most rigid mortification; and this entirely of herself: for Mr Elliston, though he does not forbid, by no means encourages her in it. Every hour she devotes to some occupation considered pious or meritorious by the Roman Catholics. At three in the morning, in every kind of weather, she proceeds, with a lamp in her hand, to the chapel. Sometimes, as a mortification to her natural feelings of repugnance to such exercises, she obliges herself to pass with naked feet across the rough court of the chapel, and along its cold marble pavement. I may, in recounting them, misplace her different acts of devotion; but, if I recollect aright, she first repeats what is termed a litany before the picture of the Virgin Mary, or some saint. Her favourite is, I believe, one named St Catherine, as she herself hopes to be. To this litany some prayers are added called matins; and, if I mistake not, they too are directed to the Virgin. Indeed, excepting some Paternosters, which are all in Latin, I do not recollect that Maria mentioned to me one prayer, in all her sister's devotions, which was addressed to God. Those prayers continue an hour, at the close of which Catherine retires to bed, sometimes, she tells her friends, so chilled, that nothing short of a miracle prevents her catching cold; but this she owes, her family and herself believe, to St Catherine."

"How deplorable!" exclaimed Ernest; "there is no rational evidence that any such person as St Catherine ever existed; and, if she did, how blasphemous is it to ascribe to a human spirit those attributes which belong to God alone: for this idol, set up by the Church of Rome, has many votaries in different and distant parts of the world, and therefore must be regarded by them as present, and able to know the wants of her many and distant petitioners at the same moment. How astonishing is it that rational people can continue in a church which teaches such unscriptural and debasing absurdities! But go on, Adeline."

"Well," resumed Adeline, "after Catherine's miraculous escape from cold,—which, however, she does not always escape, for she has had attacks of it often of late,—she returns to bed for two hours. She then rises for the day. When dressed, another hour is spent in repeating as many Paternosters and Ave Marias, and other prayers, as there are beads on a long string. This string of bead-remembrancers is called a rosary. Most, or all of these prayers are in Latin, which she does not understand."

Ernest sighed deeply. "What a mockery!" exclaimed he, sadly. "Poor thing! what a labour which can bring no improvement to the soul!—no return whatever, but a delusive hope that she has thus fulfilled a duty, while she has only been doing that which Christ positively enjoined his disciples not to do—'using vain repetitions as the heathen did, who thought they would be heard for their much speaking.' One heartfelt confession of unworthiness to Him who is ready to forgive—one ardent prayer for pardon in His name, who is the Only

Mediator and Intercessor—one believing aspiration after renovation and holiness of spirit, by the grace of the Holy Spirit—Oh how different would be the return! Adeline, we who have the Bible can scarcely conceive a mind in such a state as you have described that poor girl's to be—and you say she thinks highly of herself:—But go on."

"Forget what I have said," replied Adeline; "I am ashamed of myself."

"I will, Adeline; and also my own displeasure at her contemptuous treatment. So pray go on."

"Still," resumed Adeline, "she has another religious service to attend before breakfast—that is Mass. But Maria said little to me regarding that, except that it was performed every morning. I believe, since old Mr Clarenham's death, there are some additional observances which are to benefit him in some way; but I could not, you know, ask any questions on that point."

"No, certainly," answered Ernest; "but we all know what effects Roman Catholics ascribe to that service when performed for the dead.

But does Catherine spend the whole day in such acts of devotion ?"

"No; the forenoon is dedicated to deeds of charity. Immediately after breakfast she repairs to the cottages of one class of poor people at Hallern village—those afflicted with sores. I need not tell you that the people of that village are remarkably poor, and almost all Roman Catholics. Many of them are pensioners of the Clarenhams, and are in some measure portioned out to the different members of the family. Those afflicted with sores have been selected by Catherine, since her return home, because she is very easily disgusted and made sick by any object that is loathsome: and because she finds herself particularly so just after breakfast, that is the time she chooses to commence her attendance on her poor patients. She is frequently obliged, Maria tells me, to leave their cottages when she has only opened the dressings from a sore, to breathe the air for a moment, and then returns just to be obliged to go out again. She, however, perseveres, and some days is able to perform what she wishes. So anxious is she to overcome these, as she considers them, uncharitable and sinful feelings, that she has left nothing untried that she could think of for that purpose; and I really cannot help feeling admiration for that part of her conduct."

"All depends on the motive in such actions," replied Ernest. "If Catherine's motive is love to Christ, and, for his sake, to poor Christians, then it shall be said to her—'Inasmuch as ye have done it unto one of the least of these my brethren, ye have done it unto me.' But if she hopes, by such acts of kindness to the poor, to merit heaven, or atone for her sins, which is the common opinion amongst Roman Catholics,—then she is putting them in the place of Jesus Christ, whose blood alone atones for sin, and whose merits alone are sufficient to deserve heaven."

"I do not know her motives," replied Adeline; "but Maria believes that such deeds not only secure the salvation of the person who performs them,—if that person belongs to the Romish Church,—but that if he performs very many of them, that is, more than God is supposed to require of one individual, it is in the power of the church to transfer the overplus to another person to add to his merits; and, out of that fund of the surplus merits of saints, which the church falls heir to, she draws those indulgences which she grants. Maria has told me all this, though she now begins to be ashamed of it as part of her creed, she saw that it struck me as so utterly ridiculous."

"So utterly impious," observed Ernest. This doctrine of the Romish Church at once sets at nought God's whole method of salvation. Does poor Maria really believe what is so completely irrational, and so utterly without the foundation of authority from Scripture, which is directly opposed to it, from beginning to end, both in letter and spirit."

"I ought rather to say, that Maria once believed it," replied Adeline. "I think her faith has been staggered on many points since she has ventured to listen to my quotations from the Bible, and to converse freely on the subject."

"Do you think she mentions those conversations in her confessions to Mr Elliston?"

"She does not confess often. That omission is one of the sins for which Catherine reproves her, even before me. Maria has acknowledged to me, that she has had an invincible repugnance to confession ever since she began to consider herself bound to perform it as a duty: and that nothing but Mr Elliston's affectionate kindness to her could have made it tolerable. She has always been his favourite of the whole family, and is much attached to him. She has determined to confess to him before he goes. That was the purport of the note you brought from her to me this morning."

Adeline gave her brother the note, which was as follows:—

"Do come and see me to-morrow, dearest Adeline. Come in the evening. Basil and I shall walk home with you, and we shall together see the sun set from the hill. I say the evening, because I shall confess to-morrow, and know not at what hour I may get Father Dennis; and to him I must confess before he goes, for I every day more and more dread Father Clement, who, on his part, I think, already regards me with suspicion respecting my devotedness to the authority of the priests. Your brother has just been saying strange things in our chapel. Ever yours, "M. C."

"Will you meet us on the hill to-morrow evening, Ernest?" asked Adeline.

"I will with pleasure, if you assure me of being welcome to all."

"I can assure you of welcome; and do put your Greek Testament in your pocket. Maria will soon lead to the subject, and Basil may not listen to our translation."

"You are very ardent in proselyting, dear Adeline."

"Oh Ernest! if you loved Basil as I love Maria, you would feel what a continual weight upon the heart the idea is, that the soul of your most beloved friend may not be safe."

Ernest made no reply for an instant. Adeline had touched on one of those subjects which led to a train of thought, in the depths and mysteries of which he too often found himself involved. "You are surely right in using the means, Adeline," said he at last. "The effects are with God."

"Were you pleased with young Clarenham?" asked Adeline.

"Extremely so. He is very prepossessing, both in manners and appearance."

"Ah! then I hope you will soon feel as deeply interested in him as I do in Maria."

"And poor Catherine!" said Ernest, smiling.

"She is so fenced round by the good opinion she has of herself," replied Adeline, "and so full of contempt for us poor heretics, who dare read the Bible, that I do not feel at all inclined to attempt meddling with her opinions—but if you do—"

"I would far rather make a convert of Mr Dormer," replied Ernest. "But this is a foolish way of talking; and now I think it must be late, the sun has got so low."

It was indeed getting late, and Ernest and his sister hastened homewards, as it was Sir Herbert's invariable custom to proceed with whatever was the stated occupation of the hour in his family, whoever might be absent; and they dreaded that family worship might be commenced before their return. It was indeed the hour at which it usually commenced ere they came in sight of the house; but, to their great surprise, on leaving a wooded, and now almost dark little path, they had chosen as the nearest, they perceived Sir Herbert and Dr Lowther at a short distance, leisurely approaching on horseback.

"What on earth can be the matter !" exclaimed Adeline. "My father detests riding at this hour, and Dr Lowther always spends it alone, and will not suffer himself to be disturbed. Something must have happened."

Both parties reached the house together. Ernest held the bridle of his father's horse while he dismounted.

"My dear Sir, this is a very unusual hour for you to ride."

"And I have been at very unusual business," replied Sir Herbert.

"Not unpleasant, Sir, I hope."

"Less so than I expected.—Dick, take the horse," turning to the groom,—then looking at his watch, "just lead them all to the stable, and return yourself, for it is the hour for family worship." Sir Herbert then put his hand kindly on Ernest's shoulder, as they entered the house, but continued silent.

Adeline had been more successful with Dr Lowther, who told her that Sir Herbert, having discovered that old Mr Elliston was to leave Hallern Castle in three or four days, had sent to say that he and Dr Lowther wished to see him in private for half an hour, and would call at any time he appointed. He had fixed that evening.

" And we have just been with him, my dear Miss Adeline," continued Dr Lowther, " to acknowledge our faults, and ask his forgiveness, as you heard Sir Herbert say this morning he was determined to do."

" But surely, dear Sir, Mr Elliston had more cause to ask yours and my father's forgiveness."

" That was not to prevent us, my dear, from acknowledging that we had acted unsuitably to our profession. We must not leave those sins which we are led into by our own pride and evil passions to be charged on our religion."

" But how did Mr Elliston receive my father? My dear father!—I can scarcely conceive his submitting to—and you, dear Dr Lowther—and that old priest does at times look so haughty."

" I have not time to tell you now, my dear

Miss Adeline, but he was not haughty—at least not after he knew the nature of our visit. But we must now join Sir Herbert."

Family worship occupied rather more time in those days than it usually does now, as it was then thought essential, at least amongst Presbyterians and the descendants of non-conformists, to train their young people, and those they considered under their charge, by a much more laborious and deep course of religious study than is thought necessary in our more enlightened days: and young people, or those who had but recently begun to take an interest in religious subjects, from this notion, that time and study were necessary to the acquirement of knowledge on that, as on other subjects, were sadly kept back, and prevented in those dark times of systematic and heavy divinity, from teaching, and deciding, and dictating on disputed points, as they do now, with so much benefit to others, and to themselves.

Ernest and Adeline took notes of the explanation given by Dr Lowther to the passage of Scripture he had selected for the evening, and into the meaning of which he entered at considerable length, and apparently with much interest and anxiety that it should impress his hearers. Lady Montague also took notes occasionally; and even Sir Herbert recorded on his tablets two or three strong and original remarks made by his old friend: while the domestics listened with looks of intelligent attention: and, when the service was over, it did not seem as if it had been an interruption, from which every one afterwards returned to more congenial occupation, but to have so arrested the attention, and engaged the mind and feelings, as to impress its own character on what followed.

"How true your remark was, my dear friend," said Sir Herbert to Dr Lowther, referring to a part of his recent lecture,—"that the pain attendant on performing any plain duty, is not in the act, but in the imaginary evils which precede it."

"The duty of this evening has not then proved painful," said Lady Montague, looking more to the well known expressions of Sir Herbert's countenance for an answer than listening to his words.

"No, my love," replied he, with that softness of expression which his countenance never wore to any but to herself, and with a smile which conveyed to her that she should afterwards know whatever she chose of his least expressible feelings.

Adeline had seated herself next to her father, and now unconsciously watched his countenance. He continued to converse with Dr Lowther and her mother without seeming to observe her. At last turning abruptly round, and looking her full in the face, "Well, Adeline, you have studied my looks for the last half hour, what have you discovered?"

"Nothing, Sir," replied Adeline, casting down her eyes and blushing.

"At least nothing you wish to discover, Addy. But, come now, confess the truth; you can think of nothing else from your anxiety to know how your father made out to ask forgiveness of an old Jesuit priest."

"I have discovered, Sir, that it has made him look so mild and benignant," replied Adeline archly, "that I am in hopes he will gratify my curiosity."

Sir Herbert smiled: "Well, Addy, I will tell you thus far,—you need never dread doing what is right; for you may trust that if you are determined to deny yourself, and obey God, he will make your way plain and smooth before you." Then turning to Ernest, "You are right, my dear boy, in trying to discover what is attractive, or worthy of a rational being's love in those religions which differ from your own. We are too apt to consider those who oppose us, fools and hypocrites. Poor old Elliston! I am sure he is neither. Yet I have thought him a hypocrite for the last twenty years, because I could not conceive that a man of his sense and shrewdness really credited all the nonsense taught by his church: but I must now lay the blame elsewhere, for I am certain he himself is deceived.

"How did he receive you, Sir;" asked Ernest.

"He supposed we had come with some complaint or threat about his attempt to proselyte the labourers who have lately come to the new cottages near my stone quarry, and received us very stiffly. I was rather at a loss how to commence what I had to say, and he began the conversation by saying rather haughtily:—"I suppose, Sir Herbert, you and Dr Lowther are come to accuse me of the crime of having attempted to bring some of the heretics on your domains back to the true church."

"Provoking old fellow!" said Rowley indignantly. "I wonder you could proceed, Sir."

"I felt more hurt than angry, Rowley, because I meant kindness only. I just said, that I had not come to complain of any part of his conduct; but, before his departure, to acknowledge how sensible we were of having on some occasions acted in a very unchristian manner towards him, and to ask his forgiveness: And then what a change there was in the old man's looks and manner!" Sir Herbert seemed moved even at the recollection.

"Certainly I never witnessed such a change," said Dr Lowther; "and when Sir Herbert held out his hand and asked his forgiveness, the old man wept. He tried to overcome his softness, and said he had prepared himself for a scene so different—that he was already moved by the thoughts of so soon parting from a family who were too dear to a man who had taken the vows he had—and then he had so many confessions to make of unchristian conduct towards us;—and, in the fulness of his softened heart, acknowledged that the very intention of instituting his order was to reclaim heretics. That their vows tended to that one point: and that on their success depended all they valued;—and then he asked our forgiveness so earnestly —in short, my dear madam," said Dr Lowther, addressing Lady Montague, "Sir Herbert, Mr Elliston, and I, parted like brothers."

"And does he go so soon as we heard he did?" asked Lady Montague.

"The day after to-morrow is what they call Good Friday," replied Dr Lowther. "It is a busy day with Roman Catholics: so is the Sabbath following; and on Monday Mr Elliston leaves the castle. He is appointed confessor to a rich old English gentleman, who resides generally at Florence.

"Poor old man!" said Sir Herbert, compassionately; "How cruel to remove him from those young people whom he must feel for as if they were his own. What an iniquitous system that is which denies to the minister of God that relation to any creature which the Divine Being has marked out as so honourable, by constantly appropriating the character to himself—that of a father. Did you remark the expression of poor old Elliston's countenance, Dr Lowther, when he asked you for your sons and daughters, and how many grandchildren you had?"

"I did—there was a strange mixture of sarcasm and sadness in it."

The reader must be informed, that though Dr Lowther now generally resided at Illerton-Hall, he had done so only for two years. Previous to that period he had dwelt in his own house near his church. A few months before that time, however, he had lost his wife. His three sons had been honourably settled in different situations before their mother's death, and his two daughters happily married in his own parish. When his home thus became sad and lonely, Sir Herbert had tried every means to induce him to reside at Illerton. He had got his books carried thither, and, by degrees, prevailed on him to prolong his visits, till at last, though he still considered his own house his home, he was never suffered to be there, but spent his time either with some member of his own family, or as chaplain at Illerton-Hall.

CHAPTER IV.

"Imperocche Dio e uno, uno anche il mediatore tra Dio, e gli uomini, uomo Christo Gesu." *Martini's Trans.*—1 Tim. ii. 5.

It was still two hours from sunset on the following day, when Ernest proceeded to the appointed hill where he was to meet Adeline and the two young Clarenhams. He walked slowly and thoughtfully to the place of meeting, his whole soul absorbed by one subject of desire and hope—the conversion of his young relations and of their interesting chaplain. The conversion of the last seemed almost hopeless: and Ernest, when he recollected, in his modest estimation of himself, how little he knew of those arguments by which Roman Catholics defended their faith, shrunk from the idea of entering on the subject with one whose appearance and manner conveyed so much sincerity and devotion, and who, he had heard, was as eminent for learning and talents as for sanctity. Not that he felt a doubt as to his being in error; "for any argument must be sophistry," reasoned he, "however subtile, which defends a system, the basis of which is so utterly unscriptural as that of the Romish faith.—Denying free access to the word of God—ordaining prayers to be offered up in a language not understood by the people—praying to departed spirits—setting up images and pictures in the churches for the people to prostrate themselves before. No argument could prove these to be agreeable to the Scriptures." Ernest walked slowly as he thus reasoned, his arms crossed on his breast, and his eyes fixed on the ground. "Impossible! no argument could prove it;" said he aloud. Some one passed as he spoke, he looked up, and saw—Dormer.

Ernest started and stopt. Dormer also stopt. He looked slightly embarrassed, but said, with his usual mildness—

"I beg pardon, Mr Montague. I have interrupted you. The extreme beauty of the views seen from this hill has perhaps led me too far. Am I beyond the bounds which separate the domains of Illerton from Hallern? I do not yet exactly know them."

"If you were, Mr Dormer, surely you cannot possibly suppose that you are not perfectly welcome."

"I can suppose nothing of Mr Montague but what is benevolent and kind," replied Dormer, feelingly. Then smiling,—"I perceive I have passed the boundary."

"It is at the top of the hill," replied Ernest; "but one of the finest views is seen a little lower down on this side. If you will permit me, I will conduct you to the place."

Dormer seemed to hesitate.

"I assure you it is finer than any you have yet seen," said Ernest.

"I doubt not that," replied Dormer; "but whether I ought to indulge myself by encroaching on your time and kindness."

There was something so perfectly simple in Dormer's manner, polished as it was, that it conveyed the most irresistible conviction of sincerity; and Ernest now replied, with warmth, that no way in which he could at that moment employ his time would give him equal pleasure —and the next instant he found himself walking arm in arm with that same most interesting Jesuit priest who had so deeply engaged his thoughts a few minutes before. They walked on for a time in silence. Ernest felt embarrassed—and Dormer seemed not quite at ease. At last Dormer broke the silence—

"I think, Mr Montague, I ought in honesty to tell you how much I overheard of what you, in the depth of thought, and you supposed in solitude, said as I passed you a little ago. Your words were—'Impossible! no argument could prove it.'—I heard no more."

"I was indeed very deep in thought," replied Ernest, reddening as he recollected on what subject.

"Your family are Calvinists, I believe, Mr Montague?"

"They are," replied Ernest. "They profess the doctrines of the Church of Scotland."

"And of Holland and Geneva?" said Dormer.

"Yes—and of the puritans and non-conformists of England and America."

"It is, I know, a wide-spread creed," replied Dormer; "and I have remarked that those who are educated in its doctrines, if they take an interest in religion, learn to be very deep thinkers."

"It is not surprising they should," replied Ernest. "They are early led to the contemplation of very deep mysteries. It was not any doctrine of my own church, however, which occupied my thoughts when I met you, Mr Dormer. It was——" Ernest hesitated for a moment, then said frankly, "I was endeavouring to discover what could be said in defence of some of the doctrines of your church."

Dormer looked surprised but pleased. "In defence of them!" repeated he.

"Yes," replied Ernest. "I am acquainted with what, by Protestants, are considered the erroneous doctrines of your church: but I do not believe I am acquainted with what wise and good men of the Romish faith say in their defence."

"Do you, a Protestant and a Calvinist, believe that there are wise and good men at this day in the church of Rome?"

"I assuredly do."

"And men of real religion?" asked Dormer. Ernest was silent.

"You cannot go so far," said Dormer.

"That was the very difficulty I was attempting to solve," replied Ernest. "I must believe that there have certainly been truly religious men in the Romish church. Who can read the writings of Fenelon and Pascal and not believe it."

A slight motion of Dormer's arm made Ernest look in his face. There was a passing expression of displeasure, but he said nothing; and Ernest instantly recollected how little agreeable to a Jesuit it could be to hear Pascal singled out for praise. Ernest felt confused—"I certainly cannot doubt that there have been, and consequently still may be, truly religious men in the church of Rome. But, Mr Dormer, may I ask you the same question: Do you believe that there are men of real religion among Protestants?"

"I will answer you with perfect frankness, Mr Montague," replied Dormer, "though I would rather you had not, so early in our acquaintance, asked me that question, lest the answer I must give you should lead you to suspect me of bigotry. But let me ask you,—do you think there is more than one *right* way of understanding any subject?"

"Certainly not."

"And whatever deviation is made from that one right way is error?"

"Certainly."

"And you are not one of those, Mr Montague, who regard error in religious principles of no moment, provided your conduct to your fellow-men is irreproachable?"

"I am not. I look upon sound religious principles in the soul as the only source from whence conduct acceptable to God can proceed."

"Yes, *sound* principles of religion; but if those which are supposed so are in fact erroneous, is the person who is guided by them safe?"

"Certainly not."

"Then I will answer your question. I cannot suppose that Protestants are safe, because I believe they are guided by a system of error. I cannot think a man, however I may love him, and desire his salvation, can be a truly religious man while his religion is error: and I think Protestants are strangely inconsistent when they say that the Catholic church is full of corruptions and errors, and yet allow that her members may be safe.

"We do not say," replied Ernest, "that those who are guided by the corruptions and errors of the Church of Rome are safe; but that, corrupt as that church is, it still teaches, though deeply mingled with error, those truths which, if believed and obeyed, save the soul. In the writings of those members of your church whom I have mentioned, they profess to rest their hopes of salvation on those truths: We therefore, in charity, hope that they, and all such as they in the Romish church, are safe. It is, however, difficult for a Protestant to conceive that state of mind, which, at the same time can believe the truths taught in the Bible, and admit some of those doctrines and observances insisted on by your church."

"May I ask you to mention one of those doctrines or observances?"

"I need only remind you of what I witnessed in your chapel yesterday," replied Ernest.

"St Paul says expressly—'there is one God, and one Mediator between God and man, the man Christ Jesus.'* The church of Rome teaches the first great truth of this passage,—'there is one God;' but, in direct contradiction to the inspired apostle, says, that there are hundreds of mediators—angels—the departed spirits of men and women."

"But not in the same sense that Christ is mediator," interrupted Dormer, mildly.

"Allowing the distinction," said Ernest, "which, however, Roman Catholics themselves admit is not always made by the ignorant,—and such in their communion always constitutes the majority;—allowing such mediators in any sense is utterly an invention of the church of Rome—without one word or one example in Scripture to authorise it—and corrupts, and weakens, and dishonours those plain Scripture doctrines, on the belief and right understanding of which our salvation depends."

"I cannot perceive that it does," replied Dormer, with the same perfect gentleness.—"Were Mr Montague a member of the Catholic

* 1 Tim. ii. 5.

and apostolic church, I have already heard so much of his extreme kindness to the poor—of his anxiety to make all around him good and happy—and I have seen so much of his zeal for what he considers truth—and felt so grateful for his benevolent kindness to a stranger, for whom all the prejudices of his education must have taught him to feel the contrary;—that I should humbly ask the benefit of his prayers: and surely the prayers of the saints in heaven may be intreated."

Ernest remained silent—not from being satisfied with Dormer's reply, for nothing could be less satisfactory; but from the modesty of his nature, and the kindness of his heart. Had he yielded to the last, he could almost have embraced the interesting stranger who seemed so grateful for common civilities; but such direct praise of himself, mingled with a defence so weak, of what appeared to Ernest gross superstition in his church, checked his kinder feelings, and reminded him that his companion was a Romish priest and a Jesuit.

"Forgive me, Mr Montague," said Dormer, "if I have treated the subject we were talking of, as of less importance than it appears to you."

"You certainly have—but now we have reached the spot I mentioned," replied Ernest, as he and Dormer got clear of some straggling trees and underwood through which they had been passing, and pointing to the widely extended view which now lay before them. "I hope we shall not now differ in opinion." Ernest retired a step or two, and looked in a different direction from that to which Dormer's attention seemed immediately to be fixed, not so much to contemplate the view as to watch the looks of his companion.

Ernest was an enthusiastic admirer of the beauties and sublimities of nature, so much so, that an absence of the same taste in others led him, in the common rashness of youth, to regard such as deficient in all the lovelier qualities of the human character. Dormer in this, however, did not disappoint him ; but seemed as deeply susceptible of those beauties as himself. His looks—his words—his gestures,—all expressed that deep feeling of admiration which is produced by natural taste joined to adoration of that glorious Being who has still left traces of his character wherever we look around us on our sinful world. There was one point, however, to which Dormer's looks still returned, and that point Ernest considered the least beautiful of the whole landscape. Dormer seemed to forget Ernest's presence—every thing—while, as he looked earnestly in that direction, his countenance gradually assumed an expression of extreme melancholy. At last recollecting himself—" I was not aware," said he, " that those hills," pointing in the direction to which his attention had been so earnestly fixed, " could have been seen from hence. Amongst them is my birth-place, and the place in which I spent my youth. I supposed that fifteen years' absence had deadened every feeling of attachment to its scenery; but, at this moment, it is all before me; and the effect is strangely powerful."

" You have not, then, visited it since your return?" said Ernest.

" No: nor shall I visit it. Strangers possess it now. The part my family took for their church and king was too open and decided to leave them with lands and fortunes, while the one is oppressed at home, and the other in exile abroad. They are all dispersed. For my own part, I ought to rejoice, that, for many years, I have been separated from all natural ties to this world. I ought the more perfectly to feel myself what I profess to be, 'A stranger and a pilgrim on the earth.'"

Ernest made no answer. He was plain and sincere on all occasions; but his feelings of interest and sympathy for Dormer could not lessen his dislike to that cause for which his family had suffered; and which was, in his opinion, as bad as a weak, corrupt, and arbitrary government, and a false and intolerant religion, could make it.

"You do not think the cause worth the sacrifice, I perceive?" said Dormer.

"I certainly do not in either case," replied Ernest. "Yet I hope you will believe I can feel for those who do."

"I certainly cannot disbelieve it," said Dormer; "but I must not encroach longer on your time and kindness."

"We may return together," said Ernest.

"I promised to meet my sister at the boundary before sun-set; and may I beg of you, Mr Dormer, to have a better opinion of us than to believe we should not be gratified by your finding it agreeable to you to walk or ride on any part of the Illerton grounds."

Dormer expressed his gratitude—looked again earnestly towards the hills, and sighed deeply; then, putting his arm within Ernest's, they turned towards the path to re-ascend the hill.

"May I invite you, Mr Montague," said Dormer, as they walked, "to witness the service in Hallern Chapel to-morrow? I think your once doing so would have more effect in convincing you that the Catholic church has judged wisely in exciting the devotion of her children, by those representations you seemed so much to condemn yesterday, than any thing I could say."

"I wish much to witness the service," replied Ernest, "and shall willingly be present to-morrow; but hope I shall meet with nothing to reconcile me to what is expressly prohibited in the word of God."

"We do not adore the representation," replied Dormer; "we adore the reality only. We do not, therefore, transgress any law of God."

"Your distinctions are too nice," said Ernest. "The words of the commandment are, 'Thou shalt not make unto thee the likeness of any thing in the heaven above, or in the earth beneath. Thou shalt not bow thyself to them, nor worship them.'"

"Bow thyself to them, to adore them, is the translation of the church," said Dormer; "and we do not transgress that law."

"Even allowing that translation, which is not literal, why thus come on the very verge of disobedience? Why teach that which all Roman Catholics allow may be so misunderstood as to lead the ignorant into the commission of that sin, more condemned than any other in Scripture, and consequently most dangerous to their souls,—idolatry? Why are the Romish clergy so determinately bent on this, that where it is possible the people may never discover that there is a law of God on the subject, they suppress that law altogether?

Is it possible for Protestants, with the Bible in their hands, containing the law, to know this, and not regard the clergy of the Church of Rome with distrust—and to apply to them the words of Christ, 'In vain do they worship me, teaching for doctrines the commandments of men.'"

"Protestants misunderstand us," replied Dormer, with unchanged gentleness, though Ernest had become warm;—"Come to-morrow to our chapel, Mr Montague, and judge for yourself."

Ernest again promised, and, soon after, he observed his sister and her young friends approaching to meet him; and, much to his surprise, accompanied by Catherine, who walked apparently in a very friendly manner, with her arm within that of Adeline Montague.

Ernest was met by young Clarenham with increased cordiality and kindness, and by Maria with the same unaffected expressions of pleasure with which she had received him the day before. He bowed to Catherine, but scarcely looked at her, and was therefore unconscious of the change in her manner when she returned his salutation.

"How prettily you have kept your appointment, Mr Ernest," said Adeline.

"I imagined I was keeping it."

"Look at the sun."

Ernest looked, and saw that it had sunk beneath the horizon. "I had no idea it was so late."

"You must blame me, Miss Montague," said Dormer; "your brother had, I believe, nearly reached the appointed place of meeting when he met me wandering, I did not know whither, and became my guide to view the most attractive scenery I have looked upon for many years."

"O, I forgive *you*, Mr Dormer; but Ernest always finds means to spend his time with the wisest and gravest people—" Adeline stopt and blushed—"I do not mean to say that those were not wise with whom I have passed my time, but it was scarcely fair in you, Ernest, to leave one to combat three."

"Combat!" repeated Dormer.

"One against three, Father," said Maria Clarenham quickly. "Surely we ought to make converts; for strength of numbers, at least, is always on our side."

"I wish you all success from my heart, daughter," replied Dormer, looking calmly and gravely at Maria. "I trust you do not forget how serious the subject is to which you allude?"

"I hope not," replied Maria, reddening; "and I must say," continued she, "that we have been only two against one." Catherine joined not in the argument.

"No," said Catherine. "I venture not on such ground. I listen not to the words of Inspiration but as they are imparted to me by a priest. I presume not to use my own judgment in matters so sacred. Yet I desire, as much as any one, the return of heretics to the church—and most particularly the return of my cousins."

There was an air of elevation and enthusiasm in Catherine's manner as she spoke, and, on ceasing, she approached Ernest, and, lightly touching his arm, said, "Follow me. I have a message for you." Then turning, she again put her arm within Adeline's, walked to a little distance from the rest of the party, and stopt. Ernest followed; and now Adeline and he looked at each other, while Catherine, withdrawing her arm from Adeline's, placed herself before them—one hand raised—and an expression of intense thought gathering on her young brow.

"I will tell the truth," said she at last—"Yes, the whole truth. Adeline, you have thought me an unfeeling bigot."

"No, no, dear Catherine, only an euthusiast," said Adeline, affectionately.

"Do not interrupt me. You are not quite sincere. You at least thought I regarded myself as right; and, while I was satisfied you were in dangerous error, instead of pitying, only felt for you contempt and dislike. You thought the truth. I saw the ridicule with which you regarded all the pains I took to work out my own salvation. I knew that Maria had acquainted you with my most secret religious acts, because I had given her leave to do so—still you seemed only to feel that all were ridiculous. It is strange that I should have felt so painfully my want of success in convincing you of the superiority of that sanctity practised by the religious of our church; but when I saw that you would not be convinced—when I saw that you esteemed Maria's regard far more highly than mine—that you even thought her more truly religious—that you felt my society an interruption,—I did not feel, as I ought to have done, sorrow for you as a heretic, but displeasure at you and dislike of you. Since yesterday, there has been the most wonderful change in my feelings. It is a miracle. I know it is. Yesterday," addressing Ernest, "when you entered the chapel, I was displeased that a heretic—a brother of the scoffing Adeline, should have been brought into our very sanctuary. I could not prevent it, but determined that I at least should not join in welcoming you. I kept my uncharitable resolution in the very presence of the cross. I saw that I had wounded your feelings, and it gave me pleasure—but only for a time. You remained and condemned our worship—but there was no ridicule, no scorn in what you said. It seemed, even to me, calm, sober, unanswerable truth. I was certain you were in error, and that I only needed instruction from my confessor to be convinced you were; yet I felt the deepest compassion for you taking possession of my mind. Shame for my reception of you made me avoid looking at you as you retired, but I saw your parting bow to Father Clement, and felt sure that you did not scorn us. From that moment, the thought of your's and of Adeline's conversion has occupied my every thought. It prevented my sleeping; and I rose an hour earlier than usual to bestow that hour in saying Ave Marias for you to the virgin. Adeline, I see you ready to smile, but I will nevertheless tell you the truth."

"You are unjust to me, Catherine," said Adeline.—"Who could feel any thing but gratitude for intentions so kind?"

"No one could, indeed," said Ernest.

"Well, listen," continued Catherine.—"I had been thus employed for nearly the hour, and a sweet calm seemed to be breathed into my soul, while I so earnestly longed for your conversion. A current of morning air came along the aisles so as to blow upon the lamp, and I looked away for a moment from the face of the virgin to place it differently. Now listen:—When I looked again, there was a smile upon her lips—I am sure there was—and that smile approved of my wish for your salvation, and is an assurance to you that she will mediate for you, and that she longs to regard you as her children. Will you refuse her? Will you not be pursuaded, even by a miracle, to return into the bosom of the true church? Oh, surely you will?"

Ernest and Adeline were both silent from surprise, and from compassion for the young visionary."

"You do not believe that I saw the virgin smile?" said she to Ernest.

"I believe, my dear cousin," replied he, "that you supposed you saw your most kind and amiable feelings reflected in the countenance of the painting. I should make a most unworthy return for the interest you take in us, were I to say I believed more."

"You do not believe my word because I am a Catholic?"

"I do believe your word, Catherine. I believe that you felt natural displeasure when you supposed Adeline treated with ridicule those observances which you held sacred. I believe that you really desire to have your mind in that state which is most pleasing to God, and that you therefore most readily admitted the first kind feeling which entered it on behalf of your cousins. I believe also that this kind feeling was much more agreeable than unkind feelings had been, and produced that sweet calm of soul you mentioned; but I think the state of your mind, and the belief that such things had happened before, led you to suppose you saw the painting smile. I cannot believe that a piece of canvass smiled."

"But it was a miracle. Many such happened to me in the convent; and Father Ignatius, my confessor, in most instances, assured me I was not mistaken."

"Did you mention this last miracle to Mr Elliston?"

"I did."

"And did he say you were not mistaken?"

"He said I was right in wishing for the return of my cousins into the church; and that I was also right to pray to the virgin for them,—and did not say I was mistaken."

"Then, Catherine," said Ernest, solemnly, "that priest has your blood on his head if you perish. He knows that God, in his word, has said, 'There is none other name under heaven, or among men, by which we can be saved,' but the name of Jesus.* Yet he teaches you to pray to the spirit of a woman—a creature. He knows that the same inspired word declares,—that there is one mediator between God and man, the Man Christ Jesus; and no where speaks of any other mediator. Yet he encourages you to hope in the effectual mediation of a creature; and to believe that miracles are performed to support the gross delusion. These, my dear Catherine, are all inventions—mere groundless fables of your priests, entirely contrary to the Bible. Jesus Christ himself says, 'God so loved the world that he gave his only begotten Son, that whosoever believeth in him should not perish, but have eternal life.'† 'This is life eternal, that they might know thee

* Acts iv, 12. † John iii, 16.

the only true God, and Jesus Christ whom thou hast sent.'* 'He that believeth on the Son,' said John the Baptist, 'hath everlasting life.'†—And St Paul says, 'Ye are all the children of God by faith in Christ Jesus.'‡ The Bible is full of passages to the same purpose; while there is not one, from its beginning to its end, which authorises praying to any departed spirits, or asking their intercession, or any thing of the kind; but, on the contrary, the most severe denunciations against every species of worship that is not addressed to the only true God."

"The church believes in the Son of God," said Catherine, looking bewildered, and half-alarmed.

"Yes, my dear Catherine; but your church greatly dishonours him, by representing him as made more propitious by intermediate intercessions. This is utterly opposite to the Bible. He there invites all to come unto him—reproaches men for not coming to him, in words of kindness and sorrow—'Ye will not come unto me that ye may have life.' His office is that of a Saviour. The office of his ministers is to

* John xvii, 3. † John iii, 36. ‡ Gal. iii, 26.

preach him as the Saviour: and, believe me, dear Catherine, they have not an adequate knowledge of his character who join creature-mediation with the all-perfect mediation of the Son of God."

Clarenham now approached—"We must leave you, Catherine. It is getting so late and chilly, that Maria can wait no longer."

Catherine looked towards the darkening sky. "How rapidly time passes in such conversation!" said she.

The party then took an affectionate leave of each other: Adeline and Ernest to hasten home to evening worship—their cousins and Dormer to return more leisurely through the Park to the Castle.

The moon was just beginning to be seen above the woods to the east, and its light gradually becoming brighter than that produced by the glow in the western sky.

"What on earth were you saying with so much earnestness to the Montagues, Catherine?" asked Maria. "Two days ago you would scarcely speak to Adeline, and to-day you seem quite to love her—and now so long a secret for these two heretics."

"I was wrong in not wishing to speak to Adeline," said Catherine. "I am sure Father Clement will say so; as my only motive was her being a heretic, and her regarding my religion with that scorn which her education had taught her to do."

"You were wrong certainly, daughter," said Dormer; "yet you ought to be cautious of bringing scorn justly on your profession, by changes so rapid, and which, to those who may not know your motives, must appear at least whimsical."

"But I told my motives. I told the whole truth."

"And what was the truth, dear Catherine?" asked Clarenham.

"I wish to have no secrets from any of the present party," replied Catherine; "and they I know, will believe me." She then told the story of the Virgin smiling.

"And did you tell that to the young Montagues?" asked Dormer, with alarm.

"I did. I thought truth would have more effect than any thing I could say."

"How imprudent! How miserably ill-judged!" exclaimed Dormer, with displeasure. "Did you not know, Miss Catherine, that such things ought never to be mentioned to any one till they have been communicated to your confessor that he may judge whether or not the whole has been a work of the imagination?"

"I did know it, Father, and told the whole to Father Dennis at confession this morning."

"And did he permit you to divulge it?"

"He did not forbid me; and commended my wish for the return of my cousins into the true church."

Dormer made no answer, and the party walked on for a time in silence.

"If I have erred, Father," said Catherine at last, "I beg you may tell me, that I may do penance before to-morrow."

"I interfere not, daughter. Father Dennis is your spiritual guide while he remains here. You cannot require to do penance if he approved of you."

No more was said on the subject, and each one

of the party seemed willing to remain silent, as they passed, by the calm moonlight, over the rough and now damp grass.

Mrs Clarenham, surprised at their lateness, sat at a window watching their return; and, before they could explain the cause of their delay, anxiously hurried them away to change those parts of their dress which she supposed might be damp, and, in their absence, had a large fire prepared to do away all effects of cold.

A repast followed—not such as was usual at that hour. It was a fast. Clarenham, slight in form, and scarcely yet in the strength of manhood, but now looking animated, and the glow of recent exercise in his countenance, eat sparingly of vegetables: Catherine equally sparingly.—Maria, who, in every thing of which she could see no use or spiritual benefit, was a bad Roman Catholic, made a hearty meal of such fare as the table afforded. Mrs Clarenham seemed scarcely to know what she ate; and Dormer, with the fast and service of the following day before him, supped on a little sallad. Elliston was less abstemious, and reminded Dormer of the long fast which must follow. Dormer thanked him, but only said, "I have strength for it, Father."

After the spare repast was over, and the family rose to separate for the night, Dormer requested Elliston to remain for a few minutes, and then repeated to him what had passed respecting the miracle.

"The child told me of no miracle," said Elliston.

"Strange! she assured me you had received her confession this morning—that she had informed you of what she believed she had seen, and that you had not forbidden her to regard it as a miracle, or to mention it as such."

Elliston thought for an instant. "I have sinned, brother. I now have a confused recollection of her mentioning something of rising earlier than usual to pray to the Virgin for her cousins; but the truth is, my thoughts were far distant. I know not what she confessed. Her confessions hitherto have shown her heart so true to the church, and have been so like each other, that——but I need not extenuate my fault. I have sinned, and grieve for the consequences."

"It may be possible to prevent farther evil, Father. This does not appear to me to have been a miracle."

"A miracle!" repeated Elliston, looking with surprise at his brother priest—"If you listen to that child you will hear of a miracle every day."

"I think not, Father," replied Dormer, rather coldly.

"Well, well," said Elliston—"perhaps she may become less of a saint under your güidance than she has been considered hitherto;—but, let me tell you, brother, if you suffer the intimacy which seems again commencing so ardently with the young Montagues, to proceed, you will soon have neither saints nor Catholics among the young Clarenhams."

"I should rather hope to have, by that means, both Clarenhams and Montagues," replied Dormer.

"You do not know that family, brother, or the man who has reared them in heresy," replied Elliston.

"The true church ought not to shrink from those who are in error, as if error was stronger than truth," said Dormer. "Young Montague seems most amiably disposed, and, though prejudiced against the church, yet willing to listen candidly to whatever is advanced in her behalf: and I already have his promise to be present at our service to-morrow."

"It will make no impression, brother," replied Elliston. "The boy is what he ever was, thoughtful and clear-headed, mild, feeling, and sensible, with rather a disposition to melancholy. I have studied him from his childhood; and for long his conversion was one of my most anxious wishes: But he has been nurtured on the Bible—he is intimate with the languages in which it was originally written—his disposition has led him to study it deeply; and the Protestant system in which he has been educated is the one, of all others, most opposed to Catholicism."

"I know it is," replied Dormer, "and therefore feel the more ardently desirous to deliver him from its errors."

"Well," said Elliston, with rather a sneer on his countenance; "you can try, brother. Experience is not often trusted to by any but those who can no longer profit by it;—but surely every member of our church might know by this time, that there is no heresy so deep-rooted and insurmountable as that wrought in the mind by the free use of the Scriptures, with the right of private judgment of their contents. But good night, brother; I shall do away the evil effects of my negligence this morning as far as I can—but if the Montagues are to be the daily companions of my poor children, it signifies little to attempt any thing. That girl Adeline would ridicule the relics of St Peter. There is no hope of any of them but the younger boy. He has no head for their deep doctrines—and no heart for their strict practice—and wearies to death of Dr Lowther's long preachings. He might be attracted by the splendour of our service,—but good night, brother. You must take your own way."

CHAPTER V.

"Iddio e spirito: e quei, che l'adorano, adorar lo debbono in ispirito, e verita."
Martini's Trans.—John iv. 24.

The service in Hallern Chapel, next day, had been some time commenced before Ernest entered the small private gallery which had been shown to him by young Clarenham. This gallery was in a dark recess, and had curtains so disposed as to conceal the persons in it from the congregation below, while all that passed in the chapel was perfectly seen by those in the gallery.

When Ernest entered the chapel, all was so still that he imagined the service was not begun. On softly approaching the front of the gallery, however, he was most forcibly struck with the scene below. The chapel was nearly full of people,—all, at that moment, kneeling on the pavement in profound silence—every eye turned with apparently intense devotion on the painting over the altar. It was that crucifixion which had so powerfully moved Ernest's feelings on his former visit to the chapel. Amongst the worshippers were Mrs Clarenham, her son, and two daughters, kneeling also devoutly on the pavement, with their eyes fixed on the painting. Dormer knelt near the altar—his hands clasped on his breast, and his eyes fixed with an expression of adoration on the suffering, but beautifully resigned and affecting countenance of the picture. Elliston was in the pulpit. He stood with his hands also clasped on his breast, and apparently adoring the representation.

The whole scene was powerfully imposing; but, after the first moments of novelty, Ernest found it oppressively painful. It was impossible not to believe that the feelings he saw so powerfully depicted on every countenance were real. He could scarcely bear even to look at Dormer. His countenance—his attitude—all expressed the most ardent, the most unaffected feelings of devotion; and yet,—superior in intellect as he was,—he could thus, in submission to the authority of his fellow-men, bend and limit his soul to a worship so little spiritual. Ernest thought of that glorious Being who has promised *Himself* to be present, wherever two or three are gathered together in his name, to bless them, and to do them good: and he could feel no sympathy with those who sought to worship him—a present God,—through a medium so unworthy; and yet Roman Catholics themselves defend the use of these representations only on the ground that they excite and inspire devotion. "Is it possible," thought Ernest, "that one thought of His glory, who fills eternity, would not have more effect, when recollecting what he chose to suffer for our sakes, than those unworthy attempts to move, not our souls, but our senses!"

Ernest's thoughts were at last interrupted, and the profound silence in the chapel broken, by Dormer, as he knelt, repeating, in a voice of thrilling power, the words addressed to the thief upon the cross:—"Verily I say unto thee, to-day shalt thou be with me in Paradise."—Elliston then began, in a strain of most vehement declamation, to call the attention of the people to these words. Some things he said were good, and Ernest listened to them with pleasure; but the old man, before he concluded, had worked up his own and the people's feeling to a state with which Ernest could feel no emotion of sympathy. He and they were in tears; and the chapel resounded with audible sobs. Dormer, he however observed, was not moved: neither were Clarenham and Maria: but Catherine and her mother were deeply so.

Just as Elliston finished, the chapel began to darken. Ernest looked towards the large Gothic window by which it was lighted, and saw a thick curtain gradually descending over it. This, he supposed, was meant to represent that miraculous darkness which accompanied the last sufferings on the cross; and he felt shocked by an imitation which appeared to him so profane. Soon all was in the gloom of departing twilight —all but the painting. A lamp suspended above it, which Ernest had not before observed, now shed its pale rays on the countenance, giving it still more the expression of suffering and exhaustion, and throwing on the figure the pallidness of death. The darkness seemed to affect the people as if it had been real. A sensation among them, as if gathering together, had a powerful effect on Ernest's feelings. This was increased by Dormer's voice proceeding from the darkened altar, and pronouncing the next sacred words uttered by Christ. These again called forth a vehement burst of declamation from Elliston. Another and another sentence was thus pronounced by Dormer, and declaimed on by Elliston; and Ernest began to feel wearied of the sameness of his exaggerated expressions,—and thought of retiring, when, after another pause of deep silence, the next sentence was pronounced, not by Dormer, but by Elliston; and then Dormer began, not like old Elliston, with vehement, and unstudied, and ineloquent appeals to the feelings of his hearers, but in a voice, calm, low, and thrilling, to explain the words, and point out the instruction to be derived from them. Ernest's attention was completely arrested: but it required more than even Dormer's eloquence,—though every sentence seemed the result of study and of conviction,—to prove what he attempted to prove. The words he preached on were those addressed by Christ to his disciple John, on consigning to him the care of his mother :—" Behold thy mother." The Evangelist simply adds, as the consequence of this charge—" And from that hour that disciple took her unto his own home."* Dormer, from these words, attempted to defend the worship of the Virgin Mary; and this, apparently, with the most perfect sincerity. Perhaps he might not have chosen this subject as the first on which his young friend should hear him preach; but it was a part of a service he wished him to witness, and could not be avoided; and he attempted to prove his doctrine from the words of Scripture. The salutation of the angel to Mary—" Hail, highly-favoured!"† he said was evidently worship. But Ernest recollected that Christ had used the same form of salutation to his disciples after his resurrection " All hail!"‡ And words implying still greater favour than the words—" highly-favoured," had been addressed on three occasions to Daniel :—" Thou art greatly beloved—O Daniel! a man greatly

* John xix. 27. † Luke i. 28. ‡ Matth. xxviii. 9.

beloved—O man, greatly beloved!"* David, also, had been called—"The man after God's own heart."† And Abraham—"The friend of God."‡ Dormer therefore spent eloquence in vain, to prove, to one acquainted with the Bible, that such words implied worship.—Again the words—"The Lord is with thee," Dormer attempted to prove had the same meaning. But the same words were addressed to Gideon;§ and those—"Blessed art thou among women,"‖ was said of Jael.

Though Ernest could not agree in any thing Dormer said on this point, still he felt no inclination to depart. At last he was rewarded for his long attendance. Elliston pronounced the words—"It is finished." And never in his life before had Ernest heard eloquence so powerful, as that by which Dormer clearly, and from Scripture, proved, that, at the moment these words were uttered, the stupendous work of redemption was finished. Ernest covered his face with his hands, that he might see none of those degrading appeals to the senses, by which

* Daniel ix; 23. x. 19; and x. 11. † Acts xiii. 22. ‡ Isaiah xli. 8. § Judges vi. 12. ‖ Judges v. 24.

the powerful preacher was surrounded. When he again raised his eyes, on Dormer's concluding, the darkness was dispelled. The congregation still knelt; and, as if to do away the impression produced by the Scriptural and instructive truths he had just uttered, Dormer began to repeat rapidly some Latin prayers, while his fine and expressive countenance, which had been lighted up by the deep feeling of those important truths, gradually sunk into an expression of the most excessive exhaustion and languor; and Ernest, supposing the service near a close, softly left the gallery, and, deep in thought, bent his steps homewards.

"What a mixture of error and truth!" thought he, as he slowly crossed the park. "How fatally dangerous to give up the soul to any doctrine taught only by man! That Dormer!—who could resist his eloquence, was it always on the side of truth? And that man, with such powers to attract and win the soul and affections, instead of devoting those powers to proclaim the message of God—the Gospel—His mercy and glory whom he calls his Master, bends his soul to the wretched unprofitable slavery of rhyming over a list of prayers not understood by the starving immortal souls who wait on his lips for instruction. Oh! if the Romish clergy would throw their idols, and their vain repetitions to the winds, and preach as that man did this day! Not once in the year—not mingled with the poison of error—but all—all their system is so hopelessly full of error!" Ernest groaned aloud—and then almost smiled at his own feelings. "But that system," thought he, "powerful, complicated, —so sanctioned by a mixture of truth, as to make the thraldom of the soul a thousand-fold more hopeless: that corrupt system shall one day be destroyed by the brightness of His coming, who is 'Truth.'"

Several days passed without any further intercourse between the two families. During that time Elliston left the castle, and Dormer took his place as chaplain.

In the Romish church, as well as in the Protestant, there are those amongst the clergy, who, though they profess to believe the same creed, and are admitted into orders by the same forms, yet whose influence over their flocks, putting out of the question all mere external powers of attraction, is altogether different. The one leaves his people unimpressed, and at ease, in the most careless state of worldly-mindedness. The other rouses, and alarms, and forces those under his charge to remember they have souls which must live for ever. Poor old Elliston was of the first description: Dormer was of the last. All his arrangements, as chaplain, and, in fact, as guide and ruler, at Hallern Castle, convinced every inmate of the family that the strictest discipline of his church should be enforced. The young master of the family was prepared to second all his wishes. Had he not been secure of this, Dormer, dearly as he loved him, would not have been permitted by his order, who well knew his powers, to bury himself in the family of the half-ruined Clarenhams. But England was too valuable ground to be deserted, and too cultivated to be any longer trusted to priests of the common order; and the only way, at that period open to the Church of Rome, was to insinuate her doctrines into the knowledge, and attention, and good will of those amongst whom she could find means to place her clergy. It was at that time well known, that the end principally proposed by the Order of Jesuits was to gain converts to the Church of Rome, with which view they had dispersed themselves in every country and nation; and with unceasing industry and address pursued the end of their institution. No difficulty was considered too great for them to overcome—no danger too imminent for them to meet—no crime, in the service of their cause, of which they were not considered capable. The professed fathers of this Order take the three solemn vows of religion publicly; and to these add a special vow of obedience to the head of the church, as to what regards missions, heretics, and other matters.

Dormer was a professed father of this Order; though the abhorrence in which the society was at that period held in England led the Clarenhams to conceal the circumstance where it was possible. Other members of the Order were placed in English families; and also a superior or provincial, through whose means there was continual, direct, and rapid intercourse with their General at Rome. All this was but partially known, even to the Catholic families where those priests resided; but their system of proselyting was zealously pursued, and every impediment attempted to be taken out of the way, while their well-laid and cautious plans were carefully concealed; and it was scarcely known that any confessor, in any family, did more than the simple duties of his humble station.

Frequent confession was one of those duties most strongly urged by Dormer; and, ere a week had passed, after old Elliston's departure, each member of the family, except Maria, had confessed to him. Maria confessed not—neither did she join in that admiration of Dormer's sanctity, which was the constant theme in her family whenever he was not present: neither did she listen to him as an oracle when she was: and though she saw that he carefully sought an opportunity to converse with her alone, she, with equal care, avoided giving him one. She was not insensible, however, to the energy and zeal with which he had commenced his care of souls, not only at Hallern Castle, but at the village, and wherever any one resided, however poor, or in the meanest hovel, in the neighbourhood. Dormer had already visited them all—appointed different houses, where the old and infirm, or sickly, might with ease come to him to confess. Particular times were set apart for one or other mode of instruction in the Romish faith: in short, nothing was heard of at the Castle, or in the village, or amongst the cottagers, but the zeal and sanctity of the new chaplain. The extreme strictness of his personal devotion was guessed to be equal to his zeal for the souls of his flock,—but of this he made no display. It was known only to himself and to his God. No inmate of the Castle, however, though perhaps detained to a late hour out of bed, ever saw the light in Dormer's window extinguished; and the attendant who performed the few services he required, however early he offered them in the morning, found him already at study or devotion. Maria knew all this, yet still was grave and cold when appealed to by the other members of her family, to join in praise of Dormer. Her mother ascribed this coldness to her grief at parting from her old friend Mr Elliston: but Dormer seemed to judge more truly; and seeing all his efforts to obtain a private conversation fail, at last, in his usual manner of gentle, but calm authority, said one morning, as the family were retiring from the breakfast room, and Maria had inadvertently remained the last:

"Daughter, I must beg of you to allow me a few moments' conversation with you."

Maria stopt, and became as pale as death.

"I feel rather surprised, Miss Clarenham," said Dormer mildly, but with great seriousness, "that, of all the souls committed to my charge at Hallern, you should seem most careless of those things necessary to your salvation. I cannot feel that I am fulfilling my duty here, unless I warn you of the danger of such carelessness. I must ask you, daughter, whether you confessed to Father Dennis immediately previous to his leaving the Castle?"

"I did not, Father. I intended to do so, but always found him engaged with some one else at the time I wished to confess."

"Strange!" said Dormer. "Surely Father

Dennis"—he stopt—then asked how long it was since she had confessed?

Maria hesitated. "Not for a very long time, Father. The truth is," added she, a little recovered from her alarm at finding herself at last compelled to have a private conversation with Dormer,—"the truth is, Father, that I have ever had the greatest repugnance to confession. I could scarcely overcome it with good old Father Dennis, whom I regarded as a parent."

"That repugnance is sinful, my daughter; and, like other sins, the more you indulge it, the more difficulty you will find in subduing it."

"But, Father, if I confess my sins to God? —He only can pardon them."

"God pardons those in his Church through the medium of his priests, daughter. The Church says expressly—'A penitent person can have no remission of sins but by supplication to the priest.'

"Does the Bible say so, Father?"

Dormer looked surprised, but said mildly—"I am not in the habit of hearing it asked whether the Church is supported by any authority in its decrees but its own."

"But if the Church decrees what is contrary to the Bible?"

Dormer looked still more surprised. "You are on dangerous ground, daughter. I have suspected that some serious error withheld you from attending to your Christian duties. I now perceive the cause of your unwillingness to confess; but beware, my daughter, of suffering your heart to be hardened by unbelieving thoughts regarding the power of the Church. Remember that Christ Himself said to his apostles,—'Whose soever sins ye remit, they are remitted;' and also, 'whose soever sins ye retain, they are retained.' That power is still in the Church; and how awful must the state of that person be, on whose own guilty head the Church retains his sins."

These words, but still more, the solemn tone in which Dormer pronounced them, made Maria cold all over, and her limbs tremble.

Dormer perceived the impression his words had made, and continued: "How dangerous, my daughter, is the very first step in error! Some enemy of the truth has sown the poisonous seed of unbelief in your heart. I have seen you, daughter, delighted with the cavils of a heretic. I have seen you turn looks of contempt on the pictures of those saints who now reign in heaven: and, last of all, you have scorned the ministrations of the priest commissioned by the Church to teach you the way of life. Daughter, you ought to tremble."

Maria, however, trembled no longer; but looking at Dormer with an expression of restored calmness and elevation—"That enemy of the truth, Father," said she, "who has sown the poisonous seed of unbelief in the power of the Church, in my soul, is the Bible! Those words of the heretic, to which I listened with delight, were words from the Bible; and knowledge of the Bible has taught me to look with contempt on those pictures—those idols which the Bible has forbidden: and I have not confessed to a priest, because there is no command in the Bible to confess to a priest; and because the Bible says none can forgive sins but God. Those apostles, to whom Christ imparted the power of remitting and retaining sins, also received the Holy Ghost, by whose power alone they always professed to act, and by whom they wrote those Scriptures, by the belief or disbelief of which our sins are still remitted or retained."

The exertion of making this confession almost overpowered Maria, and she sank, pale and trembling, on the nearest seat. Dormer did not utter a word; but, after looking for a moment or two at her agitated countenance, turned from her, and walked slowly, and appearing unconscious of what he did, towards a window, where he stood for some minutes in deep thought. Maria also thought deeply and painfully. The consequences of the avowal she had made rose before her,—above all, her mother's sorrow: for well she knew how deep-rooted her devotion was to the Romish Church; and she was on the point of intreating Dormer not to impart to her mother what she had revealed to him, when he returned from the window, to the place where she still sat.

"Miss Clarenham," said he, "are you aware of the terms on which you are considered the eldest daughter in your family?"

"I am, Father," replied Maria, "but confess I did not expect to hear *you* remind me of a circumstance so altogether worldly at this moment."

Dormer reddened.

"I know, Father," continued Maria, "that my uncle left his fortune to the eldest daughter of my father, provided that, on her coming of age, she declared herself a Roman Catholic. I know that I must forfeit that fortune if I leave the church, or marry any but a Catholic, or at any time change my faith. I know all this, Father; but the Bible says, 'What shall it profit a man if he gain the whole world, and lose his own soul?'"

"True, indeed:" said Dormer emphatically. He then asked whether the Bible Maria had learnt so much from was an English one?

"It is," replied Maria.

"But you surely must know, Miss Clarenham, that the English Bible is so translated as to favour the Protestant heresy, with regard to those passages respecting which Protestants are at variance with the Church of Rome."

"I thought so, Father," replied Maria; and, until Basil's return, I supposed those passages which seemed to me to give a character so different to the true church, from that in which I had been educated, must have been changed by Protestants; but since Basil's return, I asked him to translate some of those passages literally from the Greek, for me. He has also told me the translation of the church; but allowed, that, as far as he knew, the same words, when occurring in profane authors, were never translated as the church translated them."

"I should like to know some of those passages you mentioned to him?" said Dormer.

"I have mentioned several," replied Maria. "For instance, some of those which the church translates—'Do penance:' and from which our clergy assume the right of enjoining penances. The English Bible translates the word—'Repent;' and Basil says, that is the universal meaning put upon the word, except by the church."

"It may," replied Dormer; "but the church, in her heavenly wisdom, has given a depth of meaning to that word which the common translation cannot convey. 'Do penance,' includes both the internal and external act of repentance."

"Very often only the external act, I assure you, Father," said Maria.

Dormer's thoughts seemed absent, while he now conversed with Maria. He looked half displeased, half sad.

"And so your brother has been your assistant in learning error?" said he at last, sighing heavily as he spoke.

"He has answered my questions," replied Maria, "but he is still devoted to the church."

"Still!" replied Dormer, fixing his eyes on Maria, as if to read her very soul; "but you hope he too will soon be perverted. You perhaps know of plans for his perversion, as there probably have been for yours."

"I know of no plan, Father," replied Maria, "but to induce him to read the Bible. That is my plan. O Father!" added she earnestly, "Surely that church must be in error which shuts up the word of God from the people."

"You are now intimate with the Protestant Bible, daughter," said Dormer. "Do you remember the words of Christ, 'Upon this rock will I build my church, and the gates of hell shall not prevail against it?'"

"I do, Father."

"Do you believe them?"

"Assuredly."

"Yet you seem disposed to be led astray by the errors of Protestants. Now where was the Protestant church two hundred years ago." If the gates of hell never were to prevail against the true church, where had it vanished to for the fourteen hundred years before it came to light in the form of the Protestant Church?"

Maria hesitated, and then remained silent; for she could not answer the question.

Dormer stood patiently before her, waiting for her reply.

"Father, I cannot tell where it was," said Maria.

"Neither can Protestants," answered Dormer; an expression of pleasure brightening his countenance. "And will you, daughter, lightly conclude that the Catholic Church can be in error—that church which has descended regularly from the apostles—which has been the mother of martyrs and saints innumerable; and against which the machinations of a thousand heresies have never prevailed?"

"Father," replied Maria, "You must be aware that in that *Church* alone, situated as I am, can I look for this world's happiness. My mother is devoted to it. My whole family are so. If I leave it I shall be without fortune. I shall be regarded in my own home as an alien from all they love and value in this world, and from the hopes of heaven. If you will convince me, Father, that ours is the true church of the Bible, I shall not cease to thank God for the day in which you were sent to Hallern: but though I cannot answer your last question, neither can I, at the command of the church, part with the Bible; for it is impossible for me to believe that the true church would prevent its members from knowing and searching the revealed will of God."

"The church does not prevent her children from knowing the revealed will of God, daughter; she only guides them, particularly the young and ignorant, into the right meaning of that will. Is it possible, daughter," added Dormer, with extreme gentleness, "that you can suppose the meaning, which you, almost a child, and almost on a first reading, put on the words of Inspiration, can be equally just with that which has been the result of the study of councils, and fathers, and martyrs of the church?"

"Perhaps I ought not, Father."

"Most assuredly you ought not, indeed, daughter."

"I shall then, if you please, Father, consult you on those passages which do not appear to me to agree with what is taught by our church."

"Would it not be better for you, daughter, humbly to receive those instructions from Scripture which the church thinks fit to impart to the young and weak in the faith?"

"Father, you must allow me to think over this in private."

"I would indulge you, daughter, with pleasure, did I think it for your soul's good; but you have already trusted too much to your private judgment. That judgment has led you into much presumptuous error. Could I be performing my duty, as your spiritual father, if I left you to be further misled by it?"

"What then, Father, must I do?"

"You must return from the error of your

ways, and again submit to the holy guidance of the church."

"I desire to do so," said Maria, breathing a deep sigh as she spoke.

"Not with your whole heart, I perceive, daughter."

"Father, are you permitted to read the whole Bible, as freely as you choose?"

"I am," replied Dormer. "Every priest is."

"And in reading it, Father, do you always find your judgment agree with that of the church?"

"I think, daughter, that question tends more to the gratification of idle curiosity than to profit," replied Dormer, with some severity.

"No! no, indeed, Father!" said Maria earnestly, and her eyes filling with tears; "Nor would I care what answer some who are considered saints might give to my question; but if you would condescend to answer me, Father, perhaps I might attempt to do what you have found succeed with yourself."

Dormer seemed doubtful of complying with her request. At last he said, gently, "I desire your confidence on religious subjects, my daughter. I begin to hope, too, that your errors have proceeded less from presumption than from a real interest on the subject of religion; and an earnest, but ill-directed desire for knowledge. This desire is most natural, particularly in youth; but it is also most dangerous, if without an infallible guide. In answer to your question,—Priests do not receive permission to read the Scriptures freely, till they have sworn their belief respecting the proper interpretation of them. Every priest does so on his entering into holy orders; and also takes a most solemn oath, not only that he himself thus believes, but that he will maintain, defend, and teach the same to the people under his charge."

"And what is your belief respecting the proper interpretation of Scripture, Father?"

"I have sworn solemnly, that I do admit the Holy Scriptures, in the sense that holy Mother Church doth, whose business it is to judge of the true sense and interpretation of them. These are the words of the vow which every priest takes on this point."

"And if your judgment differs from the church, Father?"

"I know it errs, daughter, and seek earnestly to bring it into subjection."

"And does it ever differ?" asked Maria earnestly.

"But too frequently. Pride, and arrogance, and self-will, are too natural to every heart: but the church does not leave us ignorant of those methods by which such sins may be mortified and subdued."

Maria gratefully thanked Dormer for having answered her question; and then begged him to point out the course she ought to pursue.

"I think, daughter, in order to mortify that anxiety for knowledge, which has led you for a time to cast off the authority of the church, I must insist on your first delivering to me that English Bible, which you have so misunderstood as to wrest some of its passages, as 'the ignorant and unlearned,' always do, to lead you into the path of destruction."

Maria started. All that Adeline had ever said to her on the necessity of keeping up the Scriptures from the people, if their Priests would prevent their leaving the Romish Church, flashed upon her memory. Dormer, however, did not seem to observe her, and proceeded,—

"I know not from whom you received that Bible: but those who are so anxious to distract the church, by introducing their heresies into her bosom, ought to show first their own title to the name of a church. But I shall know more of all this, daughter, when I receive your confession, which I shall be ready to do before mass to-morrow morning. And now," added he gently, "do not detain me. I shall wait till your return, but must meet my poor people a quarter of an hour hence." He then turned away, and Maria left the room; and, hurrying to her own, opened her most secret depository, and from thence took her small Protestant Bible. This Bible she had got without the knowledge of any one—not even of Adeline Montague.

There was in the village of Illerton a small shop, which contained a great variety of very heterogeneous goods for sale. This shop was kept by a Protestant, an excellent pious man: and the Rector of Illerton, and Dr Lowther, took care that one part of it should be appropriated to a good stock of Bibles, which the man was directed to dispose of to whosoever should wish for them, without asking any questions. Of this Maria had been informed by Adeline, and soon after had written for a New Testament, and sent a half-ideot boy to fulfil her commission, she herself waiting for him as near the place as she dared venture to be seen. This had happened about a month before Dormer's arrival at Hallern Castle; and every spare moment since that time had Maria spent in reading this heavenly, but forbidden treasure. At first, she had done so with a feeling of guilt; but that feeling had soon given place to others of a far different character—to anxiety respecting the safety of her soul—to doubts which soon arose to certainty, that, if the word of God was truth, she had been educated in gross error. To love and adoration of that Saviour, of whom she read there all that was calculated to draw the sinner to trust his salvation simply, joyfully to Him—but of whom she had heard in her own church, as a Saviour indeed, and as the son of God—but as a distant Saviour—One whose death had purchased, for those who were baptized, salvation from the sin of their natures, and grace, with which, if they used it aright, they might work out their own salvation,—a Saviour who would be more propitious, if approached through other mediators. Of all this she found nothing in the New Testament; and now these thoughts, and the character she had there found of that all-glorious Saviour, returned to her recollection with overwhelming force. She, however, could not stop. Dormer's mild, earnest, sincere, and authoritative manner, and, above all, the confidence he had reposed in her, could not be resisted; and, taking the sacred little volume, she hurried back to the apartment where Dormer waited for her. The words of St Paul to the Galatians, "Though we, or an angel from heaven, preach any other gospel unto you than that which we have preached unto you, let him be accursed,"—returned to her recollection. "How, then," thought she, "dare any church preach things as matters of faith, so absolutely different from what St Paul preached, as our church does?" Her hand was on the lock of the door as she thought thus; and, while she paused, she heard Dormer's step approaching within. He opened the door. " Daughter, I thought I should have been obliged to go before your return." He held out his hand for the Bible, saying, " Do not be late to-morrow morning. I may have much to say to you."

Maria put the Bible into his hand, saying, in a voice almost inaudible from emotion, " Father, if I sin in parting with this, my sin must be on you."

" Fear not," replied Dormer, with extreme gentleness: " Humility, submission to the church, cannot be sin." He then put the little volume in his pocket, bowed, and left her.

Maria instantly hastened to her own room—locked her door—and, kneeling down in the place where she for some time previous had knelt to read her Bible, she covered her face, and burst into an agony of tears. She could not pray, however; for He to whom she had been learning to pray, in the language and spirit of the New Testament, she had given up—had forsaken. She had consented to deprive herself of that pure instruction, which she had learnt from his own blessed word, and which she had felt so powerfully effectual, and again to subject her mind to the guidance of a fellow-sinner. She remembered the words of Christ, " In vain do they worship me, teaching for doctrines the commandments of men;" and she recollected that those observances most insisted on in the Romish Church, were only 'commandments of men,' and without any authority whatever from Scripture. Such was confession to a priest, on which Dormer so determinately insisted. On this point Maria had searched her New Testament with the most persevering earnestness; and from its beginning to its close, had found—not one precept—not one injunction—not one single word on the subject. The only passage which seemed even to have a reference to it, was the following from St. James :—" Confess your faults, one to another, and pray, one for another, that ye may be healed;"*—and here no priest, no minister of religion was mentioned. The injunction was addressed to all believers. With

* James v. 16.

regard to confession of sin to God, and His method of remission, all, on the other hand, was clear and simple. "If we say we have no sin, we deceive ourselves, and the truth is not in us. If we confess our sins, God is faithful and just to forgive us our sins, and to cleanse us from all unrighteousness."*—"My little children, these things write I unto you, that ye sin not. And if any man sin, we have an Advocate with the Father, Jesus Christ the righteous; and He is the propitiation for our sins." †—"The blood of Jesus Christ cleanseth from all sin."‡

As Maria remembered these words, they were as a healing balm to her agitated spirit. She wrote them down, and recalling other passages to the same effect, wrote all she distinctly remembered; and now they seemed more than ever precious.

"I have sinned, grievously sinned," thought she. "How shall I approach that Holy God, whose word I have put away from me, even when I was feeling its sacred power? I have

* 1st Epistle of John i. 8. † 1 John ii. 1.
‡ 1 John i. 7.

an Advocate with the Father—an Advocate whom the Father heareth always—an Advocate who has himself suffered as a propitiation for my sins, whose blood cleanseth from all sin."

Maria was soon again on her knees; and, while she confessed, and searched her heart, that she might not leave one sinful thought or wish unconfessed, she felt how suitable, how attractive, how softening and purifying that way of returning to God was which he himself had appointed;—how sweet the peace which followed;—how calm and secure that state of mind in which God alone was exalted and glorified; and the sinful spirit relying in love and confidence on His word alone for His promised cleansing and forgiveness;—how wonderful the fulfilment of that promise in the taking away of the sense of guilt, and in restoring peace, and strength, and activity to the soul.

"Never shall I confess to any but God," said Maria, as she rose from her knees. She then sat down to write. "I must find an answer to Father Clement's question. I shall not again venture to converse with him. He is in the habit of ruling and commanding. He overawes me,—and yet he surely is sincere. He struggles to resist those doubts which rise in his mind. He believes, or seeks earnestly to believe, all he asks me to believe; and, if *he* seeks to subject his powerful mind to what the higher teachers of the church impose, shall I dare to use my poor judgment?"

Maria was staggered by this consideration, till she again recollected some passages in her precious New Testament. It was *the poor* to whom the gospel was effectually preached—the poor in spirit. It was the *common people* who heard Christ gladly. The Scribes and Pharisees, and teachers of the people, rejected Him. It was of them Christ had given that character which struck her as so forcibly applying to her own clergy—"They taught for commandments the doctrines of men,"—and, therefore, he pronounced their worship to be "vain!" It was they of whom Christ had said, "They made the commandments of God of none effect, by their traditions."* "O!" thought Maria, "if

* Matth. xv. 6.

Christ was now on earth, what could he say more applicable to our church?"—She remembered, too, that Christ had returned thanks to God, "Because He had hidden those things from the wise and prudent, and had revealed them unto babes."

All these recollections, however, did not assist Maria in finding an answer to Dormer's question,—"Where was the Protestant Church two centuries before?" All her knowledge of history could not furnish her with this answer. She had, indeed, learned from thence,—though Elliston had, from her childhood, been the only person from whom she was suffered to receive books,—that her church had found it necessary to combat heresy by force of arms; and, when she had read St Paul's words, "The weapons of our warfare are not carnal, but mighty, through God, to the pulling down of strongholds; casting down imaginations, and every high thing that exalteth itself against the knowledge of God, and bringing into captivity every thought to the obedience of Christ;"*—when

* 2 Cor. x. 4, 5.

she read that description of St. Paul's method of warring with error, she could not suppress her feelings of indignant contempt for the empty pretensions of her own church, which, having no power from God to bring down strong holds, of what they called error, or to bring any thought into the obedience of what they called truth, fought *only* with carnal weapons to any effect, and made war only after the flesh,—yet she could not venture to meet Dormer on this ground. At last, after in vain attempting herself to find any answer to his question, it struck her, that, though Dormer had said Protestants could not answer it, he could only mean, in such a way as to convince Roman Catholics; for, otherwise, so many good and sensible people could not remain Protestants. No sooner had this idea struck her, than she determined to apply to Dr Lowther for a solution of her difficulty: and, full of this plan, she soon after, with a mind almost at ease, obeyed the summons to meet the other members of the family at dinner.

All stood round the dinner table, while Father Clement said rather a long grace, in a tone of voice and attitude of deep devotion—but it was in Latin; and Maria ventured to thank God for his continued bounty, in her heart, and in the language in which she thought and spoke.

"I have not seen you all the morning, Maria," said Mrs Clarenham. "Have you been visiting your cousins?"

"No, mamma. I have been in my own room all the morning. I have been very deeply engaged there. I shall, if you please, tell you regarding what at another time."

Maria glanced at Dormer as she spoke.

"Miss Clarenham has, I believe, been very properly engaged this morning," said Dormer.

"I rejoice to hear you say so, Father," said Mrs Clarenham, looking affectionately at Maria.

That kind and confiding look brought tears into Maria's eyes, and it was with difficulty she could swallow what she had taken on her plate.

Dormer seemed to observe her emotion, and changing the subject, soon attracted every one's attention away from her. She felt grateful to him; but this rather added to the difficulty she felt in overcoming the saddening thoughts which crowded on her mind. Dormer's conversation, however, increased in interest; and, at last, she completely forgot all other subjects while listening to him. He seemed particularly anxious to gain her attention; and, though there was, as there ever was, a constant something in his manner, and in all he said, which reminded others that he was of a different class of beings, so to speak, separated from common feelings, and common sympathies; and also that he expected, as a matter of course, to guide in all opinions which were in any way whatever connected with religion, —yet, on this day, he was so unusually cheerful—so animated—and discovered so much skill in drawing those he addressed into interesting and agreeable conversation, that even Maria felt regret, when at last, with apparent reluctance, he rose to leave the circle, on discovering that the hour was come for one of his many ministrations amongst his poor.

"And I, too, am forgetting an appointment," said Basil, "and also a message to you,

Maria. I promised to spend this afternoon at Illerton; and also to persuade you to accompany me."

"I shall go with the greatest pleasure," said Maria, joyfully. She glanced at Dormer, and saw that the expression of his countenance immediately changed.

"I think Mrs Clarenham regretted your absence all the morning," said he gently.

"Yes," replied Maria, hesitatingly.

"Oh, do not mind me, my love," said Mrs Clarenham. "Catherine is at home. I shall not miss you."

"I do not wish to go; only wait, dear Basil, till I write a few lines to Adeline—that will do much better," said Maria. "I shall return with my note in an instant."

Dormer opened the door to let her depart; and, as she passed, said, "You will not regret this self-denial, daughter."

"Oh, Father, I am not acting from the motive you suppose," replied Maria earnestly. "I would not deceive you, Father, for a single moment. I am not in the state of mind you imagine," and she hurried past him to her own apartment, and there wrote to her friend :—

" I intreat you, dearest Adeline, while Basil is with you this evening, to request Dr Lowther to write a short, but strong reply for me to the following question,—' Where was the Protestant Church two hundred years ago?' Tell dear, excellent, kind Dr Lowther, that I venture to intrude on his precious time to give me this answer, because I have learnt from the Protestant Bible, that a minister of Christ is instructed by his Lord to be ' patient, and apt to teach,'—and I am sure he is a true and faithful servant of his Divine Master.

" Ever yours, M. C."

Maria delivered her note to Basil, and took his promise that he would not return without bringing her an answer.

When again left with her mother and Catherine, they began, as usual, to praise Dormer.

" Surely," said Mrs Clarenham, " we shall all have much to answer for, if we do not benefit by the instructions of a spiritual director so highly gifted."

"Maria seems at last to have discovered his merits," observed Catherine; "and he seems wonderfully anxious to obtain her regard and confidence." Catherine said this with some displeasure of manner.

"A good shepherd tries to make the fold pleasant to all his lambs," said Mrs Clarenham, soothingly.

"And those poor lambs, who already love it, and have given up all for it, must be satisfied without the kindness of the shepherd, I suppose," replied Catherine, an indignant tear starting into her eye.

"Catherine! my love! Is it possible you can feel any thing but pleasure in seeing Father Clement's anxiety to gain that place in your sister's confidence which has hitherto been possessed by Father Dennis? He cannot disapprove of her regret at parting from her kind old confessor. He knows you have been less at home, and were, consequently, less attached to our good old friend; he has, therefore, found no difficulty in supplying his place to you. Surely he is most right and kind in trying, by such winning gentleness, to lead your sister to confide in him as the guide of her soul,—the appointed shepherd over his little persecuted flock."

"Ah," said Maria, "he is a poor shepherd for souls, who has not love, and attention, and kindness enough to satisfy all the flock. Dear mamma—dear Catherine—there is but one Shepherd, who is *Infinite* in all these—infinite in love—infinite in compassion—infinite in tenderness—infinite in power—ever present. Surely, surely, mamma, we Catholics subject our minds too decidedly to the guidance of our fellow-sinners?"

"Fellow-sinners!" repeated Mrs Clarenham with astonishment. "We do not subject our minds to the guidance of sinful men, my love, but as they are ordained and commissioned by that church which cannot err. It is to the church we submit, my dear. You seem getting into strange errors."

"And what is the church, mamma, but a number of men and women, redeemed by Christ, and prepared, by His sanctifying Spirit, gradually overcoming their sinful natures, to abide for ever with Him ?"

"Well, my love, allowing it to be so ?"

"Well, mamma, how can any of that sinful number be infallible ?"

"They are not infallible as individuals, my dear, but from situation. Infallibility was bestowed on the rulers of the church by Christ, and does not depend on the character of those who fill the situation."

"Do not the rulers of our church appeal to Scripture for the truth of all that, mamma ?"

"Assuredly, my love."

"But mamma, did it never strike you, that it looks very like a system of—what shall I call it ? deception—a design to keep up something they are conscious they have no very plain authority for in Scripture, their making it a point of conscience that none but priests—none but those whose interest it is to keep up the delusion, shall read, and judge of those Scriptures on which they pretend to build their authority ?"

Here Catherine rose from her seat. "Mamma, may I ask your permission to retire ?" said she, formally. "It is painful to me to hear Maria talk in that manner."

"You had better put me right, then, Catherine," observed Maria, smiling.

"No," said Mrs Clarenham, "we shall leave that to Father Clement—and you need not leave the room, Catherine, for such conversation is also very painful to me. I have had too much of it to-day. Basil talked in the same strain to me for more than an hour before dinner. One or two conversations with his cousin, Ernest Montague, seems to have regained to him that influence over the mind of your brother, which he had so completely established when they were boys; and, to do away which, I consented to be separate from my only son for five years. What may happen next I dread to think."

"Do you mean on the subject of religion, mamma?" asked Maria.

"Certainly, my dear. On what other subject could I dread Ernest Montague's influence? On every other point, I know of no young man who bears so high a character—one at least which I consider so."

"Perhaps the ascendency you mention, mamma, is the ascendency of truth over error?"

"You pay a compliment to my judgment when you say so, certainly, Maria," replied Mrs Clarenham. "I, too, have a very dear friend, who is a Protestant. Often, often have we discussed, and argued, and differed, but never has Protestant truth overcome my Catholic errors. I hoped my children would have been equally steady to their faith—I begin to dread the reverse."

"Mamma, may I ask you one question?"

"Certainly, my love."

"Is there a single individual, Catholic or Protestant, in the whole circle of your acquaintance, whom, putting her religion—the principle from which she acts, out of view—you think, in every point, more truly good and amiable than Lady Montague?"

"I will answer you at once, my love: there is not. And I will not ask you to put her religion out of view, for Lady Montague's character could not be what it is on any other principles than those of the Christian religion. Humility—that is, a real, ever-present sense of unworthiness and weakness; earnest, devoted love to God her Saviour; and a singleness of purpose to do His will, and seek His glory in all she does,—are the leading and principal features of her character, and become more and more so every day."

Here Catherine rose and left the room.

"Your sister loves not to hear me thus praise a heretic," continued Mrs Clarenham; "but I cannot in justice answer your question otherwise."

"And, dear mamma, may I ask you one other question?"

"Whatever you will, love."

"Do you really believe, then, mamma, that Lady Montague, loving God so devotedly—so humbly trusting in Christ—so single-hearted in seeking to obey Him—so kind to all—so unboundedly charitable to the poor,—do you believe that, because she cannot, when she reads the Scriptures for herself, perceive those grounds on which our church claims to be the only true and infallible church, and therefore rejects her pretensions; and will receive no doctrines, taught by her, which she finds not in the

Scriptures—do you believe that, for thus closely adhering to the revelation from God, she will perish for ever?"

"I hope, my dear, that, before she is called to another state, she may be led to see her error in this, and return into the bosom of the true church."

"But if not, mamma?"

"My love, you will believe me when I tell you, that, respecting one I so dearly love, I have often, often anxiously attempted to find an answer to that question. Father Dennis always evaded giving me a direct one, which I knew proceeded from his unwillingness to pain me, but which plainly showed me his opinion. I have already consulted Father Clement on the subject. He read to me the decision of the church on this point, which is, that there is no salvation out of the Roman Catholic faith. He would not enter into the subject farther. To him it seemed extremely painful; and he urged me not to seek to draw aside that veil which God had, in mercy, placed between us and the future, but to pray earnestly and perseveringly for my friend, and leave the rest to God."

"But, dear mamma, it is not God who draws that veil over the future, on a subject so interesting and momentous. The word of God says expressly, that those who believe in Christ shall never perish; and St Paul exhorts those, whose friends have fallen asleep in Jesus, not to mourn as those who have no hope—for, 'When Christ shall appear, they shall appear with him in glory.' And the possession of that 'faith which worketh by love,' is the only character given of that person's state, who, in the New Testament, is considered a child of God. Indeed, indeed mamma, our church teaches many painful things which are not contained in the Bible."

"My dear child," said Mrs Clarenham affectionately, "I intreat you to guard against that self-sufficiency so natural to young people. You have learnt a few passages of Scripture from your cousins, and suppose you are now capable to judge of matters the most profoundly difficult and mysterious. Open your whole mind to Father Clement. Have no reserves with him in spiritual matters. You will soon learn, my love, that you are a mere babe in knowledge. But we shall speak no more on this subject."

Maria submitted with reluctance to this prohibition, for no other subject had now any interest for her; and the time seemed unusually long, while, with her thoughts constantly returning to it, she attempted to converse on other matters.

When the evening had nearly closed, she seated herself near a window to watch for Basil's return; but though she continued straining her eyes, that she might see his approach from the most distant verge of the park—twilight, and then bright moonlight, succeeded, ere she saw any living creature cross the lonely distance. At last two figures slowly approached, their long shadows for a time leaving her uncertain whether there were not many more. They frequently stopped, and seemed in earnest conversation. They thus continued approaching, and then stopping to converse, till they were within a few steps of the house, when one of the two, after showing, by the energy of his gesticulations, that the subject on which they conversed had been of deep interest, shook hands warmly with his companion, and, turning back, hastened across the park. The other stood looking after him.

"It is Basil," said Maria, as she left the room to meet him, and receive the anxiously-looked-for answer to her question from Dr Lowther. Basil was slowly coming up the steps, as she opened the hall door.

"How late you are, dear Basil. Have you brought an answer for me? Who was that who came so far with you?"

I have brought an answer—It was my friend—it was Ernest Montague who came with me. Here is your answer."

Maria eagerly took it, and retired to her own apartment. It was a large packet; and, on opening it, she found a note from Adeline—a letter from Dr Lowther—and a New Testament.

Maria melted into tears on opening the last. It seemed as if it had been sent by a forgiving God; and she instantly knelt down, and returned her ardent thanks—then carefully depositing it where she had kept the one she had given up, she opened Dr Lowther's letter, which was as follows:—

"Do not ask, my dear Miss Clarenham, where the *Protestant* Church was two hundred years ago, but ask, where is to be found the character of that church which God himself has declared to be the true church—that church, which in spirit and in truth worships Him. The true church, my dear young lady, must ever bear one and the same character. God has not left us without ample means to know what that character is. His spirit has, in the Scriptures of truth, most plainly described it: and though various denominations of men assume to themselves the exclusive claim to it, that description of the character of those who alone compose it is still the same, and will try all pretensions at that day when each of us shall stand at the judgment-seat of Christ.

"Protestant, my dear young lady, is merely a name which was attached at the beginning of the sixteenth century, (1529,) to those Christians who protested against the unscriptural corruptions of the Church of Rome. Such witnesses for the truth have existed ever since it was first preached; and the apostate Church of Rome has the blood of thousands, and tens of thousands, of such to answer for, at the great day of account: Yet that fallen church, with the whole power of which she was once in possession, has not prevailed against the truth.

"I know, my dear Miss Clarenham, that the question you have applied to me to answer is made a difficulty, by the Romish clergy, in the way of those who begin to perceive the want of Scripture authority for many of the doctrines of the Church of Rome. Her priests cannot produce authority from Scripture: they therefore appeal to tradition and antiquity, and thus, in many cases, find a short and easy method to stop all further inquiry. For what a task presents itself, if it is necessary, before deciding on this important point, to get acquainted with the controversies of fourteen centuries. To a female this is impossible. I think very few words will be sufficient, however, to convince you how weak that religious cause must be, which grounds its chief claim on antiquity. If antiquity be a proof of truth, the pretensions of Mahomet are just about the same in antiquity with those of the Bishop of Rome to supremacy over the other Christian churches. Both began in the seventh century: and the superstition of Mahomet is of far higher antiquity than many of the doctrines now taught as a part of the creed necessary to salvation by the Romish church. The mass and purgatory are two of those lately-discovered doctrines.

"Again: If numbers, unity, and power to suppress, by persecution to death, the profession of a different belief, proves that any set of men are in possession of the truth, all these can, in a greater degree, be claimed by the followers of Mahomet than by the Church of Rome. How absurd then is it to claim the character of the true church, on grounds so altogether unsubstantial, and which may equally be urged by the worst systems of delusion! How much more absurd, when those very Scriptures, on which the Romish Church rests her first claim to the very character of a church, are in the hands of those who oppose her apostasies and corruptions, and prove their accusations from those very Scriptures, while she finds it necessary to her very existence to prevent her people from reading those Scriptures.

"Your spiritual guide will probably tell you, my dear young lady, that the Church of Rome has transmitted the truth in a direct line from the Apostles, particularly from St Peter, who, he will tell you, was Bishop of Rome, and imparted the power he received from Christ to his successors,—the Bishops of Rome. Protestants allow of none of all this. They even defy the Romish Church to prove that St Peter was ever bishop or pastor at Rome: and Protestants, my dear Miss Clarenham, are quite as learned, and as capable of discerning the truth, as Roman Catholics are.

"Perhaps I ought to remind a Catholic that there is but one way of coming to the truth on such points—that of historic evidence. The Romish Church no longer ventures to appeal to miracles in arguing with Protestants. Such deceptions are now confined to convents, or to the most ignorant of their own people. On this historic evidence, Protestants positively deny that the Church of Rome has for many centuries,—and, on the knowledge of its present state,—that it does now, bear any resemblance to the primitive church; and, in proof of this, appeal only to the account of the primitive Church given in the New Testament : and the clergy of the church of Rome subject themselves to strong suspicions, when they refuse their people the right of judging of their pretensions by that rule. Protestant clergy desire to be judged by no other.

"You must, I think, my dear Miss Clarenham, perceive in what very different situations this places the Protestant and the Popish pastor. The Protestant teacher appeals,—for the truth of all he inculcates, for his title to demand your belief, and for authority to demand your obedience,—to the word of God. The Popish pastor appeals only to the authority of his church, or of the Scriptures as explained by that church. And what is the church according to a Roman Catholic priest? Ask your spiritual guide this question. He may not, however, chuse to tell you, that whatever unity may be demanded from the people with regard to the reception of those doctrines which the rulers of the Romish church have agreed to impose upon them, there is no unity amongst those rulers themselves regarding the answer to this question. Where does the authority and infallibility of the church of Rome reside? Some of the clergy assert that it resides in the pope; others, in general councils approved by the pope; and others, in general councils, whether approven of by the Pope or not. But to prove that the rulers of the Romish church do not themselves really believe that infallibility resides in any of these: —Popes with councils have rejected the decrees of preceding Popes with councils: Popes without councils have done the same; and also councils without Popes. Yet, my dear Miss Clarenham, this undefined infallibility, this imposing delusion, is what your spiritual guide asks you to subject your mind to instead of those Scriptures which all your clergy allow to be a revelation from God. Read these Scriptures, my dear young lady: Read them for yourself. They are not addressed only to the learned. Were they so, a very large number of those priests of the Romish Church, to whom the guidance of souls is committed, ought to be excluded from their perusal; for any well-educated person,—your brother, Mrs Clarenham, you yourself,—are, I am sure, far better informed than many of them are. Do not be imposed on by high-sounding pretensions. Were you, my dear Miss Clarenham, really and intimately acquainted with the Bible, and had imbibed its pure and unearthly spirit, the whole structure of the Church of Rome would appear to you, as it does to all Bible Christians, a system of the grossest worldliness, supported by earthly power,—made attractive by earthly splendour,—governing by earthly means,—holding out earthly lures to the ambition of its ministers; and, the higher they attain in its rank, surrounding them with more and more of what is altogether earthly, until at last they reach that preëminence of gross earthliness, where we find him, who styles himself the head of the Church, the vicar of Christ, the representative of Him 'who had not where to lay his head,'—in the most gorgeous of palaces,—the representative of Him 'who is of purer eyes than to behold iniquity,' surrounded by all that painting and sculpture can represent, addressed to depraved sense,—all that heathen art could do to clothe in attraction the crimes of their idols, or the real abominations of men whom they had deified. Thus surrounded, the head of the Romish Church reigns over her; and is regarded by Bible Christians as the most deplorable of all self-deceivers,—as the weak instrument of the prince of darkness,—or as the most profane and audacious of charlatans.

"I inclose you a New Testament. Remember, my dear young lady, that every word in it was inspired by God. The way of salvation revealed in it is the only way revealed by God. It is a plain way: search it yourself. Search first for any commission given by Christ to his Apostles, or by those the Apostles appointed to succeed them in feeding the flock of Christ, by which they are directed to withhold the Scriptures from the people; and when you find St Peter,—he whom your church unscripturally exalts above his brother Apostles,—when you find him saying to those to whom he addressed his first epistle, 'As new-born babes, desire the sincere milk of the word, that you may grow thereby;'—judge yourself whether your spiritual guide holds out the same nourishment for your soul. You have only to ask yourself this question,—'Shall I trust God's own word, as it was written by His inspired servants, to direct me to the knowledge of His character and will; or shall I rather trust to the word of my priest, who tells me he gives me the right meaning of the word of God, but will not allow me to read it for myself, neither can tell me satisfactorily where that infallibility of interpretation resides, on which he insists that I shall rest the salvation of my soul?'

"I intreat you earnestly, my dear Miss Clarenham, to pray to God that He may enable you to make the right choice. I shall join my prayers to yours, that He may enable you to make that choice which is agreeable to his will, and give you strength to abide by it. I commend you to His love and guidance. 'He loves those who love Him;' and has promised in His word, that 'those who seek Him early *shall* find him.' Your sincere friend,

"THOMAS LOWTHER."

Maria read this letter quickly, but with deep attention; her resolution, after finishing it, was soon taken. "I shall certainly not confess," said she; and instantly wrote to Mr Dormer:—

"Forgive me, Father, if I led you to suppose I meant to meet you at confession to-morrow morning. I cannot. I must do what appears to me the will of God, whatever follows. I ought also to inform you, that I have, I think providentially, received another New Testament. I wish not to deceive you, Father. Oh that you would yourself instruct me from that sacred source!

"MARIA CLARENHAM."

It was so late when Maria finished this note, that she every moment expected to hear the bell ring for evening prayers. It did not, however; and she still had time to read Adeline's also:—

"I gave your request to Dr Lowther, dear Maria, and he has just sent his answer to your brother. He tells me that he has sent you a New Testament. Dear Maria, will you read it? I intreat you do. You cannot, I am sure, otherwise understand what Dr Lowther has written. O my dearest friend, how inconceivable it seems to me, that any one should know that there is a revelation from God! the Creator! the Preserver! the Judge of all! and yet rest satisfied without having read, and searched, and earnestly studied that revelation. David said of that small portion of it which existed in his day, that it was 'a lamp to his feet, and a light unto his path;' that 'it converted the soul, and made the simple wise;' that 'the words of the Lord were pure words, as silver tried in a furnace of earth, purified seven times;' and 'were sweeter than honey, and the honey-comb, and rejoiced the heart.' How much fuller and more precious is that revelation in our day!

"Forgive Dr Lowther, dearest Maria, if he has said harsh things of your church. I am afraid he may; as he always, from principle, says what he thinks the truth concerning it, to whomsoever he may mention the subject. Again adieu! dearest Maria. Ever your's,

"Adeline Montague."

Maria had scarcely concluded this note, when the bell rang; and putting up Dr Lowther's letter, and taking her note for Dormer, she hastened to the chapel.

Here all the family, and several of the people who resided near the Castle, were assembled. Dormer, with much devotion of voice and manner, read prayers for about half-an-hour. The people seemed to listen in the posture of worship: but with all, except Basil and Dormer, the heart and understanding were unemployed, for almost every prayer was in Latin. Maria's thoughts were most busily engaged, as probably those of all present were, except Dormer's and Basil's, by the subjects which had been most interesting before worship began.

At last the unprofitable service was finished, and all slowly retired from the chapel.

Dormer rarely joined the family after evening prayers. On this night, as he politely took leave of all, Maria put the note she had written into his hand, and hurried past, that she might avoid answering any question he might ask.

CHAPTER VI.

"Ne vogliate chiamare alcuno sulla terra vostro Padre; imperocche il solo Padre vostro e quegli, che sta ne' cieli."

Martini's Trans.— Matth. xxiii. 9.

During prayers in the chapel next morning, Maria never lifted her eyes: and when afterwards seated at the breakfast table, carefully avoided meeting Dormer's looks. She, however, remarked that he was almost entirely silent. Basil, too, was unusually so; but he sat next to Dormer, and she dared not raise her eyes in that direction to read his looks. Mrs Clarenham and Catherine attempted to draw Dormer into conversation; but though his replies bespoke attention to what they had said, and were in his usual mild tone of voice, yet they were short; and soon the party sunk almost into silence. The instant that breakfast seemed concluded, Dormer rose, and after returning thanks in Latin, requested Mrs Clarenham not to wait dinner should he be absent at the usual hour. He was going, he said, to Sir Thomas

Carysford's, and might be detained till the evening. He then bowed politely to all, and left the room.

"Did you ever see any thing so grave as Father Clement is this morning?" exclaimed Catherine. "You really ought to ask him, mamma, if any thing painful has happened? Perhaps some of the Carysfords are ill."

"Oh no," said Basil, "I am sure they are not. Young Carysford passed the Chapel while we were at prayers. Did you not hear his dogs?"

"I heard dogs, but how could I know they were his?"

"But I saw them from the side window," said Basil. "He galloped past, accompanied by Rowley Montague."

"Young Carysford naturally feels himself at home in our grounds," said Mrs Clarenham, looking at Maria.

Maria rose and turned away. This was a painful subject to her. From her childhood it had been understood in the families of Clarenham and Carysford, that when she should come of age, and, according to her uncle's will, declare herself a Roman Catholic, she was to be, on his making the same declaration, united to the young heir of the Carysfords. While younger, the pleasure with which this union was always hinted at by her own family; the great respect with which all the neighbouring Roman Catholic families regarded the Carysfords; the universal acknowledgment that they were the first family in the country of that faith; their large fortune and high connexions; and the superiority which the confessor in that family assumed over his brother priests,—had dazzled her young imagination, while the unceasing and indulgent kindness with which young Carysford was everywhere received; the interest and anxiety expressed by all concerning him as the future leader of their decreasing party, and their exaggerated details of whatever appeared promising to their cause in his character and conduct,—increased her pride, and gave her a feeling of self-exaltation in the prospect of sharing with him the distinguished place he seemed destined to hold amongst those whose regard she most highly valued. Now, when she looked forward to this hitherto-supposed happy lot, all was changed in her feelings. The prospect had lost many of its attractions; and Carysford's pursuits and character were gradually sinking in her esteem. Her thoughts on the subject, however, were confused and painful; and as it was, she supposed, still two years before she must decide, she generally got rid of them as soon as she could: and now seeing Basil about to leave the room, she followed him into the hall, and putting her arm within his,—

"My dear Basil, is there any thing the matter? Perhaps I can guess one cause for Father Clement's looking so grave—but you—I hope nothing has happened to annoy you?"

"Yes—much, dear Maria." They walked towards the hall door, which was open, and a groom in attendance near it, with a horse for Dormer. "I have displeased Father Clement," continued Basil, "and if you knew what cause I have to love him, you would be able to judge how painful it is to me to do so."

"But is he so unforgiving?"

"Oh no, no. I have his forgiveness—his kindest affection—he is all gentleness and goodness to me, but I see I have deeply distressed him."

"How, dear Basil?"

"Let us go out and I shall tell you all. You, too, Maria, have grieved him."

Dormer himself at this moment approached: "Do not allow me to interrupt you," said he politely, and, passing quickly, mounted his horse, bowed again with an expression of mild kindness in his looks, and then rode off.

We shall leave Basil to tell his story to his sister, and follow Dormer.

There is not, perhaps, a greater contrast in any two states of mind where both are seeking to know and serve God, than between those of a thorough Roman Catholic and a Protestant. So great is the contrast, that it is not wonderful either should be unwilling to allow that the other does indeed worship acceptably, or love acceptably, or serve acceptably, the same God whom he loves and serves. There are some points, however, in which truly pious Catholics, and truly pious Protestants, would they allow themselves to listen candidly to each other, would find they could agree. Each would acknowledge the deep, the profound awe, with which he regarded the character of that "High and Holy One who inhabiteth eternity." Each would allow, that, at times, his inmost soul trembled at the remembrance of his holiness—his justice—his power—his omniscience. Each would acknowledge, that, in his own eyes, he was utterly unholy; and conscious that, if God should enter into judgment with him, he could not answer for one of a thousand of his thoughts, his words, or actions. They would also find, that, to both, the character of God was infinitely, adorably attractive. That those very attributes, the remembrance of which made them tremble, still appeared to them altogether lovely and excellent, and that they esteemed the favour of this all-holy, all-just, all-glorious God, to be better than life. Thus far Protestants and Catholics, if really the children of God, are of one mind: but, in the solving of that most important of all questions—How is that favour to be obtained? or rather—How are apostate, fallen creatures to be restored to that favour? their difference of opinion becomes almost irreconcilable. Thus far Dormer felt and believed, as every child of God at some period of his progress does; but at this point he became entirely Roman Catholic, and suffered much of what is frequently suffered by sincerely pious Roman Catholics, while labouring, as it were, "in the very fire," to *merit* that favour which Protestants, at least truly pious Protestants believe, is bestowed only through the merits of Him who took the nature of fallen man, that He might, in that nature, and in the place of fallen man, fulfil that law men cannot fulfil, and "bring in for men an everlasting righteousness." This was not a doctrine taught by Dormer's church; and if at any time the comfort it was calculated to convey to a mind agonizing under a sense of sin, flashed upon his, he would reject it as unauthorized by his church, and as a temptation of the enemy of his soul to lure him from the path of self-denial. *His* church taught, that it was in the power of fallen man himself to merit favour from God. She taught, that good works, done for the love of Jesus Christ, are available for the remission of sins—that they obtain from God an increase of grace in this life and the reward of everlasting happiness hereafter. What these good works were she also taught. Fasts, penances, mortifications, repetitions of prayers;—such were the works by which Dormer hoped to attain to everlasting life. His church taught also, that it was in the power of fallen apostate man to do even more of such works than were necessary for salvation; but Dormer's conscience demanded far more than he ever could perform. No mortifications, however strict, which he imposed upon himself, could prevent thoughts and wishes, which, when on his knees before a holy God, appeared to him altogether earthly and unholy. No penance, however severe, could prevent him from again, in some unguarded moment, giving way to the same feelings of pride or of ambition, or to the same indulgence of worldly dreams which his conscience had told him were unholy. No fast, however long, produced the spiritualizing effect he looked for. To him the gospel was no glad tidings. He did love Christ, ardently loved him; but, as yet, to him Christ was only his supposed Saviour; for he laboured constantly, and with a continual sense of unworthiness weighing down his spirit, to be his own saviour. The law, however, not of his church, but that law of God written on his heart, became more and more strict in its demands the more he sought to obey it.

On this day, as in deep thought he proceeded to consult the Catholic priest who resided at Sir Thomas Carysford's—self-reproach embittered and saddened his spirit. Every neglect of which he had to accuse himself during all the time that young Clarenham had been under his tuition, seemed to rise before him; and the fact, that five years' superintendence on his part seemed to have done so little that a few hours' conversation with a Protestant boy had done away its whole effect, filled him with the most painful and humbling sense of self-condemnation; while the disappointment of those sanguine hopes with which he had undertaken the spiritual guidance of the family at Hallern, depressed his spirit.

In this state of feeling Dormer was introduced into the presence of Mr Warrenne, the Roman Catholic chaplain in Sir Thomas Carysford's family; and who, though unknown to be so, even to most of the Roman Catholics in the neighbourhood, was superior over all the Jesuit priests in that part of England.

Dormer was detained for a few minutes in an antiroom, till Warrenne's own domestic should usher him into the presence of his master; for no servant in the family was permitted to intrude into his privacy.

The priest's servant soon appeared, and silently, but with much respect of manner, conducted Dormer across a long passage into another apartment, and then respectfully motioning to him to stop, advanced, and softly opening a door opposite to the one at which they had entered, just far enough to admit himself, closed it after him. In a minute or two he again appeared—held the door open for Dormer, and softly closed it immediately after he had entered.

The apartment into which Dormer was conducted, was large and handsome, and furnished with massive splendour. At the farther end of it, near a door which was a little open, sat Warrenne on a large chair covered with crimson velvet. A footstool of the same rich exterior supported one foot; and a table, also covered with crimson-velvet, stood before him, on which lay many books and papers.

Warrenne rose not on Dormer's entrance, but, bowing slightly, addressed him with the air of a superior;—"Brother, I am glad to see you."

Dormer approached, and humbly kneeling before him:—"Father, I intreat your blessing."

Warrenne laid his hand upon Dormer's head, and rapidly repeated the usual benediction, then motioned to him to be seated on a plain chair near him.

"I wish to consult you, Father," said Dormer, humbly, "on a subject, regarding which I find my own judgment too weak to decide."

"Private? or regarding our order? or the church?" asked Warrenne, his quick eye and utterance seeming to demand a brief reply.

"The church, Father."

"Heresy?"

"I fear so, Father."

"Among the Clarenhams?"

"Yes!"

"The lady or the young people?"

"The eldest son and daughter."

"The eldest son! your own pupil?"

Dormer reddened. "You know, Father, the cause of his being sent abroad. He had at that time imbibed heretical notions. The society of his Protestant cousin has again revived those notions: but Clarenham is greatly more devoted to religion now; and he will, I fear, ere long, determine to judge in this matter for himself."

"It must not be. Clarenham cannot be spared at this crisis. The example would be most injurious. Our interest in this part of England must on no account be lessened. I must hear more of this youth. A remedy suited to his temper must be discovered without delay."

Warrenne here abruptly rose—kicked the footstool aside—and entered the room the door of which was open near him. In this room two young priests were busily engaged in writing. Warrenne rapidly gave directions first to one, then to the other—turned over one or two papers they presented to him—wrote like lightning his signature to some, and a cipher to others—then returned, and closing the door on the two priests, seated himself, with his forehead resting on his hand, and his dark penetrating eyes fixed on Dormer.

"Tell me the disposition of this youth, brother".

"Extremely amiable," replied Dormer with warmth.

"Ardent?"

"No—gentle, modest, refined, delicate, fearful of inflicting the slightest uneasiness—yet firm."

Warrenne was thoughtful for an instant—"Is he thoroughly loyal to the cause of our exiled king?"

"As yet I think he is entirely so."

"And can you answer for his honour and fidelity?"

"I can unhesitatingly."

"And now, on what points has he been corrupted?"

"Principally with regard to private judgment in reading and examining the Scriptures."

"The most formidable of all—time for reflection will only increase the evil. He must be employed in some affairs suited to his disposition—and, above all, he must be instantly separated from his Protestant relations. I shall think on this matter, and send you my instructions as soon as I have decided. Now tell me of the daughter. Is it the one intended for the nunnery?"

"No, the eldest."

"Ha! the intended wife of Carysford! Brother Dennis ought to have been removed years ago. I dreaded that his partiality for those children had weakened his zeal for the church. But this too must be stopped. Have you discovered the character of the girl?"

"She is uncommonly lively and acute, with a quick sense of the ridiculous; and appears to have an ungovernable disposition for inquiry. Her understanding seems very superior to what is usual in her sex, and she has much confidence in her own judgment. All her own family—the domestics—and those people around the castle whom I have heard speak of her, seem to be ardently attached to her, and to regard her with great respect. To me she has always shown reserve and coldness."

"And what, think you, are her errors?"

"The same as those of her brother with respect to the Scriptures; but she has boldly become possessor of a New Testament which he has not ventured to do. She has also refused to confess."

"Very bad—very bad. I must think over all this. I shall send you the result of my thoughts. In the mean time, brother, if possible keep the young cousins apart. I shall now bid you good morning."

"Father, I wished to confess."

"Again, brother! Certainly, if you wish it." An expression of impatience passed over Warrenne's countenance. He, however, immediately retired with the lowly-minded Dormer, who, kneeling before him, confessed, with sorrow and contrition, those earthly feelings, and sins of thought, which weighed down his spirit, but his sorrow for which appeared, to the ambitious and worldly fellow-sinner to whom he thus humbled himself, as the morbid result of a melancholy and too sensitive temperament. Warrenne, however, advised as a superior, and concluded by pronouncing the following absolution:

"God forgive thee, my brother: the merit

of the passion of our Lord Jesus Christ, and of blessed Saint Mary, always a virgin, and of all the saints; the merit of thine order; the strictness of thy religion, the humility of thy confession, and contrition of thy heart; the good works which thou hast done, and shalt do for the love of Christ,—be unto thee available for the remission of thy sins, the increase of desert and grace, and the reward of everlasting life. Amen."

This absolution, repeated by Warrenne so rapidly as to be scarcely intelligible, was eagerly drunk in by Dormer, as that which was to lighten his soul of the load by which it was oppressed.

"You will pay a visit to the family, I hope, brother," said Warrenne. "Your first visit impressed them, and the friends who were present, very highly indeed in your favour, and has already produced two applications for chaplains from our order. It is of consequence that this favourable impression should be increased."

Dormer bowed his acquiescence, and then Warrenne rang, and left the room. His servant immediately appeared, and, at Dormer's desire, conducted him to the apartments occupied by the family.

The hour which Dormer had spent with his superior had been one of painful humiliation ; the next was of a very different character. He was received by Sir Thomas and Lady Carysford with the utmost possible respect; and every word he uttered listened to as if he had been a messenger direct from heaven ; and, as his gentle and conciliating manners won more and more upon their affections, their intreaties to prolong his visit became so urgent that it was evening before he was again on his return to Hallern Castle.

Warrenne had joined the family at dinner, and appeared much pleased again to meet his brother, to whom his manner was then entirely changed. He indeed seemed altogether a different person. The quick, impatient looks and rapid utterance were exchanged for manners and expressions of the most polished suavity; and, to domestics and common observers, Father Adrian only exhibited the character of the mild, affectionate, and indulgent chaplain. He, however, remained but a short time with the family, and Dormer had scarcely dismounted from his horse, on his return to Hallern Castle, when he was overtaken by a messenger with a dispatch from his indefatigable superior. The man, as he delivered it into Dormer's hand, said, in a low voice, "secret." Dormer put the packet into his bosom, and, after spending half-an-hour with the family, retired to his own apartment, and broke the seal. The envelope inclosed the following directions written in a peculiar cipher:—

"Brother,

"You will, as soon after receiving this as you possibly can, prepare young Clarenham to proceed with secret and important communications to the court of the exiled king; and from thence to proceed, if necessary, to Rome. You may impart what your prudence suggests respecting the present state of affairs in Scotland; and rest the high confidence reposed in him on the expectations of the suffering but lawful party from the representative of the ever-noble and honourable house of Clarenham.

"Also prepare Mrs Clarenham to hear shortly of a communication from Rome, dispensing with that part of General Clarenham's will, in which he makes it necessary that his niece should be of age before her marriage; and an advice to bring about, without delay, a union between the houses of Carysford and Clarenham. I shall put matters here in such a train as will soon produce subjects of thought for the young lady, which I have no doubt will be more attractive than religious controversy.

"In the mean time, avoid all religious discussions with the young Clarenhams; and your success in the part allotted to you, brother, in bringing back those stray lambs to the fold, may, I hope, be such as to confirm our belief, notwithstanding what has happened, in your zeal for the church."

The signature to these instructions was, to Dormer's surprise, in Warrenne's own hand.

These directions from his superior Dormer read again and again, with increasing uneasiness and alarm. About this period (1715) the rebellion in favour of the House of Stuart was on the eve of breaking forth, both in Scotland and in the north of England. Every Roman Catholic family, whether actually involved in this rebellion or not, ardently wished for its success. Priests of the same faith naturally felt deeply interested in the issue; and, from the constant and rapid intercourse which they, and particularly those of the order of Jesuits, maintained with the continent, it was ever found that intelligence was most securely and most expeditiously communicated through their means.

Dormer was perfectly informed respecting the preparations for this rebellion; and, had his superior directed him to proceed with any mission in favour of the cause, he would have undertaken it with ardour, had it been at the hazard of his life; and he would even have offered himself in the place of young Clarenham, could he have entertained the slightest hope that his offer would have been accepted: but he was well aware, that the real object of this mission was to give a new turn to Clarenham's thoughts, —to lead him from the study of religious subjects altogether,—and to involve him, while still under age, in what, were his party unsuccessful, might bring him to the scaffold; and the voice of that law written on Dormer's heart, which no recollection of the authority of the church for a time could stifle, declared the end to be daring and unjustifiable, and the means diabolical. But such thoughts Dormer struggled against, as full of guilt. He had solemnly vowed obedience to his church, and to regard her interests above all others. He had also taken a vow of obedience to the superiors of his order; and any feeling of reluctance to fulfil these vows seemed to him the abandonment of religion, and a criminal indulgence of his own unhallowed affections. The struggle was intensely severe. Young Clarenham's anxiety to submit to his guidance, which had induced him, notwithstanding his present apprehension that he was leading him into error, to refuse to read the Scriptures but with him,—all those amiable and endearing qualities which, for the last five years, had won, even more than he was aware of, upon Dormer's affections, and the unbounded confidence reposed in him by Clarenham,—were now dwelt upon in sad remembrance. The widowed mother, whose spirits seemed to have revived from day to day since the return of her feeling and most attentive son,—she, too, must be called to bear the anguish of another separation: And for what? Lest Clarenham should read the Bible, and discover that the power assumed by his church was not given her there. The thought merely flashed for a moment on Dormer's mind, and was immediately followed by the deepest sense of guilt. He threw himself upon his knees before a crucifix, which stood in that part of his small apartment where he usually performed his devotions; and as his church taught, that, by "a thorough sorrow, you may utterly destroy and put an end to sin," and that such sorrow is to be obtained "by begging it humbly and frequently through the merits of a Saviour," he ardently sought that sorrow; and, while doing so, the questions, "Why is the Romish church so eager to shut up the Scriptures from the people? Why does she discourage their close and frequent study even by the priests?" mingled with his petitions, and were regarded by him as the suggestions of the evil one. He spent nearly two hours in this state of wretchedness, and was then obliged to meet the family in the chapel, there to repeat in Latin the usual formulary. He looked exhausted and depressed; and, after the service was over, Mrs Clarenham and Basil intreated him, with the utmost kindness and urgency, to join the family and partake of some refreshment.

"You have eat nothing since dinner—I intreat you, Father, do not refuse to join us," said Basil earnestly, and following him after he had got away from the others.

"I must fast still longer, my son," replied Dormer. "This night must be spent in fasting and devotion for us both."

"Is it on my account you thus suffer, Father?" asked Basil, becoming pale as he spoke.

"It is, and for my own unsubdued feelings regarding you."

"Then, Father, allow me at least to partake in your humiliation. Suffer me to be with you."

"No Basil. I must be alone. Your presence would not lessen my disquiet. In the morning you will oblige me by joining me as early as you please. I shall then inform you of the very painful duty which awaits us both."

"Painful duty!" repeated Basil anxiously.

"Yes, my dear Clarenham, to me altogether painful—to you, if I know you, it will at least partly be so: But good night—prepare your mind to fulfil an honourable, but, in some degree, self-denying duty."

"Father," said Basil earnestly, "do not impose any duty on me that you have any suspicion may excite a scruple in my conscience. You would not, if you knew the extreme pain it gives me to dispute your guidance in any point."

"The duty is not a religious one," replied Dormer—"but again, good night. I wish not to enter on the subject till we can do it fully."

"If it is not religious," replied Basil, affectionately kissing Dormer's hand, "I am sure of having the happiness of doing as you wish."

Very early next morning, Basil was admitted to the small apartment where Dormer had passed the night without any sleep but what he had taken when quite exhausted by laying down for two hours without undressing, on the hard pallet which at all times was his only bed. He looked even more pale and depressed, and worn out than the night before. He was, however, perfectly calm, and immediately began the subject :—

"Clarenham, you still, I am persuaded, feel devoted to the cause of our absent king."

"Still, Father! Most assuredly I do. Can you suppose me so base as to desert it?"

"I hope not: but you know that, in these days, many people, who we considered good and honourable, have forsaken the cause of an unfortunate king."

"I understand you, Father; but I assure you, upon my honour, Ernest Montague—no Montague—or any person whatever, has come on the subject with me since I returned to England."

"It is well," said Dormer; for great devotion to the cause is expected, by the friends of the king, from the representative of your family, Clarenham."

"I think I shall not disappoint their expectations, Father, if devotion to the cause is all they look for from me."

"Young as you are, then, Basil, you have been fixed upon to convey intelligence of great importance to the king."

Basil's countenance brightened up. "I shall rejoice to fulfil the mission," said he, ardently. "But my poor mother,"—his looks saddened: "Is it wished that I should go immediately?"

"Immediately."

"Well, I am ready. I need not be long absent. But why, Father, did you consider this duty so painful? and, to you, why should it be painful to you?"

"Because it is accompanied with some danger to you, Clarenham. I have much to tell you; and, till you have heard all, do not make your determination."

Dormer then gave a sketch of the plan of rebellion, as far as he knew of its arrangement, carefully avoiding all allusion to the interests of the church; and only addressing those feelings of loyalty and compassion to the exiled house of Stuart, which he perceived were now powerfully awakened in the warm heart of his young pupil. Dormer did so, from that determination to deny his own feelings, and sense of right, and to submit to his church, to which he had excited himself by the severe exercises of the night; and, as he proceeded and observed his success, he alternately felt that he was acting the part of a devoted self-denying saint, and that of a deceiver and a murderer. The first feeling, however, predominated; and, amidst the conflict within, he preserved a perfect calmness of manner.

"I have but one thing further to suggest to you, Basil," said he at last. "I think it would be dangerous for you yourself to inform your cousins, the Montagues, of your intended absence. They might ask questions you would find it difficult to answer. Will you, then, if you wish to see them before your departure, do so without mentioning it?"

"I will. But, if I go soon, I need not see them again. Ernest is gone to Edinburgh, I suspect, on this very business. I thought something was the matter the last day I was at Illerton. The whole family were even more than usually kind to me; and Sir Herbert, though he generally treats me as a mere boy, reminded me that I was within less than a year of being of age, and that I already had a part to act which might mark my future character and fate; and that, in all I did, I ought to recollect that, whoever was my adviser now, I must bear the consequences hereafter."

Dormer rose abruptly and turned away. "My watch," said he, after seeming to search for it,—"O, here it is, and it is not so late as I thought. I beg your pardon for interrupting you. Sir Herbert, I fear, must have got some intelligence of what is going on. Did he say any thing more which would now lead you to suppose so?"

"No. He only reminded me, in the kindest manner, of the nearness of our relationship, and intreated me to regard him, on every occasion, as one who felt for me as a father."

Dormer was silent for a few moments, then asked what had led his young friend to suppose Ernest Montague was gone to Edinburgh on the business he had mentioned?

"Because," replied Basil, "he told me it was to receive correct information respecting some very painful intelligence which had reached his father; but, as he did not tell me what that intelligence was, I supposed it of a private nature, and did not press him on the subject:

but, after the religious conversation I have already mentioned to you, Father, I now recollect that he somehow led to the subject of civil war, and most strongly urged the misery and crimes that must ever accompany it; and the responsibility of those who in any way assisted in producing or promoting it." Basil looked thoughtful after this recollection, then said, "But our cause is so just, I cannot hesitate. I am ready whenever my services are wished for. And now, Father, may I impose on you the painful task of informing my mother. She will require to have the intelligence softened to her by the aid of religious consolations."

Dormer undertook this: and, before that mournful day had closed, he saw the widowed mother, almost heart-broken, carried in a faint to her apartment, after having strained her eyes to catch the last glimpse of her son, as he rode across the park, on his way to Sir Thomas Carysford's;—his sisters in the deepest grief; and that gloom again thrown over every countenance at Hallern Castle, which had been passing away amidst the brighter hopes which had been inspired by the presence and engaging qualities of young Clarenham.

Dormer had, early in the day, informed Warrenne of the promptness with which his young charge had undertaken his proposed mission; and had very soon received an answer, requesting Basil's immediate presence; and saying, that suspicions were already afloat; and that, unless he set out immediately, his going might be prevented altogether. Lord Derwentwater (a leader in the rebellion,) was that day to be at Sir Thomas Carysford's, and, Warrenne said, wished to meet with young Clarenham. The lure succeeded; and, though Basil's gentle nature was deeply moved by the grief his departure occasioned, still he felt gratified by the confidence which he believed was reposed in him, and attempted to lead forward the hopes of his mother and sisters to those brighter days which still awaited the house of Clarenham. "And, whatever happens," added he, "this I feel assured of, that we shall have sufficient interest with our friends to secure the Montagues from any injury."

CHAPTER VII.

"Rispose Gesu, e disse: in verita vi dico, che non v'ha alcuno, il quale abbia abbandonnato la casa, o i fratelli, o le sorelle, o il padre, o la madre, o i figliuoli, o le possessioni per me, e per vangelo, che non receva il centuplo,—e nel secolo avvenire la vita eterna."

Martini's Trans.—Mark x. 29, 30.

Weeks now passed away, and still Dormer's account of Mrs Clarenham's state of spirits and health prevented Warrenne from hoping that any proposal regarding the speedy union of the houses of Carysford and Clarenham would meet with her approval. He had himself visited her several times, and had succeeded in exciting at least a feeling of gratitude in her gentle nature. At his desire also, Lady Carysford had urged Mrs Clarenham and her daughters to pay a visit of a few days at the park. This Mrs Clarenham positively declined; and Warrenne was annoyed by discovering, that, though she thus shrunk from the society she would have met there, she seemed pleased and comforted by that of Lady Montague and her daughter, who were frequently with her.

During this period the rebels had appeared in arms, in the North of England, under Lord Derwentwater and Foster, and troops were collecting to meet them and defend the country.

At last, on some soldiers being quartered at Hallern village, and reports reaching Mrs Clarenham that others would soon be quartered at the Castle, and alarmed by the accounts related to her of their insolence and disorderly conduct, she yielded to Sir Thomas Carysford's urgent intreaties to put herself and her daughters under his protection.

On the day after giving her consent to this proposal, Mrs Clarenham, the very picture of sorrow and depression, and her daughters, with looks also full of anxiety and apprehension, left the Castle. Many of the villagers, having heard exaggerated reports of the danger which occasioned their departure, were gathered round the carriage which was to convey them away, and stood ready to add to their depression, by their affectionate, but sad and foreboding exclamations.

"Oh, our dear Lady! how pale she looks. Holy Mary bless her!" exclaimed some.

"Jesu Maria! could the Protestant wretches be so cruel-hearted as to hurt her, or the sweet young ladies?" exclaimed others.

"Blessings, blessings, from holy Mary and all the saints follow them!"

"We will defend the castle to the last," said the men. "We will not forget our kind young master."

"Oh, what will become of the poor now?" said some.

"Father Clement is to remain among you," said Maria kindly to the people. "You think too seriously of our going away. I hope we shall very soon return; and, in the meantime, Father Clement will let us know all about you."

"Blessings on you, dear Miss Clarenham. You always cheer our hearts. Blessings on holy Father Clement for staying with us."

Dormer raised his hand to motion silence, and in an instant the clamour ceased, and the old coach slowly drove away.

Mrs Clarenham had determined, on her way, to call at Illerton, herself to inform the Montagues of her removal to Sir Thomas Carysford's, and to take leave for a time of her Protestant but most beloved of all friends.

Sir Herbert and his lady were in astonishment on seeing Mrs Clarenham; and still more so on her telling the cause of her leaving that retirement, which, a few days before, they would have regarded as the most painful exertion.

"Absurd!" exclaimed Sir Herbert. "Sir Thomas must know that at present there is no danger of more soldiers coming to this neighbourhood. Those now at Hallern are to leave it to-day. Lord Derwentwater has taken the field, and all the soldiers that can be mustered will be in requisition to meet him. And, at any rate, my dear cousin, you would, at present, be much safer with us. Why not remain at Illerton? The Carysfords are no relations. Matters cannot go well with the rebels." (Mrs Clarenham became paler than she was before.) "At least," continued Sir Herbert, "it is time enough to leave us when Sir Thomas can offer a more secure protection."

"Let us leave my mother and Sir Herbert to settle that matter," said Maria Clarenham, taking her friend Adeline aside into one of those deep recesses in which it was common at that period to have the windows. "I wish from my heart," continued Maria, "that Sir Herbert had thought of proposing our coming here some days ago; but now it is too late. I have all along, Adeline, suspected that exaggerated accounts were purposely brought to us of the unsettled state of the country around this, and of the bad conduct of the few soldiers at Hallern."

"But why, dear Maria, should any one be so cruel as to add to the sufferings of your mother,—your dear, patient, gentle mother!" Adeline's eyes filled, as she glanced at Mrs Clarenham while she spoke.

"I begin to suspect who could be so cruel," replied Maria indignantly. "I may perhaps think I see more than is to be seen; but I am greatly mistaken if that wily, inquisitive, domineering Warrenne has not succeeded in sending one unsuspecting, noble-minded, dear dupe, out of the way of Protestant influence, and is now manœuvring, in a way he regards as equally secure of success, to involve another in irrevocable trammels. But he knows her not: at least I trust she now leans on a strength before which all his efforts will fall harmless. But, dear Adeline, I have a request to make to you. Dr Lowther, you know, sent me a New Testament. It is the treasure and light of my heart and soul; but it has made me desire more light. The volume he sent me has a great number of references to other parts of Scripture on the margin of every page. Those references have been of the utmost use in teaching me to understand what I read. I have found that the Bible explains itself. A passage may seem so obscure in its meaning that you may read it,—at least I found it so,—over and over, and not be able to comprehend it, when, if you turn up a few other passages, it seems as light as day: but many of these references are to the Old Testament, and I have not been able to procure one. Will you, dear Adeline, bestow an Old Testament on me?"

"Will I? dear, dear Maria!" Adeline could not speak for tears. "Come," said she at last, "I think Dr Lowther must produce an Old

Testament to suit the New one he sent you."

"We shall return immediately," said Adeline to her mother, as she accompanied Maria out of the room. They then proceeded to the door of Dr Lowther's study.

"But I cannot think of disturbing Dr Lowther," said Maria, laying her hand on Adeline's, as she was about to knock at the door. "I shall pass on, and then, if we are interrupting him, he will less scruple to tell *you* so."

"Ah! you do not know Dr Lowther," said Adeline, retaining her hand, and tapping gently at his door.

The Doctor's kind and cheerful voice answered by an invitation to enter.

"Well, my dear Miss Adeline, what is it?" asked he, without raising his head. A large Bible was before him, in which he seemed to be searching for some passage.

"Are you very busy, my dear Sir?" asked Adeline.

"Yes—very busy," replied the Doctor, in an absent manner, and glancing intently down one column, then another. "I am preparing my lecture for next Lord's Day, my dear; and there is a passage,—I am sure there is,—to the point, but it is not marked in my concordance, and I cannot find it."

"Do not let us disturb Dr Lowther," said Maria earnestly, and drawing Adeline away.

The Doctor raised his head, and put up his spectacles.

"Miss Clarenham! my dearest young lady, I beg your pardon."

"I ought to ask your forgiveness, Sir, for this intrusion."

"No apologies, I intreat you, my dear Miss Clarenham," interrupted Dr Lowther, taking Maria's hand and placing her in a chair by him; then retaining her hand in both of his, and with the manner of the kindest father—"Can I be of any service to you, my dear young lady?" asked he. "Nothing would give me greater pleasure."

Maria's heart was full, and when she attempted to speak, she could not. Dr Lowther turned to Adeline, who in few words told her friend's wish.

Dr Lowther was much moved. "It is the Lord's own work!" said he, emphatically. "O how pleasant it is to see the effect of his own powerful word upon the heart, without the intervention of human teaching! What is any teaching compared to that word applied by his Spirit? 'What is the chaff to the wheat? saith the Lord. Is not my word like as a fire? saith the Lord, and like a hammer that breaketh the rock to pieces?'* My dear young lady, may I ask—can you thus love God's word, and still join in the observances of the Romish Church?"

"I do not join in any observance, Sir, which I do not think I find inculcated, or at least permitted in the Scriptures. I have never confessed since I examined the New Testament on that point. I attempt to pray now, but never merely repeat prayers. I regard the Virgin Mary as only the most blessed among women, because she was honoured to be the mother of the human nature of my Lord; but think it idolatry to worship or pray to her, or to any of the saints; but I still attend mass and the eucharist," continued Maria, hesitatingly, and looking timidly at Dr Lowther, "because, though I

* Jer. xxiii. 28, 29.

wish the prayers were in English, still I think the Catholic Church,—as I understand the Bible,—receives that great mystery more simply and literally than the Protestants do, who explain away what appears to me the plain doctrine of the real presence."

"We do not explain away the doctrine of the real *spiritual* presence, my dear Miss Clarenham; but we say, that nothing but what is spiritual or future is in the Bible made an object of faith. The Romish church turns an object of sense into an object of faith; in other words, asks you to believe in the presence of a real substance—of real flesh and blood, contrary to the evidence of your sight—of your touch—of your taste—of all your senses."

"But, my dear Sir, Christ says—'This *is* my body.'"

"True, my dear Miss Clarenham; but when he so said, and distributed the broken symbol, his body had not been broken. He could therefore say so only in a figurative sense, as he is elsewhere designated 'The Lamb slain from the foundation of the world.'* But I do not

* Rev. xiii. 8.

wish to enter into controversy with you on this point. It is one on which the Romish Church builds so much error, while the people mingle with that error so much devotional feeling, that the heart is engaged in its defence; and many pious souls have left this world, I hope and believe, for a better, with their heads in confusion on the subject, while their hearts were wholly devoted to that Saviour in whose merits they put their only trust for salvation. Only allow me to say a very few things to you on this point, which your own mind would naturally suggest, but which, from early impressions, you might regard as profane, though they can only be so if the doctrine is true; and I think they prove it to be false. You are, I know, my dear young lady, in your books of preparation for, and devotions at, and after receiving the Eucharist, exhorted to prepare your heart; and, as one of those books says—'If you find your conscience defiled with any mortal crime, approach not this dreadful mystery till you have first purified it in the tribunal of penance: there it is the Apostle will by all means have you examine yourself before you partake of the Eucharist.' Are not such exhortations addressed to you, Miss Clarenham, both in the books given you by your spiritual guides and by themselves?"

"They are, Sir, constantly; and I perceive how unscriptural the passage you have repeated is. I remember St Paul's words—'Let a man *examine himself*, so let him eat of that bread and drink of that cup.'* There is nothing said of penance—no tribunal mentioned but that of the man's conscience before God. I have attempted to follow this direction before attending mass. Still, however, Sir, St Paul adds—'Lest, coming unworthily, he eat and drink damnation to himself, not discerning the Lord's body.' Still, my dear Sir, the real bodily presence"——

"And how, my dear Miss Clarenham, do Roman Catholics *discern* the Lord's body in the Eucharist?"

"They all firmly believe that it is really there; and shew that they do so by adoring the Host."

"But, my dear young lady, discerning and

* 1 Cor. xi. 23.

believing are not the same. Discerning means discriminating, distinguishing between one thing and another; and, if you will read the passage attentively, and putting away, as much as you can, early prejudices, you will find that St Paul was reproving the Corinthians for an improper observance of the Lord's Supper. They had partaken of it as of a common meal or feast. He says—' For, in eating, every one taketh before other his own supper, and one is hungry and another is drunken.' He then reproves sharply this profanation of the Lord's Supper, and reminds them of the real purpose of the institution, and warns them of the danger of not distinguishing between a common feast and that ordinance of the Lord in which they were to shew forth his death till he came—between that bread which was the symbol of the Lord's broken body and that used for common food. But to return to your books of devotion: you are, in them, exhorted to remember that, in the Eucharist, Christ becomes as it were incorporated with you, by giving you his flesh to eat; and you are taught, that the bodily presence of Christ in the communion is 'an extension of the incarnation.' Are you not, my dear young lady, taught all this?"

"Yes, Sir, constantly."

"And you are even told that you receive God into your heart?"

"Yes."

"Do not be shocked, my dear Miss Clarenham, when I point out the profanity of this absurd doctrine. Our Lord Himself explains the meaning of the figurative language he had used when he taught the necessity of believing in his incarnation, and of trusting to its efficacy as the very support, food, nourishment of our souls. He says—'It is the Spirit that quickeneth; the flesh profiteth nothing: the words that I speak unto you, they are spirit and they are life.'* Our Lord here plainly declares that all he had taught was spiritual; yet the Romish Church, disregarding this explanation of Christ, support this doctrine of a literal presence by those very words which our Lord Himself has declared he meant spiritually; and which, he said, when applied to the literal flesh, profited nothing.

* John vi. 63.

And mark the consequences of this literal doctrine:—The Church of Rome avers that the thousands of her communion who have partaken of the Eucharist, worthy and unworthy, have really partaken of the literal body of Jesus Christ. I shall just mention one necessary, but most profane consequence from such a doctrine. Thousands and ten thousands of Roman Catholics, who have thus received the flesh of Jesus Christ to become *incorporated* with them, have died, and become the prey of corruption. Many every day are consigned to corruption. The Scriptures say—' Thou (God) wilt not suffer thy Holy One to see corruption.'* St Peter explains this of Christ.† But the Romish Church profanely teaches a doctrine which involves the blasphemous consequence, that the real body of the Holy One of God is in a continual state of corruption. I shall say no more."

Maria looked shocked, but said—" I do not think the Church would allow that it taught this consequence."

" Certainly not," replied Dr Lowther, " but

* Psalm xvi. † Acts ii. 31.

still it so necessarily follows from what she teaches, that, to get rid of it, she must very nearly get rid of the doctrine also. She says, "Christ is not present in this Sacrament according to his natural way of existence, that is, with extension of parts, in order to place, &c. but, after a supernatural manner, one and the same in many places, and whole in every part of the symbols. This is therefore," say they, "a real, substantial, yet sacramental presence of Christ's body and blood, not exposed to the external senses, not obnoxious to corporeal contingencies." This explanation, if intelligible at all, admits that Christ received in the sacrament is Christ received by faith into the soul—that is, a spiritual reception—not the literal body and flesh of Christ, but a supernatural body and flesh—a sacramental presence—a whole Christ in every part of the symbol. Thus, you perceive, my dear Miss Clarenham, that, when obliged to explain herself, the Church of Rome no more believes in a real or literal presence than Protestants do; and that the latter teach, simply and scripturally, to all the people the spiritual doctrine taught by Christ, while the Church of

Rome blinds her votaries by pretending to teach what she is obliged, when brought to reason with those who oppose her, to explain away so as to have a meaning entirely different from that generally received by her children. As to the sacrifice which you are taught to believe is offered by the mass, it is a notion equally contrary to the Scriptures and to reason. The Scriptures say, ' Christ is not entered into the holy places made with hands, the figures of the true, but into heaven itself, now to appear in the presence of God for us; nor yet that he should offer himself often, as the High Priest (alluding to the temple service,) entereth into the holy place every year with the blood of others; for then must he have often suffered since the foundation of the world: But now, *once* in the end of the world hath he appeared to put away sin by the sacrifice of himself, and as it is appointed unto men *once* to die, but after this the judgment, so Christ was *once* offered to bear the sins of many."* St Paul continuing, in his address to the Hebrews, to

* Hebrews, ix. 24, 25, 26, 27, 28.

contrast the figurative Jewish service with the reality fulfilled in Christ, says, 'Every priest standeth daily ministering, and offering oftentimes the same sacrifices, which can never take away sins: but this man, after he had offered *one* sacrifice for sins, for ever sat down on the right hand of God. For by *one* offering He hath perfected for ever them that are sanctified.'* If we reason on the subject, let me ask you, Miss Clarenham, what we mean when we speak of a sacrifice to take away sin? Is it not constantly represented in Scripture under the character of an innocent victim, substituted in the place of a guilty being, to suffer in his stead? Does not the very idea of receiving forgiveness, in virtue of a sacrifice, denote that our sins have been transferred to the victim, our substitute? Sin, in the Scriptures, is represented as washed away only by blood—by suffering. Then where is the virtue of that sacrifice your priests pretend to offer? Christ, when 'He was *once* offered for the sins of many, was wounded for our transgressions, He was bruis-

* Hebrews x. 11, 12, 14.

ed for our iniquities; the chastisement of our peace was upon Him, and with his stripes we are healed.'* But this silly and profane invention of a corrupt church has no virtue, no meaning. They call it an unbloody sacrifice: but a bloodless is a useless sacrifice, since blood alone can wash away sin; and bowing down to adore what is thus offered is the most childish idolatry—the worshipping of the veriest unworthy trifle ever made by men's hands and set up as a god. I shall only further ask you to consider the uses to which the Romish clergy put this doctrine—their masses for the dead bought with money. But I need say no more."

Dr Lowther then sought among his books for a small old Testament with marginal references, and presented it to Maria.

"You must also accept from me the articles of belief of the different Protestant Churches," said he. "You may hear much of the want of union which exists among us, as I know that it is a point much dwelt on by those members of your church who are kept in ignorance of the truth on such subjects. Here is the Confession

* Isaiah liii. 5.

of Faith of the Church of Scotland, and also the Catechism taught in every parish-school in that country: The articles also of the Church of England. The belief of the Swiss and Dutch Church is allowed to be the same as that of Scotland. You will find that there is scarcely a shade of difference in the faith of all these Churches. The minor sects of Protestants also agree in those articles, which are by all considered as essential; and, as the Bible is the only standard of truth with all Protestants, we may hope and trust that time will do away those differences which all good men amongst us lament, and which have been produced by the pride and evil passions of those who have mingled amongst professing Protestants, and by that darkness and ignorance which a deeper acquaintance with the Bible will do away: and then that blessed time may be hoped for when true Bible Christians will alone, as they alone are, be acknowledged by all as the only true Church."

Here little Maude put in her head at the door: "Mrs Clarenham is going away, Maria, and has sent me for you."

Maria immediately rose : " Pray for me, dear Dr Lowther," said she earnestly.

" I will, from my inmost heart, my dear Miss Clarenham."

She held out her hand to him ; he took it in both of his, and, raising his eyes to heaven, prayed shortly, but with much fervour, for her as a lamb of Christ's fold ; imploring guidance, and light, and strength, and prudence in conduct while amongst those still in darkness, and peace and confidence in God.

Maria was much moved : " Precious English prayers !" exclaimed she. " Oh how different from the rapid unmeaning words with which our priests pretend to guide our devotions ! Oh that I might remain in this house ! But it must not be. Farewell—Farewell :" and she hastened away.

Mrs Clarenham and Catherine were already in the carriage : and, after a melancholy drive of several miles, during which they passed through several villages and hamlets which seemed as peaceful as usual, they arrived at the massive old gateway which led into Sir Thomas Carysford's grounds. Here Sir Thomas and his son rode up to the carriage to welcome them. Young Carysford came to the window next which Maria sat, and leaning forward, "Good news!" said he joyfully. "All the north of Scotland is in arms. Not a false heart amongst them but Argyle; and he, I hope, will share the fate of his covenanting rebellious ancestors!"

"Is Argyle against us?"

"Yes. When did a Protestant Argyle favour the house of Stuart?"

"One Protestant Argyle put the crown of Scotland on the head of a wanderer of the Stuarts when he had few friends besides, Edward," said Maria with warmth; "for which he was rewarded by losing his own when that *grateful* exile came to power."

"That is the Illerton edition of the story," replied young Carysford, rather piqued.

"Is it not the true edition?"

"He lost his head as a judgment for having signed a covenant to suppress the Catholic Church," answered Carysford, half playfully. "But now, I hope, we shall see the heretic, covenanting Presbyterians unsettled again, and the true church triumphant in their room."

"Many heads will fall in Scotland, Edward, ere the Romish Church shall raise *her's* there."

"Are you become a prophetess, Maria?"

"It is only necessary to look back, not forward, Edward, to prophecy on that point. A land thirsting for education and Bibles promises ill for the success of our church."

"Ah—all—learnt at Illerton, that vile seducing Illerton," replied Carysford, laughing good-naturedly.

"True, sincere, happy Illerton!" said Maria smiling at last also, "where every one may venture to hear, or tell, both sides of a story."

Sir Thomas had, on the other side of the carriage, been eagerly listened to by Mrs Clarenham and Catherine, while he detailed the exaggerated accounts of the state of affairs in Scotland, where, he seemed quite certain, such forces were assembling as must, at least, put the house of Stuart in possession of that country.

The news was at last told, and the coach

again moved slowly along the beautifully-kept road which led through the fine old park to the magnificent mansion of the Carysfords. All, except in extent, was in complete contrast to Hallern. Not a withered leaf was left on the smooth velvet turf. Every part of the grounds was in the most perfect state of keeping. Maria, from an early age, had been in the habit of regarding Carysford Park as the place of her future residence, and had become warmly attached to its scenery. The thought that she must no longer look forward to it as such now mingled with the many other sad thoughts which at this moment had full possession of her mind, and gave a melancholy character to the masses of foliage with which the fine old trees shaded the bright green verdure, and to the deep dells into which the park was in some places broken; and even to the smiles with which young Carysford occasionally addressed her, as he continued to rein in his horse, that he might keep pace with the heavy, old, long-tailed, broad-backed, state cavalry, which, mounted by two not very youthful postilions, dragged the massive coach along the levelled gravel.

At length the solemn procession stopt before the splendid mansion, and in an instant Lady Carysford was at the hall-door to welcome her guests. Every arrangement had been made by her with kindness and feeling; and Mrs Clarenham soon found herself mistress of a set of apartments entirely appropriated to her use, and separated from those occupied by the family; and in which, Lady Carysford assured her, she would at no time be disturbed. From these apartments a door led into a flower-garden, which she was also to consider as entirely her own. All promised peace, and liberty to occupy her time as she chose; and Mrs Clarenham warmly expressed her thanks.

"I do as I would wish my friends to do to me, my dear Mrs Clarenham," replied Lady Carysford. Nobody shall come near you. But the young people must not shut themselves up. I have engaged some companions to join them here. When you are disposed to see Sir Thomas and I, or Father Adrian, we shall make a quiet party, and let the young folks amuse themselves. Maria shall do the honours for me. Ah, my dear Mrs Clarenham, how often

I long for a daughter: every female visitor must I look after myself. Well, my time may come," looking archly at Maria: "but, my dear, I have heard strange reports about you. I shall not mention them now; but you and I must have some conversation. I am prepared for you. I do not fear a host of Protestant arguments; but I have come on the subject, which I did not intend."

So ran on Lady Carysford, but, after a few more such speeches, left her guests to go and receive some other visitors.

CHAPTER VIII.

"Chi ama suo padre, o sua madre piu di me, non e degno di me; e chi ama il figlio, o la figlia, piu di me, non e degno di me."
Martini's Trans.—Matth. x. 37.

DURING a week passed at Carysford Park it was so managed that, for a considerable part of each day, Mrs Clarenham joined Sir Thomas and Lady Carysford, and some of the elder visitors at the Park, while the young people were left to amuse themselves. Every species of amusement to be found in the country was at the command of the young party; and Carysford's high spirits and good nature made him particularly ingenious in varying and contriving entertainments for his guests. Still, however, he sought to discover what was most agreeable to Maria in all he did; and with her only he was unsuccessful. All his other young friends, including Catherine Clarenham, entered, with apparent delight, into his plans, and a scene of gaiety and enjoyment was constantly around him. Yet Maria, who had formerly been the life of every such scene,—except at short intervals, when she seemed to forget the sorrow that checked and saddened her smiles, and the lively playfulness of her fancy would give new life to all the others,—except at such short intervals, Maria was grave, and absent, and thoughtful. Sometimes she would succeed in leading her light-hearted companions to enter into the grave and melancholy kind of conversation which suited her own state of spirits. This gradually superseded, or at least always followed, gayer hours; and the two last evenings of the week, on Lady Carysford joining the young party to see that all were amused and happy, she found them sitting close together, in grave and apparently deeply interesting conversation.

"No music! no dancing!" exclaimed she, the first evening she found them thus—and then the conversation was interrupted, and music and dancing commenced; but, on the second evening, all declared that they preferred those hours of quiet conversation to any amusement.

Lady Carysford was surprised, but not pleased. It was evident that Maria had been the attraction in this grave manner of spending time. All were gathered round her, and Lady Carysford had distinguished her animated voice as she entered the room.

"What on earth can you find to converse about, that is so very agreeable?" asked Lady Carysford.

"Indeed, Madam, you would not think it so very agreeable," said Catherine. "Maria does nothing but ridicule and undervalue all those saintly virtues which Catholics look upon as most deserving of heaven. Here she has just been leading us to define what we thought most excellent and lovely in human character; and, indeed, her own descriptions have not one holy ingredient in them."

"That is, Catherine, they have no hours spent in repeating what is not understood,—no virtuous going without stockings or shoes over cold marble,—no living without food in the woods, like some of those whose stories you believe, till they become so spiritual that they are seen telling their beads on their knees a little way up in the air. I see nothing in all that, but childish fabulous nonsense."

All the young people laughed except Catherine.

"You may judge, Madam, of our conversation, from the specimen Maria has just given," said Catherine, indignantly.

"Oh, fie, fie," said Lady Carysford. "Come with me a little, my love," addressing Maria; "and the others have still a little time to dance themselves into spirits before prayers."

"Dance themselves into spirits!" thought Maria. "I wonder what they would think of that as a preparation for devotion at Illerton?" but she instantly recollected that Dormer would approve as little of such a preparation as the Montagues; and she was settling, in her own mind, how much true devotion of heart had the same effect on the conduct of all who were influenced by it, when she found herself alone with Lady Carysford in her dressing-room.

"My dear Maria," said Lady Carysford very affectionately, "I did not wish to hurt your feelings, by alluding sooner to this subject; but really, my dear, when I recollect the near tie which is to unite you to me, and the very prospect of which has already made you dearer to me than almost any other person on earth, I can refrain no longer."

"You know, my dear Madam," said Maria, "*that* connexion cannot take place, if you are at all dissatisfied with me on the point to which you allude."

"Maria! my child! my daughter! do not utter such words. You will break my heart. You will break all our hearts. You have been misled by those Protestant cousins of yours; but you are too good, too sensible, to remain long in error. And now, my love, I have got something I wish you particularly to read."

"I shall read most attentively whatever you recommend, my dear Lady Carysford."

"That is like yourself, my own dear girl. This is what I wish you to read, my love," continued Lady Carysford, drawing a large pocket-book from her ample pocket, and selecting, from many papers and letters, one paper, beautifully written, and richly gilt and emblazoned. "It is a letter, written by the Duchess of York," said she, "who was carefully educated by Protestant preceptors in the faith of the Church of England."

"My dearest Lady Carysford, I have read it a hundred times."

"Have you, my dear?"

"Yes; and you must not be angry if I say that I think it very silly."

"Silly!"

"Extremely so. She does not give one reason for changing her religion that could satisfy any sensible person really in search of truth. She says she could discern no reason why the Protestants in England separated from the Church of Rome, but because Henry VIII. chose to renounce the Pope's authority, when he would not give him leave to part with one wife that he might marry another. Now, my dear Madam, it is this sort of nonsense which we Catholics are nursed upon, and which makes us appear so ignorant, and priest-led, and childishly ridiculous in the eyes of Protestants, who, on this point, have only to ask us, while they cannot refrain from laughing at our silly credulity,—what induced so many Protestants to prefer being burnt to death rather than return to the bosom of the Church a few years after, under the reign of the pious Catholic, as we term her; but as they, I think, more justly designate her, 'the bloody Mary.' Henry VIII. took advantage of the times, when the light of the Reformation was becoming too powerful for the Church of Rome. He then succeeded in setting up his own despotic power in opposition to her's; but, as to religion, ours suited his character best, and he continued to profess himself a member of our Church to the last: and he is regarded by Protestants as a wicked, half-mad tyrant. Then those Bishops of the Church of England, whom the Duchess of York mentions having consulted, a tolerably-instructed Protestant child would tell you, that, if they believed what she says they believed, they were not Protestants. You must give me more conclusive arguments, my dear Lady Carysford, in favour of our Church, or I fear I must consider her cause a weak one indeed, when put in competition with that which appeals only to the Bible—which urges you to try its truth by God's own word—to search that word as for hid treasures—and to receive no doctrine from men but what they can plainly show you is written there."

"But, my love, our Church does not ask you to believe any thing that is not in the Bible."

"My dear Madam, she asks us to believe many things that are not in the Bible. Does she not command us to receive, as matters of faith, necessary to salvation. '*First*, What in Scripture is plain and intelligible. *Secondly*, Definitions of General Councils, on points not sufficiently explained in Scripture. *Thirdly*, Apostolical traditions, received from Christ and his apostles, (and we all know how easy it is to make that a wide belief). *Fourthly*, The practice, worship, and ceremonies of the Church in confirmation of her doctrines?'"

"My dear child, I must give you over to Father Adrian upon these matters. You have got into strange errors; but now I must return to your mother. You really have taken extraordinary fancies into your young head. But, come with me, till I find out what accounts of our cause Sir Thomas has received, that I may be able to tell your mother. He left us some time ago to receive letters from a messenger who would deliver them to none but himself. I was on my way in search of Sir Thomas when I looked in on you, and forgot every thing else on hearing what you had been conversing about."

Sir Thomas was still in the apartment in which he had received the messenger, and looked grave and dissatisfied.

"What is the matter, my dear?" asked Lady Carysford.

"Bad news—very bad news. Our friends have been obliged to lay down their arms, and are made prisoners as rebels. Our cause, for the present, is lost in England. Poor Derwentwater is a prisoner. There is little hope for him."

"How, Sir! what!" exclaimed Maria, "will he suffer as a traitor?"

"I fear—I fear too soon. They will make an example of him. There is not, I fear, one ray of hope that any mercy will be shown to him."

Maria clasped her hands. "And my brother, he will be returning to England; it may be known that he was the bearer of dispatches from Lord Derwentwater!"

"He must be prevented returning at this crisis," said Sir Thomas, anxiously. "I must see Father Adrian."

At this moment he entered the room.

"No grave looks—no gatherings together, as if some disaster had happened—no exciting of suspicion," said he, quickly. "No eye, no ear amongst the domestics must be counted on at present. Do, my dear Miss Clarenham, set the young people to dance. Let the sound of cheerful music be heard—then let us all meet, as usual, in the chapel."

"But first, Father, will my brother be returning about this time? Is there any chance of suspicion falling on him?"

"Your brother, my dear young lady! he is at Rome."

"At Rome! When did he go there, Father? Why does my mother not know?"

"He proceeded there on a confidential mission. I shall tell you all about it at another time.

You see what a mercy it was that we thought of sending him there. I shall write this very night to delay his return."

Maria looked inquisitively at Warrenne, but his countenance baffled her skill in attempting to read its expression. She was, however, relieved on hearing that Basil was, at least for the present, in safety; and went to engage her young friends to put on the semblance of mirth. She, in a few words, told them her errand; and soon the sounds of gaiety were heard, while whispers, and looks of anxiety and alarm, were interchanged by the young dancers, who were soon relieved by hearing the bell for evening prayers.

One glance at her mother's pale countenance proved to Maria that she was suffering from a new cause of alarm and anxiety. Warrenne himself repeated the prayers; which, without seeming more rapid than other priests in his utterance, he always contrived to finish in half the time.

When the service was closed, all the party, excepting Mrs Clarenham, assembled at supper. She found herself quite unable longer to wear the exterior of calmness, and retired to her own apartment. She was soon joined by Maria, and a short time after by Warrenne, who requested a few moments' conversation with her. He was immediately admitted, and hastened to inform her, as he said, of the nature of her son's mission to Rome. She listened in silent acquiescence. It was on affairs which, he said, were important to the English Catholics. She scarcely understood their nature, after his professing to explain it to her; but, if it was to advance the interests of the Church, she could not object; and she was thankful that God, in his gracious providence, had so ordered events, that, whatever she might suffer from his absence, Basil at least was safe.

While this conversation was going on, Maria intently watched the expressions of Warrenne's countenance, and saw, or thought she saw, that, while he spoke a species of cant to her mother, his thoughts were at times far away. In this supposition she was soon confirmed. After rising to take leave, Warrenne seeming as if he had suddenly recollected something,—

"Ah!" said he, "I was sure I had forgot something—but these matters are so little a part of my duty. Madam, I received, some days ago, an intimation from Rome, that, in the present state of our affairs in this unhappy erring country, every means ought to be taken to connect, by the closest ties, those families who still adhered to the ancient faith. Amongst other instructions, tending to further this fatherly plan, I am informed, that his holiness, as General Clarenham left him a power in his will to do so, chooses to dispense with that clause which makes it necessary that Miss Clarenham should be of age before the union of the two families, and wills that union to take place without delay. I have told you this, Madam, in your daughter's presence, because I know there are some clauses in General Clarenham's will, regarding which she may, perhaps, find it necessary to have some conversations with me, that I may be satisfied she is ready to comply with them."

"So I am to be deprived of all my children," said Mrs Clarenham, in a voice of the deepest dejection. " Well," added she, " My God, thy will be done."

" It is not God's will, my dearest, ever dearest, kindest mother !" exclaimed Maria. " God has commanded me to love and honour you, not to leave you in grief and solitude ; and no Pope shall oblige me to disobey the plain commands of God and the feelings of nature."

" My dear young lady," said Warrenne, soothingly, " I am sure you will be indulged in whatever you wish by Sir Thomas Carysford's family. Whatever arrangement Mrs Clarenham may propose——"

" No, no, Father," interrupted Mrs Clarenham, " I shall propose nothing. Why should I withdraw an only son, an only child from his parents? I never will. God sees that I am too, too much wrapt up in these earthly blessings ; therefore he means to wean me from them. Shall I not bow in submission to his will ?"

" Maria stood up ; and, raising her eyes to heaven with an expression of awe, remained silent for a few moments, then said solemnly, but calmly, " Hear me, Father, while I plainly declare that I cannot, in my present state of mind, fulfil my uncle's will. I cannot profess that I firmly believe in the doctrines of the Church of Rome. I cannot promise to remain in her communion. Her's does not appear to me the faith of the Bible; and I am prepared to give up my title to all my uncle left me. That I give up without a feeling of pain. I cannot say so with regard to all I must resign. I am ill prepared for a change in the feelings of those who have hitherto loved, and esteemed, and rested hopes on me; but I think I could even meet that change—all changes—death itself,—sooner than give up the Bible."

Warrenne seemed struck mute with astonishment.

"Maria! my child! what do you mean?" exclaimed Mrs Clarenham, scarcely able to believe she had heard distinctly.

"I mean to remain with you, my dearest, dearest mother. To devote myself to you. To show you what the Bible teaches those who simply obey its precepts. Catherine may possess my fortune. I will remain with you."

"It must not be, my own best, ever kindest

child. Leave us, Father Adrian. Forgive us. Our minds are weakened, and our spirits are broken by misfortune."

Warrenne bowed, and in silence left the room. And Maria, after two hours' earnest conversation with her mother, left her, though not reconciled to her change of views, yet deeply alive to the warmly devotional feelings now almost for the first time expressed by Maria in her presence, and soothed by her affection; and the hope that, for a time at least, they would not be separated.

CHAPTER IX.

—" Che giova all' uomo di guadagnare tutto il mondo, se poi perda l'anima."
Martini's Trans.—Matth. xvi. 26.

MARIA had not courage to meet the family at breakfast next morning: yet, as it was known that Mrs Clarenham, even at home, preferred spending her mornings alone, she had no excuse for her absence. After several times, however, leaving her room some steps on her way to the breakfast-room, her heart still failed, and she returned again and again to reason herself into composure. At last, finding the effort vain, she went to her sister's room, to ask her to apologise for her absence.

Catherine's life, since coming to Carysford Park, had been spent in alternate acts of devotion and scenes of amusement. Ever since Dormer had become her spiritual director, she had been gradually becoming less remarkable as a saint. He had given her spiritual direction and advice, altogether different from that she had been accustomed to receive from her foreign confessor, or from Father Dennis. He had disregarded and discouraged the visionary turn of mind which had been cherished in her convent, and to the dreams of which old Elliston had not troubled himself to listen; and had spoken to her of the danger of self-exaltation; of the necessity of self-knowledge; of the lowliness of heart which ever accompanied it; and urged her to contemplate, as the only, altogether, perfect pattern of holiness, the character of Jesus Christ. And every penance he imposed, had tended to mortify and check all those desires after the attainment of a certain species of saintship, which had hitherto been fostered by her spiritual guides. Dormer had thus succeeded in lowering Catherine's opinion of herself, but he had not taught her to pray for that new heart which alone loves the things of the Spirit. *That*, his Church taught, was bestowed in baptism; and he only urged her to *use* a power, of which poor Catherine was still destitute. When that earthly distinction at which she aimed, and the means by which she hoped to attain it, were lessened in her estimation, all that she knew of religion lost its attraction; and now she became every day less able to fulfil the round of observances she had imposed on herself.

On this morning, though it was not early, Maria found Catherine with her beads still half unsaid. She seemed vexed at being detected thus remiss, and Maria turned away, and stood at a window, with her face from her, till she had repeated the remaining prayers, not one of which she understood.

"Well, Maria," said Catherine, rather sharply, "to what am I indebted for this visit?"

"Is it not the breakfast hour, Catherine?"

"If it is, you do not usually require my assistance to reach the breakfast-room."

"No; but I am come to beg you will apologise for my not appearing there this morning."

"What, dear Maria, are you unwell?" asked Catherine, immediately softening into kindness.

"Only in mind, dear Catherine. But I cannot explain just now. Indeed, it is nothing new to you; so, good bye,"—and she kissed Catherine and left her.

Maria continued in her own room for a time, attempting, but with little success, to dissipate the cloud which had gathered on her spirits. She then joined her mother.

Here Catherine soon followed in search of her. "You must come, Maria. It was you yourself who proposed the sailing party for to-day. Every one asks for you, excepting Edward,—he, indeed, would always have you indulged."

"Do go, my love," said Mrs Clarenham. "You *must* again meet your friends."

"Did Lady Carysford say anything when I did not appear at breakfast?" asked Maria.

"I do not know what is the matter with Lady Carysford," replied Catherine. "You know Sir Thomas says nothing will make her take an interest in public affairs; yet we know of nothing distressing besides which has happened, and she looks as if she had wept all night. When she heard you were not in spirits to join the breakfast party, her eyes again filled with tears, and she rose, and said she would come to you. Sir Thomas stopt her with one of his peremptory 'No, my dears,' and down she sat again; but I thought every good thing on the table was to be sent to you."

"Dear Lady Carysford!" said Maria, in vain endeavouring to restrain her tears. She, however, got ready, and accompanied Catherine to join her young friends.

All received her as the life and joy of the party, and with kind attentions and inquiries—all but young Carysford: his address was cold and hurried; and he immediately discovered that he must, for some reason or other, go on board the boat which awaited them on the lake: nor did he return to offer his assistance to Maria, which, on similar occasions, was regarded by all as a matter of course. Another gentleman assisted her into the boat; and Carysford had placed himself to act as pilot, in order, apparently, to avoid her. Another boat, with music, kept at a little distance. The air was balm. Scarcely a breath of wind passed over the glassy lake: and the scenery which bounded its smooth expanse looked even more than usually lovely and magnificent. Maria regarded it with feelings of extreme sadness; and, at that moment, she knew something of what that suffering is, which is described by "leaving all." Exclamations of delight and admiration were every moment expressed by her young companions, while the music, softened by the distance, tended to deepen her sadness. At last she was appealed to by a young friend,—

"You are silent, Maria Clarenham. Is it possible one can become so accustomed to those scenes as to be insensible to their beauty?"

"Ah, no!" replied Maria, unconsciously speaking in a tone of voice full of sadness, "That is not the effect produced by such scenes. I am sure, wherever my lot may be cast, I shall ever regard them as the loveliest, and most attractive on the face of the earth, and only admire others as they resemble them."

"Haggerstone, Jerningham, pray how long do you mean to leave me at the helm without having the grace to offer me assistance," said young Carysford, with something of his usual cheerfulness. He looked towards Jerningham, who was seated next Maria, and his eyes met her's. He immediately looked away, but she saw that the cold distant expressions with which he had before regarded her had given place to those of happier and kindlier feelings. She was conscious of the power she possessed over his affections, and tears filled her eyes as he took Jerningham's place by her. He seemed to have observed them, for he did not address her; but his attentions, his looks, his whole manner seemed to intreat her forgiveness: and, she felt deeply and bitterly, that, however painful it may be to separate from and give up for ever what is lovely and attractive in natural scenery, it is altogether nothing when compared to the breaking up of those living attachments which have become a part of our nature. Never, till now, had she known that she felt so kindly for Carysford; but still one rapid glance into the future convinced her that she must either prepare to separate her affections from him, or give up what she no longer had the power to give up—that knowledge of truth which made it impossible for her to believe in many doctrines of his church. Such thoughts mingled with all that passed during the time the party continued on the lake. When they landed, Carysford, as usual, was at her side, and offered his arm. She accepted his offer, but felt embarrassed, and they walked on in silence. Maria, at last, on coming to a path which led to the flower garden, from whence was an entrance to her mother's apartments, withdrew her arm, saying she would shorten the distance by taking that path.

"We shall see you at dinner, I hope?" said Carysford, apparently unwilling to leave her.

"Certainly."

He walked on a few steps to open a little gate that was in her way; then observing his mother approaching, he left her.

Maria looked anxiously at Lady Carysford, as she advanced, to read in her countenance the reception she might expect to meet with from her. She seemed in deeper thought than was at all usual for her, and did not perceive Maria's approach till she had almost reached her, then tried to assume an air of coldness, and said—

"I have just been with your mother, Miss

Clarenham, and find she is determined to leave us this evening."

"So soon!" said Maria, and her eyes filled with tears.

Lady Carysford's countenance immediately softened.

"Are you sorry then to leave us after all, Maria?"

"I pray God, Lady Carysford, that no member of your family may feel half the sorrow I do," replied Maria, bursting into tears, and attempting to pass.

Lady Carysford caught her hand—"What does all this mean, my dearest Maria? You have only to say you are what you used to be—you have only to say you will give up your cousin and return to us. We shall never think more of this little estrangement—all shall be as it was before. Do not leave us—do not again see your cousin. You cannot—you do not feel for him as you soon will for Edward."

"What on earth do you mean, my dearest Lady Carysford?" interrupted Maria. "You are altogether mistaken. What"—

"My dearest girl, I will say no more about

it. I do not wish to pain you. Oh, that we might never, never, have one thought more on the subject!"

"What subject, my dear madam? Indeed I must ask you to explain what you mean. I am sure you are in some strange error."

"No, no, my dear. Do you think I am so blind as not to see what is so plain, and what it was so natural should happen? Your young cousin, Ernest Montague, is a fine youth. His character stands high in every one's opinion. Are not all the strangers who come to this part of the country taken to see Illerton village? So much industry—such admirable schools—not a pauper to be seen in all the village, while Hallern and our villages are full of them. Not an idle creature; and such fields and gardens, and so forth; and all brought to this state of perfection by the Montagues and their chaplain, but above all, by young Montague. O it was most natural that your young mind should be dazzled by such representations, and knowing too the pleasing sensible youth; but Edward will do whatever you choose in these kind of things."

"My dearest Lady Carysford," interrupted Maria, "I intreat you to hear me. My cousin Ernest is no more concerned in what I declared before Father Adrian last night than his sister is. They have led me to examine the Bible; but I have no preference whatever for Ernest, that I might not retain were I your daughter; and he never gave me the slightest cause to suppose that he regarded me in any other light than I have been regarded by all others, as the affianced daughter of your house."

Maria spoke with emphatic solemnity, and Lady Carysford listened with surprise in her looks.

"Then, my dear, what is all this? what are we differing about? You attend prayers in the chapel—you attend mass—you eat no meat on fast days—I am sure neither Sir Thomas nor I will suffer you to be prevented associating with your amiable young cousins if you choose, or from reading a few Protestant books if you wish it—or what is it you do wish?"

"You know, my dear madam, my having fortune depends entirely on my declaring myself a decided member of the Church of Rome. Now, I do attend prayers in the chapel; but when Father Adrian, or Father Clement, repeats what I do not understand, I attempt to pray to God in my heart, for it is the heart God regards. I do attend mass; for, on that point, though I begin to hesitate, I am still more of a Catholic than a Protestant; and I do not eat meat on fast days, because it is the same to me whether I do so or not; and, in a matter so perfectly insignificant, I do what those around me do: but I do not believe in the infallibility of the Romish Church. On the contrary, I begin to suspect she is the most corrupt of all the Christian churches."

"My love, how strangely you speak! All the *Christian* churches! Surely there can be but one true Christian church."

"I shall say churches professing Christianity, then, my dear madam: But you remember Christ Himself addresses the *Seven* Churches of Asia as Christian churches, and reproves and threatens several of them for the corruptions into which they had fallen, yet addresses all as if there were true Christians in each. Such, I hope, my dear Madam, is still the case with the Christian churches of our day; but I cannot partake in the sins of any of them, after I see that they are sins. The Bible has been my guide in this, and must be my guide in all things; and I cannot give up reading the Bible for myself."

"Hush, hush, my love! that will never do."

"And therefore, my dear madam, I cannot declare myself a Roman Catholic."

Lady Carysford looked much distressed.

"Father Adrian is so determined on hurrying this business," said she, "and Sir Thomas is so completely led by him—and they have been tormenting poor Edward,—proposing your sister Catherine to him, as it seems your fortune goes to her if you leave the church; and he vows, that if such a proposal is ever again made to him he will go abroad next day. He declares he can love none but you, and that he cares not for fortune—that if you choose to become a Protestant you may; and that it was neither to your religion nor to your fortune he was engaged, but to yourself: and that though you may think yourself at liberty to break that engagement, he regards it as quite as sacred as if it had been fulfilled; and that, as long as you are unmarried, no power on earth can induce him to think otherwise; and that, if you marry, he will never be happy again. In short, the poor boy was half distracted last night—and so jealous of young Montague: one time he would blow his Protestant brains out, and then he would not hurt a hair of his head, if it would give you pain: and his father was angry, and Father Adrian contemptuous. Such a scene! But Sir Thomas swore a Protestant should never be his daughter. So, my dear, what is to be done?"

Maria thought for a few moments, then said —"Edward is right; we are engaged. I have no title—I have no wish to break that engagement. I can say no more; but assure him"—

"Here he comes," said Lady Carysford.

Ernest had lingered at a distance till his mother should join him. She now motioned to him to approach, and going to meet him, said in a low voice—"It is all a mistake about Ernest Montague. Maria cares not for him. She has told me so herself. She does not wish to break her engagement with you, but she cannot declare herself a Roman Catholic."

"I cannot, indeed, Edward, for I am not one," said Maria, who had heard Lady Carysford's last words as she approached.

Pleasure beamed in young Carysford's looks, while he said, half reproachfully—"And can *you*, Maria, be so ungenerous as to desert our cause at this moment, when her friends are few, and all seems going against her. Were the church in her former state of prosperity we might then do as we chose."

"Nay, replied Maria, smiling, "were she in her former prosperity, I should be burnt."

It had become habitual to Maria, in her intercourse with young Carysford, to evade, by a kind of playful sauciness, those allusions which he was continually making to their peculiar situation; and now her lively countenance had again brightened, for a moment, into its usual playful expression.

"Well, I am rejoiced to see you both like yourselves again," exclaimed Lady Carysford with delight. "Now do not let that sad face return, Maria; for you are, next to Edward, the light, the very sunshine of my life. Say to me, my dearest child, my daughter, that you will give up these new fancies, and let us all be happy once more. Now the cloud returns—well, let us say no more. Let us wait"—

"Yes, dearest madam, let us wait," interrupted Maria. "I can say nothing."

"Yes, Maria," said Edward, "you can say you will not desert a falling cause."

"If it is a bad cause, Edward, why should it not fall?"

"But such a time to discover it to be a bad one!"

"Do you mean the cause of the Stuarts, or that of the Church of Rome?"

"Both."

"I do not desert the Stuarts. I wish them success—at least I have been in the habit of doing so, as all my friends, or at least most of them do. I have thought little on the subject, for I can neither aid nor injure them: but it is different, Edward, when the safety of the soul is at stake."

“ But even Protestants allow that members of our church may be saved.”

“ Yes ; those who, in the midst of her errors, rest their hopes on the truths she still teaches —those who have never had it in their power to know her errors ; but not those who have been made acquainted with the Bible, and yet choose to be guided by what is contrary to its precepts.”

“ Well, Maria, whatever misery it may cost me, I cannot desert our friends at such a time. I will not seek to judge for myself, and I will not listen to you on the subject—but I will do no more—you shall, in all things, be your own mistress.”

“ Stop Edward—such arrangements cannot be made by you, nor by me. We both have parents. Your mother has left us, (she had walked on,) but she has told me that Sir Thomas has sworn that he never will receive a Protestant into his family as a daughter.”

“ My father cannot keep such a resolution. I shall leave home till he changes it.”

“ Oh Edward, how wrong.”

"Why so? Is he to make me wretched, and expect me to think of nothing but his gratification? I should not have been idle here, and all our friends in arms, but for him. Can this last for ever? And he to dictate to me in the nearest ties. You leave this to-day, Maria. I go to-morrow, unless he allows me to follow you with his permission to make what arrangements you choose."

"No, no, no, Edward. I will not agree to this. I will arrange nothing. Promise to do me one favour, Edward."

"What, Maria?"

"Say not one word further on this subject, unless your friends oblige you, until my brother's return. Nothing could induce me to leave my mother till then; why, therefore, do any thing?"

"I will promise, on condition you suffer me to see you daily, and consult with you on all that passes."

"I will, provided I find your friends do not object."

"And will you make me one promise, Maria?"

"What?"

"To remember, while you are gaining more acquaintance with the Protestant religion, how long your family, our family, all our ancestors, have suffered and struggled for the ancient faith; and ask yourself whether a Clarenham ought to abandon it."

"Yes, Edward; provided you will sometimes ask yourself, whether a rational being will be able to answer, at the great day, for having, in the most momentous of all concerns, given up the mind and soul God gave him to the guidance and direction of a fellow-sinner, without ever having employed that mind to know the will of God, in that revelation of it which he has given to man?"

Edward smiled, but promised; and, shortly after, the young friends parted: and, after again meeting at dinner, where, from Sir Thomas Carysford's stiff and pompous manner, all was embarrassment and restraint, Mrs Clarenham and her daughters set out on their return to Hallern Castle.

CHAPTER X.

—" Verra tempo, che chi v' uccidera, si creda di rendere onore a Dio."

Martini's Trans.—John xvi. 2.

Several weeks passed away, during which each individual of the family at Hallern Castle was occupied with subjects of the deepest interest and anxiety. On one point, however, certainty, or peace seemed as distant as ever. There were no letters from young Clarenham—no accounts of him. Mrs Clarenham was wretched. Dormer seemed equally so; and his answers to her inquiries, though intended to remove her anxiety, were so unsatisfactory, and the expression of his countenance, whenever Basil was the subject, so mournfully grave, that, though he attempted to do away her uneasiness, she felt certain he himself participated in it. His health, too, had become wretched; and his abstemiousness increased, not from religious motives, but from utter loss of appetite. His person was becoming every day more emaciated; and the expression of his countenance, habitually melancholy, was now marked by extreme dejection.

Maria observed all this; and it increased her anxiety respecting Basil, while it excited a feeling of sympathy and regard for Dormer, which was every day increased by her observation of his unremitted exertions to fulfil all those religious duties which he considered himself bound to perform. Amidst this anxiety regarding her brother, and cares for her mother, and compassion for Dormer, Maria had to guide, and check, and soothe the unrestrained, undisciplined spirit of young Carysford. Till now he had known nothing but unbounded indulgence; and his impatience, while a doubt seemed to hang over the completion of his dearest wishes, made him, like other spoilt children, throw every other source of happiness from him, and torment himself almost into madness regarding that which seemed a thousand-fold increased in value, by the difficulty thrown in the way of its attainment. Each morning Carysford rode over to Hallern, full of some new scheme by which he was to compel his father to accede to his wishes, or some argument by which he was to persuade Maria to give up her new religion. And, again, when Maria would no longer remain absent from her mother, to converse with him, returned home, soothed—more rational—convinced that Maria alone could render him happy; and determined to imitate her in that resignation to the present arrangements of Providence, which she attempted to convince him could not be broken through, without committing sin against that God who could, in a thousand ways, compel them to wait the decisions of his will: but the evenings spent with his father and Warrenne—the one cold and dictatorial, assuming too late an authority he had never possessed,—the other acute and sarcastic, levelling his irony against Protestantism,—did away all the effects of the happier morning, and sent him back to Maria unchanged.

The evenings spent so wretchedly by Carysford were the least unhappy hours of Maria's day. Some of the Montagues spent those hours generally at Hallern. Lady Montague, carefully avoiding every point on which they could differ, was again the friend from whose society Mrs Clarenham received her chief pleasure; and Adeline spent hours in reading the Bible with Maria, and giving her Dr Lowther's explanation of those passages, which, on former evenings, they had not perfectly understood. Maria, however, was cautious in receiving any explanation which did not appear obvious to herself, and sometimes would venture to apply to Dormer to explain what appeared to her made no plainer by Dr Lowther. On such occasions, Dormer was ever ready to give the explanation put upon the passage by his church; but also seemed to consider it his duty to speak with warmth against the presumption of venturing the salvation of her soul on the decision of her own private judgment. He seemed, however, rather desirous to engage her in such conversations; and she, too, had pleasure in conversing with him: for, whatever his subjection of mind might be to his fellow-men—his superiors in the church—she felt that he was more devoted to the service of God—more lowly in heart—more fearful of the slightest levity on religious subjects—more in continual awe and recollection of the presence of a holy God, than she was.

Sometimes Dormer would remain when Lady Montague came to spend the evening with her cousin—at first for a short time, and as if to observe her style of conversation; but gradually his stay became longer. Lady Montague's lowly, fervent piety—her frank but respectful manner to himself—and her cheerfulness, seemed to overcome his reserve: and, while Maria and Adeline sought earnestly for instruction from the Bible in another apartment, the two elder ladies and Dormer conversed with openness and increasing mutual regard, on those religious subjects with which we only become acquainted by experience. The perverseness of the human heart—its deep-rooted aversion—its determined alienation from that holiness required by God;—the necessity of chastisements and afflictions to wean the affections from the world:—on such subjects Dormer spoke with a feeling, and eloquence, and experience, to which Lady Montague listened with deep and evident interest: and she could with humility acknowledge how slight her own impressions on those subjects were, compared to what they ought to be, and compared to those expressed by him. He, on his part, would listen with earnest attention when she spoke of the effects produced by belief in the love of God—that love which he manifested in Christ; of its powerful influence in subduing sin, and winning the heart to obedience: and to the receiving of every dispensation, however afflictive, as sent, in Fatherly love, to purify and prepare the heart for heaven.

Ernest Montague now frequently joined in these conversations. For a time he had been constantly and actively employed with other gentlemen in the north of England, in taking measures to secure the safety of the country, in the expectation of the Scotch rebels penetrating into England. But that alarm was now over. The cause was losing ground in every quarter; and those gentlemen, who had most ardently come forward to oppose it, were again returning to their usual quiet pursuits.

One evening, Ernest had accompanied his mother to Hallern, and had found the conversation so interesting that he asked permission to return; and, young and reserved as he was, his mind did not seem far behind those with whom he conversed, in the experience of that discipline which, in one way or other, is common to all Christians.

Ernest, on these occasions, was struck with Dormer's looks; and he and his mother agreed, that, whatever might be his errors, his heart was so evidently, so deeply, so touchingly humble and devoted to God, and his health declining so fast, that he appeared to them hastening to a better world.

During this period, Catherine spent much of her time at Carysford Park; not that it was hoped young Carysford would transfer his affections to her, at least by any but Sir Thomas,—for, ever since the idea had been suggested to him, she seemed to have become his aversion, and Lady Carysford's also: but Warrenne had a new plan in view, to which her devoted inclination was also necessary. Warrenne's plan was, to have a nunnery endowed in that part of England. He had long been aware, that unwillingness in parents to send their children, particularly their daughters, abroad for education, had exposed them to intercourse with Protestants at that age when the mind is most alive to religious impressions, and from the influence of which his church had lost many members. His plan now was, to induce Catherine to devote the fortune he foresaw, if he hurried matters, would be her's, to this purpose. He soon succeeded in obtaining the influence he desired over Catherine's mind. He became her confessor; and, in a very short time, she again was as great a saint as ever. Under the pretence of warning her against the worldly temptations that might await her, he had hinted at what were her future prospects, and set forth the merit of devoting wealth to the church; and afterwards, in conversation, praised, as the greatest saints, those who had spent their fortunes in endowing such institutions, and expatiated on the holy, happy state of a young lady abbess. All was exactly suited to Catherine's turn of mind; and visions of future eminence again rendered all her mortifications, and penances, and prayers, as easy as ever.

One evening, as Ernest Montague was proceeding in his usual thoughtful manner to Hallern Castle, deeply engaged in following out a subject he had entered upon with Dormer the last evening they had met, he was startled in the darkest part of the wooded path through which he was passing, by a man coming from among some trees, and placing himself in the path before him. The suspicious-looking stranger was completely muffled up in a large cloak, and his hat drawn over his face. Ernest paused, and stood on the defensive.

"I wish to speak to you, Mr Montague," said the man, in an under-tone of voice; "but I must, on no account, be seen here."

"Are you from Scotland?" asked Ernest, approaching nearer. "You may speak. No one is near."

The man looked around him from under his hat—then, seeming assured that he was not observed, he drew the mufflings from his face, and, to Ernest's surprise and instant alarm, discovered himself to be the confidential servant who had gone abroad with Basil Clarenham.

"Ainsworth!" exclaimed Ernest—"And your master?"

"I intreat you, Sir, be cautious. My master is lost if I am seen here."

"Lost!" repeated Ernest, in a suppressed tone of voice—"What, where is he?"

"In a prison of the Inquisition at Rome," replied Ainsworth.

Ernest was struck mute. An Englishman of the present day would smile at the supposition that a foreign Inquisition would venture to secrete an Englishman, of a well-known family, as he does at many things he hears ascribed to the Church of Rome, by those who have studied her character as it was displayed in the days of her power; but Ernest lived nearer those days, and was aware of the extreme difficulty with which deliverance was obtained from the prisons of that mysterious but powerful tribunal.

"Are you certain of what you have just told me, Ainsworth?" asked he at last in a low voice.

"Perfectly so, Sir. I myself was also a prisoner."

"But that does not prove him of whom you spoke to be so, Ainsworth. It is not the custom of that tribunal to let its actions be known to any but the individual who is the subject of them."

"True, Sir: but I know my master was in the same prison. I am not at liberty to say more; for I was liberated only on taking a solemn oath never to divulge what I witnessed there. I am a Catholic, Sir. I abhor all heresy; and I think you, Mr Ernest, have the guilt of misleading my young master—but I have been about him ever since he was a child, —they did not take my oath regarding ought but what I witnessed in the prison. If you, Mr Montague, betray my having been in this country, the intelligence will instantly be conveyed to Rome, and my master will be removed, where those who now might serve him can have no influence."

"Has your master been long where he now is?"

"He was, on his first going to Rome, lodged

in the Monastery of ——, where he soon found he was to be considered as a prisoner, until the Fathers should attempt to overcome those notions against the faith which he had learnt from you, Mr Ernest. He was, however, treated with great respect, and was permitted to amuse himself as he chose within the walls, till it was found that he spent most of his time in the library, and was detected various times reading books forbidden by the Inquisitors; and, at last, Sir, a New Testament, with the prohibitory mark of the Holy Office upon it, was found in his apartment; and, when the Fathers remonstrated with my master, and removed the book, he said they could no longer prevent his knowing its contents, for he had spent most of the time he had been in the Monastery in committing a great part of them to memory; and they now were, he said, in his heart, from whence they had entirely banished the belief that the Romish was any other than the most corrupt of churches professing Christianity. I myself heard him say so, Sir," continued Ainsworth, "and you know, Mr Ernest, where he first learnt these notions." The man seemed to struggle between indignation at Ernest and love for his young master.

"And then he was conveyed to a prison!" said Ernest, much moved. "Dear, dear Basil!"

"It is not the way to do him any good," said Ainsworth, also moved. "But I must not stay here, Sir."

"Have you seen Mr Dormer? Does he know what you have told me?"

"Seen him! No, Sir. He is the person I most dread seeing. He *must* know where my master is. He persuaded him to go abroad. He arranged every thing, and my master has constantly corresponded with him ever since he left home."

"Not directly," said Ernest sternly, on recollecting Mrs Clarenham's anxiety for letters, and Dormer's silence respecting those he was now said to have received.

"No, Sir, all letters to the priests are sent first to Father Adrian."

"Villain! hypocrite! true Jesuit!" muttered Ernest, as he thought of Dormer. "And what can be done? Who can follow the windings of such wretches?" said he aloud, and eyeing the man with looks of disgust and suspicion. "Confiding, amiable, excellent Clarenham!"

"It is all your own doing, Sir," said Aimsworth, indignantly. "Father Clement loves his soul better than his present comfort. I am not so good as he is: I can only be miserable till my master is at liberty. And now, Sir, this is all I think can be done:—You know there is what is called rebellion still in Scotland. Your family are known to have been very successful in gaining information which led to the suppression of the rising in the north of England. Father Clement will believe it, Sir, if you say you have gained certain intelligence that it was he and Father Adrian who sent my master abroad as bearer of confidential dispatches from Lord Derwentwater to the King. Say, also, that you have further information respecting Mr Basil; and that, if you are not assured solemnly that he shall return in safety in less than two months, all shall be made public. One word from Father Adrian is sufficient to release my master; and Father Clement will trust your honour, if you pledge it to reveal nothing should my master appear within the time specified. And now, Sir, I must be gone. I shall not leave England, but must depart from this neighbourhood; yet you may perhaps soon see me again." The man then turned into a by-path in the wood, and was instantly out of sight.

Ernest stood motionless for a few minutes. He knew not how to proceed, while he became more and more alive to the danger of young Clarenham's situation. Dormer's last conversations,—his pale, sad countenance, only lighted up when conversing on subjects most deeply spiritual,—his chastened manners, expressive of the most constant and severe self-government,—the benignity and kindness with which he had always treated himself, now returned with softening influence to Ernest's recollection; and, still undetermined, he again proceeded, but now at a quickened pace, towards Hallern Castle. He had not half-crossed the park, however, before he had twenty times changed his purpose,—whether at once to reproach Dormer with his abuse of the confidence reposed in him by young Clarenham and his family, and endeavour to alarm him into instant exertions for Basil's safety—or to meet him as one led, by devotion to his spiritual superiors, to do what threatened in the end to endanger the life or intellects of the being he loved most on earth, and which, from unceasing anxiety, and the struggle between supposed duty and his natural feelings, was undermining the springs of his own existence. The last supposition, on looking back, appeared to him to be the true one; and his heart readily yielded to the belief that it was so.

"Can I see Mr Dormer alone?" asked he, when a servant opened the hall-door.

The man hesitated. "Father Clement desired that he might not be disturbed for an hour, Sir," replied he. "He is particularly engaged."

"I must see him," said Ernest rather peremptorily.

The man looked surprised, for Ernest's manner was, in general, peculiarly free from every thing of the kind.

"If you must, Sir, it is not my fault. I shall tell Father Clement so." And he proceeded towards Dormer's apartment, followed by Ernest, who stopt, however, at some distance, to allow the servant to announce his approach. The man knocked gently at the door of Dormer's room. Dormer himself opened it, and, in a tone of voice so mild as to confirm Ernest in his favourable interpretation of his conduct, answered the man's half-indignant—

" Father, I would not have disobeyed your orders, if I could have helped it."

" I believe it, my son; but do not detain me, for at this moment my time is precious."

" Mr Ernest Montague will not be denied seeing you, Father."

Ernest approached. " I have business, Mr Dormer, of sufficient importance to excuse this intrusion."

" I guess its nature, I believe, Mr Montague," replied Dormer, courteously inviting him to enter.

For an instant Ernest forgot even his purpose, on glancing round the apartment of the dignified, polished Dormer. It was a small square room, in one of the towers of the Castle. The floor, which was of stone, was uncarpeted. A small iron bed-stead, without curtains, on which were a single blanket and mattress, two wooden chairs, and a table, was all the furniture it contained. One wide shelf extended along a side of the room, on which lay a good many books; and in the window which looked east was placed, as if in contrast to the bareness and poverty of the apartment, a beautifully sculptured marble slab, supporting a crucifix of the most perfect workmanship, every agonized muscle and suffering expression of which was now seen in the bright light of the evening sun, which glowed upon it from an opposite window.

Dormer placed one of the small wooden chairs for his guest, and, seating himself nearly opposite to him on the other—"I believe, Mr Montague," said he, "I have guessed the kind motive which brought you hither. You have heard of the suspicions which have fallen upon the Catholic priests in this neighbourhood, and the search that is about to take place for secret and rebellious instructions supposed to be concealed by us; and, bad as your opinion of our order is, there is still one of the number you would rather should not suffer, and you generously wish to warn him of his danger. You are silent. I see it is so, and I wish I could find means to prove my gratitude to you for this, and many, many other kindnesses you have shewn to me. Of this danger we have been apprised, and are prepared to meet it. We are accustomed to such suspicions, and must bear them as we best can for the sake of truth."

"I knew not of these suspicions," replied Ernest. "I deserve not your gratitude, Mr Dormer. My business is entirely of a different nature."

"Is it of life and death then?" asked Dormer, with one of his sad smiles,—"for, if not, I must ask you to wait till I have looked over some papers. It is wonderful what kind of things, in my situation, may be construed into treason."

"My business *may* be of life and death," said Ernest: "but I shall wait:" and he rose and turned to the cross, to look more narrowly on its ever interesting representation. Dormer followed him with a look of alarm; but, on Ernest assuring him that a short delay would be of no consequence, he took down a small portfolio from the book-shelf, and began rapidly to look over some papers it contained, while Ernest continued alternately to regard him and the crucifix; his thoughts, as usual, being soon deeply engaged with the two subjects, which, as they then were to him, have been, and still are, to informed and reflecting minds, the most powerfully interesting which can be offered for contemplation—the permission of evil, and the astonishing means employed to overcome it. In Dormer he thought he saw the most mysterious difficulties personified;—a being panting after good; yet, so under the influence of evil, as to be seeking that good in a path where he found only sorrow and disappointment so deep as to waste his very form to the pale emaciated figure which now sat before him. The setting sun shed a glow of something like health over his thin white temples as he stooped: and the representation of that which purchased redemption for man, shed a something like the light of truth over his system of religion; but neither seemed to reach his case. The expression of his countenance, as he continued to glance rapidly over his papers, was so deeply marked by mental suffering, as to betray a soul as far from peace as his person was from health. Some papers he burnt, lighting them at a taper which was placed on the hearth, for there was no fire in his room. One paper he put aside, after seeming to hesitate whether or not to burn it, and that more than once.

At last the examination was finished; and, after restoring the portfolio to its place, and putting the paper he had reserved in his bosom —" Now, Mr Montague," said he, " if it is in my power to serve you, believe me there are very few things, indeed, which would gratify me more."

" It is in your power, Mr Dormer, and, I believe, only in yours."

Dormer warmly shook hands with Ernest. " Only tell me how that I may do whatever you wish."

Ernest grasped his hand. " Even if your church should disapprove ?"

" Nay ; that I cannot promise," replied Dormer gently. " Would Mr Montague himself be led, even by his most esteemed friend, to act contrary to the dictates of his conscience?"

"I hope not, Mr Dormer, were I certain the infallible word of God was the guide of my conscience."

"The word of God is also the guide of the church," replied Dormer.

"No," said Ernest, emphatically. "The word of God plainly declares, of those who do evil that good may come, 'That their damnation is just;'* but your church teaches that the end sanctifies the means. The word of God says, 'Thou shalt do no murder;' but the church of Rome says, it is justifiable to murder thousands on thousands, provided the suppression of what she calls heresy is the end aimed at. Can *you*, Mr Dormer, in obedience to that church—can you, in the hope to produce what you call good, so blind *your* mind, as to suppose God will not require, at your hands, an account of the trust,"—Ernest stopt. He could not proceed, as he looked on Dormer's calm holy countenance, who seemed mildly to await whatever he chose to say.

* Rom. iii, 8.

"Let me understand you, Mr Montague. I thought you were going to put it in my power to serve you," said Dormer. "If you begin by attacking my church, you must allow me to vindicate her."

"Not now, Mr Dormer;" then again grasping his hand, but looking on the ground as he spoke:—"It is impossible, Mr Dormer, to vindicate a church which demands from its ministers a subjection so absolute as to compel them, rather than suffer heresy from her dogmas, to involve a confiding fatherless youth under age, the only son of his newly widowed mother, the last hope of a falling house, in a desperate rebellion,—then imprison him in a convent,—and at last give him up to the merciless tribunal of the Inquisition!"

Ernest did not venture to look at Dormer, as he concluded, but turned away, and continued to gaze intently from the window.

In proportion to what we ourselves would feel were we convicted of a deed of shame, do we sympathize with those, hitherto considered worthy of esteem, who are so convicted, and still more if we are the means of that conviction: and it was long ere Ernest could turn to look at the now silent Dormer. When, at last, he did so, his stealing glance would, to an observer, have bespoken him the criminal. Dormer, however, did not see it. He sat leaning against the table, his hands covering his face. The veins in his forehead seemed swelled to bursting, and his deep, quick, unequal respiration betrayed the tumult within; but he spoke not. Ernest regarded him with heartfelt affection and compassion, but he shrunk from breaking the silence. He felt as if by doing so he would assume the part of one superior in goodness, and entitled to reprove; and when the point seemed already so humbly yielded, who could have added one feeling of depression to the struggle that was agonising that lowly spirit.

At last Dormer raised his head. His eyes met Ernest's, and fell under them, but instantly raising them, he said, with an expression of haughtiness and resentment:

"I would wish to be alone, Mr Montague."

Ernest was instantly going, and bowed with an expression of respect more than was even usual with him, as he passed where Dormer still kept his seat. But the momentary feeling of sin was already checked. Dormer started up.

"What a moment for pride!" exclaimed he. "How determinately bad are the first impulses of the human heart where self-love is wounded! I give you cause to suppose I consider myself as guilty as you do, Mr Montague: and I can only account for the pain I feel at discovering your knowledge of what you have just mentioned, by avowing how highly I have valued your good opinion, which, as you are a Protestant, I must now lose. How you have obtained your information I cannot imagine; but since you have, I will only say, that, by divulging it to Mrs Clarenham and her family, and making it known in this neighbourhood, you may make the family miserable,—you may oblige me to quit England,—and you may throw worse suspicions than already attaches to it over the character of a Catholic priest; but you cannot secure the liberation, though you may increase the danger of your young friend."

"My information led me to believe that you

alone, Mr Dormer, could procure the release of Clarenham. I have mentioned the subject only to you. I wish to be entirely guided by you; and it is impossible for me to believe you will not aid me."

"Were you a Catholic, Mr Montague, you would believe it. I have only fulfilled the most solemn engagements in all I have done. Every feeling of my nature has struggled to overcome my sense of duty. The struggle, I feel, cannot last much longer; but I hope, whatever may happen to accelerate its end, that I may be enabled to fight the good fight, and keep the faith. There are many kinds of martyrdom, Mr Montague; and some feelings are more dreadful than any external sufferings."

"And Clarenham," said Ernest, "who loved, who trusted you more than all the world besides; who told me, the very last conversation I had with him, that he could not conceive himself happy, even in heaven, were you not there: Still so young, so amiable——"

"Stop, Mr Montague," exclaimed Dormer. "Do you not see in this emaciated body the effects of such thoughts as you suggest?

Do not at this moment urge me too far. Do you know what it is to feel on the verge of madness? Put your hand here."

Ernest gave his hand, and Dormer pressed it on his temples. The full throb seemed uncountable. Ernest felt alarmed, and Dormer looked so also, but instantly took a phial from the book-shelf, and swallowed part of its contents.

"This is a desperate remedy," said he, "but it does the business,—and the body must not be regarded, when losing the command of intellect might endanger the interests of the church." He did not say what it was he had taken, but its effects were soon visible in the languor and exhaustion which stole over his countenance and person.

"Now you may say what you will, Mr Montague, I shall not feel it deeply. At least not for a time."

"I shall say nothing, Mr Dormer, but that I wish you knew the religion of the Bible. Yours is a dreadful service."

"I know," said Dormer, in his usual gentle manner, "that Protestants, particularly Calvinists, profess to believe that their own good works cannot avail in obtaining their salvation. Theirs may therefore be an easy service: but, my dear Mr Montague, that is a tremendous error!"

"It is an error then taught by every page of the Bible," replied Ernest; "but we cannot discuss that subject now. Tell me, dear Mr Dormer, what am I to do? Must Clarenham remain in danger? I have, in some degree, been the means of bringing him into it. I intreat you for once—yield to the light of conscience—to the spirit of love and gentleness, which is the spirit of the Bible—to the dictates of honour and integrity, which your subjection to your church has led you to break through, contrary to your own better feelings. Surely, my dear Sir, if Clarenham is in error, your persuasions, your kindness, would restore him sooner than the instructions or cruelties of strangers. Who ever heard of the soul being converted by compulsion? It is an impossibility. You may compel a man to become a liar: you cannot compel him really to believe any thing."

Dormer shook his head. "Impossible—impossible, Mr Montague. I can do nothing. The church must guide in this matter. The means she has devised must be the best. I can only submit. Was it at the risk of my own soul that I could save his, you might succeed in turning me; but his soul is more safe where he now is, than were he here,—and, whatever it may cost me, I ought not to remove him."

At this moment a bustle and noise of approaching footsteps were heard near Dormer's apartment. He listened. Voices were now also distinguished under the windows; and a command to "surround the house, and let no one escape."

"It is the search I expected," said Dormer, "and this paper—"

"Intrust it to me," said Ernest quickly.

"No, I must not. It was weakness to preserve it; but I could not destroy what would secure Clarenham's safety. I was wrong—" Footsteps approached, and Ernest snatched the paper from him and secured it.

"What have I done!" exclaimed Dormer, becoming as pale as death.

"You have done nothing," said Ernest, his eyes sparkling with pleasure.

"Oh! my will was not against it. I have sinned." He raised his eyes with an expression of deep compunction to heaven—"If you would restore me to peace, Mr Montague, return it to me."

"No," replied Ernest—"I shall better secure your peace by retaining it. I shall never return it till Clarenham is safe."

At that moment the door of the room was rudely burst open, and several officers of justice entered. Their leader seemed surprised on seeing Ernest, whom he knew, and who viewed his entrance with looks of displeasure. He stopt short, and then Dormer, with his usual mild dignity of manner, asked for what he came?

The man immediately showed his warrant to search the apartments, &c. and person of Clement Dormer, Catholic priest at Hallern Castle.

Ernest also read the warrant. "My friends," said he, "you must do your duty; but remember every man in England is entitled to be considered innocent till he is found guilty; and every innocent person is entitled to respect."

The men bowed, and proceeded to examine minutely every part of Dormer's small apartment. The examination went on rapidly, till the book-shelf became its object. Then each book was examined with a suspicion and minuteness which showed that the examiners expected to find what would prove the necessity of the search. Several Greek books, after Ernest having marked their names, that they might be returned, if found to contain nothing treasonable, were delivered to the attendants, to be conveyed where they might be inspected by more learned eyes. The port-folio was also conveyed away. A small press, containing Dormer's linen, was also carefully and minutely examined; and, at last, the officer approached to search his person.

Dormer shrunk from this for a moment—then mildly prepared to submit to the indignity.

"Is this absolutely unavoidable?" asked Ernest.

"Absolutely so, Sir," replied the officer.

Dormer smiled faintly. "May I ask you not to leave me," said he to Ernest, who had turned away. He immediately resumed his place by him, and checked by his presence the rude coarseness of the officer.

"What have we here?" said the man at length, and Ernest's attention was as much arrested as his, on seeing, when the officer opened the breast of Dormer's shirt, that, beneath its white folds, he wore another of haircloth. Dormer smiled—

"Mr Montague will tell you, my friend," said he, "that such things are common among Catholics; and are no peculiar indication of treason."

Ernest did so; but the officer seemed to consider himself obliged to examine a thing so extraordinary with scrupulous attention.

"And what is this, Sir?" asked the suspicious examiner, turning out the breast of the haircloth shirt, and discovering a large cross fixed within, so as to rest upon the heart of the wearer. "It is thick. Does it open? I must examine it," said the man: and Dormer unfixed it, and put it into his hand, saying gently,

"I hope, my friend, you will one day, if you do not now, know its value."

The officer narrowly examined it, and Ernest observed that the side which had been turned inward was sharpened at the edges; and, on glancing towards the place where it had been worn, he saw on Dormer's side, next his heart, a large red scar the form of the cross,—the wound, in some places, appearing unhealed. The man at last was satisfied that the cross contained no treason, and returned it to Dormer, who devoutly kissed, and then replaced it, and the hard shirt, upon the scar.

At last the search was concluded, and Dormer restored to his usual perfectly suitable and dignified exterior, when the officer informed him that, till his books and papers had been examined by the proper authorities, it was necessary that he should submit to be confined to his apartment, with a guard over him.

Dormer mildly acquiesced; and, as he turned from the officer, Ernest observed him raise his eyes submissively to heaven, and press the sharp cross to his heart.

The officer and his attendants now departed,

excepting one strong man who was left as guard. Ernest felt inclined to remain with Dormer; for he was so well aware of the feelings by which a Roman Catholic priest was regarded by the class to which his present jailer belonged, that he believed his presence might be of use. His impatience, however, to see the paper which was to save Clarenham, that if possible he might immediately make use of it, made him hesitate.

"May I ask you, Mr Montague, to go to Mrs Clarenham?" said Dormer. "She must have been alarmed."

Ernest immediately assented; but, on drawing near to ask permission to return, the guard approached, and said his instruction obliged him to prevent any secret communications.

"May I return to you, Mr Dormer?" asked Ernest aloud.

"You would very much oblige me by doing so," replied Dormer earnestly.

Ernest instantly promised, and then proceeded to join Mrs Clarenham and the young party. He found all in a state of anxiety and alarm, which he with difficulty succeeded in calming.

Dormer had become an object of regard and interest to the whole family. The servants had watched for Ernest's leaving his room, and followed him to the apartment in which he found the family, and all joined in intreating him to return to the prisoner. Ernest declared his purpose to spend the night in his apartment, and was thanked and blessed by all for his kindness to—" Good Father Clement—dear Father Clement—holy Father Clement."

Before returning to Dormer, however, Ernest felt anxious to examine the paper in his possession, and for that purpose walked into the park, that he might be alone. On opening it, he was disappointed on finding it written in a cipher of which he was ignorant. The only part intelligible to him was the date and signature—" Carysford Park, 1715," and—" Adrian Warrenne." In vain he attempted to decipher any other part of the paper. The only person to whom he could apply to overcome this obstacle, with any hope of success, was Dr Lowther, who, he knew, had become master of some of those ciphers in secret use among the Romish Clergy: but he hesitated whether, by informing him, he might not involve Dormer in danger. Determining at last, however, to endeavour to get a promise of secrecy from Dr Lowther, before he showed him the paper, Ernest hastened towards Illerton.

The difficulty in obtaining a promise of secrecy from Dr Lowther was even greater than Ernest had anticipated: and the evening had long closed in ere the questions he had to answer, before he attained his object, were concluded; and when at last his old friend ventured, merely because he thought he might trust one in whom he had never found his confidence misplaced, and Dr Lowther gave his promise past recal, and the paper was laid before him, which he perfectly understood,—it was still some time before Ernest could escape from his remonstrances and intreaties.

The paper was that in which Warrenne had given Dormer instructions regarding young Clarenham's mission to the exiled king, and Dr Lowther conceived it to be Ernest's duty immediately to make it known to the proper authorities; and this Ernest could not consent to do. At last, after making himself master of the cipher, and intrusting it to Dr Lowther to account for his absence, he again set out for Hallern.

As he crossed the park, he observed that there were still lights in the castle; and, on approaching nearer, and looking towards the tower in which Dormer's apartment was, he observed a figure pacing slowly across the windows.

A servant was in waiting to admit him to the prisoner. He found him, with his arms folded on his breast, and an appearance of languor in his deportment which seemed to call for repose, pacing the small bounds of his apartment. Ernest apologised for his delay, and expressed surprise at not finding Dormer attempting to sleep.

" I waited for you," replied Dormer, " and have, with difficulty, resisted the call of worn-out nature for rest; but it is always short with me. Your kindness, Mr Montague, to a stranger and a Catholic, has emboldened me to encroach on your benevolence. May I ask you to remain with me while I attempt to sleep, and instantly to awaken me when what is refreshing seems past, and the misery of the mind has again regained its ascendancy over the misery of the body."

Ernest, much moved, gave his promise; and Dormer, after grasping his hand with a look expressive of the deepest feeling of his kindness, threw himself on his hard pallet. Ernest placed himself so as to screen him from the light of the lamp; and soon his sleep was so profound and still, that, as Ernest looked on his thin pale countenance, it seemed calmed into the repose of death. Not a sound broke the silence, except, at intervals, the change of posture of the guard, and even he seemed to move with caution. Whatever had passed between him and Dormer, he seemed now to regard his prisoner with compassion. He had been amply supplied with provisions, which he had evidently not spared; but, while Dormer slept, they continued on the table before him untouched. On the same table lay two pistols: the jailer's hand rested on one of them; and the light shone full on his coarse bronzed features, expressive only of the feelings of human nature in their rudest state. In the further end of the room, the light of the moon was brighter than that of the lamp, and added to the feeling of stillness. Ernest sometimes stopt breathing, to listen whether Dormer breathed.

This calm sleep continued for about two hours—Dormer then began to appear disturbed, and once or twice uttered a few indistinct words. Ernest stooped over him, and laid his hand gently on his arm.

"Yes, Yes—I am ready!" exclaimed he instantly. "Take me in his place. He is so young. Harshness never succeeded with him."

Ernest now perceived why Dormer had dreaded falling asleep when left alone with his guard, and instantly attempted to awaken him; but worn-out nature was still unsatisfied; and, before he succeeded, Dormer exclaimed—

"Is it for giving up the paper? I did not give it, Father." And again, "Will they not release him? Father Adrian will find means to compel them. Penance! I care not for penance—let it be as severe as you will—but I gave it not, though I felt joy. I confess it, Father—I felt joy. Not absolve me? Dreadful! Horrible!"

The uneasiness of awakening against the inclinations of nature rapidly supplied painful images, and when, at last, Ernest succeeded in his attempts, Dormer's countenance expressed a mixture of anguish and horror. The guard had approached, and muttered, as he stood over his now conscious prisoner—

"Ay, ay, all the same—some black popish work."

"Have you allowed me to speak?" asked Dormer, with quickness and alarm.

"Not a word that I could prevent," answered Ernest.

"Nothing that can injure you," said the guard,—"but I have heard men say, that a clean breast and the gallows before you, was easier than a foul breast though nobody knew it. Make a clean breast, Sir. It is the only thing will give you peace."

"You are right, my friend," replied Dormer, with his usual mildness. "There can be no peace with a guilty conscience; but I believe you mistake in my case."

"I hope so, Sir," answered the man, doubtingly. He, however, returned to his seat, and now began to make up for his lost time by commencing a hearty meal, keeping his eye fixed on his prisoner and Ernest. The latter was attempting to persuade Dormer again to sleep.

"No, no," replied he. "I have had all I require to prevent my being overcome by my exhausted body." He looked wretchedly ill, and acknowledged that he felt so, but positively declined again lying down.

"But you, Mr Montague," said he, "must now leave me. I never meant to deprive you of a whole night's rest; and, if you will return by the passage which leads to this room, you will find, just at its entrance, a door opening into an apartment prepared for you."

"I will not sleep to-night," answered Ernest, "unless," glancing towards the iron bed, "I try to do so on this Roman Catholic couch."

Dormer smiled, and seemed pleased, but said, "You would not sleep on a first trial."

Ernest stretched himself upon the bed, and felt that it was not only hard, but that there were bars across to render it uneven also.

"No, indeed, I could not sleep till after many trials," said he, again rising; "but is it possible, Mr Dormer, you can suppose such treatment of your body renders you more holy in the sight of God ?"

" Certainly. You know St Paul says, 'I keep under my body, and bring it into subjection.' "

" True, my dear Sir, but surely not by such means. St Paul says, ' If ye live after the flesh, ye shall die; but if ye, through the Spirit, do mortify the deeds of the flesh, ye shall live.' It was by the grace of the Spirit of God that he was enabled to govern his body, and to resist and overcome those sinful inclinations which would have impeded his course in that heaven-ward race which he was describing. Any other subjection of the body but to the guidance of the soul, influenced by the grace of God, seems to me to no purpose; and I think St Paul says the same when he speaks of ordinances of men, 'which have a show of wisdom in will worship and humility, and neglecting of the body.' "

" The subjection of the body to the spirit is assuredly the end at which all sincere Catholics aim in all their mortifications," replied Dormer. " Our objection to the Protestant view of the subject is, that they use no means to attain the end they allow to be necessary."

"You say *sincere* Catholics," said Ernest. "You must also allow me to say, that *sincere* Protestants do continually use means for the attainment of that end."

"I know no Protestant whom I should consider more perfectly sincere than Mr Montague," replied Dormer. "He has seen one of my methods of seeking that end; I should like to know one of his?"

Ernest reddened, and glanced towards the guard.

Dormer smiled. "I would not ask your confidence farther than you felt disposed to give it me, Mr Montague; but though, on that point, it was given me in the plainest English, I believe it would be as unintelligible to some ears as if it were in Greek."

"I believe so too," replied Ernest, again reddening; then, after a short pause,—"I think," said he, "Christ has mentioned two ways of avoiding sin—'watching and prayer.' If we watch what our peculiar dispositions find to be temptations to sin, and pray for grace to enable us to avoid and resist those temptations, and continue to join wathfulness with prayer, we are, I think, following the directions of Christ, and shall succeed in attaining our end; we are also, in this way, subjecting our bodies to the guidance of our spirits, while they are depending on Him, without whom, we are assured by Himself, 'we can do nothing.'"

"But *he* speaks of self-denial, and of taking up the cross daily," replied Dormer.

"Certainly: but it is the cross he sends I am to take up and bear, not one of my own creating; and I am to deny my own inclinations when they would stand in the way of obedience to Him; not to make a merit with Him by mortifying them, merely because they are my natural inclinations."

Dormer was silent.

"My idea is simply this," continued Ernest, "by believing in Christ, and receiving him as my Saviour, I receive him as a complete Saviour. He is infinitely perfect in all his works, and is so also in his character and work as a Saviour. I do not add any of my imperfect doings to that all-perfect work. I lay the accomplishment of my salvation wholly into His hands. I trust the everlasting safety of my soul entirely to him. In so far as I, from weakness of faith, or natural pride, withdraw this trust, and attempt to be my own Saviour, I dishonour him, and act as a fool; for without him, he has himself assured me, I can do nothing."

"But thus, my dear Mr Montague, you do away the necessity of good works. If Christ is to work out your whole salvation, why are you exhorted to work out your own salvation?"

"Let us have the whole passage," replied Ernest. "St Paul says to the Philippian church, 'Wherefore, my beloved, as ye have always obeyed, not as in my presence only, but now much more in my absence, work out your own salvation with fear and trembling: for it is God that worketh in you both to will and to do of his good pleasure.'* Paul exhorts this church not to rest on his presence for assistance, but to continue, as they had done in his absence, to regard the matter of salvation as between them-

* Phil. ii. 12.

selves and God. He wrought in them both *to will and to do,* and it was their part, disregarding all that man could do for them, to unite themselves with God in that work. This is exactly what I desire to do. I have received Christ as my Saviour, not, as our divines say, 'in my sins, but from my sins.' I desire to follow his guidance of me—to study his providences regarding me—to receive his chastisements—to bear his cross—to wait on him for his grace—all in order to purify and prepare me for himself—and while attempting, in dependence on his grace, to follow his footsteps, and to walk even as he walked, I am not, as our divines also say, 'working for life, but working from life.'"

Dormer was again silent and thoughtful for a time, then said emphatically: "Christians of different communions ought to associate more together. They would then know what true charity, true love for mankind is. A year ago I should not have believed it possible that I could have felt as I now do in conversing with a heretic—a Calvinist. Yet, my dear Mr Montague, I must think any error, whoever holds it, most fatally dangerous, which at all lessens the necessity of exertion on our part; and deeply as I believe you feel on the subject, and highly as I know, 'your works praise you,' yet the system you have adopted—the system of Calvinism, assuredly does so."

"Surely you misunderstand me," replied Ernest. "We do not deny the necessity of exertion on our part—we only deny that any exertion on our part can have the smallest efficacy in justifying our souls before God. We say that a perfect righteousness only can justify. That ours is never perfect; and that the perfect righteousness of Christ is that on which we rest our hopes of justification. Calvinists, too, perhaps look more into the heart, the source of action, for evidences of their state before God, than merely to their works; yet facts prove that Calvinists, and Calvinistic communities, attain to as high, or higher perfection in works than those who differ from them. The Calvinist believes that he must, as Christ says, 'be born again,' before he can see even the nature of 'the kingdom of God,' and before he can make any exertion pleasing to God. A

Calvinist, therefore, tries his own character by that given in the Bible of one who is born of the spirit. 'The fruit of the spirit is love, joy, peace, long-suffering, gentleness, goodness, faith, meekness, temperance.'* The possession of these graces and virtues are the only evidences to a Calvinist, that he is born of the spirit—that he has the spirit of Christ. And he knows that if he 'has not the spirit of Christ he is none of his.'† And that if he is not Christ's, 'he is without hope, and without God in the world.' It appears to me, my dear Sir, that the works a Calvinist regards as necessary to prove to himself that he is even in the path of safety, are more pure and spiritual than those which are regarded by your church, and by many ignorant Protestants, as sufficient to justify them in the sight of God."

Dormer held out his hand, and said, smiling, "I see you feel the necessity of good works as much as I do. I shall soon believe that real Christians differ merely in words."

Not quite perhaps at this moment," replied Ernest; "but I hope, before we leave this

* Gal. v. 22. † Rom. viii. 9.

world of darkness and error, we shall both have built our hope on that one foundation which cannot disappoint us; and if on that we have also attempted to build 'wood, hay, stubble,'— the day, 'the bright day of truth,' shall reveal to us our errors, and destroy them; but we shall, on that 'rock of ages,' still be safe."

"God grant it may be so!" said Dormer fervently.

The morning sun now shone brightly into the little apartment, gilding the edges of the crucifix as it stood between Ernest and the glowing sky. Dormer had revived while conversing on that subject which seemed for him always full of interest, but now he informed Ernest that his hour of prayer was come; and that the presence of no one must prevent his observing it. Ernest immediately, though reluctantly, took leave; and Dormer, kneeling before the crucifix in the presence of his gaoler, spent the next hours in devotion.

CHAPTER XI.

"Beati coloro, che lavan le loro stole nel sangue dell Agnello; affine d'aver dirrito all' albero della vita, e entrar per le porte nella citta."
Martini's Trans.—Rev. xxii. 14.

On Ernest returning to Hallern Castle the following forenoon, he found that, about an hour before, Dormer's books and papers had been restored to him; and as nothing had appeared to justify the suspicions entertained, he was again at liberty, and had gone out. Ernest heard also that the search made at Carysford Park had ended in the same manner. He determined, therefore, immediately to proceed thither, demand an interview with Warrenne, and insist on his instantly procuring the release of young Clarenham.

When Ernest had nearly reached the gate leading into the Carysford grounds, he observed Dormer approaching, and immediately quickened his horse's pace to meet and congratulate him. Dormer, however, seemed to feel no pleasure on perceiving him, and received his cordial congratulations as if he heard them not, and then asked anxiously—whether Ernest was proceeding to the park ?

"I am," replied Ernest; "and, if you will allow me, I shall call at Hallern on my return, and tell you what has passed."

"If you feel disposed to do so, Mr Montague, I shall be prepared to listen to whatever you have to say." Dormer seemed to wish to say more, but, after breathing a heavy sigh, or rather groan, he rode on.

Ernest felt surprised, and also proceeded on his way, attempting, as he went, to account for what had passed; and thought he had done so when he recollected that Dormer had himself probably been with Warrenne to acknowledge the loss of the paper, and that the displeasure of his superior now hung heavy on his thoughts.

On Ernest reaching the house and giving his name, he was immediately shown into an apartment, not such as that in which Warrenne had received his inferior brother, but one almost as poorly furnished as Dormer's. Here Warrenne received Ernest with extreme politeness. Two young men in clerical habits were in the apartment, busied apparently in study. Warrenne placed a chair for Ernest with his back towards them. He had, however, observed that they were two very strong, athletic-looking young men; and the thought had crossed his mind—'Will fasting and penance reduce these robust youths to the state in which Dormer now is?'

"I wished to speak to you on business of a private nature," said Ernest, coldly to Warenne.

"I believe I know its nature," replied he, with politeness, but with an air of indifference. "Mr Dormer, the priest of Hallern, has been with me. He has thought too seriously of this matter. My two young brothers were present when he was with me. His gloomy disposition has on this, as on other occasions, left an impression on his mind regarding the contents of the paper he mentioned, which they do not convey. If you understood the cipher, Mr Montague, you would be aware of this."

"The paper has been deciphered to me," replied Ernest, coldly. " Its contents, I imagine, must convey the same impression to every one."

Warrenne looked incredulous. " Dormer informed you that it would insure the object which you, Mr Montague, wish to attain; but all your information on this subject has been with a view to deceive you. It is without foundation. It is absurd."

Ernest rose. " I shall not allow myself to be deceived now," said he. " I know the contents of the paper, and shall merely say, that they shall be made known to government unless you immediately give me your written promise, witnessed by these gentlemen, that young Clarenham shall return to his friends before two months are past."

Warrenne smiled. " If you know the contents of the paper, Mr Montague, may I at least beg of you to make me acquainted with them?"

Ernest did so.

" Impossible!" exclaimed Warrenne. " I cannot believe it. Dormer has been dreaming, and your decipherer has imposed on you.— Nothing short of seeing my own signature to such a document could make me credit its existence; and even that would only convince me that my enemies had succeeded in producing what might ruin me."

"You know your own cipher, I suppose," said Ernest, taking out the paper.

The instant he unfolded it, so as to discover the cipher, his arms were seized from behind by the two young men, and Warrenne himself darted forward to snatch the paper. Ernest was, however, powerful and active in person. He firmly grasped the paper, and, with a violent struggle, freeing his right arm, levelled one of the young men to the floor; then, flinging off the other, he seized Warrenne, who was making towards a bell near where he had sat, and placing himself so as to prevent its being rung—

"I see your intended villany!" exclaimed he, "and also your consciousness of guilt; but recollect my words, for they shall be kept."

He then pushed Warrenne from him to the opposite side of the room; and seeing the young man he had knocked down again on his feet, he glanced towards the window, and, perceiving that it was near the ground, he flung open the casement, and leaped from it. His horse and servant he saw not far distant, and hurried towards them. He had scarcely mounted, when a crowd of servants issued from the house, and rushed forward to stop him: but, putting spurs to his horse, and not regarding throwing down one or two who attempted to get in front of him, he was soon clear of the grounds of Carysford Park, and began to slacken his pace, and think of what had happened.

All had passed so rapidly, it seemed scarcely a reality; and he took out the precious paper, to be certain that it was still in his possession. It now struck him that Dormer must have known of the intended plan of forcing the paper from him, should he go to Carysford Park; and, recollecting his looks, and the groan of anguish with which he had parted from him, he could again trace the struggle between his feelings and his subjection to his church: but, as Dormer seemed to regard it as a duty to confess every thing to his superior, Ernest, though he longed to tell him what had passed, as he felt certain it would only give him pleasure, thought it prudent to inform him no further till he had decided his plan of proceeding. His determination was, to proceed to Rome the instant he had procured a written promise from Warrenne to release his young friend, and himself accompany him home. For this he must gain his father's consent; and that he was sure he would not obtain unless he made him acquainted with the whole affair.

While engaged in these thoughts, Ernest, in passing through Hallern village, had a note slipped into his hand by a woman who had first attracted his notice by walking for a part of the way close to his horse. On opening the note, he discovered it to be from Ainsworth, and containing a request to meet him that evening, in the same wood in which they had formerly met. Ernest determined to proceed no further till this meeting was over: and, on returning to Illerton, attempted to gain all the information in his power from Dr Lowther, who was well acquainted with the manner of proceeding and history of the Inquisition.

Ainsworth, in the same disguise as formerly, was at the place of meeting when Ernest reached it.

"Have you done anything for my master, Sir?" was his first question.

Ernest informed him of all he thought necessary, and the poor man wept for joy.

"Oh, Sir," said he, "every thing will do but your leaving the country. You must not, Sir. Father Adrian might go abroad—he might leave Father Clement to bear all—Sir, you *must* find means to keep him in England."

"But, Ainsworth, by leaving England, and throwing all blame on Mr Dormer, he would equally ruin the cause of his order in this country."

"No, Sir, no. But you do not understand these things; and now we have not time. Father Adrian must not leave the country, Sir. My master will never come back if he does: and nothing but your written promise of secrecy regarding what has passed, and also to return his paper when my master is restored to his family, will be sufficient to make him feel secure, and remain in England; and your presence, Sir, to watch his motions. Besides, Mr Ernest, you would not know how to proceed at

Rome, and I know every thing. Trust me, Sir, to bring home my young master, and be intreated to remain on the watch here. Do not say any thing to Father Clement. Let him gain his information from Father Adrian. Believe me, Sir, the more quiet every thing is kept the better. Your absence would lead to inquiries and talking. I can be at Rome sooner than you. I know where my master is. I shall set out immediately. Ask nothing from Father Adrian, but that my master shall return. Leave the means to him, and my master's comfort to me."

Ernest thought for a little—"I believe you are right, Ainsworth. I think I may be satisfied that he cannot have one with him who loves him more devotedly."

The man was moved. "You, too, love him, Sir, but not in the right way for his soul."

It was then determined that Ainsworth should set out on his return immediately to Rome, and that Ernest should write what was necessary to Warrenne; and they separated.

In two days Ernest was in possession of Warrenne's written promise to procure the release of Clarenham; in return for which he gave his written promise of secrecy, and to restore the paper in cipher immediately after his young friend rejoined his family; and, in order to secure instant intelligence, if Warrenne made any attempt to leave the country, Ernest so far confirmed Maria Clarenham's suspicions regarding him, as to inform her, that he had reason to believe that he was, in some degree, the cause of her brother's absence, and intrusted to her the easy task of inducing young Carysford to keep a constant watch upon his motions, and instantly prevent him, should he make any attempt to leave Carysford Park.

Again all went on as before at Hallern Castle. Young Carysford was still a daily visitor, each day, to complain of his father's determination to treat him with the repulsive haughtiness of newly assumed authority, and still to be lectured or charmed into submission by Maria. Again the evenings were spent by Maria and Adeline as formerly; and Lady Montague also sought to win Mrs Clarenham's thoughts from the sad subjects by which they were occupied, by her kindness and cheerfulness; and had the happiness to observe that she succeeded in leading her cousin to brighter hopes than had hitherto been indulged by her timid and depressed spirit. Dormer and Ernest again joined Lady Montague and her friend in those conversations in which the subjects most interesting to all were alone introduced; and each felt the sweetness and profitableness of Christian communion, though each felt also the imperfection of the purest earthly intercourse, while conscious that on some points it was necessary, even in the most confidential moments, to observe silence and reserve.

Dormer and Ernest, however, now felt that they perfectly understood each other: and though each regarded his friend as in error, and in dangerous error, yet each believed in the other's perfect sincerity; and while anxious to communicate his own views, so as to convince his friend of the truth as he saw it, still the warmest affection and esteem existed on both sides. Dormer, however, seemed on the way to know first who was in the right. His strength decreased daily: still, determined to fulfil his duty as priest of Hallern, no intreaties would induce him to spare himself.

"Why should I not die at my post?" replied he to Ernest's anxious remonstrances.

"But a little rest—a little ease—would keep you longer at your post. We are not entitled to throw away life."

"The church gives no instructions such as these," replied Dormer. "I remember none in Scripture; but I read of 'working while it is called to-day,' and of that 'night coming when no man can work.'"

This conversation passed as Ernest accompanied Dormer to his apartment, after having met him returning from the village almost overpowered by weakness and fatigue.

On entering Dormer's little apartment, Ernest was startled on observing that near his iron bed there was now placed a coffin. He stood fixed, gazing upon it. For a time he resisted the admission of the thoughts inspired by the sight; and when he could no longer do so —and the truth, that Dormer felt he could not live, forced itself upon him, he was so completely overcome that he had no power to restrain his feelings.

Dormer was moved. "There was one being on earth," said he, after a few moments of silent emotion, "who, I once thought, would, for a time at least, feel a blank in the world if I was called away. His affections I have been compelled to alienate from me. It is strange to feel consolation in the belief that we excite grief in others,—yet so it is,—and at this moment, Mr Montague, I feel oppressed by a sense of gratitude to you, for kindness so undeserved on my part."

Ernest could on no occasion find words to express his deeper feelings, and now continued silent, while his flushed forehead, and firm-closed mouth, betrayed the effort he made to maintain the composure he had struggled to regain.

"I felt a strange shrinking from the foolish gloomy accompaniments of death," resumed Dormer, "in consequence, I suppose, of my weak state of body; and, as you know it is my way to use means for the attainment of the ends I wish, I had this brought here, (pointing to the coffin,) to familiarize myself to what long association has rendered so much an object of gloom: and even that association I have found wonderfully powerful in giving to this last depository the greatest effect in solemnizing the thoughts."

"It does indeed," replied Ernest, relieving his breast by a long-drawn, heavy sigh.

"Yes," continued Dormer, "when I lay myself in this coffin for my hours of rest,—and all is dark around me,—and I feel its narrow bounds,--and recollect all that is combined with being laid in it for my last long sleep—Oh! my thoughts are too, too clearly on the verge of eternity. I could sometimes pray even for annihilation—the future seems so awfully momentous! The question—Am I safe? without an answer. The past so worthless, so mispent, so inconceivably, so madly regardless of the bearing time must have upon eternity!"

Ernest fixed his eyes intently on Dormer.

"And at such moments," asked he, "on what can you rest your hope? Do those penances——those self-inflictions—those acts of charity—those pious feelings and endeavours, which your church teaches are to secure your justification at the bar of Christ return to your recollection so as to give you courage to meet your Judge, with feelings of peace and security?"

"The church teaches that it is best for the departing saint not to be secure," replied Dormer.

"But may I ask you to answer my question, at least with regard to hope, if not security," said Ernest.

"Yes, provided you do not take my answer as one which would apply to those who are really holy men in the Catholic Church. For me, no penance—no mortification—no fasting—no means I have ever attempted, and I believe few ever have attempted more, who had to support the external character imposed on our order,—nothing has succeeded. Sin still reigns, mingles, triumphs in all I do, and seems to laugh at every effort I make to overcome it. On looking back, therefore, in those awful moments, nothing returns but sin."

"In what, then, my dear Sir, do you find a refuge from despair?"

"'Tis strange," replied Dormer, "how, at such moments, one doctrine of our faith stands forth so as to throw all the others into distance and insignificance. The vastness of that sense of want felt by the soul seems instinctively to cling to the infinite vastness of the means appointed by God to supply it. The death of the Son of God seems alone sufficient to blot out sins so aggravated and innumerable:—the righteousness of the Son of God alone so spotless as to answer the demands of the perfect law of God. Christ is seen to have wrought the work alone, —and then the soul asks—for whom was it wrought? For man,—for all men,—for whosoever will: and for a time, a glorious triumphant moment, the soul forgets all but its Almighty Saviour, and its own safety,—and can say—'my Lord, my Saviour, my hope, my all. My own righteousnesses, when I remember them in the light of thy spotless holiness, appear as a covering of filthy rags. Purge away their filth as thou wilt, I lay myself wholly into thy hands.'"

"You are, my dearest Sir, in those triumphant, glorious moments, a Calvinist, a Bible Christian," exclaimed Ernest, an expression of joy lighting up his countenance. "You once asked me whether Calvinists could believe a Roman

Catholic might be truly and devotedly religious: at this moment I do."

"Nay, nay, I am no Calvinist," replied Dormer; "but if you agree in what I have just said, you are a Catholic; for I have said that I resigned my soul to that purification which your church teaches is unnecessary."

"You have said that you desired to resign your soul to Christ, as its only Saviour," said Ernest; "and that is what every Bible Christian does for both life and death."

Dormer smiled. "I do not wish to differ from you, Mr Montague; but this one thing I feel assured of, that some change must take place on my soul ere it can enter heaven. What produces that change our church has decided to be a point into which we ought not to inquire. And I am glad it has done so; because I feel pleasure in resigning its nature,—all, into the hands of Christ.'

"I should not dread the purgatory in which you believe, my dear Sir," said Ernest smiling. "Yet," added he seriously, "It is a pernicious error to teach that there is any purgatory. It is contrary to Scripture; because, if Christ's death, as you believe, was an all-sufficient atonement for sin,—to make man suffer also for that sin is either a contradiction or an assertion that more suffering is inflicted than is necessary."

"I believe you are in error on this point; but I cannot argue with you," said Dormer gently. "At this moment I would rather not differ from you about any thing."

"Speak to me, then, about your own health, my dear Sir," said Ernest. "Will you not consult a physician?"

"I have done so already," replied Dormer.

Ernest looked anxiously for his saying more.

"I will acknowledge to you, Mr Montague, that, for some days after I was informed by Father Adrian of what had passed between you and him,—that the paper was still in your possession, and that he had written letters which would restore Basil Clarenham to safety,—for some days after I knew all this, I felt such a weight, such a mortal weight taken from my mind and thoughts, that it seemed as if health, and peace, and enjoyment were restored to me; but still this relief from anxiety had no healing effect on this poor frame. The precautions I had taken against the worst of maladies, had destroyed its powers. As misery had done before, joy only increased the rapidity of their decay. I cannot sleep. I every day become weaker; and my physician gives me no hope of recovery, but from using means which I do not feel at liberty to use. Perfect idleness—complete relaxation—and such means, he confesses, only promise an uncertain cure. He has in vain endeavoured to reduce the fever which continually preys upon me; and I feel that I am hurrying on to death. I have no other wish. What charm can life have for me, or for any Catholic priest who devotes himself to his duty? All my desire is to labour incessantly while I am able. Why should I spend the little time left me, in trying, by the indulgence of this decaying body, to continue it a little longer, a clog to my soul, and a useless burden on the earth? No, no: The grave is the only place where it is not sin for a priest to indulge in rest."

Ernest made no reply—He could not.

Dormer had, on entering his room, sunk

down exhausted on his hard bed. Ernest sat beside him, and the coffin was at their feet. Ernest now stooped forward over it.

"Is this strange bed hard too?" asked he, putting aside a covering of haircloth which seemed to conceal somewhat which raised the inner part of the coffin. It was a thick layer of ashes.

Ernest looked up. "For what is this, my dear Sir?"

"A means of humiliation," replied Dormer. "You know I regard it as a duty to make the body partake sensibly of mortification. These ashes are my bed, and that haircloth is my covering, when I am employed in those meditations on death which I have described to you."

Ernest again looked thoughtfully down on the coffin and its accompaniments, then said emphatically, "How selfish is it to wish to detain you amongst these 'beggarly elements.' How inexpressibly rapturous to you will that moment be which at once will convince you that faith in Christ completely justifies—that being absent from the body is to be present with the Lord—and that to be present with Him is to be holy, to be 'like Him.'"

"How confidently you speak regarding me," replied Dormer. "How can you so greatly reprobate, so utterly condemn a church, one of whose least worthy members you believe to be far more secure of heaven than he almost can venture to hope for himself?"

"Because, my dear Sir, that member of the fallen and corrupted church of Rome has built his hope, not on what she teaches, but on that sure foundation which cannot fail him; and that, amidst so much of the darkness and error which his church teaches, that the light which he follows proves its divine origin by overcoming them all. Built on this foundation, Scripture declares the soul to be safe. You, my dear Sir, have attempted to make your hope more secure by adding your own inventions;—an iron bed,—a coffin with ashes,—a haircloth shirt,—a wounding cross,—nights without rest, subjection of your mind to your fellow-men: but when everlasting day shall dawn upon your soul, its light will shew the vanity of such trifles, when it is attempted by them to make more perfect the finished work of the Son of God; and all this painful labour shall be lost—shall require forgiveness. And those of your church who, disregarding the true foundation, build their all on this rubbish——"

"Too, too many do," interrupted Dormer.

"They are taught to do so," said Ernest.

"Not by me—never by me," interrupted Dormer warmly.

"I believe not, resumed Ernest; "but they are by the men to whom you subject the guidance of your spirit. What else does Warrenne teach? You must have observed how that poor deluded girl, Catherine Clarenham, is led by him to suppose herself a saint—a peculiar favourite of heaven, in consequence of her observance of those unscriptural trifles; while the poor thing is vain and full of self-importance, and irritable and impatient when crossed or opposed in the most unimportant matter."

"Poor child!" said Dormer, and sighed deeply, but immediately changed the subject.

CHAPTER XII.

"Un solo Signore, una sola fede—"
Martini's Trans.—Ephes. iv. 5.

DAYS and weeks again had passed away, and still each member of the family at Hallern felt, till Clarenham returned, as if waiting and hoping for that which was to relieve them from the languor and anxiety which accompanied their continued uncertainty respecting him. Still each day so much resembled the preceding one, that time passed away imperceptibly; for it is strange, but true, that those days, most full of interest and events, and during which there has been no time for weariness, seem longer in retrospect, than those in which no event or variety has occurred to mark their course.

During this period, the rebellion in Scotland

had been so powerfully opposed that the most sanguine of those who had hoped for the restoration of the Stuarts had now given up that hope. Amongst those was Sir Thomas Carysford; and as his visions of new honours and royal favour to his house gave place to less splendid realities, his hopes and affections again rested more entirely on his son; and, notwithstanding Warrenne's efforts to prevent it, he, at times, expressed to Lady Carysford his regret at losing so amiable a young creature as Maria Clarenham for a daughter. This was immediately repeated by his mother to young Carysford, whose spirits were as rapidly raised as depressed, and his affection and restored gaiety seemed to give Sir Thomas new life.

During this time of tedious anxiety to the inmates of Hallern Castle, the cloud which seemed to rest upon them was made still darker by the evident approach of the King of Terrors to deprive them of one whose ministrations amongst them had won to him the veneration and love of the whole family. Dormer, every day, became more and more weak. When no longer able to discharge his duties in the village, he made himself be carried out on the lawn to meet his people, who, crowding round his couch, listened to his solemn and affectionate expostulations—sometimes with attention so deep as to suppress all emotion, at other times with sobs and tears. The Clarenhams and Montagues were often at such times amongst the listeners; and once, when he was carried to the verge of the park, that some old people might be able to come and hear his last instructions, Sir Herbert Montague and Dr Lowther were seen stealing to the spot, and, concealed by some bushes, listening with evident emotion to the dying Catholic priest. Now, however, Dormer taught only the simple, powerful truths of the gospel. In listening to him, the Bible Christian alone could have recognised his creed.

At length this exertion was also too much for Dormer's strength, and he became too weak to leave his room. Death seemed fast approaching; and Ernest watched his couch, from day to day, with increasing feelings of interest and affection; while Dormer confided to him, without reserve, his hopes and fears—

his thoughts and feelings in moments of darkness, and also at those times when faith enabled him to view the near withdrawing of that veil which separates between time and eternity, with calmness and hope.

One day, on which Ernest had been prevented seeing him till towards evening, Dormer, after receiving him with even more than his usual kindness and confiding affection, said, "I had but one earthly wish, my dear Mr Montague. That was once more to see Clarenham. That wish will not, I think, be granted. You can tell him that I have not given him cause to abhor my memory without myself suffering. His forgiveness would have calmed my last hour as much as any thing earthly could."

"You have that forgiveness I am certain," replied Ernest; "and I hope you will still receive it from himself."

"No," replied Dormer—"No, dear Ernest—my physician has permitted me this evening to receive the last rites of the church. I desire no earthly interruption after that is over."

It was now evening; and, though the weakness and brokenness of Dormer's voice seemed to justify the opinion of his physician, yet his mind seemed so calm, and clear, and present, that Ernest could scarcely believe all was so near a change. He made no reply, but continued looking earnestly at Dormer, who lay, supported by pillows, on his hard pallet—his eyes raised to heaven, or at times speaking a few words of kindness to Ernest, or repeating aloud the Latin prayers of some holy men of his order. Ernest did not feel satisfied. He had witnessed the last moments of many dying Christians of his own church, and it now seemed unsuitable, at such a time, to abide by human forms of prayer. The words were excellent; but, to a Calvinist, no words short of inspiration seem strong enough to lean upon, when entering "the valley of the shadow of death."

Dormer's hand was in his—it was cold, and the pulse low and unequal. Ernest leant towards him, and repeated the words—"When I pass through the valley of the shadow of death I will fear no evil; because thou art with me, and thy rod and thy staff they comfort me."

Dormer turned towards him. "I am in that

valley, Ernest,—I wish I could say I fear no evil. Sin is that which gives its awful gloom to the shadow of approaching death. We know not, Ernest, what sin is till that shadow is upon us."

"But we have a promise," replied Ernest, "that as our day is, so shall our strength be. We cannot see the nature of sin so clearly as Christ saw it when he died in our room. Our seeing its vileness more clearly does not prove us more sinful; it only ought to make us cling more closely to Him whose blood cleanseth from all sin, and who makes his grace sufficient to meet every situation in which he places his people."

"Yes," replied Dormer, "if they are of those who merit that grace."

"Merit grace!" repeated Ernest: "My dear Sir, what do you mean? What you *merit* is no more grace, it is debt. What can you mean?"

"I mean that I look for nothing, because I deserve nothing. I humbly resign myself as a lost sinner to Christ, to save me as he will. My mind is at this moment more vividly clear than ever. It suffers a dreadful struggle between terror and hope. Oh! what a tremendous thought is that of judgment! Final judgment! A sentence for eternity! To appear before Omniscient Purity! To give an account of the deeds done in the body! To give an account of my ministry,—the care I have taken of souls—of immortal souls! If I have deceived—if I have misled,—to have their blood upon me! Oh! who would undertake such a charge, if he saw its importance as I now see it."

Ernest paused before he replied. Dormer's state of mind was new to him; and, while he wished to speak comfort, he felt at a loss how to proceed. During his evening conversations with him, he had constantly been distressed by observing the confusion which prevailed in his mind on that most important of all points, the justification of the soul before God. This proceeded from the variance which existed between what he learned from Scripture, amply confirmed by his own experience, and the dogmas taught by his church. At one time Dormer would, in language every word of which was felt and understood by Ernest, declare his hope of salvation to rest on the atonement and merits of the Son of God: at another he would express as much dread and anxiety at the thought of appearing at the judgment-seat of Christ, as if his salvation depended entirely on the account he could then give of his own works. Often had Ernest laboured to prove the inconsistency of his faith and of his fears. "If your justification shall depend on its being found that you have obeyed any law," he would say, "then shall you have saved yourself. If Christ is your Saviour, then must he be a complete Saviour. If you venture to the judgment-seat of Christ, to be judged according to his pure law, then you must perish, 'for by the deeds of the law shall no flesh be justified in his sight.' If you believe in Christ for your justification, then are you dead to the law: It can demand nothing from you. Faith in Christ makes you one with Him. He died not for himself: He died for you. He obeyed the law in your place: 'You are complete in Him.' All you have to do is to examine, on Scripture grounds, whether you believe in Him. 'To those who believe, Christ is precious.' Is he precious to you? Those who believe, 'delight in the law of God, after the inner man;' and though they know the truth too well to say 'we have no sin,' yet it is their load. 'They groan' under its influence, 'being burdened.' They cry out with St Paul, 'Oh wretched man that I am, who shall deliver me from the body of this death.'"

Dormer would listen with delight while Ernest thus spoke to the feelings and experience of his mind, and would thankfully acknowledge the possession of those evidences of faith: But still his church taught, in direct contradiction to St Paul's plainest declarations, that it was a dangerous error to believe that faith alone justified the soul. St Paul says, 'We being justified by faith, have peace with God.'—'By grace are ye saved, through faith.'—'Ye are all the children of God, through faith in Christ Jesus.' And Christ's own words are,—'He that believeth in me shall never perish. This is the work of God, that ye believe in Him whom he hath sent. He that believeth in me is not condemned. He that believeth in me hath passed from death unto life.'

Dormer's church, however, not giving her

members the Scriptures to judge for themselves, have also given the character, favourable to their own usurpation of power over their consciences, to the doctrine of faith. The Bible teaches that the faith which unites the soul to Christ, and justifies, necessarily receives from that union His spirit to produce that new heart whose nature it is to bring forth good works. But the Church of Rome confounds the faith which justifies, with its effects; and teaches, that, in addition to resting your faith on Christ's finished work for salvation, you must do so and so yourself. Dormer had subjected his mind to these unscriptural doctrines of his church; and, while his awakened conscience shewed him the imperfections of his best performances, and his heart clung in love and adoration to the Saviour of sinners, still his church demanded from him a round of observances, which he had indeed attempted to fulfil, but which, on looking back, had been accompanied by so many sins of heart, that he dared not plead them as having any merit before him who looked only to the heart.

Ernest now again attempted to combat these

dangerous errors,—errors which have made most miserable the last days of many awakened Catholics. Dormer listened, while Ernest easily proved to him, what he so powerfully felt, that every attempt to rest our hopes on our own sinful works must fail at the hour of death, when the soul knows any thing of the comprehensiveness and holiness of the law of God. Our own works are then "shorter than a man can stretch himself upon them, narrower than that he can wrap himself in them."

Dormer agreed, and was listening to the truths of the gospel brought forward by Ernest, with ejaculations to heaven that he might be found interested in their peace-giving declarations, when a servant softly entered to say that Father Adrian was come.

"Why suffer him to disturb you, my dear Sir," said Ernest, rising as the servant retired, and leaning in sorrow over Dormer: "Oh! trust your soul to Him who can alone prepare it for Himself."

"Scripture commands this last unction," replied Dormer, looking with an expression of mingled affection and sorrow at Ernest. "Farewell. After Father Adrian has been with me, I shall regard myself as separated from all in this world. Farewell, kind, dear, Ernest." He held out his arms, and made an effort to embrace Ernest, who folded his arms around him and wept upon his breast. Dormer laid his hand upon his head, and prayed that God would keep him in the truth,—or lead him into it where he still might err,—and again unite them to each other, where there was no more darkness, no more sorrow, no more separation.

Footsteps were heard approaching; Ernest started up. "Must I leave you?" asked he.

"I shall confess," replied Dormer.

"To a man! My dear, dear Sir, what can he do for you?"

"I shall soon know, Ernest. Once more I shall confess to a priest; and, if I am in error, I must lay all on Him who will not 'cast me out.' I cannot think or decide now: life is ebbing fast. You need not leave the room. Go to the further window; and when I want support, give me your breast."

The door opened, and Warrenne entered the room, accompanied by three other priests, bearing various articles concealed under rich coverings.

"Father, I shall confess."

Warenne approached. "This young friend wishes to be a witness of the last rites of our church," said Dormer.

"Certainly," replied Warrenne, apparently unconscious of what he said, while he looked with an expression of awe on Dormer, as he lay with that last paleness on his countenance, the sight of which appals the most worldly and thoughtless, and particularly a worldly clergyman.

"Father," said Dormer, fixing his eyes on him, "eternity opens an awful prespect on the soul."

"Yes, brother; to him who is not in the true church, or whose sins are mortal, or unconfessed, it is an awful thing to die; but to you, a member of our holy mother church—a priest—one whose life has evinced such evangelical purity—whose confessions, and fasts, and penances—whose charity—whose self-denial, and unwearied exertions for the faith, are so well known to the true church—to you death ought to have no terrors. We shall offer masses; for we cannot withdraw the veil to know whether they are unnecessary; though, I think, you may rest satisfied that few indeed are required for you."

"Oh, father, you know me not," said Dormer. "Whatever is required to purge away sin is necessary for my soul. You know me not."

"Would to God I could exchange with you, Dormer!" exclaimed Warrenne, as from his inmost soul:—then recollecting himself—"Did you say you would confess?"

"I did, Father."

Ernest and the other priests retired to the farther end of the small apartment, while Warrenne bent over Dormer, and received his whispered confession. It was short, and the absolution was pronounced by Warrenne. Dormer's eyes were, however, raised to heaven; and, to Ernest, he seemed praying for absolution to Him who alone could give it. The priests then approached; and, after some other prayers and ceremonies, all partook of the eucharist.

Dormer, after this, seemed much exhausted. He looked towards Ernest, who immediately went near. Dormer smiled, and held out his hand. "Raise my head," said he, faintly.

Ernest did so, and supported him on his breast. The door of the room was open opposite to the bed; for the oppression of death was on the patient's breast, and the priests, as they brought near the sacred apparatus, knelt on the coffin.

Warrenne himself anointed the dying sufferer. He repeated the words in Latin from whence the institution is taken by the Romish church: "Is any sick among you, let him call for the elders of the church; and let them pray over him, anointing him with oil in the name of the Lord; and the prayer of faith shall save the sick, and the Lord shall raise him up; and if he has committed sins they shall be forgiven him."

Ernest listened to these words, so evidently alluding to the gifts of healing imparted to the first Christians, but so unmeaning in the Church of Rome, where none of the effects followed which are ascribed by the Apostle to the observance, where the sick becomes more sick, and, instead of being raised up, goes down into the grave. Warrenne, however, rapidly pronounced the words, and repeated some Latin prayers, then touched, with the sacred oil, the eyes, the lips, the hands; whatever had been the means of seeing, of hearing, of speaking, of doing evil.

Ernest supported Dormer's head on his breast while Warrenne proceeded, repeating prayers each time he applied the chrism.

At last all was concluded, and the last words supposed to prepare for entering an eternity were about to be said, when Dormer, starting forward, gazed earnestly towards the door, and exclaimed "Clarenham!" then immediately fell back into Ernest's arms.

It was Clarenham, and in an instant he was at the side of Dormer's bed.

"Father! dearest Father!" He threw himself on his knees on the coffin. "Father, have you forgiven me? Oh, if I could have spared you all you have suffered! But you, Father—you made me what I am—you taught me to love truth." He would have taken Dormer's hand, but Warrenne pushed his away.

"The holy oil is upon that hand, Mr Clarenham—it must not be polluted by the touch of a heretic." The priests drew farther away from Clarenham, and removed their things.

"Do you not forgive me, Father?" asked Clarenham, in a voice of despair.

Dormer looked earnestly at him. "I thought I required *your* forgiveness, Basil."

Clarenham threw himself on the bed. "Oh, my beloved Father." He could say no more, but burst into an agony of grief.

"The service is not over, Mr Clarenham," said Warrenne, with displeasure.

Clarenham heeded him not.

"My son—my dear son," said Dormer, "I have no time to lose. Suffer Father Adrian to proceed."

Clarenham immediately rose and stood by Ernest, endeavouring to be calm. Ainsworth now stood near Dormer's bed; and other faces were seen in the dark passage which led into his room.

Dormer himself, however, seemed now unconscious of what was passing. His eyes were closed;—an expression of heavenly calm was on his countenance: the motions of his clasped hands shewed that he prayed mentally, but he spoke not.

All stood in profound silence, every eye fixed on the dying countenance. The last prayer was said, but no one stirred.

" Brother, in what faith do you die?" asked Warrenne, with unaffected solemnity.

" In the faith of the only true church—the church of Jesus Christ;" answered Dormer in a calm, low tone of voice.

" You mean, brother, in the only true and apostolic church of Rome?"

" The church of Christ," said Dormer, quickly.

" Yes, brother; but there are those now present who regard other communions as churches of Christ."

Dormer answered not—his thoughts seemed away; and, for a time, all again was silence. The expression of his countenance at length changed, and he opened his eyes and raised them to heaven with that fearfully-anxious look which so forcibly expresses the helplessness of the soul as life recedes and eternity must be entered.

" Lay me in the ashes," said he quickly.

"Why, why, dear Sir?" asked Ernest, in a whisper.

Warrenne beckoned to the priests, who immediately took the lid from the coffin, and prepared to obey him.

"You will hasten his departure," said Ernest to them.

"You shall not," exclaimed Clarenham.

"Lay me in the ashes—in the coffin," said Dormer, with a look of agony.

The priests approached, and Clarenham no longer opposed them, while they wrapped him in his blanket, and laid him in the coffin. Ernest, however, did not leave his place, but himself supported his head, and, kneeling down again, laid it on his breast. The priests looked at him, and at Warrenne; but the latter did not seem disposed to dispute his doing what he would.

For a few minutes Dormer seemed insensible; he then asked in a voice scarcely audible, "Does Ernest still support my head?"

"Yes, dearest Sir," replied Ernest, leaning forward.

"Dear Ernest—dear Clarenham, farewell."

"My dear Sir, is all peace?" asked Ernest in a whisper.

"Yes—now."

"What disturbed you?"

"One look to the past—Sin, Sin."

"But these ashes—what can they do?"

"Nothing, nothing. It was a moment of darkness."

Warrenne approached. "Brother, you have not distinctly declared your faith—at least you may be misunderstood."

"I die the most unworthy—the lowest, the least profitable of all—yet a member of the one true church—saved only by Christ."

"The Church of Rome?" asked Warrenne, putting his face close to Dormer's.

Dormer answered not. There were a few long breathings, and then all was at rest for ever.

For some minutes every one remained as still as him on whom they gazed. At last Ernest laid his hand on the pale forehead. The chill of death was upon it. He then closed the eyes, —for an instant pressed the lifeless form to his heart—kissed the cold cheek; then gently resigned the body to its last narrow house.

Clarenham knelt down, and would have embraced the remains, but Warrenne seemed on the watch to prevent him.

"No, Mr Clarenham. The church must prevent the pollution of that pure body: though in the sleep of death, still united to the one holy Catholic communion."

Clarenham would have broken from Warrenne's restraining hold; but, after an effort, fell back senseless into Ernest's arms. Ernest immediately had him conveyed from the apartment. The servants were just entering to have a last look of one whom they all had revered and loved; and were now prepared to approach with that veneration with which the Romish Church regards the remains of departed saints. The sight of their young master, pale and insensible, instantly changed the object of their attention and anxiety, and all crowded round him as Ernest had him conveyed to the hall. Maria Clarenham, who had been anxiously on the watch, while at the same time attempting to conceal from her mother the melancholy rites which were performing in Dormer's apartment, now also appeared. She had sufficient presence of mind to restrain every exclamation of alarm and anxiety on the part of the domestics, and herself, pale and trembling, stood over her brother, and assisted Ernest in his attempts to restore animation. At last Clarenham opened his eyes.

"What has happened? where am I?" exclaimed he, attempting to start away from Ernest, and looking wildly around.

"Dear Clarenham, recollect yourself," said Ernest, gently.

"Basil—dearest Basil—you are at home—you are with those who love you," said Maria, soothingly.

He thought for a moment—then turning away, as if all on earth had lost its power to attract him—"And Father Clement"—

"Is at last where there is no sorrow," said Ernest, gently but solemnly.

Clarenham immediately became calm—"Yes, yes—how selfish to wish it otherwise!" He looked at Ernest—then threw himself upon his breast, and both wept, regardless of all around them.

The servants now returned to the apartment, where the priests were busied in performing the last ceremonies over the dead: and Clarenham, Maria, and Ernest, proceeded to inform Mrs Clarenham of the event. And so deep had been her veneration for Dormer—so enlightening, and consoling, and heavenly had been his instructions and ministrations, that even the return of her son could not overcome her sorrow, though she humbly and thankfully acknowledged how graciously mercy and goodness were mingled in every affliction sent by her heavenly Father. Clarenham's appearance, however, excited her alarm and anxiety. He was pale and thin to a degree. His health seemed greatly injured; and to every question she asked regarding it, his answer was—"I am already better than I was, my dearest mother; but ask me no questions, for I am under the most solemn vow to answer none."

Ernest, at Clarenham's request, continued with him and his family during the remainder of the evening—all joining in deep and sincere grief, but finding comfort in the recollection of those many evidences, which all had witnessed, of his devotedness and holiness, whose spirit they now believed had entered into everlasting joy.

At night, before Ernest's departure, he went, accompanied by Basil, once more to contemplate that countenance in which he had, for the last few months, looked for the expressions of that mind and heart which had become more interesting and attractive to him than any other he had yet met on earth.

The little apartment was already hung with black, and lighted with large wax tapers, two of which stood on the table with the crucifix. The coffin was placed upon the bed; and the body clothed in rich vestments, but so disposed as to display the haircloth shirt beneath, and also the ashes on which it lay. The sharp cross which Dormer had worn in secret on his heart was now fixed outside, and its edges displayed. His hands were clasped upon his breast, and between them was placed a crucifix. The face, however, was in the profound peacefulness—the indescribable calmness of death: The expression—that of complete relief from suffering and sorrow. This had never been its living expression; and Ernest and Clarenham felt its calm enter into their own souls. And when at last the hour came in which the priests, and Roman Catholic domestics, who knelt around the dead, began to repeat the prayers of their Church, and Ernest and his friend left the apartment, the last impression of that countenance remained on their memories as indelibly as that of his holiness, and his gentleness, and his kindness, did upon their affections.

CHAPTER XIII.

"— quell'iniquo cui il Signore Gesu uccidera col fiato della sua bocca, e lo annichilera con lo splendore di sua venuta."

Martini's Trans.—2 Thessal. ii. 8.

For one week all were left undisturbed at Hallern Castle. During that week Dormer's remains had been laid in the chapel, and his grave continued to be surrounded by his flock, who, kneeling there, implored his intercession with heaven. Warrenne favoured this, and took pains, by his encomiums on the dead, to convince the people that he had joined that assembly of saints, to whom it is the strange policy of the Romish church to direct the devotions of her members.

Before this week had closed, Basil Clarenham had publicly received the communion from Dr Lowther, and abjured the Romish faith. To his mother he declared that the perusal of the Scriptures had convinced him of the errors of her church. To Ernest he acknowledged his sense of gratitude to heaven in having removed him from one to whom he felt pleasure in subjecting his mind—and placing him where the degree of corruption into which the Romish church had fallen was so awfully evident that he no longer could resist the command: "Come out of her, my people, that ye be not partakers of her sins, and that ye receive not of her plagues."—"Though," added he, "before I left the Inquisition, I was induced to take an oath of secrecy respecting all I had witnessed there, too solemn ever to be forgotten or infringed."

Mrs Clarenham seemed less grieved at this change than her son expected, and positively declined, for the time, Warrenne's proposal to appoint a successor to Dormer. "My son is now master here," said she. "If he continues a Protestant, I must try to understand what Protestantism is, at least so far as to learn its doctrines of charity."

At the end of that week of peace which followed Dormer's death, Warrenne asked a conference with Mrs Clarenham and Maria; and then read to them his instructions from the court of Rome. These declared—that as the heirs of General Clarenham had been left under the guardianship of certain churchmen, subject in their decisions to the court of Rome, it had been decided, that, as heresy had entered the family, both should be called on to profess their faith, that their guardians might act accordingly.

Maria instantly declared her willingness to answer this call. The day was fixed; and, in the presence of Warrenne and several of his brother priests, she avowed her determination to receive her faith only from the Bible, read by herself, in a language she understood.

On the same day Catherine professed herself a humble member of the church of Rome.

In a few weeks it was decided that Maria was no longer heiress of her uncle's fortune—which devolved on Catherine.

Three years after this decision, a convent was endowed by Catherine, of which she, a year or two afterwards, became the lady abbess, and, in her own opinion, the first of saints, and most perfect example and guide of the young sisters of her order. In the opinion of Warrenne, the most easily managed of all his tools. In her convent many miracles were performed in those days, of which it was found equally easy to make her the subject, or the witness to their truth.

While Catherine enjoyed her authority, and her own good opinion as lady abbess of the convent in ——shire, Maria was, as the wife of young Carysford, learning, from her own experience, that to the heart which seeks to know God, and humbly to love and serve him, His grace renders all situations means of discipline and improvement. Maria had considered herself bound to fulfil her early engagement as soon as Sir Thomas Carysford gave his consent; and had been received into his family—with rapture by young Carysford—with unfeigned joy and affection by his mother—with pompous stiffness of manner, but real pleasure, by Sir Thomas—with pretended satisfaction by Warrenne—and with unbounded joy by the domestics and people on the estate, who all knew how much she was beloved by those of their own class at Hallern.

Maria was of a character warmly to feel and participate in the joy and affection she inspired, —but her heart could not rest satisfied with nothing more: and now she felt indeed her dependence on that grace which could alone enable her so to act as to bring no reproach on that purer faith she professed amongst those who regarded that profession as her only fault. These considerations kept her close to her Bible, and to prayer; and gradually her lowliness and gentleness amongst so many surrounding temptations to pride and self-importance— her engaging attentions to Sir Thomas—her anxiety to be all a daughter could be to Lady Carysford—the use she made of her unbounded power over the affections of young Carysford, to win him into a course of actions the most beneficial to all around him, and honourable to himself:— her talents and information, and evident superiority, at least in holiness of principles and knowledge of Scripture, when conversing with Warrenne, rendered her soon the person in the family to whom each other member looked with most affection and esteem, or dread.

The case was the same with the domestics and the people: The good and well-intentioned loved and esteemed—the ill-disposed and bad feared their lady.

Perhaps some descendant of such a family, as that we have described under the name of Carysford, may be reminded of one whose character has descended to them under the appellation of the Good Lady—whose son was the first Protestant representative of the family; and whose grave they may have often visited, to admire the exquisite beauty of the monument and epitaph, as it is still seen in the chapel near the mansion, once Roman Catholic, now reserved as the lonely place of repose for the dead. Perhaps the epitaph has been read by some of the travellers permitted to view the now ivy-covered little chapel; and perhaps, if they have visited a still more beautiful chapel in the neighbourhood, a grave and monument may have been pointed out to them, to which, in the memory of the grandfathers of those who showed it, "the poor ignorant papists used to come to worship, till the young gentleman at the Castle, and his young friend at the hall went into the chapel and read the Bible aloud to the pilgrims—and then their priests would not suffer them to come."

The Protestant traveller would recognise the spirit which dictated this only justifiable method of attempting to prevent an erroneous approach to God. The Roman Catholic traveller would sigh as he remembered, that in Britain his church is almost forgotten; her places of worship in ruins; or, stript of the character they once bore, now dedicated to another faith; her services regarded as unmeaning ceremonies; her doctrines held as too absurd to be professed by rational men, therefore explained away by those who wish to regard her few remaining members as brothers and fellow-countrymen; her claim to unchangeableness and infallibility charged as an illiberal accusation of her enemies; and his church in her thus fallen state considered as justly complimented by being characterised as having advanced in improvement with society, and with other churches.

The true Christian will pray that the light of

truth—the light of Divine revelation—may continue to extend its beams till it overcomes all darkness, Protestant and Romish, and unites all in the one only true church, of which Christ is the living Head, to whom every living member is united by that "faith which purifieth the heart," and worketh by love.

THE END.

Edinburgh : Printed by A. Allardice.

FATHER OSWALD

Bibliographical note:

this facsimile has been made from a copy in the
Bodleian Library of Oxford University

FATHER OSWALD;

A

GENUINE CATHOLIC STORY.

"And other sheep I have that are not of this fold: them also I must bring, and they shall hear my voice: and there shall be one fold and one shepherd."—John x. 16.

LONDON:

CHARLES DOLMAN, 61, NEW BOND STREET.

1842.

Printed by J. L. Cox & Sons, 75, Great Queen Street,
Lincoln's-Inn Fields.

DEDICATION.

TO THE BRITISH PUBLIC.

The following pages are respectfully dedicated to the British Public, by one who ardently hopes, and earnestly prays, that the light of the true faith may perfectly and finally dispel the mists and clouds of prejudice and ignorance which obscure the understandings of so many noble and generous individuals in the British Isles, on the vital and all-important subject of Religion, which, unless it is known and practised pure and undefiled, can neither produce happiness here or hereafter.

PREFACE.

HAVING observed with much pain, several years ago, the harm done against the truth by the publication of "Father Clement" and many similar productions, I was induced, at the instances of a much and highly-respected friend, to sketch the following story, the outlines of which I have filled up by the aid of various sources of information and assistance.

I have freely made use of all the means of information which lay in my way, whether published or unpublished; from the beautiful gardens of many distinguished authors I have culled a flower here and there, and endeavoured to weave them into a garland, offered to the greater honour and glory of God. To these authors I beg to return my most grateful thanks once for all, and I trust they will not take it ill if I have not referred to them, which I must have done in almost every page. This story, as a novel, has little to recommend itself to the mere novel-reader, who seeks only the passing excitement of the moment. But this was not the object of the present work: its only aim has been to present an antidote to the baneful production of "Father Clement."

Hence, all the objections against the Catholic faith are taken *verbatim* from that work, and therefore I earnestly beg the admirers of "Father Clement," if they have any candour in them, to read "Father Oswald." If there is much repetition in many of the objections and answers, all I can say is, that it is the fault of "Father Clement;" but it is, nevertheless, a fact, that Protestants frequently repeat the same objections over and over again, although they have been previously refuted a hundred times.

The theological part of this work has been submitted to the censure of a competent Ecclesiastic, to whom I express my respectful and grateful thanks, as well as to all others from whom I have, known or unknown to themselves, received assistance in this little undertaking, which has been performed entirely from motives of love to God and to my neighbour. Gentle reader, receive it in the spirit with which it has been written.

SUNDAY,
January 24th, 1841.

FATHER OSWALD,

&c.

CHAPTER I.

> "Fishing and fiddling were his arts; at times,
> He altered sermons, or he tried at rhymes."
>
> CRABBE.

"WHITHER have you been strolling, my dearest Emma?" said Edward Sefton to his lovely wife, as he met her one delicious summer evening returning along the lawn to their happy home.

"I have been to visit poor William Smith; I think he will not be now long for this world," answered she, putting her arm within that of her husband.

"Poor fellow! I am sorry for it: he was always an honest industrious creature. I hope our good friend Dr. Davison has been to see him."

"Indeed, Edward, I don't believe he has," answered Emma, with rather a melancholy smile.

"And why not, pray?" said Edward; "surely, when the poor man is likely so soon to be called to his awful account, he requires the succours of religion."

"So he thought, and so I thought; but so did *not* think Dr. Davison."

"Impossible! But has Smith ever sent for him?"

"Yes," answered Emma, "he sent for him, I think it will be now three months ago."

"And why did he not go to him?"

"He did go then—one visit," answered Emma; "I remember it quite well; and he told Smith he could do nothing for him."

"Nothing for him!" interrupted Mr. Sefton; "I have a good mind to report him to the bishop. It will be well for him if his gown is not pulled over his head. Nothing for him! and so I presume he thinks Christians are to die like dogs, as if they had no souls at all."

"I was visiting poor Smith at the time he called, and he said to him, 'Dr. Davison, I have for many years prayed to God to make a good death, for I have felt the disease coming on; and now you tell me you can do nothing for me: yet I have read in my Bible that St. James says, "When any one is sick amongst you, let him bring in the priests of the church:"* to which Davison answered, 'It is no use wasting my time in talking about it, Smith, because the Archbishop of X—— has quite settled the point some time ago: but read your Bible, and, as I have known you for some time to be a good kind of man, I will tell my wife to come and read you a chapter now and then.'"

"Tell his wife, indeed! a pretty idea of his duties as a clergyman. Did not you remonstrate, Emma?"

"Yes; but to all I could say he only answered, that there was nothing more he could do, and that he was too busy with his studies, and with the composition of a little work on angling."

"Too busy with his studies! I never knew him put forward his studies as a barrier to a good dinner party, or a general *battue* of the preserves of Lord B——. His art of angling, to be sure, if practice makes perfect, will be a valuable acquisition to amateurs of that sport, for he is truly an indefatigable whipper of the stream, and a cunning artist in fly-making. If the devil himself were a trout, he could scarce, I think, escape being hooked by one of his murderous flies: after all, fishing

* James v. 14.

is an innocent amusement; the Apostles, you know, Emma, were fishermen."

"Yes, Edward; but you forget that when they were called to be fishers of men, they left their nets to follow Christ. I can conceive that fishing and field-sports are very innocent and healthy amusements when used with moderation, and as a relaxation from more serious duties, as you are wont to do; but to make them the all-important and sole business of life, ill becomes a Christian, and still worse a clergyman."

"Your observation is just, and the conduct of our clerical Nimrod has often given me pain; but surely he sometimes calls in to see poor Smith?"

"He has never been near Smith since; and I remember quite well thinking to myself, that I hoped Dr. Davison would not have the cure when I shall be called to my long home."

"Well, I cannot understand it," said Edward, rising from the bench on which they had been reposing; "it would not have been so in good old Mr. Robson's time. I declare I will write to the Bishop of D—— about it."

"It is no use to write to the bishop about it, if an archbishop has already settled it. I think it is very sad to depend on the individual opinions of different clergymen on such an important point."

"Ah, do not be sad about it, dearest," said Edward; "you know we do not depend upon the opinion of any clergyman: we can all read the Bible, and have a right to interpret it according to our own unbiassed opinion."

Emma suppressed a rising sigh, and Sefton continued:

"Now I think it clear that poor Smith, in his ignorance, has mistaken the meaning of the Apostle's words: for James is evidently speaking of the miraculous gift of *healing*, which was given to the Apostles. But miracles, you know, my dear, have long since ceased."

"So we are *taught*," said Emma anxiously, "but I never heard upon what scriptural evidence. Did not Christ say, if we had faith, 'as a grain of mustard seed, we might move mountains;'* and on another occasion, did he not say, 'He that believeth in me, the works that I do, he also shall do, and greater than these shall he do?'† Now, I never read that these promises were limited to time, or place, or persons."

"Your reasoning is specious, Emma; but all reasoning is of no avail against a positive fact: for when do we now see a miracle?"

"I think that is rather a negative fact, which seems to me to argue rather a deficiency of faith on our part, than a failure of promise on the part of Christ," answered Mrs. Sefton.

"Pooh, pooh! Emma; put that foolish notion out of your head. The fact is, miracles have ceased, and no more need be said about it."

This evasive answer noways satisfied the mind of Mrs. Sefton; but she could not, or rather durst not, then pursue the question further; so turning the discourse, she gently replied—

"I do not think that poor Smith expects a miracle; but having read the words of St. James, he has it fixed in his mind, that the priest ought to be called in, to pray over him, and to anoint him with oil; for, somehow or other, he fancies it may do him good, and that 'his sins will be forgiven him.'"

"What gross ignorance!" exclaimed her husband, "to think of such a superstitious practice in this enlightened age! But all this comes from the fellow's continually running from one fanatical meeting-house to another. He had much better have attended to his own lawful minister, Dr. Davison."

"You just now observed, Edward, that we are not obliged to follow the opinions of any clergyman. Now, I am sure poor Smith has read his Bible with assiduity and great earnestness to find out the truth, and if he thinks differently from us, we ought not to blame him: besides, his own minister tells him that he can do him no good."

"In that Davison is wrong; we have in the common

* Matt. xvii. 19. † John xiv. 12.

prayer-book an express ordinance for the visitation of the sick."

"That ordinance, you know, love, prescribes nothing for the 'anointing with oil.' Now, this it is which molests poor Smith the most."

"A foolish and superstitious fancy, Emma, and the fellow does not understand the Scripture."

"Dr. Davison understands it better, of course, and is, therefore, right when he says he can do him no good."

"I did not say that; he might, at least, pray over him, and—"

"But," interrupted Emma, "does the archbishop understand the Scripture better on this important point?"

"It seems not," answered her husband; "it is a subject, however, well worth thought and investigation, and I will sift it to the bottom—depend upon that."

By this time the sun was down, and the last golden ray of evening hung lingering on the horizon; they entered the door of their home. Edward retired to his study, and Emma went to her nursery, each musing, somewhat painfully, on what had passed.

At the opening of this narrative, Mr. and Mrs. Sefton had been married about five years, and were the happy parents of three little boys and an infant girl. Mr. Sefton was a *strict* Protestant, a man of deep feeling and deep prejudice; very affectionate and very firm; warmly attached to his wife, and towards all but her more inclined to severity than mildness; he was well educated, well read, and made literature his principal pursuit. Mrs. Sefton was the only daughter of a Catholic gentleman, who died when she was a year old; she was carefully educated by a Protestant mother, who survived her daughter's marriage but a few months Emma was an affectionate wife and mother, good, gentle, and amiable to all around her; but with a great fund of firmness and disinterestedness of character when called upon to act; possessing a cultivated mind, much inclined to religion, and exercising herself assiduously in charity to the poor and infirm. Mr. and Mrs. Sefton were tenderly attached to each other, and happy in their own domestic circle, endeavouring to diffuse amongst their numerous tenantry peace and content, and to relieve, with ample generosity, the sufferings and wants of the unfortunate; often did they feel peace and consolation in the remembrance of those emphatic words of Scripture, "Charity covers a multitude of sins."

CHAPTER II.

"Another had charge sick persons to attend,
And comfort those in point of death which lay;
For them most needed comfort in the end,
When sin, and hell, and death, doe most dismay
The feeble soul, departing hence away."
SPENSER.

THE individual William Smith, mentioned in the first chapter, was one of Mr. Sefton's tenants, the father of a small family, and, as has been hinted, dying of consumption. During the progress of this insidious and flattering disease, the poor man had abundant time to reflect on the importance of an hereafter, and he often felt in his mind a little doubt, or trembling half-formed fear, whether he was in the "strait way that leads to life," and amongst the few whom the Scripture says, "find it." He felt the yearnings of his soul towards its Creator; the desire of spending his eternity with Him, and the fears that he might be rejected before the awful judgment of God for not being in the right path of salvation, often threw him into the painful agonies of a doubtful and distracted spirit. He was a well-meaning man, much inclined to religion, and whilst in health had often gone to places of different worship, of which there are so many in England, and there of course he had heard many and most contradictory doctrines; and now, on his death-bed, all these things came to his mind, coupled with the importance of the "one thing necessary." He tried to find relief in his Bible, but when he met with texts like these: "There is one faith, one baptism, one God;"* "There shall be one fold, and one shepherd;"† "Without faith it is impossible to please God,"‡ his perplexity and anxiety of mind increased. One day he in his extreme agony pricked into his Bible, as many will do when their minds are ill at ease, and his eye fell on the following text:—"Is any man sick amongst you? Let him bring in the priests of the Church, and let them pray over him, anointing him with oil in the name of the Lord; and the prayer of *faith* shall save the sick man; and the Lord shall raise him up, and if he be in sins, they shall be forgiven him:"§ a ray of light seemed to beam on his soul; he called instantly to his wife, and desired her to go for Dr. Davison: she went, and the result of his visit has already been detailed. From that time the poor man's troubles of mind daily increased, and he in vain tried to account to himself for the reasons of that text being written at all, when his own clergyman told him he could do nothing for him. God is ever good to those who seek him with an upright heart. One evening, while his poor wife was endeavouring with all the anxiety of a woman's love to soothe his mental and bodily anguish, she said to him, "God knows I have no time to read the Bible as you have, William, but I have heard that text, 'Ask, and you shall receive; seek, and you shall find; knock, and it shall be opened to you,'|| and I have asked for you, that God may give you peace."

"Oh! Mary," answered he, "and so have I often asked it; but He does not!"

"Well, Willie, do you know what I have been thinking? Shall I go and call Mr. Ebenezer, the Methodist preacher?"

"No, no, Mary, by no means. I have often heard him preach, but I never found peace to my soul; I always came away with a heart as heavy and as cold as a stone."

"How so? Thou usedst to call him a wonderful man."

* Eph. iv. 5. † John x. 16. ‡ Heb. xi. 6.
§ James v. 14, 15. || Luke xi. 9.

"Aye, so I thought for a time; but when I found he was always hammering into us, that God made some few men to be saved, and all the rest to be damned, I could bear it no longer."

"Why, that was making God a cruel tyrant."

"So I thought; and then that 'saving assurance,' which he said all God's elect must have, I could never feel, so my heart fell within me, and I was wellnigh going into despair."

"Well, then, I will go and ask that man who they say is so holy, to come and see thee, and talk to thee."

"What man?" said he, anxiously raising his head from his painful pillow.

"Why, Mr. Oswald, to be sure, the priest at the Catholic chapel. I have heard him preach, and I have seen him visit the sick, and comfort them, and who knows but he might make thee quiet?"

"But, Mary, he would not come to me; he would say I was a heretic—but no; there can be no harm in seeking to know the truth. I will do so. Go directly, Mary, that I may sleep in peace."

She was off in an instant; and shortly returned with Father Oswald.

Father Oswald was eminent for his great talents, and still more so for his great piety and sanctity; he was a professed Father of the Society of Jesus, about fifty, of a fine majestic exterior, and open, engaging countenance; with a peculiar mixture in his deportment and manner of what is calculated to win and to awe, of gentleness and compassion, of zeal and of fervour; but that which forcibly struck even the most casual observer, was the evident superiority and power his spirit maintained over its earthly tenement, and the great sincerity with which he seemed to feel and to practise the love of God and of his neighbour. In a few minutes he was seated by the sick man's side, anxiously inquiring if he could be of any use to him. Poor Smith looked up in his face, and, encouraged by the beam of compassion in it, said—

"I have sent for you, Sir, because I am very wretched. I hope you will forgive me, for I am not a Catholic;

but my own clergyman says he can do nothing for me, and so my wife persuaded me to speak to you."

"She did very well; part of my ministry is to visit the sick, and comfort the afflicted. Now, tell me a little in what way I can serve you. I fear you seem ill in body."

"Yes, Sir, very ill, but my mind is worse; I fear I am not in the right way to go to Heaven. Dr. Davison says he can do nothing for me, and yet I find this text (pointing with his finger to the passage quoted above). Now, what is the use of its being there if they quite neglect it? I wish to serve God in the right way, but in the Bible I cannot see quite clearly which it is, and I am very miserable about it." There he paused for want of breath, and Father Oswald answered:

"My son, be of good heart, and you will soon be quite happy; it is not from the Scripture that you or any individual can find out which is the right way. Tell me, my good man, do you know the Apostles' Creed?"

"I suppose, Sir, you mean the 'I believe in God?'"

"Exactly so."

"I did learn it when I was young; but I have not thought much about it since I began to read the Bible."

"Do you believe all the things contained in that creed?"

"I did believe them when I was a lad, and I think I have always believed them, and do now believe them."

"Why do you believe them?"

"I believe them because I was *taught* to believe them, and I have never seen any reason to doubt of them."

"Who made the Apostles' Creed?"

"I cannot exactly tell, but I guess the Apostles must have made it. But I do not remember ever to have read it in the Bible."

"Certainly not; but tell me, why do you believe the Bible?"

"I have always believed the Bible because I have been *taught* that it is the Word of God."

"Exactly so: now, my good friend, you see that

the Apostles' Creed and the Bible have the same authority; for you believe both on the same motive—because you have been so *taught* to believe, and that is as it should be; for you remember the Bible says, that Christ sent his Apostles '*to teach* all nations.'"*

"I see, I see," said Smith, after some reflection; "it must be so. But there are so many teachers, teaching such different doctrines, that I do not know whom to believe. And Christ tells us to 'beware of false prophets;'† and St. Peter, I think it is, says, 'There shall be amongst you lying teachers.'‡ How, then, is a poor man to know the true teachers?"

"Nothing more easy, as I trust I shall be able to shew you; for as Christ calls all to the truth, the way to find it must be so plain and easy, that the poor and ignorant, if they will not blindly shut their eyes, cannot miss it; just as the prophet Isaiah foretold of the Church of Christ, 'And a path and a way shall be there, and it shall be called the holy way: the unclean shall not pass over it; and this shall be unto you a straight way, so that fools shall not err therein.'§ But let us take one thing at a time, and go on with the Apostles' Creed. From whom did you learn the creed?"

"I learnt it from my mother, poor soul."

"And from whom did she learn it?"

"Why, I reckon from her father or mother, or from the parson."

"Exactly so; and thus we go back from son to father, for three hundred years, when we come to the first Protestants. Now, I ask you, from whom did the first Protestants get it?"

"Eh! I see what you would be at," said the sick man, with a ghastly, yet artless smile upon his lips. "Why, they must have got it from the Catholics."

"So they did, just as they got the Bible; and the Catholics received the Apostles' Creed and the Bible equally from the Apostles, and have handed them down from father to son, to the present day; while the pas-

* Matt. xxviii. 19. † Matt. vii. 15. ‡ 2 Peter ii. 1.
§ Is. xxxv. 8.

tors of the Church took care that nothing should be changed in the one or the other, and this handing down Catholics call tradition; without which, you see, you could not be sure of your Bible."

"I see, I see," said Smith, musing as if a new light had broken in upon his mind. After a considerable pause, the sick man, casting a wistful look towards the father, said—

"Pray, Sir, go on, if it be not too troublesome for you."

"With the greatest pleasure, my good friend. Do you remember one article of the Apostles' Creed, where it is said, 'I believe the Holy Catholic Church?'"

"I remember it very well, and I have often wondered why we Protestants were taught to believe the Holy Catholic Church, while they tell us that the old Catholic Church was corrupted by all sorts of abominations."

"I will tell you," said Father Oswald; "the creed was too well known by all the people, and they could not change it. Now, if the creed be as true as the Bible, there was always a *Holy* Catholic Church; how, then, could a *Holy* Church be filled with all sorts of abominations?"

"That could not be, it stands to reason," said Smith.

"And if we are *to believe* that Church," continued Father Oswald, "it could not lead us into error, otherwise we should be obliged to believe a lie."

"True, I see it now clearer than ever, and I long very much to know something more about the Catholic Church, or, as the creed calls it, the *Holy* Catholic Church, for I begin to see it must be the right Church."

"I will satisfy your pious curiosity immediately. Christ being God, is truth itself, his words can therefore never fail. He founded the true and only Church, and commissioned St. Peter and the Apostles to preach and teach his gospel to all nations, promising to be with them 'all days,' and promising to send on them the Holy Ghost, to teach them all things, and to lead them into *all truth*: now, with the successors of St. Peter and the Apostles must remain the true faith, and it is to them we must apply to find it."

"And where are we to turn to find them?" said Smith, anxiously.

"To the ministers of the Holy Catholic Church, mentioned in the creed, and which existed fifteen hundred years before Protestants were heard of: this Church teaches the same truths the Apostles taught; it is founded on a rock, and Jesus has declared, 'The gates of hell shall never prevail against it;' and it is by its decisions we are to know what is true faith, and not by our own explanations of the Bible; that is, as we receive the Bible from the Church, we must receive the true sense of the Bible from the same Church, for if we give a wrong sense to the Bible, it is no longer the Word of God, but the word of man."

"Aye," said Smith, "that stands to reason; and now I see why so many Protestant ministers, all pretending to the Bible, preach such different doctrines, that a poor man knows not which is right and which is wrong. It must be that they preach their own conceits, and not the Word of God."

"So it is, unfortunately," replied the father; "but from this you may learn a useful lesson; that it is more necessary to have an unerring authority to hand down to us the true sense of the Bible, than to hand down to us the Bible itself."

"That certainly seems very plain," said Smith, thoughtfully; "for there can be but one truth, and the true Word of God cannot say yea and nay, black and white, of the same thing; and yet Protestants and Methodists, and so many others with the Bible in their hand, all think quite different one from another."

"Exactly so; but Catholics all think alike; with them there is but one faith through all the nations under the sun, because they do not follow their own wild interpretations of the Scripture, but that sense which has been always held by the Holy Catholic Church."

"It stands to reason," said Smith, "that if we cannot find the true sense of the Bible, it would be better to have no Bible at all." Then, looking earnestly in the father's face, he continued, "Do you then think, Sir, that you can be of use to me on my death-bed, and teach me the sure way of going to Heaven?"

"I am sure of it, my son; as sure of it as I am of my own existence. I will willingly come and visit you, and explain to you the Catholic doctrines; and I think when you have heard a little more, you will soon be much happier than you are now."

"Oh! Sir, I can never thank you enough, and if I should be satisfied with what you tell me, you will then, perhaps, do for me what St. James has ordered."

"I trust that may not be yet necessary; but should it be so, I will not fail, please God, to give you all the comforts and helps that the Catholic Church administers to her departing children. What St. James describes here is extreme unction, which is one of the sacraments of the Church administered to dying persons; but now I will leave you, and return to-morrow morning. In the meantime be of good courage, and may God Almighty bless you."

Smith clasped his hands, but could not speak. After the father's departure, he remained, as it were, in a profound reverie for nearly an hour; but a peace and a calm were at his heart which in his whole life he had never experienced, and in that state he fell asleep, sweetly reposing in the arms of Divine Providence.

CHAPTER III.

"—— Still thou errest, nor end wilt find
Of erring, from the path of truth remote."
MILTON.

THE next day Smith looked with an ardent wish for the hour which Father Oswald had appointed to return; the hour came and passed, and another and another hour succeeded, and no Father Oswald appeared. The evening shades began to lengthen, and a cloud of despondency passed across the mind of the sick man; he thought himself abandoned by all. At length Father Oswald made his appearance.

"Oh! Sir," exclaimed Smith, "how glad I am to see you, I began to think you would not come again, because I am a heretic."

"My son," said the father gently, "I have been unexpectedly detained by other pressing duties; but do not think I consider you a heretic. I can distinguish between a poor man who errs through ignorance while he earnestly seeks the truth, and the man to whom the truth has been sufficiently made known, yet obstinately adheres to his errors, and shuts his eyes against the midday sun. This latter only I call a heretic."

"God knows, Sir, I have honestly sought after the truth," said Smith, sighing.

"And God will bring you to it," added the father.

"I hope so, indeed!" ejaculated Smith. "Well, Sir, I have been considering all this long day on what you told me yesterday about the Catholic Church: but I do not know exactly the right meaning of *Catholic.* I have been thinking—"

"Catholic, my good friend, means *universal.*"

"Aye, so I have been taught; but, then, if it be universal, it must take in all sorts of Christians, Church of England, Presbyterians, Independents, Baptists, Methodists, Quakers, Shakers, Ranters, Jumpers, and five or six score more."

"I think," said Father Oswald, smiling, "you will find it rather difficult to cram all these into one Church, or to pen them into one fold. Were you to attempt such a union, you would only build up a new Babel of jarring opinions and confused tongues. But then tell me, how could you *believe* such a mass of contradictions?"

"True, true," said Smith, after a little reflection. "We cannot believe yea and nay of the same thing, that's certain; but I was not thinking of that word *believe.*"

"Now, Sir, since my notion of a universal church cannot stand, pray tell me its true meaning."

"I will tell you from your Bible. Let us turn to the commission which Jesus Christ gave to his Apostles, to plant and propagate his Church, and we shall soon see in what sense he intended it to be Catholic, or universal. 'All power is given to me in heaven and in earth. Going, therefore, teach ye *all nations;* baptizing them in the name of the Father, and of the Son, and of the Holy Ghost; teaching them to observe *all things* whatsoever I have commanded you: and, behold, I am with you *all days*, even to the consummation of the world.'* First, the Church established by Jesus Christ must be Catholic or universal with respect to *place.* 'Teach all nations.'"

"I see, I see," said Smith, "and I see, moreover, that no Protestant sect is spread over all nations."

"Secondly, the Church must be Catholic in *doctrine,* 'teaching them to observe all things.'"

"I see it, I see it; but to be able to teach all things,

* Matt. xxviii. 18.

it must know all things; now I am sure the Protestant sects either do not know, or do not teach all things which Christ commanded to be observed, otherwise they would agree in all things, and not teach such contradictions and lies."

Thirdly, the Church must be Catholic with respect *to time:* 'Behold, I am with you all days, even to the consummation of the world.'"

"Let me see," said Smith, "I think the first Protestants began about three hundred years since. Nay, I remember some beginning: the Ranters, the New-lights, and the Old-lights, and Johanna Southcote and Dr. Irving, and half a score more; and I have heard my father tell of a dozen more in his time. None of these can belong to the Catholic Church established by Jesus Christ."

"Your reflections," said the father, "are just and natural, and I would not interrupt you: but take notice of another thing. Christ promises to be with his Apostles '*all days*, even unto the end of time.' Now, as the Apostles all died in due time, the promise of Christ extends unto all their successors, the *teachers* of the Church through all days: consequently, as long as Christ is with the great body of the teachers of the Church, they cannot go wrong, nor lead us into error; so that the *doctrine* of the Church never stands in need of reform."

"I see it clearly," said Smith; "so that all that a poor man has to do is to inquire what the Church teaches, and he is sure to learn the truth. But, Sir, can you tell me why we are called Protestants?"

"It is a name of your own choosing. Your forefathers called themselves Protestants because they protested against the doctrine of the Holy Catholic Church; against the doctrine of that Church which had existed fifteen hundred years in the quiet possession of the promises of Christ."

"Ah! Sir, that was an ugly beginning; I will never be called a Protestant again, but I think I never *protested*."

"Formally you never did, for that reason I never called you a heretic; I only considered you as erring through ignorance. But mind, if you blindly shut your eyes against the light of truth, which you now begin to see, you may easily become an obstinate heretic."

"I trust in God," said Smith with a deep sigh, "that will never become my misfortune."

"I am confident it never will," said Father Oswald, rising, "but it is growing late; to-morrow I hope to see you at an earlier hour; so, good night, and may God bless you."

From that day Father Oswald continued daily to visit William Smith, and to explain to him simply and distinctly the faith and doctrines of the Catholic Church. It was not long before Smith, with a full conviction of the truth of that Church, was received into its bosom. He made the confession of his sins and his abjuration with great courage; and having received the Holy Communion and Confirmation, had only to regret not having known the truth, nor had these consolations before. He had sought the true faith with a simple and upright heart, and to such God never denies the knowledge of it; his intellect was not obscured by worldliness and vice, nor warped by human respects; so that when the truth of the Catholic faith was clearly apprehended by his understanding, his will joyfully embraced it. Many there are, alas! a countless many, who know and feel where the *one* true faith is, and refuse, or neglect, or delay to embrace it, from human respects, from fear of what the world may say, or from the numberless impediments of worldliness, luxury, and vice; but when eternity succeeds to time, how will they then bitterly regret not having embraced the 'one faith of the one God!' Emma Sefton continued her visits of charity to Smith, and in his humble cottage she met and became acquainted with Father Oswald. She often sat awhile, and listened to his explanations and instructions, and she was much surprised to perceive the extreme change there was in Smith after he became a Catholic. The air of tranquillity, calm, and peace which beamed in his every word and look, even amidst great suffering, struck her forcibly in contrast with the restlessness and misery of mind which she had continually observed in him but a few short months before. She said in her own heart, I wonder what can be the cause of this? and I wonder, too, that Father Oswald, and even Smith now, seem so *quite* certain that the *Catholic faith* is the only true and real one. I wish I could feel so very very certain as they seem to be, that the Church of England is the only true Church—but, after all, it is not of such great consequence whether one is a Protestant or a Catholic, as long as one is good; Harriet always says so. My father, to be sure, was a Catholic, but my mother was a Protestant, and my husband is an excellent Protestant, and, of course, I ought to be what he is; however, if I feel more uneasy, I will ask him about it, or perhaps Dr. Davison. The Harriet to whom in her soliloquy she alluded was sister to Mr. Sefton, and lived with them; she was an easy-tempered, fat, contented lady, about forty, who, when religion was the topic, always said, "It is little matter of what religion people are, as long as they are Christians and do no harm." Her idea of Christianity was most comprehensive; it did not exclude the Jew or the Mussulman, or even the Papist, provided they lived up to their principles, and did no harm to any one. She had, moreover, a strong tinge of superstition in her character, and readily gave credit to omens, dreams, and fortune-tellers. Hence, her opinion on religion had not much weight with Emma; but when man is in want of an argument to support his opinion, he will sometimes condescend to cling to a straw. The point which had most struck Mrs. Sefton in what little she had heard Father Oswald explain of the Catholic faith, was the doctrine of the real presence of the Saviour in the Eucharist and of Transubstantiation. She, with the generality of Protestants, had always looked upon the sacrament as a commemoration, and when she had taken it, her simple idea was that she had done a pious action, to put her in mind of the Redeemer. To be sure, she had heard some Protestants, and even some of the clergy, say, that they believed some sort of a real presence, not easily defined; but she had never reflected on the foundations of their opinion, and had always turned away her thoughts from it as a most revolting idea. When she heard Father Oswald clearly explain and maintain, that unless "we eat *the flesh* and drink *the blood* of the Son of God, we cannot have life in us,"* she felt extremely uneasy, and began to wonder how it happened that it had never struck her in that way before, though she had read the Scripture so often. She was timid of speaking to her husband about it, because his prejudices against Popery were very violent, and her father having been a Catholic, made her still more backward to open her mind to him; she had several of her father's books, and she determined to examine them for further explanation. Amongst them she found some books of controversy, and the explanations of the doctrine of Transubstantiation found therein were so clear, that her difficulties about the Protestant opinion, instead of being dispersed, were redoubled. She was, at this time, in daily expectation of the arrival of her uncle, General Russell, from the Peninsula, where he had been absent in the wars more than twenty years. The general was a Catholic, and a very staunch one; in early life, he had the misfortune to lose a wife and only child, to whom he was fondly attached. To divert his grief, he entered the army, where he soon became distinguished by his bravery. Now he wished to return, to end his days at his hereditary estate, ten miles distant from Sefton Hall. The general was of a generous and open character, the avowed enemy of all irreligion; having all his life openly practised and defended his own faith, and the rites of his own church, he would as soon have surrendered to the enemy the outworks of the fortress under his command as he would have yielded the practices of crosses, beads, relics, and holy-water, to his Protestant antagonist. He used to say to the divines of his own church, "Take you charge of the citadel; leave the

* John vi. 54.

advance posts to my defence; I can easily disperse the rabble scouts of the enemy." He had employed much both of his leizure and talents in detecting the absurdities and inconsistencies of Protestantism, which, from his possessing naturally an uncommonly quick perception of the absurd and ridiculous, caused the follies of the Reformation frequently to come under his good-natured, though keen and just sarcasm. From the time Emma began to feel uneasy on the subject of faith, she became still more anxious for the arrival of her uncle; and about a month from the commencement of her acquaintance with Father Oswald, he actually did arrive, to the no small joy of both parties,—he at seeing again the niece whom he had left a laughing sportive child, and who was now almost his only relative; and she, because she hoped to find in him a friend and adviser in many difficulties, being nearly the only relative remaining to her since the death of her mother. But we must leave the general to speak for himself in the next chapter.

CHAPTER IV.

"A merrier man,
Within the limits of becoming mirth,
I never spent an hour's talk withal."
SHAKSPEARE.

BESIDES the general and Harriet, there dined at Sefton Hall next day Dr. Davison. It was not unusual with the parson, who was a sleek, rosy, pompous personage, to visit the better classes of his parishioners about the hour of dinner: so it happened this day, and as Mr. Sefton had long wished to give him a hint about Smith, he was not sorry for it. During dinner, the general entertained Mr. and Mrs. Sefton with many interesting accounts of what he had seen and observed in Portugal and Spain, whilst Dr. Davison as closely interested Harriet with an account of his morning sport, and particularly by describing with what masterly art he had hooked a fine salmon-trout, and fought with it for an hour, regretting very much he had not sent it to the Hall for this joyful occasion. Harriet, in a sort of half-confidential tone, consulted the doctor on a strange dream which she had had a few nights before, and which, she greatly feared, foreboded no good. The doctor tried to turn off the discourse, but was obliged to listen to the whole details. He became quite fidgety, and in his hurry to get rid of the annoyance, overturned the salt. "Be not alarmed," said he in a low tone, observing Harriet change colour; "you see the salt fell towards me, so to me the evil betides." This assurance re-assured the good lady, and

Mr. Sefton, challenging him to a glass of wine, commenced his premeditated attack about Smith.

"It has given me great concern, my dear Dr. Davison," said he, "that you should have lost one of your parishioners."

"Indeed! I was not aware of it; who is gone to the next world now?"

"Not to the next world, not to the next world; worse than that—gone over to Popery!"

"Oh, my dear Sir," said the doctor, "I understand you now—you mean that man, Smith. Well, well, no great loss; he was never a strict Protestant; but was always poking his nose into some meeting-house, or chapel, or conventicle."

"Well, Sir," said Edward firmly, "if you had visited him, as he so particularly wished, during his illness, the parish would not have had this scandal; it is an occurrence infinitely to be regretted."

The doctor turned very red, but before his mouth was sufficiently empty to answer, Emma said, soothingly—

"It was very natural, I think, that the poor man should become a Catholic, considering the great and kind attentions paid to him by Father Oswald."

"Call no man on earth, in that sense, Father, Ma'am," said the doctor gravely; "these are words of Scripture."

Emma blushed.

"I beg pardon, Doctor, Mr.——; really, Sir, I know not how to call you," exclaimed the general; "for Christ forbids me in the same place to call you malibi, that is, doctor or master."

"Humph," said the doctor gruffly.

"You forget, General," interrupted Edward, "that the Lord hath given some doctors to his Church, and Paul calls himself the doctor of the Gentiles."

"True," answered the general; "and he calls himself the only Father of the Corinthians in very energetic terms."*

* 1 Cor. iv. 15.

The doctor reddened with anger.

"You profane the Scripture."

"I only follow your example, my good friend," answered the general. "Now, tell me, Doctor, would you scruple to be called the Right Reverend Father in God the Lord Bishop of so-and-so, if such a windfall were to happen?"

Dr. Davison put on a sanctified face, and was about to answer, when Edward interrupted him by saying—

"Before you answer that puzzling question, Dr. Davison, perhaps you will explain to me your objection to visiting the sick."

"My dear Mr. Sefton," exclaimed the doctor, "what objection can I have to visit the sick, especially at the last, if they should wish to take the sacrament; but what more can one do for them? besides, they have their Bibles, and Christ orders them to 'search the Scriptures.'"

"Oh! oh!" said the general, "but if people are to search the Scriptures for themselves, of what use are the parsons?"

Harriet laughed.

"But I understand you well enough," continued he; "you gentlemen of the clerical gown consider that text as the broad stone on which your Protestant fortress is built."

"Yes, General Russell," said the doctor, getting quite roused, "it is the broad stone of Protestantism on which our impregnable Church is built."

"Well, Dr. Davison," said the general quietly, "I belong to a Church which Christ founded on a very different rock; I should feel very little scruple in sapping your foundation, and laying a train of gunpowder under it."

"Aye, aye," exclaimed the doctor, "that's always the way with you Papists; all your arguments end in blowing up with gunpowder."

"I imagine, Doctor," interposed Mr. Sefton, "the general was only speaking metaphorically."

"Metaphorically, to be sure," said the general; "in the style of an old soldier."

"Nevertheless," continued Mr. Sefton, "I have always considered that text of Scripture as an unanswerable argument in support of the Protestant right to read the Bible, and of course to form his own opinion of what he reads."

"Yes," said the doctor, pompously raising his voice with all the dignity of self-sufficiency; "the Bible, the Bible alone is the religion of Protestants; as long as the Protestant shall hold the Bible, the palladium of his liberty, so long may he defy the efforts of hell and popery! That is the charter of his rights, sealed with the broad seal of Heaven, and bearing impressed in indelible characters the high behest of God, 'Search the Scriptures.'"

"Hold, my good friend," called out the general; "let not your enthusiasm carry you beyond the bounds of discretion; allow me to put in a word or two. If I understand you rightly, you maintain that Christ in these words gives an express *command* to all men, women, and children, to the learned divine and to the unwashed artificer, to search the Scripture, and consequently to judge for himself, to form his own creed, to believe or to disbelieve whatever he may think conformable or contrary to that sacred code, otherwise the search would be to no purpose?"

"Certainly, certainly," said the doctor.

"Excepting," interrupted Edward, "that all strict Protestants must believe the Thirty-nine Articles."

"Now, it appears to me," continued the general, "that the obvious and fatal consequences of such a mode of proceeding suffices to make a prudent mind doubt, if Christ, in his wisdom, ever gave such a command."

"But it is written in the Scripture, Sir, said Emma."

"Yes, my dear niece, it is written there, and having heard so many Protestants quote it, I have particularly examined this passage with a learned Catholic divine: now, in the English version, the verb *search* is rendered in the imperative mood, which *may* indeed, but *does not* absolutely, imply a command: in the Greek original, the verb is of such a form, that it is the same in the indicative and in the imperative mood. I have now a choice before me, and the Latin Vulgate, which often throws a light upon the ambiguous expressions of the Greek, unfortunately in this instance is equally ambiguous with the Greek; so, both being equally mute, I cannot catch from either the tone of command which might determine me to receive the text in the imperative mood. I am now left to conjecture: I study the context, and find that either mood fits in wonderfully well. I am therefore left to a free choice; but as our choice is usually influenced by our liking or our prejudices, I prefer to render the passage in the indicative mood thus: 'Ye search the Scriptures; for in them ye think ye have eternal life; and they are they which testify of me, and ye will not come unto me, that ye might have life.' Now, in this form it looks much more like a severe reproach to the learned Rabbis of the Synagogue, than a command to Christians; therefore, Sir, before I admit *your command*, you must prove to me that my version is wrong; this I defy you to do, and until you have done it, you must consider the broad seal of your charter torn away, and the broad stone of your Protestant fortress blown up to the devil."

"Oh! dear uncle," exclaimed Mrs. Sefton, "do not use that wicked word."

"Emma," said the general, "I know of no respect due to the devil's name. Really, I do not know whither I can more properly send the whole system, 'which changes the truth of God into a lie,' than to its own father."*

Mrs. Sefton blushed, half mortified at the rebuke and half conscious that she had been "straining at a gnat, and swallowing a camel."

"But," said Edward, "according to what you say, the Catholic version renders the text in the imperative mood."

"The Catholic version gives both, and leaves us the free choice of either, because Catholics do not build their faith on the ambiguous reading of a Greek or Latin verb."

* Rom. i. 25.

"You allow at least, that the Protestant version may be right?" said Edward.

"Most freely; but I cannot allow that any man acts wisely, who grounds his faith or risks his salvation on the toss up of a shilling, where there is an equal chance of its turning up heads or tails," answered the general.

"What, exclaimed Doctor Davison angrily, "do you deny that a man who searches the Scriptures with a sincere heart will find therein eternal life?"

"It is not for me to judge the sincerity of any man's heart," answered the general coolly, "nor to set limits to the mercy of God. I am only now contending that to search the Scripture in the Protestant meaning is *no command* of God, but attended with very fatal consequences."

"That I defy you or any other Papist to prove," said the doctor doggedly. "But, my dear Sir," continued the general, "daily experience sufficiently proves these fatal consequences; are not thousands continually searching the Scriptures, 'ever learning and never attaining to the knowledge of the truth?'* But come; for the sake of argument, as the chances are equal, I will suppose that the Protestant version is right."

"Bravo!" exclaimed Edward.

"Bravo!" reiterated the doctor.

"But, remember," continued the general, "this supposition affords but quaggy ground to lay a foundation on. However, we will read, 'Search the Scriptures:' still, I can see in these words of Christ nothing like a *command* laid on any Christian to read and search the Scriptures, and I defy any Protestant to prove such a command."

"Why, my dear Sir," said the doctor, "the words are as clear as the noon-day sun."

"No doubt," said the general, "but to whom were they addressed?"

"To all men: who can doubt it?" answered the doctor decidedly.

"I doubt it," said the general, "and you shall hear

* 2 Tim. iii. 7.

my reasons for doubting it. Read with attention the whole context. Jesus had healed the infirm man at the probatic pond, on the Sabbath day. For this the *Jews* persecuted Jesus, 'because he did not only break the Sabbath, but also said God was His Father, making Himself equal to God.' Christ asserts His divinity in the most unequivocal manner. John had given testimony to this truth; but Christ received not, needed not the testimony of man, not even that of the Baptist. But he appealed to the testimony of God manifested by *miracles* and *prophesy:* 'But I have a greater testimony than that of John. For the works which the Father hath given me to perfect, the works themselves which I do *give testimony of me*, that the Father hath sent me.' He then appeals to the Scriptures, to Moses and the Prophets, who had foretold so many things concerning him: 'Search the Scriptures, for you think in them to have life everlasting, and the same are they *that give testimony of me.*' Now, in all this I can see nothing but a simple appeal to the evidences of the Old Testament, the authority of which the Jews admitted; or, if I must admit a command, it was given to the Jews, to the Scribes and Pharisees who persecuted Jesus, and who neither believed in the Saviour on the testimony of his miracles, nor on the testimony of Moses: 'For if you did believe Moses, you would perhaps believe me also; for he wrote of me;' but in all this I can see nothing applicable to *Christians.*"

The doctor groaned.

"The Saviour," continued the general, "is not addressing his Apostles as disciples; he lays down no rule of doctrine, either how they are to find out the truth themselves, or how they are to teach it to others; to them and to all Christians he holds a very different language: 'Go and *teach* all nations;' 'He who hears you, hears me;' 'He who will not hear the Church, let him be to thee as the heathen and the publican.'"

"You have certainly taken a new view of the subject," said Edward thoughtfully; "I should not have suspected you, Sir, of being so conversant with the Bible."

The general bowed and continued: "You should also reflect that Christ only addressed the learned amongst the Jews, for the bulk of the people, like the greatest portion of Christians for many centuries, did not know how to read, and therefore could not search the Scriptures. Certainly, there were no Sunday-schools in those dark ages," added he with a smile.

"What a pity," said Mrs. Sefton, half earnestly, half archly; "but I fear there are no records of such things in those early times."

"No," answered her uncle, "you are right, my dear; and did not the Jews when they heard Jesus teaching, whom they thought to be the son of a humble mechanic, express their wonder, 'saying, How doth this man know letters, having never learned?'* It is therefore evident that Jesus Christ did not make this appeal to the great mass of the illiterate Jews; neither can I conceive any reason why Protestants continually din into the ears of the illiterate crowd, 'Search the Scriptures,' unless it be to dupe and deceive them. Had Jesus Christ intended that the world should learn his doctrine from a book, he would have written the book himself in a plain, easy, clear style, and intelligible to the meanest capacity. Instead of sending his Apostles to *preach* and *teach*, he would have given them the commission to teach the ignorant their A B C, and when they had learned to read, to put his divine book into their hands, and leave them to themselves. Then we should have read in the Acts of the Apostles, and in their Epistles, splendid examples of their zeal and exertions in establishing everywhere Sunday-schools, and day-schools, and Bible societies! Unfortunately, we find no traces of all this in our present Bible. Nay, more, Jesus Christ should have instructed his disciples in the useful art of paper-making, and, above all, he should have revealed to them the powerful engine of the printing-press; for the demand for Bibles would have been

* John vii. 15.

so great, that without these two grand discoveries, it would have been impossible to furnish a sufficient supply. He should have left an authentic copy of his divine work in every language that then existed, or ever would exist to the end of time, and not left it to the ignorance or malice of translators to impose upon the credulous their own productions for his Word."

Here Harriet could no longer refrain from laughing outright; and the doctor exclaimed in an angry tone—

"Stop, Sir, I think you are carrying the joke too far; the subject is too serious for a jest, and I cannot condescend to treat it in so light a manner. It is not for us to determine what Jesus Christ should, or should not have done; we ought to be content with what he has done."

"I perfectly agree with you," answered the general; "we ought to be content *with what he has done;* that is precisely the point in question; namely, whether Jesus Christ has commanded us to search the Scriptures or to hear the Church; yet I can see no joke in demonstrating the absurd consequences which necessarily flow from the Protestant principle; but why do you not answer the reasons I have brought against it from Scripture?"

"Why, really, Sir," said Edward, "there is something plausible in them, which, I confess at this moment, I am not prepared to answer." Then glancing at Dr. Davison, he added—"but I dare say the learned divines of our Church could very easily expose the sophistry of them."

"I am so persuaded," said the doctor, in a tone of considerable effrontery, "of the wisdom and holiness of our principle, that I shall ever think it my duty to bring to the home of every poor man the pure Word of God; he can derive nothing but holiness and salvation from that source of eternal truth."

"My dear doctor," said the general, smiling, "I am always delighted when I catch a glimpse of Protestantism in reading the Bible; and here we are undoubtedly fallen upon real Biblicals. The Scribes and Pharisees *thought* they could find life everlasting in the holy Scriptures. Such, undoubtedly, was their opinion, as it is the opinion of modern Protestants. But what certainty had they of the truth of that opinion? It strikes me that Christ reproves their overweening confidence in that opinion, when he says, '*Ye think* in them to have everlasting life;' if Christ meant to approve of their system, he would naturally have said, Ye know, or ye ought to know."

"General, your observations are rather caustic," said Mr. Sefton, evidently nettled, "and we cannot receive it as a compliment to be compared with the Scribes and Pharisees."

"I mean no offence, I assure you; but I cannot help drawing comparisons where I see a striking likeness."

"It is wonderful," observed Mrs. Sefton, with a half suppressed sigh, "that the learned Jewish doctors, who were so attached to the holy Scriptures, and so studious of their contents were yet unable to understand the testimonies which they bore to Christ; how, then, shall we poor creatures ever comprehend them?"

"Madam," said the doctor, glad of the occasion to change the line of argument, "the Jewish doctors could not understand, because they would not. They had formed to themselves a false notion of the expected Messiah, and therefore wrested the plainest texts of Scripture to their own preconceived notions."

"Alas!" said Mrs. Sefton, "is not this evidently the case with many Protestant sects?"

"Undoubtedly it is," replied Dr. Davison, "because they pay no attention to the luminous expositions of the Bible, which have been given by the learned divines of our Church."

"It is a frightful spectacle," said Mr. Sefton with an air and tone of deep regret, "to behold so many swarms of new sects, that rise up daily around us. In every village new meeting-houses are erected, and every illiterate fanatic quits the loom or the anvil, and, with all self-sufficiency, mounts the pulpit to explain to the stupid crowd the deep mysteries of revelation."

"Aye," said the doctor, "that is the greatest plague that infests the land: it bodes no good to the Establishment. Why cannot the idiots be contented to read the Bible to themselves?"

"So, gentlemen," exclaimed the general, highly delighted at these acknowledged evils of indiscriminate Bible reading, "you abandon the Scripture when it testifies clearly against you, and seek for refuge in the learning of your divines! This is the usual inconsistency of Protestantism. But since you are determined to read the Bible, and to put it into the hands of every *unlearned* and *unstable* mechanic, you must abide by the necessary consequences. Allow me to address you in scriptural language: 'Search the Scriptures, for *you think* in them to have life everlasting, and the same are they that give testimony against you.' Read what St. Peter says of St. Paul's epistles, in which are certain things *hard to be understood*, which the unlearned and unstable wrest, as they do also *the other scriptures*, to their own destruction.* 'There is one that accuseth you, *Peter*, in whom you trust; for if you did believe *Peter*, you would perhaps believe me also.' After this, go and spread your Bibles through the land; put a copy into every work-shop and every hovel, and tell the gulled and gaping multitude, that they will find therein eternal life; from my soul I pity them; I pity such folly and blindness, convinced as I am that ninety-nine in a hundred are either *unlearned* or *unstable*, and therefore must meet with their own destruction."

"Bah! bah!" replied the doctor contemptuously; "that is all mighty fine! but it only proves the cruel and persecuting spirit of popery, that would keep the people in ignorance and darkness by depriving them of God's Word; but the day has already dawned, when, by the glorious efforts of the schoolmaster and the Bible Society, the world shall open its eyes to the blaze of truth, and disdain the brutalizing yoke of papal authority, imposture, and priestcraft."

"Sir, I have done," said the general, with firmness

* 2 Peter iii. 16.

and dignity. "I doubt not your mind is too much cultivated not to know that the rant of fanaticism carries with it no conviction; it may mislead the vulgar, who never reflect; but, upon a thinking mind, it can produce no effect; yet," added he, in a melancholy tone, "I ought to have known that neither the clearest evidence of Scripture, nor the dictates of common sense, nor the fatal experience of every day, were ever able to pluck up a deep-rooted prejudice. I shall only add this one word of St. Paul's, 'And when they *agreed not among themselves*, they departed;' Paul speaking this one word: 'Well did the Holy Ghost speak to our fathers by Isaias, the Prophet, saying, Go to this people, and say to them, With the ear you shall hear, and shall not understand; and seeing, you shall see, and shall not perceive. For the heart of this people is grown gross, and with their ears have they heard heavily, and their eyes they have shut, lest, perhaps, they should see with their eyes, and hear with their ears, and understand with their heart, and should be converted, and I should heal them.'"*

There was a dead silence, and Mrs. Sefton proposed their adjourning to the lawn to take coffee. As Dr. Davison led her out, he muttered, in a half whisper to her, "If I were you, Mrs. Sefton, I should forbid controversy at my table, for it sadly spoils the taste of the viands, and the flavour of the wines."

Emma coloured, and smiled rather contemptuously; for the doctor seemed to her to have made but a miserable figure. The arguments she had just heard her uncle use appeared to her conclusive against searching Scripture for ourselves, and interpreting it according to our individual judgment. The question, then, naturally suggested itself to her mind—Where are we to find an unerring interpreter of the divine word? and who is it that is appointed to explain to us, with authority from God, what is the true faith which he requires of us? Before she retired to rest that night, she resolved to take means of clearing up her doubts on this point.

* Acts xxviii. 25.

CHAPTER V.

> "Why should this worthless tegument endure,
> If its undying guest be lost for ever?
> O let us keep the soul embalmed and pure,
> In living virtue, that when both must sever,
> Although corruption may our frame consume,
> The immortal spirit in the skies may bloom."
>
> NEW MONTHLY MAG.

A FEW weeks after this, as Mrs. Sefton and Harriet were strolling along the village one beautiful evening, they perceived the door of Smith's cottage closed, and lights gleaming from the window. This circumstance surprised them, as the sun was still high above the horizon, and the evening very bright. Emma proposed paying the sick man a visit, to which Harriet readily consented. When they entered, they were struck with awe at beholding poor Smith evidently drawing to his last moment, and Father Oswald arrayed in his sacerdotal habits holding the Blessed Sacrament in his hand, in the act of administering it to the dying man as his viaticum. There was an odour of incense in the room, near the bed-side was a small table covered with a clean napkin, and two wax-candles burning on either side of a crucifix, before which was placed the pyx in which the Blessed Sacrament had been brought; there were also the sacred vessels containing the holy oils for extreme unction. Around the bed of the dying man were kneeling a few pious Catholics, with lighted tapers in their hands. Emma felt irresistibly impelled to kneel also, which she did, and shortly after Harriet followed her example, as if ashamed to be seen standing alone. After Smith had received the viaticum, the father knelt by the little table in silent prayer for a few minutes; nor was this solemn pause interrupted by the slightest noise from any of the assistants; the awful stillness which was there, seemed as the forerunner of that still more awful one which was soon to follow. Father Oswald then rose, and, approaching the sick man, administered to him the sacrament of extreme unction; he anointed with the holy oil his eyes, ears, and lips, and his hands and feet, repeating, as he made each application, the beautiful and appropriate form of prayers used by the Church on these affecting occasions. 'May our Lord by this holy anointing, and his own most tender mercy, pardon thee whatever thou hast sinned by seeing;' and so of the other senses. During the whole imposing rite, Smith was in perfect possession of his senses, and answered and attended to the prayers with the deepest sentiments of devotion; his heart seemed overflowing with comfort and hope, and his countenance wore an expression of the most perfect calm and resignation. When the holy rite was finished, Smith called his wife to his bed-side, took her hand in both his, and, in a faltering voice, said, "Promise me one thing, Mary, before we part. Wilt thou get thyself instructed in the holy Catholic religion?"

"Oh! Willie," replied she, in accents broken by her sobs, "I have heard and seen too much in thy long sickness, not to wish to make as good an end—I promise thee."

"I believe thee: thou wast always faithful to thy word—and thou wilt take our poor children to learn their catechism from Father Oswald?"

"I will." She could say no more, for her heart was full.

"Then I die content. Thanks be to God," said the poor sufferer.

After a few minutes, during which Smith seemed to be absorbed in prayer, he stretched out his hand towards

Mrs. Sefton, which she perceiving, approached the dying man, and asked him what she could do for him.

"Thank you, Madam, thank you; you have been very good to me, God reward you—you are not angry at my change—you have told me so. Do not forget my poor orphans."

"I will take charge of them, William; think no more of that."

"Thank you—thank you. God—" and his voice failed him.

"Tell me, William," said Mrs. Sefton, while the big tear trickled down her cheek, "do you die quite happy?"

"Happy! oh, yes, yes. Oh! Madam, if you knew." His strength failed him, and he could utter no more. For some time he continued to move his lips as in prayer, but nothing more was distinguishable, but from time to time, the sacred names, Jesus—Saviour—Mary mother.

It was evident to all present that a few minutes more would liberate the soul from its sinking tenement. Father Oswald seated himself to support the head of the expiring Christian, and from time to time presented the crucifix to his lips, suggesting brief acts of faith, hope, the love of God, contrition, resignation, and fervent aspirations, "to be dissolved and be with Christ." The assistants all knelt round the bed, and recited the Litanies for the recommendation of the soul, and Father Oswald continued the touching prayers which follow them, beginning—"Depart, Christian soul, out of this world, in the name of God the Father Almighty, who created thee; in the name of Jesus Christ, the Son of the living God, who suffered for thee; in the name of the Holy Ghost, who sanctified thee." When he came to the words, "May Jesus Christ, the Son of the living God, place thee in the ever verdant lawns of his paradise, and may He, the true Shepherd, acknowledge thee for one of his flock," a slight, a very slight sigh was heard, and Emma, whose eyes were fixed on Smith, saw that he had expired. At that moment the last and richest gleam of the setting sun shone into the poor cottage, and reposed on the face of the departed Christian, rendering, if possible, with its vivid ray, still more vivid the ardent expression of faith, and hope, and love, which had not yet died off from the countenance of the cold and still remains of the dead. There was a mournful silence of some minutes, broken only by the sobs of his poor wife and children. Father Oswald then recited in a low and tremulous voice the "De profundis" and some other short prayers for the repose of the soul just fled to eternity; he then rose, and addressed a few words appropriate to the occasion to those around him: "You have," said he, "just witnessed the entrance of a poor but good man into the house of eternity. How calm, how peaceful, how full of bright hope was his departure hence. I cannot doubt of the merciful reception which he has met in the presence of his God. This blessed confidence he received from the holy faith, which he so lately found and embraced. You have all long known our deceased brother to have been an upright and honest man, blameless in his conduct, and of great good sense. He had a long time indeed wandered from sect to sect, from error to error, but this was the effect of his ardour and sincerity in the search after truth. For many years he was 'tossed to and fro with every wind of doctrine,' until God, hearing his prayer and seeing the simplicity of heart which existed in him, conducted him to that haven, where alone he could cast the anchor of his faith on a solid rock. There he found peace and repose to his soul. Well, then, may we bless God, saying, 'Thou hast hid these things from the wise and prudent, and hast revealed them to little ones.'"* The dying accents of Smith and the few words of the Father sunk deep into the heart of Mrs. Sefton. The little assembly dispersed in mournful silence, leaving Father Oswald endeavouring to soothe the sorrows of the poor widow and orphans. Before Emma left the humble roof, she asked him in a whisper to stop for a moment at the Hall in his way home, to which he willingly assented, and she

* Matt. xi. 25.

and Harriet slowly retired. When they had proceeded a few steps, Emma exclaimed with a deep sigh, "What a most affecting, what a most touching scene! Oh! Harriet, I do think—I am sure, indeed, I should like to die a Catholic."

"Certainly, I never saw such a scene before, though I have seen many Protestants die," replied her companion thoughtfully.

"And so have I," returned Emma; "but it was a very different kind of thing indeed."

"Those I have seen," continued Harriet, "all, however, died very quietly, and did not seem to have any fear about saving their souls: how can one account for that, if they were not in the right way?"

"I think I can account for it this way," said Emma, "without discussing which is the right way, and which is the wrong. There are a great many people of all persuasions who are vicious, and whose hearts are quite blinded and indifferent to all religion, and do not believe in a future state of existence; or if they do believe that the soul survives the dissolution of the body, persuade themselves that it can only be in a state of happiness. Now, it strikes me, such persons would be very likely to die without much remorse or fear."

"Well, I do not understand it of a wicked person without religion," said Harriet, "but of good moral Protestants I do, because I don't see what they have to fear: has not Christ died for the sins of all?"

"No doubt," said Mrs. Sefton, "but may not Christ require something on our part?"

"I do not see why he should. Is not his redemption all-sufficient? Are not our efforts worse than nothing? When a man's conscience is at ease, what has he to fear? Why, I remember my brother told me some years since, that he was at the death of Lord ***, who you may have heard had a criminal connection with another man's wife: well, when he came to be actually dying, this creature was sitting by his bed-side, and a few minutes before he expired, he turned to Edward, and said, 'He thanked God he did not recollect ever having offended his Maker in his life.'"

"How very horrid!" said Emma, shuddering; "but you know there are some men who have 'a seared conscience,' and 'whom God has given up to a reprobate sense.' Now, if he had been a Catholic, he would have known that he had been living in the constant violation of one or more of God's commandments; that he was then in the state of mortal sin, that is, in the state of damnation, and this reflection alone would fill him with fear and trembling."

"I think, with horror and despair," said Harriet.

"Not so," replied Mrs. Sefton; "for as Father Oswald explained, there is no time in this life in which a man ought to despair; and he cited the words of St. Peter, 'Repent, therefore, and be converted, that your sins may be blotted out.'* So that he must repent of his sins, and confess them too, to the priest who has authority to absolve him. Therefore, I cannot but think that the Catholic religion gives one much more help and consolation than any other."

"It may be so," said Harriet, "for I am not clever at these matters, but I think the main point is to be good, whatever one is. I am sure that good old soul, Mrs. Crump, who was as constant a church-goer as ever I saw, and as good a creature too, died like a lamb; and why should she not? I dare say she went straight to Heaven: so, Emma, if you will take my advice, you will not bother your head any more with such troublesome thoughts; for, depend upon it, it is little matter what we believe, if we are only good and sincere Christians."

"Indeed, Harriet, I cannot agree with you, and I think you are much too easy on those points; nor do I see how any one can be a *good* and *sincere* Christian who does not hold the true and entire faith revealed by Christ. You know, dear Harriet, that 'faith is *one*, and that without this *one* faith it is impossible to please God.' We must therefore hold the true faith in order

* Acts iii. 19.

to be *good* Christians; and we must use all the means in our power to find out the true faith, in order to be *sincere* Christians."

"I do not see," said Harriet, "why the goodness or sincerity of any Christian should be doubted while he follows what appears to him to be right."

"Pardon me," replied Emma, earnestly; "there can be no good in believing falsehood for a revealed truth of God, nor much sincerity in blindly following a preconceived opinion without examining whether it be true or false. Why, according to your notion, Quakers without baptism have just as much right and chance of going to Heaven as good Protestants, who believe in the necessity of baptism, because to them it appears so plainly ordered in the Bible."

"Well, who knows but they do go to Heaven? they are a good, moral set of folks, though they are Quakers."

"I cannot think faith is a matter of indifference," said Emma decidedly, "because truth is one on all subjects; and reason itself tells us that God, who is truth itself, cannot reveal to the Quakers one thing and to the Protestants another thing on the same subject, and yet there are some Protestants of my acquaintance who do not believe in the necessity of baptism, and that is because they happen to have different views of the same passage in Scripture. Now this is very puzzling, and it has frequently struck me that God ought to have appointed some infallible umpire, who could not err in interpreting his Word; I am very uneasy about it."

"If you listen to the Romish Catholics," said Harriet, laughing, "they will tell you that their pope, or their Church, or themselves altogether are infallible; but for God's sake, Emma, don't go and make yourself a papist; not that I should think worse of you for it," added she affectionately, "but I know *who* would, and so do you."

Emma sighed: by that time they had reached the Hall door, and she hastened to her husband, who, with

General Russell, was in the library, to tell him all that had happened, and to ask him how they could best assist the widow and orphans.

Shortly after, Father Oswald arrived, as he had agreed, and the party consigned to him their charitable donations for the surviving sufferers. Since General Russell's return, the father had been frequently seen at the Hall—at least, frequently for him, whose numerous duties and labours left him short moments of leisure. The general and he had been schoolfellows for their whole college-career, and the heart-felt friendship formed in youth had continued with increased strength and constancy during manhood. At first, Mr. Sefton did not like to see Father Oswald calling on the General; for, besides his deep-rooted prejudices against Catholics as a body, these prejudices were doubly strong against their clergy, and especially against Jesuits; but, by degrees, the extreme urbanity and winning gentleness of Father Oswald's manners made him frequently forget he was talking to one, until the father, by some profound observation, or a little display of the universal erudition with which his vast mind was adorned, again roused his latent prejudices, and put him on his guard against one of an order which he had ever considered as dark, designing, and mysterious, whose members would not hesitate to commit any crime for the service of their cause. Still there was a something in Father Oswald's manners and observations which piqued his curiosity and his love of literature. Moreover, Edward's love of discussion caused him to feel a certain pleasure in the company of this member of the Society of Jesus which he could not, however he wished it, conceal from himself. Emma had just given him the account of her having seen the administration of extreme unction, and Edward could not resist the desire of attacking Father Oswald on this point.

"It seems to me, Sir," said he, "that you Catholics take a most erroneous view of what you call the sacrament of extreme unction; because, as it is mentioned in the New Testament, it evidently refers to the gift of healing; whereas, now, none of the effects follow which are ascribed by the Apostle; for, does he not say that the sick man shall be raised up again? and I have just been told that your sick man, after you gave him extreme unction, became more sick, and, instead of being raised up, is gone down into the grave."

"My dear Mr. Sefton," replied Father Oswald mildly, "according to your explanation of this text, no one would have died in the time of the Apostles; for, certainly, if by calling in the *Elders* of the Church, as you translate the word, not very wisely, I think, who would have neglected such an easy means of recovery from corporal infirmity? but this mystery, as you justly observe, is considered by the Catholic Church as amongst her sacraments."

"I should like much to know, however, how you can prove it so," interrupted Edward.

"We have in it," said Father Oswald, "an *outward* sign or symbol, 'anointing him,' namely, the sick person, 'with oil, in the name of the Lord,' and a promise of *inward* grace, 'and the prayer of faith shall save the sick man, and the Lord shall raise him up; and if he be in sins, they shall be forgiven him.' Two effects of this outward sign are distinctly specified: first, sanctifying grace with the remission of sins, which is the principal effect of the sacrament; and secondly, the raising up or healing of the sick man, when it shall be for his spiritual advantage; but this secondary effect does not always take place, neither did it in the time of the Apostles, as I have just observed; Catholic priests, however, who administer this sacrament, know well that this *secondary* effect often occurs even now. The 'prayer of faith' is the form of the sacrament used by the priest when he 'anoints the sick man;' it is a deprecatory form, and derives its efficacy from the faith of the Church in the Word and promise of Christ."

"Yes, yes," said Sefton thoughtfully, "faith of the Church is the means by which you papists get out of many difficulties, be they ever so contrary to common sense."

"I cannot see any thing contrary to common sense in this explanation of the text in question," replied Father Oswald; "much less do I see any thing contrary to common sense in us weak mortals submitting our understandings and our often-erring reason to the God of all truth, who cannot have revealed to us that which is false."

"No, no," exclaimed Edward eagerly; "I grant you there is nothing contrary to common sense in submitting our reason to the God of truth; it is not that I object to by any means, but by blindly giving up the use of our understandings to fellow-sinners like ourselves: for I believe it is the Catholic doctrine, that when once their Church has decided a thing to be an article of faith, that you are all obliged, under pain of damnation, to believe it."

"Yes, we are," answered the father calmly; "but in thus submitting our understandings to the Church, we do not submit them to a *human*, but to a *divine* authority; and in so doing, it is my poor opinion that we shew a great deal of common sense."

"How so?" said Emma hesitatingly.

"Because, my dear Madam, as we believe the Gospel of Christ to be a divine book, so we believe that none but a divine authority can expound the same," said Father Oswald; "and in this we are confirmed by St. Peter, who says, that 'no prophecy of the Scripture is made by private interpretation.'* Now, Mr. Sefton, will you tell me candidly if you believe in the divinity of Jesus Christ, or not?"

"Most certainly I do," said Edward, colouring; "how can you doubt it?"

"Because many of our countrymen who read the Bible with as much assiduity as you do, not only doubt, but deny the divinity of Jesus Christ. Now, if you believe that Jesus Christ is God, you will acknowledge that His promises must be infallible, and must be fulfilled."

"Naturally, I must believe so," said Sefton, "for,

* 2 Peter i. 20.

being God, His words must always and ever have the same truth as they had the moment He uttered them."

"Then," continued Father Oswald emphatically, "you must, according to common sense, believe the Redeemer when he says to St. Peter, 'Upon this rock I will build my Church, and the gates of Hell shall not prevail against it.'* If the Church could possibly teach damnable errors or fail in the true interpretation of Scripture, then the gates of Hell could prevail against her, contrary to the above promise, and contrary to Christ's express words, when he says, 'Go ye, and teach all nations, baptizing them in the name of the Father, and of the Son, and of the Holy Ghost, teaching them to observe all things whatsoever I have commanded you; and, behold, I am with you *all days*, even to the consummation of the world.'"†

"According to that," said Mrs. Sefton timidly, "there never would have been any need of the Reformation."

"Certainly not, my dear lady; there never was and never will be any need of it," answered Father Oswald.

Edward looked sternly at his wife, and then said, "The Catholic Church teaches many painful things not contained in the Bible, and contrary to the plain sense of it."

"Egad!" exclaimed the general sarcastically, "there are many painful things that Protestants cannot find in the Scripture, such as 'denying themselves, and taking up their cross daily;'‡ 'crucifying their flesh with their vices and concupiscences;'§ 'mortifying the deeds of the flesh;'|| and a few other such unpleasant things, which do not sound very gratifying to reformed ears."

"If the Church is directed by the 'Spirit of truth,' and if Christ be with his Church '*all days*,' it cannot teach that which is contrary to Scripture, as we have just proved," said Father Oswald, rising; "it cannot teach that which is false, either concerning things contained in the Scriptures or concerning things handed

* Matt. xv. 18. † Matt. xxviii. 19, 20. ‡ Luke ix. 23.
§ Gal. v. 24. || Rom. viii. 13.

down to us by tradition, however painful they may appear to human nature."

"Do not leave us yet, Sir," said Edward, "for I assure you I have not finished with you. I understand, that after you sent your sick man to the grave, you sent him on to purgatory; now, this is certainly a doctrine quite contrary to Scripture, and never heard of in the first ages of Christianity, till the Church became full of corruptions."

"Gently, gently, my good friend," said Father Oswald, "the Church could never become full of corruptions, and never will become full of corruptions, otherwise Christ's promises are good for nothing; some other day you will, perhaps, tell me your objections to the doctrine of purgatory; but now it is late, and there are some poor people waiting for me." So saying, he took his leave, making the most grateful acknowledgments for their benevolent contributions for the poor widow, and breathing a fervent prayer, that the same Lord who has promised 'a reward for a cup of cold water given in his name,' would pour down upon them his choicest blessings.

Edward exclaimed, as he closed the door after him, "What a thousand pities it is that such a fine soul as that man possesses should have been obscured by the errors and bigotry of the Church of Rome!"

CHAPTER VI.

"To comfort man, to whisper hope
Whene'er his faith is dim:
For who so careth for the flowers,
Will much more care for Him."

HOWITT.

THE next morning, while Mrs. Sefton was working in her flower-garden, which was a very wilderness of luxuriant beauty and rural enchantment, her mind frequently reverted to the conversation of the previous evening. Two of her infant children were bounding around her in their innocence and joy, sporting, like beautiful butterflies, from flower to flower. The very spirit of love and beauty, with which God created flowers, those tender and gratuitous emblems of his pure benevolence towards us, seemed as if it were pausing and gazing on that lovely spot; but Emma's heart was not at rest; and the Spirit of the Almighty was speaking to it in another and a different language. She heeded not her children, she heeded not her flowers. Smith's death-bed, the conversations she had lately heard, but more especially a sermon of Father Oswald's on the blessed Eucharist, which she had attended in the Catholic chapel, had made deep impressions on her, and had opened her understanding to a wide field of thought, and doubt, and *hope*. God had gifted her with a great perspicuity of intellect: in this sermon she had heard Father Oswald clearly explain the Catholic doctrine of the real presence of our Saviour in the

Eucharist. She had heard him prove this dogma from the most clear and copious passages of Holy Scripture, as well as from the perpetual faith and practice of the Church from the days of the Apostles down to our own times; so that she had not a doubt of the divine mystery. But she was deeply penetrated with the explicit declaration of the Redeemer, 'That unless we eat the flesh of the Son of God, and drink His blood, we cannot have life in us;'* her reason consequently very soon came to the conclusion that this being true, it was then *necessary* for her, before she could possess eternal life, to belong to a Church which believed in this dogma as Christ had taught it; and which could moreover administer to her this rite so absolutely necessary for her eternal salvation. Her first thought, then, was to become a Catholic; and this thought was accompanied by a touch of divine love, so sensible to her heart, and at the same time so gentle and so strong, that it soothed all the previous agitation of her soul; the thought of partaking of the sacrament of love was touched with a beam of hope almost tinged with rapture. She mentioned some of her reflections to her husband, but his manner was so marked with displeasure at them, and his dissent from them was so decided, that all her interior perturbation and anxiety returned. While she was externally employed at her rural labours, her mind was intent on these thoughts. Her good sense told her that the bold denial and cold sarcasm of her husband was no answer to the luminous arguments of Father Oswald; that the doctrine of the real presence was supported by innumerable texts of Holy Scripture, taken in the plain, obvious, and literal sense, in which every unprejudiced and single-hearted reader must necessarily understand them, while not one single text could be adduced by Protestants in refutation of it. If, thought she to herself, Scripture alone is to be my guide, as I have always been taught, I must believe with Catholics on this point. But how can I believe and commune with Catholics on this point without ceasing to be a

* John vi. 54.

Protestant? How can I cease to be a Protestant without inflicting a deadly wound on the kindest, the warmest, the most generous of hearts? Merciful God! into what straits hast thou brought me! Her swelling heart beat in her breast as though it would have burst its confinement, until a gush of tears came to her relief; when suddenly, before she was aware of it, she heard her uncle's voice close to her, and, looking up, saw him standing by her side. The tears were flowing from her eyes; she tried to conceal them, but the general had perceived them and noticed them to her: her only answer to him was, "Uncle, may I ask you a question?"

"Yes, my dear Emma, a hundred, if you will."

"But you will not tell Edward that I have asked it of you?" said she hesitatingly.

"My dearest child," said the general, "cannot you trust me, who love you as though you were my own!"

"Well then, uncle, do you think a person cannot be saved out of the Catholic Church?"

"That is the truth," answered the general, "and it is the docrine of the Catholic: it is the doctrine of Christ himself. For he has revealed a code of doctrines to be believed, and he has added, 'He that believeth not shall be condemned,' or 'damned,' as your Bible renders it.* Now as the Catholic Church most firmly holds and proves that she alone is the true Church of Christ, she must hold this doctrine of exclusive salvation as the doctrine of Christ, or surrender her title to the true Church. Hence it is only in cases of invincible ignorance that a person can be saved out of the pale of the Catholic Church; and even then, we cannot say strictly that such a person is out of the pale of the Church; for every child that is baptized is made a member of the one, holy, Catholic Church; and though he should have the misfortune to be brought up in error, and to make an open profession of erroneous doctrines, he ceases indeed to belong to the external body of the Church, but as long as his error is invincible he still belongs to the spirit of the Church, and to the com-

* Mark xvi. 16.

munion of Saints, until by grievous sin he loses the vivifying spirit of divine grace."

There was a pause of some moments; at length, Emma looked up from her fairy work, and said, "I fear, Sir, I am not invincibly ignorant, since I have heard that sermon of Father Oswald's upon the Eucharist."

"My dear child, do not say you *fear* you are not invincibly ignorant; but rather say, 'I thank God I am not invincibly ignorant;' for to be brought to the knowledge of the truth is the first and greatest blessing of God's saving love."

"But, uncle, if I were to become a Catholic, Edward would be so *very* angry, I do not think I could bear it; and then he is so clever, and knows so much, and tells me he himself is quite convinced that a person who is a good Protestant will go to Heaven; so I think I may be quite satisfied with St. Paul's order to wives to obey their husbands."

The general shook his head mournfully, and said, "Emma, I see the strong workings of your heart, and I wish I could relieve them. The Apostle does not preach implicit obedience to the husband in all things; for remember, 'If any woman have a husband that believeth not' . . . most assuredly he does not send her to learn of him what she is to believe: for though St. Paul allows her to dwell in peace with him, yet he adds, 'If the unbeliever depart, let him depart, for a brother or sister is not under servitude in such cases.'"*

"But you do not call Edward an unbeliever, uncle?"

"In similar cases," replied the general, "I believe the Apostle would make no distinction between an unbeliever and a misbeliever."

"But, uncle," continued Mrs. Sefton in an imploring tone, "would you have me make my husband so very miserable? If it were not for him, I think I should certainly inform myself more about the Catholic religion."

"If you have any doubt on your mind, my dearest Emma, you are bound to clear it up. Doubt is incom-

* 1 Cor. vii. 13.

patible with divine faith; it is criminal to doubt of a revealed truth; it is impious to reject it, when you know it to be revealed. How wicked, then, must it be to shut your eyes against the light, when it begins to dawn upon you!"

"But, surely, you do not think I am obliged to sacrifice all my peace in this world, when my husband, who has studied so much about religion, tells me I can be quite as well saved, if I am a good Protestant."

"Tell me, Emma, is your husband, with all his learning, infallible? May he not err, and lead you into error? Are there not many others equally learned, who widely differ in opinion from him on several essential and important points? what certainty, then, can you have that he alone is right?"

Emma sighed deeply. "Alas!" said she, "how often have I, with the most poignant misgivings of my heart, observed the great differences of opinions, even amongst those who are esteemed the best Protestants; but is not this the unavoidable lot of human nature? and, since all men are subject to error, may we not as safely follow one as another?"

"If faith," replied the general, "were the result of human speculation, or a mere human opinion, your conclusions would be just; it would then be your duty to follow the opinion of your husband. But *faith* is a voluntary submission of our understandings to the revealed truth of God, grounded on His divine authority alone; human authority can be no ground for an act of divine faith. You must then seek for some authority superior to that of man, that you may not err in matters of faith."

"Have we not the Bible?" exclaimed Mrs. Sefton, with an air of triumph.

"No doubt we have, answered the general; "but you know too well that the Bible, the infallible Word of God, is made to speak a thousand different languages, and is wrested into a thousand different meanings, and thus, only expresses the vague opinions of men. The Word of God, when misinterpreted by man, ceases to be the

Word of God, and becomes the deceitful word of man. In fine, it is not sufficient to know that God has revealed a system of divine truths, but we must know with equal certainty, and upon the same divine authority, what those truths are. Now, seek where you will, you will never find that certainty, but in the perpetual and living authority which Christ, from the beginning, communicated to *His Church*."

Mrs. Sefton sighed. "I must acknowledge," said she, "that I have often felt the necessity of such a guide; and often have I envied the peace and security of Catholics, who believe themselves guided by an infallible authority. Oh! how often have I felt my heart sink within me, when I have thought who will tell *me* what is truth? what is error? And yet, dear uncle, now that I am opening my heart to you, and speaking as to a friend, I must acknowledge to you, these questions seem to me both unavoidable and unanswerable; and then I think there can be but one source of truth in the world, and that the Bible."

"But, my dear niece, if the Bible is the only source of truth, how does it happen that so many people draw such totally contradictory doctrines from the same source? The Protestant believeth 'every spirit,' and particularly his own: hence the ten thousand of errors and contradictions into which they fall. The Catholic follows a more simple, and perfectly secure rule, namely, the authority of the Church, by listening to those whom Christ commanded all 'to hear' as himself, and to whom was given the infallible promise, that the Spirit of truth should abide with them '*for ever*,' and should teach them '*all truth*.'"*

"But how shall we know that it is to the Catholic Church this promise is made, Sir?"

"By following the directions which St. John gives us in order to distinguish between truth and error," replied the general.

"What directions?" said Emma, "I do not remember ever to have heard them."

* John xiv. 16; xvi. 13.

"Does not St. John say," answered the general, "'We are of God. He that knoweth God *heareth us*. He that is not of God *heareth us not*. By this we know the spirit of truth and the spirit of error'?* Now, from the time of St. John, down to the present moment, every Catholic has heard, and does hear, and believe the Church; that is, he hears and believes the lawful successors of the Apostles whom Christ commanded 'to teach all nations,' and promised 'to be with them all days, even to the consummation of the world.' You Protestants, Emma, do not think it necessary to believe the parsons in matters of faith; and no wonder, as they very *liberally* grant each individual permission to judge for himself about the interpretation of the Bible: now if the Bible be the only source of truth in the world, how happens it, that so many draw such fatal errors from it?"

"Because, I suppose," said Mrs. Sefton timidly, "Christ has not promised to each individual person to teach them all truth to the end of the world, but he has only promised it to the teachers of his Church, I mean to the successors of the Apostles."

"Exactly so, my dear child, and without an unerring guide, the Bible is more frequently the source of error than of truth."

"But tell me, uncle, if I try to love God with my whole heart, and strive to serve him as well as I can in my present circumstances, may I not rest secure in His mercy?"

"Emma," replied the general, "I must not conceal the truth. God is our Sovereign Lord, and demands the homage not only of our whole *heart*, but of our whole *mind* also, and I cannot see how you may be said to love, or to serve him with your whole mind, while you refuse him the entire obedience of *faith*, by firmly holding all and every article which he hath revealed; for to doubt of one, the least, would be to question his veracity equally as to doubt of all."

"Oh," said Mrs. Sefton, "it is enough for me to

* 1 John iv. 6.

know that Christ my Lord and my God has spoken; I do believe every word."

"That is not enough," continued the general; "we *must* at every cost confess our faith before men, if we would not be denied by Christ before the Father who is in Heaven; he has forewarned us that a man's enemies shall 'be they of his own household.'"*

"What!" exclaimed Mrs. Sefton, clasping her hands in an agony of despair, "is it necessary to save my soul, that I should come to such extremities as these! Oh, uncle! you little know what Edward is capable of, if he thinks it right to shew sternness and determination. Alas! alas! I dare not trust myself to think what would be the consequences of my making myself a Catholic."

"I would fain spare your feelings, my dearest niece, if I could; but you have asked me to tell you the truth, and I should ill repay the confidence reposed in me by deceiving you; it would not be deceiving you in a matter of indifference, but deceiving you in what concerns your *eternal* happiness or misery. Our Saviour himself says, 'If any man come to me, and hate not his father and mother, and wife, and children, and brother and sister, yea, and his own life also, he cannot be my disciple.'† To become a disciple of Christ is to embrace and profess his doctrine; no worldly considerations, however dear, must withhold us from it. The trial is severe, but God will reward the generous sacrifice a hundred fold."

At this moment the nurse came to call the little children to their dinner; they ran to kiss their mamma before they went and gazed with innocent surprise in her face at seeing it covered with tears; the next moment they were running after their nurse, forgetful of all but the sunshine in their own light hearts. Emma took the general's arm, and they slowly followed the children to the house. Mrs. Sefton felt convinced of the truth of the Catholic religion, and would have freely and joyfully embraced it but for the obstacles already men-

* Matt. x. 39. † Luke xiv. 26.

tioned. The struggle in her mind between the sense of duty and the apprehensions she entertained of what might be the consequences of her acting up to that duty, made her very unhappy. This unhappiness affected her naturally cheerful spirits, and it was not long before her husband perceived it; he observed her conduct closely, in order to find what might be the cause of this alteration in one so dear to him; but he could discover no cause; he saw the innocence of her manners and pursuits the same as it ever was; he saw the daily tenour of her life fulfilled with the same simplicity and urbanity to all around her; the same attention to the feelings of others; the same tenderness to her children and to himself; the same kind-heartedness to every one. He had sometimes perceived, that when she was fondly gazing on her little ones, her fine blue eyes would become suffused with unbidden tears, and that she would strive to smother a scarce audible sigh in the caresses of her baby. Edward felt much pain from these circumstances, and he resolved to endeavour to win her confidence. Once, when he perceived her more affected than usual, he pressed her tenderly to his breast, and entreated her to open her heart to him, and to tell him if there was aught which caused her affliction. At first she hesitated, but at length succeeded, and she opened her whole heart to him. Then he was by turns agitated by sorrow, by anger, and by scorn; finally pushing her from him, he exclaimed—

"No, Emma; never will I take to my bosom a Catholic bigot, an idolatress! Never shall my children suck in the abominations of popery with their mother's milk! I warn you once for all; and never shall my lips mention the subject again; if you should ever, Emma, dare to take this step, I shall think it my bounden duty before God to have my children placed in other hands, and I shall not fail to act in consequence. But no, my own, my beloved wife, you cannot, you will not, thus utterly cut up and destroy the happiness of one who does truly dedicate his whole heart to you; to you, who are the solace and the delight of his very existence? Answer me, Emma, my love—answer me."

But Emma could not answer him; the weight of her emotion was too great, and he abruptly left her. Alas! she knew too well the firm, unbending nature of his character when he thought he was acting from a point of duty; and her very heart sunk within her when she repassed in her poor distracted mind the terrible words he had just uttered. It was not till some hours after the sun had gone down on their emotions, that the hearts of Edward and Emma were at all restored to calm; but when they met at supper, it was more in sorrow than in anger; and he saluted her with so much kindness, although shaded by a tinge of sadness, and shewed her so many little attentions, that Emma's trembling heart was again re-assured, and she felt it almost quite calm, as she said within herself, "Whether I am a Catholic or a Protestant, with *me* it will never make any difference in my love to my husband."

Before she retired to rest she examined her heart before God, and earnestly implored him to direct her how to act, and to give her strength to do that which was right. Nor did she rise from her prayer before she felt her soul perfectly at peace.

CHAPTER VII.

" Danger may gather round thee, like the cloud
Round one of Heaven's pure stars, thou'lt hold
Within thy course unsullied."

By this time Weetwood, the ancient seat of General Russell's ancestors, was ready for the reception of its master, and the general had taken up his residence there, amid the beautiful and romantic scenery of his " careless childhood." The house was ancient, but in excellent repair, and the old chapel still preserved its Gothic windows, with rich painted glass, casting hues of gold and purple over the beautiful pavement and altar which remained, remnants of times gone by, a sweet relic of the taste of our ancestors in the ages of faith, when the Catholic religion was the only one in England, and when the *old* religion of the Apostles was thought to be sufficient; before the intellectual pride of man had poured forth in Proteus form a brood of discordant sects which now overspread the land. This hallowed sanctuary had, in fact, withstood the storms of the Reformation, and time had so slightly swept its sculptured treasures, that his touch seemed but to have mellowed and enhanced the exquisite beauty of the chiselled ornaments which so profusely and appropriately adorned it. The paintings, too, were in the finest preservation, gems from the chaste and luxuriant pencils of Guido and Murillo. The general loved this spot, and never, during the long years of his absence from it, was its remembrance effaced from his mind; often and often, in the toil and turmoil of war and when danger threatened him nearest, did he wish himself before its holy altars, which were associated in his remembrances with all the feelings he had experienced in his infancy and early manhood; feelings of piety, and peace, and holiness, associated, too, with the memory of his long lost and lamented wife, who had shared with him, during their brief union, all those soothing and holy sentiments which do honour to the man and to the Christian. Weetwood was ten miles from Sefton Hall, and after the general had been settled there some little time he wrote to beg Mr. and Mrs. Sefton to come with their family to visit him; this they accordingly did, and during the first month of their visit saw a great deal of society, all the neighbouring families coming to renew their old acquaintance with General Russell. At the end of a month Mr. Sefton was suddenly called to Devonshire, on business relating to some property he possessed there. At the general's earnest request, he left his wife and children at Weetwood, where they remained during his absence. It was during this period that Mrs. Sefton obtained, by observation, much information on the Catholic religion, which, owing to her particular situation, she would almost have feared to have sought for; but though her will remained wavering in this state of irresolution, her understanding became daily more convinced, and her heart daily more uneasy; how often did the thought come to her mind, What will it avail me if I enjoy all the happiness this world can give, and lose my own soul? this was frequently her waking thought, and if she chanced not to sleep during the night, her thoughts, in spite of herself, constantly recurred to the same subject. She felt a void in every thing, an uneasiness and distaste in the discharge even of those duties dearest to her heart; she felt a want of something, and a shrinking, timid fear of investigating her own conscience as to what this something was. If she tried to say her prayers, she felt a distraction, a hardness and dryness of heart, which was very painful to her. She could not endure this agonizing state long, and she sought an opportunity of opening her mind to some one. About this time, there came to Weetwood the Catholic bishop of the diocese, Dr. Thornton; the object of his visit was to confirm the children of the congregation, and to administer to them their first communion; there were about thirty of them. Emma witnessed this touching ceremony, and she felt her very heart melt with tenderness at the sight of these little tender innocents approaching the holy altar to receive their God and their Saviour. "And can I never do so?" exclaimed she, covering her face with her hands, to conceal the tears which gushed from her eyes as she knelt in the little chapel looking at this beautiful spectacle: the anguish of her heart became too intense and oppressive to endure, and she determined that evening to open her mind to the bishop. She accordingly told her uncle she wished to speak alone to the bishop. The general seemed affected, but not surprised at her request; he bade her follow him, and conducted her to the sacristy belonging to the chapel, telling her to wait there. This little sacristy was of the same architecture as the chapel, though not so much ornamented, and its arched roof was at once simple and striking; the window was of very rich painted glass, representing the last supper, the glowing luxuriancy of the tints casting a mellow and sombre light into the interior of this building, calculated to promote thoughts of calmness and recollection. Emma had never been into it before; and though she was very much agitated during the time she was waiting, she could not help remarking the air of calmness and beauty that reigned within its walls. At length, the door opened, and the bishop entered: he was a venerable-looking prelate, of about sixty years of age, with perfectly white hair, and a countenance beaming with piety and benevolence. He approached Mrs. Sefton, and seeing her extreme agitation, he begged her to sit down, and placed himself nearer, saying—

"Your uncle, my dear Madam, told me you wished to speak to me; in what can I serve you?"

"You are very good, my Lord; I wished to speak to you indeed; because I am very unhappy; you know I am a Protestant."

" So I have been told; but from your constant attendance in the chapel, I should have thought you were a Catholic."

" No, I am not a Catholic; my father was one, but my mother was a very good Protestant, and brought me up in that Church; still, though I am not a Catholic, I have no objection to the Catholic religion, and I think I should like very much to become one, if it was not for an insurmountable objection."

" My dear child, there can be no insurmountable objection which the grace of God cannot overcome; do you know I was once a Protestant?"

" You, my Lord!" exclaimed Emma in great surprise.

" Yes; I was a Protestant till I was one-and-twenty years of age."

" And why, then, did you change your religion?"

" Because I was convinced that the Catholic religion is the only true one."

" But how, Sir, did you get courage to take the decided step; or perhaps there was no one who opposed you?"

" Yes, my dear Madam, I met with great opposition from my parents, for I was their eldest son; but Almighty God gave me the strength I needed."

" Oh, that the same God would give me strength!" exclaimed Mrs. Sefton, " Oh, that he would enable me to do what is right! but I have difficulties, *very* very great difficulties."

" What is impossible with man is possible with God," said the bishop; if you like to mention to me your difficulties, perhaps I may be able to be of some service to you."

Mrs. Sefton then stated to him all her difficulties, the sum of which was the fear of her husband; and she ended by asking him, if in his conscience he thought she could not be saved by leading a moral, good life, without openly embracing the Catholic doctrines."

" My dear child," answered the bishop, " every thing in religion is connected and linked together; the morality of the Gospel cannot be separated from its doctrines, they reciprocally support and enforce one another. We are to obey the precepts of Jesus Christ, not only because they appear to us conformable to reason and truly sublime, but because they have been enjoined by Him who is the sovereign truth, and has an uncontrovertible right to command our ready and unreserved obedience. Now, my dear Madam, from what you tell me, you seem quite convinced, I think, that the Catholic religion is the true and only religion founded by Jesus Christ. Is it not so?"

"Yes, my Lord, you have expressed what I feel."

"Well, then, I am bound to tell you, that you cannot save your immortal soul without giving to Jesus Christ the obedience of faith which he requires of you; but take courage, there is nothing so difficult in this. Did you ever read the History of St. Perpetua and St. Felicitas?"

"No, Sir, I never did."

"Well, they were both married women, and Perpetua of a noble family; at the time of her martyrdom, for she gave her life in defence of her faith, she had an infant at the breast, and suffered much from her father on account of her constancy to Jesus Christ; the parting from her infant, you may imagine, was most sensible to her tender heart. Felicitas became a mother in the prison where they were both detained for the faith, and she and Perpetua shortly after suffered a cruel martyrdom with the greatest courage and constancy. Now, my dear child, these were delicate females like yourself, wives and mothers, who gave that which was dearest to them in this world, namely, their lives, for Jesus Christ, and not only they, but hundreds and thousands of others did the same; for, rather than *deny* Jesus Christ, they left their husbands, and wives, and fathers, and mothers, and children, and every thing else that was dearest to them; but I recommend you to read the whole account of St. Perpetua and St. Felicitas in the Lives of the Saints."

"But these, Sir, were the martyrs, and that all happened in the first ages of Christianity."

"Assuredly they were the martyrs; but if you reflect a little, you will perceive that if it was necessary to part with one's life rather than one's *faith* in the *first* ages of Christianity, in order to obtain eternal salvation, the very same obligation exists *now*; because the religion that Jesus Christ founded, the religion that existed in the first ages of Christianity, and the religion taught by the Catholic Church now, is all one and the same thing; and as you have read a great deal in the Holy Scriptures, you may recollect our Saviour's words when he says, 'Every one therefore that shall confess me before men, I will also confess him before my Father, who is in Heaven. But he that shall deny me before men, I will also deny him before my Father who is in Heaven.'"* Mrs. Sefton sighed, and the bishop continued: "You will remember also what St. Paul says, 'With the heart we believe unto justice; but with the mouth confession is made unto salvation;'† you see therefore, my dear lady, that to be saved, it is not sufficient that we hold the right faith in the heart, but we must openly with our lips profess it to the world, as the martyrs did."

"But there are no martyrs in our times?" said Emma, inquiringly.

"I beg your pardon; there are many, even in the present day; though of course not so many as in the first ages of the Church, because Christianity has almost in every part of the known world triumphed over paganism and idolatry. I can shew you several interesting accounts of different Catholic missions, in which you will find more than one martyr mentioned."

"Thank you, my Lord, I should like very much to see these accounts; but, after all, the martyrs must have had a very great and extraordinary help from God, to give them so much courage," said Mrs. Sefton, with an anxious sigh.

"The same God that gave them courage, can give

* Matt. x. 32, 33.

† Rom. x. 10.

you courage," replied the bishop with emotion; "besides, you are not required to give your *life* for Christ, but only to bear, for his sake, the displeasure of your husband, supposing him even to be seriously displeased with you."

"God only knows," said Emma, in a tone of great agitation, "what I shall have to bear, if I attempt to do this."

"But do we not serve a tender and a loving Father?" said the bishop. "Nay, I am convinced that, however he may permit you to be afflicted for a while, he will console you in due time. Act generously with him, and he will not be outdone with generosity. From the very evil which you dread the most, he will draw the greatest good. Take courage, then, and joyfully embrace the cross from which you recoil, for the sake of that Saviour, who, to save your immortal soul, died upon a cross amid the most cruel and protracted torments. Yes, my dear child, in order that you may possess eternal bliss, he became the 'man of sorrows.'"

Emma wept.

"Go now," continued the bishop, opening the door which led to the chapel, and leading her to the Altar of the Blessed Sacrament, "go now, and ask that Saviour, in whose divine and real presence you believe, to give you the courage you want; go, and ask Jesus to give you one spark of that divine love which burnt in the breasts of the martyrs."

Emma knelt down before the altar, and the bishop retired, and left her alone with her God.

She did pray; and she prayed so fervently from her heart, that He who has said, "Ask, and you shall receive; seek, and you shall find; knock, and it shall be opened to you,"* did give her the courage she so humbly asked for. In three weeks from that time Emma was a Catholic. Father Oswald, by her particular wish, came over, from time to time, from his mission, and instructed her in the practical duties of the Catholic religion, for of her faith he had no doubt; she had received that pre-

* Luke xi. 9.

cious gift from God, and, with the docility of a child, submitted her understanding to every dogma taught by the Church; he also received her abjuration, and heard her confession. This, indeed, was a severe trial for Mrs. Sefton; for, although in the eyes of the world the whole tenour of her life had been irreproachable, and she had ever been esteemed a model of virtue and innocence, yet her tender conscience smote her inwardly for many and, as she thought, grievous transgressions of the law of God. To manifest these misgivings of her inward soul to a sinful man, appeared to her yet unsubdued pride an intolerable task. But after she had been instructed by Father Oswald of the divine precept, and had been made sensible of its reasonableness, she strengthened herself with fervent prayer, and approached, with trembling limbs, to the sacred tribunal: for some time she could not open her lips; but, being encouraged by the kind exhortations of the good father, at length summoning courage, she mentioned those things which lay heaviest on her conscience; a flood of tears followed the avowal, and in an instant she found her heart relieved from an unsupportable burthen. Father Oswald, with the kindness of a parent, consoled and encouraged her; then, enjoining a small penance of some vocal prayers, absolved and dismissed her. Then, for the first time in her life, did she feel truly happy, and learned from experience how sweet is the yoke, how light the burthen of our merciful Redeemer. The good bishop shortly after confirmed her, and administered to her for the first time the Holy Eucharist. Then Emma was happy indeed; she felt within her breast a satiety of peace and a fulness of hope, of which before she had not the slightest idea. When she was a Protestant, she had always felt with regard to her religion, that there was a something wanting, and that there was an undefinable uncertainty of ideas in her mind, a painful uneasiness lurking about her heart, which prevented her ever being able to say, with decision and without doubt, I am *certain* that I am in the right road to Heaven. But now it was quite otherwise; there were no misgivings in her heart, no vagueness in her ideas; both her heart and her understanding told her she was in possession of the right faith, and this certainty produced an indescribable peace and happiness through her whole soul. She knew now there was but one faith, one baptism, one God, and she wondered within herself that she could have remained so long in the trying state of interior doubts, and uncertainties, and sufferings, which she had endured for many months past. Now all was light, and peace, and joy in her soul: her innocent pleasure and zest in all her daily duties and occupations returned double fold; she seemed to be blessed with a new existence. Sometimes, to be sure, the thoughts of what Edward might say came across her mind; but her faith was so firm in that God "who tempers the wind to the shorn lamb," that she abandoned herself with a full and entire confidence into the arms of her heavenly Father; and placed all her hopes for defence and protection in "Him who slumbereth not, nor sleepeth."

CHAPTER VIII.

"Sweetest Saviour, richest blessing,
Thou the wounded heart caressing,
Driest, ere it fall, the tear.
All, save thee, will but deceive us;
All, save thee, can only grieve us;
Let the world of all bereave us,
With thy love we know no fear."

CATHOLIC HYMN.

A FEW weeks more, and Edward returned. He was delighted to clasp again to his breast his wife and little ones, and he was particularly rejoiced to perceive such an evident improvement as had taken place in Emma's spirits and appearance. All her natural amiable vivacity and sweet cheerfulness had returned; her eye, which had latterly become downcast, was again lit up with its dove-like lustre; and her cheek, which for some months had been pallid, had again resumed the returning bloom of happiness; she had never appeared to the eyes of her husband more lovely nor more interesting. The general would keep them a little longer, and these were to Emma days of pure and delicious happiness. At length the day of parting came, and they returned to Sefton Hall. Emma knew that she had an obligation of hearing mass on all Sundays and holidays, from which nothing could exempt her but sickness or serious inconvenience; she felt very much embarrassed at thinking how she could fulfil this duty without attracting Edward's notice and anger. The first Sunday that occurred after their return home, she made an excuse of visiting a lady, a Catholic friend of hers, who lived in the neighbouring town of D——, to go there, and thus, besides paying her visit, was able to hear mass also. The next Sunday she did not find it so easy, as Edward asked her to go with him to church; however, she determined that when they had arrived at D—— she would make a plea of being rather tired, and remain with her friend while her husband went to church: she did so, and thus was able to hear mass another time, without exciting suspicion. During the ensuing week, Edward mentioned to her that he thought it would be better they should take the sacrament the following Sunday, as they had been some time from home. Emma changed colour, and felt very much frightened; but as Edward was writing a letter when he made this observation, he neither observed her confusion, nor noticed that she had given him no answer. Emma felt very uneasy all the week; but she prayed a great deal that God would give her strength to act rightly, and not to deny her faith. On the last day of the week, Mr. Sefton after breakfast said to his wife—

"I will thank you, Emma, to mention in the family that to-morrow is Sacrament Sunday; and to give orders for Thomas to have the horses at the door by nine o'clock, because it will be better to go a little earlier, you know, love."

"Edward, I do not think I shall be able to go with you to-morrow," said Emma timidly.

"Why not, love? I trust you do not feel yourself ill?"

"No, I am not ill, but..." here she seemed overcome, "but..."

"But what? what objection on earth can you have to go with me to-morrow?"

Emma hesitated.

"It is some time now since you have been to church, Emma, and I must beg you as a favour to go with me there to-morrow."

Emma was silent.

"This is not like your usual conduct, Emma. I need scarcely tell you, I think that not approaching the temple of the Lord and appearing sometimes in church is a bad example to others; but I shall say no more about it, for my Emma never opposes her husband's wishes," said he, kissing her, "so it is all arranged."

Emma looked up in his face with an imploring gaze; then timidly cast down her eyes, and said faintly, "My Edward, I cannot go."

"What is all this?" said he, looking at her sternly; while a vague suspicion of the truth suddenly flashed across his mind.

Emma looked terrified, and was silent.

"These are some nonsensical popish ideas you have got into your head," continued he; "come, come, let me hear them, and I will soon settle them for you."

Emma was still silent.

"Now, Emma," said Mr. Sefton, with a determined air, "will you go with me to church to-morrow?"

"I cannot, Edward."

"And what is the reason that you cannot, Emma?"

"My conscience forbids me."

"Why does your conscience forbid you? I cannot understand; you must explain yourself," said Edward, much agitated.

"Oh! Edward, do not be angry at me!"

"I am not angry at you, Emma, but I must know what all this is about; why does your conscience forbid you? answer me that."

"I do not think the Protestant religion is the right one."

"Not the right one! what nonsense: it is the papists who have put all this stuff into your head. I insist upon your going to church with me to-morrow."

"I cannot," said Emma, bursting into tears; "I can never more join in Protestant worship."

"No! and why not?" exclaimed her husband, fixing his gaze intently on her.

"Because I have embraced the Catholic religion," said she, in a mingled tone of firmness and anguish.

"You a Catholic!" answered Edward, turning pale; "what do I hear? Oh my God!...Emma, you have not dared, no, surely you have not dared to do such an act as this. But no, my poor dear wife! they have deceived you, they have deluded you. You little know what papists are; they are capable of any thing to make proselytes."

"No; I have neither been deceived nor deluded," said Mrs. Sefton firmly; "it has been the act of my own free will, on the firmest conviction of the truth."

"But when, and how, and where could you accomplish this?" said Edward with increased agitation.

"I became a Catholic when you left me at Weetwood."

"It is, then," said Mr. Sefton indignantly, "as I suspected; it has been the work of your uncle. Would to God he had never returned! No doubt he was aided too, by that Jesuit, Oswald! You have had communication with him, I am certain of it; tell me the truth."

"Yes; he instructed me in the Catholic religion, but it was by my own desire."

"Villain! hypocrite! true Jesuit! Who can follow the windings of such wretches?" exclaimed Edward with great warmth.

Emma was shocked at his violence, and, summoning courage, said with something of a sarcastic smile, "Methinks the best way of stopping their audacity would be to follow them through all the subtleties of their arguments, and openly expose their sophistry; when a person begins to scold, and abuse, and use harsh words, one cannot help having a little suspicion that there is a tough adversary to deal with, and that they have nothing better to give him in reply."

Edward was still more provoked. "Do not talk such nonsense to me," said he; "you little know the arts of Catholics and Jesuits; but it is not yet too late; this sad affair has not yet become publicly known, and therefore, if you appear with me at church to-morrow, it will all yet be well."

"Edward," said Emma firmly, and with unwonted energy, "I have become a Catholic from conviction. I have abjured the errors of the pretended Reformation, and been received into the bosom of the Catholic Church, and I will not deny Jesus Christ before men, or He will deny me before his Father, who is in Heaven."

"This is all religious enthusiasm—all Catholic cant. I give you one hour, Emma, to make up your mind, and to give me your answer; but beware," said he sternly, "for if you continue in your obstinacy, you will have to rue it to the last day of your life."

When Mr. Sefton had left the room, Emma sunk on her knees: she trembled so, that she could not stand—she held both her hands tightly over her throbbing heart—she scarcely knew where she was, nor what she felt, so great was the sense of oppression and terror which overwhelmed her. After a few minutes, a deep sigh burst from her, and, clasping her hands, she lifted them to heaven, and said with intense fervour, "Jesus Christ, Lord of all things, thou seest my heart—thou knowest my desire, possess alone all that I am. I am thy sheep, thou art my Shepherd; I was thy strayed and lost sheep; out of thy pure goodness and tender mercy thou hast sought and brought me back, like the good shepherd, to thy own fold. Oh! speak to my soul, for I am willing to hear thy voice, and give me strength to overcome the wiles of the enemy, the allurements of the flesh, and the strong attachments of my nature. Let no earthly considerations ever separate me from thy love. Be thou my God, my protector, my salvation." She continued in ardent prayer during that fearfully anxious hour which passed before her husband's return; and He, who never forsakes those that trust in Him, did hear her humble cry, and he filled her heart with a calm and a courage of which she could never have believed it capable. When Edward re-entered the room, Emma rose from her knees, and stood meekly before him. He drew her kindly towards him, and placed her on the sofa, where he seated himself close to her. "I am come," said he, "to hear from the lips of my own Emma, that she will be to me all she has ever been; to hear her tell me, that the wife of my bosom and the mother of my children will realize, as she has hitherto done, all the fond and ardent dreams of my first affection."

Emma threw her arms passionately round her husband's neck; his voice faltered as he added, "To-morrow you will go with me to receive the Lord's Supper, and then all will be forgotten and forgiven."

Emma looked wistfully in his face, and she saw that the tears were falling from his eyes: she had never in her life seen Edward weep, and all a woman's tenderness and love rushed with a thrill of anguish to her heart; she clasped her hands in agony. "Oh! my God," exclaimed she, "help me." And then, after a pause of deep and fearful agitation, she said in a low, but firm and calm voice—

"Listen to me, my own husband, I have but *one* soul, and if I lose that, I shall be damned for ever; to save your life, or to procure your salvation, I would willingly give my life at this moment, but *I* must answer to God for the immortal soul He has given to me, and which is created to love him through an endless eternity. It is *God* who will demand my soul of me at the last day, the day of judgment, and not *you*. I am convinced, after much prayer and deliberation, and mature examination and reflection, that the religion I have embraced is the only true religion, and that to save my soul I must live and die a Catholic."

Edward started up; she threw herself on her knees, and tried to cling to him; he spurned her from him, and rushed out of the room.

In a few minutes, she heard a horse galloping past the windows, a crowd of vague and indefinable terrors passed through her mind; she remained motionless on the spot where Edward had left her, till she was roused by the cries of her little infant, whom the nurse brought to be suckled. She took the child and mechanically placed it at her breast; the nurse seeing there was something the matter, immediately retired, and left her alone with her baby. When she had had it a little while in her arms, her tears began to flow, which gave her some relief; she pressed the child so tightly to her heart, that the little innocent bit her breast, and then paused in its sweet labour to gaze in its mother's face;

but seeing her smile upon it through her tears, it again closed its little eyes, and abandoned itself to all the luxury of infantine love. "And when thou shalt be a man, wilt thou too spurn thy mother!" said she, fondly caressing it, "but now, oh! now at least, thou lovest me entirely, and I am all to thee."

What a long, long day did that seem to poor Emma. Mr. Sefton did not return, and a thousand distracting thoughts and fears racked her brain. At length, late, very late at night, she put her babe into its cradle, and gave it the last kiss for the night. Alas! little did she think it was for the last time; it slept with its nurse in a little room next to hers, that she might hear it if it cried in the night; but she did not hear it all that night: for, worn out by mental exertion and anxiety, she fell into a profound sleep, and did not awake till late the next morning. She immediately rung for her child; but when the door opened, it was not the nurse and her baby who entered, but her own maid, Mrs. Ashton. Mrs. Ashton had received Emma into her arms when she was born, and had never after been separated from her; it would have been difficult to have found a more faithful and attached domestic than she was. The moment Emma saw her face, she knew something was wrong.

"Ashton," said she, in a voice of alarm, "what is the matter? How are the children? Where is my baby?"

"Oh, my poor child! oh, my dear Madam!" exclaimed Ashton, wringing her hands, "be calm; do not for God's sake alarm yourself."

"I will not alarm myself," said Emma firmly; "but do you tell me the plain truth instantly."

"Then, Madam, my master came back early this morning with two carriages, and took away the children and the nurses."

"Not the baby?"

"Yes, Madam, all, all!"

"Merciful God!" exclaimed Emma, "can it be true?" and she sunk in a swoon in the arms of her attendant.

Mrs. Ashton rung for assistance, and when Emma's senses returned, she said, in a low and tremulous voice, taking hold of poor Ashton's hand, who was tearfully watching over her, "Send directly for my uncle."

Mrs. Ashton did as she was desired to do; and did also the best in her power to restore and comfort her poor young mistress; but Emma spoke no more; in her heart she thanked God that he had given her strength to go through this bitter trial without denying Him. She repeated over and over to herself, 'Thy will be done on earth as it is in Heaven,' with an humble and calm hope within her soul that God would not leave her without support in whatever trials he might please to appoint her yet to endure. In a few hours, violent fever naturally succeeded, and when her uncle arrived, she did not know him, and was as totally insensible of his presence as she was of the remembrance of the injustice and violence, which had caused her the sudden and dangerous illness, that confined her to her bed for many long and tedious weeks.

CHAPTER IX.

> "Alas! we listen to our own fond hopes,
> Even till they seem no more our fancy's children;
> We put them on a prophet's robes, endow them
> With prophet's voices, and then Heaven speaks in them;
> And that which we would have be, surely shall be."

WHEN the events related in the last chapter occurred, Harriet was not at Sefton Hall, but some forty miles distant, on a visit to a friend. She was extremely surprised and concerned at receiving one morning a letter from her brother. She opened it with a trembling hand, fully persuaded that it would announce some dire event; for a croaking raven had flown across her path in her evening walk the preceding day. Her superstitious fears, however, were somewhat abated when she read that Emma had declared herself a Catholic, and that her brother had in consequence thought it right to remove the children from her; adding, that he had placed them at Eaglenest Cottage, on his property in Devonshire, being resolved to try what rigour would do, to induce his wife to retract the errors and abominatious of popery. He concluded by begging Harriet to return as *soon* as possible to Sefton Hall, in order to report to him the exact state of things there, and to assist in bringing Emma back to her duty. This letter both surprised and grieved Harriet; it surprised her, because, though she knew the sternness of her brother's character, she never could have imagined he would have shewn such unreasonable severity towards a wife to whom he was devotedly attached; it grieved her, because she herself loved Emma with the affection of a sister, and knew well her excellent and exemplary conduct as a wife, a mother, and a friend. Harriet's ideas of liberty of conscience were very extensive, and she could in nowise reconcile it to her ideas of right and wrong, that any one ought to be restrained in their own opinions on religious matters, more especially those who did no harm to their fellow-creatures; and not only did she know that Mrs. Sefton did no harm to any one, but she was fully aware that she did much good, and, moreover, made all around her happy. "Well," said she to herself, as she slowly refolded her brother's letter, "I am very sorry for all this; but certainly I thought that raven note foreboded something worse; I never heard a raven croak on my left hand that something ill did not happen; and, now I recollect, both the cats turned their tails to the fire last night, and I never knew that fail to produce some *imbrolio* or another; still I think there is much to do about nothing. It seems to me the best thing I can do is, to go immediately to poor Emma; besides, if I write to my brother, only having heard his side of the question, I shall probably give myself a great deal of useless trouble to no purpose: for I hate writing letters at any time, especially on other people's concerns. But then, again, how vexatious it is to have to leave my friend in such a bustle! when I thought I was quite comfortably settled here, with nothing to do but enjoy myself for another month at least to come. Out upon the raven! Fie upon the cats! Well, I must have patience. I have heard it said, one cannot go to Heaven in a feather-bed; so I suppose there is no help for it. Let me see, to-morrow is Thursday—that is a lucky day. I would not set out on the following day for all the world." So saying, she gave orders for her departure, and before eight o'clock the next morning was on the road to Sefton Hall. This promptness in Harriet was really an exertion of friendship; for being a lady of considerable *embonpoint*, and habitually indolent and passive in her disposition, it required a strong impulse to produce any exertion above the ordinary routine of a very easy and quiet life. Her dislike to mental exertion was in the same ratio as her disinclination to locomotion, and hence arose her favourite maxim of every one thinking and acting as they pleased, and her frequent surprise at what appeared to her the useless trouble people often took to maintain their opinions, even on matters of indifference; whereas a quiet acquiescence, or simple silence, in all things where there was no evident crime, was what she always employed, and recommended to the practice of others. Alas! in the land of Bibles and of religious license, she had frequent occasion to exercise her patience. The nearer she approached to Sefton Hall, the more anxious she felt; it was a bitter cold wintry day, the ground covered with snow, and the northern blast howling through the trees. As she drove through the long avenue, she passed General Russell, who was pacing slowly towards the house, with his arms folded and his eyes on the ground. At the sound of the carriage wheels, he looked up: there was a deep melancholy on his brow, but a smile of pleasure and surprise lit up his countenance when he recognized Harriet, and he quickened his steps to follow the carriage to the Hall. Harriet was painfully struck with the air of melancholy desolation about the place; nearly all the windows in the house were closed, and when the old butler opened the door, and she found herself within the fine old Hall, she saw there was no blazing fire within its ample chimney, nor sign of comfort, nor welcome, as was wont to be.

"Oh, Miss Harriet! is it you?" said old Wilkins. "I am right glad to see you, Madam: but, Lord bless me! your rooms will be as cold as the North Park; there has not been a fire in them these weeks and weeks past."

"Never mind that," said Harriet impatiently; "that inconvenience is easily remedied, my good Wilkins; but how is Mrs. Sefton? Where is she? Pray shew me into her room immediately."

"Oh, Miss! sad changes since you were gone. My poor master—who could have ever thought it—would you believe, Miss Harriet? *popery*, rank popery, in his own house."

Harriet made a move to pass him, saying, "I have heard my sister is ill, and I wish immediately to see her," muttering at the same time to herself, "I knew there was ill foreboded by that unlucky raven."

"To be sure, Ma'am, to be sure," said the old butler with deference; "and then I will tell the housekeeper to put your rooms in order as soon as may be. My poor mistress is still confined to her bed, Miss," continued the good butler, tapping very gently at her door.

Mrs. Ashton came out, and started when she saw Harriet.

"Oh, Ma'am! God bless you; my poor mistress! We have need of comfort here; but I had best speak to her before you come close to the bed, Miss."

"Yes, do so," said Harriet, scarcely able to articulate.

Harriet approached the bed, and Emma made an effort of joyful surprise to raise herself up to fold her in her arms, but sank exhausted on her pillow; and Harriet burst into an agony of tears, when she beheld the emaciated form that lay before her: she was obliged to leave the room, and it was some time ere the sisters could see one another without mutual agitation and emotion.

"I will write to my brother, indeed, an account of the state I find her in," said Harriet to the General, "and try to persuade him of the folly of his conduct."

"Rather say of the cruelty, injustice, and bigotry of his conduct," exclaimed the General indignantly.

"Nay, nay, my good General, not so bad as that neither; for Emma certainly ought not to have taken the step she has done, knowing, as she did, how displeasing it was sure to be to Edward."

"So you would have had her lose her soul to please her husband! but, putting that *trifling* consequence of her rejecting the truth aside, Miss Sefton must be aware, that one essential part of the Protestant religion is liberty of conscience in the free interpretation of Scripture: now, if my niece chose to interpret some of the most forcible texts of Scripture in favour of the Catholic Church, I should like to know what *consistent* Protestant has a right to persecute her?"

"Very true, General; very true," said Harriet,

alarmed at the idea of a discussion; for my part, I think all religions are equally good, if a person only lives up to them; and I am sure no one could be a better Christian than Emma was, nor a better wife, nor mother; and my opinion is, there is much to do about nothing, and so I shall take care and tell Edward."

Harriet accordingly wrote a letter to Mr. Sefton, remonstrating with him on his conduct towards his innocent wife, and describing in very pathetic terms the state to which his unkindness had reduced her. Mr. Sefton was much affected by this letter, and as he could not help feeling the truth of some of his sister's reproaches, it made him very uncomfortable and angry at himself, and consequently still more angry at poor Emma. But knowing his sister's easy sentiments on religion, he sophistically reasoned himself into a belief, that her opinions on this point ought not to be attended to, and that it was his duty to steel his heart to every sentiment of compassion arising from his wife's illness. In this frame of mind, he wrote to Harriet, expressing his displeasure at her indifference as to what tenets of faith a person held, and exhorting her to use her utmost endeavours to recal Emma to the reformed Church, expressing also his decided wish that Dr. Davison should visit her, and endeavour by instruction to reclaim the lost sheep from the errors of popery. To this end, he wrote a most zealous letter to Dr. Davison, entreating him to do his duty, and to give him detailed accounts of his interviews with Mrs. Sefton; he wrote lastly to poor Emma herself, a letter beginning with upbraidings and reproaches, and ending with lamentations and expressions of affection. Many a tear did Emma shed over this letter; but she was yet too weak to answer it; she revolved what she should say in return, over and over again in her mind and in the inward recesses of her afflicted spirit; and this increased her anxiety and habitual fever. The General and Father Oswald, who constantly attended her, soon perceived she was labouring under some additional uneasiness; it was not long ere she told them the reason of her anxiety, and her pain at not being able to answer her husband's letter: that which had not occurred to her in her weak and agitated state, immediately occurred to her two friends, namely, for her uncle to write at her dictation. The letter she dictated was both touching and firm; touching, because it expressed the sentiments of a heart, which, though deeply wounded, yet yearned and overflowed with affection towards him whom she had chosen for her friend and protector during this mortal pilgrimage; and firm, inasmuch as it expressed her fixed determination to be faithful to her God, and to live and die in the faith to which God in His mercy had brought her. When this letter was sent, she seemed much relieved, and the affectionate care of Harriet, united to the unremitting attentions of the General and Father Oswald, contributed not a little to place her in a convalescent state. In the meantime, Dr. Davison received Mr. Sefton's letter, desiring him to go to Sefton Hall, and endeavour by every effort to reclaim his wife from the errors of popery; when this letter was brought to the good parson, he was sitting after his dinner dozing over a large fire, with the "Sportsman's Annals" in his hand, or rather on his knees, whither it had inadvertently slipt, after many vain endeavours to keep his attention fixed on its animating contents. "The Lord be merciful to me, a sinner!" muttered he, with an indescribable groan of dismay, as he perused the zealous contents of Mr. Sefton's letter.

"Did you tell me to ring for the tea, my dear?" said his wife, who was sitting with her back to her worthy mate, engaged on a tambour-frame.

"I did not say so, Mrs. Davison, I did not say so," said the Doctor shaking his head, "though God knows I have need of something to keep up my courage at this particular trying moment; a fine job cut out for me, indeed! as if I could do any good! as if I could stop popery, or hinder folks following their own mad ideas! but he always was, and always will be a fiery zealot."

"Doctor Davison, are you raving, or are you dreaming?" said his wife, who not having perceived the entrance of the letter, really thought the worthy Doctor was suffering from uneasy dozing.

"I am neither raving nor dreaming," answered he, "I wish I was: but here is a letter from that hot-headed zealot, Edward Sefton, who wants me to neither more nor less than go and bring that poor wife of his back again from popery."

"Oh!" said Mrs. Davison, "she has too much popish blood in her veins."

"Yes; her father was a Catholic."

"However," said Mrs. Davison, "you know she had a worthy, pious mother, who gave her an excellent Protestant education."

"Aye, aye, and great trouble had I in securing that point; you remember her mother promised her husband on his death-bed, to send their only daughter to a nunnery for her education, and how I had to labour before I could quiet her scruples. But all labour in vain! What is bred in the bone, will never be out of the flesh. What hopes, then, can there be of her conversion? Now, my dear, think of my difficulties, think of the folly of attempting such a thing; ill as she is, too, and, what is worse, guarded by that Cerberus of an uncle, whose very bark is enough to terrify one."

"Aye, and what is still worse," said his wife, "constantly visited, as I am informed, by that sly, hypocritical Jesuit, Father Oswald, as they call him! however, for all that, Dr. Davison, I should certainly think it my duty, were I in your place, to make a trial at least, to bring her poor deluded soul back from the horrors of popery."

"Bless me! how you talk, Mrs. Davison; you had best take the Bible to her yourself, I think. How unfortunate is this business, just at the time when the grand coursing match is to come off; I should be sorry to lose that; for you know our greyhound, Spanker, is entered, and I must be there to see fair play. I will thank you, however, to order my tea; that will perhaps throw some light on this difficult matter."

Mrs. Davison did as she was desired to do, and called out to Jenny at the top of her voice to bring the tea, and, added she, "bring also, Jenny, at the same time, the Doctor's Cogniac."

After a few cups of the refreshing beverage had been consumed, Mrs. Davison recommenced her observations.

"Well, Doctor, and what line of conduct do you mean to adopt in this very difficult matter?"

"Why, Mrs. Davison, something I must do, that is certain, or I fear Mr. Sefton is capable of going to the Bishop about it. I will write to him, however, and endeavour to soothe him, and persuade him that I will do my best; and I really think, my dear, the most prudent way to begin, will be for you to go and call on Mrs. Sefton first, as it might be to inquire after her health."

"Well, I think so too," answered his wife, "and I will take at the same time the Bible with me, in case an opportunity should occur."

"No, my dear, no," interrupted the Doctor, "the Bible at the first visit, no; it requires the greatest possible prudence, Mrs. Davison: for, betwixt ourselves, I may tell you, I cannot approve of that mania for Bible reading which has seized upon the people of the present day so universally."

"How so?" exclaimed his wife, with a look of great astonishment.

"Why, do you not perceive that the Church is in danger; that it is frittered away into a thousand discordant sects? and, believe me, the true cause of all this is the imprudent distribution of the Bible amongst the illiterate and vulgar. Every madcap reads it, and invents a new religion for himself and his silly neighbours! No, no; it is high time we should exert the authority of the Church to put down these accursed heretics."

"Really, Doctor Davison, you astonish and confound me, to hear you talk in this style; why, I thought to read the Bible was the glorious privilege of Protestants."

"No doubt, no doubt, as far as reading goes I can have no objection; but then people should read it in the sense of the Church."

"Well, really, I can see no use in reading the Bible at

all, unless people try to understand it, and form their own judgment on it," interrupted Mrs. Davison; "and pray, Doctor," continued she, "how can you bring authority to bear upon Mrs. Sefton?"

"Aye, there is the rub," replied the Doctor with a sigh; "truly, we live in awful and perilous times. If we proclaim authority, the Papists silence us in a moment. If we assert the right of private judgment, the sectaries must undermine us. The Church has been brought into a false position, and I do not see how it can stand long."

"Come, come, Doctor, do not let your courage down; I can see a remedy. Why, can you not harass the Papists with the Bible, and awe the Dissenters with authority?"

"Humph," groaned the Doctor, "that is an awkward business; yet I see no other way of proceeding."

"Well, then, I will take the Bible with me to Mrs. Sefton."

"No, no, that will not do at all; Mrs. Sefton has read the Bible for years; and she will tell you she understands it as well as yourself. Besides, I should not wonder if that red-hot General was to throw the pure translation of the Word of God in the Protestant Bible out of the window. I have heard him say such things on that subject; you little know him, I assure you."

"Well, my dear, I will be guided by you; only I would not wish to act too tamely in such a cause," answered his wife.

The next day, Doctor Davison wrote a long letter to Edward, assuring him of his grief at Mrs. Sefton's falling off from the pure doctrines of the Reformation to the bigotry of Catholicism, and concluding with warm assurances, that he would exert all his learning and authority to bring her back from the horrors of popery. Mr. Sefton was much pleased with this letter, and fondly flattered himself that the Doctor would succeed; he could not imagine that Emma, separated from her little ones and from him, would be long ere she made up her mind to grant the wished-for concession; for he knew well that theory and practice are very different, and that the courage and perseverance of the happy and contented wife and mother might be very different to the courage and perseverance of the bereaved mother and comfortless wife; in fine, he fully persuaded himself that he should succeed, and anticipated a speedy and happy return to his own home. How far his hopes were realized must be related in another chapter.

CHAPTER X.

" Mark you this, Bassanio,
The Devil can cite Scripture for his purpose."
SHAKSPEARE.

A DAY or two after Doctor Davison had despatched his letter to Devonshire, his favourite little poney, Mouse, was harnessed to the poney-cart, and Mrs. Davison, dressed in her best, proceeded to make her intended visit at Sefton Hall. Emma was now able to sit up, and though, when Mrs. Davison was announced, she felt both nervous and frightened, yet, with her usual urbanity, she yielded to Harriet's wish that she should be received.

Mrs. Davison was much struck with the change in Emma's appearance, and being a personage who had not much command over her feelings, she involuntarily exclaimed—

" Good God, Mrs. Sefton, how you are changed!"

" Yes," said Emma faintly, and trying to conceal her emotion, " I dare say I am changed, for I have been very ill since I saw you last."

" Mrs. Sefton is much better now, Madam, and I trust will soon be entirely restored to her usual health," said Harriet rather dryly.

" I hope so indeed, Miss Sefton; but when the mind is ill at ease, the body will not mend. I know that Ma'am; so, for that reason, I made nothing of coming a couple of miles this bitter cold day, to see how matters were going on, and to see also if I could be of any use, or Doctor Davison either; how sorry will he be to hear the way I have found kind, excellent Mrs. Sefton in; but all is not lost that is hid, and while there is life there is hope; so we must trust the Doctor will soon be able to bring all things quietly about."

"The hectic of a moment" flushed Emma's pallid cheek, as she attempted to answer the bustling volubility of Mrs. Davison; it was but a passing emotion of wounded feeling instantly repressed, and in a gentle and calm tone, she said—

"I thank you, my good friend, for your kind interest about me. I am now daily recovering my health, and as to my mind, it is, thank God, in perfect peace."

"In perfect peace! that cannot be; you can never persuade me of that," exclaimed Mrs. Davison, her zeal getting the better of all prudence, compassion, and politeness.

"And why not?" said Emma timidly.

"Because," answered Mrs. Davison, "the pitiable idolatrous practices of the Catholic Religion which you have unfortunately embraced, can never bring peace to the mind, I am sure."

"They are pitiable visionaries, and certainly not interesting fanatics, who think so," replied Emma, with something of her natural spirit. "I should have thought few people in this enlightened century could yet believe such fables; idolatry could certainly never bring peace; but the knowledge of the true religion can bring true peace, and has brought peace to me."

"Yes, yes, I dare say your new friends keep their grossest superstitions out of your sight for fear of startling you too soon; but I pray God it may not yet be too late to bring you back to the pure and primitive religion of the Bible."

"I do not know what you mean, Ma'am, by speaking in that manner: the Catholic religion condemns superstition as much as you can do, and to be guilty of superstition is to render oneself culpable before God; but, perhaps, you will tell me what you mean by superstition?"

"I mean, my dear Mrs. Sefton, picture-worship, the dreadful idolatry of the mass, holy water. I mean, I mean—in fine, all the abominations of the corrupt Church of Rome."

Harriet laughed outright. "I thought, Ma'am," she said, "you would have preached about omens, and dreams, and charms, and the innocent observance of birds and beasts. Edward used to call that superstition: now I am glad to find he was mistaken."

"Superstition, according to Johnson, is religious reverence paid to things which are not worthy of such reverence," exclaimed General Russell, appearing from behind a large Indian screen, where he had been sitting, reading the newspapers, in no very good humour at Mrs. Davison's interruption; "or, still more accurately, Madam," continued he, "superstition is an inordinate worship of the true or of a false divinity. This is the definition of it given by all divines, which, with due deference to the wisdom of the parson in petticoats, is, I think, quite as correct as the one I have just heard."

"Lord bless me! General, is it you?" exclaimed Mrs. Davison, starting, "why you have put me into a tremble from head to foot."

"To accuse us of superstition," continued the General, without minding Mrs. Davison's tremble as she called it, "is then to say, that we either worship the true God in an inordinate manner, or that we worship false gods, or that perchance we are guilty of both: now, will you tell me, Mrs. Davison, to which of the tenets of the Catholic Church does any of these three modes of superstition apply?"

"Really, General, you make such a bluster and a fuss, that you quite bewilder my poor head," drawled out Mrs. Davison; "it would require the Doctor himself, with his Bible in his hand, to answer all your quirks and quibbles, and learned sentences."

"Well, then, Ma'am, as you cannot defend, it is rash in you to attack; but as you are aware that my niece has been dangerously ill, you must excuse me if I request you to accompany Miss Sefton and myself to the dining-room, where luncheon will no doubt by this time be ready."

Mrs. Davison very reluctantly withdrew, telling Emma at the same time, "that as she was now able to sit up, she should take an early opportunity of returning, accompanied by Dr. Davison, who would be most rejoiced to see her convalescent."

At length Harriet and the General succeeded in getting the loquacious old lady into the dining-room, where she consoled herself with a good luncheon for the mortification she had experienced from what she called the General's rudeness. When they had left the room, poor Emma hid her face in her hands, and burst into tears. Mrs. Davison's visit had been quite unexpected, and the attack on her religion still more so; neither she nor her uncle had the least idea of Edward's plan of reconversion; for Harriet's sympathy with her sister-in-law was so sincere, that she carefully abstained from giving the least hint on the subject, and expressed in her letters to her brother her opinion, that his project was both cruel and useless. Emma felt all the painful delicacy of her situation in being separated from her husband, and the thoughts of what the world and those who were ignorant of the cause of this separation would say and think, caused her many an anxious moment: at these times she would offer up her keen suffering to God, and say to Him, "Accept this most painful sacrifice, O my God, in union with the dreadful mental agony my Saviour suffered in the garden of Gethsemani;" and then, though the sense of her suffering still continued, she felt a calm and peace in her soul, and an unspeakable consolation in knowing she was submitting herself to the will of God, and bearing this humiliation for His sake. It was therefore quite true what she had told Mrs. Davison, namely, that she had found perfect peace after she had embraced the Catholic religion, though that lady could not understand it. Dr. Davison was not at all satisfied with the account his wife gave of her mission, and accused her both of imprudence, and of having made matters worse instead of better; he knew enough of human nature to feel satisfied, that open opposition was never the way to reclaim any one from what they considered a high sense of duty, and, therefore, resolved to try other means to perform this to him disagreeable office. From time to time he called on Mrs. Sefton, and sometimes asked a question of explanation on different Catholic practices, listening to hers or the General's explanations quietly, with an air more of curiosity than opposition. This implied deference encouraged Emma to feel gradually an interest in conversing with him, as at least she did so without the fear and vexation she felt at his first visit. Still he saw he was gaining nothing, and wrote to Edward stating how things were going on. Edward suggested he should for a few weeks go and reside at the Hall, under the pretext of having access to the library, on account of a work he had in hand. Edward, therefore, wrote to his wife to that effect, and she of course made no objection; nor, indeed, had she the slightest suspicion of the real motives for such a residence. Not so the General, who began to see through the matter; but as it was not his house, he could only vent his vexation by grumbling to himself, and now and then expressing his impatience to Harriet.

"I knew that no good could come from this visit," observed Harriet; "for, ever since the Doctor entered this house, I have heard an owl hooting before my windows every night."

"Pooh! pooh!" said the General, smiling, "don't make such vain, senseless observations. The owl would have hooted just the same, although the Doctor had been a hundred miles away."

"I do not know that," replied Harriet, with a solemn shake of her head; "I never heard hooting of owl which did not bring me some trouble."

"Come, come, take courage, Miss Sefton, the Doctor and I hear the hooting as well as you, so the trouble may be meant for him, or me, or perchance we may all share it together."

Mrs. Sefton was not yet able to leave her sofa, or even to stand, but her friends often in the evening assembled round her couch to beguile the tedium of convalescence; on one of these evenings, in attempting to change her position, a rosary fell from her sofa upon the ground.

Dr. Davison, who was sitting the nearest to her, picked it up, and held it very deliberately in his hands for a few minutes, as if to examine its construction; in giving it back to Mrs. Sefton, who coloured a little in taking it, he said, "Is not this the thing which Catholics call Beads?"

"Yes; it is a Rosary," replied Emma.

"And is it possible that you, my dear Mrs. Sefton, can be guilty of such a mockery!" said the Doctor solemnly.

"Oh, Sir! indeed, the Rosary is not a mockery," exclaimed Emma eagerly; "but, on the contrary, it is a source of the most tender and solid devotion."

"Tender and solid devotion! Good God! what abuse of terms," said the Doctor, somewhat angrily.

"Yes," replied Mrs. Sefton firmly; "I repeat what I said; for, in reciting the Pater Nosters and Ave Marias, Catholics are taught to call to mind and contemplate the great mysteries of man's redemption in the life, and sufferings, and glories of Jesus Christ."

"Stuff and nonsense," said the Doctor contemptuously.

"Protestants who scoff at the rosary, understand it not," exclaimed the General indignantly; "but, 'blaspheming those things which they know not, shall perish in their corruption.'"*

"Softly, softly, General," said Harriet, smiling; "but it is contrary to our Saviour's positive commands, you know, to use repetitions in our prayers; I love to say short prayers."

"Indeed," said the General, dryly; "I never heard of such a command."

"Perhaps not, Sir," said the Doctor, with an air of triumph; "yet, verily, it is expressly recorded in the Bible."

"Where?" asked the General.

The Doctor took out a pocket Bible, and, turning over the leaves, read, "When ye pray, use not vain repeti-

* 2 Peter ii. 12.

tions, as the heathens do."* "There, General, what say you to that?"

"I say that it is a shamefully false translation; in the original Greek there is not one word importing 'vain repetitions.'"

"Pray, Sir, how do you render the Greek?" inquired the Doctor.

"Thus: 'When ye pray, gabble not like the heathen.'"

"Nevertheless," replied the Doctor, in a grumbling tone, "I prefer our own authorized translation."

"Though false?"

"Yes; because it is more explicit;" and, turning towards Harriet, "what is much worse, we have here repetitions of that idolatrous prayer called the Hail Mary."

"Away with such cant about repetitions!" interrupted the General. "If repetitions in prayer be vain, what shall we say of the inspired David, who, in one psalm, repeats twenty-seven times the same words: 'For his mercy endureth for ever,'† that is, once in every verse? What shall we say of the Seraphim, who rested not night and day, saying, "Holy, holy, holy, Lord God Almighty, who was, and who is, and who is to come?"‡ What shall we say to the example of our Redeemer, who, in his fervent and prolonged prayer in the garden, 'prayed the third time, saying the self-same words?'"§

"What shall we say, indeed, to that most touching example," said Emma, sighing, "in Him who was perfection itself?"

"This seems plausible enough," replied Harriet thoughtfully; "but still I think the repetition of all those prayers in Latin must be a labour which can bring no improvement to the soul."

"If any one does not understand Latin, let him say his prayers in English," answered the General: "the rosary is translated into all languages; however, most

* Matt. vi. 7. † Psalm cxxxv. ‡ Apoc. iv. 8; Is. vi. 2.
§ Matt. xxvi. 44.

good Catholics have a deep-felt consolation in understanding a little of the universal language of the Church, and in being able to join in it, in those prayers and psalms which are in common and daily use amongst us. You would be astonished frequently in Italy and Spain to hear the most illiterate and uneducated amongst the peasants and common people answering even to antiphons and psalms which occur but once or twice in the year."

"But they do not understand what they thus repeat with their lips in a language different to their own; how can they?" asked the Doctor.

"To be sure they understand it; and much better, I think, than your people understand the Hosannas and Alleluias which you teach them to sing, and which, you know, are expressions of a far more difficult language. Catholics suck in with their mothers' milk many Latin phrases, of which they learn the meaning as they learn the meaning of their own vernacular tongue; one is just as easy as the other to the infant mind. They are taught these little prayers with their catechisms, and they *daily* hear and join, more or less, in the Church service. Catholic churches are not shut up like Protestant places of worship, every day but Sunday; in Catholic countries, religion is one of the daily and hourly concerns of life; and it is not by these good, simple souls thought sufficient for them to hear a dry sermon on Sundays and read a chapter in the Bible. No, no, they know well enough, that unless religion is *daily* practised and thought of, it will not sink into the heart, and be to them a support in the distresses of life, and a solace in their lighter moments."

"Well, I cannot but think Catholic service unprofitable," said Harriet.

"Catholics are the best judges of what is profitable to their own souls," said the General dryly.

"Humph!" said the Doctor, "but you cannot, I think, so easily evade, Sir, the fact, that this devotion of the Rosary must necessarily be idolatrous, because I understand it is all composed of Hail Marys addressed to the Virgin?"

"I do not *evade* the fact, Doctor Davison," said the General, "but I do *deny* it; namely, that the Hail Mary, or any other prayer addressed by Catholics to the Blessed Virgin, Mother of God, are idolatrous. She is not an object of idolatry to us, but an object of the deepest respect and veneration; neither will I insult your understanding by answering further to a charge against Catholics, which, I am convinced, you do not seriously believe. You must keep in mind, that the Rosary is said as much, or I should say more, in honour of Christ than of Mary; for in every decade we commemorate in spirit and in affection some great mystery of our redemption; and nothing can be more grateful to the truly Christian soul than the pious recollection of what Jesus has done for us, and the part his holy Mother bore in most of the mysteries."

"It must be very difficult, I should think," said Harriet, "to say the words to the Virgin, and reflect on a mystery at the same time. I am sure it is more than I could do."

"And yet nothing is more easy," continued the General, "to excite that reflection, than a momentary pause in the Ave-Maria after the word, Jesus, with a mental recollection of the mystery we are meditating; such as 'Who was made man for us, who was born for us,' and so on. Indeed, devotion to our Lady can never be separated from devotion to our Lord, as long as the relation between mother and son shall subsist."

"Oh! indeed, Harriet—indeed, Dr. Davison," exclaimed Emma, "this devotion of the Rosary is a most sweet and solid devotion, and full of heavenly consolations. I thank God for the day on which I first learnt it."

"I am glad, my dear Madam, at whatever gives you consolation," said the Doctor, shaking his head; "but you must excuse me, if I still think counting one's prayers by beads is a very foolish and childish practice, besides being a great innovation."

"Oh! there, Doctor, you are mistaken or misinformed," said Mrs. Sefton, "for I have read in a book that my uncle lent me, that it was the custom amongst the very first Saints in the earliest ages, to count their prayers and ejaculations by little round pebbles or stones used for that purpose; now, I think it is a great improvement, if, since the time of Saint Dominic, these little pebbles, or beads, or stones, have been bored and hung on a string. You are very fond of improvements, Sir, in sciences, and even in angling; now why should we object to improvements in the way of counting our prayers? The holy solitaries in the first ages did not move much from their cells; but we who lead more active lives, might be losing our little pebbles, if they were loose."

The Doctor smiled. "But I cannot see," said he, "what good there is in people counting their prayers at all."

"However, you see the saints, who were more learned in the ways of salvation than we are, thought otherwise," replied Emma; "and I am not afraid of imitating them, especially as the Church holds them up for our example and veneration."

"Yes, yes, believe me, the Apostles, Martyrs, Confessors, and Monks knew how to pray quite as well as we do," said the General. "Now really, Doctor, it seems to me that to number our prayers, is neither so foolish nor so childish as when you, in your convivial meetings, Hip, hip, hip, with three times three."

"Humph," said the Doctor, "but that is done on a very different occasion, and is only meant to preserve a certain degree of order and decorum."

"As for the decorum, let that pass," replied the General; "but surely a certain degree of order in our devotions cannot be displeasing to the God of all order, 'who has ordered all things in measure, and number, and weight.'* Besides, if it be *childish* to number our prayers, why I like it all the better for that; for Jesus has taught us to humble ourselves like little children, if we would enter into the kingdom of heaven: and if it be *foolish*, so much the better; for 'the foolish things of

* Wis. xi. 21.

the world hath God chosen, that he may confound the wise.' "*

Mrs. Sefton kissed her beads with renewed affection, and placed them in her reticule.

"Humph, humph," growled the Doctor, "a great deal of nonsense in all that."

"There you and I differ, my good friend," replied the General; "but I am aware that some people now-a-days pride themselves on certain studied compositions, which they seem to consider perfect models of prayer. Certainly no one can object to these forms on the ground of their not being sufficiently clear, as far as the words themselves go, which are very precise; or, of their omissions, for every want that can be conceived is specified; but I doubt whether our ancestors would have altogether approved of them; they did not like long, wordy narrations in addressing God, and even considered it an indication of the divine Spirit when nothing nominally was sought in prayer; the repetition of ejaculations, or accumulated epithets, such as, 'misericordia mea,' 'refugium meum,' 'liberator meus,' and so on, is so much the more full of internal delights as it is imperfect in external expression: for affection has this property, that the more fervent it is within the heart, the less can it be developed externally by the voice. Did not St. Francis Xavier spend whole nights in repeating only 'Deus meus, et omnia'?"

"To be sure," said Harriet hesitatingly, "the Lord's Prayer contains much more than is expressed; and the sick that were healed by Jesus as related in the gospel, expressed themselves in very short and simple sentences."

"Yes, and often repeated them, too," said the General. "Witness the blind man of Jericho, who could not be made to hold his peace, but kept *repeating* and crying out, 'Jesus, Son of David, have mercy on me.' But Emma, my dear," continued he, observing his niece seemed exhausted, "we will not talk more now, but leave you to go quietly to bed; I fear we have kept you up a little too long."

* 1 Cor. i. 27.

Dr. Davison wished Mrs. Sefton kindly good-night, but added, "that he thought she would find it very difficult to explain away the absurdity of many of the devotions used by the Catholic Church."

"Doctor, I defy you," said the General with much gravity; "I challenge you to-morrow to name any Catholic devotion you please, and I will clear it of the charge of absurdity: let us see what an old soldier can do, when pitted against a learned Divine."

"I accept the challenge," said the Doctor stoutly and good-humouredly, as he closed the door after them, leaving Mrs. Sefton to repose.

"Good-night, Miss Harriet," said the General, smiling, "and don't fear the hooting of the owl: you see the trouble has fallen on the Doctor this evening, at least."

CHAPTER XI.

The literal sense is hard to flesh and blood ;
But nonsense never could be understood."
DRYDEN.

DOCTOR Davison reflected a good deal during the course of the following morning, what point against the Catholic religion it would be advisable for him to bring forward in his evening conference with the General: he thought of picture-worship, using images of the Cross, and especially of the Saints of churches; but he had a sort of vague idea in his mind, that these charges against Catholics, as far as the accusation of idolatry went, were not altogether true, and he feared, if he brought them forward, the General's sarcasm and ridicule. No, said he to himself, I will go on more solid and serious ground; I will boldly attack at once the idolatry of the Mass. Accordingly, he spent most of the morning in the library, fumbling over the Protestant divines most likely to refresh his memory; he believed all that he had ever read or heard against Catholics on this point, and had no doubt but that he should make an impression on Mrs. Sefton at least, if he should even fail with the General. "Yes," exclaimed he triumphantly to Harriet, rubbing his hands with exultation, as they returned from their walk before dinner, "you will see what a drubbing I will give that old General this evening."

"Don't be too sure of that," observed Harriet; "he is not at all easy to deal with."

"But my attack to-night will be so well managed," persisted the Doctor, "that he will at least have to beat a retreat."

"I see something that is in your favour," said Harriet, "or I am much mistaken."

"What do you mean? I don't understand."

"Why, Doctor, do but look at that fallow field to the right."

"Well, I see the field, and two chattering magpies; that is all."

"And plenty too, I think," said Harriet; "don't you know what that signifies?"

"Not I; they are picking out the grubs, I suppose, as I hope to pick out the General's superstitions."

"No, no; no such thing: the old proverb gives, speaking of pies, that is, magpies, the following rule:—

One of sorrow,
Two of mirth,
Three a wedding,
And four a birth;

that is, seeing them in these numbers signifies those things."

"Pshaw! pshaw!' tush! tush! stuff and nonsense, Miss Harriet; how can you believe such idle sayings?"

"I do believe it though," continued Harriet, as she slowly ascended the stairs to arrange her dress for dinner, "for I have often and often seen it come true."

In the evening the Doctor was the last to join the little circle round Emma's fireside; as he approached with a serious and mysterious face, the General flourished his snuff-box in the air, exclaiming, as he offered his antagonist a pinch, "You have made the ladies wait, Reverend Sir; you have made them wait."

"The seriousness of the subject I am going to bring forward must claim your indulgence, ladies, for this delay," answered the Doctor gravely.

"Well, said Emma, smiling, no excuse is necessary. I understand from Harriet you have been very busy brushing up your arms for the combat all this day."

"Yes, Ma'am, I have been in the library most of the morning, notwithstanding there are a brace or more of woodcocks in the copse, about the cress spring, which was very tempting. You will soon see now, however, the success of my more serious morning's work."

"Don't sound the trumpet before you have gained the victory, Sir," said the General; "but let us hear the accusation against us this evening."

"Well, then, the accusation I bring against Catholics is, that they worship the veriest unworthy trifle ever made by men's hands, and set up as a God, which is childish idolatry; namely, the Mass; the silly and profane invention of a corrupt Church, which has no meaning, a bloodless sacrifice being useless, since blood alone can wash away sin."

"My dear Sir," said the General, when the Doctor had paused, "there seems to be a strange jumble in your accusation: in the first place, the sacrifice of the Mass follows from a right notion of the real presence; in the second place, it is not a *bloodless* sacrifice, but an *unbloody* sacrifice. In the sacrifice of the Mass, there is the real blood of Christ, which is surely enough to wash away the sins of the whole world, shed in a mystical and unbloody manner, not in the bloody manner in which it was once shed upon the Cross."

"Really, Sir," said the Doctor, "I cannot comprehend your mystery, unbloody and *bloodless*; where is the difference?"

"Much the same," replied the General, "as that between the living soldier and one shot through the heart."

"Humph!" growled the Doctor; "I do not see the comparison."

"Perhaps not; but I will try to explain myself. You remember that St. Paul, speaking of the Eucharist, says, that 'as often as you shall eat this bread, and drink the chalice, you shall shew the death of the Lord;'* now, in the sacrifice of the Mass we do this in a most wonderful manner, by the separate consecration of his body and blood, under two distinct species; for by virtue of the words of consecration, the substance of the bread is changed into his body, and the substance of the wine into his blood; but as 'Christ now dies no more,' the body and

* 1 Cor. xi. 20.

blood are not really separated; for where the body is, there also is the blood, not by the change of bread into the blood, but by concomitancy: so the bread is not changed into the soul and divinity of Christ, but where-ever his body is, it is necessarily accompanied by his blood, soul, and divinity. So, when the wine is changed into his blood, his body, soul, and divinity are also present; now, by this *mysticcl* separation of the body and blood, the death of the Lord, which consisted in the real separation of the two, is represented to us in a most lively and almost visible manner. The essence of the Christian sacrifice consists in this mystical separation."

The Doctor looked puzzled. "But you presuppose, Sir, that *I believe* in what you call the real presence; now, I do *not believe* in any such thing; nay, in the very text which you have quoted, does not the Apostle Paul say, that we eat the *bread* and drink the *cup*?"

"No doubt he does," replied the General; "but if you read the next verse, you may make a shrewd guess of his meaning: 'whosoever shall eat this bread and drink the chalice of the Lord unworthily, shall be guilty of the *body* and *blood* of the Lord.' Now, you must tell me, how eating bread and drinking wine in any unworthy manner, can make a man guilty of such a heinous sacrilege?"

"Why, to be sure," said the Doctor; "it is the profanation of a most holy rite and ordinance."

"Suppose," said the General, "a man were to profane the Word of God, baptism, or any other divine ordinance, would he thereby become guilty of the body and blood of the Lord?"

"Humph!" said the Doctor; "that is nothing to the purpose. I asserted that *I* did not believe in the real presence, and, what is more, I believe the Church of Rome, when obliged to explain herself, believes no more in a real and literal presence than Protestants do."

"Oh, fie! what an assertion, Sir," said Mrs. Sefton with evident surprise.

At this moment Mrs. Ashton entered the room, and told her mistress that Father Oswald had just called.

"Then let him come in, Ashton," replied Mrs. Sefton; "it always does me good," added she, "to see that truly apostolic man."

"I think I had better retire," said the Doctor hastily, looking rather foolish; "perhaps I intrude."

"No, Sir, by no means," answered Emma earnestly; "you do not intrude, I assure you."

Father Oswald entered, and explained that he had a sick call at some distance, and it being late, and a very stormy night, he had ventured to call, and ask hospitality at the Hall. Hospitality was warmly and joyfully offered, and the good missioner was soon seated by the blazing fire. After the preliminary compliments had passed, the General bluntly told him their evening's occupation, and that Doctor Davison had just extremely surprised them, by asserting that Catholics do not believe in the real presence.

"Indeed!" said Father Oswald, with something of an arch smile; "there is novelty in that assertion: perhaps the Doctor would be kind enough to tell us what *he* believes, or rather what he disbelieves on this subject."

"I believe," said the Doctor solemnly, "and Protestants believe, the *spiritual* presence of Christ in the Eucharist. Now, the Romish Church turns an object of sense into an object of *faith*. When Christ distributed the broken symbol, his body had not then been broken; he could, therefore, only have spoken in a figurative sense, as he elsewhere designates, 'the Lamb slain from the foundations of the world.'"

"A *spiritual* presence is a *real* absence, my dear Sir," answered Father Oswald, "and you wrong Catholics by asserting that their belief is any thing like what you have just expressed."

"What, then, is your belief, Sir?"

"Catholics hold," answered Father Oswald, with much seriousness in his manner, "that Jesus Christ is really, truly, and substantially present under the exterior appearance of bread and wine; and no dogma of the Christian religion is so clearly and distinctly revealed in the New Testament as this. This is the object of our faith, and a sublime mystery of faith it is. What you mean by changing an object of sense into an object of faith, I know not. When the disciples saw Jesus on the earth, they certainly had an object of sense before their eyes; but they believed that what they saw was the eternal Son of God made man; this was the object of their faith. Can you tell me what you mean by broken symbol?"

"Why," said the Doctor, "a symbol, I take it, is a representation of one thing by another."

"But," observed the General, "it is not a Scriptural phrase, nor is there the slightest indication of a symbol or figure in the Scripture when speaking of the Eucharist, and therefore we may give it to the winds."

"Certainly," continued Father Oswald, "Christ broke the bread; before consecration, it was not yet changed into his body. In the English Protestant version of St. Paul's account, we read 'This is my body, which *is broken* for you,' and so it stands in some Greek editions. This reading is preferred by the Protestant translators, because they imagine they can build an argument upon it against the Catholic doctrine of the real presence. Thus they say, when Christ spoke the words, his body was not yet broken; therefore, that which he gave them to eat, was *not* his real body."

"To be sure, Sir,—to be sure!" exclaimed the Doctor triumphantly; "there you have got yourself into a dilemma, from which you will not so easily extricate yourself."

"I don't know that, Doctor," said Father Oswald, smiling good-humouredly. "In the first place, I answer, that this conclusion is in direct contradiction to the express assertion of Christ, who says, 'This *is* my body,' and therefore I cannot admit it. In the next place, although many editions have *broken*, others have *bruised*, and the most recent and correct editions have *given*, as it stands in St. Luke: so that we must look for some authority superior to that of editors, in order to ascertain the true reading. Again, admitting the word *broken*, I ask, what does it signify? Christ's body was not properly broken; and surely the *bread* was neither broken nor bruised, nor given *for us*. The Lamb was slain from the beginning of the world, not in reality, but in the foreknowledge of God; and in view of the future sacrifice of the Lamb, God conferred all his graces on the saints of the old law."

"Very true, Sir," said Harriet; "what does it signify, as you observe, whether the word be *broken*, or not? there is, I am sure, much to do about nothing. I, for my part, think good Queen Bess's opinion was the safest and easiest:—

> 'Christ took the bread and brake it;
> And what his Word did make it,
> That I believe, and take it.'"

"Sound Christian doctrine," said the Doctor; "and if all men would quietly adopt it, there would be an end of all disputes, and we might live in peace and brotherly love."

"Sound Christian doctrine," echoed the General, "if we could only understand it. But how can I believe, whilst I know not, 'what his Word did make it?'"

"I see no need of bothering our heads about it," replied Harriet. "It is enough to think it must be what Christ intended it should be, and he intended, no doubt, to leave us in this holy ordinance a symbol of his body and blood."

"Very right," echoed the General, "it must be what Christ intended it to be, and he intended to leave us his real body and blood, if there be any meaning in his divine words"

"Oh!" said Harriet, "I do not think the Scripture is so clear, or men would not differ so much about its meaning."

"Your *Saint* Luther did not think, it seems, however, as you do," said Emma, laughing. "He tried all in his power to rid himself of his faith in the real presence, as he himself tells us, but could not; and then says, as well as I can remember, 'the text of the Gospel is so clear, as not to be susceptible of misconstruction.'"

"You remember the sentence quite rightly, my dear,

and have quoted it correctly," said the General; "you may also tell Miss Sefton, and the Doctor too, that Archbishop Cranmer owns, 'that Christ may be in the bread and wine, as also in the doors that were shut.' John Fox says, 'Christ abiding in heaven is no let but he may be in the sacrament also;' and then, again, Melancthon: 'I had rather,' says he, 'die than affirm that Christ's body can be but in one place.'"

"Well, Sir, and suppose the difference of opinion which you state to exist between the doctrines of some of the first reformers and those of the present day, it is quite consistent, considering we have the Bible, which strikes one person in one way, and another in another."

"But," said Emma, "truth can be but one: God, who is truth, cannot reveal contradictory doctrines on the same point, and this a point, too, on which our eternal salvation depends. Is it not written, 'He that eateth and drinketh unworthily, eateth and drinketh damnation to himself, not discerning the body of the Lord?' namely, in the true sense which he intended, under the dreadful penalty of eternal damnation. There must be no trifling on this important point."

"God forbid," said the Doctor seriously, "we should ever trifle on this, or any other Scriptural doctrine."

"Well, then," subjoined Father Oswald with a good-natured smile, "if you are so disposed, I do not care if once in my life I join 'a tea and Bible' party."

Harriet took the hint, and in a few minutes the hissing urn was on the table, and the grateful odour of that refreshing beverage soon filled the room. While sipping the tea, Father Oswald proposed to discuss the sixth chapter of St. John. Dr. Davison did not relish the proposition so much as his cup of tea; and, somehow or other, even that seemed to have lost much of its wonted flavour. He felt himself in an awkward predicament, and sought to avoid the contest, if he could do it with honour to himself. Asking Harriet for a second cup, he turned to Father Oswald and said—

"I think, Sir, this subject too serious and too abstruse to be discussed before this company."

"I am no friend," said Father Oswald, "to such Biblical discussions as I am told are often exhibited over the tea-table. I have a different way of teaching religious truths."

"Well, then," said the Doctor, "suppose we drop the subject?"

"With all my heart," replied the Father.

"No, no, Doctor," exclaimed the General, who had overheard the conversation; "you have chosen the subject and the ground; I cannot allow you to sculk from your post, and suspiciously seek safety in flight at the first appearance of danger. Come, on the faith of an old soldier, you shall have fair play."

The Doctor saw that the retreat was now impossible, and, mustering courage from the readiness which Father Oswald had shewn to retire from the contest, he opened a large Bible, which he had deposited on the table when he entered the room, and began to read with all solemnity the sixth chapter of St. John. The first part of the chapter afforded little subject of discussion, though frequently interrupted by their reciprocal observations. Father Oswald observed, that the miracle of the five barley loaves was in many points an admirable illustration of the Holy Eucharist; the Doctor could see no connection between the two. Father Oswald observed, that Christ's walking on the waters was a clear demonstration, that His body when he pleased could be exempted from the most universal laws of nature. But the contest became more animated at the twenty-seventh verse, when Father Oswald observed, that Christ promised to give food superior to the barley loaves—meat which endureth unto life everlasting. He propounds the means to obtain it, faith in his divinity, which the Jews had not. He promises to give bread from Heaven, superior to the manna. He declares that he himself is the bread of life, the living bread which giveth life to the world. The Doctor fought a good fight, stoutly maintaining that nothing more was meant than faith in Christ, and scouted the distinction which the Father made between the promised bread, and the condition required in those who were to receive it. But the heat of war began at the fifty-second verse. Father Oswald observed, that hitherto Christ had used the word *bread* in a figurative sense, as the Doctor admitted, but that now he explains the figure, "The *bread* which I will give is *my flesh*." The Doctor twisted the expression into a hundred shapes, to make it signify, The bread which I will give is a *symbol* of my flesh. "Nothing is easier," replied the Father, dryly, "than to make the Scripture say any thing, by introducing one or two extraneous words."

"Fight fair," exclaimed the General. "Let us have Scripture, without note or comment."

The Doctor, finding himself sorely pressed, changed his sentiment, and thought the meaning might be, The *bread* which I will give is *faith* in my flesh; that is, in my incarnation.

"Bravo!" said the General; "then it was faith in the incarnation, and not his real flesh, which he gave for the life of the world; and this faith we must *eat* with our mouths, just as the Israelites eat the manna."

"Read on, good Sir," said Father Oswald gently; "we shall then see how the Jews to whom Jesus spoke understood him."

The Doctor read, "How can this man give us his flesh to eat?"

"Ha!" exclaimed Harriet, "how often have I heard the same question asked!"

"Yes, yes," said the General; "there were good Protestants, you see, even amongst the Jews."

Harriet laughed, nor could Mrs. Sefton suppress a smile: the Doctor was piqued, and observed—

"It cannot be denied, that the Jews understood Christ's words in their literal sense; but what wonder? they were a wilful, carnal, sottish race."

"No doubt," subjoined Father Oswald; "but our merciful Redeemer will correct their error; if not for their sake, for the sake of millions of faithful believers, who he foresaw would take his words in their plain, obvious, literal sense. Pray read on."

"Amen, amen, I say unto you, Except you *eat the flesh* of the Son of Man and *drink his blood*, you shall not have life in you."

"Now, mark," said Father Oswald, "the solemn asseverations 'amen, amen,' with which our Saviour expresses the importance and truth of what he is about to say. So far from modifying his former words, he reasserts them in the strongest terms. To the eating of his flesh, he now adds the drinking of his blood, which, far from diminishing the objection of the Jews, must have shocked them still more, from their being prohibited by their law even to taste the blood of animals, much more human blood."

The Doctor remained silent for some time, as if recollecting and arranging in his mind the various and discordant comments which he had read on this celebrated passage; his ideas rose in such a medley array, that his confusion remained only worse confounded: at length he spoke, with much hesitation and frequent interruption, and occasional contradiction, as one or other system of figurative interpretation occurred to his mind. "To eat and to drink signified simply to believe, and he wondered much that the Jews could not so understand the words after the preceding part of Christ's discourse. Again, reflecting that Christ afterwards said, 'My flesh is meat indeed, and my blood is drink indeed,' he thought that to eat and drink might be taken in the literal sense, and that flesh and blood must be taken in a figurative sense, and could signify nothing more than bread and wine, the symbols of his flesh and blood."

"Perhaps, Doctor," said Father Oswald, "you would do better to read the four following verses, and consider them all together; for then we shall see that five times Jesus confirmed the literal meaning of that sentence which gave so much offence to the disbelieving Jews; and each assertion is more expressive and significant than the preceding."

The Doctor began to hem, and his confusion and irritation increased so much, that he in vain attempted to proceed.

"Come," said the General, "I promised you fair play, and I must relieve you. I will do justice to your cause."

The General then, assuming a most serious and sanctimonious, but dogmatic tone, began to read thus: "Verily, verily, I say unto you, you quite mistake my meaning: I would only say, Except you eat *bread, not* my flesh, and drink *wine, not* my blood, you shall not have life in you. He that eateth *bread, not* my flesh, and drinketh *wine, not* my blood, hath everlasting life, and I will raise him up on the last day. For *bread, not* my flesh, is meat indeed, and *wine, not* my blood, is drink indeed."

The Doctor could contain himself no longer, and launched out on the impious profanation of God's Holy Word.

"Truly," said Father Oswald, "the sacrilegious impiety is too obvious; but I conceive the General, in his humour, has only given your own interpretation."

"Precisely so," replied the General; "for half a dozen *nots* and a few words interpolated, has made the Protestant sense evident to the dullest capacity."

The Doctor chafed again with ire, and his eyes sparkled with indignation, "It is really too bad," said he; "the very words of Scripture itself profaned."

"A truce, good Doctor," said the General; "promise me never more to speak of *bread*, or *wine*, or *symbol*, or *figure*, or *faith*, of which there is not one word in the passage, and I will promise to unsay all that has given you offence."

"A truce, a truce," muttered the Doctor, trying to suppress his impatience. "Still, I think I am authorized to put a spiritual meaning on the text."

"Put what spiritual meaning you please on the text, and then you will authorize me to introduce my negatives, to contradict the literal sense."

"But," said the Doctor, addressing Father Oswald, "does not Christ himself sanction a spiritual meaning when he says, 'It is the spirit which quickeneth; the flesh profiteth nothing; the words that I speak unto you, *they* are spirit and *they* are life'?"

"I remark," said Father Oswald, "the emphasis which you lay on the two pronouns *they;* you are aware, I presume, that they are superfluous, and not found in the original Greek?"

"Yes, yes," said the General, "they are foisted in, to the detriment of the Queen's English, and to the cheating and puzzling the intellects of her liege subjects."

"Humph!" said the Doctor, "that is no answer to my argument."

"Now," said Father Oswald, "allow me to propose a question. Is Jesus Christ speaking of his own flesh, or of flesh in general?"

The Doctor was not prepared for such a question; after some hesitation he replied, "Of his own flesh:" for he saw, if he answered of flesh in general, then there was an end of his argument, and because Jesus Christ had said all along, *my flesh, my blood.*

"Be it so," said the Father; "then the quickening spirit will be his soul. The sense is now clear; dead flesh separated from the quickening spirit, divided, mangled, and consumed in the gross manner which you have imagined, would indeed profit you nothing; not so my *living* flesh, quickened by my soul, and united to the divinity. The words that I have spoken to you imply 'spirit and life.' I have spoken to you of the *living* and *life-giving bread;* I have said, 'That he who eateth me, shall *live* by me as I *live* by the Father.'"

"Plausible enough," grumbled the Doctor, fanning himself with his pocket-handkerchief, to relieve the heat he had worked himself into, "very plausible to the weak and unlearned; but believe me, ladies, there is much jesuitical sophistry in all this. To-morrow—another day—gracious me, how hot it is! I am sure, Mrs. Sefton, you must find this room too close and oppressive; don't you find it very hot, Miss Harriet?"

"Not particularly so," said Harriet, suppressing a titter, "particularly on this cold December night."

"Allow me," continued Father Oswald, "to make one more observation, and I have done. Those disciples who had found the words of Jesus *a hard saying*, saw nothing in this supposed explanation to soften the doctrine, and therefore abandoned their master and 'walked no more with him.'"

"Mark that, Doctor," said the General; "sound Protestants even amongst the disciples of Jesus! faith, I shall begin to think there is more Scripture for Protestantism than I had imagined."

"Humph—hem—stuff—sophistry," said the Doctor in considerable agitation.

Harriet could resist no longer, and laughed most heartily; as soon as she had a little regained her composure, she said, "I told you, Doctor, that the two magpies foretold us mirth."

"A plague on the magpies, and the mirth too," muttered the Doctor; "how can you talk such stuff, Miss Harriet?"

Harriet laughed again, but more pleased at the confusion of the Doctor, than at her own skill in augury.

"Nevertheless," said the Doctor, rallying, and speaking in rather a high and angry tone, "I do maintain, that the doctrine which Catholics hold, that the bodily presence is an extension of the Incarnation, and that they actually receive God into their hearts, is an absurd and profane doctrine."

"Prove the absurdity, and we will try to give you an answer," said the General; "but will you tell me, Doctor, if you object to believe that the incarnation of Jesus Christ was wrought by supernatural means? namely, that He was the Son of God, and not of St. Joseph?"

"Of course, General, I believe His incarnation to have been the work of the Holy Ghost, and that the order of nature was not followed in it; how can you doubt it?"

"Then," replied the General, "if you believe that in the mystery of the incarnation and birth of our Saviour, the Almighty could and did suspend the ordinary course of nature, why do you object to believe that He may, if

He pleases, do the same thing with regard to the mystery of the blessed Eucharist? If you acknowledge the mystery in one case, I cannot conceive what can be your objection to acknowledge the mystery in the other."

"Because," said Doctor Davison, after a pause, "I think that blasphemous and profane consequences follow the doctrine of the real presence: namely, that the body of our Saviour is in a state of constant corruption, in consequence of our deaths, after having partaken of it."

"The Catholic Church teaches no such blasphemy, Sir," said Father Oswald warmly; "you speak of the glorified and immortal body of the Lord Jesus Christ as if it were subject to the same laws as our frail, miserable, corruptible frames; *you* should know, that, amongst other privileges of a glorified body, one is impassibility."

"I know that, Sir, as well as you do," said the Doctor; "but when our Lord says, 'it is the spirit that quickeneth,' he means, that what he taught both of the Incarnation and Eucharist, he taught and meant in a figurative and spiritual sense."

"What! was Christ incarnated only in a spiritual sense, and not in reality?" said Mrs. Sefton, in evident amazement; "I thought you told us, only a minute ago, that you believed in the Incarnation; now, if Christ's body was *spiritual*, and not *real*, when it was born, I should think one could not call it an incarnation at all."

"Pooh! pooh! my dear Madam, what can you know about such high things as these?" said the Doctor; "you should submit to be taught."

"You say very rightly, Doctor Davison, said Emma with spirit; "what can we poor laical sinners know about the mysteries of God! and for that very reason I have submitted my judgment in all matters of faith to that Church which has received authority to teach; but, nevertheless, the Catholic Church takes good care to instruct her children on all points that are necessary to salvation, as far as the subject can be explained; therefore, I do understand what it is necessary I should understand on the mysteries of the Incarnation and blessed Eucharist. St. Paul, you know, says, we ought to be 'able to give a reason for the hope that is in us.'"

"There's a rap over the knuckles for you, my worthy Doctor," said the General, stirring the fire.

The Doctor looked very angry.

"God forbid, my dear Sir, that we should say the flesh of Christ profits nothing," said Father Oswald earnestly; "that would, indeed, be a blasphemy."

"Well," said Harriet, "I had no idea till this evening, that Catholics could give such a rational account of the Mass, because I always thought, and I was always taught to think, that it was contrary to the Scripture and to reason; but if one believes in the real presence, which we may do if we choose, the apparent absurdity immediately vanishes."

"The Mass is neither contrary to reason nor the Scripture, my dear Miss Sefton," said Father Oswald, smiling; "the Holy Sacrifice of the Mass is the greatest act of religion that can be performed; indeed, the only one perfectly worthy of God; therefore, it is most reasonable we should offer it to him: it is not contrary to Scripture, but expressly enjoined therein by Christ himself, 'Do this in commemoration of me.'"

"There I have you," said the Doctor hastily, "*there* I will nail you to your own admission. We here see in the words of the institution, that Christ establishes a perpetual memorial of himself, 'Do this *in remembrance* of me.'"

"Let us not jump too rapidly to conclusions," said the Father gently: "let us first settle the previous question: Christ says, 'Do this.' What are we to do? that is the question."

"We must do what Christ did," replied the Doctor; "we must take bread and wine, and bless, and break, and eat and drink in remembrance of Him; nothing can be clearer."

"No doubt we must do what Christ did," continued Father Oswald, "but the question again recurs, *what* did Christ do? Did he give to his disciples bread and wine simply, or did he give them, as his words import, His body and His blood? When this previous question is settled, we shall readily agree *why* we are to do it."

"That is a sophistical distinction," said the Doctor.

"No sophistry at all," interposed the General, "but a plain straightforward question; too difficult, I perceive, for a straightforward answer. But as you have asserted in the beginning of our conversation, that the Mass is a silly and profane invention of a corrupt Church, I have a right to demand an answer to another question. When, where, and by whom was this invention made?"

"In the dark ages, to be sure," said the Doctor boldly; "those ages of ignorance and superstition; there is no need of fixing the precise date, place, or person; it came in gradually; it was unknown in the early ages."

"A blessing on the dark ages!" ejaculated the General, "they always afford a safe retreat to a worsted foe. But the dark ages will not profit you in this case; for we have the testimony of the Fathers, that Mass was celebrated in the earliest and brightest days of Christianity; and we still possess the liturgies which they used. Nay, we have historical evidence that the Apostles themselves celebrated Mass. I have seen myself in Rome the altar on which St. Peter offered the Holy Sacrifice; it is preserved in the church of St. Pudenyiana. The words of St. Andrew the Apostle, when Ægeas the judge exhorted him to sacrifice to idols, are very remarkable: 'I every day,' says he, 'sacrifice to the Almighty, the only one and true God; not the flesh of oxen or the blood of goats, but the immaculate Lamb, upon the altar, whose *flesh* is given to the faithful to eat; the Lamb thus sacrificed remains whole and alive.'"

"Those are indeed remarkable words," said Harriet thoughtfully. "I should think if persons once bring themselves to believe implicitly what the Church teaches them, and nothing more nor less, they must be very happy; it must save them a world of trouble."

"Miss Harriet, Miss Harriet, beware how you express such a sentiment as that," exclaimed Doctor Davison, glad to turn the discourse from the subject in dispute; "how can a rational being answer for his soul at the last day, if he has given the guidance of it to a fellow-sinner, without having employed his mind to know the will of God in that revelation of it which he has given to man?"

"Now, I venture to answer to Miss Sefton," said Father Oswald, "though it is foreign to the point we had in hand, that the Catholic acts very rationally and very securely in giving the guidance of his soul to those who have received authority from God to guide him; consequently, he very much promotes his own happiness; 'He hears the Church;' he hears the ministers of the Church, as Christ has commanded him to hear them, and as he would hear Christ himself, and on this score he is under no apprehension of not being able to render a good account at the last day."

"Yes, yes," exclaimed the General, rubbing his hands, "we must leave the Biblical to settle his own account as well as he may; but I fear if 'he heareth not the Church,' his lot will be likely to be with 'the heathen and the publican.' 'If he despiseth the ministers of the Church, he despiseth Christ himself; and he that despiseth Christ, despiseth the Father who sent Him.'"

"But for what reason has God, then, given us understanding, if we will not employ it in knowing the will of God on religion, which is the most important of all concerns?" expostulated the Doctor.

"The Catholic does employ his reason to know the Will of God, and the true sense of His revelation; only he goes a different way about it," said Father Oswald; "he takes the straightforward path, pointed out to him by Christ, such as it was foretold by the prophet: 'And a path, and a way shall be there, and it shall be called the *holy way;* the unclean shall not pass over it; and it shall be to you a *straight way*, so that the fool shall not err therein.'"*

"But how can you make this applicable," said the

* Is. xxxv. 8.

Doctor earnestly, "to those who rule themselves by the pure Word of God expressed in the Scriptures?"

"Because," answered Father Oswald, "daily experience too clearly proves that Bible readers have widely deviated from this 'straight and holy way,' each one running his own tortuous career, and crying out with all his might, 'Here is Christ,' and 'There is Christ.' The Catholic pities their blindness, and jogs on his straight way, nor turns to the right nor to the left."

"Well," said the Doctor with great pomposity," I do seriously think that Catholics will not be saved, if, being acquainted with the Bible, they still continue to let themselves be guided by the Church in what is contrary to the precepts of the Bible!"

Oh! oh! so we are to go to the regions below, because we will not come into your mad scheme," exclaimed the General, laughing; "it were not very difficult to retort the compliment; but I shall be content to send you to Bedlam; I wish and pray that your ignorance may plead excuse in another world; but I have a difficulty to propose, to which I expect an answer: for the affair of salvation is too serious a one to be trifled with."

"Then do, my good General, keep your difficulty till to-morrow," interrupted Harriet, "for I am sure we have had quite seriousness enough for to-night."

"I think so too," said the Doctor, rising, "but I shall be happy to solve your difficulty to-morrow, Sir," continued he, casting a side glance at Father Oswald.

The Father rose also, and having given his blessing to Emma, they all retired to supper, leaving her somewhat exhausted with the varied emotions of the evening.

CHAPTER XII.

"As long as words a different sense will bear,
And each may be his own interpreter,
Our airy faith will no foundation find,
The word 's a weathercock for every wind."
DRYDEN.

IN the middle of the night, when Father Oswald was in a sound sleep, after the fatigues of a well-spent day, he was suddenly roused by the drowsy voice of John the footman, who drawled out that there was a countryman making a great noise at the back door, who begged him for the love of God to tell the priest that the sick person he had visited the day before was worse, and not likely to last many hours.

"I did my best, Sir," added John, "to keep the man quiet till the morning, for there can be nothing wanting, I take it, since you saw the poor creature but yesterday: such manners! coming and rousing good folks out of their warm beds such a night as this, when one would not send a dog to the door; but there's no beating manners into such bumpkins as them, and the more I argued the louder he got, so I e'en feared he would be disturbing the mistress, poor thing."

By the time John had finished this tirade, Father Oswald was nearly dressed.

"We must have patience, you see, John, with these poor people, for they have souls to save as well as we have," said he mildly, as he took the candle from the shivering lad's hand.

"Souls! yes, they have souls, no doubt, but they may contrive to save them without worrying their neighbours in this guise," muttered John.

"We must trust, John, that God will reward you for your charity in helping to get assistance for this poor person, when you come to be lying on your death-bed," observed Father Oswald.

"The Lord be merciful to us, Sir!" said John, quickening his pace to keep up with the Father, who was descending the stairs; "don't be talking about dying at this uncanny time of night; I was always timorous of gaists and hobgoblins."

"A little holy water would be the best remedy for you in this case, John," said the Father, unable to suppress a smile.

"And would it indeed, Sir? how can you explain that, now?"

"I have not time to explain it now," said Father Oswald, as they reached the door where the countryman was impatiently waiting for them. "Good-night to you, my lad," continued he, "and many thanks for your trouble. Keep a clear conscience, and that is a remedy against all fears," added he, as John closed the doors after him, as soon as he saw that Father Oswald had recognized the messenger who had come in search of him.

The next morning, when breakfast was half over, Dr. Davison asked Harriet what had become of the Jesuit, expressing a hope he was by that time safe at his own house.

"I don't know indeed, Sir," answered Harriet. "I suppose he will be arriving ere long: or, perhaps, he does not breakfast at all. I have heard that Jesuits make great fasts. I don't think he will have gone home, because I heard Emma say she wished to speak to him a little later."

"I can tell you where he is," said the General, laying down the newspaper; "he has returned to that sick person at the Mills, where he was yesterday; he will, I hope, be back for dinner."

"What a deal of useless trouble!" said Harriet; "I should have thought one visit was quite enough."

"The poor creature was worse in the night, and sen for him," said the General.

"In the night!" exclaimed Harriet. "How extra ordinary! Why, it was an awful night: every time wakened, I heard the snow pelting and the win howling."

"However, he went in the night, for all that," sai the General quietly, "as was his precise duty. John i my authority, and I imagine he did not dream it. Mis Harriet, may I beg another cup of tea?"

"Well," said Doctor Davison, helping himself t another slice of ham and a buttered muffin, "I canno conceive what charm life can have for any Catholi priest who devotes himself to his duty."

"None at all," said the General bluntly; "it would be a pity it should have: he would then neglect hi duties."

"It seems the grave is the only place where it is no sin for a priest to indulge in rest," said Harriet compassionately.

"But, Miss Harriet," answered the General, "he has his consolations of a higher order: 'he seeks the things that are above, he minds the things that are above, not the things that are upon the earth; for he is dead, and his life is hid with Christ in God.' His treasure is in Heaven, and there is his heart fixed."

The Doctor had ordered his dog and gun to be in readiness after breakfast, but it snowed so hard that he unwillingly counterordered them; he sauntered into the billiard-room; but the General seemed so occupied with a new French publication he had just received, that he durst not venture to propose a match at billiards. He then tried the library, but found it difficult to fix his attention. Whatever book he opened, the troublesome thought occurred to his mind, of what might be the nature of the difficulty with which the General was going to torment him that evening. "I wish I was safely out of this house," said he to himself; "nothing can be more disagreeable to me than this sort of work;

to be sure, I am comfortable enough: good table, good library, and the society mighty pleasant, if it was not for this plaguy controversy. Well, well, I am doing my duty, and a stout one it is." So musing, he replaced the book he had in his hand in the shelves, and dawdled into the sitting-room, where he was soon established by Harriet's work-table, reading aloud to her the last new novel. The dinner was half over before Father Oswald made his appearance, and when he had eat a little, and got himself thawed from the state of freezing in which he seemed, Harriet proceeded to ask how he had left the sick person.

"The sick person, my good Madam," replied he, "is gone to another and a better world."

"Indeed!" said Harriet, "then that fully accounts for it. I heard the death-watch all last night close to my bed-head."

"What is the death-watch?" said Father Oswald in some surprise.

"Don't *you* know what the death-watch is?" retorted Harriet. "That does surprise me; well, I can tell you: it is a little tick-tacking noise, which occurs at regular intervals, very slowly, somewhere in the room; it is difficult to find out exactly in which part it is; and whenever one hears this, it is a certain forewarning that there is death in the house or neighbourhood."

"Upon my word, Miss Sefton," said the General, laughing," I wonder how a lady of your sense can talk such arrant nonsense! It was probably your own watch, or your own pulse, or, at the utmost, a certain little spider which makes that said noise."

Harriet shook her head incredulously. "I know better than that," said she in a mysterious voice.

"It is superstition, my good lady, to hold such opinions as those," said Father Oswald.

"To be sure it is," said the Doctor triumphantly; "so I have often told Miss Harriet."

Harriet smiled, and only said, "Remember the magpies, Doctor."

In the evening the little party assembled as usual in Emma's room, and the General was not long ere he sounded the signal of war in the Doctor's ear.

"Well, Doctor," said he, "I mean to come to close quarters with you this evening, so let us take up our ground fairly in the beginning."

The Doctor groaned internally, but declared he was ready to answer the General's difficulty to the best of his poor abilities.

"Well, then," replied the General, "in the first place we are agreed, that Christ has revealed a code of religious doctrines to be believed by all men, under the pain of eternal damnation: for, when he sent his Apostles to preach the Gospel to every creature, he added these words, 'He that believeth and is baptized shall be saved; but he that believeth not, shall be condemned.'"*

"Certainly; I agree to that."

"Then," continued the General, "since 'God our Saviour will have *all men* to be saved, and come to the knowledge of the truth,'† it follows that He has provided easy, secure, and certain means, by which *all men*, the learned and the unlearned, the wise and the ignorant, may know all things which God has revealed, and they are bound to believe."

"Undoubtedly."

"What are these means?"

"The Bible, which contains God's infallible Word."

"Is that means easy?"

"Nothing more easy; every man can read the Bible, or hear it read."

"Nothing more easy," continued the General; "but when the unlearned read the Bible, or hear it read, is it easy for them to understand it?"

"I suppose so," said the Doctor.

"I think not," replied the General. "But is it a secure means to find out the truth?"

"What can be more secure than the infallible Word of God?"

"But what security can a man have in his own

* Mark xvi. 16. † 1 Tim. ii. 4.

opinion, when he finds his neighbour of a different opinion?"

"Humph!" muttered the Doctor. "If they read with simplicity and prayer, they will agree in all essentials."

"I doubt that much," replied the General; "there can be no security when there is no certainty. No man can be certain that his private opinion is true, unless he presumptuously supposes himself gifted with more acumen, more light, and more knowledge than his neighbour. But let us come a little more closely to the point. You tell me to search the Scriptures, to read the Bible, to judge for myself. Why, then, do you come to dictate to me, and hurl the thunders of God's wrath against me, if I come to a different conclusion to what you do?"

"Why, my good General, your difficulty vanishes like snow before the mid-day sun," said the Doctor, seeming much relieved. "You can never come to the same fair and proper conclusions that we do, because you Catholics do not read the Bible, and are not allowed to read it, and—"

"I beg your pardon, I beg your pardon, Sir," interrupted the General; "be it known to you, that I have read the Bible and thumbed it through and through, and the more I search it, the more am I convinced that the Catholic Church is the only true Church of Christ, 'without spot or wrinkle,' and that all the supposed abuses and abominations are the visionary workings of a disturbed brain, or the malignant inventions of a perverted heart."

"Hold, hold," cried the Doctor; "there is much to be said before you can convince me, or any other sound Bible reader, that the Catholic is the true Church, and that we do not find there that she is full of abominations."

"Well, Sir," said the General, "have a little patience, at least. What you state is one of *your* conclusions; but allow me to state the result of my Biblical observations quietly, and then we shall see."

"By all means, by all means, General; as quietly as you like," said the Doctor; "I am a great friend to quietness in discussion."

"Well, then, I was going to state," continued the General, "that I am convinced from my soul, and that I have come to the conclusion after the most cool and mature deliberation, that out of the pale of the Catholic Church there is no salvation for my soul; and that those 'who separate themselves' from it are sensual men, 'having not the Spirit,'* and 'revolt and not continue in the doctrine of Christ,† and, therefore, they have not God.' Now, this being the case, and my own conviction, grounded, as it appears to me, upon the clearest testimonies of Holy Scripture, am I to renounce it, and embrace your conviction, grounded, you honestly believe, upon more solid testimony? If I renounce my own conviction of the truth, I am damned; if I do not renounce it, you are equally convinced I am damned. This is truly a sad dilemma; who shall help us out of it? Thank God! *I* have a way out of it; but my solicitude is for you: you have made your last appeal to Scripture, you have no further resource."

"Yes, you see, General, we have both studied Scripture, and I can answer for my own intentions being pure, so you need not be uneasy about me, my good friend," said the Doctor.

"But if I am really your good friend," said the General earnestly, "it is very natural I should be uneasy about you: for we have, as you observe, both studied Scripture with the purest intention of 'attaining to the knowledge of the truth,' and we have arrived at conclusions diametrically contradictory on many most important points of salvation. One of us must be involved in damnable error. What is now to be done? I wait for your reply."

The Doctor hesitated, and then replied rather doggedly, "I suppose you Catholics would have recourse to the old story of Mother Church and her infallibility; but we Protestants think she fell into error."

* Jude 19. † 2 John 9.

"Gently, gently," cried the General; "that is no answer to my difficulty. Let us have no more of this random skirmishing; stick to the point; leave *me* to take refuge in Mother Church, if you like; but here is the Presbyterian, the Methodist, the Baptist, the Socinian, one and all read the Bible with the purest intention, all earnestly pray for light to understand it, all seek the 'truth as it is in Jesus;' tell me, now, candidly, do they all find the truth?"

"Certainly not."

"Then you must allow, Dr. Davison, that the Bible alone affords no secure means of finding out the truth."

"Humph!" said the Doctor with a sort of indescribable groan. "I allow that the authority of the primitive Church may help us to the right understanding of the Bible."

"If you appeal to the authority of the primitive Church, you yield the question; for whatever authority the Church had in the beginning, she retains to the present day."

"Not so," said the Doctor; "for we can shew from the Bible that the Roman Church has erred, and thereby lost her authority."

"By the same rule," replied the General, "the Dissenters prove that the Church of England has fallen into damnable errors; so, you see, we can make no progress with an authority liable to error."

"Humph! Hem! I cannot allow the authority of any Church to be infallible," persisted the Doctor.

"My dear Sir," replied the General with great emotion, "consider seriously if it be not a false and absurd supposition, that the Church of Christ, which St. Paul says is 'the pillar and ground of the truth,'* can possibly guide her children into what is contrary to the doctrine of the Bible. From a false supposition the most monstrous consequences may be drawn; as an example, if I lay it down as a certain principle, that you are mad, it would be a logical conclusion, that all

* 1 Tim. iii. 15.

your outpourings were the sheer ravings of a distracted mind."

"Of course, any one understanding any thing of logic must acknowledge," said the Doctor, "that from a false supposition false consequences must follow; but still, Sir, though you say *you* have read the Bible, yet you cannot interpret it as you wish or as you please, but *must*, according to your own acknowledgment, abide by the decisions of the Church."

"Certainly," answered the General; "and so must every Christian who can understand the plainest precept in the Bible, 'He that heareth you heareth me, and he that despiseth you despiseth me;'* again, 'Obey your prelates, and be subject to them.'† When Christ commanded the Apostles and their successors to 'teach all nations,' he exacted obedience to their doctrine from all men who were *to be taught*, and he propounded a sufficient motive for such obedience, when he promised to be with those teachers '*all* days, even unto the consummation of the world;' so that you see our subjection to the decisions of the teaching Church is both rational and Scriptural. Observe particularly, I pray you, that Christ has promised to be with the Church *teaching*, but has nowhere promised to be with each private individual reading his Bible. The Bible is a divine book, and must have a divine interpreter; but my being obliged to submit to the decisions of the Church in matters of faith, does not in any degree alter what seems to my own convictions and common sense the truth, any more than it alters the mathematically demonstrative truth, that two sides of a triangle are always longer than a third, because I am convinced of the same fact from my own observation and from common sense."

The Doctor hemmed, and, after a little hesitation and a pause, continued: "Then, Sir, according to you, the Catholic says, the interpretation of the Word of God must belong to the Church; private judgment may, and often does err in a matter so difficult. Why, then, is it said of the Jews of Berea, to whom one of the

* Luke x. 16. † Heb. xiii. 17.

Apostles himself preached, 'These were more noble than those of Thessalonica, in that they received the Word with all readiness of mind. and *searched the Scriptures daily*, whether those things were so; therefore many of them believed'?* Do not these words point out the duty of the teacher and of the hearer, and the result to be expected when both are fulfilled?"

"But, Sir," said Father Oswald, "in order to understand this passage of the Acts, we must not separate it from the preceding context; perhaps you would be kind enough to favour us with that, before we proceed further?"

"By all means, Sir," said the Doctor eagerly. "Where are my spectacles? Where is the Bible?"

"The Bible you left behind you yesterday, Sir," said Emma; "it is on the table near the window; but where your spectacles are, I know not."

"I do though," said Harriet; "they are in my reticule; you left them, Sir, on the work-table in the sitting-room."

"Well, well, give them here," said Dr. Davison, settling them on his nose, and opening the Bible; when he had found the 17th chapter of the Acts, he read it in a pompous voice from the beginning, till he came to the text in question, when he paused.

"Now, Sir," said Father Oswald, "please to observe that from this it appears, that St. Paul had previously preached to the Jews at Thessalonica, and, appealing to their own Scriptures, proved to them 'that the Christ was to suffer, and rise again from the dead; and that this is Jesus Christ, whom I preach to you.' Now, some of the Jews believed on the preaching of St. Paul, without searching the Scriptures, and a great multitude of the Gentiles, who certainly did not search the Scriptures, which they did not possess. The more fiery zealots persecute the Apostles, and drive him from the city."

"Egad!" ejaculated the General, "those Jews were genuine Protestants; they chose to read their Bible in

* Acts xvii. 11.

their own way, and preferred their own to St. Paul's interpretation."

"St. Paul next proceeds to Berea," continued Father Oswald, "and there in the synagogue of the Jews, *preaches* the same doctrine. The Bereans gave him a kinder reception, 'and receive *the Word* with all eagerness;' for this St. Luke says, 'they were more noble than those in Thessalonica;' and having received the Word, they very laudably consulted those passages of the Prophets which the Apostle had quoted, and thereby confirmed their faith in the Word received."

"There's for you, Dr. Davison! What have you to say to that?" exclaimed the General, rubbing his hands. "It is difficult, I think, from these premises, to conceive by what magical logic a Protestant can jump to the conclusion, that therefore every man, woman, and child must read, search, and expound the Scripture for himself. Oh! how I would laud the Protestant who, without passion and prejudice, would open the Prophets and the Apostles, and search and study those passages which a Catholic divine would point out to him, and prove the unity, the indefectibility, and the infallible authority of the Church of Christ."

"What a noise you do make, General!" exclaimed the Doctor, putting his hands to his ears, "I'm sure you must quite distract poor Mrs. Sefton's head."

"Oh! no, Dr. Davison," replied Emma, laughing; "I have not got the head-ache, thank you: besides, I am accustomed to my uncle's ways."

"But, you observe, Sir," said Father Oswald mildly, "that St. Paul *expounded* the Scriptures to the Bereans: the Catholic pastors imitate his example, and expound them to their flock. St. Paul did not leave it to the Bereans to question his authority or his exposition, nor would he have lauded them, had they, exercising the pretended right of private judgment, come to a different conclusion. No doubt, many did so."

"Like free-born Protestants," subjoined the General. "Egad! the Scriptures are full of them."

"In like manner," continued the Father, "the Catholic

pastors do not leave it to their flock to question the same authority which they have inherited from the Apostles, under the guidance of the same unerring Spirit. Such of the Bereans who searched the Scriptures, and received not the word, were not praised by St. Luke; neither can we praise the Protestants, who search the Scriptures, and receive not the word of the authorized preachers."

"But," said the Doctor boldly, "the basis of the Roman faith and its doctrines are utterly unscriptural."

"It is easy, Sir, to make a bold assertion; but there is no need to receive every bold assertion as an infallible oracle," replied Father Oswald; "a shrewd man, like yourself, Doctor," added he, smiling, "may often ask an awkward question; pray, how do you prove your assertion?"

"Don't sophisticate, Sir," said the Doctor in an angry tone; "it would be easy enough to prove what I assert."

"But, my good friend," continued the Father, "it is really not fair to call an argument sophistry, when you are unable to answer it; there is no system of religion, besides the Catholic, which, as a whole, and in every part, harmonizes completely with Holy Scripture. With good reason, we call upon the Bible readers to harmonize amongst themselves, from the thousand and one discordant sects into which they are divided, one complete system, in which all agree. We might then form a comparison, and see which most chimed in with Scripture. As matters stand at present, we cannot believe that the Word of God will answer to such jarring notes."

"And what wonder," said Harriet, "if they don't all agree! The Church is fallible, being only a number of men and women, gradually overcoming their sinful natures."

"This is really a novel definition of the Church," replied Father Oswald, looking at Harriet with surprise, "and would comprehend many honest Pagans, Mussulmen, and Jews, who, by the light of natural reason, know their own weakness and proneness to sin, and often make efforts to correct their passions. The question, my dear Miss Sefton, is not of the infallibility of individuals, but, whether the whole body of Pastors, under the guidance of the Holy Ghost, can go astray."

"Well, Sir, I should say, and indeed I feel convinced," said Harriet, "that it is sufficient simply to lead a good life, whatever one may be, either Jew or Mussulman, and much so in a Christian *to believe* in Christ, with love, to be saved."

The Doctor shook his head, but said nothing: the General was not so easily satisfied, and exclaimed with great warmth, "To believe in Christ! Good God! how Thy sacred word is 'wrested by unlearned and unstable men to their own perdition!' There is not a man bearing the name of Christian, however foolish, visionary, or impious his opinions may be, that does not profess 'to believe in Christ,' and with this vain, vague, undefinable faith, he flatters his self-love, that he is secure of salvation."

"I see no self-love in it," said Harriet, somewhat piqued. "I hate disputing, but I do sometimes read my Bible quietly of a Sunday, and I have often remarked that soothing sentence which is expressed in many forms; 'God so loved the world, as to give his only begotten Son, that whosoever believeth in Him may not perish, but may have life everlasting.'* And, therefore, as I do believe in Him, I am fully persuaded that I may sit myself down, without further bother, in perfect security."

"But, Harriet, did you never ask yourself the question, what *is it* 'to believe in Christ?'" said Emma earnestly.

"Not I, dear Emma," said Harriet, clasping her hands on her lap, and twirling her thumbs. "I never ask myself troublesome questions."

"It's a very necessary question though," said Father Oswald seriously, "however troublesome it may seem to you."

"Can you answer it then, Sir?" said Harriet with a yawn.

"I think I can," replied Father Oswald: "to believe

* John iii. 16.

in Christ, in the first place, is to believe that he is the eternal and only begotton Son of the Father, sent into this world and made man for the instruction and salvation of mankind; and, in the next place, to believe in the *whole* of his doctrine: for he who denies one iota of it, questions the veracity of Christ, and thereby denies his divinity."

"Well, however, we all believe that," interposed the Doctor.

"However, *you*, my good Sir, cannot be ignorant," said Father Oswald, "that there are some who call themselves Christians, and many even of the dignitaries of your own Church, who, though diligent Bible readers, yet deny the divinity of the Redeemer."

"Then, Mr. Oswald, they do not deserve the name of Christians; they subvert the foundations of all faith," exclaimed the Doctor indignantly.

"No doubt they do," replied Father Oswald; "for 'they deny the Lord who bought them, bringing upon themselves swift destruction.'* But there are other 'lying teachers who bring in sects of perdition;' such teachers cannot, I presume, be said to believe in Christ unto salvation, whatever their pretensions may be."

"Certainly not," replied the Doctor; "but I hope the sects of perdition are few; and certainly the national Churches of England and Scotland cannot be accounted amongst them: for, however they may differ in some minor circumstances, they all believe in Jesus Christ, their Redeemer."

"I dare not flatter you," said Father Oswald sorrowfully, "with assenting to that proposition; they, too, have the brand of perdition too deeply marked upon them; 'they are they who separate themselves.'† They no longer 'keep the unity of spirit;' they have severed 'the bond of peace;' they form no longer 'one body and one spirit;' they no longer hold 'the *one faith*;' and, therefore, I must conclude, they no longer believe in the 'one Lord.'"‡

* 2 Peter ii. 1. † Jude 19.
‡ Eph. iv. 3.

"How, Sir; how so, Sir?" said the Doctor, much ruffled; "what do you mean? I beg you will explain yourself."

"I will, Sir," said Father Oswald patiently; "does not St. John say, 'Whosoever revolteth, and continueth not in the doctrine of Christ, hath not God?'* now, all the Protestant Churches have revolted from the doctrine of Christ: because they have revolted from that Church which was in possession of 'the faith once delivered to the saints.'"†

"But, Sir, the Church fell into error; into gross and damnable errors and abuses," said the Doctor passionately; "hence, the first reformers did well to separate from her, and form a new fold for themselves."

"Aye," said the General, "and take the old reprobate, Harry, for their own shepherd."

"Excuse me, Doctor Davison," said Father Oswald firmly, and drawing himself up with great dignity, "but to say that the Church has erred, is to give the lie to Christ, who has declared that it shall never err; and who has promised to remain with his Church *all days*. Whoever asserts that the Church has erred, and that the gates of Hell have prevailed against her, impugns the *veracity* of Christ; and certainly cannot be said to believe in him, because to *believe in Christ* is to receive, with humble docility of heart, and an entire submission of the understanding, *all* the divine truths which he has revealed to his Church, and to give an entire and undivided assent to every thing that she teaches in his name."

"Yes, Sir, yes," growled the Doctor; "the Gospel no doubt contains the compendium of those truths."

"But the Gospel," rejoined Father Oswald, "must be *preached* and *taught* by men who have authority. The Apostles and their legitimate successors have received this authority from Christ himself: 'Go, teach all nations, teaching them to observe *all things* whatsoever I have commanded.' The Gospel of Christ is essentially one; when, therefore, 'lying teachers' come

* 2 John 9. † Jude 3.

amongst us, and announce new, perverse, and contradictory *opinions* as the doctrines of Christ, we say to them, You announce 'another gospel, which is not another, only there are some that trouble you, and would pervert the Gospel of Christ. But though we, or an angel from Heaven, preached a gospel to you besides that which we have preached to you, let him be anathema.'"*

There was a pause; all seemed struck with the words they had just heard, and the impressive manner in which they were uttered; but, in a few minutes, the Doctor, rallying his scattered forces and scattered intellects, said, in a hurried manner—

"But I maintain that the Roman Church is fallen and apostate, and her priests not being able to produce Scripture authority for all they teach, appeal to tradition and antiquity: the religion which founds its chief claim on antiquity must be weak."

"Why, Doctor," exclaimed the General, "you called in antiquity to your own aid just now! Do be consistent, at least."

"But," said Harriet, coming forward to support the Doctor, "if antiquity is a proof of truth, Mahometans have more right to it than Catholics, and more claim to numbers, power, and unity; many of the doctrines of Mahomet being more ancient than the *newly* discovered doctrines of Mass and Purgatory."

"Besides," interposed the Doctor, "the supremacy of the Pope began only in the seventh century."

"My friends, my friends, what a confusion of accusations, and a jumble of ideas!" exclaimed the General; "just listen one moment: it seems to me, that if an antiquity, which extends in one unbroken chain up to the Apostles themselves, be not a proof of the true Church of Christ, I know not what is. Again, Mass and Purgatory, and every other dogma of the Catholic Church, are proved by the testimony of Fathers who lived long before Mahomet; if it had not been a lady who had made these observations, I should have said, what ignorance!"

* Gal. i. 6, 7, 8.

Harriet bit her lip.

"But, Sir, I would have you to understand clearly," persisted the Doctor, "that Protestants deny the succession of the popes from St. Peter, or, that St. Peter ever was Bishop of Rome; Protestants are quite as capable of discerning truth as Catholics: there is no means of getting at truth on such points, but historic evidence."

"Pshaw! pshaw! Doctor, stuff and nonsense!" cried the General, offering him a pinch of snuff, "well-informed Protestants are now ashamed of such an old wife's fable. St. Ireneus, who lived in the second century, the disciple of St. Policarp, who was the disciple of St. John the Apostle, has given us the list of the popes down to his own days, beginning with St. Peter."

"Nothing can be plainer than that, I think," said Emma.

"But from historic evidence, my dear Mrs. Sefton," replied the Doctor, "Protestants deny that the Church of Rome has for many centuries, or does now resemble the primitive Church, as described in the New Testament."

Mrs. Sefton smiled.

"Faith!" said the General, laughing, "the Protestant clergy rolling in wealth, ease, and luxury, would cut a sorry figure, if compared with the primitive preachers of the Gospel. It would be a most edifying spectacle, to see the Protestant laity selling their posessions, and uniting their property for the common use of all. Thousands and tens of thousands of Catholics of both sexes follow this primitive rule to the letter in religious communities, even to the present day."

The Doctor looked very angry. "Well, I am convinced," persisted he, "that the Catholic Church teaches many painful things not contained in the Bible."

"No, Doctor, it does not," said Father Oswald; "the voluntary poverty of so many individuals in the Catholic Church is one of those *painful* things, I suppose!"

"Well, I as a sound Protestant divine," said the Doctor solemnly, "maintain that no doctrines ought to be received, but what can be plainly shewn in the Bible."

"Then we must turn Jews," said Emma, laughing, "and keep the sabbath-day on Saturday. But how do you prove your assertion? You must prove it to me from your Bible; for really I cannot admit it on your word, Doctor."

The Doctor looked puzzled, but after a pause said, "Mrs. Sefton, I prove it in this way, that the observances most insisted on in the Roman Church, as, confession, mass, purgatory, and such like fond inventions, are only commandments of men."

"Then," said Mrs. Sefton, "you have just proved nothing at all, but only added to a bold assertion, a new accusation."

"If you call confession a commandment of men," said Father Oswald, "will you tell me, by what man it was first given? and also by what extraordinary power he could prevail upon all Christians to submit themselves to such a grievous, and till then unheard-of yoke?"

"Oh! no doubt," said the Doctor, "it was introduced gradually in the dark ages."

"Still," replied Father Oswald, "some Pope, Bishop, or Parish Priest must have begun the innovation; did he meet with no opposition?"

"What opposition could he meet with," answered the Doctor, "from the ignorant and superstitious men of those times?"

"Doctor," interposed the General, "*you* have, methinks, a congregation consisting of as ignorant and superstitious a set of bumpkins, as ever disgraced a Christian congregation in a Christian country; I will bet a hundred pounds to a sixpence, that in twelve months you will not persuade one to come to confession to you."

"I shall never make the experiment, General, I promise you," said the Doctor.

"But, my good Sir," said Father Oswald, "you must surely have read St. John's Gospel, in which he relates our Saviour's words, 'When He said this, he breathed upon them; and he said to them, Receive ye the Holy Ghost: whose sins you shall forgive, they are forgiven them; and whose sins you shall retain, they are retained.'* Here we see the commission stamped by the broad seal of Heaven, by virtue of which the Pastors of Christ's Church absolve repenting sinners upon their confession."

"But there is not a word about confession there," interrupted the Doctor; "I know there is a text in St. James, which says, 'Confess your faults one to another,' and so forth,† but in this text there is not a word said about a priest, or minister of religion."

"Quote correctly, my good Doctor, quote correctly," cried the General; "the text is this: 'Confess *therefore* your sins one to another; and pray for one another that you may be saved;'‡ now, this little word *therefore* refers to what the Apostle had just mentioned in the verses fifteen and fourteen of the same chapter, in which he had ordered the priests of the Church to be called for, and brought in to the sick."

"Certainly," said Father Oswald; "and as we have already seen from the words of St. John, that Christ our Lord gave to his Apostles, and their successors in the ministry, the power to *forgive* and to *retain* sins, nothing can be more clear than the consequences which must follow from this discretionary power, namely, that we must confess our sins, and make known the state of our consciences to the ministers of Christ, before they can possibly know whose sins they are to forgive, and whose they are to retain."

"Most disagreeable doctrine, indeed!" muttered Harriet; "I wonder how any one can bring themselves to take such a deal of useless trouble."

"For the sake of their immortal souls," said the General.

"Yes," continued Father Oswald; "we have all our sins: one condition is requisite to obtain pardon; we must *confess our sins*, and then God is faithful and just in his promises, and he will cleanse us, through the sacrament of penance, of all our iniquities. Jesus Christ is

* John xx. 22, 23. † James v. 16.
‡ James v. 16.

then our Advocate with the Father. He is the propitiation for our sins. His blood cleanseth us from them all. Of this we cannot doubt; for the efficacy of the sacrament is derived from the blood of Christ; but that blood must be applied to our souls through those channels which he has opened, one of which the Apostle most clearly points out, namely, '*if* we confess our sins,'* so clearly, that none but the wilfully blind can mistake it."

"Do you ever recollect, Doctor," said Emma with an arch smile, "to have read in the works of St. Martin Luther himself these words?—'Sooner,' says he, 'would I submit to the papal tyranny, than let confession be abolished.'"

"Some spurious edition, no doubt," said the Doctor, rising and taking his candle; "but I must wish you good-night, Mrs. Sefton, I have a letter to write for to-morrow's post; but you, my good lady, are grossly deceived if you think the Roman Catholic Church has power to forgive sins; no, she has no such power: none but God can forgive sins. No command exists in the Bible to confess to priests, at least that I can interpret in that light."

"Hold, Doctor," cried the General; "we cannot let you off in that style; sit down a few minutes longer."

"Excuse me, General," replied the Doctor, walking towards the door, "it is a letter of importance, and must be ready."

"Will you stick to your charge then, Doctor, for four-and-twenty hours, and stand fire to-morrow evening: remember, Sir, you have given no answer to my objection; so, in order that you may have something to ponder upon, if you should chance to wake in the night, I will state it again briefly. Two serious Bible readers come to two contradictory conclusions on some great mystery of faith affecting their eternal salvation; which is to yield to the other? or how is the question to be settled? Has Christ commanded us to believe all that he has revealed under the pain of eternal damnation, and

* 1 John i. 9.

provided no easy, secure, and certain means of knowing what he has revealed? think of that, Doctor Davison."

"As to that, General Russell, I have given my answer: it is not likely I shall change my mind to-morrow, and I am not afraid of your fire, I can assure you; but the morrow will provide for itself, 'sufficient for the day is the evil thereof,' says Holy Scripture," muttered he to himself, as he walked along the corridor to his room.

In a few minutes, Harriet took her candle also, and retired. When she had closed the door after her, Mrs. Sefton asked her uncle, with a sigh, how long he thought Dr. Davison was going to stay."

"I don't know, my dear; the shorter the better," said he bluntly.

"Long or short," said Father Oswald kindly, "don't let this little trial disturb you, my dear child; God will strengthen and protect you in all your difficulties, if you place your whole trust in Him; but you have been quite long enough disturbed this evening; so good-night, and God bless you."

CHAPTER XIII.

> " 'Heathens,' they said, 'can tell us right from wrong,
> But to the Christian higher points belong.'
> Yet Jacques proceeded, void of fear and shame,
> In his old method, and obtained the name
> Of *Moral Preacher*. Yet they all agreed,
> Whatever error had defiled his creed,
> His life was pure; and him they could commend,
> Not as their *guide* indeed, but as their friend."
>
> CRABBE.

Doctor Davison had his letter ready for the post the next morning, as he had announced was his intention so to do the previous evening; but to his great disappointment the post could not go. The snow had increased so much during the night, that all the roads from the Hall were completely blocked up. The letter was to Mr. Sefton, complaining bitterly of the disagreeable circumstances in which he found himself placed; and his entire conviction, that he could be of no use whatever to Mrs. Sefton in the way of bringing her back to Protestantism; he failed not to hint at his own zealous exertions in the cause in which Mr. Sefton had so deep an interest, and to produce two or three well-turned sentences of regret at the hopeless obstinacy of the strayed sheep; he concluded by recommending measures of conciliation, and by giving his opinion, that mildness would do more than violence and persecution to carry conviction to the heart. The Doctor had determined, moreover, to return immediately to the parsonage, and there wait for the answer to his letter; the unexpected increase of the snow-storm was therefore a considerable annoyance to him, as he could not help anticipating a few more dull days and wearisome evenings. In vain he looked out of the window, and then consulted the thermometer; the snow seemed every moment to increase, and the whole air was darkened with the constant and quiet succession of brilliant flakes, as they silently descended to feed the dazzling mass of snow which covered the whole surface of the landscape several feet deep, as far as the eye could reach to the utmost bounds of the horizon. There was no resource for the Doctor but returning to the fire-side, and endeavouring to find some occupation to divert his mind from the tedium of his involuntary captivity; at length, he settled himself to write a letter to Mrs. Davison, to have the pleasure of complaining at least of all his annoyances, trusting that the road would soon be sufficiently cut to allow a passage for the little boy, who carried the post-bag to the next town and passed the door of the parsonage in his route. Father Oswald was compelled also to remain, but not unwillingly; for he saw he could in this moment be of use and comfort to the new convert; besides, he knew his flock at his little Mission could not suffer, as there was one of the superiors of his Order staying there for a time on business of the Society. Mrs. Sefton felt the influence of the severe storm, and was not well enough to see her friends in the evening, which was a great relief to the worthy Doctor, though he affected to lament the circumstance much, and neglected not to send most polite inquiries after the invalid by Harriet and Mrs. Ashton; in the evening, the General challenged him to a game at chess, and failed not now and then to remind him, that he came off much better in that battle, than it was likely he would have done, in his controversial attack, which he begged him to remember stood over for the next meeting in his niece's room. This meeting the Doctor promised himself would never take place; for he had determined to urge business of importance, and escape to the parsonage the moment the road was safe; but this determination, like so many of our more important ones, vanished before the influence of circumstances. In a few days, Mrs. Sefton was able to receive them, and the Doctor was still snow-bound; he could not in common politeness avoid joining the party, though somewhat late in the evening. The Doctor did his utmost to keep the conversation on general topics, in which Father Oswald seconded him, and amused them with some very interesting literary anecdotes; for he did not think these controversial discussions were good either for Mrs. Sefton's health or spirits, in her present convalescent state. But the General was not to be baulked of his evening's amusement; besides, he thought the sooner the Doctor got a good drubbing, as he called it, the sooner the matter would be finished, and the sooner they would be released from his presence; therefore, the moment there was a convenient pause in the conversation, he commenced, "Well, Doctor, and do you still stick to your charge, that the Church has no power to remit sins, and that there is no command to that effect in the Bible?"

"Yes, General," said the Doctor very reluctantly; "I do repeat what I said some evenings since; it is *my* creed, that none but God can forgive sins."

"On my word! and a very easy way have you chosen to get rid of your sins," replied the General; "you have only to believe in the Scriptures according to your creed, and the job is done; now let me try the experiment. Suppose my conscience is burthened with sin, I make an act of faith, I most firmly believe that Christ died for me, and made full atonement to the justice of God for all my sins; I believe this on the infallible Word of God, as I read it in the Scriptures, lo! my sins are blotted out; nothing more comfortable!"

"Very comfortable, indeed," said Harriet.

"Wait a little, Miss Sefton," continued the General. "I open the Scriptures again, and they tell me, I must confess my sins to a man who has received power to forgive them, and, lo! my sins stare me again in the face! not quite so comfortable after all, you see, Miss Harriet."

"Blaspheme not, Sir," said the Doctor, turning very red; "this is not a fit subject for jesting with."

"I beg your pardon, Dr. Davison, I never was more serious in my life," replied the General; "but let me finish my sentence. Well, I now run to confession, and when I have got over the rough work of declaring my sins, of blushing at my iniquities, of detesting them from my heart, and repenting of the grievous offence I have given to God, and proposing, on no consideration, ever more to relapse into them, I receive absolution, or the pardon and remission of all my sins; and then I rise up from the feet of the Confessor, with well-founded confidence that my iniquities have been really forgiven. Now, indeed, I do feel comfortable, and the more so, that I have carried my faith in Scripture into faithful execution. That no one but God can forgive sins is very true and sound Catholic doctrine; but it is equally true that God can prescribe what conditions He, in His wisdom, mercy, and justice, shall deem proper; and that He can exercise this His supreme power through any minister on whom He pleases to confer it."

"But, Sir," said the Doctor emphatically, "has God conferred such power on man? has He given this, His supreme power, to weak, sinful man as His delegates?"

"Yes, He has," said Father Oswald firmly; "Christ our Saviour wrought a miracle to prove that God can do this."

"How is that, Sir? I do not remember any such thing in Scripture," said the Doctor.

"And yet St. Matthew relates it thus: 'And behold, they brought to Him one sick of the palsy, lying in a bed. And Jesus, seeing their faith, said to the man sick of the palsy, Be of good heart, son, thy sins are forgiven thee. And behold, some of the Scribes said within themselves, He blasphemeth. And Jesus, seeing their thoughts, said, Why do you think evil in your hearts? Whether is it easier to say, Thy sins are forgiven thee, or to say, Arise, and walk? But that you may know that the *Son of man* hath power *on earth* to forgive sins (then said He to the man, sick of the palsy), Arise, take up thy bed, and go into thy house. And he arose, and went into his house. And the multitudes, seeing it, feared and glorified God, that gave *such power to men.*'* We now and then meet with a glimpse of Protestantism in Holy Scripture. The Scribes in this passage are fair representations of them; for, like them, they say, 'He blasphemeth.'"

"Egad!" exclaimed the General, "true Protestants again; the Bible swarms with them."

"It is too much, Sir, it is too much," said the Doctor very indignantly.

"Not at all too much, my good friend," replied Father Oswald quietly; you made use of those very words yourself, not three minutes ago, to the General. But observe, Dr. Davison, Christ promised to confer this power of forgiving sins, first upon Peter alone, with the plenitude of all jurisdiction: 'I will give *to thee* the keys of the kingdom of Heaven. And whatsoever thou shalt bind upon earth, it shall be bound also in Heaven; and whatsoever thou shalt loose on earth, it shall be loosed also in Heaven.'† Next, He gave it to all the Apostles in a body: 'Amen, I say to you, whatsoever you shall bind upon earth, shall be bound also in Heaven; and whatsoever you shall loose upon earth, shall be loosed also in Heaven.'‡ At length He actually conferred that power as fully as He had received it from the Father: 'As the Father hath sent me, I also send you. When he had said this, he *breathed* upon them, and he said to them, Receive ye the Holy Ghost! whose *sins* you shall forgive, they are forgiven them; and whose *sins* you shall retain, they are retained.'§ It is evident from this very explicit text, that Christ constituted his Apostles judges over the consciences of men; for they are to determine, who is fit to have his sins forgiven, or who is not fit, and must have his sins retained. Now, it is impossible that the ministers of Christ can come to this knowledge but by the candid confession of the penitent."

"But," said Harriet doubtingly, "supposing Christ did give this power to his Apostles, it does not follow

* Matt. ix. 2, 8. † Matt. xvi. 19. ‡ Matt. xviii. 18.
§ John xx. 21.

that it exists in the Catholic Church now: it certainly is not practised in the Protestant Church, and if the power exists at all, is considered as a dead letter."

"My dear Miss Sefton," replied Father Oswald, "the powers which Christ gave to his Apostles, when he *sent* them, are transmitted to their successors in the ministry until the end of days: 'Behold I am with you *all days*, even to the consummation of the world.'* Confession is daily practised *now* in the Catholic Church, and with us it is no dead letter. The primitive Christians practised confession: 'And many of them that believed came, *confessing and declaring their deeds*, and many of them who had followed curious arts, brought together their books, and burnt them before all; and counting the price of them, they found the money to be fifty thousand pieces of silver.'† Now, the faithful came not to boast of their good deeds, but to confess and manifest their evil deeds, as is evident from the fruit of their confession in burning their wicked books."

"This certainly seems curious," said Harriet, "and difficult to explain in any other way."

"The Apostles," continued Father Oswald, "exhorted their converts to approach the sacrament of reconciliation, in language perfectly understood and familiar to Catholics of the present day: 'But all things are of God, who hath reconciled us to Himself by Christ, and hath given to us the *ministry of reconciliation*. For God indeed was in Christ, reconciling the world to himself, not imputing to them their sins; and he hath placed *in us* the word of reconciliation. For Christ, therefore, we are ambassadors, God as it were exhorting by us. For Christ, we beseech you, *be reconciled* to God.'"‡

"Mighty sophistical!" said the Doctor contemptuously; "I cannot see the application."

"Why, it is as clear as the sun at noonday, Doctor," said the General; "take a pinch of snuff to

* Matt. xxviii. 20. † Acts xix. 18, 19.
‡ 2 Cor. v. 18, 19, 20.

brighten your intellects; I fear they are somewhat offuscated."

"You see," said Father Oswald patiently, "the Apostle in this passage expressly says, that Christ has established in his Church a ministry of reconciliation for the forgiveness of sins; that his ministers are the ambassadors or delegates of God, holding the word of reconciliation or the power of absolution. Again, St. John exhorts also to confession: 'If we say that we have no sin, we deceive ourselves, and the truth is not in us. If we *confess* our *sins*, he is faithful and just to forgive us our sins, and cleanse us from all iniquity.'* St. James is equally earnest on this point: '*Confess*, therefore, your sins one to another;'† there can be no doubt the Apostle means, to those who, we have just seen, have power to *forgive* them or to *retain* them."

"Well," said Harriet, "what you have stated is certainly very strong; still this confession is a most severe law to flesh and blood; and then the trouble and bother of it! to say nothing of the shame one must feel to tell all one's faults to a man; dear me, I am sure I never could bring my mind to do it; would it be absolutely necessary, Sir, before one could be made a Catholic?"

"You have seen," said Father Oswald, smiling, "that St. Peter holds the keys of the kingdom of Heaven; we must be content to enter there on the conditions our Saviour has attached to unlocking the door."

"Besides, Harriet," said Emma, "though it does seem at first a very hard and disagreeable thing to a Protestant, yet, I do assure you, that the inexpressible peace and comfort which succeeds to the performance of this duty, repays a thousand-fold whatever there is humiliating and painful in it. Before I took the final determination of becoming a Catholic, it was one of the things which worried and frightened me more than any other; it used to occur to my waking thoughts and to my nightly dreams; and in the midst of my most pleasing occupations it brought a pang to my heart, which I cannot describe. I thought it would be impossible to

* 1 John i. 8, 9. † James v. 16.

get over this great difficulty. I prayed to God to help me, and then I began to think of it with less apprehension; I resolved to do it, whatever it might cost me, for the love of God; when I came to the execution of my resolve, my fears and horror of it redoubled; but God had compassion on me, and gave me grace to kneel down at the feet of the priest, and to confess my sins; then all the difficulties vanished, and in a few moments, instead of feeling one of the most frightened and miserable of beings, I felt one of the most consoled and most joyful. Since then I have had no difficulty; but every time I approach this sacrament, I feel an increase of peace and spiritual consolation."

Doctor Davison looked touched, and sighed deeply.

"Yes," observed the General musingly; "it is this bugbear of confession which prevents hundreds from coming to the point, and embracing the Catholic religion, though they perfectly feel the conviction that it is the only true one; they cannot brook the humiliation of telling their sins to a fellow-man, though that man is bound by all laws, divine and human, to perpetual secrecy. You can never, my dear niece, sufficiently thank God, who gave you the grace to overcome your natural repugnance, for I will acknowledge it is a very natural repugnance, to this act of penance, and who enabled you to embrace the humiliation of the Cross."

"I should not so much object," said the Doctor rather slowly, "to the humiliation of the act; it is not *that* I should mind so much; but I object to the system altogether, as tyrannical and galling, nay, even as demoralizing, and being capable of producing great abuses."

"Halt, halt, for Heaven's sake!" cried the General; "those who tax a law which Jesus Christ himself has given us with being tyrannical, galling, and demoralizing, are rash indeed, and should tremble, lest they may not incur the guilt of blasphemy."

"Oh, no," said Mrs. Sefton earnestly; "that is not *your* objection to confession, nor that of any other Protestant who professes to believe in the divinity of Christ; for God could never give us a law which was tyrannical and demoralizing; rather confess candidly that it is the *humiliation* and *penance*."

"Pray, tell me, Doctor," interposed the General, "do you ever hear the confessions of your parishioners?"

"Never," answered the Doctor with emphasis.

"Yet it is prescribed in your Common Prayer-book, in the Visitation of the Sick."

"That," said the Doctor, "is quite optional to the sick person. In the beginning of the Reformation it was necessary to quiet the scruples of the people, who had been accustomed to it under popery. Now the people know better, and no one needs it."

"Then, I suppose," said the General with a malicious smile, "you consider the Bishop to be acting a notable farce, when he lays his hands on your head, and says, 'Whose sins you shall forgive, they are forgiven them,' and so forth."

"Speak more reverently, Sir, if you please," exclaimed the Doctor; "those are the words of Holy Scripture."

"And most irreverently applied, my good Doctor, if they mean nothing."

"They have their meaning," responded the Doctor; "but what have they to do with penance? there is no such a word in Scripture."

"And yet, what says St. John the Baptist? 'Do penance; for the kingdom of Heaven is at hand,'"* added the General.

"There I entirely differ from you, General Russell," replied the Doctor warmly; "for the Catholic Bible is wrong translated, as in this instance; instead of *do penance*, the Protestant Bible translates it *repent*, from the Greek."

"But, Doctor Davison, did you never observe," said Father Oswald, "that the English Catholic Bible purports to be, in its title-page, a translation of the Latin Vulgate, and so it is a most faithful one? Therefore, 'to do penance' is the expression of the Vulgate: now, are we to be told that the translators of the Greek text into Latin, eighteen hundred years ago, did not understand

* Matt. iii. 2.

the meaning of the Greek word, but that its true meaning was reserved for the sagacity of the Protestant sciolists? fie upon them! let them consult the Greek Fathers; let them ask the Greek Christians of the present day, how they understand the word, and these Protestant quibblers will find that the Greeks agree with the English Catholic version."

"Yes," added the General; "for, in fact, 'to do penance,' implies *repentance*, and something more; for, no man proceeds to inflict upon himself external acts of penance, until he has acquired an internal change of heart. Penance was always hateful to Protestants, who, for the most part, walk so, that we may say with the Apostle, 'that they are enemies of the Cross of Christ; whose end is destruction, whose God is their belly, and whose glory is in their shame; who mind earthly things.'"*

"You are too severe, General," said the Doctor, reddening; "Protestants, I can tell you, see no religion in fasting, mortifications, and penances; more especially fasting in public at stated times, fasting as commanded by the Church, or exceeding what the Church commands, are absolutely contrary to Scripture."

"Oh! yes," said the General, laughing; "it is very natural that Protestants should see no religion in fasting, mortifications, and penances. They have inherited the dislike to such things from their great ancestor, Martin Luther, the profligacy of whose life sufficiently proves his abhorrence of such uncomfortable practices; he was wont to say, 'I cannot bear this Jerome, he is perpetually canting about fasting and continence.'†

"Yes," said the Doctor, "Luther had seen how liable such things are to introduce bad consequences, such as hypocrisy and licentiousness, particularly among the Clergy, so he wisely reformed those abuses."

"We must not lay aside a good practice, Doctor, because it may be abused; otherwise, we should be reduced to strange straits," said Father Oswald; "Catholics, on the contrary, believing that 'Christ also

* Phil. iii. 18.

† Serv. Arb.

suffered for us, leaving you an example, that you should follow His steps,'* and knowing that 'Christ did not please Himself;'† think only of His forty days' fast, His vigils by night, His having no place whereon to lay His head, His humiliations, His sufferings, as so many striking examples given to the world, which at a great distance they try to imitate; they are encouraged in their efforts by the practice of the Apostle, who says, 'I chastise my body, and bring it into subjection.'"‡

"But," said Harriet, "has not Christ reprobated fasting, when He says, 'When you fast, be not as the hypocrites, sad, for they disfigure their faces, that they may appear unto men to fast. But thou, when thou fastest, anoint thy head, and wash thy face'?"§

"What a singular instance of Bible reading when viewed through a pair of Protestant spectacles!" said the General, with surprise.

"I beg your pardon, Sir," replied Harriet, colouring and drawing herself up; "I do not wear spectacles,—at least, very, very, very seldom, and that only when I am doing open hem by candlelight."

"Well, my dear Miss Sefton, no offence," said the General, in an apologetic tone; "however, the Doctor does; so it comes much to the same thing. I only want to prove to you, that these said *Protestant* spectacles obscure the Bible reader in his views of Scripture truths rather than aid him; for if you had read another verse, you would have found these words, 'and the Father will repay thee,' so that you see there is some profit in fasting; moreover, by the same reasoning, it follows from the context, that Christ equally reprobates prayer and *almsdeeds*. Because the hypocrites, you tell me, 'disfigure their faces, that they may appear unto men to fast, but thou when thou fastest anoint thy head and wash thy face,' therefore there is no religion in fasting and corporal penances. Now, listen to the purity of such reasoning. Because the hypocrites love to stand and pray in the synagogues, and corners of the streets, therefore there

* 1 Peter ii. 21. † Rom. xv. 3. ‡ 1 Cor. ix. 27.
§ Matt. vi. 16, 17.

is no religion in frequenting the churches, or the conventicle, or prayer-meeting, where much speaking and long-winded orisons are poured forth. Because the hypocrites sound a trumpet before them in the synagogues and in the streets, therefore there is no religion in the jingle and glitter of coin dropped into the open plate at the conventicle door, or in the names trumpetted in the subscription lists of Bible Societies, Missionary Societies, Reformation Societies, *et cetera, et cetera.* Strange Bible commentators these! Christ, in the passage you have just mentioned, reprobates equally prayer, fasting, and almsdeeds, when done through a motive of hypocrisy, 'that they may be seen by men;' but he equally commends to his disciples, and enjoins also, fasting, as well as prayer and almsdeeds, when done for the pure and sole motive of pleasing God."

"Bless me, General! what a rout you do make just about a simple, innocent observation," exclaimed Harriet in a pet. "I always hated controversy; I never could endure it; and what unlucky sprite put it into my head to speak, I know not. But I knew something vexatious was sure to happen, when you were clumsy enough to spill that nasty salt close to my plate at dinner."

Emma laughed outright, neither could Father Oswald keep his countenance. The General attempted an apology for his awkwardness, but the Doctor, with much gravity said, "No, Miss Sefton, it was neither an unlucky sprite, nor the spilling of a little salt, which caused you to speak forth in the good cause of truth, and to exercise your right reason in free discussion. Whatever Catholics may say, I maintain, that watching and praying, and bearing the crosses God sends us, and resisting our inclinations, when contrary to our obedience to God, is sufficient, without mortifying our inclinations, merely because they are natural inclinations."

"What!" said the General, with unfeigned surprise, "are *watching* and prayer, and *bearing crosses*, and resisting evil inclinations, any ways requisite? A little while since you told us all this was perfectly useless! nay, even that it was contrary to Holy Scripture. From my perusal of the Bible, particularly the New Testament, I have inferred that to *resist* the evil inclinations of nature, yes, and to *subdue* them too, is the primary duty of every Christian, and the great triumph of grace over corrupted nature."

"To be sure," said the Doctor, "there can be little doubt but that Christians ought to try, as I just observed, to resist their evil inclinations; but God knows how difficult it is, and almost impossible, in the sense in which you Catholics mean it."

"We know very well," replied Father Oswald, "that in this warfare of the flesh against the spirit, of ourselves we can do nothing, but with the grace of God we can do every thing. I say *we can do* nothing by our own unaided strength, but fortified by the grace of Christ we can do much, therefore *we* must co-operate with the grace of God. These exertions on our part are of two sorts, internal and external; the internal consist in the acts of the free will, always strengthened by divine grace, by which we promptly repress the first rising emotions of our passions, and these I am willing to allow are the more perfect acts of virtue: the external consist in the mortification of the senses, and sensible pains inflicted on the body. These acts of themselves are of no avail, unless accompanied by the internal acts of the soul; but so accompanied, they are powerful to subjugate the passions, and render 'the members as instruments of justice unto God.'"*

"Inflicting pains on the body to make an impression on the soul!" said Harriet contemptuously; "what arrant nonsense, and how perfectly useless."

"No; it is by no means useless," continued Father Oswald mildly, "it is very salutary, however you may dislike it; for, if to pamper the body, to indulge the senses, to loll in ease and luxury, and feast sumptuously every day, are powerful incentives to concupiscence and sin, it follows of necessity, that 'to crucify the flesh,' to 'mortify the members,' to check the appetites, to watch, to fast, to pray, are powerful means to acquire the

* Rom. vi. 13.

dominion of the spirit over the body. So whosoever does these things with the pure motive of pleasing God, does works highly acceptable to Him, and 'He will repay him.' There is another motive for external mortification, which is 'to do penance for our sins;' a still more sublime motive, which has animated the saints to the most heroic deeds of penance, is to render themselves in some sort 'conformable to the image of His Son.'* But these are motives," added the Father, sighing, "which none but Catholics can understand."

"Luckily for us, we cannot understand any such curious ideas," said Harriet, whose horror at the very thought of the trouble and disagreeableness of doing penance, had quite roused her. "I once opened a book I found on Emma's table, called, I think, 'The Lives of the Saints.' Well, to be sure, I never read such curious things in my life. I went reading and reading on, for I dare say a couple of hours; it really quite interested me. Such penances! it was something so new to me. Such accounts of hair shirts, and disciplines, and spending whole hours in saying their prayers. Oh me! I could not help pitying them, and feeling sorry they had given themselves such a deal of useless trouble, to say the least of it, for some of them must have been quite blinded by enthusiasm. However, I suppose such things don't take place now-a-days."

"Indeed they do," said Emma; "Catholics still many of them take the discipline, wear hair shirts, and do penances; and as to the saints, they need not your pity, but ought rather to excite your envy; for now they are glorified spirits in Heaven, reaping the rich reward of their penances and good works, done for the love of God here below."

"Well, I cannot envy them their penances," said Harriet, "for I hope to get a bed in Heaven at a much cheaper rate: I am quite satisfied there is no need of mortifications to subdue our evil inclinations, the guidance of the soul with the grace of God being sufficient."

* Rom. viii. 29.

"St. Paul," replied Emma, "the vessel of election, had surely the guidance of the soul; but, perhaps you mean conscience, by this strange expression: and St. Paul had also the grace of God, yet he did not think this quite sufficient to preserve him from reprobation; for he says, 'but I *chastise my body*, and bring it into subjection; lest perhaps, when I have preached to others, I myself should become a castaway.'"*

Harriet looked a little uneasy, but said, "Well, well, Emma, you will see, that penance can do nothing for us at the hour of death."

"It is quite enough for us if it can do something for us before that time," replied Emma; "few think of doing much penance at that awful moment. It is enough *then* for the pious Christian to bow in humble submission to the divine will, and kiss the hand that inflicts the greatest chastisement of sin, 'for by sin death entered into the world.'"

"You have thought much more about these things than I have," said Harriet, somewhat pensively.

"There is but one thing necessary, dearest Harriet," answered Emma, with a slight sigh.

"Come, my dear, it is high time you were in bed," said the General, looking at his watch.

"Indeed it is," added Father Oswald, "so God bless you, my dear Madam."

"Have you got that book by you, Mrs. Sefton, which Miss Harriet was just now mentioning?" said Doctor Davison; "the 'Lives of the Saints,' I think. I should just like to have a look at it."

"It is in the library, Sir; it belonged to my poor father; my uncle will shew you the shelf where you will find it."

"Thank you, Madam, and good-night," replied the Doctor, following General Russell into the library.

* 1 Cor. ix. 27.

CHAPTER XIV.

"A hideous figure of their foes they draw:
Nor lines, nor looks, nor shades, nor colours true;
And this grotesque design expose to view,
And yet the daubing pleases!"

DRYDEN.

"WELL, Doctor Davison," said Mrs. Sefton, after the little party round her fire-side had finished their tea the following evening, "and what do you think of the 'Lives of the Saints,' which you asked me to lend you last night?"

"Yes," said Harriet eagerly; "what do you think of them, Sir? did not I say truly, what a curious production it is?"

"Ladies," said the Doctor solemnly, "my opinion of the singular work I have been perusing this morning may not be agreeable to all parties here present; so I had best, I think, keep it to myself."

"I think that is scarcely fair upon us, Sir," said Harriet, somewhat disappointed.

"Fair! no, indeed it is not fair," said the General; "come, Doctor, out with it; we shall be able to stand the shock, I dare say."

"Well, then," answered the Doctor, "I must in candour own, that there are many very interesting, and even heroic and edifying actions related of these pious individuals whom you call Saints: but there are many things mentioned of them, which seem to me so enthusiastic and so extraordinary, that I can scarcely believe them: indeed, some of them, I think, are perfectly incredible."

"An act of divine faith is not required by the Church from her members for *all* the actions which are related of the saints," said Father Oswald, "but merely a human faith, such as we give to historical facts, when founded on what seems to us good and unobjectionable evidence of the truth of what we read there; but I think from what you say, Sir, you are altogether pleased with the work you have been skimming through this morning."

"Those were my first *impressions*, Sir," replied the Doctor, "but the result of my *reflections* on them I have not yet told you."

"Perhaps you will favour us with them, Sir," said Emma.

"They may seem strange to you, Madam, who probably have not reflected much on the subject; but to me it seems very evident that our Saviour being a complete Saviour, we have no business to add any of our imperfect doings to that all-perfect work: we must trust our salvation wholly into his hands: for attempting to help ourselves is acting as fools, and dishonouring Christ, for without him we can do nothing."

"No doubt," answered Father Oswald, "Christ is a complete Saviour, and nothing is wanting on his part to make his redemption most plenteous. But," added he, "is nothing wanting on our part, in order to be made partakers of his redemption? did not St. Paul say, 'I fill up those things that are *wanting* of the sufferings of Christ in my flesh'?"*

"Yes, yes; the Doctor has only put the thought which I tried to express yesterday in a clearer point of view," exclaimed Harriet, triumphantly, "namely, that at the hour of death, penances, good works, and piety will give no courage to meet our Judge: all will seem a covering of filthy rags, and the righteousness of Christ *alone* will be seen to have wrought the work of salvation."

"Well, Miss Sefton," said the General gravely, "you have certainly chalked out for yourself a much easier path to Heaven than St. Paul seemed to think advis-

* Col. i. 24.

able; beware lest you may be deceiving yourself. *I* always thought that 'to lay up treasures in Heaven,'* by prayer, fasting, and almsdeeds, as recommended by Jesus Christ himself in his sermon on the mount, would give some secure hope to a poor mortal, when on the point of appearing before the tribunal of the just Judge, who will take special account of such good works. Why! does not Jesus promise the Kingdom of Heaven as a reward to those who do good works? 'For I was hungry, and you gave me to eat, *et cetera*.'† Alas! this vehement spite of evangelicals against good works shews too clearly whence they all spring."

"I am not an evangelical, General Russell, I would have you to know," retorted Harriet.

"You know best what you are, my dear lady," replied the General; "you express their sentiments however."

"Nevertheless, the sentiments are good sentiments," interposed the Doctor, "and sound doctrine too; for when the day of eternity comes, we shall see the vanity of such trifles as mortifications, penances, and watchings; and we shall require forgiveness for attempting to add such rubbish to make more perfect the finished work of the Son of God; for these said good works, fasts, mortifications, penances, and prayers, are of no merit nor use; there is no favour to be expected from God, nor increase of grace gained, nor help towards Heaven acquired by them, but by the sole merits of Christ, who has merited and done all for us."

"I can see no inference to be drawn from this," said the General: "that as Christ has merited and done all for us, we have nothing to do ourselves! If it be so, why keep the people in ignorance? Why not preach a farewell sermon to them, and speak to them openly at once, somewhat in this style?—My dearly beloved brethren, I am come to announce to you this morning tidings of great joy: the Salvation of Israel is come: he has made wide the narrow gate, he has opened broad the strait way: enter ye in at the widened portal; you

* Matt. vi. 20. † Matt. xxv. 35.

are no longer to labour, and be burthened: for Christ hath refreshed you; he has washed you from all your iniquities, he has cleansed you from all your sins. Rejoice always in the Lord; I say again, rejoice. Eat, drink, and be merry; above all things, never mortify your members, with their vices and concupiscences: it is all to no purpose: you are only covering yourself with filthy rags; never presume to add such rubbish to make perfect the finished work of the Son of God. Christ has done all for you; to think the contrary is a vile popish superstition: for they, poor fools, think there is something 'wanting in the sufferings of Christ,' which they fondly imagine they can fill up in their own flesh; nothing can be more opposed to the Scriptural scheme of man's redemption. How much more comfortable it is to know and to feel assured, that our salvation is finished! We have got above all law; we have attained Christian liberty: sin and death have lost all dominion over us, and therefore it is quite useless trouble in us to pray and to preach; let us shut up our churches, or rather let us clear away these lumbering benches; turn the building into a ball-room, and call in the pipe and tabor. As for me, I never intend to preach again: for that is quite useless; you have all the Bible, and you can read it, if you like, from beginning to end: you will find my doctrine true. But as some men of gloomy dispositions may easily mistake certain obscure passages of the Bible, which the Papists are continually putting forth against the clearest evidence, that Christ has done every thing for us; but what say ye, my beloved brethren, to our burning the Bibles altogether in a heap, and henceforward passing our days in jollity and fun! for, truly, there can be little use in reading the Bible, that being a trouble which cannot help us one step towards Heaven, seeing that Christ having done every thing for us, we have no need to do any thing for ourselves; rejoice, therefore, my brethren; rejoice always in the Lord; again I say, rejoice."

"Really you are a great deal too bad, General Russel," said Doctor Davison very indignantly; "ridicule is no argument."

"But it sets things in a clear point of view sometimes," answered the General good-humouredly; "however, to be serious in answer to what you assert, namely, that by good works and penance we try to become our own Saviour, I must, in the first place, assure you, that no Catholic tries to become his own Saviour; for he knows, as well as any Biblical can tell him, that Jesus is the only Saviour, 'Neither is there salvation in any other. For there is no other name under Heaven given to man, whereby we must be saved.'* In the second place, he knows also, and better it seems than Biblicals know, that he cannot arrive at salvation but by the narrow path which Christ has pointed out to him. Good God! one would think that the Calvinistical Bible readers had never opened the first pages of the Gospel, when they raise their voices against good works."

"Indeed one would," said Father Oswald, shaking his head; "yet, what can they make of the sermon on the mount? it is but an exhortation to the practice of every species of good works: prayer, fasting, almsdeeds, patience, humility, self-mortification, *et cetera;* and, though Jesus reprobates the hypocrisy of those who seek the applause of men, yet he tells his disciples, 'So let your light shine before men, that they may see *your good works*, and glorify your Father who is in Heaven.'"†

"That is rather strong, to be sure," said Harriet, looking fidgetty.

"Then, again," continued Father Oswald, "there is not an epistle of the Apostle, in which he does not exhort the faithful to the practice of good works, springing out of faith, and the grace of our Lord Jesus Christ. The whole of St. James's epistle is written to prove the *necessity* of them. Hence, the solicitude of Catholics to abound in them; for they are taught, and they know 'that Christ gave himself for us, that he might redeem

* Acts iv. 12. † Matt. v. 16.

us from all iniquity, and might cleanse us to himself a people acceptable, a *pursuer of good works.'** 'It is a faithful saying, and these things I will have thee affirm constantly; that they who believe in God, may be careful to excel in *good works.* These things are *good* and *profitable* unto men;'† and again, in writing to the Corinthians, the Apostle continues, 'Now, this I say: he who soweth sparingly, shall also reap sparingly; and he who soweth in blessings, shall also reap in blessings; and God is able to make all grace abound in you; that ye always having all sufficiency in all things, may abound in *every good work.*' "‡

"Bless me, Sir!" interrupted Harriet, "you have given us texts enough to make one uncomfortable for a month; I am sure I do not remember to have seen one of them in the Scripture."

"Nevertheless, they may all be found there, Miss Sefton," said Father Oswald, smiling; "now, Catholics knowing all this, and much more to the same purpose, 'we labour the more, that by *good works* we may make our calling and election sure;'§ for, as Christ says, God will 'render to every man according to his works.' "||

"You speak very strongly, Sir," said the Doctor, "but you are not aware, perhaps, that Calvinists judge more of the state of their souls before God by their *feelings*, than by their works; still they attain to a high degree of perfection in works: we must be born again before we can see the Kingdom of God, or make any exertion to please him; therefore we must try our characters by the one given in the Bible, of those born of the *Spirit;* if we possess the fruits of the Spirit,¶ we have the only evidence we can have, that we belong to Christ. The works, therefore, a Calvinist requires to prove he is even in the path of safety, are more pure and spiritual than Catholics and ignorant Protestants regard as sufficient to justify them in the sight of God."

"Bless me, Doctor!" said the General, "I never knew you were a Calvinist before!"

* Tit. ii. 16. † Tit. iii. 8. ‡ 2 Cor. ix. 6.
§ 2 Peter i. 10. || Matt. xvi. 27. ¶ Gal. v. 22.

"Neither am I, Sir," answered the Doctor gruffly; "but after I had finished my course of divinity at Oxford, I travelled for a couple of years with a young nobleman: we spent much of our time at Geneva, and I made acquaintance with some of the most leading Calvinistical divines there: I imbibed many of their opinions, to which I am still in a great degree inclined, though I acknowledge that you might live with me long before you made the discovery, on account of my endeavouring, as St. Paul says, 'to make myself constantly all to all.'"

"Humph!" said the General slowly, and taking a very large pinch of snuff.

"That is no answer to my difficulty, Sir," said the Doctor, rather impatiently.

"All in good time, Doctor," said the General, deliberately finishing his pinch of snuff. "You state, I think, that Calvinists judge more of the state of their souls before God, by their *feelings* than by their *works*; now, I answer, that I conceive feeling to be a very uncertain and delusive criterion of truth. Our feelings are often too apt to warp our judgment. The wild fanatic, and in this land of Bibles, every day some new one starts up, *feels* himself called by God to promulgate to the gaping multitude his crude conceits as the Gospel of the Redeemer: the deluded enthusiast *feels* himself overwhelmed at once by a *saving assurance*. The proud Pharisees judged by their feelings, to whom Christ said, "You are they who justify themselves before men; but God knoweth your hearts: for that which is high to men, is an abomination before God.'"*

"Yes," said Emma; "and I think St. Paul did not judge himself by his *feelings* when he says, 'I am not *conscious* to myself of any thing, yet I am not hereby *justified;* but he that judges me is the Lord.'"†

"Believe me, Sir," said Father Oswald, "a much safer and better criterion is to judge ourselves by our works; it is the rule laid down by Jesus Christ himself: 'A good tree cannot bring forth evil fruit, neither can

* Luke xvi. 15. † 1 Cor. iv. 4.

an evil tree bring forth good fruit. Every tree that bringeth not forth good fruit, shall be cut down and shall be cast into the fire; wherefore by their fruits ye shall know them.'* According to this rule, no man, Protestant or Catholic, can appeal to 'the fruits of the Spirit until he has purged his soul from all the works of the flesh; for a bad tree cannot bring forth good fruits.' This is the natural order of proceeding. St. Paul observes this order: 'Now the works of the flesh are manifest,'† and I need not enumerate them. I shall only recommend to the special consideration of the Bible reader the one of *heresy;* for that is reckoned amongst the works of the flesh, and with good reason, heresy having always sprung from men, whose minds were darkened, and hearts corrupted by the grossest works of the flesh. Now, as long as a man is involved in heresy, that is, in an *obstinate error* against faith, 'he shall not obtain the Kingdom of God,' however much he may boast to me of the fruits of the Spirit."

"Then what is meant by the expression, 'To be born of the Spirit?'" said Harriet petulantly.

"'To be born of the Spirit,'" replied Father Oswald, "signifies to receive a new life of grace, either by baptism or penance. Does not Christ say, 'Unless a man be born again of *water* and the Holy Ghost, he cannot enter into the kingdom of God'?"‡

"You are pleased to be severe, Sir," said the Doctor, waving his hand majestically; "but the Bible teaches, the faith that unites the soul to Christ and justifies, necessarily receives from that union his Spirit to produce that new heart, whose nature it is to bring forth good works; but the Church of Rome confounds the faith which justifies with its effects, and teaches that in addition to resting your faith on Christ's finished work of salvation, you must do so and so yourself; all unscriptural doctrines of the Church of Rome."

"The Catholic Church," replied Father Oswald, "teaches that the ground of all justification is faith in Christ and in all his doctrines, without which all

* Matt. vii. 18, 19, 20. † Gal. v. 19. ‡ John iii. 5.

justification is impossible, and that all good works spring from the grace of God, which is infused into our souls. She teaches, moreover, that grace will produce its effects without the consent and co-operation of the free will of man."

"Prove your words, Sir, if you please," interrupted the Doctor.

"Why, Sir," continued Father Oswald, "is not the Scripture full of exhortations to men 'to hear his voice and harden not their hearts?' Does not Christ lay it down as a distinguishing mark of his sheep, 'that they follow him, because they know his voice?'* Read the tender lament of Jesus over the obstinate city of Jerusalem.† Hence, 'many are called,' but, because many resist the motions of grace within their souls, 'few are chosen.'"

"What, then, can be the meaning of justifying grace?" said Harriet with a sort of half groan.

"Vocation to the *true faith* is the first great gift, or grace of God; but man is not thereby justified," replied Father Oswald; "faith alone, though it were great enough to move mountains, will never justify a man. Man is justified by the grace of God alone, poured into his soul through the channels of the sacraments; though the man without faith cannot receive justifying grace."

"Oh me! how very puzzling," said Harriet; "I am sure I shall never understand it."

"Have a little patience," said the Father quietly; "there is no confusion of ideas in the exposition I have just given; no confusion of cause with effects: the grace of God is the primary cause of faith, justification, and good works; but the grace of God would remain without effect, if man refused his assent; hence the Apostle says, 'And we helping do exhort you, that you receive not the grace of God in vain.'‡ Christ is the vine-stock which supplies all the sap and vigour to the branches, and enables *them* to produce the good fruit. This doctrine, so far from detracting from the perfect redemp-

* John x. 4. † Matt. xxiii. 37. ‡ 2 Cor. vi. 1.

tion of Christ, greatly enhances it; for Christ our Head still continues to merit in his members, and will one day, as St. Austin has it, 'crown in us his own gifts.'"

Father Oswald paused.

"You have certainly explained it very clearly," said Harriet; "even I, who am but dull at these matters, can understand it."

"The fundamental error of the Protestant system of justification," said Father Oswald, "consists in this; you conceive that the stain of original and actual sin remains indelible on the soul of fallen man, and that man is justified by the righteousness of Christ, covering over, as with a garment, not obliterating, the odious stain. It follows, of course, on this system, that the best works of man are vitiated by the original canker of his soul; and it would be difficult to assign a moral difference between the faith of Peter and the treachery of Judas; hence you are led to question the efficacy of the sacraments. Truly it is this system which lessens, if it does not subvert, the perfect redemption of Jesus Christ."

"Allow me to ask, Sir, what is the Catholic belief on this very intricate subject?" said the Doctor somewhat brusquely.

"We hold with St. John," replied Father Oswald, "that 'the blood of Jesus Christ *cleanseth us from all sin*.'* And with St. Peter, 'Repent, therefore, and be converted, that your sins may be *blotted* out.'† And with Ananias, who said to St. Paul, 'Rise up and be baptized, and *wash away* thy sins.'‡ *To cleanse*, to *blot* out, to *wash away*, and many similar expressions in Holy Scripture, convey to the Catholic mind the idea of a perfect purgation, and abolition of the stain of sin. Nor can we conceive how the guilt of sin, as long as it exists, can be concealed from the penetrating eye of God; nor how the soul, marked with the plague-spot of sin, can be just, holy, and acceptable to God. Hence, we believe in the efficacy of the sacraments of baptism and penance, as the channels instituted by Christ to

* 1 John i. 7. † Acts iii. 19. ‡ Acts xxii. 16.

convey his justifying grace to our souls; thus being cleansed by the operation of sacraments, and sanctified by 'the charity of God poured forth in our hearts,'* we are considered capable of producing holy and meritorious works; and this indeed places the perfection of redemption in its brightest light."

"I think I have understood all you have said," added Harriet thoughtfully.

"But what shall I say," continued the Father, "of the contradictions and confusion of ideas in the heads of these Evangelicals? They tell me that 'faith alone justifies me.' But this faith in Christ, this believing in Christ, is an act of my own soul."

"To be sure, Sir, to be sure, Sir; it is an act of each individual soul," said Doctor Davison eagerly.

"But how is that act excited and produced in the soul?" said Father Oswald. "Is it by my own exertions solely, or by the co-operation of my soul with the grace of God; or by the grace of God solely? If you answer, by my own exertions solely, then I become my own saviour; if by the grace of God solely, then it is the grace of God, and not faith, that justifies; and as I can do nothing of myself, it is useless to make any exertion, it is in vain for you to exhort; I have nothing more to do than to sit down quietly, and enjoy myself, until it shall please the Almighty to send me down this saving assurance. If you answer, by the co-operation of my soul with the grace of God, why then you become Catholics."

"But, my good Sir," persisted the Doctor, "we cannot merit grace, we cannot merit grace. No exertions on our part can have the slightest efficacy in justifying our souls before God. A perfect righteousness only can justify; ours is never perfect; therefore it is on the perfect righteousness of Christ that we can rest our hopes of justification."

"Grace," replied Father Oswald "is no doubt a gratuitous gift of God, noways due to any preceding works. 'If by grace, it is not now by works; other-

* Rom. v. 5.

wise grace is no more grace.'* Though no man can merit the grace of justification by his own works, Christ has merited it for all men, 'For all have sinned, and do need the glory of God, being justified *freely* by His grace, through the redemption that is in Christ Jesus.'† God, through the merits of Jesus Christ, gives to all men sufficient grace to bring them, if they reject not the grace, 'to the knowledge of the truth,' and to justification by *faith* and *baptism*."

"How very beautiful the Catholic doctrine is on this subject," exclaimed Emma.

"When once justified," continued the Father, "that is, brought into the state of habitual grace, they still need the influx of actual grace to excite them, and help them to the performance of good works, 'For it is God who worketh both to will and to accomplish, according to His good will.'‡ The good works now done in the state of grace are meritorious, as proceeding from the fructifying grace of Jesus Christ; and merit an increase of grace in this world, and a crown of glory in the next. But if by mortal sin a man falls from the state of grace, all his works are again dead, and he again stands in need of a gratuitous help from God, to bring him to repentance."

"If a person's justification," said the Doctor, "depends on their having been found to obey *any law*, then they have saved themselves; but if Christ is their Saviour, then He must be a complete Saviour. If a person ventures to the judgment-seat to be judged by the pure law of Christ, he *must* perish. If we believe in Christ for our justification, then we are dead to the law, as He has obeyed it for us, and we are all complete in Him."

"Bravo! bravissimo!" exclaimed the General, rubbing his hands; "here is, indeed, a glorious emancipation from all law! just what I said in my sermon. I knew I was preaching the right doctrine, to say nothing of the pure law of Christ; for if we presume to observe *that*, we are just told we must all perish. Yet I

* Rom. xi. 6. † Rom. iii. 23. ‡ Phil. ii. 12.

thought at least the ten commandments were obligatory on all men, even Evangelicals. But, no; I have quite mistaken the whole Gospel, and God's perfect method of saving souls. The next new edition of the Bible will require many corrections; but I particularly recommend to the care of the printer's devil, to put in the little word *not*, where any thing good is commended, and to leave it *out*, where any thing evil is prohibited. By observing this rule, he will hardly add or take away a single iota from the Word of God. It will then be very pleasant to read: 'Thou shalt kill. Thou shalt commit adultery. Thou shalt steal. Or more compendiously, 'If thou wilt enter into life, keep *not* the commandments.'"

"Really, General Russell, your boisterous sallies carry you beyond all bounds of discretion," interrupted the Doctor warmly; "it's too bad to speak of such serious matters in so light and absurd a tone."

"I beg your pardon, my good friend," replied the General; "I have said nothing half so absurd as your propositions. I have only said what I could in my poor way, to shew you the fatal consequences of the said foolish propositions."

"Yes," said Father Oswald firmly; "it is from these misunderstood ideas of justification and predestination, that have flowed the most dreadful crimes which have disgraced human nature. Who can recount the wild enthusiasm, the desponding insanity, the fearful despair, the dreadful suicides, of which they have been the teeming parents? Happy are those, who repose in the bosom of the true Church, and are content to work out their salvation with 'fear and trembling.'"

> "'No more;—where ignorance is bliss,
> 'Tis folly to be wise!'"

exclaimed Harriet; "I always thought that good works were not available in obtaining salvation, and that *faith* in Christ was sufficient to save the soul; this is what I call comfortable doctrine; and now you Catholics tell me this is an error, in contradiction to St. Paul's plainest declaration, that *faith* in Christ alone is sufficient."

"St. Paul nowhere says," replied the General, that

faith in Christ *alone* is sufficient to save us. Martin Luther, indeed, the fifth Evangelist of Wirtemberg, says so in his German Bible. Of course he knew better than St. Paul!"

"And," added Father Oswald, "what says St. James? 'What shall it profit, my brethren, if a man say he hath faith, but hath not works? shall faith be able to save him?'"*

"And, oh! dearest Harriet," said Emma very earnestly, "do not say it is bliss to be ignorant of the only one thing necessary for you; do not wilfully shut your eyes to the light of divine grace, which is now beaming around you. Follow it steadily; it will conduct you to the true Church, out of which there is no salvation for the wilful heretic. Alas! if you reject the grace now offered you, you may rue it for a long, long eternity of woe."

"Dear Emma," said Harriet, "if I really thought that would be the certain consequence, I would give myself a little trouble about it; but you may depend upon it, all real Christians differ merely in words."

"Catholics of course are excluded," said the General, smiling, "from the denomination of *real* Christian; and if I do not much mistake, Biblicals alone are comprehended. Now, as these all agree *in the words* of Holy Scripture, while each one has the high privilege of understanding them as he pleases, there can be no difference amongst *them* in *words* merely; but if 'contentions, quarrels, dissensions,' and other works of the flesh, rise amongst them, it must be about *the things* signified by the words."

"Well," said Harriet thoughtfully, "I was born and bred in the Protestant Church to be sure, and I never have thought very much about the matter; but sometimes it has come into my head, that all our ancestors, and we have a good long pedigree, were Catholics. They never changed before two or three hundred years ago; but now it is another story: there are very few Catholics, I believe, in Britain, in proportion to the number of

* James ii. 14.

Protestants and Dissenters: now there must be some reason for that."

"To be sure," said the General, "there is a very good reason for it; because they like the broad and flowery road that leadeth to destruction, and not the 'narrow path,' which the Lord Jesus tells us, leads to life. But with regard to the number of Catholics in Britain, Miss Sefton, I think you are labouring under a mistake; they are much more numerous than you think, and are every year rapidly increasing. No, no; believe me, that in Britain, the Roman Catholic faith is not yet forgotten; though her ancient, fine, and magnificent places of worship be in ruins, they are not yet stript of the character they once bore, and though dedicated to another worship, they retain too much of their ancient form, not to recal continually the ancient faith: her doctrines are held, I know, as too absurd to be professed by those, 'who blaspheme what they do not know,' and who look upon her ancient and magnificent service as unmeaning ceremonies; but she is ever ready to explain them to those who wish to regard her increasing members as brothers and fellow-countrymen, and boldly to defend her claim to unchangeableness and infallibility against the accusations of her enemies; for the Catholic Church exhibits even in her thus humbled state, the brightest evidence of an Almighty power, that has borne her triumphant through three centuries of the bitterest persecution."

"The sight of those fine old cathedrals, and the splendid ruins of so many beautiful monasteries, which were built by Catholics and originally belonged to them, has certainly very often struck me," said Harriet; "I once knew a person who became a Catholic in consequence of going over the Cathedral of Durham, which you know is a beautiful specimen of fine old Saxon architecture: well, the beadle of the church was shewing all the curiosities to this acquaintance of mine, and, amongst other things, the vestments and priests' copes, I think you call them, which had belonged to the Catholics; she asked him what use was made of these things: he answered, none, that they belonged to the *old* religion; now my friend thought about this, and came to the conclusion, that the *old* religion was more likely to be the true religion than the *new* one, and she went to a Catholic priest to ask him the difference between the old religion and the new one, and in a few weeks she became a Catholic."

"Go you, my dear lady, and do likewise," said Father Oswald, smiling very benignantly; "and oh! let all true Christians pray that the light of truth, the light of divine revelation, may continue to extend its beams, till it overcomes all the darkness of Protestants and infidels, dispelling from their understandings the clouds of ignorance and prejudice; and that divine grace may soften their hearts and render them docile to the truth, so that they may be reunited to the only true Catholic and Apostolic Church, of which Christ is the living Head, to whom every living member is united by that 'faith which purifieth the heart, and worketh by love.'"

There was a pause, interrupted only by Doctor Davison rising, wishing them good-night, and taking his candle; in which operation he let fall the snuffers and extinguisher, and fumbled for them so long under the table, that Harriet at length offered to assist him. Emma and her uncle exchanged glances; a few minutes after the Doctor had made his exit, the clock struck eleven, and the little party dispersed for the night.

CHAPTER XV.

"Ye good distressed!
Ye noble few! who here unbending stand
Beneath life's pressure, yet bear up a while,
And what your bounded view, which only saw
A little part, deemed evil, is no more;
The storms of wintry Time will quickly pass,
And one unbounded Spring encircle all."

THOMSON.

IN a few days the severity of the weather was sensibly mitigated, and the much wished-for thaw rapidly followed. The Doctor lost no time in profiting of the first moment in which the roads became passable, and with great glee took leave of the little party at the Hall, to return to the parsonage. He had already received a letter from Mr. Sefton, thanking him for his exertions, and hinting at Church promotion, if he could but succeed in the much-desired object of bringing back his wife to Protestantism; he mentioned also that he wished her as a last experiment to have an interview with his very particular friend, the Lord Bishop of S——, who he expected would pass by Sefton Hall in a short time, on his way to the North, to look after the tithes of a rich rectory worth £2,000 a year, which he held in commendam. Though the Doctor received this letter before he left the Hall, he said not one word about it, from the fear that Harriet might wish him to remain longer to help her to receive the Bishop. When he was safely and snugly seated by his own fire-side, he wrote to Mr. Sefton, saying he had been obliged to return to the parsonage, and expressing his hopes that the Bishop of S—— might be more successful with Mrs. Sefton than he had been; at the same time, maintaining his decided opinion, that she never would relinquish the religion she had embraced, and recommending conciliating measures as he had previously done. In a few weeks from this time, Harriet received a letter from her brother, which both provoked and annoyed her extremely; inasmuch as it announced the arrival in a few days of the Lord Bishop of S—— and his lady, Mrs. Boren, with all the little Borens, and their nursery-maids, lady's-maids, footmen, valets, coachmen and horses, to pass a night at Sefton Hall on their road to the North, and expressing his desire, that they should be all treated with the greatest attention and hospitality.

"Upon my word! and a nice little modest suite too for a Bishop; quite apostolic," said the General, laughing, as Harriet, in order to give vent to her vexation, read aloud to him at breakfast that paragraph of her brother's letter.

"I really think my brother has gone out of his mind," added she; "what is to be done, General? And then the disturbance it will be to poor Emma, now especially that she is really beginning to get a little better."

"Say nothing to her about it, Miss Harriet, till they are all in the house, or going out of it; and then pass it off as an accidental occurrence."

"Not so easily done as you think, my good General," said Harriet with a perplexed air; "you don't know what this Bishop is coming here for."

"To make this house an inn in his way to the North, I suppose?"

"No, no," said Harriet, smiling; "that may perhaps be one reason; but the principal object of this invasion is to make Mrs. Sefton renounce Catholicity."

"Folly! worse than folly!" exclaimed the General indignantly; "as you yourself must ere this be fully aware."

"Yes; I think any other attempt in that respect is quite useless," replied Harriet with a slight sigh.

"I'll tell you what, Miss Sefton," said the General,

"I am quite determined upon one thing, and it is this; that if your brother makes no conciliatory advances towards reconciliation with his wife, the moment she is strong enough to bear the motion of a carriage, I shall have her removed to Weetwood, and take charge of her myself, till such times as Mr. Sefton comes to his senses."

"Oh! dear Sir," said Harriet with a look of great distress, "it will only widen the breach, and make matters worse."

"I am of a different opinion, my dear Madam."

At this moment John opened the door, and told the General that his mistress wished to speak to him when breakfast was finished. When the General answered the summons, he found Emma in tears, with an open letter in her hand—she gave it to her uncle to read; it was couched in severe terms, reproaching her for the little attention she had paid to Dr. Davison's exhortations, and consequently the little affection and care she had for her husband and his happiness; and concluded with offering her, as a *last* alternative, the retraction of her errors privately in the hands of his very particular friend the Bishop of S——, whom he had commissioned to bring him her final determination on the subject. There was not a single touch of tenderness to mitigate the harshness of the whole of this letter. And poor Emma's feelings were deeply wounded. Her uncle did all in his power to compose and encourage her under this severe trial; but he saw she was not then susceptible of human consolation, and therefore wisely only endeavoured to excite her submission to the divine will, and to animate her courage to receive and embrace, for the love of God, this naked Cross dipped in gall; he took down the little crucifix, which hung by her bed-side, and placed it on her breast; and then quietly retiring from the room, left her to seek her consolation from Jesus alone. In the afternoon he returned, and though he found her very pale, and extremely exhausted, yet she seemed perfectly calm, and even cheerful. She conversed with him on the subject of the letter, and asked his advice, whether she should answer it or not: he advised her not to write, but to give her final answer to the Bishop for her husband, as he wished it so; adding, that it was his opinion she would do well to make her interview with the Bishop as short and decided as possible. The General then told her his wish: that she should go and reside with him at Weetwood, until such time as a reconciliation could be brought about. Emma looked up, and smiled at him gratefully through her tears, which flowed at the thoughts of leaving the home of which she had been so lately the happy mistress; but she agreed to accept his kind proposal as soon as she was well enough to travel. In the meantime, Harriet informed the butler and housekeeper of the expected intrusion, and of their master's orders, that the guests should be treated with distinction; all was soon bustle, and grumble, and preparation, and Harriet could not resist, from time to time, venting her vexation with most sincere sympathy in Emma's room at all this useless trouble and commotion. In a day or two from this time, the expected party arrived for a seven o'clock dinner, which, however, they were not ready for till near eight, as Mrs. Boren had to see that all the little Borens had a proper allowance of bread and milk, and were in train for going to bed, before she could make her appearance in the dining-room. The Bishop was a man about fifty, of a grave aspect, and somewhat pompous in his manners and words. The dinner went off rather stiffly, for Harriet was out of humour, and the General did not care to make himself agreeable. After dinner, as the Prelate was sipping his rosolio, he inquired if Mrs. Sefton would wish to see him that evening, adding, in the same sentence, that he thought the visit might, perhaps, be more convenient to the lady if made the next day.

"You cannot possibly see my niece to-night, my Lord," said the General bluntly; "she is, no doubt, by this time in bed, and I am just going up-stairs to wish her good-night."

"I'm afraid we are rather late, indeed," said Mrs. Boren carelessly; "the roads were in such a horrid state, and the Bishop does not like travelling early."

The General left the room, and the Bishop, turning to Harriet, said, "Miss Sefton, do you think you could accommodate us with a pack of cards? It is an invariable custom with myself and Mrs. Boren to play every evening a game at picquet: it has been our custom ever since our union, and there is nothing like keeping up good old customs; besides, these little mutual condescensions are of infinite use in preserving the amiable sociabilities of the marriage state."

Mrs. Boren simpered.

Harriet rose, and slowly opening the drawer of a little cabinet, produced cards and counters; she then rung for the servant to arrange the card-table, and settled herself to her work. While the Bishop was shuffling the cards, he put sundry queries to Harriet concerning Mrs. Sefton's state of health, which she answered as laconically as was consistent with politeness.

"Before seeing this unfortunate, misled lady," continued the Prelate, "I should wish to have your unbiassed opinion, Miss Sefton, as to any probability of success in the delicate commission consigned to my execution by my excellent and zealous friend, Sefton; you, my dear Madam, I am given to understand, are fully aware of its vital importance."

"I understand, my Lord, that my brother has commissioned you to receive Mrs. Sefton's answer as to whether she is willing to renounce the Catholic religion, or not," answered Harriet coolly.

"Precisely so, Miss Sefton, precisely so," answered the Bishop; "now do you think I have any reasonable chance of success, or not?"

"I think," said Harriet, looking up from her work, and shaking her head, "to answer you in the words of a good old English proverb, 'you may save your breath to cool your porridge.'"

The Lord Bishop of S—— looked surprised. "How, Madam? I do not understand you," said he, laying down his cards.

"To explain myself seriously then," continued Harriet, "I do not think that Mrs. Sefton will ever renounce the Catholic religion, which she has embraced from the conscientious conviction that it is the only true one."

"No, no, Ma'am," interrupted the Prelate, "Mrs. Sefton has not become a Catholic from any solid conviction of the truth; that can never be; but from the foolish perversion of a weak understanding. She has allowed herself to be led astray by the specious sophistry of some crafty priest. If she were better informed of the errors of Popery, and the purity of the reformed religion, it might be otherwise. I fear Dr. Davison has been very negligent, or he would have opened her eyes before this to the evident illusions into which she has been led by deep, designing, and dangerous people."

"I can assure you, my Lord Bishop," said Harriet warmly, "your surmises are any thing but right. In the first place, I know Mrs. Sefton is a well-informed woman, of sound judgment and acute penetration. She has read much, and is well instructed in religious matters, so that I am persuaded she has not taken her resolution, and sacrificed all her earthly feelings, without the fullest conviction. In the next place, I know that Dr. Davison has taken immense pains and trouble in the matter, and has exerted all the strength of reason and authority to convince her of her errors, but in vain; Dr. Davison cannot be blamed, I assure you."

Harriet said this with great feeling, anxious to exculpate her old friend.

"Well, my dear Miss Sefton," subjoined the Bishop, "granting for a moment what you say to be true, she has still been under the influence of her uncle, and, what is much worse, under the influence of a certain Jesuit, who lives, I understand, somewhere in this neighbourood, of the name of Oswald."

"I know Mr. Oswald very well; he is a very clever, pious, and charitable man," replied Harriet, "and, I am sure, a very sincere and good Christian. General Russell, to be sure, is rather a rough antagonist, and I can assure you, Sir, it was very distressing for me to behold Dr. Davison knocked about like a shuttlecock between two battledoors; still, I am certain of one thing, that no human influence made Emma become a Catholic, poor thing! and no one shall ever persuade me to the contrary."

"You little know the wiles of Jesuitism, Madam," said the Bishop warmly, as he dealt the cards.

"Take care, my love, or you will miss the deal," said Mrs. Boren.

"I hope, Miss Sefton," continued the Bishop, "their sophistry has not undermined your faith."

"No fear of that, my Lord," said Harriet, "for I do not think it matters much what opinions we hold, provided we live a good life. This I can assure your Lordship, that while Dr. Davison was speaking I was fully persuaded he was in the right; then, when Mr. Oswald was speaking, it seemed to me he was also in the right. How could I judge between them? so methought it was best not to trouble myself about it."

"Beware, Miss Sefton," replied the Bishop; "it is astonishing and most alarming, the incalculable damage done to the Church by the active fanaticism of those missionary Jesuits."

"Yes," lisped out Mrs. Boren; "they will not hesitate to commit any crime for the service of their cause."

"You are pleased to be complimentary, my good lady," exclaimed the General, who had, unperceived by her, at that moment entered the room; "if the poor Jesuits heard you, I fear you would make them proud; they are too apt to rejoice 'when they are counted worthy to suffer reproach for the name of Jesus.'"*

"La!" said Mrs. Boren. "I thought, Sir, you had gone to wish Mrs. Sefton good-night."

"And I have done so, Ma'am," said the General, "and she desires me to express her wishes that you and the Bishop will ask for whatever you want for yourselves and your family."

"I am sure we are infinitely obliged," said the lady.

"Point, quint, and quartorze!" exclaimed the Bishop, displaying his cards.

The clock struck eleven, and Harriet proposed to the

* Acts v. 41.

travellers to retire, as they might probably be fatigued with their journey.

The next morning the Bishop of S—— had an interview with Mrs. Sefton. He was not a little surprised at the calm and simple dignity with which she received him. The Bishop began in a mild manner to expostulate with her on the infatuation, as he called it, of plunging herself and family into an abyss of misery, and of forcing her worthy husband to flee from her presence, and from his own house.

"Ah! Sir," said Mrs. Sefton with great meekness, but with evident emotion, as the big tear started from her eye, "no one could feel the cruel pang more deeply than I do myself; yet the sufferings of this brief life, however acute, must weigh as a feather when placed in the balance with the interests of eternity."

"Do not deceive yourself," said the Bishop with a kind and soothing tone of voice; "may not the interests of eternity be sadly compromised by a wilful and obstinate disobedience to him, to whom you have bound yourself by your marriage vow?"

"My conscience," said Emma with meek firmness, "does not reproach me with disobedience in any one thing that a husband may command. God knows my heart, how ready I am at this moment to render him in a tenfold degree, all the love, respect, and obedience that I have hitherto rendered him, if he would only permit me to enjoy the liberty of conscience which he himself so loudly vindicates."

"Perhaps, my dear Madam," insinuated the Bishop in the same bland manner, "you may mistake the true nature of liberty of conscience; a licentiousness of thought and conduct is often cloaked under that name. You must be aware, that God himself cannot sanction in man the profession of error and superstition."

"That, Sir, is precisely the reason which determined me to renounce the errors of Protestantism, and to embrace the truth of Catholicism."

"Madam," replied the Bishop with some degree of warmth, "you misname things egregiously; what you call errors are pure Gospel truths ; what you deem truths, are the pernicious errors of Popery, rank idolatry, and frightful blasphemy ; such you would have found them, had you read your Bible with attention."

"I have read the Bible, Sir, and studied it to the best of my power, and the more I read, the more I am convinced of the truth of Catholicity."

"You ought not, my dear Madam," said the Bishop more soothingly, "to rely too much on your own judgment ; your too vivid imagination may too easily lead you astray. On such an important step, you ought to have listened to the voice of your legitimate pastors, who have been placed by the Holy Ghost to rule the Church of God."

"For that very reason," said Emma, smiling somewhat archly, "I applied to the legitimate pastors of that Church, which received the divine commission fifteen hundred years before the self-constituted pastors of Protestantism were heard of."

The Bishop seeing he had no chance of making any impression on her, rose to withdraw, and then Mrs. Sefton declared to him in the most formal terms, her firm and final determination to live and die a Catholic. The Bishop, fully convinced he could do no more, was secretly as much desirous of shortening the interview as herself. Mrs. Sefton then begged him to interpose his good offices with her husband, to induce him to a reconciliation, but he gave her little hopes of succeeding, and thus the meeting ended. After a hot luncheon, the whole episcopal suite were again in progress towards the North, to the no small relief of Harriet and the General.

This additional mortification retarded the convalescence of Emma, and her natural yearnings towards her children and daily anxiety about them she endured with resignation to the will of God as a Christian, but she could never feel them mitigated as a mother. She often and often tried to persuade Harriet to go and join her brother in Devonshire, and then she would add with a sigh, "perhaps I might suffer less about my babies if they were under your eye;" and Harriet would reply smiling, "You know, dearest Emma, I am not fond of children, but if you would only make haste and get well, I don't know what I might do to please you."

Harriet flattered herself, as people will flatter themselves through the medium of a little self-love, that if *she* could see her brother, she might have influence enough with him to induce him to consent to a reconciliation with his wife. In the meanwhile, Emma's health improved so much, that about the middle of March, she was able to be removed to Weetwood, to the great satisfaction of the General, who did all in his power to settle her there as comfortably and peaceably as the circumstances would permit; her mind, too, was much soothed and relieved by the kindness of Harriet, who, immediately on her removal, left Sefton Hall, and joined her brother and his little family at Eaglenest Cottage, in Devonshire.

CHAPTER XVI.

"What stronger breast-plate than a heart untainted?
Thrice is he armed that hath his quarrel just;
And he but naked, though locked up in steel,
Whose conscience with injustice is corrupted."
SHAKSPEARE.

The thread of our story obliges us now to follow the devious wanderings of Mr. Sefton, while we leave his afflicted and abandoned wife to pursue the even tenour of her life under the hospitable roof of Weetwood. There she offered up daily at the throne of mercy her fervent supplications for the welfare of her husband and of her children; many and many a time in the day and night would the ardent aspiration burst from her heart, that the Father of lights might in his mercy pour down on him and on them his first best gift, the knowledge of the truth; that they might with one heart and one mind worship together at the same altar, and live again in holy peace and happiness.

The arrival of Harriet at Eaglenest Cottage, caused Mr. Sefton many painful and conflicting emotions, for he had never seen her since his separation from his wife; and Harriet did not fail to speak her mind very freely to him on the entire disapprobation she felt of his conduct. However he might be sensible of the truth of his sister's remarks, his pride prevented him from acknowledging himself in the wrong; he became every day more and more unhappy. In the secret of his inmost heart, he wished to forgive Emma, but the thoughts that the world might attribute this lenity to weakness, and that his more rigid Protestant friends might not approve, chilled the justice of his better feelings. He sternly resolved not to forgive her; but this resolution, instead of bringing him peace as he had hoped, made him positively miserable, and had an evident effect in producing moroseness in his manners, and irritation in his temper. He loved Emma even passionately, and the yearnings of his affection towards her caused him frequently excessive mental anguish and regret; in vain he struggled with his feelings; the more he tried to persuade himself he was acting rightly, the more miserable he was; he could scarcely bear the sight of his children, and when the little prattlers named "Mamma," he would rush out of the house, and pace for hours along the sea-shore in the greatest agitation. One day he heard his friend the Bishop of S—— mention his intention of making a tour on the Continent, for the benefit of giving a travelling finish to his eldest son and daughter, the former a captain in the army, having obtained a few months' leave of absence. The idea suddenly struck Sefton, that it would be an excellent step for himself to make; that travelling would divert and improve his mind, and that his absence from England would be a still greater trial to Emma. Accordingly, a few days after he resolved to travel, and he promised the Bishop to meet him in the sunny garden of Europe ere the Autumn was over. Sefton persuaded Harriet to take charge of his babes, and in less than a fortnight from the time he had first thought on the subject, he was sailing on the 'sunny sea,' between Dover and Calais. True it is, that his heart was sunk in a profound melancholy, and that his conscience bitterly reproached him with abandoning his wife and family in that manner; but still the novelty of the scenes around him diverted his imagination in spite of himself. When he landed on the French shore, he was forcibly struck by the characteristic and national difference in the persons, manners, and dress of all around him. He stood gazing on the scenes that passed rapidly before him, in a sort of a dreaming philosophical study upon what might be the origin and cause of so striking a difference in the inhabitants of the Gallic and British shores, separated by so short a distance, until he was roused by the rueful face of his valet, who inquired if he would not like to go to the hotel. The poor valet had suffered from the sea, and seemed to think the most sensible and practical philosophy at that time would consist in the comfort to be drawn from a good basin of French soup. At the same moment Sefton was attacked by some half-dozen of dirty ragged French porters, all solicitous for the honour of his employment; some trying to attract his attention in one way, some in another; some stuffing cards into his hands, recommending the hotels by which they were employed, others declaring this way was the way Monsieur ought to go, and others that Monsieur ought to go the opposite way, or that Monsieur would be sure to be imposed upon and ill served. At length Luigi succeeded in obtaining something like silence, and in making his master understand that his luggage had already been conveyed to Dessin's Hotel. With some difficulty Sefton escaped from his zealous pursuers, and soon found himself in a quiet and elegant little apartment, with Monsieur Dessin before him making his best bow, and offering every imaginable kind of civility. Sefton ordered a late dinner, and having done so, soon after left the hotel, to explore the curiosities and peculiarities of Calais; he amused himself with walking in all directions for a couple of hours, and then began to think of retracing his steps to the inn. As he passed through one of the quaint and narrow streets, he observed a low and antique-looking building, the sounds of music issued from its opened door; Edward's curiosity was excited, and he entered. It was a church; the Blessed Sacrament was exposed on the high altar, incense was circling in clouds around it, and the last dying strains of the "Tantum Ergo" were falling from the lips of the assembled peasants. It was the first time Edward had been in a Catholic church: he was surprised to see the religion he so thoroughly hated and despised publicly professed and respected; and, in spite of his mingled sentiments of pride and dislike, he could not help being struck with the air of tender piety and respectful awe of all around him. When the religious rites were ended, he examined the church with curious eyes, and not a few mental aspirations of contempt at what he conceived superstitious objects; as he drew near the door, he observed a French female peasant about thirty, with a high Normandy cap and sunburnt cheeks, kneeling before an altar over which was placed an antique marble image of the Blessed Virgin and her Divine Son, upon which the rich golden rays of the setting sun were casting their last effulgent beams through one of the gothic windows at the top of the church. The peasant was teaching her little girl to join her hands in prayer before the image of Jesus and Mary. Edward approached them, and asked in a low voice what holiday it was.

"It is no holiday at all, Sir," answered the young woman, without raising her eyes.

"No holiday! then why is the church open?"

"In order that we may praise the good God, and pray to him."

"But what is all this ceremony I have just seen?"

"It is the evening benediction," said the peasant, raising her dark eyes to look at her interrogator, while a slight smile of pity, mingled with a little satire, dimpled round her lips as she added, "Monsieur must know that good Christians should pray to God on Mondays as well as on Sundays."

Edward felt a little confused; he knew not why; he bowed slightly to his new acquaintance, and hastily left the church.

"What a pity, Mamma," said the little French child to her mother, "that such a fine gentleman does not know his Catechism better!"

"Hush, my dear," replied the good countrywoman, "let us recommend him to our Lady," and they breathed a silent prayer to the mother of divine love for the salvation of the passing stranger.

When Edward reached his hotel, he found the dinner ready, and a blazing wood fire in the chimney; every thing was excellent, even elegant, but he felt an indescribable melancholy. Emma and he had often anticipated the pleasures of a short excursion to the Continent: Edward was now enjoying that pleasure, but Emma was not with him; and why was not the loved one with him? he stifled the thought without answering it; but memory was busy in recalling her gentle and lovely form, and imagination in suggesting what pleasure he should have had in the enjoyment of her bland and lively conversation. With an involuntary sigh he took up the last French papers and seated himself by the fire. It was a time of great public interest in France, being early in the spring of 1830, when every thing was ripening for the approaching crisis. Edward determined to observe the progress of events, but not to mingle in politics, a resolution more easily made than easily kept by one of his ardent character and temperament; happy for him if he had adhered to this prudent resolve, "car les occasions ne nous rendent pas fragiles, mais elles font voir combien nous le sommes." The Church clock struck eleven; Sefton took his candle, and, ordering Luigi to call him at seven o'clock, he retired to rest. Very early the following morning he was roused by the ringing of bells and the hum of busy voices, and, opening the window-shutter, was surprised to see that though it was still dusk, the street was thronged with people. He tried to sleep again, but could not, and, in the vexation of his spirit muttered to himself, "If such a nuisance existed in England, it would soon be indicted." At length Luigi appeared, and his master called out in no very patient voice to know what holiday it was which occasioned such an early noise and bustle amongst the inhabitants?

"It is no holiday, Sir," answered Luigi; "the bells are only ringing for the first masses."

"What stuff, what nonsense, what humbug!" exclaimed Edward indignantly.

"But, Sir, the poor people like to hear mass before they go to their day's work," expostulated Luigi.

"Pshaw! stuff and nonsense! bring some hot water,

and get ready to start for Paris immediately; I have had quite enough of this vile place."

Luigi was an Italian and a Catholic, and he could not help giving a slight, a very slight shrug of his shoulder at his master's burst of indignation against the good practice of hearing mass in the morning; however, he said nothing, but quietly withdrew, to execute the orders he had just received.

Mr. Sefton had no idea that his valet was a Catholic; he had desired one of his fashionable London acquaintances to recommend him a good travelling servant, and had forgotten to inquire about the religious part of his character: so much for consistency. In a few more hours, he was travelling as fast as four French horses would canter on the road to Paris.

Soon after Mr. Sefton's arrival in the gay metropolis, whither he journeyed to drown his own reflections, he settled himself in a comfortable and elegant lodging in the Rue de la Paix, and the day after, delivered the letters of introduction which he had brought for several French and English families of distinction. Amongst these letters there was one for a Monsieur La Harpe, an eminent literary character, and a relation of the celebrated La Harpe, who figured in the Revolution of 1792, and afterwards atoned for his fanaticism and his errors to the best of his power by his exertions in the cause of religion and literature. With the gentleman to whom he presented his letter, Edward soon formed a considerable intimacy, and many of their mornings were spent together. Monsieur La Harpe accompanied him to the churches and institutions the best worth seeing in Paris, to St. Denis, and to Père La Chaise; still there was such a total dissimilarity in their opinions and sentiments on religion and politics, that it prevented their acquaintance ripening into the more congenial feelings of friendship. La Harpe was strongly in favour of the reigning sovereign, and he trembled for the fate of religion and his country in the political and infidel ferment which he knew to be silently but surely working for its destruction. Sefton laughed at his apprehensions, and spared not the most bitter sarcasms against those who wished to maintain what he conceived an erroneous system of religion: he was by principle a royalist, and abhorred the idea of a revolution, unless it could be effected quietly, and solely for the subversion of despotism and bigotry.

Monsieur La Harpe was also frequently piqued and annoyed with the unsparing and even harsh manner in which Mr. Sefton criticised and abused every thing relative to the Catholic religion; he was astonished, too, at his gross ignorance of the customs, rites, and history of that religion, which, nevertheless, he seemed to have such a peculiar zest in maligning. At first La Harpe endeavoured to explain things to him, and then Edward proceeded from objections to sheer abuse, which very much disgusted his new acquaintance, and thus their intercourse gradually became less frequent; not, however, without the secret regret of Edward, who, notwithstanding his errors and prejudices, had a great and natural admiration for talent wherever he met with it. To drown recollection, Sefton next tried gaiety, and plunged into the dissipations of the highest circles, and all the heartless trifling of what is especially styled the "beau monde;" he sedulously frequented assemblies, dinners, routs, and theatres; but a few weeks of this life soon disgusted him: neither had the round of senseless gaiety in which he indulged power to touch his heart or interest his understanding; he felt a void and weariness in every thing; and the importuning thoughts which beset his memory with redoubled force became each day more vivid and more difficult to banish. He resolved to try literature: he frequented all the libraries, museums, and lectures, of any note, either public or private; but when the first ardour of pursuit was over, and the pleasure of novelty had ceased, he felt that he was more unhappy than ever, and further from the peace of mind and repose of heart which he so much coveted, and which he had once enjoyed, but which he now had lost, it seemed to him, for ever. "And why have I lost this treasure?" he would sometimes say to himself; "and why do I now find no interest in any thing?" He did not dare to seek for the answer, though he knew that it lay in his inmost soul; for, as often as he turned his mental eye inwards, he was startled with the image of his injured, persecuted, and deserted wife. He strove in vain to banish the accusing thought; but, night and day, it ever haunted him, and embittered every hour of his life.

CHAPTER XVII.

"The march of intellect! What know we now
Of moral, or of thought and sentiment,
Which was not known two thousand years ago?
It is an empty boast, a vain conceit
Of folly, ignorance, and base intent."

EGERTON BRYDGES.

ONE day, as Sefton was passing along the boulevards, he accidently met with an old acquaintance; this was a young man of the name of Le Sage, the son of a French emigré, who had been born and educated in England. Edward had known him at Cambridge. They had not met for twelve years; Le Sage was delighted to see again his old friend, and welcomed him with all the animated warmth of the French character.

"Ah! Sefton!" exclaimed he, "and can it be you! thrice welcome to Paris and to my roof."

Sefton thanked him for his kindness; but a forced smile, belying the melancholy of his brow, betrayed to the quick eye of his friend some secret sorrow that lay rankling at his heart. Le Sage perceived it, but prudently forebore to probe it too deeply, lest he might irritate it the more. He only asked Sefton if he had come alone.

"Quite alone," replied Edward rather shortly.

"I hope nothing has occurred to render my friend unhappy?" inquired Le Sage in a tone of interest.

Sefton gave no answer, but sighed deeply.

"My dear Sefton," continued Le Sage, "unburthen at once the sorrow of your heart into the bosom of a faithful friend, who would willingly bear a portion of your grief, and do any thing in his power to serve you."

Sefton became still more agitated.

"Alas! perhaps cruel fate has robbed you of some dear object of your affections?"

Sefton almost groaned.

"Come, cheer up, my friend; we cannot reverse the decrees of fate; death is only an eternal repose, and your poor wife—"

"Is not dead," exclaimed Sefton with vehemence; "would to God she had died before she brought disgrace upon herself, and misery on me and my family!"

"Oh! oh!" replied Le Sage with a sarcastic smile, "I understand you; so your once, no doubt, incomparable wife, has proved herself as frail as any other fair one."

Sefton's countenance burned with an honest blush: he was conscious that his own unguarded expression had cast an unmerited stain on Emma's name; he bit his lip, he vainly tried to suppress his indignation, his eye kindled and flashed with emotion, his irritated feelings burst through all control.

"My God!" exclaimed he, "what have you dared to insinuate! you wrong her, Sir, you wrong her grossly; the withering breath of scandal has never tarnished her spotless name, and never shall, with impunity, in my presence."

"Heavens and earth! my dear Sefton," said Le Sage, quite astonished at his agitation; "pardon me, I pray, if, unintentionally, I have caused you any pain; I can assure you I meant no offence. If I have offended by a rash suspicion, it was yourself who led me into error; you spoke of disgrace and misery on yourself and family; what else could I infer?"

"Any thing but that dreadful suspicion."

"Sefton, be calm; tell me the extent of your misfortune, for I am quite bewildered."

Sefton's indignation now turned against himself; he blushed more intensely at his own hasty expression. "To cut short every other suspicion," said he more calmly, "she is become a Papist."

Le Sage could with difficulty prevent himself from laughing; but, seeing the emotions of his friend, he tried to soothe him.

"Come, come, Sefton, lay aside this morbid humour; banish melancholy; if this be the only cause of your grief, all will soon be well. A short run in Paris will soon inspire you with wiser notions. We manage these matters much better in France; we allow our wives and daughters to amuse themselves with these bagatelles just as they please; they must have something to occupy their busy imaginations, and we do not find them less dutiful or less amiable because they are more devout. Why you know that I was born a Papist, and am generally esteemed one now."

"Yes," replied Sefton, "I know you are nominally a Papist, because such is the predominant sect of your country; but thanks to your English education, you have imbibed more rational ideas; you can neither believe nor practise the vile superstitions of that abominable system."

"You would hardly believe it, Sefton, yet I actually went to mass almost every day as long as my poor mother lived: a more kind, a more indulgent mother, no child ever had. But while she, poor dear soul, was fumbling her beads, and mumbling her aves, I stood behind her, paying my fervent devotions to the more visible deities of flesh and blood, which flitted by me in all the bloom of youth and loveliness. Since her death, I do not think I have seen the interior of a church; in fact, no man of sense goes to church now-a-days."

Sefton felt an internal disgust at the light manner with which Le Sage treated religion; but regarding it as the natural result of Popery, and feeling thereby doubly proud of the superior purity of his own religion, he observed that it was but natural that he should have acted thus, for, continued he, "I am not in the least surprised that a man of your sound sense, and blessed with the advantages of an English education, should be ill satisfied with the empty forms of your national church, but I think you might have found some rational consolation for your soul in the more solid service of the Protestant temple."

"Bah! bah!" exclaimed Le Sage; "how little do you understand the activity of the French mind! No sooner do we take leave of Notre Dame, than we seek refuge in the temple of reason and universal philanthropy. No half-way house can for a moment detain us in our ardent career. In one word, Sefton, we see intuitively the final conclusions of your admirable principles; for, to do you justice, we cannot but allow that the true principles of philosophy—independence of thought, and freedom from the trammels of authority, passed from Britain into France; but you on your part must acknowledge, that in regenerated France they have produced the most abundant fruits."

Sefton did not feel flattered at this compliment, and observed drily, "The best things may be abused when carried to excess; even good itself in that way may be perverted into evil. Still I cannot see how, from any English principle, you can deduce French infidelity."

"Nothing more logical," replied Le Sage. "You maintain that it is the unalienable right of man, to hold and express his own free opinions on all religious and political subjects: nay more, you assert that no man can believe what he does not understand; on these principles you very justly protest against *a few* of the obsolete dogmas of Catholicity; we protest against them *all*. Thus we are more consistent and more perfect Protestants than yourself; so that if the orthodoxy of Protestantism is to be measured by the extent of protestation, we are the most orthodox Protestants on the face of the earth."

Edward was thunderstruck at hearing such language from his friend,—at finding infidelity ascribed as the natural consequence of Protestant principles: he found himself unprepared to refute the reasons of Le Sage. What he had just heard surprised him the more, as he had known him in his younger days rather piously inclined, and, as he then thought, too much attached in secret to Catholic superstitions; and far too scrupulous in declining to conform to the Protestant practices of devotion. In fact, Le Sage had received a pious education from his religious parents; but after his return to France, he had fallen into the company of the gay, vicious, corrupted youth of Paris; he was soon whirled away in the vortex of reckless dissipation; his conscience for a while reproached him; his faith held out to him the prospect of a miserable eternity, and haunted him in the midst of his pleasures with continued terrors. He could bear the conflict no longer, and sought every means to free himself from this intolerable burden. Reasoning from some of those plausible principles which by dint of repetition he had imbibed at Cambridge, but without questioning the soundness of them, he drew all the consequences of the French sophists; "he made shipwreck of the faith," and soon persuaded himself that Revelation was a fable, as repugnant to human reason as subversive of the noble passions which the Creator had implanted in the nature of man.

When Sefton had a little recovered from his astonishment, he asked Le Sage, if he had really become a deist.

"Deist or atheist, call me what you will. I regard such appellations merely as the frothy but harmless venom of expiring bigotry. I am ambitious only of the name of philosopher; but come, I must shew you the lions of Paris. You have been rusticating too long in your northern clime: you are literally an age behind the world in your ideas. To-morrow you shall dine with me at a select party, *l'élite de la jeune France.*"

"I am much obliged to you, I am sure," said Sefton, "you do me too much honour."

"Not in the least, my good friend," said Le Sage; "our dinner hour is seven: give me your address, and I will call for you; for the present I must wish you good morning, as I have an engagement at our club."

The two friends separated, and Sefton strolled on in melancholy mood, reflecting deeply on what he had heard, and seeking in vain for reasonable refutations of the strange system of Le Sage. Since his residence in

Paris he had involuntarily heard many explanations and observations on the Catholic religion, which had sometimes raised a passing thought, whether that system had not more claims to be the religion founded by Christ than Protestantism. True it is, that these intrusive thoughts were generally rejected with disdain; but there were moments when the bare idea that Protestantism might not perhaps be the true religion caused him intense mental irritation, and never before had he felt that pang more acutely; surely, thought he, if the principles of Protestantism lead to deism, as they seem to have done in France, there must be something rotten at the core; he rejected, however, this idea with as much horror as he would have rejected a temptation to commit any dreadful crime. It was too humiliating to think that his private judgment could have erred so egregiously in a matter of such vital moment; it was too galling to self-conceit to think for a moment that the religion for which he had sacrificed so much that was dear to his heart, might have been the work of Satan and not of God; he therefore concluded that the infidelity of France must somehow or other be more connected with Catholicity than with genuine Protestantism, although he could not yet discover the connection; consequently, he therefore hated and despised the Catholic faith more than ever, and did all in his power to thicken the mist of prejudice in which his understanding had so long been enveloped. The evening of the day on which Sefton renewed his acquaintance with Le Sage he retired to rest harassed with doubts and difficulties which he was unable to resolve; nor could all his efforts to combat or banish the subject of his uneasy doubts procure him one hour of the rest and tranquillity he sought. The following day, as the hour of dinner approached, Le Sage drove to Sefton's lodging and took him in his cabriolet to the hotel, which was the place of rendezvous for the dinner to which he had invited him. The hotel was magnificent, and the saloon into which Sefton was conducted by his friend was furnished in the most fashionable and luxurious style: there they found assembled about forty or fifty young men between the ages of fifteen and twenty-five, and three or four others of more mature age, who seemed to exercise a sort of tacit superiority over the rest. They were all dressed in the most exquisite fashion, and the whole place and company breathed luxury and novelty. Soon after the usual compliments and introductions had passed the dinner was announced, and the company were soon seated in the dining-room at a splendid banquet, consisting of every luxury and delicacy of the season, prepared under the inspection of the first *artiste* in Paris. Sefton was placed at the right hand of the president, and received the most flattering attentions from all around him. Several toasts were given and drunk with the greatest enthusiasm: "*Vive la jeune France*," "*Vive la Patrie*," "*A bas la Calotte, à bas la tyrannie.*" As the wines circulated, the conversation became more animated; they talked of the wonderful progress of civilization, and of the high destinies towards which the European nations were rapidly advancing. Sefton listened with conscious pride and the most pleasing satisfaction to the high encomiums which were passed on the free institutions of England, the liberty of the press, and the freedom of thought and speech which that favoured people enjoyed; and ardent were the aspirations and fervent were the vows that young France would soon equal or surpass her. With animated eloquence Sefton's new friends explained to him that France indeed was at present under a cloud, a hateful dynasty having been forced upon her by the bayonets of foreign nations; but that they were all hope and confidence that the sun of liberty would again break forth. Some late measures of the ministry were severely criticised, unsparingly condemned, and denounced as perfidious, and as tending to the suppression of public opinion, and to the enslavement of the press. Sefton expressed a little dissent of opinion on this, but they maintained that every thing that had been done for the last fifteen years, proved demonstratively a plan for the gradual restoration of ancient despotism and bigotry. These liberal sentiments met with a warm response from the heart and lips of Sefton, although once or twice his high notions of loyalty were not a little startled at the vulgar abuse, low murmurs, and loud menaces, which were poured out on the devoted head of Charles Dix. However, he soon became reconciled to this unceremonious warmth of expression, when they had convinced him, that the hoary monarch was a mere tool of the *partie-prêtre;* a very puppet in the hands of an ambitious and intriguing priesthood; that Charles himself had actually taken orders, and said mass every morning privately in his cabinet. In proof of the fact, or at least of the public opinion, some five-franc pieces were handed about, on which the *calotte* had been ingeniously stamped on the head of the king. Nay, the president gravely assured Sefton, that Charles X. was a Jesuit in disguise, *à robe courte*. Sefton's blood was fired at these discoveries; and he no longer hesitated to pronounce, that it was a holy cause to conspire against such superstition and tyranny. He was assured that there was not a generous young heart in France that did not ardently long for the moment to shake off this intolerable yolk; and that a favourable occasion of manifesting themselves could not be far distant. The party at length broke up, and Sefton received pressing invitations to the houses of the most distinguished leaders of the *soi-disant* liberals; he became deeply interested and involved in their machinations, more from ignorance of the fatal consequences of their schemes and principles than from malice of heart. In all revolutions, the most abandoned, wicked, and idle characters, are ever the most ready to join; they have nothing to lose, and their want of religion and good principle, make them totally regardless of the real happiness of their fellow-men. With some of the most worthless and desperate of these characters did Edward connect himself; but many amongst his new associates found he had too much belief in Revelation for their purposes, and therefore they endeavoured, not unsuccessfully, alas! to undermine his belief in Christianity. Edward sedulously frequented the saloons and clubs, and there he met with infidels: he heard their blasphemies against Christ and his religion; he was horror-struck, and he attempted to refute them on Protestant principles; his companions laughed at him, and shewed him that Protestant principles lead logically to deism. He appealed to his Bible, to prove the Trinity and Incarnation; the deists pointed out to him the texts by which Catholics prove the real presence; these he rejected, because he did not comprehend the mystery; because the testimony of his senses deposed against it: his deistical companions then pointed out to him, that the three in one, and one in three, is a greater mystery, and more contradictory to the senses; that a God suffering and dying was as absurd as any fable of ancient mythology; they fearlessly asserted, indeed, that the very idea of Revelation is absurd; the great Author of the universe having endowed man with free will to act, and having given him reason for his guide, there can be no need of any other rule of conduct. It was in vain that Sefton observed, that reason itself dictates to us the justice and obligation of submitting our judgment and will to the supreme reason and will of our Creator. They urged the absurdity of supposing God to have given reason to man for his guide and then to have given him Revelation for a guide which destroyed the former one. Sefton replied, that the second and more perfect guide does not destroy the first, but perfects it; for by original sin the human understanding was darkened, and free will impaired, and that therefore Revelation was necessary to enlighten the one, and fortify the other. Original sin! replied the deists, sneeringly, bah! a shallow invention of the dark ages; the understanding darkened! Why, witness the noble efforts it has exerted in these later ages! What does the genius of Newton and La Place owe to Revelation? and yet what sublime mysteries of nature have they not opened to our wondering eyes! What has taught the modern chemists to unravel the most hidden secrets of nature? The unshackled reason of man. This it is which has taught him to subdue the elements, and make them subservient to his use or amusement; to impel the rapid steam-boat through the stormy ocean, as to employ the same wondrous power in spinning the finest gossamer. Look at these stupendous triumphs of the human mind, and on a thousand others, and then say which of all these Revelation imparted to us.

The human mind has, indeed, been too long benighted, but it was the night of ignorance and superstition; knowledge, at length, shone forth, and knowledge has imparted power. Sefton was not prepared to answer these arguments. It did not occur to his mind that all the glorious discoveries of modern science do not extend beyond the limits of the material world, nor advance one step into the spiritual world. They disclose no new ray of the divinity; they teach us nothing of our origin, nothing of the ultimate term of our creation; they teach us nothing of the spirituality and immortality of the human soul; they explain not the war of passions in the human breast, and afford no aid to regulate or subdue them. Striking facts had been instanced, which could not be denied, and Sefton was too enthusiastic an admirer of the progress of science to venture a reply. His mind was confounded, and his faith, which rested on his own reason, tottered to the ground. He revolved, in his own mind, various texts of his Bible, which hitherto had appeared to him sufficiently clear on the foundation of Christianity, the original fall of man, *et cetera;* they now seemed to him obscure, ambiguous, and inconclusive. He would still have hesitated to acknowledge himself a Deist; but if he had dared to examine his interior sentiments, he would have found that he was nothing better; hence, he no longer refused to associate with the impious, and to join in all their orgies, profane and political; he involved himself deeply in the plots of the revolution, which shortly after exploded; he took up arms against the reigning dynasty, and distinguished himself during the three *glorious* days by his rashness and by his violence; he felt a sense of desperation about him, and he fought recklessly. Towards the end of the third day he received a sabre slash on the left arm, and a musket shot passed through his right shoulder, while in the thickest of the fray on the Boulevard. He fell to the ground, and was soon trampled on, and nearly stifled by heaps of dead and dying; his wounds bled profusely; he felt a sense of hopeless feebleness creep over him; the roar and tumult around him seemed gradually to fade away from his hearing and sight, and, in a few minutes, Edward Sefton was as stiff, and cold, and insensible to all around him, as were the green trees that rejoiced in the bright sun above him to the carnage, fury, rage, and passions of the poor human beings who fought so wildly and so desperately under their calm, cool shade.

CHAPTER XVIII.

Oh! when will the ages of faith e'er return,
  To gladden the nations again?
Oh! when shall the flame of sweet Charity burn,
  To warm the cold bosoms of men?

When the angel of vengeance hath sheathed his sword,
  And his vials have drenched the land;
When the pride of the sophist hath bent to the Lord,
  And trembled beneath his strong hand.

FRAGMENT.

How oft have the enemies of faith torn the bosom of France! How oft have the unbelievers and the impious united to crush the Catholic religion, and to annihilate the churches and the altars of Jesus crucified! The pride of the sophist cannot understand, and will not bow to the humility of the Cross; still, amidst these bitter blasts, Providence has yet protected the scattered and humble followers of the Man-God; and, like the lowly and sweet-scented violet, they have still, unheeded and unperceived, contrived to cast around the odour of their good works, and of their heroic endurance, and of their unshaken belief. Hope whispers, that the spark of divine faith, which has been almost hidden so long, will one day yet burst forth into a glorious and universal blaze, which will scare the infidel and the profane from the land, and leave religion once more in possession of France, to receive to her tender bosom her erring and misled children; to point out to them the path of happiness, and to

"Bind the heart long broke with weeping."

For several days after the tumult, which occurred in Paris at the end of July, was over, Edward's servant

Luigi continued to make indefatigable inquiries after his master, but all in vain ; from no one could he obtain the slightest intelligence about him, excepting that he had been seen in the contest. At length Luigi came to the conclusion that Mr. Sefton must either have perished in the general slaughter, or have left Paris, and that he had probably returned to England. In either case, the good valet thought he could not do better than to take his place in the diligence, and return as soon as possible to London. There, again, his inquiries were vain. He then hastened to Eaglenest Cottage to inquire for his master there, and not finding him at his own house, he told Miss Sefton all he knew about her brother, which very much frightened and agitated her. She lost no time in sending an express to Weetwood, thinking he might have gone there on the excitement of the moment, if by chance he had escaped destruction. But he was not at Weetwood. It is impossible to describe the terror and anguish of Emma, or the anxiety of the General. Poor Emma! she knew not but that she might be at that moment a widow, and every grief and every sorrow bled afresh. . . . And where was Edward? Edward was in an hospital in the heart of Paris, whither he had been carried along with the rest of the wounded; and there he lay gasping between life and death, surrounded by the sick and dying, some of whom uttered the most horrible imprecations and shrieks of despair. His bodily sufferings were intense, but his mental agony and horror were a thousand times more acute and intolerable. When he recovered from his swoon, after his removal to the hospital, his first effort was with much difficulty to feel for a small miniature of Emma, set in rubies, which he always wore round his neck—it was gone; his watch and his ring, her gifts, also were gone. "O my God!" exclaimed he bitterly, "I have deserved this!" He inquired in vain for them of the attendants round his poor pallet; they only smiled, and sarcastically observed that these trinkets no doubt were in safe keeping. Remonstrance was in vain, nor had he time to think on the subject, for he heard the young medical students observe to one another, that it was a thousand to one whether he would recover or not. Death was before his eyes; the remembrance of his wife and children pierced his heart to the very quick; he would have given worlds to have had his injured Emma by his side in that moment of bereavement; the thoughts of the injustice he had offered to her conscience by denying her that liberty which every Protestant claims to himself, and by causing her the grief and sufferings he had done, were daggers to his very soul. How different do we see things in the hour of death to what we do in health, and in the ordinary routine of daily life: those only who have experienced this can know and feel how strikingly true it is. Sefton continued hoping for several days that some of his new associates would come to see him, but they came not; not even Le Sage, though an old friend, made his appearance. Surely, thought Edward, our old intimacy, so lately renewed with every expression of eternal attachment, ought to have taught him some compassion for one who is suffering on his account, in a common hospital, in a strange country, and far removed from any dearer connection. Were all his assurances unmeaning, hollow, deceitful? Alas! what avails us the friendship of this world, if we are deprived of it in the hour of our greatest distress? Perhaps Le Sage himself has perished! cut off in his infidelity, with all his sins upon his head! Oh! it is horrible to think upon. And I also doomed to share the same fate! God have mercy on my poor soul! In the meantime Sefton got worse; the thought of God and eternity haunted his mind, but he could not feel the consolations of faith, for he no longer believed. He wished to believe, but he could not; he knew not what to believe; his anguish became extreme. He entreated those around him to give him a Bible—but the infidels had their emissaries even there, and instead of a Bible they put into his hands the impious and ribald comments of Voltaire on the sacred text. . . . He reads, and his horrors increase. O God! he knows not which way to turn his terror-sticken heart; he sees no ray of comfort or hope, either for this world or the next . . . . his tortured and weakened frame sinks under the intense agony of mental anguish; despair seizes him, and in a few hours more he is in the wild phrenzy of a dreadful delirium. For many long days and tedious nights he hung between life and death, insensible to all external impressions, and his soul and brain racked with remorse, and with appalling and hideous ravings of God, His awful judgments, and of a never-ending eternity of endless and unutterable woes. . . . At length the God of all mercy had compassion on His poor, suffering creature. The physicians consulted, and administered a powerful opiate to produce a crisis of sleep, which for fifteen days had not closed his wearied eye-lids; it was a desperate remedy, which would either kill or cure. Ten minutes after he had taken it, he closed his lurid and raving eye, and his throbbing and beating brow sunk calm and tranquil on the pillow. Poor Edward! he slept in peace and balmy tranquillity for several hours. When he awoke the fever had left him; he gazed around him with a vacant eye, as if trying to recollect where he was; he saw that he was in a small but neat white-washed room; the partitions which formed the walls did not reach to the ceiling nor to the bottom. There was a window opposite to his bed, the casement of which was open, and the freshness of the morning air circulated through the little apartment; seated near the window there was a slightly-formed female figure, dressed in a religious habit, with a crucifix fastened to her girdle; the folds of her black gauze veil concealed her countenance as she leaned over a book on her knees, which she was intently perusing. Edward endeavoured to raise himself in his bed, but he found he could not move; the unnatural strength produced by fever had left him, and he was weak and helpless as an infant. The rustling he made in attempting to move, caused the Sister of Charity, for such she was, to turn her face towards him; she was of a fair and delicate complexion, with large, expressive blue eyes, lit up by a touching and sublime tinge of feeling and devotion, but shaded and tempered by the modesty of their long dark lashes. She rose and advanced quietly towards the bed.

"Do you feel yourself a little better now?" said she, in a compassionate and soothing tone.

"Where am I?" exclaimed Edward, still more bewildered at hearing himself addressed in his mother-tongue.

"You are with those who will take care of you, and will not suffer you to be neglected nor abandoned," said Sister Angela, in accents of kindness; "but you have been ill, very ill, and we must thank God that the fatal crisis is past."

She knelt down by the bed-side, and uttered aloud a fervent prayer of thanksgiving to God and the Blessed Virgin for the amelioration which had taken place. Edward joined in it with all his heart, and as the sister rose from her knees, he looked fixedly and earnestly in her face, and said, "Give me, I entreat you, something to drink."

There was a jug of barley-water on the little table by the bed, and she began to pour some of it into a glass.

"Give me the jug," said Edward, in a languid voice.

Sister Angela approached it to his lips, and called at the same time to a person, who then appeared at one of the open divisions at the bottom of the room; this was a stout-looking lay sister, somewhat advanced in years, with a most benevolent countenance. At a sign from Sister Angela, she quietly raised Edward's head, so that he could drink conveniently; he emptied the jug at one draught, and then instantly sunk back into another profound slumber. He dreamt of peace and domestic happiness: he thought he was in his own beautiful woods at Sefton, and that Emma was giving him to drink, water from the coolest fountains, and that his little ones were gathering him grapes and fruits. During the height of his delirium, Edward had been removed to the fever ward of the same hospital, for his frantic ravings disturbed those who were recovering from their wounds. The fever ward was more especially under the care of the Sisters of Charity, and the greatest attention, both to soul and body, was paid to the patients under their care, by these admirable and heroic females. Under the direction of such compassionate and skilful nurses, Edward's convalescence continued to make favourable progress, and in the course of a week, he was able to sit up a little in his bed, and the wound in the left arm was nearly healed. During this week, he had gradually recovered the recollection of all that had occurred to him before his delirium began. As he regained strength, Sister Angela observed that he seemed daily to become more uneasy in his mind; he often sighed deeply, and would sometimes put wild and incoherent questions to her about religion, and the belief in Revelation; frequently, too, when he was slumbering, he uttered the name of Emma, and called upon his children. Sister Angela was an English lady of good family, who had very young embraced a religious life, and dedicated herself to the service of Jesus crucified, in serving His sick members. She had been sent by her superiors, on some business, to Paris, and while serving in the hospital there, heard that there was then in it an Englishman, severely wounded and dying; she was sent to visit him, as in his ravings he spoke nothing but English, and the attendants on the wounded gladly accepted her proposal, to take the charge of nursing him in the fever ward. This was all she knew of Edward's history, but she by degrees endeavoured to gain his confidence, in hopes of being able to alleviate the weight of woe, which seemed to press on his heart. She so far succeeded, that ere a fortnight had elapsed, he had related to her his whole story. She soothed and comforted him, and raised his hopes that brighter days were yet in store for him, telling him, that now that he had experienced a little of the horrors of infidelity, he would more readily turn with true repentance to his God. He half promised to examine carefully the Catholic religion, and to write to Emma. Though Sister Angela perceived that whenever she pressed these subjects a little, there was a fierce working of passions still in his breast, yet she continued, with firm and undaunted charity, to urge him to write kindly to his wife.

"If you will write a few affectionate lines," said she, "I will narrate to her, in a postscript, how ill you have been, and how well your convalescence is going on; you will feel much more peace in your mind when you have done so."

"Well, I will do so then," said Edward, still half hesitating; "but will not Emma think it odd to hear from you?"

"Oh! no," answered Sister Angela, smiling, as she placed the writing materials on his bed: "your good and excellent wife will require no apology for an act of Christian charity, and I promise you I will say nothing about the events which brought you here—you shall read what I write."

"Oh! no, no," replied Edward, half ashamed—"I am quite satisfied, I assure you."

The letter was written, and it was a very affectionate one, and it expressed that his sentiments towards Catholics, individually, were much changed. There was enough in it to console Emma greatly, in the state of anxious agony and bereavement in which she was; but there was not enough to give her any hopes that his prejudices towards the Catholic religion itself were in any material degree changed. Sister Angela added her postscript, and then prepared to take the letter to the post.

"I do feel certainly much relieved," said Edward, as he gave it into her hand. "Poor Emma! I have often been sorry I wrote that last harsh letter to her."

"You have done what you can, now, to atone for any little unkindness you may have expressed to her before," said Sister Angela; "and I think that you will ere long give her more solid subject for consolation: therefore, remain in peace, and trust in God."

"Oh! no; I shall never be a Catholic," said he, with an incredulous smile, "if that is what you mean."

"You think so now, no doubt," replied Sister Angela; "but make no rash resolutions. The hand of

God is not shortened, and I cannot persuade myself that he has delivered you so miraculously from the most imminent death unless he had other graces in store for you. All I ask of you is, not to resist these graces, and then I fear not the result."

Sefton was touched with this observation, and replied, with great emotion, "I trust I shall be ever more faithful to the calls of my God."

"I ask no more from you at present."

"How good God has been," said Sefton, with a sigh, "to deliver me from this abyss of misery; how little I have deserved it! How can I ever requite it?"

"I think," said the nun, "there is one to whom, under God, you are most indebted for this mercy."

"To whom?" asked Sefton eagerly.

"To your wife; to whose pious prayers and tears God has lent a willing ear."

Sefton hid his face for confusion beneath the clothes, and sobbed audibly. After a few minutes, he again raised his countenance, bathed in tears; but Sister Angela had already left the room, and Edward could only say to himself, "I would give a great deal to have the calm conscience and the peace of mind of that truly angelic being." He turned round to arrange his pillows, and, in so doing, he observed that his nurse had inadvertently left on the table near him, a little black book, in which she often read for a long time. He had frequently wished to know what this book was, but his respect for her had prevented him asking her. He eagerly took it up: it was "The Imitation of Christ." Edward had never before seen it; he opened it with avidity, and his astonishment increased as he read, and felt the unction of that precious book penetrate his soul.

"Can you lend me this beautiful little book?" said he to Sister Angela, as soon as she returned in the evening to put things in order for him, before she went to her convent for the night.

"Certainly, if you wish it," answered she; "it is a wonderful little book, and contains most sublime lessons of Christian perfection, and profound sentiments of true philosophy."

"May I ask, Sister Angela, what is that large book I have seen you sometimes read, when you have done what is to be done so kindly in the room, and think I am going to sleep?"

"Oh, that is my office book," said she gaily.

"What is an office book?"

"It is composed of the book of Psalms and select lessons from the holy Scripture, with several hymns and prayers: these we religious have to say daily; all the clergy have an obligation of saying it also."

"Really!" said Edward, "I did not think Catholics had so much to do with the Bible."

Sister Angela laughed; she and the lay sister, Sœur Clotilde, were dressing the gun-shot wound in his shoulder, or perhaps Edward might have laughed also.

"Well," added he, when they had finished, "you Catholics do certainly say a great many prayers, and take a great deal of pains to get to Heaven; but do you not feel that the life you have chosen is a very hard one?"

"Oh! no, no," answered she with enthusiasm; "I find no hardships in it; the love of God sweetens every thing; and besides," added she, crossing her hands gracefully over her breast, "I have a peace and joy here, which the world can neither give nor take away."

Edward looked touched, and Sister Angela and her companion, wishing him kindly good evening, left him in the care of the person appointed to watch during the night, and returned to their convent.

CHAPTER XIX.

"There are more things in heaven and earth, Horatio,
Than e'er were dreamt of in thy philosophy."
SHAKSPEARE.

ONE day, while Edward's convalescence was making its tedious progress, the governor of the hospital came into his room, and told him there was a tall, elderly gentleman, with an order, of the name of La Harpe, who wished to speak to him. Edward desired he might be admitted. When La Harpe saw him, he was so struck with the ravages sickness had made in his appearance, that he could not help testifying his surprise by an involuntary start. Edward held out his hand to him. "This is kind in you, very kind," said he, "to come and see the poor wounded man; it is more than I have deserved from you, Monsieur La Harpe," added he, with evident emotion.

"Oh, I should have been with you long ago, could I but have found you. I have sought you, and inquired after you in so many places," answered La Harpe; "and now that I have the happiness of finding you alive, before I hear your story, I must discharge my conscience of a trust which has been reposed in it."

Saying this, he drew from his breast a small packet, and placed it in Edward's hand; "That," said he, "is your property, or I am much mistaken; you once shewed it to me in happier days."

"O my God!" exclaimed Edward—"it is the lost miniature of my beloved Emma;" and he kissed it rapturously, and pressed it to his heart. "I never thought

I should have seen it again: and the rubies, too, are all untouched! But how could it possibly have fallen into your hands?"

"You must ask no questions," said his friend. "I can only tell this much: it was given to me by a poor missionary priest, who knew I was acquainted with you; he received it, in confession, from a person since dead of his wounds, who was deeply implicated in the late commotion."

"If restitution of ill-gotten goods is a fruit of confession, I am sure I feel the benefit of it at present," said Edward, smiling.

"No Catholic priest can grant absolution to his penitent without such restitution," answered Monsieur La Harpe: "but tell me now all that has happened to you since we parted."

Edward then detailed all his miseries and adventures, touching, however, as lightly as he could upon his connection with his deistical friends, and not failing to abuse them most vehemently for having at such a time completely abandoned him. "If it had not been for that angel, the Sister of Charity," added he, "God knows I should have been laid low enough by this time."

"What could you expect from infidels?" said La Harpe indignantly: "in no circumstances can one place real reliance on any, but on those actuated in their lives by motives of pure religion. But you must now be removed from the hospital, and made more comfortable."

"No, no," said Edward; "I had rather remain where I am, till I am able to rise; but Monsieur La Harpe could do me a great kindness by sending to my old lodgings in the Rue de la Paix for my servant, and bidding him to bring my clothes and the other things belonging to me. If it had not been for the coarse but clean linen with which the liberality and charity of this hospital has furnished me," said he, pointing to the homely materials with which he was surrounded, "I should have been badly off indeed."

"I will go instantly," said La Harpe, rising, "and will return this evening with your servant, if he is to be found—I am surprised he has not yet visited you—and you shall have all your things, if possible."

He accordingly went to the lodging, and found that the servant had departed: the landlord had sealed up all Edward's effects until he could by more diligent inquiry ascertain how he was to dispose of them. He accompanied Monsieur La Harpe to the hospital, where in the pale and altered Edward he recognized his former lodger. By the kind and attentive influence of his friend, Edward was soon supplied with many of those little necessaries and comforts which so materially aid the advancement of convalescence; he called to see him almost daily, and brought him newspapers and literature to divert his tedium. Sefton felt very grateful to him, and though they often talked on religion, his tone was much less offensive to the ears of La Harpe than it used to be. One day he even went so far as to say—

"I have often felt, my dear La Harpe, during this my severe illness, very sorry for the things I have said to you about your religion; but do not think it is that I like it a bit better than I did—no, certainly not; but, somehow or other, though Catholics are really much more inflexible in matters of faith than those of other creeds, still I think they are more individually compassionate and tolerant towards their fellow-men than we are."

"That is the practical effect of their religion," said La Harpe: "we condemn the error, but pity and cherish the individual who has the misfortune to be deluded by it."

"Yes," said Edward, musing; "it must certainly be the daily earnestness about religion, and the real Christian virtues I have seen practised by some Catholics, many of them virtues, too, very painful for human nature to practise, which I candidly own have made me think with less disgust than I used to do of that religion."

"Well," said his friend, laughing, "we shall certainly not die of vanity, in consequence of the magnitude of your concessions in our favour."

Sefton coloured a little, and sighed slightly.

"We learn our practical lessons of charity and Christianity," continued La Harpe, without noticing his emotion, "from the study of our crucifix, and we find there all the lessons we need."

"I have often thought, my good friend, do you know," said Sefton, looking at him earnestly, "that I would make a serious study of the different existing religions; but, somehow or other, my mind is so unhinged now, I don't know what to say to it."

"As a Protestant, you are bound to inquire, and to examine, you know. As I understand it, you ought to take nothing on credit; being accountable for your individual *opinions*, for *faith* I cannot call it."

"It is astonishing what odd ideas you French people have of Protestantism," said Edward, smiling bitterly; "but the subject makes me sad," added he, unwilling to acknowledge the exact state of his feelings. "Tell me how things are getting on, and what is the news of the day."

La Harpe detailed to him the progress of events, and concluded by expressing his fear for the consequences of the agitated state of his poor country. "Alas! you yourself have seen," said he, "some of the set of deistical and unprincipled vultures who are gnawing at her vitals; it will not be their fault if religion is not destroyed, and anarchy and confusion overspread again the land. The same infidel and blasphemous maxims were promulgated by those who paved the way for the great and awful revolution of '92; and who can answer that the consequences may not be most frightful at present?"

"Not so bad as that, my good friend," said Edward; "your ideas are too highly wrought, though I will acknowledge to you, that what I have seen of that sort of society has, more especially on reflection, caused me both surprise and horror; and I, as a most warm and sincere patriot, would rather die, than see the British throne surrounded by such a set of unbelieving blasphemers as I have met with since I came to Paris. Still we must not condemn all indiscriminately, nor consider every liberal idea as an innovation: we must allow 'La jeune France' to shew a little spirit; and remember, too, that the schoolmaster is abroad."

"I hope I shall never live to see the consequences of the spirit of 'La jeune France,'" said La Harpe despondingly; "there are many very clever and excellent people who predict no good of it."

"Stuff and nonsense, my good friend: some of these excellent and clever people are the most timorous foreboders in the world. What can they know about it? Experience has surely taught 'La jeune France' not to go too far, but to prune the tree without rooting it up."

"Time will shew," said La Harpe. "There is a Providence over every thing; and we may form a pretty correct idea of what is to come, by what has been. But, alas! one of the peculiar characteristics of this enlightened generation is, the materialism which denies all supernatural agency and interference of an active Providence in the affairs of men."

"My dear Monsieur La Harpe, do not be superstitious, for God's sake," exclaimed Edward with energy; "I really gave you credit for more sense!"

"Sefton," said La Harpe quietly, "did you never hear of a celebrated prophetic conversation which took place a little before that terrible revolution which so many enlightened men had foreseen and announced?"

"Not I," said Edward; "I dare say it was some old woman's twaddle, or some vile priestcraft, published to mislead the simple;" but seeing his friend looked hurt, he added, "Come, La Harpe, let me have it—it will serve well to while away an hour."

"Oh! it is nothing to jest about," answered La Harpe, dashing a tear hastily away from his expressive light-blue eye; "it was related to me by my celebrated namesake and relative after he had become a sincere convert: he was present himself when it occurred. He often said that the impression this conversation, which I am going to tell you, made upon him, was as vivid as if he had heard it but the previous day, though it took place at the beginning of the year 1788."

"Then an eye-witness related it to your relation?" said Sefton.

"No, he heard it himself," answered La Harpe, musing: "it occurred at a grand dinner given by one of the academicians, a person of distinction, and a man of talent. This dinner consisted of a mixed and numerous society of courtiers, lawyers, literati, academicians, *et cetera*. Every thing was, as usual, in the greatest luxury, and the most exquisite wines added to the conviviality of good society that sort of liberty in which its tone is not always preserved. At that time the world was so little fastidious, that every thing which might occasion mirth was permitted. Chamfort was one of the party, and, to use my relation's words, had just read some of his impious and libertine tales, to which even the high-born ladies there present listened without having recourse to their fans. Thence followed a deluge of witticisms on religion. One person cited a trait from 'La Pucelle,' another recalled and applauded the philosophical verses of Diderot:

> 'Et des boyaux du dernier prêtre,
> Serrez le cou du dernier roi.'

A third rose, and holding a bumper in his hand, exclaimed, 'Yes, gentlemen, I am as certain that there is no God, as I am certain Homer was a fool;' and, in fact, he was quite as sure of one as he was of the other. The conversation then became more serious, and every one expatiated with enthusiastic admiration on the revolution brought about by Voltaire, all agreeing that his most glorious title to distinction was founded on that. 'Yes,' continued they triumphantly, 'it is *he* who has given the spirit to his age. He has diffused his works through the anteroom as well as in the cabinet.' One of the guests related an anecdote of his barber, who, while he was powdering him, exclaimed, 'Depend upon it, Sir, though I am but a poor devil of a barber, I have not a bit more religion than any one else.' The company then came to the conclusion that the consummation of the revolution could not be far distant; because it was certain that superstition and fanaticism must give place to philosophy, and they calculated the probabilities of when that epoch might be, and who out of that society would live to see the reign of Reason. The old complained that they could not flatter themselves so far as to expect to see it, and the young rejoiced that there was every probable hope, at least, for them. They congratulated the Academy especially, as having been the stronghold, centre, and promoter of liberty of thought. Amidst all the conviviality of this conversation, one person only amongst the guests had taken no share in it, and had even quietly slid in some little jokes at the eager enthusiasm of the moment; this person was Monsieur Cazotte, an amiable and original character. At length, taking up the discourse, 'Gentlemen,' said he in a most serious manner, 'you may all be satisfied, for you will all see this grand and sublime revolution which you so much desire. You know I am a little bit of a prophet, and I repeat to you, you will all see it.'

"They answered him with the well-known ditty, 'No need to be a great wizard to foretell that.'

"'Perhaps so,' continued Cazotte; 'but it may be necessary to be a little more of a prophet than you seem to imagine, to tell you what remains to be told. Do you know what will come to pass in consequence of this revolution, and what will happen to each one individually of you here present? what will be its undeniably acknowledged effects, and immediate consequences?'

"'Capital! do let us hear,' said Condorcet, with his sullen and stupid air; 'a philosopher cannot be afraid of meeting with a prophet.'

"'Well, then,' said Cazotte, 'you, Monsieur de Condorcet, will expire on the floor of a prison. You will die by poison, which you will swallow, in order to escape from the hands of the executioner, by that poison which those happy days will force you always to carry about you.'

"Great, at first, was the astonishment of the company at these words; but they soon recollected that the worthy Monsieur Cazotte was subject to day dreams, and renewing their merriment, exclaimed, 'Monsieur Cazotte, the tale you are telling us now is not so amusing as your "Diable Amoureux;" but what devil can have put into your head prison, poison, and executioners? What connection can there possibly be between these things and the reign of Reason and philosophy?'

"'It is precisely that connection which I am pointing out to you,' replied Cazotte: 'it is in the name of philosophy, of humanity, of liberty, under the reign of Reason, that your career will finish thus; and it will be truly then the reign of Reason, for at that time temples will be raised to her, and to her alone, throughout all France.'

"'By my faith,' said Chamfort with a sarcastic laugh, 'you will not be one of her priests then!'

"'I hope not,' replied Cazotte: 'but you, Monsieur de Chamfort, who will be one, and most worthy of the dignity too—you will slash your veins twenty-two times with a razor, and, nevertheless, you will not die of this until some months after.'

"The company looked at each other, and laughed again.

"'You, Monsieur Vie d'Azir,' continued Cazotte, 'will not open your veins yourself, but to make more sure of your fate, you will, after an attack of gout, cause them to be opened six times, and you will die in the night. You, Monsieur de Nicolai, will die on the scaffold; and you, Monsieur Bailly, also on the scaffold.'

"'Well, God be praised!' cried Roucher: 'it seems that Monsieur Cazotte takes vengeance only on the Academicians; he has made a terrible execution of them; What will become of me, please God?—'

"'You, Monsieur Roucher?' replied Cazotte—'you will likewise expire on the scaffold.'

"'Oh!' cried every one simultaneously, 'he has laid a wager; he has sworn to exterminate us all.'

"'No: it is not I, who have sworn it,' said Cazotte mournfully.

"'Well, then, we are to be exterminated by the Turks and Tartars!' exclaimed they with one voice.

"'By no means,' replied Monsieur Cazotte. 'Once more I repeat it; you will then be all governed by

Reason alone. Those who will treat you thus will be all philosophers, and will have continually in their mouths the same phrases which you have been using for this last hour past; they will repeat all your maxims, they will quote like you the verses of Diderot, and those of La Pucelle —'

"The guests whispered to each other, 'that it was evident Cazotte had lost his head,' for he looked all this time as serious as possible; 'but,' said they, 'we know he is only joking, and that his jokes are always mingled with the marvellous.' 'Yes,' observed Champart, 'but his marvellous is not gay; he is too ominous; but can you tell us, Monsieur Cazotte, when all this will happen?' asked he.

"'Six years will not pass before all I have predicted to you shall be accomplished,' said Cazotte calmly.

"'Why, these are really miracles!' exclaimed my relative himself; 'but you count me for nothing amongst them.'

"'You, Monsieur La Harpe,' replied Cazotte, 'will be quite as great and extraordinary a miracle as any of them, for you will then be a Christian.'

"The table rung with exclamations."

"'Bravo! bravissimo!' cried Chamfort; 'I am quite happy again; for if we are not to perish till La Harpe is a Christian, we shall be immortal.'

"'Well,' said Madame La Duchesse de Grammont, 'we ladies are very happy in being overlooked in these revolutions. When I say overlooked, I don't mean that we do not sometimes meddle with them a little; but, as a matter of course, we are exempted from the consequences thereof, and our sex —"

"'Your sex, Madame,' interrupted Cazotte, 'will not protect you this time, and it will be in vain for you not to meddle with any thing; you will be treated like the stronger sex, without any distinction whatsoever.'

"'But what, in the name of patience, are you saying, Monsieur Cazotte?' expostulated the Duchess: 'it must be the end of the world you are preaching to us methinks.'

" 'I know nothing about that,' answered he drily, 'but what I do know is, that you, Madame La Duchesse de Grammont, will be conducted to the scaffold on the executioner's car; you and several other ladies at the same time, with your hands tied behind you.'

" 'Upon my word! At all events, in such a case, I trust I should at least be indulged with a mourning coach,' said the Duchess.

" 'No, Madame,' replied Cazotte; 'and ladies of higher rank than yourself will, like you, go on a car; and like you, have their hands bound.'

" 'Ladies of higher rank!—what, the princesses of the blood!' exclaimed the Duchess.

" 'Ladies of higher rank still,' added Cazotte.

" Here a sensible agitation thrilled through the company, and the countenance of the master of the house fell, for every one seemed to think the joke was carried a little too far. Madame de Grammont, to disperse this little shade of displeasure, did not insist on the last answer, and satisfied herself with observing, in the most light manner, 'You will see now he won't even allow me a confessor.'

" 'No, Madame,' said the impenetrable prophet; 'you will not have one, neither will any one else; the last person executed, who will have one, and that by a particular favour, will be' .... Here he paused a moment.

" 'Well! who is the happy mortal that will have this prerogative?' asked many voices.

" 'It will be the last prerogative which will remain to him; *it will be the King of France*,' said Cazotte mournfully.

" The master of the house rose abruptly, and every one with him; he approached Cazotte, and said to him in a marked tone, 'My dear Monsieur Cazotte, this melancholy fancy has lasted quite long enough, and you carry it too far, so as to compromise both yourself and us.'

" Monsieur Cazotte made no answer, but prepared to take his leave, when Madame de Grammont, who always delighted in banishing reflection by gaiety, advanced towards him, saying, 'Monsieur le Prophet has told us all our fortunes very well, but he does not tell us a word about his own.'

"Cazotte cast his eyes on the ground and was silent for some time; at length he said, 'Did you ever read the siege of Jerusalem, by Josephus, Madame?'

"'Oh, to be sure; who has not read it?' answered she, laughing. 'However, fancy to yourself I have not.'

"'Well then, Madame,' continued Cazotte, 'during that siege, there was a man who for seven days continually walked the round of the ramparts, in the sight of the besiegers and the besieged, crying incessantly in an ominous and thundering tone, "Woe to Jerusalem! woe to myself!" when, in the twinkling of an eye, an enormous stone, hurled from the engine of the enemy, reached him, and crushed him to atoms.' Having said this, Cazotte made his bow, and withdrew."

La Harpe ceased speaking, and Edward seemed much struck. "But," said he, in a hesitating tone, "were these predictions verified?"

"To a tittle."

"Aye, aye," said Sefton with a self-complacent smile; "it is very easy to write a prophecy after the events have taken place."

"I expected that objection," replied La Harpe; "and in answer to it, I can only allege the known integrity of my illustrious kinsman, and my own conviction that he was incapable of retailing and publishing such a story, if it was not literally true. Besides, many are still living, who have heard the account from his own lips, and never doubted his veracity."

"Do you really then believe it?" subjoined Sefton.

"As firmly as I believe any other gentleman on his word, who has no motive to deceive me, or to disgrace himself."

"Certainly, it is very extraordinary," said Edward; "but how did Cazotte terminate his career?"

"He died on the scaffold," answered La Harpe; "and before the fatal blow was struck, he turned to the assembled crowd, and said in a distinct voice, 'I die, as I have lived, faithful to my God and to my king.'"

"Then he was not what you term an infidel?" inquired Sefton.

"By no means: he always preserved his faith, and was a constant enemy to the disorders of the revolution. He was always much connected with the philosophers, who courted him for his talents. He was finally condemned, having been betrayed before a tribunal of assassins, and lost his life on the scaffold, as I have mentioned."

"Poor man! How horrid!"

"He found means, however, to get an hour's interview with a priest," continued La Harpe, "and wrote to his wife and children, begging them not to weep for him, adding, 'and above all things, remember never to offend God.'"

Edward made no observation, but seemed musing, and La Harpe, who felt himself much affected by the train of recollections he had roused, rose, and holding out his hand to his friend, silently took leave of him

CHAPTER XX.

> "Hast thou a charm to stay the morning star
> In his steep course? so long he seems to pause
> On thy bald awful head, O Sovren Blanc;
> O dread and silent mount, I gazed upon thee,
> Till thou, still present to the bodily sense,
> Didst vanish from my thought; entranced in prayer,
> I worshipped the Invisible alone."
>
> COLRIDGE.

As Edward's convalescence advanced, and he regained corporeal health and vigour, so in the same proportion returned and increased the sorrows and regrets of his heart, and the doubts, agitations and misery of his mind, on matters of religion. He was a hundred times inclined to return to his home, and allow his wife the same liberty of conscience he claimed for himself; but pride, and the difficulty he felt in making what he thought would be now the first advances, always checked the more just and generous feelings of his heart; "besides," said he to himself, "I really am so unhappy in my own mind about where true faith is to be found, or whether any particular form of faith is at all required of us, that I feel I have no chance of regaining any peace of soul, till I can make up my mind one way or another. After all the horrible ideas I have heard expressed by that vile set to which Le Sage introduced me, it seems clear enough, that *if* faith be necessary for a man's salvation, it is not to be found in Protestantism at least, which, if what they say is true, would be, after all my pains, quite as likely to conduct me to the Devil as not: though, by the way, they do not believe in the Devil at all, most of them; for if they believed in him, they would believe in revealed religion, or otherwise we should know something of the existence of the said devil; certainly, though I have tried, I find it extremely difficult to bring my mind *satisfactorily to believe*, and to be *happy* in believing, that there is no revealed religion. Without revealed religion, a thousand difficulties present themselves in explaining the moral and mental state of man; and if there is a religion revealed by God to man, that religion must exist somewhere *now* exactly as it was at first revealed, for God is truth, and can neither change what he has once revealed, nor reveal contradictory things to different sets of people. . . . Where, then, is this religion? . . . and why may not Protestantism be it? . . . I have often heard Dr. Davison speak of the purity of the Protestant religion in Geneva; I have a good mind to go thither, and examine into the matter myself; however, I shall keep an unprejudiced eye of observation on all the Catholic superstitions I may meet with, if it were but to refute them to poor dear Emma; how she could ever imagine she had found the truth in that most superstitious of all superstitious faiths, is beyond my comprehension. I used to think she had a very clear judgment, and it is most strange how she can have got so bewildered in this most important affair, for important it is, after all, as I know too well by the terrors my soul was in when I was at the point of death, not very many weeks ago: no, no, it is highly necessary to make up one's mind upon the faith we ought to live in before we come to the awful moment of giving up our soul into the terrible hands of the living God, so I will e'en lose no more time about it, but begin and sift the matter thoroughly, and may God grant me the grace to embrace the truth, and live up to it when I find it." Having come to this resolve, Edward felt his heart lighter than he had done for some time past; he rung the bell, and gave orders to Luigi, to prepare for their immediate departure for Switzerland. Luigi had rejoined his master about a week before this, and rejoiced now no little at the prospect of their being once more *en voyage*, after their disastrous visit to Paris.

The next day, Monsieur La Harpe called, and Sefton told him that he should be off in a few days to Switzerland. La Harpe was fearful that his friend was going to expose his scarcely regained strength too soon, and tried in vain to retain him a little longer in Paris. At length, the kindly feelings of the affectionate old man induced him to offer to accompany Sefton as far as Geneva, where he said he had some old friends, whom he would be glad to visit; another and a stronger motive he had, which made him wish to retreat from the turbulent and unsettled state of Paris; within a few days, he had witnessed the most outrageous insults offered to religion: churches sacrilegiously desecrated, the archbishop expelled, and narrowly escaping destruction, his palace demolished, the image of the crucified Redeemer broken, insulted, and even dragged through the filthy channels; his heart sickened, and he heartily wished himself many leagues away from these disgusting scenes. Sefton gladly accepted his proposal, for he had already experienced the loneliness of feeling caused by travelling without a companion. Before he took his departure from Paris, he called at the convent of the Sisters of Charity, to thank sister Angela for all the anxious care and kind attention she had shewn him, for so many tedious days of his illness; at the same time, he wished to make an acknowledgment to the convent, of his esteem and gratitude, and he presented them with a check on his banker for a very handsome sum of money. The Superioress gracefully declined it, alleging for excuse, that they were not accustomed to look for any temporal reward for the offices of charity which they performed.

"Receive it, then, as an alms to your convent," said Sefton, "for I am informed you do sometimes receive alms; and when I look about here, and see the nakedness and poverty of your habitation, I am convinced your receipts do not overbound."

"On that title," replied the Superioress with dignified courtesy, "I will thankfully receive it. Our community is large, and our means scanty. The grateful prayers of the sisterhood shall not be wanting for the generous Englishman."

"I feel convinced," said Sefton with some emotion, "that the God of mercy and of love can never reject the prayers of these, his ministering angels of charity."

Sister Angela then approached, and presented to Sefton a silver medal of the Blessed Virgin, attached to a silken cord, begging of him to accept and wear it in his bosom, in honour of her whose image was there expressed. Sefton was taken by surprise; he knew not how either to receive or to decline the proffered gift. After a short pause, during which his countenance betrayed his perplexity, he at length said with some trepidation—

"Sister Angela, there is nothing I would not do to gratify you as far as conscience might allow me; but, pardon me, I cannot bring myself to promise you to wear that medal in honour of the Virgin. I have been accustomed too long to consider that a superstitious practice."

"Rather pardon me," said sister Angela, "for making the proposal, but I really thought your good sense was superior to such an idle fancy."

"How so?"

"I observed in the hospital with what raptures you received again the restored miniature of your wife; kissing it, and pressing it to your bosom, without any scruple of superstition."

"True," replied Sefton with a deep blush of confusion, "but there is a great difference between the two."

"I see no difference," said sister Angela, "but in the object of these external marks of respect. You wear the image of your beloved wife next to your heart; you cherish it there, out of affection to her; the action is simple and natural, and springs from a kindly and holy motive. Now, I only ask you to wear this medal out of affection to the Mother of the Redeemer; where is the superstition in that?"

"Pardon me, sister Angela, I do not feel that affection for the Virgin which I feel for my wife; I respect, and even venerate her, as the mother of Jesus Christ, but I cannot love her so as to put my trust in her."

"Well, well," said the nun, smiling, "at least wear the medal out of respect and veneration to her."

"Excuse me, it is impossible; I really cannot do it. Bid me wear it for your sake, as a token of my obligations to you, as a memorial of your kindness, and I will accept it, I will press it to my heart, that the remembrance of you may never be cancelled thence."

"Well, then, wear it for my sake, and as often as you cast your eyes upon it, remember that there is a poor nun whose humble prayers shall be daily offered for your eternal welfare; she will invoke the Holy Virgin's protection for you, and in the hour of affliction or distress perhaps at the sight of the medal you may be induced to seek aid where it was never sought in vain."

A tear struggled in the eye of Sefton as he held out his hand to receive the medal; he threw the cord round his neck, and promised to wear the medal for the sake of Angela: he then took his leave of the religious, and in a few days left Paris. The change of scene and air performed wonders in recruiting the invalid, and his spirits rose with the hope of soon being able to rub up his Protestantism, and have his mind set at rest on religious matters. One day, while they were changing horses in a small village, Sefton, struck with its picturesque situation, got out of the carriage to examine it more carefully; he observed there was no church, which was a rare thing, even in France: he asked an old man who was seated at his cabin door, whereabouts the church might be.

"Alas! Sir," answered the peasant, sighing, "we have no church in our little hamlet."

"How is that, my friend?" inquired Sefton.

"Because," said the poor man, with a tremulous quiver of his lip, "the guillotine was placed in our beautiful little church during the reign of terror; and every thing that was sacred and holy in it was profaned and destroyed."

"Oh, my God! how horrible!" exclaimed Sefton; "I cannot conceive such licentious barbarity."

"Alas! that was not all, Sir," said the old man, while the tear trickled down his rugged cheek; "in that very church, and by that very guillotine, I lost the wife of my bosom, and my two only sons; executed, martyred, I may say, on the very spot where they were baptized."

"How very shocking! poor old man! I wonder not at your grief," said Edward compassionately; "but for what supposed crime were you thus bereft of those so near and dear to you?"

"Because in those days it was a crime to be religious, and it was against reason to believe in God and the holy Catholic faith: our poor old Curate's life was sought; he was sheltered in our house, but he was soon discovered and beheaded, and my wife and sons massacred because they had sought to save the life of an innocent fellow-creature."

"How contrary to all reason and justice!" said Edward with much emotion.

"Yes, Sir; they talked of liberty, but they would not allow a poor Catholic to have the liberty of believing the words of the Son of God, nor of practising the divine religion taught by Him: and what did they offer us in return? the horrors of incredulity, and the practice of every species of the most horrible crimes."

The old man paused, and wrung his hands, "And now," said he, "I, who once was well off, happy, and content with my country and religion, am a poor, miserable, beggared outcast, deprived of all the comforts of life, and the consolations of my faith; our once beautiful church is now a stable, and before I can hear Mass or receive the Sacraments, I have to walk sometimes ten, sometimes fifteen miles."

The poor man sunk down on the stone bench by the cabin door, and covered his face with his withered hands. At this moment the carriage, with the fresh horses, came galloping up. Edward, breathing a few words of comfort to the poor old man, and putting into his hand a liberal alms, jumped into it, and they were out of sight in an instant.

"Well," said Sefton eagerly, "I do grant you one concession, La Harpe; namely, that the spirit of revolutionary liberty appears better in theory than it works in practice."

"And when did you make that wonderful discovery?" said La Harpe, laughing, and looking up from the travelling map over which he was poring.

"Just now: I often have doubted it, and discussed the point in my own mind, but now I am convinced: such horrors as I have just heard! enough to make one's blood run cold."

Sefton then related to his friend the little episode of the old French peasant: "Now," continued he, "what was the consequence in practice of this revolutionary liberty and this pretended reason in destroying all religion, but crime, and injustice, and misery: crime in the perpetrators of such horrid massacres, injustice in the destroying of public property, and individual liberty and right, and misery to those individuals as well as to the perpetrators themselves? for I am convinced those revolutionary tigers must have had a very Hell of remorse within their own souls."

"Yes," observed La Harpe mournfully; "incredulity does not produce peace of mind."

"No," continued Sefton; "I know that full well, from the slight taste I have had of it: one might almost draw an inference from the feeling of uncertain horror which seems to darken the soul, and the anxiety and troubles of spirit which wither all the generous and tranquil sensibilities of the heart, that scepticism is not suited to man."

"There can be no doubt," said Monsieur La Harpe, "but that absolute incredulity, which reduces a soul to the lowest degree of degradation, brings with it a kind of Hell. I remember one day hearing Monsieur Viennet say to Monsieur Benjamin-Constant, 'I find myself very unhappy in believing nothing; if I had children, I would preserve them from this misfortune by giving them a Christian education, and if there were still Jesuits, I think I should place them in one of their colleges.' 'It is the same with me,' replied Monsieur Benjamin-Constant. 'I am a perfect sceptic; and this scepticism is a feeling which wears me. I wish I could believe in any thing, were it only in magnetism; but I cannot believe in that more than in any thing else, and this feeling causes me an indescribable torment.' Now, does not this acknowledgment which they made," continued La Harpe, "and which truth has so often drawn from the most incredulous, prove to demonstration, that without religious faith, man can never be happy?"

"It seems so, indeed," said Sefton, sighing, "and it proves also the truth of Montesquieu's observation, when he says, 'It is a wonderful thing that the Christian religion, which seems only to have for its object our felicity in the next world, should nevertheless constitute our happiness in this.'"

"It is a very true and a very just observation," answered La Harpe.

"Again, on the other hand," continued Sefton, musing, "if what Montesquieu says be true, how can we account for the misery and unhappiness occasioned by religious differences amongst the various classes and sects of Christians?"

"It is the abuse of religion, and not its use, which occasions the unhappy consequences you mention," answered La Harpe; "it is because these different sects are all in error on matters of faith that they are unhappy; they do not feel certain that what they believe is that which God has revealed, and which it is the will of God men should believe; hence arise the unhappiness and disagreements you refer to."

"How, then, are we to know exactly what it is the will of God man should believe?" exclaimed Edward bitterly. "All Christian sects believe that they alone possess the truth; and all profess to ground their faith on the infallible Word of God. How can this be? How can God permit weak man to become thus the sport of his own imagination? How can this be reconciled with the perfections of the Deity? Oh! surely contemplating the governing will of God in all things must necessarily lead to melancholy; because seeing the existence of evil, causes the mind to apprehend and doubt of the perfection of the divine goodness."

"The permission of evil is a question too abstruse for me to enter into at this moment," replied La Harpe, "but I think it is sufficient for us to know that God is infinitely good, just, and wise; and if he permits evil, it is for the wisest purpose, and to draw good from evil itself. The permission of evil is a necessary consequence of the fact, that God in his wisdom and goodness created man free, 'and left him in the hand of his own counsel, to choose life or death, good or evil.'* It is an impious folly in man to call God to account for what he has done. He will one day justify his ways before men. If on our part we avoid evil, and do good, we have no reason to be melancholy. Catholics, who are all perfectly certain of the truth of their own faith, are never melancholy on that score, and are everywhere more cheerful than the notoriously gloomy Calvinist or sanctimonious Methodist."

"It certainly is something surprising to observe," answered Sefton, "how every Catholic is so satisfied with his own religion, at least every Catholic that I have yet seen."

"They have every reason to be perfectly satisfied, my good friend," said La Harpe, smiling, "as you would find were you to act up to your own principles as a Protestant, and thoroughly examine the foundations upon which the Catholic faith is grounded."

"I fear I should be a long while in arriving at the foundations through the mass of superstition and bigotry which surrounds them," said Sefton sarcastically; "no, no, when we get to Geneva, I intend to examine the foundations of the Protestant faith thoroughly, which will be much more to the purpose."

La Harpe smiled and shook his head. "I deny en-

* Eccl. xv. 14.

tirely that you Protestants have any *faith* at all: you have nothing but *opinion*. Now, 'without faith it is impossible to please God,' are the words inspired by Truth itself."

"Why, what is any man's faith but his opinion or persuasion?" asked Sefton.

"Opinion," replied La Harpe, "is the persuasion of man's mind grounded upon probable, though not certain motives. Hence, we frequently change our opinions as we see more or less of probability in the motives. Divine faith, on the contrary, is grounded on the certain and infallible Word of God, which can never suffer change. You Protestants often change your opinions, as you see more or less of probability in your interpretation of the Bible; hence, I say, you have opinion, not faith."

At this moment Luigi turned towards them with an air of mysterious triumph, and exclaimed in a low but audible voice, "Gentlemen, Mont Blanc."

They both looked in the direction in which Luigi pointed, and gazed on the snow-covered mountain which appeared in the blue distance. A succession of beautiful scenery now wrapt their attention in delighted wonder and admiration for several hours, and Sefton exclaimed, as they approached the little inn where they were to pass the night, "After all, adoring the Deity in his wonderful works is worth a thousand controversial differences, and who knows but that adoration of the heart, accompanied with a good life, may not be all He requires of us?"

"I know for one," said La Harpe; "because the inspired Apostle himself has said, 'without faith it is impossible to please God;'* and simply to adore God, and lead what you call a moral life, would but reduce us to the condition of those enlightened Athenians who worshipped the unknown God."

Sefton groaned.

"Examine, examine thoroughly, that is all I ask of you," said La Harpe.

* Heb. xi. 6.

"I will, my friend, I will," said Sefton; "wait till we get to Geneva, I hope to find the truth there."

La Harpe smiled incredulously; Luigi opened the carriage door, and they entered the lowly threshold of the Mountain Inn, where they were to find shelter for the night.

CHAPTER XXI.

We now reject each mystic creed,
To common sense a scandal;
We 're more enlightened—yes, indeed,
The Devil holds the candle.

EPIGRAM.

THE next morning, the travellers were off early, and enjoyed a day of delicious mountain scenery. Sefton was even more gratified with Switzerland than he had anticipated, and the ten days they spent in travelling over the different Cantons and exploring their ever-varying beauties seemed to fly with fairy speed. When they arrived at Geneva, Sefton's first visit was to the post-office, where he found, as he had expected, letters of introduction from Dr. Davison to some of the principal professors and literati, whom the latter had known in his youth at Geneva. Edward was delighted, and the next morning, after breakfast, made his round of visits: he was particularly struck with the appearance of Professor Spielmann; he was an old man of venerable appearance, and there was something in his manners which invited confidence; accordingly Sefton contrived to turn the conversation on that which was now uppermost in his mind—religion, and mentioned, as if casually, some of the difficulties upon Protestantism which he had heard in Paris, particularly upon the Trinity.

"Well, well, my excellent young friend," said the Professor, with two or three slow and patronizing nods of his head, "I think you take these matters too seriously—indeed, I am sure of it; you will find many, very many excellent and worthy divines in Geneva, who rationally enough do not think it necessary to believe several of the antiquated dogmas which Protestants at first acquiesced in without sufficient examination; more light has by degrees gleamed on these subjects, particularly with regard to the superior nature of Christ, the personality of the Holy Spirit, the Incarnation, and the Atonement, with its attendant mysteries. I assure you, you will find that a great mass of Protestants of all denominations have cast off these dogmas as fictions and absurdities, unworthy of an enlightened age."

Sefton could not repress his astonishment, and both his look and manner testified pain and surprise.

"I did not say that I exactly agreed with all the explanations given by *rational* Protestants on the dogmas I have just mentioned," continued the Professor, observing the agitated expression on Sefton's speaking countenance; "but with regard to the Trinity, upon which you seem to have had some difficulties, it is my opinion that that dogma may be removed without scruple from religious instruction, as being a new doctrine, without foundation and contrary to reason; but," added he, lowering his voice and shaking his head solemnly, "it must be done with great circumspection, that weak Christians may not take scandal at it, or make it a pretext to reject all religion, for you must be aware that the greatest part of our people are not yet sufficiently enlightened to look upon the truth in its naked simplicity. They have been too long accustomed to regard religion through the mist of mystery. We must humour their prejudices for a while. Our hope is in the rising generation, which a better system of education is preparing for brighter days."

Sefton felt both indignation and disgust; however, he suppressed the rising emotion, and observed as calmly as he could, that Dr. Davison, who had studied much of his theology at Geneva, held and preached very different tenets.

"I do not doubt it, my good Sir, in the least," answered the Professor; "poor Davison! he was always a good-natured, simple soul: a great ally of mine at one time, but too apt to take things on credit; however, it is not his fault if his mind has not marched with the age. Intercourse with some of the enlightened spirits of modern times would be of infinite service to him."

"But, Sir," said Edward dryly, "after all, belief in the Trinity is one of the Thirty-nine Articles of the Church of England."

"Whew! whew!" said the Professor, putting his fore finger to his nose, and shutting one of his eyes with an inexpressibly sly wink, "You surely know it is nowise necessary for a good *rational* Protestant to believe in the Thirty-nine Articles of your Church; we of Geneva never admitted them from the beginning, and we know quite well that the most learned of your Churchmen are heartily sick of them."

"Luther and Calvin, I imagine, believed in the Trinity at least," observed Sefton coolly.

"Luther believed, too, in a real presence in the Sacrament," said the Professor sarcastically, "which smells far too strong of Popery to be endured; if he was wrong in one article, he might be wrong in another. But perhaps I am wronging the grand patriarch of Protestantism. I have been long persuaded in my own mind, that both Luther and Calvin, and most of their co-operators, were too clear-headed not to see the ultimate consequences of their immortal principle, that every man must judge for himself in matters of faith, and therefore no man can believe what he cannot comprehend. Mysteries and miracles must therefore be eliminated from rational faith."

Sefton was confounded; he knew not what to reply, for in his disputes with Catholics he had often urged the same maxim, that a man could not be obliged to believe what he did not understand. At length he ventured upon a reply which he had often heard from Catholics.

"I think, Sir," said he, "we act very rationally in believing whatever God has revealed to us, for that must necessarily be true, however it may surpass our very limited comprehension; let me once clearly *understand* that God has revealed a truth, and then *I must* and *will* most gratefully bow every power of my soul to receive and adore it."

"Oh, oh!" said the Doctor, "I see which way the wind sets. I tell you, young man, if you once renounce the rights of your own judgment, if you once hoodwink reason, some sly knave or other will soon lead you into all the mazes of Popish superstition."

"No fear of that," replied Sefton, "for there is a wide difference between submitting humbly to the incomprehensible mysteries of God, really revealed, and following blindly the superstitions of Rome, which are the fond inventions of men."

"Beware," said the Professor; "you do not know the craftiness of the Roman clergy; they are not such fools as to propose at first to your implicit belief any silly superstitious mystery or miracle until they have inveigled you by their sophisms into the belief that God has so revealed it; if you give up the right of judging for yourself, you will cease to be a Protestant."

"That I shall never do," replied Sefton with earnestness; "yet, in exercising the free right of my own judgment, I must be allowed to think, that God may reveal, and really has revealed many things which I cannot fathom. I am sure that the first fathers of the Reformation, and the best and wisest men that have adorned it, admitted many unsearchable mysteries, such as the Trinity, Incarnation, and the like."

"The works of the great fathers of Protestantism," replied Professor Spielmann, "have not been sufficiently studied by their followers, nor sufficient allowance made for the times and circumstances in which they appeared. The bright light of reason did not burst upon them all at once, but gradually developed itself, and, one by one, chased away the shadows of their earlier education; and when they did see the light in noon-tide blaze, they prudently withheld it from the gaze of their benighted followers and cotemporaries, which would then have only dazzled, not allured them to the truth. They were contented to be the harbingers of more glorious days which we now enjoy. Hence, at first they really did believe, and afterwards affected to believe, though not without insinuating many serious doubts, several of the mysteries of the ancient doctrine. They sowed, indeed, the fruitful seed, and we live to reap the abundant harvest."

Sefton sickened in his inmost soul, as he listened to this extraordinary avowal of a learned Doctor and Professor in the first chair of Protestant theology in Europe. He was unable to make a reply.

"Come, come," continued the Doctor, seeing that Sefton looked puzzled, "I will take you to-morrow, as it is Sunday, to hear one of the finest preachers we have in Geneva, Dr. Untersteken; he is a profound divine, and a most liberal and enlightened man. I am sure you will be delighted with him."

Sefton thanked him, and gladly accepted the offer. He then took his leave, and promised to be with the Professor the next morning at ten o'clock. He returned to his hotel with a very heavy heart; his mind was more confused than ever. He in vain tried to fix his attention on the book he was reading; it wandered every moment back to Professor Spielmann, and his extraordinary conversation. He attempted to write to Emma, but it would not do. At length dinner-time came, and Monsieur La Harpe, who had been paying visits during the morning, made his appearance. During dinner Edward was silent and gloomy; he made several ineffectual attempts to shake off his uneasiness, but the whole burden of the conversation was sustained by La Harpe, who observed his friend's uneasiness, but prudently forbore noticing it. At length, when the servants had withdrawn, and they were left alone with their dessert, Sefton told La Harpe the whole history of his visit to Professor Spielmann, and concluded by expressing his extreme surprise at what he termed such heterodox and latitudinarian principles of faith.

"I am not at all surprised at the Professor," said La Harpe quietly; "I told you before that you Protestants had no divine faith at all, merely human opinion. They believe to-day what they opine to be true, and to-morrow they change their faith with their opinion. Now, it seems to me, consistently speaking, that Professor Spielmann has as much right to deny the Trinity if he thinks fit, as you have to deny the real presence in the blessed Eucharist. You know the Apostle affirms, that without *faith* it is impossible to please God; therefore I am not at all surprised that any reflecting Protestant, who examines his own religion, should be uneasy, and very uneasy too, when he comes to see the sandy foundations on which it rests, and the dangers to which it exposes him."

"Dangers! what dangers?"

"Why, the danger of becoming sceptics and infidels, and thus displeasing God, and losing their immortal souls. These ministers at Geneva have already passed the irrevocable barrier; they have held out the hand of fellowship to Deists, and to the enemies of the faith. They even blush to make mention in their catechisms of original sin, without which the incarnation of the Eternal Word is no longer necessary."

"Very extraordinary!" muttered Sefton; "I had no idea of it."

"I have known that a long time," answered La Harpe; "why, you may remember that even in Rousseau's time the opinions of the Genevese Protestants had conducted them pretty far; for he says in one of his letters, 'when they are asked if Jesus Christ is God, they do not dare to answer; when asked what mysteries they admit, they still do not dare to answer; a philosopher,' continues he, 'casts upon them a rapid glance, and penetrates them at once; he sees they are Arians, Socinians, *et cetera*.'"

"Where, then, is to be found *faith*, what you call faith, without which it is impossible to please God?" said Sefton despondingly.

"In the Church founded by Jesus Christ himself," answered La Harpe; "the Church to which He has promised to teach all truths to the end of the world; but you will not find it in Protestantism, which is a nonentity of a religion. Protestants are entirely separated from the Church of Jesus Christ, and consequently are separated from Jesus Christ himself, who, as St. Paul says, purchased to himself a Holy Church at the price of His blood. Protestants despise the Pope, the bishops, and all the ministers of the Church of Jesus Christ, and consequently they despise Jesus Christ himself, who has said, 'He who despises you, despises me.'"*

"You are too severe, Sir, much too severe!" exclaimed Sefton, colouring; "Protestants do not despise Jesus Christ."

"Perhaps not in theory, but in practice, which is worse," said La Harpe; "it is too obvious from their refusal to comply with his words. Far be it from me," added he with emotion, "to be severe on any one; but you ask me where true faith is to be found, and I should not be your friend if I gave you a prevaricating answer. According to what you have yourself stated to me, Protestants have no fixed belief, or rather they believe nothing: neither have they the slightest regard to the order which Jesus Christ gave to the ministers of his Church, 'to teach all nations,' since they make no account of what the Church teaches, decides, and prescribes in virtue of that divine mission; but, on the contrary, each individual may regulate his belief by his own opinion, and change it according to his fancy, or deny any thing according to his own caprice, incurring thus the anathema pronounced by Jesus Christ, 'He that believes not, shall be condemned.'"†

"In other words," interrupted Sefton impatiently, "you mean to tell me, that the Catholic Church is the Church founded by Jesus Christ, and that true faith is to be found only in that Church."

"Exactly so," said La Harpe.

Sefton was silent for a few minutes, and then said vehemently, "I never will believe that Jesus Christ requires us to give credit to all the gross superstitions and traditions of the Catholic Church, nor that He ever revealed them, or sanctioned them."

"Perhaps," replied La Harpe, "what you call super-

* Luke x. 16. † Mark xvi. 16.

stitions are not really superstitious, but very well founded pious practices, which you might even approve of if you understood them; and as to the traditions received by the Church, if you took the trouble to examine them, you would find them commanded in the Bible to be observed. Listen to Saint Paul: 'Therefore, brethren, stand fast; and hold the *traditions* which you have learned, whether *by word*, or by our *epistle*.* Thus, we are exhorted to hold the same steadfast faith, whether it be handed down to us by word of mouth, or by a written document. And surely it is as easy to God to preserve the purity of faith in His Church by one means as by the other."

"I cannot think so;" said Sefton, "do we not see daily the most simple story wonderfully changed and metamorphosed when it has run through the editions of three or four mouths?"

"No doubt," said La Harpe quietly, "where there is no promise of the Spirit of truth to guide it."

"Well, give me the Bible after all; that cannot be changed."

"No doubt, as long as the same Spirit of truth watches over its preservation."

"Well, well, I must be greatly changed indeed," said Sefton bitterly, "before I can receive the traditions of your Church; it would require a miracle, I think, to make me a Catholic: no, no; that is not very likely."

"Every thing is possible to the grace of God," said La Harpe feelingly.

"I do not desire such a grace, I am sure!" exclaimed Sefton vehemently; "but no," added he, suddenly stopping, "I do desire that God would enable me to find out the truth, because I really wish to believe what is right, and to save my soul; but if I feel certain of any thing in this world, it is of the corruption of the Catholic Church."

"Bravo!" exclaimed La Harpe, laughing; "only examine, but examine with that candour and sincerity which the importance of the matter requires. Remember, that salvation depends upon a right determination.

* 2 Thes. ii. 14.

Let no human consideration bias your resolution; keep steadily in your mind the maxim of our Lord, 'What will it avail a man if he gain the world and lose his own soul?' but again, I entreat you to examine."

"That I certainly intend to do, were it only to amuse myself, and enable me to reclaim my poor deluded Emma," replied Edward with a sigh, and an expression of regret and melancholy on his fine countenance, which quite went to La Harpe's heart. Sefton rose and took his candle, saying he wished to finish a letter to her for the morrow's post.

CHAPTER XXII.

"The spirit that I have seen
May be a devil; and the devil hath power
To assume a pleasing shape."
SHAKSPEARE.

THE next morning at ten o'clock, Edward, punctual to his engagement, called on Professor Spielmann, who accompanied him to hear the sermon of the celebrated Doctor Untersteken. Sefton was all anxiety, and listened with absorbing and intense attention, in the eager hope of hearing the Word of God delivered in its most pure and perfect truth, and in the full expectation of finding some repose for his agitated conscience. The exterior of the preacher was by no means prepossessing, but he was eloquent, and his style had something in it which rivetted the attention; his discourse could scarcely be called a sermon, as it was rather a review of the ancient and new dogmas of the Christian faith, in which he very coolly set aside the Trinity, Original Sin, Justification, the Satisfaction of Christ, Baptism, and the Lord's Supper, as taught in his own Church. He took particular pains to sift the doctrinal part of the New Testament of its *irrationalism;* but the main aim of his discourse was evidently to reconcile to the laws of reason and nature those deviations from the course of both which its recorded miracles present: he endeavoured to shew, that many of these miracles were mere exaggerations of natural phenomena; that the wonderful cures performed by Christ might be the effects of animal magnetism, or some other natural, though occult power; he even went so far as to assert, that though Christ seemed to the bystanders to expire on the cross, yet he probably only swooned from loss of blood, and after a few hours, being given up to the sedulous care of his friends, he returned to a conscious state, and lay concealed until the third day. Thus, the most rational way of accounting for the resurrection, as detailed by the Evangelists, was to consider it as a sort of poetic mythus, which was to be received in some moral or allegorical sense; this being clear from the epistles of Paul, who continually applies it to that purpose. No words can describe the astonishment of Edward, nor the dryness and oppression of heart which he experienced as he hurried out of the church; he disembarrassed himself of the company of Professor Spielmann by a marked and haughty bow at the church door, and hastened back to the hotel, where he had promised to rejoin La Harpe after the service, that they might together explore some of the environs of Geneva. Sefton was partly in hopes that his friend would not ask him any thing about the sermon; but in this he was mistaken; for as soon as they were fairly out of the town, La Harpe said to him, "Well, my good friend, and how did you like your celebrated preacher?"

Sefton hesitated a little, and then said in a careless tone, "I can't say I was so much pleased with Doctor Untersteken as I expected; still he is certainly eloquent."

"Then it was the matter which did not please, I imagine?" replied La Harpe.

Sefton paused a moment, and then said, "Well, Sir, to speak candidly, I have been very much disappointed and disgusted."

Sefton then gave him a detailed account of the sermon, and added with a deep sigh—

"I fear from all this, revealed religion is at a very low ebb indeed at Geneva: truly, if I had shut my eyes, I might have fancied myself in a Jewish synagogue, or listening to the effusions of some philosopher in Paris. Indeed, I should be puzzled to draw a line of demarkation between the rationalists of Switzerland and the Deists of France."

"Oh! my dear Sefton, you see again clearly the dire effects of the Protestant principle pushed to its full extent. There is, in fact, no distinction between rationalism and Deism: of the two, the Deists are the more honest; they have no pretensions to religion, while the rationalists wear the mask; alas! I fear it will not be long before you will have plenty of them in England."

"I trust not," replied Edward; "but then to deny the miracles of the Redeemer, which established and confirmed His divine mission, seems to me the very essence of inconsistency, if they admit, as they pretend, the authenticity of the Bible, or that in his person were fulfilled the prophecies of the Old Testament."

"Truly," said La Harpe, smiling, "the Protestants of these enlightened times are very happy in their orthodoxy! I wonder how the poor, ignorant, primitive Christians could find the way to Heaven. They lived near the times of Christ and his Apostles. They highly valued and diligently read the Scriptures, and some of them wrote commentaries upon them; but yet it seems they knew little or nothing of their religion!"

Sefton groaned aloud.

"And then again," continued La Harpe, "these enlightened rationalists seem quite to forget the pains so many of the incredulous Jews took to discredit our Saviour's miracles, to deny his divinity, and more especially the great and vital miracle of the Resurrection, upon the truth of which depended the establishment of his divinity and the truth of his doctrines; but it would not do even in those days, when the personal and bitter enemies of the Saviour did their utmost to prevent the establishment of his divine religion."

"Yes, it cannot be denied but that the real truths taught by our Saviour, and which ought to be the objects of our firm faith if we hope to be saved, were established by miracles wrought both by Christ and his Apostles. Now, if miracles had not long ago ceased, one might amidst the chaos of all the different sects of Christians know yet where to find the *one* true faith, the same as it existed in the time of Christ and his Apostles: for God certainly would not work a miracle to establish and propagate a falsehood. But there are no miracles now; and truth does indeed lie at the bottom of a well."

"Miracles have *not ceased*," said La Harpe, "nor is the promise of our Saviour null and void, when He assures his followers that they 'who believe in him shall work even greater miracles than he himself.'* Now that promise was not limited to any time; and in all ages miracles have taken place, and still do take place, amongst the faithful believers in Christ."

"I'll tell you what, La Harpe," exclaimed Sefton fervently, "if I could once be fully convinced of the existence of a real miracle taking place in these days, in confirmation of the faith of any sect of Christians, I would instantly embrace that faith: but there is no such thing now; and what you call miracles, are no doubt the twaddle and superstition of a set of foolish old men and women."

"Surely," said La Harpe, "you cannot question the recent miracle at Migné, so well attested by three or four thousand eye-witnesses?"

"What miracle was that, pray?"

"Did you never hear of a luminous cross which appeared in the sky a little after night-fall?"

"Yes; now I recollect the English newspapers related the fact, and easily explained it by appealing to the effect of the magic lantern; a paltry trick played upon the ignorance of the poor peasants."

"The man who advanced such an explanation, only betrays his own ignorance," said La Harpe. "Whoever has the slightest notion of the laws of light, must know that the thing itself is impossible. No magic lantern can throw an image on the vacant air. What, then, must we think of the gullibility of Englishmen, who can content themselves with such silly reasons?"

"You are right in your philosophy," replied Sefton. "But what was the object of such an extraordinary portent?"

"It is not for us to search too closely into the coun-

* John xiv. 12.

sels of God, but to adore with profound humility whenever we see his mighty arm erected. You may remember that a mission had just been concluded with the ceremony of erecting a cross in the churchyard. The Missionary, standing at the foot of it, was haranguing a numerous audience, and took occasion to appeal to the glorious cross which appeared to Constantine. Twilight was just closing, the sky was serene, and at that moment a bright and well-defined cross, about sixty feet in length, appeared in the air in a horizontal position, extending from the end of the church. The vision lasted for half an hour, and then gradually faded. Many at the time foreboded evil to France. Three years have scarcely elapsed, and we have seen Paris deluged with blood; altars profaned; and the sacred image of the crucified Redeemer insulted, broken, and dragged through the kennels of the city. We may surely suppose that God in his mercy gave this warning to his faithful servants, that they might rely upon his protection when the day of trial should arrive."

Sefton listened with fixed attention and deep interest, and after a short pause he observed, "Admitting the reality of the fact—and I do not see how it can be denied—and considering that it cannot be explained on physical principles, we must confess that 'the finger of God was there.' Yet I do not see that this prodigy makes more for Catholicity than for Christianity in general."

"Consider, however, all the circumstances," replied La Harpe. "A cross is erected; veneration is paid to it by a prostrate multitude; a zealous missionary exhorts them ever to continue in their holy sentiments; and he assures them that, like Constantine, 'in this sign they shall conquer.' Now, these acts and sentiments are peculiarly Catholic, and God sanctioned them by an evident miracle."

Sefton was silent, and La Harpe continued: "I could appeal to many other modern and well-authenticated miracles, but I will only mention one, and that is the standing miracle of the liquefaction of the blood of St. Januarius in Naples, which takes place twice or thrice in every year."

"Stuff and nonsense! my good Sir, that at least is a mere trick; I do not doubt that the mad enthusiasm of the common people make them fancy they see it liquify; but I shall never believe any such humbug."

"Supposing you were to see it with your own eyes," asked La Harpe, inquiringly, "what would you say then?"

"I shall never see any such thing," said Sefton, "and therefore I need not trouble myself about what would be the result of such a sight; I think I should sooner doubt my own eye-sight, and believe I was deluded by some trick."

"You had better examine the matter, I think," said La Harpe.

"To be sure, I intend to examine it," replied Sefton, "in order that I may have the satisfaction of contradicting all the false statements about it which I have so often heard mentioned."

"Well, I am content if you fairly examine it," said La Harpe; "but tell me candidly, Sefton, did you ever hear of Luther or Calvin working miracles?"

"No, I certainly never did," answered he, unable to suppress a smile, "nor old Harry the Eighth either; he was not quite saint enough for that, with his six wives."

"Nor Luther, with his Catherine Bore; and yet they pretended they had a mission from Heaven to deny and change the divine truths revealed to mankind by the Son of the living God."

Edward seemed struck with this remark, and La Harpe continued, "Did you ever read the history of the introduction of Christianity into the East, by Saint Francis Xavier?"

"Yes," said Edward, "I have read his life, by Dryden, and very beautifully written it is."

"Well, there are many miracles related of him,

wrought in confirmation of his mission: now, what religion did he establish there?"

"It was the Catholic religion, I believe," said Sefton, looking a little foolish, "but that is ages ago."

"It was just about the time of the Reformation," observed La Harpe, "and at the very time God established the truth of the Catholic religion in Asia by *miracles*, Luther, Calvin, and Henry the Eighth, for the gratification of their own passions, thought proper to change it, and to declare that the Catholic Church had fallen into error."

At this point of their conversation, they turned the sharp corner of a projecting rock, and came suddenly upon a party seated on the grass, who were busily engaged in demolishing a *déjeuné à la fourchette*. To Sefton's agreeable surprise, he recognized amongst them his old friend, the Bishop of S——, who introduced him to Mrs. Boren, and also to Captain Boren, and his sister Lavinia, his eldest son and daughter. La Harpe and Sefton joined the luncheon party, and they spent the remainder of the day together. The Bishop and his family were on their way to Rome, where they proposed passing the winter; he insisted on Sefton and his friend dining with them on the following day, which they accordingly did. In the evening, the captain and the ladies went to the theatre, and Sefton took that opportunity of relating to the Bishop the observations he had made on religion since his arrival in Geneva, particularly insisting on Doctor Untersteken's sermon.

"It is an alarming degree of incredulity," observed the Bishop, "but it does not surprise me; it only convinces me more of the wisdom of what some people are pleased to term a new sect of Protestants, to which Oxford has had the honour of giving birth, and to which I am much inclined myself."

"Ah! indeed; I have not heard of it," said Edward eagerly.

"Great caution is requisite in any change or modification of doctrines," said the Bishop solemnly; "but when we have such men as Pusey, Newman, and Keble, as supporters, I think we need not much fear error."

"What are the doctrines of this new sect, my Lord?" asked Sefton, looking at the same time a little uneasily in the direction where La Harpe was seated, reading a newspaper.

"Why," answered the Bishop, "they principally contend that the Church is the sole depository of divine truth, which is not merely in the Bible, but in tradition, as handed down to us in the writings of the early Christian Fathers, and that in their works we must seek for the true exposition of the Scriptures, and the primitive practice of all Christian ordinances. The Church, and not the Bible, should be the guide in matters of faith and practice: for the interpretation put upon the Scriptures by the Bishops, who are the legitimate successors of the Apostles, divinely appointed to teach and govern the Church, must necessarily be the correct one, because they have inherited the promises of the unerring Spirit, and therefore it is wrong to put any other construction, or to inquire further into the matter. They object also to the indiscriminate reading of the Bible; they deny that it is the guide of the laity, contending that it should be restricted to the Clergy, and to the learned; in short, they virtually prohibit the reading of the Bible to the people, pronounce the Church infallible, and declare, that through it only can Divine truth be attained."

"A deal of Catholicity in those doctrines," said La Harpe, looking up from his newspaper.

"Too much so by half for my taste," exclaimed Sefton scornfully.

"We must not be rash and hasty, my good friend," replied the Bishop; "liberty of conscience is a precious Protestant right, of which we may all lawfully avail ourselves."

"Have all the Bishops agreed upon this doctrine?" inquired La Harpe.

"By no means, Sir, by no manner of means," said

Doctor Boren; "in England, Monsieur La Harpe, every one may enjoy liberty of conscience."

"I wish them joy of it," said La Harpe, laughing; "your new sect will not be likely to be very uniform in the interpretation of the Bible, if the heads cannot yet think in concert."

The Bishop looked annoyed, and they shortly after took their leave.

La Harpe could not help rallying Edward a little as they walked home on the new Protestant sect; but as he seemed hurt and out of spirits, he forebore further discourse on the subject, and turned the conversation. Poor Sefton retired to bed more puzzled and anxious than ever. He passed a sleepless night; his soul was tossed about on a sea of doubts and difficulties. On one hand, he saw the dark abyss of rationalism and Deism into which the unrestricted right of private judgment must necessarily plunge the Christian world; on the other, he trembled at the apparent necessity of interposing authority as a guide to the truth; for that must lead directly to Catholicity, a consummation to his mind as frightful as rationalism. Yet he could devise no middle course. His good sense told him, that any authority less than one absolute, supreme, without appeal, and consequently infallible, could be no authority at all in deciding questions of faith, and he recoiled from the idea of subjecting his free-born soul to any such bondage.

CHAPTER XXIII.

"God of evening's yellow ray!
God of yonder dawning day,
That rises from the distant sea,
Like breathing of Eternity!
Thine the flaming sphere of light,
Thine the darkness of the night!
Thine are all the gems of even,
God of Angels, God of Heaven!
God of life, that fade shall never,
Glory to thy name for ever!"

HOGG.

THE wonderful works of God in the beauties of nature have generally a powerful influence on characters of an ardent temperament, in raising the mind from sublunary things to contemplate the ineffable wonders and glories of the Creator, in soothing grief, in dissipating melancholy, and calming fierce and consuming passion. Sefton rose before it was light the following morning; the agitated and desponding state of his mind prevented him sleeping: before dawn he was on the borders of the beautiful lake of Geneva, to watch the glories of the rising sun. He spent that day in musing melancholy, and in silent communing with his troubled spirit, now listlessly stretched on the grass at the verge of the blue Leman, now abandoned in a little skiff on its calm waters, absorbed and entranced in admiration at the beautiful scenery around him. It was during the stillness of that passive day that Sefton ardently prayed to the great God of nature from the inward recesses of his heart, to direct him in the ways of salvation, and implored the Almighty, that if He had really established a revealed religion on earth, to enable him to find it; it was during the calmness of that day, spent on the bosom of the lake of Geneva, that he vowed to his own soul to spare no pains in search of truth, and generously and instantly to embrace it when found. Twilight had succeeded the rich and glowing beams of the setting sun, and he had felt peace and calm in his heart ere he rejoined La Harpe at the hotel; his friend with pleasure remarked, in silence, that though there was a shade of pensive melancholy in Sefton's eye, yet, still his manner and conversation were more calm and cheerful than he had ever observed from the first period of their acquaintance. In the evening, Edward proposed that they should set out the next morning to visit Mont Blanc and the valley Chamouni, which they accordingly did, and the succeeding week was spent in ever-varying emotions of wonder and rapture, at the stupendous and splendid beauties of nature which they witnessed. On their return to Geneva, Monsieur La Harpe joined the friends whom it had been his intention to visit when he left Paris, and Sefton set off towards Italy; they parted with regret, and not without mutual promises of renewing their acquaintance again at some future period. As the Bishop of S—— and his family proposed remaining another fortnight at Geneva, and did not wish to reach Rome till Christmas, Edward had no fancy to wait for them, and was thus forced to the disagreeable alternative of travelling alone; he amused himself as best he could by "guide books" and "classical tours," and when he felt gloomy or oppressed, he consoled his heart by reading the little "Following of Christ," which sister Angela had given him; or in meditating on the sublime and wonderful truths and events recorded in the New Testament, which had been a parting gift from his friend La Harpe. He made the passage of the Alps across the Simplon, the beauties of which infinitely surpassed his most ardent anticipations. He visited on his route the celebrated university of Pavia, and its exquisite Certosa, and spent a little time at the Lago Maggiore, and the Borromian Isles. In Milan, Parma, Florence, and Siena, he failed not to examine all that was curious and interesting. Yet how often did he during this journey wish for the society of his poor Emma; yes, how often did he even sorrow and grieve at their separation, and yearn towards her with feelings of deep affection. Nor could he stifle the pangs of remorse which he often endured at his conduct towards her. Frequently would he draw from his bosom her miniature, gaze on it for a while with the fondest emotion, press it to his lips, and bathe it with his tears; and still would he gaze, until he found relief. As often as he replaced it nearest to his heart, the sight of the medal would recal the grateful remembrance of sister Angela, and he again thanked God, who had sent him in the hour of his utmost need so kind a benefactress. As Edward approached nearer to Rome, his desire to behold the Eternal City increased every moment; he sedulously recalled to his imagination all his schoolboy associations with that classic spot; he reflected how Rome had ever from immemorial ages been an object of the most vivid interest to all nations and countries; and how every citizen of the world could claim it as his home; he repassed in his mind all he had ever heard of its unrivalled antiquities, of its classic lore, and of its splendid churches, and he concluded with a sigh of regret that this queen of the universal world should now be the very citadel of bigotry and superstition. "Yes," added he to himself, "I shall there see the Pope in all his splendour, and the Catholic religion in all its vain pomp and magnificence, and shall have a golden opportunity of fully convincing myself that Catholicity at least is not the religion founded by the Divine Saviour of mankind." During the last post from Ronciglione, he was all eagerness to catch the first glimpse of this long desired object; but on the approach to Rome from the Tuscan road, it certainly does not burst upon the traveller in that collected splendour which early associations and an ardent imagination may lead him to anticipate. The dome of St. Peter's is first visible, and as one approaches nearer to the desired object of so much expectation, to the city which has such claims on the recollections of the classic, and such ties on the heart and feelings of the Christian, the surrounding objects of Nature, the very ground, the trees, the whole scene seems to assume a majestic character of still calmness, which one sensibly and deeply feels. It was nearly dusk when Sefton entered the Porta del Popolo; but the moment he alighted at Serny's Hotel, he ordered a carriage, and drove direct to St. Peter's, that he might at least gratify himself by gazing on its magnificent exterior, its splendid colonnades, its eternal fountains; the church was shut, and therefore he had to wait for the further gratification of his curiosity till the next morning. The following day he returned early, eager beyond expression to behold the interior of this immortal edifice; nor was he disappointed: it is in truth magnificent! and Edward felt penetrated with holy awe as he stood gazing on its vastness; it seemed to him he had never before felt how holy the Almighty is, and he raised his heart to Him in a profound act of adoration, while he was lost in wonder at the splendour of such a sanctuary, raised to the Creator in this earthly vale, by the weak hands of puny man. It is impossible to imagine that the magnificence and richness of the materials employed, and the splendour of the details of each individual part taken separately, could have been combined together with more taste and judgment than has been displayed to produce the wonderful harmony, beauty, and keeping which pervades the whole of this rich and immense temple. Sefton approached the Confession of St. Peter; then, raising his eyes to the stupendous dome that overshadows it, he exclaimed, "What a magnificent Mausoleum, raised to a poor fisherman of Galilee! This still remains increasing in grandeur and splendour, while those of the mighty Cæsars are mouldering into dust. Oh divine Religion! thou alone couldst inspire and execute this more than mortal work! Yes! were I certain that this gorgeous tomb really incloses the remains of the great Apostle, I too could fall down and venerate, aye, and kiss the stones too, like those simple but fervent pilgrims; and am not I also a pilgrim at this holy shrine? Why, then, should I hesitate? But no, it must not be;" and he turned away, Protestant prejudice damping at once the natural effusion of a generous soul. Edward felt very happy as he gazed on this grand object; wandering from beauty to beauty in the detail of its integral parts, now stopping, lost in admiration at its unrivalled mosaics, now absorbed in wonder and amazement at the proportion and beauty preserved amidst its prodigious extent. Had he been a Catholic, he would have felt, too, all the deep enthusiasm and enraptured devotion which a Christian must feel in such a temple, raised to the awful Being that created and preserves him. Yes; that heart must be cold and cynical indeed, which can find aught to cavil at in the incentives to devotion which exist in St. Peter's; and the Catholic full well knows, that besides the extrinsic beauty and value of all that surrounds him, their real and intrinsic value consists in their being stamped with the history of his religion from the time of Christ himself, and in the means which they offer and afford him for the pure and perfect practice of it. Sefton left St. Peter's with his mind full of admiration, and a determination often to return and study it in all its details. He wrote to Emma by that day's post, and gave her an account of all he had seen, adding that he should now have an opportunity of more fully observing the Catholic religion; he expressed more tenderness towards her than he had yet done since their separation, and when he had sent this letter off, he felt his heart a little relieved, knowing that she would receive from it pleasure and consolation.

CHAPTER XXIV.

"Oh, Reason! who shall say what spells renew,
When least we look for it, thy broken clue!
Through what small vistas o'er the darkened brain,
Thy intellectual day-beams burst again.
And how like forts, to which beleaguers win
Unhoped for entrance, through some friend within,
One clear idea, wakened in the breast,
By Memory's magic lets in all the rest."

THE next week was passed by Edward in taking a rapid review of the antiquities, churches, palaces, and other objects of interest in Rome. He was both delighted and surprised with what he saw; he had very good introductions to many of the noble Roman families and resident English, and resolved to avail himself of the urbanity with which he was received to obtain solid information on the objects which most excited his curiosity and interest. Finding the churches always open in the mornings, he generally visited them early, and spent his afternoon amongst the antiquities. One morning, as he was going from church to church with his guide-book in his hand, diligently examining the numberless fine pictures, and marbles, and sculptured treasures which exist in them, he entered the church of St. Augustine, and was soon struck with admiration at the beautiful *fresco* of the Prophet Isaiah by Rafaelle. As he was earnestly gazing at it, his attention was distracted by some one sobbing near him; he turned to the other side of the pillar whence the sound came, and saw a young woman surrounded by a group of little children, apparently in the most abject poverty, kneeling before a statue of the Madonna and Child: the poor woman was in earnest prayer, with her arms extended towards the image. Sefton looked at her compassionately. "She seems in great distress," thought he to himself. "What a pity she should be wasting her prayers before that dumb idol, instead of praying to God to help her." He approached nearer to her, and asked what distressed her: "Alas! Sir," said she, endeavouring to subdue her sobs so as to answer him, "my husband is laying on his death-bed: neither I nor my poor children tasted food all yesterday, and we are come to ask some for to-day of the Madonna, and that she may cure my poor Carlo."

"You had better ask it of God," said Sefton.

"So I am asking it of God," answered the poor woman; "for our Lady can obtain all she wishes of her Divine Son, and she will obtain it for me, I am certain."

Edward looked up at the Madonna; the statue is a very ordinary production of art; but he was struck with the enormous quantities of votives of all kinds with which it, and the surrounding walls and pillars near it, are covered.

"What is the meaning of all these things?" said he in a half-musing tone to the poor woman.

"They are votives, Sir, brought to the Madonna by those for whom she has worked miracles and obtained favours."

"Miracles! stuff and nonsense! what gross superstition!"

The poor woman looked bewildered, and returned with renewed ardour to her prayers.

"But where do you live, my poor woman?" said Sefton, looking at her wan features and weeping children with sincere sentiments of commiseration. She told him where she lived, and he noted it down, that he might send Luigi to see after her and her poor sick husband; in the meantime, he put into her hand a couple of scudi.

It would be impossible to describe the mingled look of gratitude and surprise with which the poor creature gazed at him when she saw what he had given her; she clasped her hands together with fervent thanksgiving, and exclaimed, "Did I not tell you, Sir, that the Madonna *could* grant me the favour if she would?"

Sefton smiled at her simplicity, and felt a confused feeling of pleasure at having relieved her, and of vague wonder at her attributing it to the Madonna, which it would have been difficult to have analyzed. He hastily left the church, and walked on without minding what route he was taking; at length he found himself in the Piazza del Gesù, and seeing the façade of a handsome church before him, he entered it, and having ascertained that it was called the Gesù, he was soon busily employed in admiring Baccici's frescos with which it is adorned, and the many rich and beautiful treasures by which it is distinguished. Sefton observed that the church was very full of people; that there were Masses going on at most of the altars; that there were priests in the different confessionals, surrounded by groups of penitents confessing their sins; and that there were several people continually approaching to the high altar to receive the Holy Communion; he was struck by the silence and order which prevailed amidst all these various acts of piety, and particularly by the devout and serious demeanour of the people. "I have some idea," said he to himself, "that this church belongs to the Jesuits; I think I will go into the sacristy to ask." On inquiry, he found his conjecture right, and was told there that there was in the house an English Father of the name of Oswald, if it chanced that it was he whom he was in search of. Edward was again surprised, and having sent up his card, was soon admitted to the Father's room, who had lately arrived in Rome on business of his order. Father Oswald was pleased to see an old acquaintance, and Sefton felt at the same time mingled sentiments of pain and pleasure; pain, because it was principally to Father Oswald's influence that he attributed his wife's having become a Catholic, and pleasure, because he was an old acquaintance whom he could not help both admiring and esteeming. When they had conversed together a little of times gone by, of England, and of Emma, Father Oswald offered to shew him the rest of the house, which offer Edward gladly accepted; "For," said he, "I never was in a house of Religious in my life before now."

"You must not fail, then, to visit some of the monasteries and convents existing in Italy," said Father Oswald, "for you will find in them many curious and interesting objects, which will gratify your taste for literature."

Sefton bowed. He visited with much interest the library and refectory, the poor and simple apartments of the religious, and the chapel of St. Ignatius, formed of the room in which that great and holy man died; and near to which there exists the celebrated piece of prospective by Padre Pozzi. As he accompanied Father Oswald to his own room, they passed by a beautiful Madonna in the corridor. Edward had already remarked a large crucifix at the bottom of the stairs, and he could not help asking the Father why they were placed in the passages.

"To raise the mind to Heaven, and to promote religious recollection," answered he.

"It seems very odd to me, Sir, I assure you, to see the great use made of all these kind of things in Catholic countries."

"When you understand a little better the explanation and use of many things you see in our churches, your surprise will wear off; nay, perhaps even admiration may succeed to it," replied Father Oswald.

"It will be a long time first, I believe," said Sefton.

When they were reseated in Father Oswald's room, Edward told him the adventure at St. Augustine's, and concluded by a long tirade against the folly and superstition of the people, fancying that miracles take place now-a-days; and, particularly, against the credulity of the poor woman, in thinking the Madonna had any thing to do with his alms.

"Perhaps the woman was a better Christian philosopher than you imagine," said Father Oswald, smiling.

"How do you make that out?" said Sefton.

"Because the poor woman, overlooking all secondary causes, referred the benefit she had received to the first great cause, 'to the Giver of all good gifts.' She remembered, no doubt, what she had often been taught, that 'not a sparrow falls on the ground without the Father,'* and so she wisely concluded that God had heard her prayer, or rather the prayer of the Blessed Virgin for her, and had sent her relief through your hands."

"There was both wisdom and piety in that sentiment," replied Sefton, "I must allow it, if I could persuade myself she was capable of such a reflection."

"I think her very actions ought to convince you of it. The simple lessons of the Gospel to which I have alluded are not beyond the capacity of the most simple understanding."

"True," said Sefton, "the lessons of the Gospel are well adapted to satisfy a pious and simple soul; still *you* must allow that the providence of God over man is a very dark and mysterious problem to the philosopher."

"All Christian philosophers," replied Father Oswald, "ought to know that there is a double order of providence; one the order of grace, the other the order of nature; one that regulates the distribution of graces to the souls of men, by which they are disposed, and prepared, and helped forward, if they choose to correspond by their own free will, to a supernatural state of glory; the other, the disposition of secondary causes, by which God brings about all the changes in the material world, which, for his own purposes, he has determined from the beginning, or, to speak more accurately, which he *determines* from eternity; for with God there is no past or future, all is one immovable present. Now the providence of God, in the order of grace, inspired into your soul the desire to give an alms to that poor woman."

"But there was no miracle in that," interrupted Sefton.

"No, it was no miracle, though a direct interference

* Matt. x. 29.

of the Divinity with the soul of man ; it was no miracle, because it was in the ordinary course of providence, in the supernatural order of grace."

"But I object," said Sefton, "to the Divinity exercising any direct interference with the soul of man; it seems to me men have little or no other motive of action than visible objects."

"Unfortunately, most men have not," replied Father Oswald, "yet I know too much of your character not to be certain that that is not your philosophy ; it is a principle worthy only of those who have been brought up in the school of Epicurus. Indeed, to doubt of the interference of God in the concerns of man, is to doubt the necessity and efficacy of prayer; and in vain would Christ and His Apostles have exhorted us to earnest and persevering prayer, with faith and confidence that our prayer would be heard, if all things where to happen in an unchangeable order, whether we prayed or not."

"There is deep reason in that," said Sefton, musing.

"The person who can adopt the principle that we act only on sensible motives," continued the Father, "must never have looked into himself; never have consulted the motives of his own heart. Did such a one never make a pious reflection, never conceive a holy desire, never experience a salutary consolation, never form a pious resolution to practise virtue and avoid vice, unless he had been excited thereunto by some sensible object?"

"I cannot say that of myself," replied Sefton, "for I have very often made good resolutions, and felt interior consolations too, without the influence of sensible objects."

"I am fully aware of that," answered Father Oswald, "but others there are, who, perhaps though rarely, have not; and more are they to be pitied: but then did they never feel a sudden alarm, an inward trouble, a secret remorse for deeds done in the gratification of sense? if they have, what is all this but the voice of God that speaks to the heart; a direct interference of the Divinity with the soul of man?"

"It seems like it, certainly," said Edward.

"No concatenation of secondary causes, no material, sensible object enters here," pursued Father Oswald; "'To-day, if you shall hear his voice, harden not your hearts.' It is not said, to-day if you hear the thunder roll, or the earth groan beneath your feet, 'harden not your hearts:' no, but when you hear *His* small, still, powerful, but gentle voice which whispers in your heart, then you are warned to listen to, and receive it: still there is no miracle in that, because, as I observed before, it is in the ordinary course of providence, in the supernatural order of grace. When St. Paul was struck down from his horse, when the thief was converted on the cross, when Magdalen threw herself at the feet of Jesus, when Augustine heard 'Tolle, lege,' and a hundred other instances of special and extraordinary interference, we readily admit a miracle in the supernatural order of grace. It is equally true that God often ordains the course of nature in such a special order, as to co-operate with his providence in the order of grace. He disposes secondary causes, so as to produce plague, famine, earthquakes, *et cetera;* and general and individual misfortunes to awaken men from the lethargy of sin, and make them more attentive to his call; but all these sensible motives will never produce of themselves one salutary act; grace alone can do that; all these misfortunes may be brought about by a concatenation of secondary causes, or they may be produced by a direct miracle; it is very difficult easily to determine by which. But the effect is the same, for all proceed from the same directing hand."

"But miracles have ceased," said Sefton; "and it is my opinion, that God in the beginning fixed and determined a concatenation of secondary causes, according to which every event is foreseen and preordained to happen according to a preordained and immutable law."

"Taken in a limited and general sense, what you say is true," said Father Oswald; "and it is wonderful how God, in all the possible orders of succession, selected that order which does not in the least control the free will of man. But you are egregiously wrong in supposing that the law of physical causes cannot be changed. It seems to me little less than blasphemy to pretend to subject God to the physical laws of matter. What! could not, or did not God, when he established those laws, reserve to himself the right to interfere in them, when and where he foresaw that it would be for his own glory, or even for the good of his creatures?"

"It is easier, I think, Sir, to assert that than to prove it," said Sefton.

"There is no difficulty in proving it," replied Father Oswald mildly. "Did not God *suspend* the laws of nature when the waters of the Red Sea stood as walls on each side of the Israelites; when the Jordan opened to them a passage, when the sun and moon stood still at the voice of Joshua, when the head of the axe rose to the surface of the water, and when Christ and Peter walked upon the sea? Did not God *reverse* the laws of nature when the shadow of the dial went back, when Elias ascended in the fiery chariot, when the dead man returned to life at the touch of the Prophet's bones; and when Christ and his Apostles recalled the dead to life, and gave light to the blind? Has He not *changed* the law of nature when the substance of the rod of Moses was changed into a serpent, when the Prophet multiplied the widow's oil, and when Christ changed water into wine, and multiplied the bread and fishes in the desert? All these are pregnant instances of the divine interference in the laws of nature, and can never be explained by any possible concatenation of second causes; therefore my conclusion is, that God did reserve to himself the right of interfering when, and where, and how he pleased."

"Well," said Sefton, "I will grant you that this interference did exist in the theocracy of the Jews, and also in the miracles wrought to prove the mission of Jesus Christ."

"Then," said Father Oswald, "if you admit miracles at all, the question is now reduced to very narrow limits; namely, have they ceased?"

"I say they have," replied Sefton; "and so I imagine do most rational people."

"Remember," said Father Oswald, "that God distinguished his chosen people by an uninterrupted series of miracles from the beginning unto the very end of the synagogue. In our Saviour's time we read, that at stated periods the angel descended and moved the waters of the Probatic pond;* now, can we for a moment imagine, that Christ has left the Church, his beloved spouse, without this precious mark of his predilection? Has he not expressly promised it?—'Amen, amen, I say unto you, He that believeth in me, the works that I do, he also shall do, and greater than these shall he do.'"†

"Your reasoning, Sir," said Sefton, "is very plausible and specious, but of no avail against the notorious fact, that since the days of the Apostles no well-authenticated miracle has ever taken place."

"Really," replied Father Oswald, "it requires an extraordinary degree of scepticism to call in doubt the words of ecclesiastical history which bear the most irrefragable evidence to an uninterrupted succession of miracles in every age: weigh well the promises of Christ; he prefixes his most solemn asseveration, and no ways limited to time, place, or person, that miracles shall be wrought alone in his Church; faith alone is wanted. 'Amen, I say unto you, If you have faith as a grain of mustard seed, you shall say to this mountain, Remove from hence hither, and it shall remove, and nothing shall be impossible to you."‡ Now, in his Church, true faith shall always be found; shall we then be told that miracles have ceased? Well, then, I say the promises of Christ have failed, and you give a fair pretext for infidels to reject the Bible altogether."

Sefton coloured deeply; "But," persisted he, "as we see no miracles in these enlightened ages, therefore they must have ceased."

"There are none so blind as those who will not see," replied Father Oswald; "real miracles have never

* John v. 4. † John xiv. 12. ‡ Matt. xvii. 19.

ceased in the Church of Christ, and it is one of the most convincing proofs of the truth of the Catholic religion."

"No doubt it would be so if they did exist," replied Sefton very seriously, "but there is the point."

At this moment some one knocked at the door. Father Oswald called out, "Come in," and a tall young man, about thirty, in a clerical dress, with a fine Roman face, and mild and sensible countenance, entered; he said a few words to Father Oswald in Italian, who shortly after introduced him to Sefton, as Monsignor Guidi. After the usual compliments of politeness, Edward rose, and took his leave, fearful of intruding by a longer visit, as he perceived they had business together.

CHAPTER XXV.

"As when on the ivory tablet we view
The features of father or friend,
The bosom heaves high, and, like evening dew,
Soft tears on the tablet descend.

"Even so when thy Cross, O Saviour! I see,
And thy head thus drooping with pain,
The sigh of my heart shall whisper to Thee,
Thou shalt not thus love me in vain!

"Oft shall my tears, as in silence they steal
On thy wounds thus bleeding for me,
The sigh, the resolve, at my heart reveal
To cling, aye, for ever to Thee!

"We call Thee Father, but thou art far more,
Far dearer than father or friend;
Oh! teach then 'thy child' to love and adore
Thee, Father, Redeemer, and End."

CATHOLIC HYMN.

THE following day, Monsignor Guidi called upon Sefton, and they were mutually pleased with each other on a further acquaintance. Monsignor Guidi was an ecclesiastic equally distinguished by his rank and talents; he united to great sensibility of heart and mildness of manner, a cultivated understanding, and a profound erudition. He very sincerely offered to be of any use to Sefton in his literary and religious researches; which offer was gratefully accepted, and they examined together most of the antiquities and objects of interest to be met with in Rome. One morning, as Sefton was seated at breakfast, Monsignor Guidi was announced: "I have come," said he, "to ask if you have yet seen the Pope?"

"No," replied Sefton, "I have not. I suppose it is considered necessary, or I had just as soon be excused."

"You perfectly astonish me!"

"How so?" inquired Sefton; "it is my opinion that the Pope is the most deplorable of self-deceivers, a weak instrument of the Devil, and the most profane and audacious charletan."

The Prelate held up his hands in amazement.

"Don't be alarmed, my dear Guidi," said Sefton, "but the truth of it is, that to all Bible Christians, the Church of Rome appears a system of the grossest worldliness, supported by splendour, and governed by earthly means."

"I know not what you exactly mean by Bible Christians," said Monsignor Guidi; "but if that is the view they take of the Catholic religion, I am sure should they look at the moon through a pair of green spectacles, they would swear it was made of green cheese. I would not be so unpolite as to turn the tables, though perhaps it might not be very difficult, upon the splendour, luxury, and iniquity of most of the royal heads of the Church of England and Kirk of Scotland; but I imagine from what you have just said, you do not wish to see his Holiness."

Sefton looked a little foolish. "I did not exactly say that," replied Sefton; "travellers are accustomed to see many wonderful things."

"Well, then," said Monsignor Guidi, "there will be this afternoon the first vespers of 'All Saints,' in the chapel of the Pope's palace. This chapel, which is called the Sixtine, is adorned by Michael Angelo's finest paintings. His Holiness will himself assist at the vespers, and thus you will have an opportunity of seeing him."

"I am much obliged to you, I am sure," said Sefton, "and shall be most happy to accompany you; but do tell me what, in the name of patience, you mean by 'All Saints,' for to me the worship of the Saints and their intercession, one and all, seems the grossest ignorance and idolatry."

"Methinks Catholics have great reason to be obliged to Protestants for the good opinion they have of their piety and judgment," said Monsignor Guidi a little sarcastically. "I can assure you we are neither stupid, nor so grossly ignorant, as to idolize the Saints: we pay them not the worship which is due to God alone; we honour them only as the special friends of their Creator, who are already admitted to the Heaven which we hope one day to attain; in the meanwhile, we believe with a firm faith that they are not now less charitable than they were when living in this world, that they interest themselves for us and pray to God for us; if we only reflect a moment, we cannot imagine that the rich man buried in Hell should evince solicitude for the salvation of his brethren,* and the Saints in Heaven should have no care for the salvation of their fellow-combatants, still on earth. It is on the day called 'All Saints' that we honour them altogether, and recommend ourselves and all the world to their prayers."

"But do you really imagine," said Sefton, "that you have any rational ground for believing that such honour paid to created beings is pleasing to God? Can you shew any Scriptural authority for such a practice?"

"Nothing can be more rational or more Scriptural," replied Monsignor Guidi, "than that we should pray for one another here on earth. Does not St. Paul in all his epistles desire the prayers of the faithful for himself? Have you never reflected on these his words, 'I desire therefore first of all that supplications, prayers, intercessions, and thanksgivings be made for all men, for this is good and acceptable in the sight of God our Saviour?'† and does not St. James also say, 'Pray one for another, that you may be saved, for the continual prayer of a just man availeth much'?"*

"Well, but we suppose the Apostles to have been men really inspired and guided by God," said Sefton.

"Certainly they were," replied Guidi, "and yet you see they ask for the prayers of the faithful; now surely the prayers and intercession of his blessed Saints in

* Luke xvi. 27. † 1 Tim. ii. 1. ‡ Jas. v. 16.

Heaven are not less good and acceptable in his divine presence, and surely they must avail more than the prayers of souls on earth, not yet made perfect."

" Sefton remained silent for some time, as one in deep reflection ; at length he said, " Indeed, Monsignore, your reasoning appears very specious ; I know not exactly how to answer it: for if the prayers of poor sinful mortals, when offered up for other men, 'are good and acceptable to God,' we cannot doubt that 'the spirits of the just made perfect' may intercede for us with still greater efficacy ; yet it is strange we have no direct evidence of it in Holy Scripture."

"I am glad," replied Monsignor Guidi, "that you acknowledge the practice of invoking the intercession of the Saints to be at least rational. Still you seek for Scriptural evidence, and we are not without that ; yet you must allow me to protest against your mistaken principle, that every thing practically pious and holy is to be found in the Scriptures: if the thing in question be rational and pious in itself, it behoveth you to shew that it is forbidden by Scripture before you condemn it in your neighbour."

"Well, well," answered Sefton, "you may perhaps be right in that also, but let me hear your Scriptural evidence for the intercession of Saints."

"We read in the book of Maccabees, that Onias, who had been the high priest, and had been martyred, appeared to Judas Maccabæus, and 'holding up his hands, *prayed* for all the people of the Jews :' after this, there appeared also another man, admirable for age and glory, and environed with great beauty and majesty. Then Onias answering, said, 'This is a lover of his brethren and of the people, and for all the holy city, Jeremiah the Prophet of God.' "*

"That passage, no doubt, would be decisive of the question," answered Sefton, "if it were really canonical Scripture : but you know, Monsignore, that we consider the Maccabees as apocryphal."

" A very ready way of getting over a difficulty !

* 2 Mac. xv. 11.

Luther denied the authenticity of the epistle of St. James, and pronounced it unworthy of an apostle, because, forsooth, it reprobates his system of salvation by faith alone, without good works."

"But you are aware," continued Sefton, "that the Jews do not admit the authenticity of these books."

"We look not to the Jews for the authenticity of our Scriptures," said Monsignor Guidi, "otherwise we must reject the whole New Testament: we look to the authority of the Church to decide what is, and what is not, the revealed Word of God; and from the earliest ages, the Church has regarded the books of Maccabees as divinely inspired; St. Augustine teaches us this fact: but the ancient Jews did not reject these books."

"How so?" said Sefton with some surprise.

"Perhaps," replied the Prelate, "you are not aware that the canon of the Jewish Scriptures was fixed by Esdras, and that the books of Maccabees were written three hundred years later, and therefore could not be inserted in his canon. The Jews waited for another Esdras, or prophet, to pronounce on the authenticity of those books. The Christian Church, in her general councils, has pronounced the sentence as she has upon the books of the New Testament: if you reject that authority, I know not upon what ground you can admit the New Testament."

"I will not enter at present into that question," replied Sefton, "for I fear I should be involved in inextricable difficulties. But you must allow, Sir, that the legends of many of your Saints are silly, blasphemous, and disgusting."

"You use strong language, Sir, and I can only attribute it to your ignorance; but that which appears silly before the wise of this world, may be wisdom before God. I have read the histories of many of our Saints, but I never found any thing blasphemous in them. That their poverty, humility, fastings, and mortifications, may be disgusting to sensual men, I will not deny; but to the truly pious, and to the lovers of the Cross, they produce a very different effect."

"What!" exclaimed Sefton, "would you have me believe all the absurd stories which are related of your saints?"

"By no means; I only wish you to examine, without prejudice, the evidence on which such histories are grounded: if that evidence does not satisfy your judgment, you are then at full liberty to reject them; we pretend to no higher authority for them, than what is due to well-authenticated historical facts."

"I thought," said Sefton, "that all Catholics were bound to believe them, under pain of excommunication for heresy."

"Another instance," observed Monsignore Guidi, "of the gross misconceptions which most Protestants entertain of the Catholic faith. The acts and gests of the saints, like all other historical facts, rest entirely on human testimony, and, consequently, can never become the objects of divine faith, and they claim no further credit than is warranted by the weight of the evidence in their favour."

"Are you then allowed to examine them critically?" asked Sefton.

"No doubt we are; and I need only refer you to the great work of the Bolandists, where you will find a most laborious collection of monuments and documents regarding the lives of all the saints, accompanied with the most acute criticism and free judgment in determining the certain from the dubious; truth from falsehood."

"I had no notion of that," said Sefton; "still I must say it would be no easy task to remove my doubts."

"It is the genuine spirit of Protestantism to *doubt* of every thing but the visions of their own brains," said the Prelate, sighing. "You cannot think how such assertions surprise Catholics; for, from my poor experience, I find there is no historical fact, however well authenticated, if it tends to throw a lustre on the Catholic religion, which they will not boldly deny or egregiously misrepresent, as there is no story, true or false, that reflects on the character of the Catholic Priest, that they do not credulously devour."

"You are very severe, Monsignore," said Sefton, smiling; "but there is one point of your doctrine of which I am not yet convinced. Though I were to grant that the saints in heaven feel an interest in our welfare, and may pray for us; yet I do not see how we can invoke them, without attributing to them a sort of ubiquity, which no doubt is blasphemous."

"There is surely no more blasphemy in believing that 'the spirits of the just made perfect in the company of many thousands of angels'* can communicate with their votaries on earth, than that 'there shall be joy before the angels of God, upon one sinner doing penance.'† Catholics are neither taught, nor believe, that any saint or angel is endowed with the divine attribute of ubiquity; but they know, though Bible readers may not know it, that the rich man in Hell could hold a conversation with Abraham, when he was *afar off*, and Lazarus in his bosom, although 'there was fixed between them *a great chaos*.'‡ Therefore, there is no need that the saints should move from the place of their repose, in order to know the prayers of their votaries on earth. Oh! if Protestants knew the heartfelt consolation of having so many heavenly friends and intercessors, they would rather envy us, than revile and despise us."

"Perhaps," said Sefton, "you will next justify your adoration of the statues of saints; that at least is rank idolatry."

"I will not justify such a charge," exclaimed Monsignore Guidi earnestly, "but I will deny it: the essential part of idolatrous worship, the abomination so much detested and reprobated in Holy Scripture, consisted in offering sacrifices to idols, or, as the Apostle expresses it, to devils. Now, surely, you will not accuse Catholics of such infatuation? Has the Gospel of Christ been preached to them for eighteen hundred years to no better effect? The person who can really seriously think idolatry possible amongst Christians, must have a mean idea of the efficacy of the Gospel."

"From what I have heard, and from what I have

* Heb. xii. 22. † Luke xv. 10. ‡ Luke xvi. 23.

myself seen," replied Sefton, "I certainly cannot but think that, at all events, the common people are guilty of idolatry; perhaps not you, Monsignore, nor really well-instructed Catholics either; but, depend upon it, it is very prevalent amongst the lower classes."

"My dear Mr. Sefton, I must really again positively contradict you," said the Prelate. "It is difficult for me to imagine how you can have been so completely misinformed upon this subject; but I do assure you that the greatest veneration, adoration, or worship, that any Catholic ever paid to the image of a saint, never came up to the veneration and awe which the Israelites, by the command of God, paid to the Ark of the Covenant, the workmanship of man's hand. I could shew you a hundred texts to prove this; but you may recollect with what precaution, and sacrifices, and ceremonies, the High Priest was to approach it once a year, and 'he commanded him, saying, that he enter not at all into the sanctuary which is within the veil before the propitiatory with which the Ark is covered, lest he die; for I will appear as a cloud over the oracle unless he first do these things.'* Remember, too, what reverence Josue taught the people to pay to the Ark: 'And let there be between you and the Ark the space of two thousand cubits, that you may see it afar off . . . . and take care you come not near the Ark.'"†

"There is a shadow of reason in what you say, Sir," replied Sefton; "but that was in the Old Law."

"The Old Law was not destroyed, but fulfilled," said the Prelate; "and what was commanded then, cannot be unlawful now; what was pious then, cannot be impious now: however, there is something approaching nearer to worship or adoration of the likeness of something in Heaven or on earth in this example: 'And Josue rent his garments, and fell flat on the ground before the Ark of the Lord until the evening, both he and all the ancients of Israel, and they put dust upon their heads.'‡ Again, the chastisements of the Philistines, and the fate of Oza for irreverence shewn to the

* Lev. xvi. 2. † Jos. iii. 4. ‡ Jos. vii. 6.

Ark of the Lord, and the pomp and jubilee with which David carried it in procession, are striking instances of respect shewn even to inanimate created objects. While the princes and anointed of the people gave this example of veneration and respect to a wooden box, and to the graven and golden cherubins on its lid, with what awe and terror must the vulgar have been stricken, particularly when they saw that worship sanctioned by God with the most evident miracles!"

"But," said Sefton earnestly, "I have always understood that the Catholic Church suppresses one of the commandments altogether, and divides another into two, to blind the people, and support the image-worship."

"How you must have been misinformed," said Monsignore Guidi; "the Catholic Church suppresses nothing of the Ten Commandments: she divides them—for in the Bible there is no division of first, second, third, and so forth—as the Fathers in the earliest ages divided them. Every thing that regards the worship of God, and the prohibition of idolatry, are comprehended in one and the first commandment, because they regard one and the same object. It would be an easy matter for a finical Bible reader to make three commandments out of the first. 1st. Thou shalt not have strange gods before me. 2nd. Thou shalt not make to thyself a graven thing. 3rd. Thou shalt not adore them. Now, if it be forbidden *to make* 'the likeness of any thing that is in Heaven above, or the Earth beneath,' how many precious monuments of the fine arts must be destroyed! how many portly figures and darling miniatures must be cast into the flames!"

"I am sure," persisted Sefton, "I always had the impression, that the use of paintings, sculpture, and images in churches, was contrary to Scripture, and that it was positively forbidden there."

"Yet it was by the *command* of God that two images of cherubins were made and placed on the Ark,"* said the Prelate; "and did not the Israelites venerate the brazen serpent as a type, or figure of Christ?"†

* Exod. xxv. † Numb. xxi.

Catholics venerate the images of Christ, of the Blessed Virgin, and of the saints, on account of their prototypes. None of them are so stupid as to believe that any divinity, any power or virtue, resides in any of these images."

"I wish I could persuade myself of that," said Sefton; "for though, as I observed before, the learned and educated may make that distinction, yet I feel sure the poor ignorant Catholics are incapable of it; and I cannot but fear they really adore the images as much as the Pagans did their idols."

"Pardon me," replied Monsignore Guidi; "the poor Catholics are better instructed in their Catechism than you imagine, and certainly know much more of the nature and unity of God, than the gross-minded Israelites, who adored the golden calves, as the gods which had brought them out of Egypt. You have, no doubt, traversed the splendid galleries of the Vatican, filled with splendid and countless statues?"

"To be sure: what of that?"

"You may have observed the poor ignorant Catholics wrapt in the contemplation of those precious monuments of art?"

"Yes: what then?"

"Did you ever see any of them fall down and adore them?"

"No, certainly; but remove them into your churches, and they would soon be crowded with votaries."

"Our churches are adorned with innumerable statues, as in the monuments of the Popes, and other great men; did you ever see votaries bending before them?"

"I certainly never did," replied Sefton doggedly.

"Then the poor ignorant Catholic knows how to distinguish between an image and its prototype. But, my dear Sir, reason a little more consistently. I am told that, at the Reformation, when you pulled down the images of the crucified Redeemer, and his holy Mother, you erected in their stead the royal arms, the lion and the unicorn; nay, that St. Paul's and Westminster Abbey are crowded at this day with statues of all the

Heathen divinities: now, is not all this a greater violation of the first commandment, than the Catholic images ever were?"

"But we do not make them the objects of any religious veneration or worship," said Sefton somewhat haughtily.

"I do not charge *you*," replied the Prelate, "with such gross idolatry; still, I think a fitter place might be found for them than the house of the living God. You will not find such unseemly objects in a Catholic temple."

"They are only used as allegorical representations of the prowess, renown, and virtues of departed worthies."

"It may be so; but we also employ allegorical representations, and yet contrive to keep out of our churches all Pagan deities."

"Still," urged Sefton, "you pay adoration to the statues of your saints, if you do not to your allegorical statues."

"There is a great difference betwixt the two," answered Monsignore Guidi. "Suppose I were to cast upon the ground the image of the crucified Redeemer, and bid you trample on it, would you do it?"

"No, certainly."

"Why not? It is nothing but an image."

"Because I have too much respect for my Redeemer, to offer him an insult even in his image."

"Your sentiment is Catholic; we only carry our respect a little further: far from trampling on it, we raise it with veneration, press it to our hearts, kiss it with our lips, and contemplating in the image what the prototype suffered for us, bathe it with our tears."

Sefton was silent.

"It is a beautiful day," said Monsignore Guidi; "do you feel inclined to drive as far as the tomb of Cecilia Metalla, on the Via Appia, and study the antiquities in that quarter?"

"I shall like nothing better," said Sefton, and off they set. Edward was delighted with all he saw; the balmy softness of the air, the calm repose of the Campagnia, and the views of Tivoli and Frascati, on their undulating and olive-covered hills, heightened the sense of pleasure with which they wandered over Roma Vecchia, and visited the sepulchres of the ancient Romans and heroes of antiquity.

CHAPTER XXVI.

That no lambkin might wander in error benighted,
But homeward the true path may hold,
The Redeemer ordained that in one faith united,
One Shepherd shall govern the fold.

FRAGMENT.

AT the appointed hour, the two friends found themselves ascending the magnificent staircase of the Vatican to attend the vespers, as already agreed. Edward could not help feeling a deep interest in the scene around him; the venerable assemblage of Cardinals, the throng of religious and secular Clergy, the unrivalled music, the benign and dignified presence of the Sovereign Pontiff, and the crowds of strangers from all parts of the world, assembled to gaze and to admire, struck him almost with reverential awe; as the vespers went on, he felt a desire to know what kind of a devotion it might be which he was listening to: he asked Monsignore Guidi, in a whisper, what was meant by vespers. The Prelate gave him a book, from which he found that vespers consist in five psalms, taken from the Book of Psalms, differing according to the different festivals; these psalms are followed by a little chapter, and a hymn, after which is chanted to music, the Magnificat, or Song of the Blessed Virgin Mary,* the whole terminating with some short commemorations and prayers. Edward was surprised to find by this book, lent him by his friend, that the vespers were translated into English, so that those not understanding Latin could nevertheless follow, and perfectly enter into the

* Luke i. 46.

spirit of the service. He left the chapel, much impressed with what he had heard and seen, excepting that he was both mortified and ashamed by the misbehaviour of many of his own countrymen, who seemed to consider themselves rather in a theatre than in the house of God. He attempted an awkward apology to Monsignore Guidi, by observing that they must have been some ill-bred churls, who had the bad taste to scoff at what they did not understand, or wanted the common sense to stay away, if they could not assist with decency and respect in the presence at least of a temporal sovereign.

"It has been often observed," said Monsignore Guidi somewhat sarcastically, "that you English shew more respect to the mosques of Constantinople, and to the temple of Juggernaut, than to the Christian temples of Rome."

Sefton smarted a little at this reflection, but he made no observation, and asked Monsignore Guidi to call and take him the following morning to the High Mass, which was to be celebrated in the same chapel. At the appointed time they arrived at the Sistine Chapel, where, before the service commenced, they had time to admire the beauty of Michael Angelo's immortal paintings. If Sefton had been struck with the soothing piety of the vespers the evening before, he was still more impressed by the solemnity of the High Mass, which he now witnessed. It had been with a half kind of scruple that he had expressed a wish to attend it, for he very simply believed that the Mass was the quintessence of Catholic idolatry, and it was only in consequence of a clear explanation from Monsignore Guidi of the Catholic faith on the point of the real presence of Jesus Christ Himself, God and Man, in the Sacrament, that this difficulty was surmounted. If such be the belief of Catholics, he thought within himself, the adoration which they pay to the host cannot be idolatrous. They may be mistaken; still they adore not a bit of bread. Their adoration is given to Jesus Christ, God and Man, who, they feel persuaded, is there really present under the form and appearance of bread. But then, how can our clergy swear that such a practice is idolatrous and blasphemous? I cannot comprehend it; there must be something rotten in all this. He listened very attentively to the Mass as it proceeded; he was touched with the plaintive notes of the Kyrie eleison, and the rapturous burst of praise and adoration in the 'Gloria in excelsis Deo.' When this was followed by the Epistle, Gradual, and Gospel, taken word for word from the Bible itself, including Old and New Testaments, he could not conceal his surprise, and he whispered to his friend, "I had not the most distant idea of this! Little did I think to hear the eight beatitudes recited in the very middle of a Popish Mass;" and then he thought in his own mind that perhaps Emma might not be quite so wrong as he had imagined. His attention was now called to the beautiful music of the Nicene Creed. He found the words of it were exactly the same as those repeated every Sunday in the Protestant church, and he wondered he had never before remarked that he had all his life been repeating his belief in the 'One, Holy, Catholic, and Apostolic Church;' 'Et Unam, Sanctam, Catholicam, et Apostolicam Ecclesiam:' surely, thought he, there must have been some strange inconsistency or mistake amongst the first reformers, to let such a glaring profession of Catholicity remain in the Protestant ritual; and he determined within himself to remonstrate with the Bishop of S—— on that subject, when he should arrive. After the Credo follows the solemn offering of the bread and wine; the incensing of the sacrifice; the 'Lavabo,' and other prayers, succeeded by the glorious burst of adoration chanted in the preface. The officiating priest then proceeded in secret with the solemn canon of the Mass, during which he commemorated the Church militant and the Church triumphant, preparatory to the awful consecration of the bread and wine into the body and blood of the Lord Jesus Christ. Immediately after the consecration the priest raises the host and the chalice for the adoration of the people: and all kneel, and adore in profound silence their Lord and God really present amongst them. Sefton did not kneel; he stood quite upright, though he felt in his heart a pang of regret that he could not join in the impressive and touching devotion of all around him. He could not, because he did not yet believe in the real presence of his Saviour; still he remained convinced that those who did believe in that mystery, however they might mistake, could not be condemned for idolatry. He even felt he wished he could believe, for how sublime would then be the worship of the Mass! how worthy of the Divinity! how far superior to any worship offered by Pagans, Jews, or Protestants! The Mass proceeded in silence, and by referring to the missal he had in his hand, he found that after the celebrant had offered this awful sacrifice to the Divinity, he prayed for the dead, and again commemorated the saints in Heaven. He then chanted the Lord's Prayer aloud, succeeded by the 'Agnus Dei,' and 'Domine, non sum dignus,' previous to consummating the sacrifice, by receiving in communion the body and blood of his Saviour, which he had a little before consecrated; the communion being followed by prayers of thanksgiving and the blessing, the Mass terminated with the beginning of the Gospel of St. John. The Sovereign Pontiff retired, and the assistants dispersed, descending in crowds the splendid stairs of the Vatican. Sefton was silent for some time; at length Monsignore Guidi asked him if he had been pleased with what he had witnessed.

"I have been extremely surprised," answered Sefton; "I find that the Mass is so very different to what I had thought it. Are all Masses the same as this?"

"Yes; excepting that the prayers, lessons, and gospels are different, according to the different festivals."

"To those who believe in the real presence of Jesus Christ, it must be a most awful and most consoling act of worship," observed Sefton.

"Doubtless it is so," replied the Prelate.

"Still," said Sefton, "I have always believed that the Mass at best is but a human institution, and was not known in the first ages of the Church."

" The first Mass," said Monsignore Guidi, " was celebrated by our Lord Jesus Christ himself when he instituted the Eucharist, and offered himself a sacrifice for the sins of mankind: does he not say, ' This is My body which is *given* for you'? which words clearly indicate a present offering of his body, a present shedding of his blood; ' This is My blood which *is shed* for you'? and in obedience to his command, ' Do ye this in remembrance of Me,' the Apostles offered the holy sacrifice in every region of the earth to which they were sent; and from the rising to the setting sun the clean oblation has been ever offered, as the Prophet Malachy had foretold. Nay, the altar-stone upon which St. Peter celebrated exists still in the church of Sta. Pudenyiana here in Rome; and from the time of St. Peter down to the present Pope, Mass has always been celebrated in the Catholic Church, and ever will continue to be so to the end of the world."

" But, my dear Monsignore, you must be aware that the Protestants deny that St. Peter was ever Bishop of Rome, or that the Saviour instituted any primacy of jurisdiction in him."

" That is flying from one point to another," said Monsignore Guidi, " as I find Protestants continually do; but a bold denial is not sufficient to bring conviction with it. That St. Peter was the first Bishop of Rome, and ended his days there, are historical facts, as well or better authenticated than that Julius Cæsar was slain in the senate-house. That Christ conferred on St. Peter a primacy of jurisdiction over the other Apostles, and consequently over the whole Church, is as clear in the Scripture as words can make them."

" How so?"

" Because to St. Peter alone our Blessed Saviour said, ' *Thou* art Peter (a rock), and upon this rock I will build my Church.'* To St. Peter alone our Blessed Saviour said, ' I will give *to thee* the keys of the Kingdom of Heaven;' to Peter alone our Blessed Saviour said, ' I have prayed *for thee*, that *thy* faith fail not,

* Matt. xvi. 18.

and thou being once converted, confirm thy brethren;'* to Peter alone he committed the care of his whole flock, 'Feed my lambs, feed my sheep.'† Now this primacy of jurisdiction which was given to St. Peter, we acknowledge in the successors of St. Peter, the Bishops of Rome, down to the present day. In every age of the Church, the successor of St. Peter in the See of Rome has been ever acknowledged as the supreme head of the Church of Christ. In the nature of things, a centre of unity, a centre of faith and of charity, is absolutely necessary. This very necessity is itself a sufficient reason to believe that Christ has provided his Church with such centre of union. Did he not pray for this union of his followers? 'Holy Father, keep them in Thy name whom Thou hast given Me, that they may *be one*, as We also are.'‡ We search in vain for such a centre out of the See of Rome; no other See ever pretended to this prerogative, and this prerogative has been conceded to the Chair of Peter by every other See of the Christian world."

"We nowhere read," said Sefton, "that Peter ever exercised this primacy."

"Although there were no record that he ever exercised it, that would be no proof that he never did so exercise it. Having shewn that this high commission was given by Christ unto Peter, it is natural to suppose that he would be called upon occasionally to exert it. In fact, there is in Scripture sufficient evidence that he did so."

"Pray, Sir, on what occasion?"

"First, immediately after the Ascension, when the Apostles and Disciples were assembled together, Peter proposes the election of a successor to Judas in the Apostleship, and evidently presides and directs the whole proceedings."§

"So, so," replied Sefton, laughing; "I see you would make Peter play the Pope at a very early hour, in appointing a Bishop, a successor to an Apostle."

* Luke xxii. 32. † John xxi. 15. ‡ John xvii. 11.
§ Acts i. 15.

"I only mention the fact, and leave the inference to your own good sense," said the Prelate. "But to proceed. When 'no small contest' was raised among the Christians of Antioch, whether they were bound to observe the Mosaic law, 'the Apostles and Ancients assembled to consider of this matter; and when there had been *much disputing*,' Peter arose and pronounced a definitive sentence. He had no sooner spoken, when 'all the multitude held their peace.'"*

"I must allow," said Sefton, "that looks very much like an authoritative decision of the Papal See."

"Nothing less, I assure you. Peter speaks, and the cause is decided: every opposing voice is hushed; all submit, and the contest is ended. It is worthy also of your serious reflection, that neither Paul nor Barnabas, though both Apostles, could of themselves decide the controversy of Antioch, but were obliged to repair to Jerusalem, where Peter was, to have the matter settled. This fact indicates clearly that Peter exercised a supremacy over the Apostles and over the whole Church."

Sefton was sensibly moved, and briefly answered: "I feel the full force of your remark, and I do not exactly see how it is to be answered."

"St. Paul," continued the Prelate, "did not begin his apostolic labours before he had visited Peter, for he tells us, 'After three years I went to Jerusalem to see Peter, and I tarried with him fifteen days'† The object of his visit, it can hardly be doubted, was to confer with him upon the Gospel which he had to preach among the Gentiles.‡ Thus we see that St. Paul, though called by God himself to the Apostleship, did not presume to enter into his mission without the approbation of Peter. Moreover, we find Peter pronouncing on the writings of St. Paul as one having authority: 'As also our most dear brother Paul, according to the wisdom given him, hath written to you; as also in all his Epistles, . . . in which are certain things hard to be understood, which the unlearned and unstable wrest, as they do the other scriptures, to their own destruction;'§ as if the Apostle

* Acts xv. † Gal. i. 18. ‡ Gal. ii. 2. § 2 Peter iii. 15.

had in view the presumptuous abuse of modern Bible readers."

"I grant," said Sefton, "there is a good deal of force in your argument, on the supposition that Christ really conferred a primacy on Peter."

"That supposition rests on the most explicit words of Christ himself, as I have already proved," replied Monsignore Guidi.

"But how can it be proved that the present Popes of Rome are the successors of St. Peter?" asked Sefton.

"Their names are all upon record; and any person versed in the history of the Church and the writings of the holy Fathers, will candidly confess that a primacy of jurisdiction has always been acknowledged in the Bishops of Rome: I refer you to St. Irenæus, St. Cyprian, St. Basil, in the second, third, and fourth ages, and to a host of others. The written Word is very plain on this subject, 'There shall be one fold and *one* shepherd.'"*

"But, Monsignore," said Sefton, "is it not both presumptuous and ambitious in the Popes being styled, and taking the title of *Vicar of Christ* on earth?"

"I cannot see it in that light," answered Monsignore Guidi quietly. "A Vicar is one who holds the place of another, and is subordinate to him; such is the Pope with respect to Jesus Christ. Our blessed Redeemer, under the amiable figure of the good shepherd, says, 'Other sheep I have who are not of this fold;' that is, the Gentiles, to whom Christ never preached; 'them also I must bring, and they shall hear my voice, and there shall be one fold, and one shepherd.' It is evident that Christ has but one fold, collected together from all nations, of which He is the one supreme shepherd; that is the one Church, of which he is the one supreme head."

"But what has that to do with my objection?" said Sefton.

"Because," continued the Prelate, "when the Saviour was about to leave this earth, he would not leave his one flock without a visible head. For this office he

* John x. 16.

selected Peter, to whom he had already promised the 'keys of the Kingdom of Heaven;' that is, the supreme jurisdiction and government of his Church, and now he fulfils his promise. 'When, therefore, they had dined, Jesus saith to Simon Peter: Simon, son of John, lovest thou me more than these? He saith to him, Feed my lambs. He saith to him again, Simon, son of John, lovest thou me? He saith to him, Yes, Lord; thou knowest that I love thee. He saith to him, Feed my lambs. He saith to him the third time, Simon, son of John, lovest thou me? Peter was grieved, because he had said to him the third time, Lovest thou me? And he saith to him, Lord, thou knowest all things: thou knowest that I love thee. He said to him, Feed my sheep.'* Here Christ, in the most formal and explicit manner, gives to Peter, the predecessor of the Popes, the care of his whole flock, great as well as little, sheep as well as lambs, all the Pastors who feed the flock, as well as the flock itself; and this vicegerent authority has passed to all the successors of Peter, and fully entitles them to the venerable appellation of *Vicar of Christ* on earth."

"In that sense," replied Sefton, "each Bishop in his diocese may be considered the Vicar of Christ."

"In a limited sense, with respect to their immediate subjects and subordination to their head, the Pope, the expression may be admitted, as all the Apostles were truly 'the ambassadors of Christ;' but still there is need of one supreme head, without which there could be no centre of unity, no bond of peace to keep the Church united in the '*one faith*;' to gather the sheep and lambs into the '*one fold*.' Nothing can shew the necessity of this union more than the innumerable dissensions into which every sect that has broken loose from the fold of Peter has miserably split. I appeal to the history, past and present, of your own Church."

"I cannot deny," answered Sefton with some hesitation, and a blush of conscious weakness, "but that our Church has been too much harassed by turbulent inno-

* John xxi. 15, 16, 17.

vators, and that we have no efficacious means of suppressing them."

"Such being the necessity of the case," replied Monsignore Guidi, "as your own experience proves, you must allow that Christ, as a wise legislator, has provided a remedy for the evil. You have sought for it in vain for three hundred years. We shew it in the supremacy of Peter, as the Catholic Church has enjoyed it for eighteen centuries."

"That bond of union," said Sefton, "is not so strong as not to have been frequently snapped asunder."

"It is, however, sufficiently strong," replied Monsignore Guidi, "to hold those who have the good-will to be directed by the ordinance of eternal wisdom. God constrains no man; and if he chooses to swerve from the way appointed by Christ, his own perdition must fall on his own head."

"Aye, there again," exclaimed Sefton, "your odious illiberality bursts forth. Catholics certainly are the most intolerant set of people on the face of the earth: they never will allow salvation to be found in any Church but their own."

"Truth, my dear Sir," said the Prelate, "is ever intolerant of falsehood. Possessed of the truth, we must necessarily reprobate error; but we know how to pity the erring, and the first effect of our compassion is to admonish them charitably of their danger. We tell them that we cannot be more lenient than Christ himself. Now, who said, 'He that believeth not shall be condemned?'* was it not the Saviour himself?"

"I believe it was," muttered Sefton.

"Yes; and the Catholic Church teaches that Jesus established but one Church for the salvation of man, and that out of that one Church salvation is not to be had; reason tells us that Christ, 'the way, the truth, and the life,' could never be the author of two contradictory systems of faith, and the Apostle expressly declares that there is but 'one Lord, one faith, one baptism.'† Invincible ignorance, indeed, may save a soul, but how

* Mark xvi. 16. † Ephes. iv. 5.

many Protestants are there who know far too much to lay claim to that privilege; and Oh! my dear Sefton," added he earnestly, "think of those most emphatic words of the Redeemer himself, 'and other sheep I have that are not of this fold; them also I must bring, and they shall *hear my voice*, and there shall be *one* fold and *one* shepherd.'"

Sefton sighed.

"From this," continued Monsignore Guidi, "it appears there are many sheep straying widely from the fold, which he earnestly wishes to bring back. You, my dear Sir, have seen and heard enough to make you doubt lest you be one of these strayed sheep. Oh! listen to his voice, and harden not your heart; but return to that fold, over which Christ has placed the one shepherd, his Vicar on earth."

Sefton looked disturbed, but he endeavoured to conceal his emotions. By this time they had arrived at the hotel, and the friends separated, having engaged to meet the following morning at the same hour.

CHAPTER XXVII.

" I am thy father's spirit,
Doomed for a certain term to walk the night,
And for the day, confined to fast in fire,
Till the foul crimes, done in my days of nature,
Are burnt and purged away."

SHAKSPEARE.

EVERY one, who has been in Rome during the first week of November, must have been struck with the pensive melancholy, and the lugubrious tone of the church service during that time; the slow and solemn tolling of the bells, the monotonous chant of the office for the dead, the sombre hue of the church ornaments and hangings, and, above all, the innumerable quantity of Masses celebrated in black vestments, as expiatory sacrifices for those relations, and friends, and fellow-creatures, who have gone before us to be judged at the awful tribunal of the living God. Who, that has a heart alive to the tender affections and sympathies of humanity, has not been struck with this? In every street, at every church door, the poor and the children remind us to pray for the friends we have lost; and who were, perhaps, but a few fleeting months ago, all the world to us. Those beloved lost ones! to our partial and doating eyes they seemed, perhaps, as near perfection as human nature is capable of; but who shall encounter the glance of the living God, and not be found covered with blemishes? If even the very Seraphims tremble in His sight, shall not the just man, 'who falls seven times,' tremble also? Great God! how few there are, who rush from Thy tribunal to Thy bosom. Other friends, too, we may, perchance, have lost, who, though dear to us as our heart's blood, yet we knew were careless livers, and full of frailties. We cannot think a just and merciful God will condemn them to everlasting torments, for frailties so much counterbalanced by their redeeming faith, and many virtues. No! no! they are but suffering, and suffering for a time, and it is in our power to help them, if we will; perhaps, even, it depends on us to be the means of placing them in eternal repose at any moment. Can we have the heart to shut our ears to their entreaties to us for help in their utmost need? certainly not: and what tongue can tell their joy, their peace, their repose, when, by our prayers, we have moved God to release them from their excruciating torments? what tongue can tell their gratitude to us for this last and tender act of charity towards them? But stay; there are some people who will not perform this act of charity; and why? Perhaps they have lost no friends: it must be so. Oh! no, that is not the reason of their negligence; they have lost, alas! too many. Some of them, perhaps, in early youth, while yet in invincible ignorance, like some tender snow-drop buried under deep, freezing snow; others, wavering in their faith, sincerely, yet feebly, resolving to embrace the truth, if found; whom God, in His inscrutable ways, snatched from amongst the living ere they brought their good resolutions to bear fruit; and these dear lost ones were most tenderly beloved, and the relations they have left in this earthly vale have tender and most compassionate hearts; but *they* say 'there is *no* Purgatory;' and thus they leave their poor friends suffering and lingering in the reality of its torments, while they excuse themselves from succouring them by a *bold assertion* that Purgatory is a vile Popish superstition; and they eat, and drink, and enjoy themselves, while those, that were nearest and dearest to them, are agonizing in their utmost need: so much for Protestant charity and liberality. Oh! would to God they could be induced calmly to investigate, whether *their assertion* is not more chimerical than the existence of a Purgatory.

Sefton attended the High Mass celebrated for the

repose of the souls of the faithful departed in the Sistine Chapel, and the mournful and pathetic strains of the 'Dies iræ, dies illa,' surpassed even his already excited anticipation. The Pope's choir, which consists of the finest voices, who sing without the aid of instrumental music, is peculiarly calculated for the execution of music of a solemn and plaintive description. There is a wild and melancholy cadence, produced by this union of human voices in perfect harmony, which cannot, perhaps, be imitated by any other combination of sounds in nature, but which fully and surpassingly express the deepest and most agonizing feelings of the soul. During this unrivalled execution of the simple and sublime 'Dies iræ,' Sefton was rivetted in enchanted attention, and the whole of the prayers and lessons which he heard, and which have all reference to the suffering state of our fellow-creatures who have already entered eternity, struck him as peculiarly beautiful and appropriate; and he thought within himself, that had he believed in a middle state of souls, they would have been consoling too. As they descended the staircase of the Vatican, after the service was finished, Sefton was agreeably surprised to meet his friend, the Bishop of S——, and his family. A warm meeting ensued; but as Sefton had engaged to go with Monsignore Guidi to visit some of the principal sculptors in Rome, he made the Bishop and his family promise to come and dine with him in the evening. Monsignore Guidi agreed to join the party, though he was somewhat startled at Mrs. Boren being introduced as the Bishop's wife; but a moment's reflection recalled to his mind, that the good Bishop had, in reality, as slight a title to *holy orders* as any young seminary student, who had merely taken the tonsure, and still retained the liberty of choosing a wife instead of a breviary as his companion for life, if so the fancy took him. At six o'clock, they all met at Serny's Hotel. Before they sat down to table, to Edward's unspeakable vexation and shame, for he coloured deeply, Monsignore Guidi said grace, and made the sign of the Cross. The Bishop stared; the Captain and Lavinia exchanged glances, and Mrs. Boren looked bewildered. The Prelate, quite unconscious that he had done any thing extraordinary, quietly eat his soup. After dinner, while coffee was serving, the Bishop turned to Monsignore Guidi, and said, "I understand, Sir, there was some extremely fine music this morning at the Vatican. I was, unfortunately, too late for it."

"Yes, it was very fine," replied Monsignore Guidi, "and well worth the notice of a traveller."

"What was it particularly?" said Miss Lavinia.

"It was the 'Dies iræ,'" said Sefton, "and one of the most beautiful pieces of music I ever heard."

"You will have an opportunity, my Lord, of hearing it to-morrow, though perhaps not so fine as it was to-day," said the Prelate; "to-morrow, Mass is celebrated for the souls of the deceased Popes."

"The souls of the Popes! how very ridiculous!" exclaimed the Captain.

"What a queer idea!" tittered Lavinia.

"A very cruel one, I think," drawled out Mrs. Boren. "I think the Catholic religion, instead of lessening sorrow, aggravates it, sending its members to Purgatory. The poor old Popes! I wonder how long they are left to fry there."

Miss Lavinia giggled out loud.

"I suppose, Ma'am, you think," said Monsignore Guidi sternly, "the doctrine held by many modern Protestants, that the torments of hell are *not eternal*, a much more consoling and comfortable dogma. No doubt it is for hardened sinners, to whom it is thus no longer 'a fearful thing to fall into the hands of the living God.'"*

"I never mentioned, nor thought of such a frightful, disagreeable place, I am sure, Sir," said Mrs. Boren, with a look of horror; "but God is very good, and who knows how it may be?"

"Yes, it cannot be denied," continued Monsignore Guidi, "that Protestants began by denying Purgatory, and many of them have ended by changing Hell into Purgatory: to be sure, this is well calculated to assuage

* Heb. x. 31.

sorrow, and dissipate all the superstitious horrors of a future state, and therefore must be a more perfect form of Protestantism than that which still keeps its votaries in the horrid dread of eternal flames. It may not, to be sure, be quite so conformable to the letter of Holy Scripture, but then it is more *rational;* in the meantime, I have doubts whether 'the God of revenge' will approve of this doctrine."

"You are pleased to be severe, Sir," said the Bishop, pompously. "Now I simply state it as my conviction, that Purgatory is contrary to Scripture, and never heard of in the Christian Church till it became full of corruptions."

"Then," answered Monsignore Guidi, "how can you account for the fact that all the Fathers of the four or five first ages, when I suppose the abominations of Popery had not yet made much progress in the Church, concur in the doctrine of a middle state?"

"Is that really true, Sir?" said Sefton eagerly.

"In all the earliest Liturgies prayers are offered for the dead," answered Monsignore Guidi, "and this practice of the primitive Church proves its faith."

"My dear Sefton," interposed the Bishop, "I do assure you Purgatory is a most pernicious error, and, moreover, contrary to Scripture: because as Christ's death was an all-sufficient atonement for sin, to make man suffer also for that sin, is either a contradiction, or an assertion that more suffering is inflicted than is necessary."

Sefton looked puzzled.

"The atonement of Christ," said the Prelate, "is all-sufficient for the sins of the whole world; yet man is still condemned to suffer for his sins: what is poverty, toil, labour, sickness and death, but the punishment of God inflicted on sin? If no sufferings be necessary on the part of sinful man, after the all-sufficient atonement of Christ, why are not all the miseries of life and death itself abolished? That is a question I should like to hear you solve on your own principles. For my part, I say, happy the man who can discharge the debt of punishment due to his sins, by these temporary inflictions; for such a happy soul there is no Purgatory."

"The strongest argument a Catholic can bring in favour of Purgatory," said the Bishop, waving his hand, "is from the books of the Maccabees; but our Reformation rejects that."

"I am perfectly aware that your Reformation rejects the Maccabees," answered Monsignore Guidi; "but you will permit me to observe, that this rejection made by modern reformers can bear no weight when made in opposition to all antiquity, in opposition to the universal Church, the only one extant at the time of the pretended Reformation, excepting the Greek schismatics, who believe in Purgatory. Your Lordship must also permit me to deny that the Catholic draws his strongest argument in favour of Purgatory from the books of the Maccabees: Let us even suppose them to bear no weight, still the belief of a middle state is supported by many other texts of the Old and New Testament."

"How so, Sir—how so?" said the Bishop impatiently.

"Is it not written," replied Monsignore Guidi, "'Thou also, by the blood of thy Testament, has sent forth thy prisoners out of the pit wherein is no water?'* Now that pit cannot be Hell, as out of Hell there is no redemption. Consequently, it must be a place of temporal punishment, from which redemption is had by the blood of the Testament."

"Pretty strong," cried the Captain; "that's the pit for me, then; for if I remember rightly what was thumped into my head at school, they used to tell me that from the *other pit* there is no redemption."

"Silence, young man," said his father, frowning.

"But," continued the Prelate, "what St. Paul says is yet stronger: 'Every man's work shall be made manifest; for the day of the Lord shall declare it, because it shall be revealed by fire; and the fire shall try every man's work of what sort it is. If any man's work abide, which he has built thereupon, he shall receive a reward.

* Zach. ix. 11.

If any man's work burn, he shall suffer loss; but he himself shall be saved, yet so as by fire.'* Now this text hardly requires any comment: from it it appears plainly that, although the works of man have been substantially good and pleasing to Almighty God, yet, on account of many deformities, the effects of human frailty and corruption, man must be cleansed by a purging and punishing, yet saving fire, before he can be admitted into that sanctuary into which 'nothing defiled can enter.'"†

"Well and good," said the Bishop; "if such is your faith, be satisfied, but excuse me from entering further into the subject; controversy, in my opinion, is extremely disagreeable in society, especially when one wishes to enjoy a social evening: come, Sefton," continued he, "cannot you furnish us with a pack of cards, that I and Mrs. Boren may have our usual game?"

Sefton rung for the cards, but he was by no means either pleased or satisfied at the Bishop's having beat a retreat in that style. Monsignore Guidi's observation, that the practice of the Church in its primitive ages, of praying for the dead, proved its faith in Purgatory, even in the very earliest period of Christianity, had struck him forcibly, and he would willingly have dived deeper into the subject had not his fear of annoying the Bishop of S—— prevented him. After the party had broken up, he sat musing over the expiring embers of the fire, until he had made up his mind to call the next day on Father Oswald, to hear all that could be stated on the subject; for, thought he, if the Catholics of the present day coincide with the first Christians so exactly on this point, they may do so in others also; it is certainly very singular. I cannot well see what induced the first reformers to object to Purgatory, and I think it is but justice to both parties to have my mind satisfied on this subject. I shall, moreover, ask at the same time, the grounds Catholics pretend to have for that odious custom of making the sign of the Cross, especially at meal times. I prefer asking him to asking Guidi, because Guidi might think it personal. The next day, according

* 1 Cor. iii. 13, 14, 15. † Apoc. xxi. 27.

to this resolve, Sefton called on Father Oswald, and, after a little conversation on general topics, he, with a slight degree of embarrassment in his manner, mentioned the object of his visit. "I heard, Sir, yesterday," said he, "a conversation on Purgatory, which interested me much; but as some circumstances interrupted this conversation, I have taken the liberty of coming to ask you the *real* Catholic opinion on this point."

"My dear friend," said Father Oswald gently, "the Catholic has no *opinion* on this point, he has *faith*. The Catholic Church, the supreme tribunal of our faith, teaches that there is a Purgatory or place of temporal punishment after death, and that the souls therein detained are helped by the prayers of the faithful, and especially by the holy sacrifice of the Mass.* This decree of the Church, in general council met, is sufficient for a Catholic to regulate his faith on the present subject, and convince him more forcibly of the existence of a Purgatory and of the usefulness of prayers for the dead, than all the arguments drawn from Scripture or from reason; still it is a satisfaction to a Catholic, already convinced by the authority of the Church, to find that even the plain words of Scripture, and the plainest dictates of reason, are in perfect union with the declaration of the Church."

"If such be the case," said Sefton, "no doubt a Catholic may be satisfied; but the Council of Trent, you know, is a very modern concern in comparison to the duration of Christianity; but what I want to know is, if the first Christians in the ages immediately following the life of the Saviour, held and practised the same faith and doctrines on Purgatory as the Catholics existing now in the present day?"

"Most assuredly they did," said Father Oswald.

"Well, now, how can you prove it?"

"The writings of the holy Fathers, of both the eastern and western Church, most clearly prove, that from the earliest dawn of Christianity, the belief of a Purgatory was general in the Church. Tertullian, the famous

* Con. Tri. Sess. 25. Decret. de Purg.

champion of the Christian religion, who lived in the second age, says, 'No man will doubt but that the soul doth recompense something in the places below.'* And again, in his book De Corona Militis, 'We make yearly oblations for the dead.' St. Clement, in the same age, tells us, St. Peter taught them, amongst other works of mercy, to bury the dead, and diligently perform their funeral rites, and also to pray, and give alms for them."†

"That is a striking passage, certainly, and clearly traces the practice up to the Apostles," replied Sefton.

"Undoubtedly," said Father Oswald; "and St. Cyprian says, 'It is one thing being cast into prison, not to go out thence till he pay the utmost farthing, another presently to receive the reward of faith; one thing being afflicted with long pains for sins to be mended, and purged long with fire; another to have purged all sins by sufferings.'‡ In the fourth age St. Ambrose says, 'But, whereas St. Paul says *yet so as by fire*, he shews, indeed, that he shall be saved, but yet shall suffer the punishment of fire; that being purged by fire, he may be saved, and not tormented for ever, as the infidels are, with everlasting fire.'§ Again, in the same age, St. Jerome says, 'This is that which he saith, Thou shalt not go out of prison till thou shalt pay even thy little sins;‖ in the same age, St. Cyril, of Jerusalem, says, 'We beseech God for all those who have died before us believing the observation of that holy and dreadful sacrifice, which is put on the altar to be the greatest help of the souls for which it is offered.' "¶

"It appears, then," said Sefton thoughtfully, "that from the earliest times Mass was also offered for the dead, as it is now?"

"To be sure it was: does not St. Jerome say, 'These things were not in vain ordained by *the Apostles;* that in the venerable and dreadful mysteries of the Mass, there should be made a memory of those who have departed this life; they knew much benefit would hence accrue to

* Lib. de Anima, c. 58. † Epis. i. de S. Petro.
‡ Epis. 52, ad Anton. § Cap. 3, Epis. ad Cor. ‖ c. v. Matt.
¶ Catech. Myst. 5.

them'?* It would fill volumes to quote all those passages from the holy Fathers, which prove the belief in the third place, and prayers for the dead to be coeval with Christianity; those I have quoted lived twelve, thirteen, and fourteen centuries before the pretended Reformation, and were of course better judges of genuine apostolical tradition, than the late reformers could be. Yes, my good friend, rest assured that 'it is therefore a holy and wholesome thought to pray for the dead, that they may be loosed from their sins.'"†

"Oh! now you are coming over me with the Maccabees," said Sefton, smiling; "the Protestant reformers reject them, you know."

"Nevertheless," said Father Oswald, "in the earliest ages of Christianity, we find the holy Fathers quoting the Maccabees, as well as other Scripture. Witness St. Clement of Alexandria, Origen, St. Cyprian, St. Jerome, and St. Augustine; the books of the Maccabees are by the Church of Christ honoured and proclaimed as divine books. The third Council of Carthage, and the General Council of Trent,‡ declare the two books of Maccabees to be divinely inspired: and surely the Church of Christ has as much authority as the Jewish Synagogue to pronouce on the authenticity of Holy Scripture."

"Well, but," said Sefton, "even putting out of the question these two disputed books, there is a sentence from Ecclesiastes, which book is received by both parties, which is very strong against Purgatory: I think it says, 'If the tree fall to the south, or to the north, in what place soever it shall fall, there shall it be.'" §

"Admitting," said the Father, "that the Scripture here speaks of the soul after death, which, indeed, is highly probable, how does this make against Purgatory? We believe that there are only two *eternal* states after death; namely, the state of glory, and the state of damnation. If the soul departs in the state of grace, it shall be for ever in that state, although it may have

* Homil. 3, in Epist. ad Philip.

† 2 Macc. xii. 43, 46.

‡ Sess. 4.

§ Eccles. xi. 3.

some venial sins to satisfy for, which may for a time retard the consummation of its happiness. If it dies in the state of mortal sin, and an enemy of God, it shall be for ever in torments. Here are two everlasting states, which may be meant by the north and south of the above text. If this interpretation is not satisfactory, you must prove it to me to be false. Used as we are to submit in religious matters to none but an infallible authority, we cannot be put off by mere opinions."

"But," said Sefton, "does not this doctine of Purgatory cast a reproach on Christ as a Saviour of sinners, representing his obedience and sufferings as insufficient to atone for their sins?"

"This objection, my dear Sir, will appear very trifling to you," answered Father Oswald, "when you know, that the Catholic Church teaches, that the merits of Jesus Christ are of themselves far more than sufficient to atone for all the sins of mankind."

"Now, Sir, your objection proves too much, and therefore proves nothing. For, considering the sufficiency of Christ's sufferings *only*, it would follow that no man can be damned."

"But Jesus Christ requires our co-operation," replied the Father, "and it depends upon the degree of our co-operation, whether those infinite merits of Christ are applied to us in a more or less abundant measure. It is in the order of grace, as in the order of nature. 'In the sweat of thy brow, shalt thou eat thy bread.* God's omnipotence alone gives growth to our grain; yet without casting a reproach on that omnipotence, we may safely assert, that in proportion as we plough, manure, and sow, in that proportion we shall reap. So likewise, although Christ's merits and satisfaction for sinners are of infinite value, yet the benefits we shall reap of those infinite merits will be proportionate to our endeavours, in subduing our corrupt nature and sinful inclinations, and in conforming ourselves in all things to the will of God. 'He who soweth sparingly, shall reap sparingly; and he who soweth in blessings, shall also reap of bless-

* Gen. iii. 19.

ings.'* He, then, who soweth so sparingly in this world, as to remain in his dying moment indebted to the divine justice, will after his death be compelled to pay to the last farthing, what by more serious endeavours he might have paid in this world."

There was a pause: at length Sefton said, "I certainly cannot quite see what motives could have induced the first reformers to reject Purgatory; it appears so very reasonable."

"Nor I either," said Father Oswald quietly; "the greatest part of mankind, all those who believe in revelation, excepting the followers of the late *soi-disant* reformers, and numbers of those who are guided by reason alone, agree in the belief of a place of temporal punishment, and in the practice of praying for the dead. If, then, the Protestant continues to assert that he cannot find Purgatory in Scripture, nor the practice of praying for the dead, the Catholic Church and the Greek Church answer, that they find both the doctrine and the practice very clearly in Holy Scripture: if the Protestant peremptorily decides that the belief in a Purgatory is absurd, and the practice of praying for the dead ridiculous, we in our sober senses, possessed of common sense, as well as our good Protestant neighbours, enlightened by a liberal education, as well as many of them, endowed by genius and talents, capable of the most profound disquisitions, in short, many of us adorned with all the perfections of the understanding, which nature can give or education improve, we answer that we find the belief of a place of temporal punishment and the practice of praying for the dead perfectly reasonable."

"The truth of what you say cannot be denied," said Sefton slowly.

"Well, then," continued the Father, "here is reason opposed to reason; common sense, to common sense; genius and talents, to genius and talents; but the reason, common sense, and talents of the very many in favour of Purgatory, opposed to the reason, and common sense,

* 2 Cor. ix. 6.

and talents, of the comparatively few against Purgatory: now who shall decide; and decide so as to put the question for ever at rest?"

"Oh! that is the point," exclaimed Sefton eagerly.

"None," said Father Oswald, reverently raising the clerical cap from his head, "can decide but the great tribunal, which Jesus Christ established on earth more than eighteen hundred years ago. When infusing into his ministers the Spirit of truth, he promised that that Spirit should never depart from them to the end of time. This tribunal, as I have already stated, has decided in our favour, and it is because that supreme and infallible tribunal has decided so, that we believe as we do."

Sefton sighed deeply. "There is much to reflect on, Sir," said he, "in the information you have given me, and I thank you much for it. I trust, however, you will excuse me if I trouble you on one subject more; and that is, the practice which Catholics have of making so often what they are pleased to call the sign of the Cross; especially at meal times: now, my dear Sir, you have no idea how foolish and superstitious this does seem to Protestants!"

"Really! and why, pray?"

"Oh! it is so singular and childish; this monk's trick at least can assuredly never have received any sanction from the orthodox Christians of the early Church."

"I beg your pardon," said the Father, smiling, "what, then, can St. Cyprian mean, when he says, 'Let us not be ashamed to confess Him who was crucified; let the sign of the Cross be confidently made upon the forehead with the finger'?"

"I should like much to see that passage, Sir," said Sefton somewhat doubtingly.

"Nothing easier," replied Father Oswald, rising, "if you will accompany me to the library."

"Most willingly," answered Sefton: and to the library they adjourned, where Father Oswald shewed him not only that, but the following passage in Tertullian: 'We sign ourselves with the sign of the Cross on the forehead, whenever we go from home, or return, when we put on our clothes, or our shoes, when we go to the bath, or *sit down to meat*, when we light our candles, when we lie down, and when we sit.' Sefton read, and was surprised; he mused a little, and adroitly turned the conversation on general literature; and as the shades of evening closed in, he left the library of the Gesù with real regret, and not without threatening Father Oswald with another visit: "Yes," thought he to himself, as he reached Serny's door, "if I act candidly, I certainly ought to inquire more particularly into the real tenets of Catholicity, for I have heard some extraordinary statements to-day.—May God give me the grace to do that which is right!" added he, sighing involuntarily as he rung the bell for candles.

CHAPTER XXVIII.

"Ave Maria! Mother blest,
To whom caressing and caressed,
Clings the eternal Child;
Favoured beyond Archangel's dream,
When first on thee, with tenderest gleam,
Thy new-born Saviour smiled.

"Ave Maria! Thou whose name,
All but adoring love may claim,
Yet may we reach thy shrine;
For He, thy Son and Saviour, vows
To crown all lowly, lofty brows,
With love and joy like thine."

Christian Year.—KEBLE.

"MY dear Sefton," said the Bishop, "you must come and eat your Christmas dinner with me to-morrow, that we may keep up good old English customs, even in this strange land."

"Yes," added Mrs. Boren; "from what I am given to understand, a good dinner will be very acceptable after all the fatigues of the previous night. I am told people are up all night, to see the rocking of the cradle, and going from one church to another, to see the gross superstition of the people."

"That is to say," said Monsignore Guidi gravely, "the Protestant part of the world who happen to be in Rome at this holy time, choose to make a night of dissipation of it; hurrying from one church to another, and even eating and drinking, and doing many indecorous things in the sanctuary of God, to the no small scandal and annoyance of Catholics."

"And pray, Sir, why should they not go from one

church to another?" interrupted Miss Lavinia; "I hope Mamma will go; I am sure it will be such capital fun to see all the ignorant superstitions of the Papists."

"The Papists are much obliged to you for your politeness," said Monsignore Guidi, bowing ironically; "but really it does argue a great perversion of the human intellect, to imagine it possible for a Christian people who have received the Gospel to relapse again into idolatry. I could more easily conceive it possible for a poor deluded Christian to adore the sun and the moon than a senseless block of stone. This reflection should make you distrust your prejudices; however, if you go this evening to St. Mary Major's, I hope you may be fortunate enough to meet some poor ignorant Catholic to explain to you what you may see."

"Oh! I hate explanations," said the young lady; "I have eyes and ears, and can judge for myself: all I care about is the fun and the novelty."

"With all your eyes and ears, Miss Lavinia," rejoined the Prelate good-humouredly, "it is very possible to see objects under a false light, and interpret accents in a false sense, particularly when a prejudiced person is predetermined to find faults where other persons see none."

Lavinia was nettled at the remark; she turned very red, and bit her lips for vexation, but did not venture a reply. Sefton said nothing, but he determined in his own mind not to join the Bishop's party in the church, for he shrewdly suspected he should only have to blush for his countrymen; he and Monsignore Guidi promised to join the Bishop at dinner on Christmas-day, and thus the party separated. Sefton attended all the ceremonies on Christmas night, in company with Monsignore Guidi, and was much struck with the beauty of the service, and the splendid illumination of the church of St. Mary Major. He was also much pleased with the piety of the crowds who flocked to this beautiful temple, to do honour to the Infant Saviour and His Virgin Mother. Sefton still had about his person the medal of the Blessed Virgin, given him by Sister Angela; many a time a scruple crossed his mind, whether he was justified in conscience by so doing. As often, however, as he was tempted to cast it from him, he appeased the misgiving by the reflection that he bore the medal as a keepsake and remembrance of a pious soul, at whose hands he had received the greatest kindness in an hour of utmost need. He had promised to wear it for her sake, and he was resolved to keep his word; there could be neither superstition nor impiety in that expression of gratitude. But in that auspicious night he reflected that he owed more to Mary, who had given birth to the Saviour of his soul, than to Angela, who had only ministered to the health of his body. From that moment his scruples of superstition vanished. With the remembrance of the benefits received from Sister Angela, he joined a greater veneration for the Mother of Jesus, from whom he had received the greater benefit, and whose lovely image the medal bore. His respect and affection increased as he gazed, almost with a feeling of enthusiasm, on the devotion of the multitudes around him, who thronged on this hallowed night to her sanctuary, to join with the angelic choirs in praising the Almighty for the birth of the Infant Saviour, "Glory be to God on high, and peace on earth to men of good will." "After all," thought Sefton to himself, "Mary is the mother of Jesus, really and truly; even Protestants allow that. When they were both living amongst men in this world, she, by her intercession, induced Him to work His first miracle at the marriage feast of Cana, and to anticipate His hour, which, as he said, 'was not yet come.' I cannot really see that there is any thing so very unreasonable in thinking she may interest herself for us now, though she is in Heaven; and still less is it reasonable, I think, to imagine that her Son would refuse her any request which she might present Him for us, seeing how dearly our redemption cost Him." Whether Edward would have owned these reflections to his Protestant friends is doubtful; nevertheless, it is certain that he made them, and that he retired to bed in a calm and tranquil state of mind.

The Bishop's Christmas dinner was as merry a Christmas dinner as roast beef and plum-pudding could make it; and there was abundance of chat and mirth during the whole evening, and even the Bishop expressed himself delighted at the fine illuminations he had seen, and the beautiful music he had heard.

"I hope, my Lord, you were edified also at the devotion you have witnessed?" said Monsignore Guidi.

"Why, as to that, Monsignore," answered the Bishop, "it is not, to my mind, devotion of the right kind; being principally addressed to the creature, instead of the Creator; to the Mother, instead of the Son."

"For my part," said Monsignore Guidi with animation, "I cannot conceive it possible for a devout Christian to contemplate the divine Infant, laid in the manger at Bethlehem, and not associate with him the humble mother who bore so great a share in the mystery."

"What his lordship observes is too true," lisped out Mrs. Boren, as she helped herself to a ham-sandwich from the tray of cold refreshments, which were to terminate the luxuries of the evening; "I cannot approve of all these images, and pictures, and illuminations, and music: they are such unworthy attempts to move, not our souls, but our senses!"

"If it be not through the *senses*, I know not by what other means we can ever reach *the soul*," said Monsignore Guidi: "and philosophers are generally agreed that the eye is a more faithful channel than the ear. A holy painting, an impressive ceremony, will often make a deeper and more lasting impression on the mind than the most elegant sermon."

"Perhaps on some gross and material natures," said Mrs. Boren contemptuously, "but not on those blessed with refinement, and enlightened by the pure light of the Reformation."

"Well, my dear Madam," replied the Prelate, "I have frequently heard you profess yourself an enthusiastic admirer of nature; now, what is this but to feed the mind and soul through the senses? why, then, should I be prohibited from filling my soul with pious affections through the same medium ?"

"There can be no doubt," interposed the Bishop, "that the sublime scenery of nature is admirably adapted to inspire the soul with awe and veneration for the great Creator."

"No doubt," said Monsignore Guidi ; "yet these sentiments are still within the bounds of natural religion ; they fit well with the devotions of the contemplative heathen. I have no doubt that the savage who traverses the interminable plains, and forests, and rocks, and floods of his native country, will often be filled with awe and veneration for the great Spirit, and will hear his voice in the howl of the tempest or the roar of the cataract ; with much more reason shall the humble Christian be moved to the more gentle sentiments of piety, gratitude, love, and devotion, while he contemplates a lively representation of any one mystery of his redemption, be it the divine Infant in the crib of Bethlehem or the expiring Man-God on Calvary. Almighty God, who formed the constitution of man, ordained a vast number of imposing ceremonies in the old law for this express purpose. The withering influence of Calvinism chills all devotion, and would rob us if it could of all external aid."

"I can assure you, Monsignore Guidi," exclaimed Mrs. Boren warmly, "you may talk about ceremonies till midnight if you choose, but you will never persuade me that the devotion I have seen paid to the Virgin since I came abroad is any thing but rank superstition."

"My good lady," replied Monsignore Guidi, "nothing is more shocking to Christian feelings than the proud, supercilious contempt which Protestants shew towards the Virgin Mother of the Redeemer. Most assuredly they can have but little love for the Son who try to disparage the Mother. The angel used a very different style when he spoke to our blessed Lady, announcing to her that she was to be the mother of the Messiah."

"It is much to be lamented, Sir," said the Bishop pompously, "how the Catholic Church has perverted the sense of Scripture in regard to the Mother of the Redeemer, who is neither more nor less than a simple creature; the salutation of the angel, 'Hail, highly-favoured!' are not words upon which the worship you pay to Mary can be founded, seeing that words implying still greater favour than the words 'highly-favoured' had been addressed on three occasions to Daniel; and to David, and to Abraham also words of higher import have been used."

"In the first place," said Monsignore Guidi, "I must protest against the new-fangled expression, 'hail, highly-favoured.' The old expression, 'hail, full of grace,' gives the sense of the Greek term full as well, or better; besides, it is a literal translation of the Latin version; which has been used in the Catholic Church these eighteen hundred years, when, no doubt, they understood the import of the Greek word full as well as they do now. Whatever expressions may have been used to honour Daniel, David, or Abraham, you must allow that no honour, prerogative, or grace was ever conferred on them that can be distantly compared to the singular privilege conferred on Mary when she conceived and bore the Son of the Most High."

"But," subjoined the Bishop, "Catholics defend their idolatrous worship of the Virgin from the words addressed by Christ to his disciple John, on consigning to him the care of his mother: 'Behold thy mother;' now, the Evangelist simply adds the consequence of this charge, 'and from that hour that disciple took her unto his own home.'"

"Excuse me, Sir," said the Prelate, "Protestants, indeed, say, 'that disciple took her unto his own *home*,' but this last word is not found either in the Greek or Latin; it is a Protestant addition to the Word of God; most probably St. John had no home, and particularly at Jerusalem; the true meaning is, he took her to himself, into his own possession; he treated her as his own mother; and it is easy to conceive with what love, respect, and veneration, when she came commended by the dying accents of his beloved Lord. Now, Catholics do the same: they love to call her mother; they beseech her to receive them as her children, as she received John for her son; in all their doubts and anxieties, in all their difficulties and dangers, they invoke her as their mother, because they are persuaded, and have experienced that her intercession with her divine Son is all-powerful; for what can such a Son deny to such a mother?"

"I must own," said Sefton firmly, "that it has frequently struck me that devotion to the Mother of God, for she really is the Mother of God, is both touching and consoling, and rational too; for, how is it possible respect to Mary should be displeasing to God, who has selected her in such a very peculiar way as the most highly favoured of his creatures?"

"Mr. Sefton, you astonish me!" said the Bishop; "I little thought to hear from your Protestant lips such a blasphemous expression as 'Mother of God' applied to any creature, however pure and highly favoured she may have been. She was the mother of the Man-Jesus, but in no sense the Mother of God."

"What!" exclaimed Monsignore Guidi with astonishment, "is it possible that you can have renewed in England the old heresy of Nestorius? do you then distinguish two persons in Jesus Christ; the one human, the other divine?"

"We pay no attention to your metaphysical distinctions of persons," said the Bishop; "we find nothing of that in Scripture; we know Jesus Christ as God and as man."

"I am astonished," replied the Prelate, "that a divine should speak so vaguely. We are agreed that there are two distinct natures, divine and human, in Jesus Christ; but the question is, whether there be two or one only Person; and on the solution of that question the very existence of Christianity depends; if Christ has a human person, as you seem to suppose, why, then, it was a human person only who suffered. What, then, becomes of the infinite merits of his atonement?"

"Pooh!" said the Bishop, "the Scripture nowhere makes these scholastic distinctions."

"I beg your pardon, my Lord; the Scripture everywhere represents to us Jesus Christ as one and the same individual person; at one time styling him 'the Son of the living God,' and the same 'the Son of Mary.' Now, that individual, who is undoubtedly God, was born of the Blessed Virgin, and, consequently, she is truly and properly called the Mother of God."

"Such distinctions only serve to confound the ideas of simple Christians," said the Bishop.

"I can see no confusion in the matter," interposed Sefton; "except what seems to exist in your lordship's own ideas."

"I certainly am extremely surprised at what his lordship has expressed," said Monsignore Guidi; for I had imagined that the Protestant divines of the established Church of England were better informed."

"Allow me," said Sefton, "to recal your lordship's attention to some of the early Christian writers for proofs of the antiquity of service, devotion, and respect paid to the Mother of God."

"Yes," said Monsignore Guidi; "it is precisely this high dignity of Mother of God that raises Mary far above all other creatures; others may have been called 'blessed among women,' but to no other was it ever said by one filled with the Holy Ghost, 'blessed art thou among women, and blessed is the fruit of thy womb; and whence is this to me that *the mother of my Lord* should come to me!'* Yes, Mother of God is a title justly due to Mary, and as such all the plenitude of grace and glory that can be conferred on a pure creature is conferred on her; less than that would be unbecoming her exalted dignity, and reflect dishonour on her divine Son. I am astonished that Protestants, who try to debase the Mother, cannot see that thereby they debase the Son."

"Because," interrupted the Bishop vehemently, "Protestants know that Catholics rob the Son of the proper devotion due to him, to give it to his Mother."

"Excuse me, my dear Sir," said Monsignore Guidi,

* Luke i. 42.

"but the Catholic Church, in all ages, has enhanced the praise and glory of Mary, knowing that thereby she magnified and extolled the more the praise and glory of her Son, from whom she has received every thing; hence has been verified her own prophecy, 'Behold, from henceforth, all generations shall call me blessed.' Protestant generations have no part in this prophecy."

The Bishop bit his lip, but said nothing.

"It is my full belief," said Mrs. Boren, "that all intermediate intercessors between us and the Son of God, is utterly opposite to the Bible."

"My dear Madam," said the Prelate, "allow me to observe, that a single text of Scripture cannot be brought, which forbids intermediate intercession between us and the Son of God; but there are many which command it; as often as we are exhorted to pray for one another; and there is even in Scripture, an instance of departed souls praying for their brethren.* But, were there nothing in Scripture to recommend a devotion so rational and so consoling, the constant practice of the universal Church is a recommendation abundantly sufficient."

"My dear Monsignore Guidi," replied Mrs. Boren impatiently, "it is absurdity that the Scriptures upon which the Romish Church rests her claims as a Church, are in the hands of her enemies, while she finds it necessary to her very existence to prevent her people reading these Scriptures."

"My dear lady," said Sefton, "this is very like shuffling out of the question, and no answer whatever to what Monsignore Guidi stated."

"All I can say," observed Monsignore Guidi, "is, that it is to the Catholic Church that her enemies are indebted for the Scriptures; and what is more, these said enemies have no other proof that the Scriptures are genuine, authentic, and inspired by the Holy Ghost, but the authority and tradition of the Catholic Church, while she never felt such a necessity for the maintenance of her existence; no, the security of the Catholic Church

* 2 Macc. xv. 11.

rests upon a better foundation, namely, on the promises of Christ."

At that moment, Mr. Sefton's carriage was announced, and he and Monsignore Guidi wished the party good-night, with that very unsatisfactory feeling which will occur, when one party is doubting, and the other certain.

CHAPTER XXIX.

> "By various text we both uphold our claim,
> Nay, often ground our titles on the same;
> After long labour lost and time's expense,
> Both grant the words, and quarrel for the sense;
> Thus all disputes for ever must depend,
> For no dumb rule can controversies end."
>
> DRYDEN.

"DID you ever read a little book called 'The Nun,' Father Oswald?" said Sefton, one day, as he was sitting in the library of the Gesù.

"Yes, I have," replied the Father, smiling.

"Well, what do you think of it?"

"Think of it, my dear Mr. Sefton? there can be but one opinion by those who know the spirit and practice of the Catholic religion: excuse me, but 'The Nun' is a specimen of the most bare-faced falsehood, that was ever presented to the enlightened English nation."

"And yet," said Sefton, "it has run through four editions."

"Only another proof of the gullibility of John Bull," said Father Oswald quietly.

"I have just been reading another in the same style, entitled, 'The Catholic Chapel.'"

"I have seen that also," replied Father Oswald; "it is a tame specimen of ignorant falsehoods and mis-statements; the darkness of the author is so dense, that he cannot see the truth; he has distorted and misrepresented every Catholic dogma which he has touched upon, and thinks, or at least would have his readers think, that he has faithfully given the doctrine of Bossuet, and the Council of Trent; it is not so violent as 'The Nun,' which is a downright insult to the common sense of mankind."

"But is it not true, Sir," inquired Sefton hesitatingly, "that the Bible is kept out of sight of all Catholics, but the Clergy?"

"My dear friend, it is a gross calumny; the Catholic Church permits all her children to read the Bible in approved versions, with explanatory notes, that they may not be tossed about by every wind of doctrine, and come to shipwreck of their faith; for she knows well that in the Scriptures there are certain things hard to be understood, 'which the unlearned and unstable wrest to their own destruction.'* Now, unquestionably, ninety-nine Bible readers in one hundred are either *unlearned* or *unstable*."

"Well, Sir," answered Sefton, "I always had a notion that the Scripture was forbidden to the laity, and, consequently, I thought that Church must be in error which shuts up the Word of God from the people."

"The Church does not shut up the Word of God from the people," said Father Oswald dryly, "only she has an old-fashioned way of her own in announcing it to them, which she is not likely to quit, in order to please the itching ears of Biblicals; she is mindful of, and carefully inculcates to her ministers the Apostolical charge given to Timothy, '*Preach the Word*, be instant in season and out of season, reprove, entreat, rebuke in all patience and doctrines. For there shall be a time when they will not endure sound doctrine, but, *according to their own desires*, they will heap to themselves teachers, having itching ears, and will indeed turn away their hearing from the truth, but will be turned unto *fables*,'† Alas! is not that fearful time come?"

"You must excuse me, Father Oswald, if I speak plainly; but it certainly appears to Protestants, that the Catholic clergy subject themselves to strong suspicions when they refuse their people the right of judging of their pretensions by the Scriptures; Protestants desire to be judged by no other rule."

* 2 Peter iii. 16.

† 2 Tim. iv. 2, 3, 4.

"Your own good sense, my dear Sir," replied the Father, "must tell you that the unlettered multitude are incapable of judging rightly by such a rule; neither can the learned of your various sects decide any one dispute by the same rule. Allow me to add, that Protestants, whatever they may pretend, never submit to their own rule when a Catholic divine produces the most explicit texts against them. These interminable disputes only prove the necessity of another rule, and that an infallible one, to determine the right sense of Scripture."

"But," said Sefton, "the rulers of the Church of Rome do not believe in its infallibility; only the common people; again, the clergy differ whether infallibility resides in the Pope alone, or in the Pope with general councils, or in councils approved by the Pope, or not."

"The Catholic Church, that is the Pastors of the Catholic Church," replied Father Oswald, "are constituted by divine authority to expound the Bible to the people, and to judge what is true or false, and what is right or wrong; therefore they can never submit to the people, who have no authority to judge, but are commanded to 'obey their prelates and be subject to them;'* and the real fact is, that even amongst yourselves, the great mass of every sect form their opinions from the expositions of their favourite preacher, while they fancy they draw them from the Scripture."

"But they may dissent if they choose from any such opinion, and there is the glorious prerogative of the Reformation."

"So much the worse for them," said Father Oswald, "for the Redeemer himself commands the people 'to *hear* the Church,' on pain of being considered 'as the heathen and the publican;'† that is the Catholic Church; for he certainly did not refer to the Protestant Church, and its swarming brood of dissenters, who allow every man to follow and listen to his own idle and inflamed fancies."

* Heb. xiii. 17. † Matt. xviii. 17.

Sefton looked perplexed.

"Again," continued the Father, "our Saviour says, 'He that heareth you, heareth me; and he that despiseth you, despiseth me; and he that despiseth me, despiseth him that sent me.'* Now, the Bishops of the Catholic Church cannot submit to be judged by every upstart mad-cap of a Biblical; it is in vain for the Protestant to appeal for judgment to the Bible; the Bible is dumb, and has never yet pronounced judgment in any cause where the condemned party assumes the right of interpreting the sentence in his own favour, that is, of appealing from the clearest texts of the Divine Word to his own private judgment. Now, observe, Mr. Sefton, the Protestant protests against all the authorities constituted by Christ in his Church, to bring all 'into the unity of faith,' and sets up a supreme and infallible tribunal in his own pride, from which there is no appeal. Amongst the thousand and one sects, into which Protestantism has been splintered, I never read of the union of any two sects brought about by Bible reading: but I have read of many new schisms in each sect produced by the same cause. When you have settled your own disputes and shewn us a model of the 'unity of faith,' it will be time enough then to invite us to follow your splendid example: till then, we shall march on in the old track of our forefathers."

"But," interrupted Sefton, "where does your infallibility exist? answer me that question, if you please."

"When people speak of the doctrine of the Catholic Church, they should first make themselves acquainted with it. Every Catholic, clergy or laity, believes in the infallibility of the Church; it is an article of divine faith, and he who doubts of it would cease to be a Catholic. All Catholics believe that when the great body of the Bishops, either congregated in general council or dispersed through the whole world, agree with their head in any one thing appertaining to faith and morals, that that agreement is an infallible rule of truth. Of this there neither is nor can be any dispute, for on the

* Luke x. 16.

rock Peter, principally, Christ promised to found the stability and indefectibility of His Church; then to Peter, and to the rest of the Apostles, as a body subordinate to its head, he promised to send upon them, 'the Spirit of truth to be with them *for ever*, to teach them all things, and bring all things to their mind whatsoever he had said to them;' in a word, 'to teach them *all truth*.'* Finally, when he gave them his last commission to 'teach all nations,' he pledged his Divine Word that he would be with them when teaching '*all days*, even unto the consummation of the world.' These are the title-deeds of the Church for her claims to infallibility; and all the powers of Hell and Protestantism combined shall never wrest them from her. You will observe, my dear Sir, that we ground the infallibility of the Church teaching, not on the fallible opinions of weak men, but on the infallible promises of Christ, and the unerring guidance of the Holy Ghost."

"I see," replied Sefton, "and I feel the full force of your argument; the texts are too clear, and if there be any meaning in them, the promises must still subsist somewhere in the Church: may we not suppose that these promises were made to all the faithful generally who search the Scriptures, with simplicity of heart and with a sincere desire of finding out the truth?"

"Whoever has a simple heart, and a sincere desire of finding out the truth and knowing it, will seek for it through those means only which God has appointed; and the smallest reflection will convince him, that these promises of Christ were made to the Apostles only as the future *teachers* of his doctrine to all nations; and as the promises were to endure 'all days, even unto the consummation of the world,' it follows, that the promises still remain with the legitimate successors of the Apostles. If the promises were made to all the faithful generally, how happens it that amongst Protestants no two can be found to agree? Is it that the Holy Ghost teaches contradictory doctrines to each individual? or can no two

* John xiv. 16, 26; xvi. 13.

individuals be found who search the Scriptures with simplicity and sincerity?"

"The dilemma is rather puzzling," said Sefton, somewhat nettled; "but you hold, I believe, that the Pope alone is infallible. Now, that is a very shocking doctrine, when we consider how many Popes have been profligate, wicked men."

"Not *many*," replied Father Oswald mildly, "when you come to read their genuine history. A few, indeed, in a long series of holy and learned men, have been a disgrace to their high station. But do not, like most Protestants, confound impeccability with infallibility. No Catholic attributes the former to any Pope. You should remember also that Balaam was a wicked Prophet, yet God forced him to prophesy the truth; and Caiphas was no saint, yet in virtue of his office he prophesied the truth also. Infallibility is a pledge given for the whole Church, and is totally independent of the merits or demerits of any individual."

"I see," said Sefton; "but do you really hold that every individual Pope is infallible?"

"That is another question," said Father Oswald, "which not being a defined article of faith, is freely agitated in Catholic schools; it is this: whether a dogmatical decision of the Pope, speaking authoritatively to the whole Church, or *ex Cathedra*, as it is expressed, be infallible or not before it has been accepted by the great body of the Pastors. The greatest number and the most learned of divines hold the affirmative, and those who question it, freely grant, that in fact there never was a dogmatical decree issued by a Pope which, sooner or later, was not agreed to by all the other Bishops; so that the dispute is reduced to a question more about the possibility of a thing than about its reality: that is to say, whether it be possible for the great body of Bishops to dissent from a dogmatical decision of their head for a considerable space of time; and the most sensible answer to the question is, that the thing is impossible as long as the promises of Christ shall stand."

"That is the best explanation on this subject I have yet heard," said Sefton musingly; "but to return to the Scriptures; you must, I think, acknowledge with me, Sir, that they are not addressed to the learned only, or else a very large number of Catholic Priests ought not to read them: for many well-educated laics are far better informed than they are."

"Undoubtedly," replied Father Oswald; "the Scriptures were never addressed to 'the unlearned and unstable, who wrest them to their own destruction,' and, therefore, the Biblemen, who thrust the Bible *indiscriminately* into the hands of all, powerfully help forward the devil's work in hurrying souls to perdition. Your insinuation about the ignorance of the Catholic clergy is too ridiculous to spend words over it: some, indeed, may be found little versed in the mechanical and chemical sciences of the day; but they are all well instructed in the science of the Saints and in the Bible; for the fact is, the Catholic clergy, learned or unlearned, read more of Holy Scripture daily, and know its genuine meaning better than the most learned Bible-mongers. They know that 'all Scripture inspired of God is profitable *to teach, to reprove, to correct, to instruct* in justice.'* Now, as these are the special duties of their vocation, they have known them like Timothy from their infancy; but they know, also, that the Scriptures can only 'instruct to salvation by *the faith* which is in Christ Jesus.' They first acquire this faith from the only source from which it can be drawn; and then they read the Bible, and understand it. The Biblicals, on the contrary, open their Bible *without faith*, for they open it to learn *what* they *are to believe*; and hence they stumble on '*questions*, rather than the edification of God, *which is in faith*.'"

"That is a very striking observation, which I do not recollect to have heard before," said Sefton.

"It is, however, quite true," continued the Father, "and, therefore, it is no wonder that, 'going astray, they are turned aside unto vain babblings; desiring to be

* 2 Tim iii. 16.

teachers of the law, understanding neither the things they say, nor whereof they affirm.'* Yes, yes; be assured, my esteemed friend, that Catholics, men, women, and children, understand more of the genuine spirit of the Bible than all your mad-cap Biblicals together. Listen to the household words which a French writer puts into the mouth of a child speaking to its mother:

' Oh! montre nous ta Bible, et les belles images,
Le ciel d'or, les saints bleus, les saintes à genoux,
L'enfant Jesus, la crêche, et le bœuf, et les mages,
Fais-nous lire du doigt dans le milieu des pages
Un peu de ce Latin qui parle à Dieu de nous.' "

Sefton looked a little foolish; but rallying his Protestant spirit of opposition and cavilling, "Well, then, Father Oswald," said he, "since you even brag of Catholics being acquainted with their Bible, what objection on earth can you have to the poor Biblical reading his?"

"One reason, and that a very serious one; and I have already stated it," replied Father Oswald: "namely, that the Biblical studies his Bible to *find out* his faith in it, and to interpret it according to his own arbitrary fancy: the Catholic studies his Bible to confirm his faith and morality; he studies it only in approved editions, and with authorized notes and explanations; and he has not, neither does he wish to have, the pernicious and false liberty of interpreting it according to his private judgment."

"Well, but, Sir," persisted Sefton, "if the Protestant translation of the Bible is correct, which, I suppose it to be, I cannot see the objection to its universal perusal."

"For the reasons I have already several times stated," said Father Oswald patiently, "we are not ordered to 'hear the Bible, but to hear the Church;' moreover, it is a notorious fact, that many Protestants complain loudly of the inaccuracy of their own translation. Catholic divines point out many passages that are *falsely* translated, and many more that are so *insidiously* rendered, as to lead many astray."

* 1 Tim. i. 4.

Sefton was silent for a few minutes, and then said, "I believe you always speak the truth—at least, what you think to be the truth, Father Oswald, without the fear of any man; now, tell me candidly, do you not think that faith in the *Church of Christ* in opposition to the Church of *Rome* sufficient for salvation?"

"Really, Sir," said Father Oswald, "I do not well understand you; you take it for granted, that the Church of Christ is in opposition to the Church of Rome. That is what we deny; the question is, which among the many Christian sects is the true Church of Christ? consequently, if the Church of *Rome* happen to be the Church of Christ, faith in any other church, which you may fancy to be the Church of Christ, will avail you little."

At this moment a lay brother knocked at the door, and summoned the Father to some urgent business. Sefton took his leave, and shaking him warmly by the hand, "I fear," said he, "I have had rather the worst of it this time; but, for all that, I shall come, and try again another day."

"Bravo!" said Father Oswald as they walked down stairs together: "you remember the old proverb, 'Truth lies at the bottom of a well,' and you must dive deep to find it. But let me recommend to your most serious attention the important text of Scripture, which says, 'Ask, and you shall receive; seek, and you shall find; knock, and it shall be opened to you.'* Earnest prayer to the Father of Lights, with a simple and docile heart, and you will not fail to obtain the first of God's graces—the knowledge of the truth."

* Matt. vii. 7.

CHAPTER XXX.

"He hath a tear for pity, and a hand
Open as day for melting charity;
Yet notwithstanding, being incensed, he's flint."
SHAKSPEARE.

ONE morning, as Sefton and the Captain mounted their horses at Serny's door, to take a ride into the country, they were accosted by a poor Capuchin, who had an empty bucket on his arm, with the usual salutation, 'Benedicite.' He then asked some small alms for his convent, 'for St. Francis' sake, and for sweet Charity.' Sefton roughly refused him, taunting him at the same time with his poverty and idleness; and then, as he vaulted on to his saddle, turned to Luigi, saying, "Who is this idle vagrant? Tell him to get out of the way."

"Bless you, Sir!" said Luigi, in an apologetic tone, "it is only poor Father Guiseppe, a most holy man; everybody knows Father Guiseppe; he is ever doing good to the poor and afflicted, and brings comfort and consolation to them on the bed of sickness. Shall I give him an alms, Sir?"

"No, by no means," answered Sefton; "I'll have no hand in encouraging hypocrisy, under the cloak of religion. Move off, fellow, and learn to earn your bread by honest labour; such idle varlets should not be tolerated." So saying, he set off on his ride, little reflecting on the pain he had, without justice or reason, inflicted on a fellow-creature.

The poor friar raised up his manly countenance, darted a glance of indignation from his kindling eye, and muttered with a trembling lip, "The time was, when I could ill have brooked such a gratuitous insult; but—" He checked himself, made a humble obeisance, and retired, while a deep blush covered his fine features, at the consciousness that the old man was not yet dead within him. Sefton had marked the indignation of the first emotion, and the subsequent humiliation, which he did not fail to attribute to a conscious feeling of having met with a well-deserved reproof. Luigi lagged behind, and, unobserved, dropt a pittance from his own pocket into the basket of the friar.

"How the government can encourage such a set of hulking, idle drones and vagabonds, I cannot make out," added the Captain, as he joined his companion.

Father Guiseppe, in the meantime, treasured in Heaven the humiliation he had received; yet wondering in his own heart, that the handsome, generous-looking young Englishman, who was known to give such abundant alms, should have treated him so roughly. Father Guiseppe was a stout, fine-looking man, about sixty, with a beard as white as snow; he was of noble birth, had moved in the highest ranks of society, and had distinguished himself by deeds of valour in the field of battle, when, reflecting on the vanities of all worldly honours, he had retired in the prime of life to the cloister, in order to gain a higher and a never-fading crown of glory. He was, as Luigi had expressed it, truly a good man; his life was hidden with God in Jesus Christ; but what was visible of it to the eyes of the world, was marked by daily deeds of mercy and humanity to his fellow-creatures. As he returned to his convent, musing on what had passed, he breathed an 'Ave Maria' for the conversion of the being who had so unthinkingly and unfeelingly wounded his feelings: yes, his feelings! for many a warm heart, and many a delicate mind, exist under the rough habit of St. Francis, contemned, unheeded, and unknown by the gay and thoughtless votaries of a vain and empty world.

Sefton and the Captain cantered out into the country, around Monte Mario, where they had appointed to join the Bishop and his party, with Monsignore Guidi, to a cold luncheon, at two o'clock. All the party met at the appointed place, and spent the afternoon in rambling about that interesting part of the environs of Rome. As sunset drew near, they seated themselves on a favourable elevation, to see the rich glories of the setting luminary over the metropolis of the Christian World; they all gazed at the glorious spectacle in silence, which was only interrupted by Mrs. Boren in a half sighing, half murmuring voice, exclaiming, "What a thousand and a thousand pities is it, that this unrivalled Rome should be the seat of such corruption; and that the Romish should be the *most* corrupt of the churches professing Christianity."

The Bishop groaned his assent, and Monsignore Guidi looked up with an air of surprise. "Easily, though not very charitably said," exclaimed he; "however, I can pity ignorance, and Christian charity teaches us to bear patiently with prejudice, while there is hope to enlighten the one, or remove the other; but what can be your reason for such bold assertions?"

Mrs. Boren coloured, and stammered, and hesitated, and at length lisped out, "I say, that the Romish Church is the *most* corrupt of *all* the Christian churches; mark, I do not deny that there may not be found some good Christians, even in the Romish Church; but you know that Christ addressed Seven Churches in Asia, yet addressed all as if there were true Christians in each, though they had *all* fallen into corruption; such is the present state of the Christian churches of our days."

Monsignore Guidi smiled. "My dear lady," said he, "I can see nothing but sheer abuse in what you have been saying; I can find no argument to grapple with; I can only see a false supposition, as if there were *many* Christian churches. Christ founded but *one* Church; the only question is which is that *one*. The different dioceses in which the one universal Church is divided, may be called churches in a restricted sense, because they are portions of Christ's one flock, congregated together under the immediate guidance of their own Bishop, but they all profess the one faith and doctrine of Christ, and are all united to the chief Shepherd, the Vicar of Christ on earth. Such were the Seven Churches of Asia; they all professed the same faith, though some rotten sheep were found amongst them."

"No, no," interrupted Mrs. Boren; "Christ addressed the Seven Churches as seven distinct, independent churches, each standing on its own foundation, and governed by its own angel, or bishop."

"Then," said Monsignore Guidi, "you must have many independent churches in England, and *your husband*, Madam, is an angel, I suppose, wedded to one of them."

Sefton and the Captain were convulsed with laughter; Mrs. Boren blushed, and the Bishop looked very awkward.

"Oh! but," said Mrs. Boren, with more animation than she usually exerted, "you will never persuade me that the Popish Church is not full of corruptions. The Word of God is not the guide of that church, because that church teaches that the end sanctifies the means, and that it is justifiable to *murder* thousands on thousands, to suppress what she calls heresy."

"Adagio, adagio," cried Monsignore Guidi; "for the sake of truth, stop, and let not your zeal outstrip all prudence. The Church teaches no such impiety; but it would seem that Biblicals are not very scrupulous about means, when they have recourse to such gross misstatements, in order to obtain their sanctified end of deluding the ignorant, and of alienating them more and more from their ancient Mother, the Church. The Church is not *guided* by the Word of God in the sense of Biblicals, that is, by the dead letter of the book, interpreted according to the wild fancy of each individual; the Church is guided by the unerring Spirit of truth; she has received the promise of the Spirit 'to abide with her *for ever*,' and 'to teach her *all truth*;'* to her is committed the Word of God, written or unwritten, the whole deposit of 'faith once delivered to the saints,' and she faithfully keeps that faith uncorrupt and incorruptible.

* John xiv. 16; xiii. 13.

It is her office to interpret and expound the Word of God, and guide her children to the right understanding of it."

"You had better take care what you say, you see, Mamma," said the Captain, laughing rather maliciously, "or you may get into the Inquisition."

"The Inquisition!" exclaimed Mrs. Boren; "for Heaven's sake, Frederick, don't talk of that merciless tribunal."

"The Inquisition!" said Miss Lavinia—"frightful monster! Gracious, brother, one's blood runs cold at its very name."

"Come! come!" said the Prelate, "do not let us shrink from a mere name: what is its meaning?"

"Its meaning!" screamed the Bishop and his lady, and the Captain and his sister, all in a breath; "its meaning! why, is it not the very sink of all that is horrible, and cruel, and bigoted, and tyrannical?"

"Order! order!" said Sefton in a deprecating tone; "fair play is a jewel, and we must allow Monsignore Guidi to answer one person at a time, and one accusation after another;" and then, after a pause, he added, "Will you tell us now, my good Sir, what is the real meaning of the Inquisition?"

"It means," said Monsignore Guidi, bowing to Sefton, "neither more nor less than a court of inquiry! Its office is to watch over the integrity of faith and morals. Its mode of proceeding is the most merciful, and the most lenient. It can take no cognizance of a man's interior thoughts and sentiments; they are removed far beyond the reach of any human tribunal—they rest between man and God. Hence, if a man, in the pride of his own heart, chooses to dissent from the faith of the Church, he is perfectly free to do so, and he will answer to God for his interior heresy or impiety. The Inquisition, then, takes cognizance only of overt acts. In this inquiry it proceeds with the greatest caution, prudence, and lenity. Suppose a man rises up to preach a new doctrine, 'another Gospel,' to disturb the people in the possession of their ancient faith, or to scandalize their piety by some gross immorality—and, by the way, delinquents of this species are far more common than those who impugn the faith—well, the faithful 'note that man, and do not keep company with him; they admonish him as a brother,'* and if he will not hear them, they tell 'the Church,'† and denounce him to the tribunal of the Inquisition."

"Yes," exclaimed the Captain indignantly; "then the hypocritical tyrants let their hell-hounds loose, and with merciless fangs they dart on their prey!"

"Not so fast, Captain, nor so fierce," said the Prelate calmly; "the sacred office never proceeds upon *one* information, as civil tribunals generally do. They must have two, three, or four unexceptionable witnesses, before they move a step. When they have these, they call the delinquent, and admonish him of his error; if he acknowledge his fault, and promise amendment, he is dismissed with a trifling penance, probably not exceeding the recital of the Seven Penitential Psalms. If, after 'a first and second admonition,' he remains obstinate in his error, he is then considered 'a heretic, to be avoided, being subverted and condemned by his own judgment,'‡ that is, by his own obstinacy in judgment, contrary to the doctrine of Christ. He is now imprisoned as a dangerous man, 'a lying teacher,' who endeavours 'to bring in sects of perdition;'§ and lead the ignorant and unwary into the ways of destruction."

"Aye, poor devil!" said the Captain; "once get him safe in prison, and his fate will be hard enough, I warrant. Such stories as I have heard of it would make your very hair stand on end."

"Nevertheless," continued Monsignore Guidi, "I can assure you as a fact, that his prison is not one of racks and torments, as you fondly imagine, but one far more lenient and comfortable than that to which is consigned the poor poacher, or the destitute vagrant, in Protestant England."

"Were you ever in England, Sir?" said the Bishop haughtily.

* 2 Thes. iii. 14. † Matt. xviii. 17. ‡ Tit. iii. 10.
§ 2 Peter ii. 1.

"Yes, my Lord," replied the Prelate, "and I have explored many of its prisons and public establishments also."

"Well, but what do they do with our imaginary delinquent when he is thus imprisoned?" said Sefton eagerly.

"He is 'reproved, entreated, rebuked, and that in all patience and doctrine;'* but if he still remains obstinate, if 'he cannot endure sound doctrine,' the tribunal then proceeds to its extreme sentence of excommunication; it pronounces its anathema, and 'delivers him up to Satan, that he may learn not to blaspheme.'† Here the Inquisition closes its proceedings, and delivers the culprit into the hands of the secular power, who do with him according to the criminal laws of the kingdom: with that the Church has nothing to do."

"What bigoted laws must those be," said the Bishop pompously, "to make a man answerable for his freedom of opinion."

"I cannot help being surprised, Sir," said the Prelate, "that you, who call yourself a Bishop of the Church of England, as *by law* established, should advance such a proposition."

"How so?"

"Because I did not conceive, that a man of judgment could persuade himself that God had given to man any freedom of opinion in matters of faith; that is, the liberty to receive or to reject, at his own caprice, whatever God has vouchsafed to reveal to mankind."

"Humph!" said the Bishop. "But what has that to do with the persecuting laws of man?"

"I do not mean," said Monsignore Guidi with a serious air, "to defend the system of civil persecution; yet I conceive it very possible for a Christian prince to deem it his duty to preserve his people from the poison of the heretic, as well as from the poniard of the assassin. Heresy and murder are equally ranked by St. Paul amongst those crimes, which 'exclude from the kingdom of God.'"‡

* 2 Tim. iv. 2. † 1 Tim. i. 20. ‡ Gal. v. 20.

"I see clearly," said the Bishop, "that you are an advocate for persecution."

"Not so, my Lord; I merely hint at motives, which, if they do not justify, may extenuate in great part the severity of the civil law. You will allow, I think, that every citizen is obliged to observe the law of the state under which he lives, and is protected, so long as the law is not contrary to the law of God."

"Undoubtedly," replied the Bishop. "I shall ever stand up for the inviolable sanctity of the law, without which neither our lives nor property would be secure."

"Well, then," continued the Prelate, "a law prohibiting the dissemination of schism and heresy amongst a people in possession of the 'faith once delivered to the saints' can never be deemed contrary to the law of God; and if such dissemination is known to produce dissensions, strife, rapine, and bloodshed, amongst a people once united, the state is undoubtedly justified in enacting such a law, under such penalties as may be judged necessary to arrest the evil. Every state in Europe has enacted such laws, under penalties of a greater or less degree of severity."

"On these principles," subjoined the Bishop, "you justify the penal laws of the British legislature, which lays certain disabilities on the Papists and Dissenters, and deprives them of some privileges."

"Pardon me, Sir," replied the Prelate, "the case is quite different: the British legislature began by establishing *the right* of each individual to frame his own creed, and thus very inconsistently and tyrannically chastises him with pains and penalties, if he dare to profess a creed different from that by law established. No Catholic state admits, or can admit, this *pretended* right. They know that every man is obliged to submit his judgment to the revealed truth of God; and they know that God has established an infallible tribunal, to decide what that truth is. You Protestants reject infallibility, and therefore have no plea to control the judgment of any man."

"But," said Sefton, "the laws in the ecclesiastical courts of England against blasphemy, and similar crimes, are not so very dissimilar: and as for persecution, England itself, even Protestant England, must blush for one of the blackest codes of persecution that ever disgraced a Christian people. Whilst we boasted of liberty of conscience, and the right of each individual to judge for himself in matters of religion, we hung, drew, and quartered the bodies of Catholics, and confiscated their property, if they dared to assert the same liberty. If your statement be true, Monsignore Guidi, it alters the case very much, and the aspect of the Inquisition is extremely different in my mind to what I had previously imagined."

"Perfectly true, my dear Sefton, I assure you; ask any well-informed Catholics you choose, and they will tell you the same thing, and confirm all I have said to you."

"And I fear," said the Bishop disdainfully, "that, notwithstanding all you have said, it will be found that in the Inquisition the degree of corruption into which the Church has fallen is so awfully evident, that there is no resisting the command, 'Come out of her, my people, that ye receive not of her plagues.'"

"Really, Sir," replied the Prelate with some spirit, "if politeness did not restrain me, I might fairly and easily retort, by saying that in the whole system of Biblicism the degree of error, confusion, and corruption into which it has fallen, and led men captive into perdition, is so evident, that it would be no great wonder if a simple, pious Catholic wished the Bible Societies, and all their Bibles, might taste a little of the wholesome corrections of the said Inquisition. We should not then have so many bewildered heads."

There was a pause: Sefton hummed a tune, and the Bishop looked unutterable things. By this time the sun had sunk, and the party returned to Rome, musing on what had passed.

CHAPTER XXXI.

> "The world is fallen into an easier way;
> This age knows better than to fast and pray."
>
> DRYDEN.

THE winter advanced, and Sefton felt as most people do who spend a winter in Rome, namely, that time seems to glide on too quickly, and that the days seem too short for all there is to see, and hear, and reflect upon. The merry carnival came in due time, and Sefton was both amused and edified: amused at the folly of the multitude, and edified at the piety of many. Mrs. Boren and her young people made the most of this glorious time of fun and merriment, and each day saw them sedulously going through the fatigues of dissipation: on the Corso by day, and at the balls, theatres, and masquerades at night. Sefton was sometimes induced to join; but before Ash-Wednesday he was heartily tired of it, and rejoiced at the idea of the people again returning to their sober senses: even the Bishop was weary of hearing of nought else from morning till night but comfits, horse races, ball-dresses, and masks and the like; and as he and his party sat indulging in the luxuries of a hot meat supper, about eleven o'clock on Tuesday night, he exclaimed with the utmost sincerity, "I never was better pleased in my life than to think all this mummery and nonsense is at an end!"

Mrs. Boren yawned.

"Well, we have had enough of it," answered the Captain; "it is capital fun though! I do pity those poor devils of Catholics who have to get up to-morrow morning to fast and pray and pity the poor."

"Poor wretches!" drawled out Miss Lavinia sympathetically.

"Yes, their delusion is very gross," said Mrs. Boren, "to imagine that fasting, and charity to the poor, are meritorious towards salvation or atonement for sin, the blood of Christ alone being sufficient to merit Heaven; and it is enough for us poor mortals to believe in Him."

"You have made such a jumble of misconceptions," said Monsignore Guidi, "that it is difficult to unravel them. Catholics hold that *faith* is the groundwork of salvation—'without faith it is impossible to please God;'* but faith alone will not save a man. 'If thou wilt enter into life, keep the commandments.'† 'Do you see that by works a man is justified, and not by faith only? For even as a body without the spirit is dead, so also faith without works is dead.'‡ 'If I should have all faith, so that I could remove mountains, and have not charity, I am nothing.'§ To sum up all in one word, we must have 'faith that *worketh* by charity.'‖ Now of these good works, so essential to salvation, the pious Catholic thinks he can never do too many: nay, all that he does appears as nothing to what he would wish to do; because he knows that his reward in Heaven will be proportioned to the extent of his good works."

"How wofully disappointed your pious Catholic will be, Monsignore," said Mrs. Boren, "when he comes to die, and finds his hands empty in consequence of the absurd doctrine of his Church, that it is in the power of fallen man himself to merit favour from God."

"What then do you suppose is meant, Madam, by these words of Scripture, 'Every man shall receive his own reward according to his labours'?"¶ said Monsignore Guidi.

"I was not aware there were such words, Sir," lisped Mrs. Boren, "but—"

"Yes! yes! my dear," interposed the Bishop hastily, "there are such words sure enough. I have preached from that text myself, Mrs. Boren, and I am far from

* Heb. xi. 6. † Matt. xix. 17. ‡ Jas. ii. 24.
§ 1 Cor. xiii. 2. ‖ Gal. v. 6. ¶ 1 Cor. iii. 8.

thinking good works are indifferent. Supposing even, however, for argument's sake, they do no positive good towards salvation, still they can do no harm; especially works of charity to the poor."

"I should be of opinion," said Sefton, "that they are positively meritorious towards salvation, seeing that at the day of judgment those who do them shall receive their reward, and those shall be condemned who have neglected them."

"Most certainly," said Monsignore Guidi; "and is it not also written as plainly as the greatest caviller on earth can wish it, that 'God will render to every man according to his works?'* Now these good works are eminently three,—prayer, fasting, and almsdeeds, so much recommended by Christ in his sermon on the mount;† for each of which he has pledged his divine word, that 'the Father will repay thee.' By prayer we understand all acts of devotion and piety, towards God; by fasting, all mortifications of our members, with their vices and concupiscences; by almsdeeds, all acts of charity and benevolence towards our neighbours."

"Still I cannot think," persisted Mrs. Boren, "how these works performed by frail man become meritorious, or deserving a reward."

"Certainly not from man himself," said Monsignore Guidi, "but from the grace of Christ; for it is written, 'Not that we are sufficient to think any thing of ourselves, as of ourselves, but our sufficiency is from God.'"‡

"Then it comes to what I maintain," said Mrs. Boren triumphantly, "that all our merits are from Christ, and we have nothing else to do but apply them: all our own efforts are trash!"

"Stay, my good lady," exclaimed Monsignore Guidi; "that is not the truth, by any means, much less the faith of Catholics; but our Saviour himself illustrates the whole doctrine in the most simple and beautiful parable of the vine, where he says, 'I am the true vine,' and further on adds, 'Abide in me: and I in you. As the

* Rom. ii. 6. † Matt. vi. ‡ 2 Cor. iii. 5.

branch cannot bear fruit of itself, unless it abide in the vine, so neither can you unless you abide in me. I am the vine; you the branches; he that abideth in me, and I in him, the same beareth much fruit; for without me you can do nothing. If any one abide not in me, he shall be cast forth as a branch, and shall wither, and they shall gather him up, and cast him into the fire, and he burneth.' Now, according to the very words of the Saviour, if a man be not united to him by faith and sanctifying grace, he is like the withered branch, incapable of bearing fruit, and fit only to be cast into the fire. He may be endowed with a kind heart, he may be actuated by a natural benevolence to succour suffering humanity; he may give his substance to the poor, and his body to the flames; nay, he may move mountains by his faith; but if he abide not in the love of Christ, in his sanctifying grace, all his works are dead, and they are not entitled to an eternal reward."

"Gracious goodness!" interrupted Miss Lavinia, "what strict doctrine! it is too bad; I had no idea Catholics thought in that way."

"Nevertheless," replied Monsignore Guidi, "this is real orthodox doctrine; those kind of natural good works, flowing from a kind heart, may indeed move God to mercy, and incline him to confer the grace of faith and conversion: such was the case with Cornelius, the first converted gentile; but the works *per se* are not entitled to an eternal reward."

Sefton sighed.

"On the contrary," added Monsignore Guidi, "the just man that abideth in the love of Christ beareth much fruit: the fruit is his, although it draw all its value from the merits of Christ: 'In this is my Father glorified, that you bring forth very much fruit: abide in my love; if you keep my commandments you shall abide in my love.' Thus the origin of faith, justification, and of all subsequent merit, is the grace of Christ; and the co-operation of man with that grace makes the merit his own. Such is the doctrine of St. Paul, speaking of his own works:

* John xv. 1, 4, 6.

'By the grace of God, *I am what I am*, and his grace in me hath not been void; but I have laboured more abundantly than all they; yet *not I*, but *the grace of God with me*.'"*

"This is certainly very clear and beautiful doctrine," said Sefton.

"Yes," continued Monsignore Guidi; "and this system is so far from depreciating the merits of Christ, that it exalts them exceedingly, and gives us a more sublime idea of their efficacy, when we see them thus fructify and increase continually in the living members of his body, of which he is the head. It is the dark and horrid doctrine of Calvin and his followers that makes void the grace of Christ, first by restricting the extension of his redemption to the elect only, and secondly, by denying its fructifying efficacy in the works of the just man."

"Granting, for argument's sake," said the Bishop pompously, "what you say to be true, still the Catholic doctrine of the communion of good works and merits is utterly impious, and quite contrary to God's whole method of salvation."

"Why, then," said Monsignore Guidi with energy, "it is utterly impious to believe 'in the communion of Saints;' which, by the way, Protestants repeat at *least once* a week in the Apostles' Creed; it is utterly impious then to believe that we are all members of the same mystical body; that we can and ought to assist one another in our spiritual as well as our temporal necessities. My dear good Sir, is it impious in the Protestant to ask the prayers of the man whom he esteems holy? But tell me, do the Calvinists never pray for one another?"

"Certainly they do," replied the Bishop.

"Then," continued Monsignore Guidi, "by this practice they acknowledge that they can share with another in the merits of one species of good works. In this they are quite scriptural. 'Pray one for another, that you may be saved, for the continual prayer of a *just*

* 1 Cor. xv. 10.

man availeth much.'* Now, Catholics see nothing repugnant to common sense, to piety, or to Scripture, in believing that they can share in the merits of other good works of the just man, whether they be fasting, or almsdeeds, taken in their most extensive sense."

"But you cannot prove that from Scripture," said Mrs. Boren angrily.

"Yes, I can," answered the Prelate quietly. "St. Paul entertained that opinion, when he says of himself, 'Who now rejoice in my sufferings *for you*, and fill up those things that are wanting of the sufferings of Christ in my flesh for *his body*, which is the Church.'† If there be any transferable merits in the sufferings of Christ, and I presume no one will be so utterly impious as to deny that, surely there must be some little also in the sufferings of the Apostle in the flesh, or he never would have rejoiced in being able to add his mite to those inestimable treasures which are dispensed to the members of Christ's body. The Apostle knew well that if his sufferings were meritorious and satisfactory, all his sufficiency came from Christ."

"My poor head quite aches," said Mrs. Boren, yawning: "what between the fatigues of the past week, and all this serious disputing at the end of it; so I shall wish you all a very good night."

"The discussion was your own bringing on, my good lady," said Monsignore Guidi; "but it is time I was off also," added he, looking at his watch; "it is nearly twelve o'clock, and I must be at the Sistine early to-morrow."

"What is there to be seen to-morrow morning?" asked Sefton.

"To-morrow is Ash-Wednesday, you know, and the solemn fast of Lent is begun by sprinkling ashes on the heads of the faithful. The Pope does this ceremony himself in his own chapel, and gives ashes to those who present themselves."

"I should like to accompany you," said Sefton; "I

* Jas. v. 16. † Col. i. 24.

was reading an account of that ancient piece of Church discipline only the other day."

The party broke up, and the next morning Sefton accompanied Monsignore Guidi to the Sistine, where he was much struck by the exact exemplification of the account he had a few days before been reading of the immemorial practice of sprinkling ashes on the heads of the faithful previous to their commencing the solemn fast of forty days, called Lent; a practice too so conformable to the Bible, and which is specified in many places of the Old Testament as one of the means of averting the wrath of an angry God. Did not the men of Nineveh do penance for their sins, fasting in sackcloth and ashes, with the hope that 'God would turn away from his fierce anger?' 'And God saw *their works*, and had mercy with regard to the evil which he had said he would do to them, and he did it not.' The more Edward reflected, the less he could see any good reason why the first founders of Protestantism had thought proper to depart from this very ancient Christian practice; he mentioned these ideas in a private conversation with the Bishop, who only shook his head, and told him laughingly, that he would find Lent mentioned in his Protestant prayer-book, and that nobody would prevent him either fasting or sprinkling his head with ashes if he pleased; but that the founders of the reformed Church were too considerate to force either themselves or their followers to such unnecessary penances, though they made no law forbidding people doing penance, if they fancied themselves called to it. Sefton sighed over this vague and unsatisfactory explanation; and the more he thought, the more he was perplexed by the many glaring inconsistencies of Protestantism.

CHAPTER XXXII.

"Do not as some ungracious Pastors do,
Shew me the steep and thorny way to Heaven,
Whilst, like a puffed and reckless libertine,
Himself the primrose path of dalliance treads,
And recks not his own creed."

SHAKSPEARE.

"HAVE you yet seen the ordinations in St. John Lateran?" said Monsignore Guidi one day to Mrs. Boren, as the party were walking up and down the avenue between that Church and Sta. Croce in Gerusalemme.

"No, Sir," answered the lady, "neither have I any desire to see them." The Prelate smiled.

"The Roman Catholic priesthood," continued Mrs. Boren, "is considered by liberal Protestants as a merely human institution."

"And the fact is," retorted Monsignore Guidi, "that Protestants consider many absurd things, and blindly believe them. The question is, Did *Christ institute* a ministry in his Church, or did He not? Did He constitute 'ministers and dispensers of the mysteries of God?' Did He 'give some apostles, and some prophets, and other some pastors and doctors, for the perfecting of the saints, for the work of the ministry, for the edifying of the body of Christ, until we all meet in the unity of the faith?'* Has 'the Holy Ghost placed bishops over the whole flock to rule the Church of God,' or has He not? What can be the meaning of these words, 'Obey your prelates, and be subject to them; for they watch, as being to render an account of your souls?'† Now if

* Eph. iv. 11. † Heb. xiii. 17.

there be any truth in these and many other explicit passages in Holy Scripture, then undoubtedly there is a ministry in the true Church of Christ, not of *human* but of *divine* institution: we shall look in vain for it elsewhere."

"You do not surely mean to insinuate," exclaimed Mrs. Boren indignantly, "that you Catholics claim a divine institution in preference to the reformed Church!"

"Well, will you tell me, Madam," replied the Prelate, "whence your husband derives his authority to govern a portion of the flock?"

"Oh! he was created by the King, who has supreme authority in the state."

"Or may be by the Queen," rejoined Monsignore Guidi, with a keen glance towards the Bishop; "in either case you are perfectly right, if you suppose and consider your ministry as a mere human institution."

"I beg your pardon, Monsignore," said the Bishop with pompous gravity; "perhaps Mrs. Boren has not expressed herself so clearly as she wished. She has no intention to assert that the clergy of the Established Church have no spiritual, or if you will, no divine authority in virtue of their ordinations; she objects only to the cruel and tyrannical system of oppression under which the Romish clergy groan."

"I must beg a little further explanation, my Lord," said Monsignore Guidi quietly, "or I may perchance mistake your meaning, as much as you say I have done that of your lady."

"I do not mean to be personal, Monsignore," answered the Bishop; "far from it; for there are many bright exceptions; amongst others, I think yourself; but, generally speaking, the system of the Catholic clergy is so iniquitous, that I am far from wishing to see more of them ordained."

"I do not understand yet," said Monsignore Guidi with unfeigned surprise; "how do you mean iniquitous?"

"Merely to mention one point," said the Bishop: "I conceive the celibacy of the clergy to be an iniquitous system: thus preventing them having children and grandchildren."

"Really, Sir, you do astonish me!" exclaimed the Prelate; "but why should I be astonished?" added he sorrowfully; "for hatred to celibacy was the prime motive of the first reformers. Good God! what an example of impure profligacy is exhibited in the lives of every one amongst them! In violation of the most solemn vows of chastity, they took to themselves wives; and Luther, to signalize his own impiety by a double sacrilege, took to himself a professed Nun."

Sefton coloured and looked a little annoyed: but the Bishop, nothing daunted, said with an air of assurance, "Well, Sir, and that was the consequences of the false and corrupt system of celibacy, laying commandments and rules upon men which it is impossible for them to keep."

"What is impossible to nature, is possible to grace," said Monsignore Guidi. "No one will deny that the Apostles were frail, weak men like ourselves, yet their conduct was very different; they left every thing, even their wives, those who had wives, to follow Christ.* St. Paul, giving directions to Timothy for the careful selection of men fit for the sacred ministry, positively requires that Bishops and Deacons, and of course Priests, should *be chaste*,† and consequently the state of celibacy is the best adapted to that holy office."

"Catholics may pretend to such perfection," interposed Mrs. Boren, "but it is unattainable; besides being a most unnatural system, which denies to the minister of God that relation to any creature, which the Divine Being has marked out as so honourable, by constantly appropriating the character to himself, namely, that of Father."

"Most certainly," added the Bishop; "Mrs. Boren has now expressed herself admirably."

Sefton smiled, and glanced with rather a significant expression at the gaily dressed lady, who was leaning on the Bishop's arm.

* Matt. xix, 27.

† 1 Tim. ii. 8.

"The Catholic Church forces no one to observe celibacy," said Monsignore Guidi; "but, following the counsel of the Apostle, as long as she can find men able and willing to bind themselves by vow to that more perfect state, she will ever select her ministers from amongst them. The Catholic Church has ever considered matrimony as a holy and honourable state, and believes it to have been exalted by Christ to the sublime dignity of a Sacrament; hence, she respects it infinitely more than Protestants do. Yet she equally holds that celibacy is a more perfect, a more holy, a more sublime state."

"It is easier to assert than to prove," said Mrs. Boren.

"Not so, my good lady," replied the Prelate; "St. Paul is so decided on this point, that it is astonishing any Bible reader should have ever perused the seventh chapter of his first epistle to the Corinthians, and entertain a doubt upon the subject. He goes a great deal further than Protestants can approve, when he says, 'I would that *all men* were even as myself—I say to the unmarried and to the widows, it is good for them if they so continue even as I.'"

"But what is the use, and end, and object of it?" said the Bishop impatiently.

"Many, many," answered Monsignore quietly. The Catholic priest considers himself wholly devoted to the service of God, and to the care of souls, who are his dearest children; and he feels bound on all occasions to sacrifice his ease, his health, his life for them; and therefore he deems it far the best that he should not be distracted from those sacred duties, by the cares and anxieties of the married state.'

"I perfectly disagree with you, Sir!" exclaimed the Bishop warmly; "and for my part, I should prefer presenting any living in my gift to a minister who was married, to one who was unmarried."

"But," interposed Monsignore Guidi, "listen for one moment to St. Paul: 'He that is without a wife, is solicitous for the things that belong to the Lord, how he may please God.' The Protestant minister prefers the marriage state. 'Tis well; 'tis better so than worse. Then comes 'the tribulation of the flesh;' the painful anxiety to provide for his wife and family, who depend upon the frail tenure of his life for their present and future subsistence; tithes must be collected, rates levied, dues exacted, the most rigid economy practised, every penny to be spared, nothing to afford to the poor. How true it is, 'He that is with a wife is solicitous for the things of the world, how he may please his wife; and he is divided.' So let him: his state is not an enviable one, to me at least."

"Really it is too much!" exclaimed Mrs. Boren angrily: "it is all envy."

Sefton laughed outright. "Remember, my dear Mrs. Boren, present company is always excepted," said he: "will you like to get into the carriage, for you seem a little fatigued, I think?" The lady suffered herself to be led to her carriage, but not before she had darted another indignant glance at the unconscious Monsignore Guidi.

As the carriage with Mrs. Boren and her party drove off, the Prelate said to Sefton, "I have been told that your own laws and customs consider the wives of Bishops and Clergymen in a very equivocal light; I have even heard that their children are hardly considered legitimate."

"Certainly," replied Sefton, "our laws and customs are very ambiguous on that question, and one cannot be surprised at it appearing odd to foreigners; for while a simple knight confers title and precedence on his lady, a Bishop can confer neither one nor the other on his wife: as for the legitimacy of their offspring, we must leave that question to be mooted by the lawyers. But when will these ordinations you were speaking of take place?"

"Next Saturday; and we will go to St. John's on that day, if you please," was the answer.

Sefton willingly agreed to this arrangement, and found himself, on the appointed day, early in the morning, in St. John Lateran, one of the most venerable and ancient churches in the world: he was forcibly struck at the imposing spectacle before him; the bright rays of the rising sun shone through the edifice, the choir of which was then filled by a crowd of young aspirants for holy orders, from the child of eight years to the young man of twenty-four; there, amongst them sat the Cardinal Vicar of Rome, eminent alike for his piety and learning, ready to ordain those who presented themselves, and evidently fully absorbed by the importance of the duty he was then engaged in. As Sefton gazed on this scene, it brought to his mind, as in a picture, all he had ever read in Church history of the ordinations in the time of St. Augustine, and in the records he had perused of still earlier periods of Christianity: "In those days, it was Catholics," thought he, "that were ordained; Catholics, too, who acknowledged the supremacy of the Pope; and this, too, is an ordination of Catholic ministers which I see now before my eyes, and, as far as I can make out, differing in nothing in faith and practice from the first Christians: surely it is more probable, even humanly speaking, that the truth is with those who have not departed from the faith and practice of the Apostles, rather than amongst the Protestant and dissenting Ministers, who separated themselves but a few hundred years ago from the rest of the Christian world, without any distinct authority from God for so doing; and who, moreover, have left out, or quite changed so many points of faith and discipline which the first Christians believed and practised, and which, as far as I can see and understand, Catholics still continue to believe and practise." These reflections made Sefton feel very melancholy; for it is a singular fact, that every heretic in the progress of arriving at the truth, feels the greatest repugnance to making an *act of faith* upon any point of Catholic doctrine, however clearly his judgment may be convinced on the subject; but let him once make an act of faith on the authority of the Catholic Church, to decide on what it is necessary to believe in order to possess eternal life, and all his repugnance, all his perplexities, all his melancholy and uneasiness will instantly vanish;

the mind of such a person becomes as different in an instant as the light at noon and the darkness at midnight. It is as necessary to make an act of faith to attain eternal life, as it is to make an act of charity; faith, like any other virtue, will lie dormant, or dead, unless brought into vigour and life by a decided act of the will. There is a wide difference between saying, as so many half-converted Protestants do, "*I wish* I could believe; I try to believe, and I can't believe," and saying generously and nobly, "*I do believe* in God and in the Church which Jesus Christ left on earth to teach me all truth." People who lead wicked lives often sigh and think, "*I wish* I could love God," but they know full well, that they never will enjoy God in Heaven, unless they say on earth, "*I do love God* with all my heart," and practise this act of charity, too, by keeping His commandments. So it is with the virtue of faith; before we can attain eternal life, we must make *an act of faith* and practise it, too, by believing all those things which are taught as necessary to salvation by the Church which Jesus Christ planted on earth, and in which He left the deposit of faith to be preserved pure and *unchanged* to the end of time. There are hundreds and thousands of Protestants who, in their search after truth, reach the same state of mind as Sefton was then in: they have seen too much and they know too much to be able to plead ignorance as an excuse for remaining in error, and yet they either draw back altogether, and wilfully shut their eyes to the light; or they remain in a state of doubt and vacillation, the misery of which no tongue can describe. Now, what can be the reasons for this? Alas, it is unnecessary to name them; sloth in some, indifference in others, but in by far the most predominant number, *human respect*, the fear of offending relations and friends, the apprehension of what the world will say and think, the want of courage to bear the reproaches and persecutions of those nearest and dearest to them. There is but one slight thread which keeps them from peace and happiness, and they will not or dare not snap it. . . . . And yet what are all the sufferings and trials of this short life to the immense glory of an endless eternity, " What will it avail a man if he gain the whole world, and lose *his own soul?*"* Let a person who has arrived at that state, never cease praying and entreating their Creator to lead them to the truth, and to give them *the courage* necessary to overcome whatever obstacle it is which keeps them from peace in this world and happiness in the next; let them continually meditate on the two important texts of Scripture, " Fear not them that kill the body, and are not able to kill the soul; but rather fear him that can destroy both body and soul in Hell;"† and that wherein St. Paul declares, that there is but " one Lord, one faith, and one baptism."‡ Let them do this, and God, who is faithful and compassionate to all our miseries, will not delay to encourage and console such a soul, and conduct it to the bright realms of eternal truth, where all is peace, and joy, and ineffable glory, through an endless eternity of love and bliss.

* Matt. xvi. 26. † Matt. x. 28. ‡ Eph. iv. 5.

CHAPTER XXXIII.

"Now, on my faith, this gear is all entangled,
Like to the yarn clew of the drowsy knitter,
Dragged by the frolic kitten through the cabin,
While the good dame sits nodding o'er the fire.
Masters attend; 'twill crave some skill to clear it."

SCOTT.

ONE day, about the beginning of March, induced by the balmy mildness of the opening Spring, the Bishop and his party accompanied by Sefton, set off with the intention of spending a few days at Albano, for the purpose of seeing Monte Cani and Grottaferrata, the Bishop and the ladies in an open barouche, and Sefton and the Captain on horseback; the extreme mildness of the weather, and the pleasure of feeling themselves in the open country and cheering sunbeams, tempted them to extend their excursion as far as Velletri and Cori. The party were extremely pleased with the fine scenery about the ancient and interesting town of Velletri, and still more so with their excursion to Cori, the road to which winds through rich vineyards and majestic mountain scenery the whole way to the steep eminence which it crowns. The peasants, in their picturesque costumes, were all engaged in the cheerful husbandry of early Spring, lightened by the hopes of future harvests, and enlivened by the gay carols of the lark winging his dizzy height in the joyous sunbeams. At Cori the party ascended its steep and fatiguing streets, till they reached the acclivity on which stands the portico of a temple to Hercules in most perfect preservation, and from whose site the prospect from horizon to horizon is exquisite. In their descent, they examined the remaining columns of a temple of Castor and Pollux, with the ancient bridge, and remnants of Cyclopian walls. As the Bishop thought it advisable to take a cold luncheon before they left Cori, it was rather late ere they were again *en route.* The Captain and Sefton had brought guns with them to have a little shooting on their way back to Velletri, and accordingly lagged behind the rest of the party to have more chance of starting birds. They stopped at a mountain pass, where many trees had lately been cut down near the road, though deep and dark woods extended for miles along the ascent towards Cori, and the naked and sharp-pointed rock Massimo. The underwood round the trees which had been cut down had been all burnt, and the black and scorched herbage testified that many months had not yet elapsed since this work of destruction had been effected.

"What is the reason that all this fine wood has been destroyed, I wonder?" said Sefton to his companion.

"On account of the banditti," answered the Captain; "there was a desperate gang not long ago in these mountain holds."

"Upon my honour, then," said Sefton, "I think if that is the case, it is rather foolish in us to be here at this time in the evening."

"Oh! there is no fear now; besides, the sun is not yet down, I believe. But silence! Sefton. I hear a rustling. Now for a good shot!"

A rustling indeed there was, and in the twinkling of an eye they were surrounded by a troop of armed bandits.

"Down to the ground! your money or your lives! your money or your lives!" resounded from every mouth.

"A sharp struggle ensued; the Captain threatened to fire, and in the scuffle his gun went off: this occasioned a momentary confusion amongst the bandits; the Captain reached his horse, was in the saddle in a moment, and, hallooing to Sefton to follow him and not to surrender, clapped spurs to his steed, and over hill and over dale, through the whizzing of shot sent after him, in a few minutes was in the high road, to rouse the nearest help to return with him to the rescue of his friend.

In the meantime Sefton made a desperate resistance, but his gun was soon wrenched from him; then, closing with his antagonist, he struggled fiercely with him for a time, until both fell together on the ground. Sefton grasped at the villain's throat as he lay beneath him, and was on the point of suffocating him, when the assassin drew from his belt a stiletto and launched a murderous blow on the breast of Sefton; the point of the poniard struck against the medal of Our Lady which he had hanging round his neck, and thus his life was saved: the bandit raised the stiletto to repeat the stroke, but his arm was arrested by another of the gang, who bade him "hold, for the life of the prisoner might be worth a ransom." Sefton let go his grasp from the ruffian's throat, and they both rose to their feet, but Sefton was instantly overpowered by numbers; he was stripped of his watch and money, his arms pinioned behind him, and rapidly hurried into the depth of the thick forest. The bandits were well aware, that in consequence of the escape of their other victim, the neighbourhood would soon he roused, and a hot pursuit succeed. In vain did Sefton entreat to be released; in vain did he promise not to betray their haunt; in vain did he offer them rewards, and voluntarily resign all right to his watch and money.

"Be silent, sirrah!" commanded the chief of the gang, "or it will be worse for you; such a rare bird as you cannot be released without a rare ransom." To enforce his order of silence, he drew a pistol, and threatened Sefton with instant death if he disobeyed.

The captain of the band was a handsome bold-looking man, about thirty, with eyes like an eagle. Having passed the forest, they rapidly dashed up a chasm formed between two high inaccessible and bleak rocks: about the middle of this pass they suddenly stopped, and forcing Sefton through a crevice in the rock just wide enough for one man at a time to pass, they made him turn to the left, and hurried him with painful velocity through a dark winding passage, and then, after another sharp turn, dropped him into a deep den; he fell with violence on the ground; he lay there stunned for some time, and only confusedly sensible to the sound of the retiring footsteps of the bandits, as they left with hurrying feet this dismal and loathsome prison.

The violence of the fall had burst asunder the cords which bound his arms, and when he could rise from the ground, he was enabled to grope along the walls and floor of this cave, where not the slightest ray of light penetrated; from the violence of his fall, he supposed it must be many feet deep. Awe, terror, anguish, a thousand terrible ideas rushed through his mind: would the robbers return, or would they leave him there to die the lingering, torturing, cruel death of famine, far from his wife, his children, his country, unheeded and unknown? As hour succeeded hour, with what eagerness did he not listen for the slightest sound! but all around him was literally as silent as the grave; he had no means of calculating how long it was he struggled with this almost frenzied state of excitement; nature was at length exhausted, and he sunk into a profound sleep. When Sefton awakened, he knew not where he was, and it was long ere he could distinctly retrace in his remembrance the events of the preceding day, and the anguish which accompanied each link of this recollection was most poignant; by this time, he began to feel the pain of hunger: he roused himself, and determined to grope round every part of his prison within his reach, but all his efforts to find any crevice or appearance of exit were in vain; he called aloud to the utmost extent of his voice, but it fell back unanswered within the damp walls of the dungeon. In his efforts, he stumbled over something on the ground, and after carefully feeling it, the horrid conviction flashed on his mind that it was a human skeleton: he hastened as far as he could from this fearful proof of the crimes and cruelties of the bandits; he sunk on the ground from inanition and terror, and, clasping his trembling hands together, made a fervent prayer to God to deliver him from this dreadful place, and from the horrors of such a lingering and frightful death. How fervently did he at that moment promise to serve God with all his heart, how sincerely did he resolve to do justice to his poor persecuted Emma, and what remorse did he not feel for his conduct towards her! The interests of his immortal soul then rose before him in all the reality of their terrifying importance. He had no faith whereon to rely; he had long since been convinced that the doctrines of the Established Church in which he had been educated were in great part false; he had felt the truth of most of the Catholic doctrines, and he groaned bitterly in spirit, that he had so long delayed to clear up his few remaining doubts. Why had he shut his eyes to the light that God had sent him? Had God punished him thus for the neglect of his graces? Was he doomed to die thus in his sins and in despair?

"God of mercy," he exclaimed, "I am unworthy to call Thee Father, yet I am Thy creature, the work of Thy hands. Oh! cast me not from Thee for ever! Rather look upon Thy beloved Son, and let his bleeding wounds plead in my behalf. Too long I have hardened my heart to the voice of Thy mercy; but Thou, my God, wilt not despise the humbled and contrite heart." He felt in his bosom for the portrait of Emma, that he might kiss it for the last time, and take a last and long farewell from her, in her image. But the portrait was gone: and he howled aloud in frenzied despair. He found, however, the medal of the Blessed Virgin, the only property which the bandits had respected. He kissed the medal, as the providential means which had saved his life from the dagger of an assassin, and at the same moment the parting words of Sister Angela flashed to his remembrance. They seemed to him to be the prophetic voice of a pure and superhuman being, and surely inspired by an ever-watchful providence. "Twice do I owe my life to thee, angelic maiden. Thou badest me invoke the Virgin, Mother of my Redeemer, in all my troubles and afflictions. I cannot do wrong in obeying thy injunctions." He clasped the medal between his hands, and bowing down with profound humility and with an incipient faith and hope that he might be heard, he thus prayed: "Virgin, Mother of my Redeemer, if it be true, as I am told, that thou hast often obtained unexpected relief to the poor and to the afflicted, shew now the power of thy intercession with thy divine Son, and succour me in this my utter distress." Sefton had scarce finished his prayer, when he found his heart relieved, and an undefinable ray of hope shot across his mind. From that moment he took a firm determination that no pride nor human respect should hinder him from embracing the true religion the moment he was satisfied where it existed. By degrees, however, his strength became weaker and weaker; he suffered acutely from famine, and gradually became perfectly senseless and unable to move: after remaining several days in this state, though he had no idea of the space of time elapsed, it seemed to him, as though in a painful dream, he beheld a light over his head, and heard the murmur of voices, and thought he beheld a ladder of rope let down into his dungeon, and a Capuchin with a long white beard descending the ladder, and approaching towards him; his weakness was so great, he seemed to wish the dream would pass, and that his insensibility would return; but the dream did not pass: for it was no dream, but really and truly Father Guiseppe, who, now leaning over Sefton, with the tenderest compassion, endeavoured to force some wine down his throat; after a few minutes he succeeded, and by degrees Sefton began to be sensible of the reality of what was going on around him.

"O my God!" exclaimed Father Guiseppe, clasping his hands, "and this is the horrid work of your reckless, wretched companions!"

The person he addressed was a young bandit, who was leaning over the top of the dungeon, and holding the upper end of the rope-ladder and a dark lantern, which cast a fitful light into the gloomy abode below.

"Come, come, Father, none of your reproaches," answered he, "for you are now in my power; if I draw up the ladder I can leave you to share his fate, and never would any one be a bit the wiser: but you see I have a spark of conscience left, or I should not have brought you here to give the poor wretch's soul a last chance. I marvel much he is alive."

"Peace, peace, my son," said the Father quietly, "add not to your weight of guilt by taking my life, but fix the ladder firmly, and extend your arms to draw this poor victim up by means of my cloak."

The bandit did as he was ordered, and, after some difficulty, Sefton was extracted from the dungeon, and dragged by him and the Capuchin along the intricate and narrow turnings by which he had been conducted to it. The influence of the open air, and a little nourishment given sparingly and at intervals, soon revived him sufficiently to enable them to bind him firmly on a stout horse. It was a fine moonlight evening, and all nature still around them; but Sefton's heart anxiously beat to know what was now to be his fate, and he was still more appalled on hearing Father Guiseppe take leave of the bandit, and commend Sefton to his care and fidelity on his route. "Good God!" thought he, "can this friar be in league with the robbers! how horrible! and what hypocrisy under a religious habit!" in a weak and scarcely articulate voice, he appealed to Father Guiseppe not to forsake him.

"Be at peace, my son," answered he, leaning over him, and he added in a low whisper, "all will yet go well. I will *not forsake you*, and you will yet, I hope, live to shew your gratitude to God for this deliverance, by loving Him with all your heart, and soul, and mind, in the one true faith."

Sefton felt a compunctious regret that he had not yet thanked God for his deliverance from the dungeon.

"I do thank my God most fervently," said he; "but why am I to go with that wretch?" added he feebly.

"Because he must conduct you to his Captain; too much bloodshed and crime would be the consequence of his disobedience; he has staked much to bring me to you; trust in God, and all will go right. Holy Mary and St. Francis guide you safely on your way!"

The name of Mary brought to the mind of Sefton the prayer he had made to the Virgin at a moment when all human hope of succour seemed to have been lost for ever, and he thought within himself, "May I not owe my deliverance to her? A Catholic would not hesitate to attribute the boon to her intercession, and why should I doubt it? If the prayer of the just man availeth much, surely the prayer of the Virgin Mother of Jesus must be all-powerful;" and he breathed a heartfelt prayer of thanksgiving to the Mother of Mercy, and with increased confidence commended himself to her protection, that she would finish the good work she had so graciously begun in his behalf; but why he was to be again consigned to bondage was all a mystery to Sefton, and the impatient voice of the bandit prevented any further discourse with Father Guiseppe, and they separated, the good religious taking his way towards his convent near Velletri, and the bandit, mounted and armed, dragging Sefton and his horse rapidly on towards the wilds of Tusculum. They passed under Monte Cuvi, and along Hannibal's camp, reposing in the broad moon-beams, ere a syllable was exchanged between them; but as they approached nearer to Tusculum, winding amid bleak and barren scenery, the bandit suddenly turned round, and striking his hand on his pistol, "Hark ye! young Englishman," said he, "it is as much as your life is worth to tell yonder crew that you have seen the Capuchin. Do you understand me?"

Sefton had no alternative, but to promise obedience.

"My name is Rinaldo," continued the bandit, "and I am next in command to the Captain; he sent me to bring you back to him for the sake of the ransom, and I left a dear pledge in their power for my fidelity. He is a hard man; but I, who like not the life over well, out of compassion for your soul, brought the Father, thinking you might be at the last gasp, and want shriving of your heresies."

Sefton groaned internally, and marvelled much at the odd mixture of good and bad in his strange companion.

"The Captain is so suspicious," continued the bandit,

"that if he knew of the Capuchin, he would surely shoot me on the spot."

Sefton reiterated his promise of silence, and shortly afterwards they arrived at the haunt of the bandits in the wilds of Tusculum. There is a spot, which is now shewn as Cicero's school, and just below it extends a vale, which reminds one of the poet's description of the vale of Paradise; it was at that moment lit up by the silvery softness of the placid moon; and Sefton gazed in admiration at the superb forest scenery which, on either side, fringed this lovely valley, as it gradually expanded and disclosed in its lengthening vista the little town of Frascati, sleeping in the silence of night; the ruined remains of Mont Dragone, and the villa Rufina, embosomed in rich woods, and reposing in the moon-beams, and far, far beyond, the broad and rich Campagnia, with all its soft, peculiar features, bounded only by the waters of the blue ocean, reflecting on its tranquil wave the refulgent queen of night. A few yards below Cicero's school, there exists now a circular clump of rich garden roses, mingled with the yellow broom, growing over a slight hollow on the green turf of a few yards' extent. At the time I am speaking of, this hollow concealed the entrance to the bandits' caves, which extended far underground, and had probably once formed the substruction of some Roman villa, and into which Sefton was soon introduced by his companion Rinaldo. The bandits were still carousing.

"Ha!" exclaimed the Captain, starting up; "Rinaldo, my good fellow, are you returned, and with our captive alive?"

"I have done your bidding," answered Rinaldo sulkily; "there's the Englishman: now, where is Vincenza? are she and the boy well?" added he hastily.

"They are where you left them," replied the Captain haughtily; "go and satisfy yourself."

Rinaldo entered into an inner cave, and in a few minutes returned apparently satisfied; then holding out his hand to the Captain, "Come," said he, "we are friends again; give me food and drink, for I have not had a bit or sup since we parted; but first you must attend to the prisoner, or you'll be likely to get small ransom for a dead body."

The Captain drew near to examine Sefton, and even his fierce stern features relented when he saw the pale emaciated face of his prisoner: he gave a low whistle, and a miserable-looking, hideous beldam stood before him. "Here, Macrina," said he, "attend to this poor wretch, and see him fed, and put to repose."

"And see you do not overfeed him, you old hag!" exclaimed Rinaldo; "to-night is the first time he has tasted food for many a day!"

The old woman obeyed, and Sefton was soon comfortably enough laid on a mattrass and covered with warm cloaks; but he could not sleep, for the bandits seemed to think that the arrival of Rinaldo was a sufficient excuse for prolonging their revels. From their conversation, he soon gathered that they had sent, by a shepherd boy, to Rome, to demand a high ransom for his safe restoration, accompanied by threats in case of refusal of inflicting immediate death: he found also that the Captain and a detachment were to set off on the morrow for the mountain passes near Itri, as travellers were shortly expected up from Naples. "And now, Rinaldo, my good fellow," said the Captain, who was nearly intoxicated, "let us have a parting song."

Rinaldo, nothing loath to keep up the merriment, readily complied.

1.

Oh! who is so gay as a jolly brigand,
  Who lives by his wits and stiletto,
His name runs like wildfire over the land,
  For the Pope never keeps it in petto.

2.

If we can't get a castle, we live in a cave,
  And banish all sorrow and spleen,
And when danger 's at hand, we are active and brave,
  And laugh at the old guillotine.

3.

Long life to the Pope, good compassionate soul!
  May he never have better police;
And good luck to ourselves, as we spring from our hole,
  The next plodding traveller to fleece.

4.

Then a fig for the fifty old worthies and Pope,
  Who govern the papal see,
For a true brigand can easily cope
  With their catch-him-who-can decree!

The applause which followed Rinaldo's ditty gradually subsided, and the bandits one by one wrapt themselves in their cloaks to sleep away the fatigues and revels of the day.

Early the next morning the Captain and his detachment set off on their foraging expedition, and the rest of the band, under the command of Rinaldo, penetrated higher up amongst the thick wood, which was almost trackless, except where it was interrupted by the ancient paved streets, and remaining vestiges of the dwellings of man. Some of the bandits were stationed under what is called the fortress, and others not far from the remains of the beautiful amphitheatre. Sefton was fettered, so that escape was impossible; and, thus secured, was allowed to wander from one beautiful spot to another, but always under the watchful eye of a guardian. Notwithstanding his anxiety as to his fate, he could not help being in admiration at the exquisite and peculiar scenery around him, especially during the magnificent sunsets he witnessed from this classic site; he enjoyed the delicious reveries and reflections produced by the recollections of the past, associated to the beauties of the present, now tinged by the most delicate fairy softness and freshness of early spring. More than a week had elapsed in this listless sort of existence, and he became daily more uneasy at the delay of the expected ransom, when one evening, as he was reposing on the broken remnants of an ancient column, now gazing on the shadowy softening of the evening sky, now contemplating the peaceful solitude of the Camaldolese monastery, which lay stretched beneath him, now listening to the silvery tones of the monk's church-bell as it rung the "Ave Maria," his attention was suddenly roused by the sound of a guitar. Sefton turned his eyes to the quarter from whence the sound proceeded, and beheld, at a little distance, Rinaldo seated near Vincenza, who was leaning over her infant boy, reposing on the ground, on the folds of a rich crimson shawl, the spoils, doubtless, of some unfortunate traveller. Vincenza herself was in the costume of Frascati, though it was composed of the most costly materials; and her head and neck adorned with necklaces and rich jewels; her figure was light and graceful, and her dark, brilliant, laughing eyes, accorded well with the lips and cheeks, that told of the sunny south; she and Rinaldo were singing, and the soft evening breeze brought the accents to Sefton, as he gazed on the picturesque group:—

1.

Ave Maria! ere yet the day's close,
For protection we beg through the forthcoming night,
As twilight, soft prelude of Nature's repose,
Steeps the senses in calmness and peaceful delight.

2.

Ave Maria! that monastery bell
Seems the prayer of all matter that's voiceless to thee,
Of the mountain and hill, of the valley and dell,
Of the rocks, and the waves of the fathomless sea.

3.

Ave Maria! that monastery bell
Bids the pilgrim so weary uncover and kneel,
It rouses the monk in his comfortless cell,
And calls forth from thousands the hallowed appeal.

4.

Ave Maria! that monastery bell
Has cited to prayer my all trembling muse,
Oh! receive of devotion the bosomful swell,
Nor a votary's humble petition refuse.

The sound ceased, and Sefton thought within himself what an incomprehensible being man was; here are these people, mused he, leading a wicked and lawless life, and then lulling their consciences by devotion to the Virgin, as if she, considering her merely as a pure and holy woman, could be pleased with accents from such lips. But Sefton rashly judged Rinaldo and Vincenza, though appearances were certainly against them.

In a few moments, Vincenza arose, and, taking her child in her arms, passed by the spot where Sefton was sitting; in passing him, she dropt a letter close to him, and said in a low voice, "If your answer to this is in the affirmative, break a broom branch, and leave it by the column on which you are sitting." She hastened on, and he took the letter; on opening it, he found, to his surprise, that it was from Father Guiseppe, who shortly informed Sefton, that he knew that the bandits had determined, in case of the non-arrival of the ransom, after two more days, to cut off one of his hands, and send it down to Rome; that he himself had stopped the ransom on its way; that Rinaldo and Vincenza had both become sincere penitents, and had, after many struggles, determined to forsake their lawless life; that they were both to be at the church of the Capuchin convent, between Tusculum and Frascati, before sunrise the next morning, to confess their sins, and be united in lawful matrimony; that he had arranged their escape to a distant province in Italy, where they were unknown, and in which country they hoped to lead a virtuous and honest life. Father Guiseppe stated at some length, how he had known and instructed Rinaldo in his childhood, how he was led by bad companions to the commission of some crime which had rendered him obnoxious to the laws, so that fleeing from justice, he had joined this lawless gang; how he had never ceased praying for him, and rousing his conscience, till, by God's grace, he was brought to true penitence, and he concluded by saying, that Rinaldo, at his earnest request, had undertaken to favour the escape of Sefton, by bringing him along with them as far as the convent already mentioned, on condition that Sefton should give him one hundred scudi towards the payment of his journey to the distant place of his retirement.

When Sefton had read this document, he fervently thanked God for such an unexpected hope of deliverance, and with great delight did he shew his acceptance of the condition, by breaking the broom branch, and leaving it as Vincenza had told him. That night he slept with his heart full of hopes, and fears, and gratitude, and the morning sun found him kneeling in the church of the Capuchins, witnessing the marriage of Rinaldo and Vincenza; Vincenza, now no longer decked in rich and ill-gotten robes, but in the simple costume of her native Frascati. Father Guiseppe had obtained the permission of the parish priest to perform the marriage, and the moment that was finished, they and their child proceeded disguised by the earliest coach to Rome, on their way to their destination.

Sefton remained concealed a few days in the Capuchin convent; he had several conversations with Father Guiseppe, on different points of Catholic faith and practice, and was greatly edified with the meek, humble, mortified, and pious demeanour of the religious community. "Surely," thought he, "if they who serve the Altar have a right to live by the Altar, these men must be actuated by an Apostolic spirit, who renounce all tithes and possessions, and depend solely on the voluntary contributions of the people, who will give only in proportion to the value and esteem they have of their services."

Before he left the convent, he gave them a copious alms, in testimony of his respect and obligation to them; he reached Rome in safety, to the joy and surprise of his anxious friends.

"Yes," said he, as he concluded the relation of his fearful adventures, "I do most fully retract having called that excellent man, Father Guiseppe, an *idle vagrant;* and I do acknowledge, that amongst the barefooted friars, there are excellent, and holy, and useful members of society."

CHAPTER XXXIV.

"Canst thou not minister to a mind diseased;
Pluck from the memory a rooted sorrow;
Raze out the written troubles of the brain;
And, with some sweet oblivious antidote,
Cleanse the foul bosom of that perilous stuff,
Which weighs upon the heart?"

SHAKSPEARE.

BEFORE Rinaldo parted from Sefton, he gave him a convincing proof of the sincerity of his conversion by restoring to him the little miniature of Emma, set in rubies, which has been already mentioned. In the division of the spoils this had fallen to his lot, and he now returned it to its rightful owner uninjured. After Sefton's return to Rome, as he was one morning fastening a new ribbon to it previous to replacing it round his neck, a letter was brought to him. The letter was from Emma, and affected him very much, as she informed him in it of the serious illness of their youngest child. This poor baby had never thriven after it had been so violently torn from the maternal breast, and now, during the period of a difficult teething, deprived of its natural nourishment, and of the watchful and tender cares which a mother alone can give, there seemed little chance of its living much longer in this vale of tears, or that it would ever more gladden its father's eye in this world. Sefton was struck with grief, for he well remembered the day that he forsook Emma, leaving it at her breast; and afterwards, when he had it with him at Eaglenest Cottage, he never could look at it without a pang in consequence of that recollection. He thought God had sent him this affliction to chastise him for his tardiness in doing what his conscience too plainly told him was right. When he reflected on this intelligence, he wondered how he could have left his innocent wife so long without any mitigation of the severity of his treatment towards her with regard to their children. Now all his paternal feelings were roused, and in him they were very strong. What to do was the next question. Should he return immediately to England? That thought did not give him peace; for his mind was yet far from being settled on the point of religion, or rather, to speak more correctly, he still felt he wanted the moral courage to act decidedly in the way his conscience whispered to him was right. It was too late to answer the letter by that day's post; therefore he determined to take a solitary walk and reflect the matter well over. He rambled as far as the fountain of Egeria, and reflected, and better reflected on the line of conduct to pursue; but all his reflections ended as they had begun, in a state of painful indecision. "I will take advice," said he, springing up from the broken stump of a tree on which he had been sitting: "I will go directly to the Gesù, and shew this letter to Father Oswald: he is interested in Emma's fate; and if I follow his advice, I think I cannot act unjustly towards her; besides, he knows all the circumstances of the case, circumstances which I should feel some little difficulty and pain in relating to any other person I know in Rome at present." Accordingly, Sefton set off, and walked as fast as he could to the Gesù, as fast as people are apt to walk sometimes, when they seem to imagine that locomotion will liberate them from unpleasant ideas. Sefton had not seen Father Oswald since his return from the mountains; he had, therefore, first to relate his adventures, and then told him of his grief: shewed him Emma's letter, and asked what steps he thought would be best to be taken, adding, "I have a particular reason for wishing to visit Naples before I return to England, and, perhaps, even Emma, poor thing! would be more satisfied I should do so, if she knew what that reason was."

"I am sure your wish to do so would be sufficient for her," said Father Oswald, smiling; "write, and tell her so, my good friend."

"The fact is," said Sefton bluntly, "I want to see that miracle, or rather to see that there is no miracle at all."

"You mean the miracle of the liquefaction of the blood of Saint Januarius," said Father Oswald somewhat archly.

"Yes; I do: I have been at some pains to find out that the reformed churches have never yet proved or produced a miracle to stamp their mission and truth; and I certainly have a little curiosity to see what pretensions this alleged miracle of the blood has to be what the Catholics pretend it is; namely, a standing testimonial of the truth of their religion. You may remember, Sir, a conversation I had with you once on the subject of miracles; well, I am still of the same opinion; if I could be convinced of the existence of miracles now in the Catholic or any other religion, it would make a great change in my mind."

"That miracles have ever existed, or still do exist in the Catholic religion, is an undoubted fact," said Father Oswald; "and it is equally a fact that they never have and never can exist in any other religion; because God never could work a miracle in confirmation of error; it would be a blasphemy to imagine so. I think Mrs. Sefton would certainly wish you to satisfy your mind on this subject previous to returning to England; but I recommend you to write, and mention your wish to her, as I said before; in the meantime, could you not permit her to go to her children? you must be aware that this kindness on your part would be a sensible consolation to her during your protracted absence; and, again, as you ask my advice, I think you ought not in conscience to deprive that sick infant of its mother's care without a sufficient reason; now, in this case, I cannot see the existence of any sufficient reason for such an act."

Sefton coloured, and fidgetted, and sighed.

"Excuse my speaking plainly, but I think that act of justice is the least you can do towards your wife and children; she has suffered a good deal on your account."

"O my God! indeed she has," exclaimed Sefton vehemently, striking his forehead with his hand. "I will do it, yes, I will do it. I will write by to-morrow's post, and tell her to go down to Devonshire, and join her children and Harriet there; but then the General," added he, stopping short: "the old man has been very kind to her; what will he say to this arrangement?"

"Let him accompany her there, and when the child is better, they can all return together, if he wishes it, to his own house. I owe my excellent friend a letter, and I will write and explain the state of the case to him, if you like."

"Well, I think it would be a good thing if you would take that trouble, Sir. I hope my poor Emma will be a little consoled by this arrangement, and I shall have time to get my own mind settled one way or another before we meet, which I feel absolutely necessary for the happiness of us both, if ever we are to be happy again," added he despondingly.

"Keep up your heart, my good friend; God never forsakes those who trust in him," said Father Oswald kindly.

Sefton shook him warmly by the hand, and hurried out of the room: he went to his lodgings, and immediately wrote a feeling and consolatory letter to Emma, mentioning his wish to see the Holy Week in Rome, and to visit Naples; but adding, that in case the child was worse, and that she wished him to return, he should think it his duty as a father so to do. He felt consoled and happy after this letter was sent off, notwithstanding his natural anxiety about his child.

It would be difficult to convey by words an idea of the grief, anxiety, and agitation, which Emma endured during this period, and more particularly after she was informed of the alarming illness of her baby; her uncle was indefatigable in his affectionate attentions, but her feeling of desolation was too great to be susceptible of human consolation, however grateful she might be to him who offered it; all her consolation, all her support was prayer; but never during the whole period of this severe trial did she once regret the generous sacrifice she had made to her God. She constantly prayed to her Saviour to support her under her afflictions, and he did not fail to mingle a drop of consolation in the bitter cup she was drinking for his sake. The General began to be seriously alarmed about her health, and many and vehement were the exclamations and interjections that escaped him on the conduct of her husband; these would have been much more frequent, had he not been aware of the pain he gave her. When Sefton's letter arrived, giving his wife permission to join her children, it would have been difficult to say whether Emma or her uncle were the most surprised; the same post brought Father Oswald's letter to the General, who, in consequence, bustled about, and exerted himself so effectually, that in less than three hours after the arrival of the letters, he and Emma were on their road to Devonshire. Harriet's joy and surprise at their arrival was very great; and as she clasped Emma in her arms, "Now," said she, "I shall be able at last to get some peace and quiet. Oh! the troubles I have had with those children! my dear Emma, now, at least, you will take all that off my hands, and I shall be able to sit still in peace and quietness."

"Too happy shall I be so to do, my dear, dear sister," replied Emma, whose emotion was so great she could scarcely speak; "now, take me to my children."

"Yes," said Harriet, turning to the General as they walked towards the nursery, "yesterday afternoon I saw two magpies on the lawn, and I was sure some good would come of it."

"Oh! Miss Harriet, Miss Harriet!" said the General, shaking his head incredulously, "that won't do, indeed!"

But Harriet was at this moment too much occupied with her own happiness at getting Emma back, to pay attention to any thing else.

The fostering care of its mother soon restored the babe to convalescence: it was seldom out of her arms, night or day; and fervently did she thank God for the consolation He had vouchsafed to give her. She wrote a letter full of affection and gratitude to Edward; she expressed her entire approbation that he should use every means to satisfy his mind on the subject of religion, though his prolonged absence could not but cause her pain. This letter drew tears from Edward's eyes, and from that time their correspondence became daily more affectionate and intimate; he proposed many of his difficulties to her, and was frequently surprised at the simple and clear manner in which she answered them. In the meantime Emma consoled herself with her children as well as she could; but all who know what a woman's love is need not be informed—while her husband was far away, and her heart divided with hopes and fears regarding her future destiny—how fitful her happiness was, nor how chequered were her nights and days with doubts, fears, and anxieties: in prayer she found her only peace and consolation, and she reposed with an entire confidence all her griefs in the bosom of her Heavenly Father. She frequently received the Holy Communion, and she then felt fully the truth of the Saviour's divine words, "Come to me, all you who labour and are heavy burthened, and I will refresh you, and you shall find rest for your souls."

CHAPTER XXXV.

"O teach me to believe Thee thus concealed,
And search no further than thyself revealed;
But her alone for my director take,
Whom thou hast promised never to forsake."

THE Lent passed swiftly away, and each day found Sefton more deeply engaged in studying and searching explanations of what he saw, that seemed to him odd or absurd in the Catholic religion; his mind was now so completely absorbed on the subject of religion, that he attended little either to the study of antiquities, or the pleasures of society. With the natural ardour and perseverance of his character, he was now determined to sift the subject thoroughly, and not to cease his efforts till his mind was quite satisfied one way or another; he still nourished the idea he had formed in Switzerland, that if he could be convinced of the continued existence of miracles, either in the Catholic religion or in any other, that that religion must be the true one: but his heart often sunk when he thought of the impossibility of ever being satisfied on that point; for he felt that the evidence he should require must be so unanswerable, that he despaired of ever meeting with it. He had determined to visit Naples, to see the asserted miracle of the liquefaction of the blood of St. Januarius; but so deeply impressed in his mind was the Protestant axiom that miracles had ceased, that he felt convinced that the whole was a complete trick; and that he had only to go and see, to be completely satisfied that it was a vile imposture of the Clergy to keep the people in ignorance and superstition.

He never alluded to his ideas regarding the possibility of the existence of a supernatural interposition of Providence in the affairs of men during the present age, except sometimes in his conversations with Father Oswald; he had read so many infidel and Protestant writers on the subject, that he was apt to imagine it was a weakness almost to be ashamed of, to suppose it possible that miracles could exist in the present day: however, as he always talked very freely with Father Oswald, their discussions on the subject of a supernatural providence were not unfrequent. Holy Week was now fast approaching, and the mysteries of the Passion were ushered in by the solemn benediction of palm branches in the Sistine Chapel, which the Pope and Cardinals bore in their hands in slow procession; while the choir sung the triumphal song of the Hebrews, "Hosanna! Blessed is he that cometh in the name of the Lord the King of Israel."* This joyful ceremony was followed immediately by the mournful chant of the Passion. The contrast made a deep impression on the heart of Sefton, and he could not help making the reflection, how fickle and worthless were the applauses of this world, when the very men, who a few days before in loud acclaim extolled the Saviour as the King of Israel, now cry out in horrid yells, "Crucify him, crucify him." Sefton went through all the touching ceremonies of that holy and solemn week with the greatest attention; he satisfied himself on the meaning and explanation of every thing he saw; and Monsignore Guidi found it required no little patience to answer all the minutiæ of his inquiries. He was astonished at the beauty and propriety of the Church service: as he became acquainted with the prayers and understood the meaning of the ceremonies, he felt their effect in exciting devotional feelings, and felt considerable regret that no vestige of them had been retained in the English service. When he was informed that the Catholics in England still keep up the practice of the same ceremonies as he was witnessing in Rome, his astonishment was unfeigned; he again wondered

* John xii. 13.

what reason could have induced the first Reformers to abolish the yearly remembrance of the sufferings of the Saviour, and the benefits of the Redemption, from their ritual, a practice so natural for a Christian, and so calculated to excite sentiments of compunctious penitence for sin, and gratitude to God. Sefton felt his heart melt within him, as he listened to the deep pathetic tones of the Miserere, and his whole soul dissolved in tenderness and compassion as, with absorbed attention, he dwelt on the prolonged deep pathos of the voices, that as from another sphere chanted the sublime account given by the Evangelists of the sufferings and death of a God-man. He was deeply moved at the solemn gloom that sat on every brow of those he met in the streets of Rome on Good Friday, as if some common calamity had fallen upon the city. "Surely," said he, "these people must think upon, and feel for the sufferings of the Lord! whence comes it that these salutary days pass over our people of England without producing the slightest change in their habits, looks, and busy pursuits? They have nothing to remind them of the holy season; perhaps not one in ten thousand think upon their crucified Redeemer. The men who abolished all external marks of sorrow, knew little of the human heart, or had little affection for Jesus." These mournful feelings swelled in his breast as he strolled through the streets of Rome, and remarked that the joyful sound of a bell was not heard during that day; and when he stepped into any church, he found every light extinguished, every Altar naked, stripped of all ornament, and a universal desolation reigning around. In the afternoon he went to St. Peter's with Monsignore Guidi, to see the pilgrims, who came in crowds on that day to the Basilica. He there saw a Cardinal approach; he was the grand penitentiary, accompanied with his officers and the Confessors of the Church. The Cardinal ascended to the elevated seat of the Confessional, which had already been prepared for him, and a golden wand was put into his hands; then the accompanying Priests, one after another, knelt humbly before him, and he laid on the head of each the golden wand. Then followed a crowd of seculars, male and female, of every class, to receive the same stroke of the rod. Sefton smiled at the ceremony, and, turning to Monsignore Guidi, asked him, " Is there any magic in that wand? is the Cardinal conjuring with it?"

"The question is natural enough from you," replied the Prelate; " it has been asked before by Protestants. Its meaning is simple, and when you have heard the explanation, I think you cannot disapprove of its piety. By that humble prostration, each individual acknowledges, in the face of the Church, that he is a poor sinner, worthy of those stripes which were laid on the shoulders of Jesus."

"The thought is just and holy," replied Sefton. "Yet I doubt if a Protestant could ever be induced to make such a public act of humiliation. Alas! who is more worthy of stripes than myself?"

Without saying another word, he pushed forward, and, kneeling reverently, received the tap of the golden wand. Many Protestants were present, and gazed with astonishment at this sight; some condemned it as an act of apostasy; others maintained it was only a sportive act of levity, performed to be the matter of future merriment. Quite different were the sentiments of Sefton; he felt consoled internally at this his first victory over his rebellious pride, and at the triumph ever all human respects. He then proceeded to the Sistine Chapel, to attend for the third time at the office of Tenebræ, with redoubled fervour and devotion. If his soul was touched and filled with holy pensiveness at these serious and affecting ceremonies, it was raised, and exalted, and rejoiced by the bursts of Alleluias and holy exultation which rung through the roof of the venerable Sistine Chapel on the morning of Holy Saturday, in anticipation of the Resurrection of the Saviour; that Resurrection, which was the fulfilment and confirmation of all the prophecies of the old law, and of the many promises of the Redeemer. Then came the glorious Pontifical of the Sovereign Pontiff in the unrivalled church of St. Peter's on the morning of Easter Sunday, when all is joy, and peace, and happiness; it filled him with wonder and delight. Sefton's admiration reached its climax at the imposing and heart-touching spectacle of the solemn, triple benediction imparted by the Pope to the whole world, from the front of the Vatican Basilica, as a seal of peace and protection given by the "One Shepherd," to His "one fold;" he was deeply affected, and he felt within himself how beautiful and how good it is for brethren to dwell together in this world in peace and charity, and mutual union. By degrees the tumult of his feelings subsided, and he gazed with a calm feeling of hope on the first soft, and then brilliant illumination of the dome and area of St. Peter's. He had experienced during the past week a variety of new emotions; but he retired to rest that night in a most calm and peaceful state of mind. One thing had annoyed and astonished Sefton extremely during the past week, and that was the ill-behaviour of the Protestants. He was frequently fairly ashamed of his fellow-countrymen and country-women. He sometimes attempted remonstrance and reproach; but both were equally unavailing. The English seemed to imagine these solemn and religious devotions were a kind of show or exhibition, got up on purpose to amuse and astonish them. They appeared for that week to have laid aside every feeling of decency, decorum, and propriety: they seemed to forget alike they were in the temple of God in a foreign land, where, though their conduct is too kindly tolerated, nevertheless, it occasions both scandal and contempt from its more polished inhabitants. What would any Protestants, whether gentle or plebeian, say, if they saw a party of Catholics behave in the same gross way as they do, and utter the same number of profane, insulting, and silly speeches in St. Paul's in London as they do in St. Peter's, and in other churches in Rome? Yes, it is unfortunately too true to be denied, that the conduct of Protestants often brings the unbidden, burning blush on the cheeks of honourable English Catholics, and of pious and high-born Italians.

CHAPTER XXXVI.

> " As I have seen a swan
> With bootless labour swim against the tide,
> And spend her strength with overmatching waves."
>
> SHAKSPEARE.

"CAN I do any thing for you in Naples, Sir?" said Sefton to Father Oswald a few days after Easter, as he was paying him a visit at the Gesù.

"Thank you," replied the Father, "but are you going to leave Rome so soon?"

"I am anxious to see Naples and its environs before the weather becomes too hot; and Easter was late this year, you know."

"Well; do not forget to go and see *the miracle*; promise me that," said Father Oswald.

"You mean the liquefaction of the blood of St. Januarius, or rather its alleged liquefaction; now, tell me, Father Oswald, candidly, do you really believe it to be a miracle yourself?"

"Most certainly I do," said Father Oswald; "I have seen it with my own eyes."

"I can assure you," said Sefton seriously, "I have been told that the Neapolitans themselves do not believe in it."

"Not believe in it!" exclaimed Father Oswald; "well, you do now really astonish me."

"Nevertheless, I have heard so," answered Sefton; "and in a work published not long ago by a person who had resided several years in Naples it is called 'the miracle of the Lazzaroni.' I do not pretend but that perhaps some of the most gross and superstitious of the lowest orders may believe in it, but certainly not Catholics of any education."

"There we quite differ," said Father Oswald quietly; "some infidels may scoffingly term it the miracle of the Lazzaroni, as the unbelieving Jews called the miracles of Christ the works of Beelzebub. I only wish you had been with me the day I had the happiness of seeing it take place. I wish you had seen the church crowded, not for one day, but for eight continuous days, with crowds of pious and well-educated people, from the king to the beggar. But go, my good friend, and see it yourself, and give not credit to such idle tales, but make use of your own excellent understanding."

"I can assure you, Sir," said Sefton, "Protestants maintain that such deceptions are now confined to convents, or to the most ignorant people, and that the Romish Church no longer dares to appeal to miracles in arguing with them."

"Does not Milner, the latest of our controvertists, appeal to recent miracles wrought in England, and of which innumerable witnesses were then living," answered Father Oswald gravely. "Was not the glorious miracle wrought in the person of Mrs. Mattingly, and in the house of the Mayor of Wishington, witnessed by thousands, and proved by the sworn affidavits of both Protestants and Catholics?"

"I never even heard of it," said Sefton; "I should like extremely to see the account of it."

"I can easily procure it for you," answered the Father. "In the true Church of Christ miracles must always be found until the Word of Christ shall pass away. For in the true Church will ever be found the true faith, and true believers, to whom Jesus has made this solemn promise in his most impressive manner: 'Amen, amen, I say to you, He that believeth in me, the works that I do, he also shall do, and greater than these shall he do.'"

"But that promise," replied Sefton, "was only for the first ages of the Church, and when the words of our Saviour wanted confirming; of course I believe in the miracles of the New Testament."

"But," said Father Oswald, "the solemn promise of Christ, which I have just repeated to you, is absolute, and not limited to time, place, or person. Miracles are one of the most striking prerogatives of the true Church, because it is the voice of God attesting the truth; and is intelligible equally to the wise and to the ignorant. I wish Protestants, who boast so much of their believing in Christ, would one day favour us with such a proof of their faith. But they find it more convenient to deny miracles altogether; in this they shew a little of the wisdom of this world. 'Tis easy to deny. The Pharisees denied the miracles of Christ, because they could not admit them without admitting His doctrine; or, when the evidence was too strong, they atributed the wonder to the Devil. Here again we have a glimpse of Protestantism in the Bible. There are some people, we know, 'who will not believe if one rise again from the dead.'"*

Sefton mused a little, and then said, "But this miracle, upon which you lay such a stress, is wrought, as far as I can understand it, on account of a saint, and must, if it be true, or if they believe it to be true, necessarily promote image-worship, and the intercession of saints; now, Protestants assert there is no mediator but Jesus Christ; the mediation of angels and saints being directly contrary to the inspired Apostle."

"It is written in the book of Moses," said Father Oswald, "'The Lord our God made a covenant with us on Horeb.......He spoke to us face-to-face in the mount out of the midst of fire. *I was the mediator*, and stood between the Lord and you at that time, to shew you His words.'† Here, then, we have another mediator between God and men; and what is better still, St. Paul acknowledges it: 'Why, then, was the law? It was set because of transgressions......being ordained by angels in the hands of a *mediator*.'"‡

"But," said Sefton eagerly, "St. Paul said also, there is but 'one Mediator of God and men, the Man, Christ Jesus.'"

"Certainly; as you curtail the text," answered Father

* Luke xvi. 31. † Deut. v. 2. ‡ Gal. iii. 19.

Oswald, "no doubt he does; but give us the whole text, and compare it with parallel texts, and then you will find no contradiction, nor any support for your sophistical argument. St. Paul says of our Lord, 'He is a *mediator of a better Testament*, which is established on better promises.'* Again: "He is the mediator of the New Testament, that, *by means of his death*, for the redemption of those transgressions which were under the former Testament, they that are called may receive the promise of eternal inheritance.'† And again: 'You are come...to Jesus, the mediator of the New Testament, and to the *sprinkling of blood*, which speaketh better than that of Abel.'"‡

"But I do not exactly see the application," said Sefton.

"However," continued Father Oswald, "it is clear from these texts of the Apostle, that he considers Moses the mediator of the Old Covenant or Testament, and Christ the mediator of the New Testament, but in a far more perfect manner, inasmuch as he established it in his own blood."

"I cannot see it yet," said Sefton triumphantly, "and I do not think you have got out of my difficulty at all."

"Well, wait a little," said Father Oswald patiently; "let us return to your text, but give it us entire; here it is in the New Testament: 'For there is one God and one mediator of God and men, the Man-Christ Jesus, *who gave himself a redemption for all*, a testimony in due times.'§ Christ indeed is the only mediator of *redemption*; Catholics are not such fools as to think that saints or angels shed their blood for our redemption; but what has all this to do with the mediation of prayer, with intercession such as we ask of the saints? It is really wonderful how blind Biblicals are! Why, if they would read the first words of this very chapter, they would find the sound principle of the Catholic tenet established most firmly by the Apostles."

"How so, Sir?" said Sefton.

* Heb. viii. 6. † Heb. ix. 15. ‡ Heb. xii. 18. § 1 Tim. ii. 5.

"Look here," replied Father Oswald, turning to the place in the book, "does not the Apostle say, 'I desire, therefore, first of all, that supplications, prayers, intercessions, and thanksgivings, be made for all men.... For this is good and acceptable in the sight of God, our Saviour'?* Now, if the prayers and intercessions of men still on earth, are no ways derogatory to the mediatorship of Jesus Christ, but, on the contrary, are good and acceptable in the sight of God, how much more so must be the prayers and intercessions of the just made perfect!"

"Granting what you say to be perhaps in a certain degree true," replied Sefton, "still I cannot but think it strange policy in the Roman Church to direct the devotion of her members to the assembly of the saints."

"What is there of policy," said Father Oswald quietly, "in imploring the intercession of a good man, whether living or dead? I see nothing that is not conformable to sound common sense and Holy Scripture."

"Perhaps in the sense *you* take it, Sir, and many well-educated Catholics also, there are not," replied Sefton, "but I am convinced it is a very different thing with the common people: why, there are many of them who will really fall down and adore any thing, and one can call them neither more nor less than idolaters!"

Father Oswald held up his hands! Really, Mr. Sefton, I am amazed at your assertion. Why, it scarce merits an answer; one of our little children might put you to the blush: no, no, my good Sir, Catholics are not idolaters. There is a wide difference between *divine worship* and honour paid to the saints. Divine worship belongs to God alone; honour and reverence may be paid to many of God's creatures, and the most ignorant and lowest of Catholic common people know that Catholics do not pay divine worship to the saints, or angels, or the Blessed Virgin, or their images, whatever wise and learned Protestants may think and assert to the contrary!"

* 1 Tim. ii. 1.

"But why cannot people apply directly to God for what they want, instead of asking it through the saints?" persisted Sefton.

"Because the Catholic is humble, and deems the prayers of the saints in Heaven more acceptable to God than his own weak efforts," answered the Father; "thus the Council of Trent teaches, that 'the saints who reign with Christ offer up their prayers to God for men, and that it is good and useful to invoke them, and in order to obtain from God blessings through his Son Jesus Christ our Lord, *who alone is our Redeemer and Saviour*, to have recourse to their prayers, help, and assistance.'* St. Paul himself says: 'I beseech you that you help me in your prayers to God for me;'† and St. John says: "I make my prayer, that thou mayest prosper as to all things, and be in health.'‡ Thus you see the Apostles, holy as they were, did not think they were guilty of derogating from any of the divine perfections in asking the intercession of, or in praying for others. Neither are we guilty of derogating from the perfections of God, when we ask one another's prayers; why, then, should we be guilty of derogating from any of the divine perfections of God by applying to the intercession of his saints and friends in Heaven?"

"But, Sir, you offer up Masses to the saints; is not that a most curious and extraordinary thing?" said Sefton; "does not one constantly hear of the Mass of a martyr, the Mass of this saint, the Mass of that saint? How can you possibly explain that?"

"If you had ever read the Council of Trent, Mr. Sefton, you would have met with the answer to your difficulty there; it says expressly: 'Although the Church does sometimes offer up Masses in honour and in memory of the saints, yet it is not to them, but to God alone who has crowned them, that the sacrifice is offered up; there the Priest does not say, I offer up this sacrifice to thee, Peter, or to thee, Paul; but to God himself, giving thanks to him for their victories, imploring their

* Conc. Trid. Sess. 25. † Rom. xv. 30. ‡ 3 John 2.

patronage, that they may vouchsafe to intercede for us in Heaven, whose memory we celebrate on earth.' "*

"Is that really in the Council of Trent?" said Sefton.

"Most certainly it is," answered the Father.

"It is rather strong," observed Sefton.

"Yes," continued Father Oswald; "every Altar in the catacombs is, in truth, a monument to some sacred hero; hence, to this day the relics of some martyrs must be deposited, in what is called the *sepulchrum* of every Catholic Altar at its consecration, and the centre of the Altar must, in every case, be of stone. Thus, in the older Basilicas, and in many modern churches, the great Altar is almost always in the form of a sarcophagus or sepulchral urn, and generally contains the ashes of some ancient martyr: this practice of honouring and praying to the saints is as ancient as Christianity, as is evident from the testimony of the holy Fathers in all ages. St. Dionysius, a disciple of the Apostles, affirms with the divine Scripture, 'that the prayers of the saints are very profitable for us in this life, after this manner: when a man is inflamed with a desire to imitate the saints, and, distrusting his own weakness, betakes himself to any saint, beseeching him to be his helper and petitioner to God for him, he shall obtain by that means very great assistance.' "†

"This refers to the very first ages of Christianity," said Sefton, sighing. "Certainly, I must own there is nothing like superstition in what St. Dionysius says."

"To be sure there is not," said Father Oswald, smiling; "it can be no superstition to believe that the saints desire our salvation, because God desires it. It can be no superstition to believe that the saints know our thoughts and desires: the Scripture declaring that the repentance of the sinner on earth causes joy among the blessed in Heaven. We have a right to expect much from the protection of those who, by the Spirit of God, are declared to be appointed ministering spirits for our salvation,‡ and who are again declared to have power,

* Conc. Trid. Sess. 22, c. 3.

† Eccles. Hierarch. c. 7, part 3, sec. 3.

‡ Heb. i.

and be rulers of nations;* believe me, it is no superstition to believe that the intercession of the saints in Heaven will be of more avail towards deciding the fate of men and nations than the intercession of ten mortals would have been in deciding the fate of a city;† or the intercession of one man, namely Job, in deciding the fate of his three friends."

"I never imagined," said Sefton musingly, "there was so much to be found in Scripture in favour of the intercession of saints."

"Nevertheless, it is perfectly true," observed Father Oswald. "The Apostles' Creed also makes mention of the 'Communion of Saints:' it is the ninth article of the said creed. Pray, will you tell me which Church it is that really, and not in words alone, holds this 'Communion of Saints' in every sense of the word?"

"Why, I suppose it is the Catholic Church," said Sefton, smiling; "it looks like it."

"Yes; it is the Catholic Church, most undoubtedly," said Father Oswald. "Protestants little know the advantages and comforts they deprive themselves of, by denying this article of the very same creed which they themselves constantly repeat, and which they have retained from the Catholics through all the other changes of their ritual; they little know what they deprive themselves of in refusing to make the friends of God their friends, those holy and heroic beings whom we hope one day to meet in Heaven, and along with them to praise God for a whole eternity!"

Sefton was silent.

"There is a beauty and harmony in the 'Communion of Saints,'" continued Father Oswald, "of which heretics have no idea; this Communion is one of the many links which connect the Church Militant on earth with the Church Triumphant in Heaven, in the same manner as the Church suffering in Purgatory is connected with the Church Militant on earth, by means of the prayers and suffrages we continually offer for our departed fellow-members there."

* Apoc. ii. † Gen. xviii.

"If the miracle of St. Januarius should really be a miracle, and really take place," said Sefton, "no doubt it would fully confirm all you have said, and that in the strongest and most undeniable manner too; for God never would so far betray his creatures as to work a miracle in support of error."

"Decidedly not," said Father Oswald; "it would be blasphemy to assert it: if the miracle of St. Januarius is a real miracle, and if it really takes place, the 'Communion of Saints' is an article of faith, and the Roman Catholic Church, as you designate it, is the only one, Holy, Catholic, and Apostolic Church, which Jesus Christ founded on earth, and to which he gave his solemn promise that he never would forsake her, or suffer the gates of Hell to prevail against her. All I ask of you, my dear friend," continued Father Oswald, his fine countenance lighting up with zeal and charity, "is to go and judge for yourself: go and see the miracle, and then come back, and tell me what you think of it."

Sefton felt much affected; he took leave of Father Oswald with strong emotion; and after he had reached his lodgings, mused deeply for some hours on the conversation that had passed; nor did he fail earnestly imploring, by prayer, light and assistance in his present agitation.

CHAPTER XXXVII.

"What weight of ancient witness can prevail,
If private reason hold the public scale?
But, gracious God! how well dost Thou provide,
For erring judgments, an unerring guide!"

DRYDEN.

In a few days after the conversation recorded in the last chapter, Sefton set off for Naples; he offered a place in his travelling carriage to Monsignore Guidi, who accepted the invitation with much pleasure. The Bishop, with his wife and children in the family coach, formed the rest of the party. As they passed the rich vale of Velletri, Sefton and the Captain commemorated their unwilling visit into its surrounding chain of mountains. The peculiar features of the Pontine Marshes, with only here and there a herd of buffaloes, or a solitary sportsman with his gun, breaking the lonely stillness of the scene, interested them much. They slept at Terracina, and the Captain and Sefton climbed the magnificent rocky height which overhangs the town. Gaeta, Fondi, Sessa, and Capua, were all explored with pleasure and interest. The beautiful Bay of Naples was hailed with rapture by the travellers as it burst on them in all its unrivalled glory at the end of their journey, and they could not weary of gazing at it from the windows of the "Crocelle," where they fixed their abode. The first weeks of their visit to Naples seemed to fly with incredible speed in the ever-varying novelties of that restless capital. The whole time, from morning till night, was taken up with visiting churches, museums, and shops, or in making excursions in the vicinity to Vesuvius, Pompeii, and Herculaneum. One week was dedicated to the more distant expeditions of Pestum, Nocera, Salerno, Castellamare, and Soroento. At Nocera, they visited the shrine of St. Alfonso, and they saw and conversed with several people, who knew and remembered that holy Bishop when living. A delightful day was passed at Benevento, where there exists the celebrated triumphal arch, erected in honour of Trajan, now called Porta Aurea, being used as one of the gates of the city. Nola interested them much, particularly Sefton, who purchased there many valuable additions to a collection of Etruscan vases which he was making, several very curious ones being found in the excavations in its vicinity. Monsignore Guidi suggested they should go from thence to Mugnano, where he promised to shew them many interesting things at the shrine of St. Filomena, which exists there, and also many beautiful views in the neighbourhood; they accordingly went, and the whole aspect of the country, and the splendid mountain scenery around Mugnano, strongly reminded Sefton of the beautiful views round the Cumberland and Westmoreland lakes: it made him melancholy; for it recalled to his mind the first months after his marriage which he had spent there with Emma, his poor Emma! whom he had now abandoned and left far from him. Monsignore Guidi conducted them to the pretty little church in which exists the shrine of St. Filomena, and to which numbers of devout people from all parts of the world resort. The body of this young martyr was discovered in the catacombs in Rome, and the numbers of extraordinary cures which have been wrought through her intercession have rendered her shrine very celebrated: there the blind have been restored to sight, and the cripple instantaneously cured. Seldom have any applied to this saint to obtain them relief from God in their necessities, whether spiritual or temporal, and have applied in vain. Numbers of living witnesses attest her kindness and her power. The wonders Sefton heard and saw in Mugnano recalled to his mind his visit to St. Winefred's Well, in Flintshire, and he could not help remarking to Monsignore Guidi "that it was only amongst Catholics, and in Catholic times, that these extraordinary interpositions of a supernatural Providence in succouring the sick and helpless were ever heard of."

"Yes," answered Monsignore Guidi; "God does not work miracles in favour of Protestants; they and other heretics have not the *faith* which merits and obtains these supernatural interpositions of a kind and watchful Providence; but observe, my dear Sefton," continued he, "what a fine religious and poetical justice there is in the fact, that these two young and tender virgins, St. Winefred and St. Filomena, who sacrificed their lives in defence of their faith and their chastity, should now be celebrated through the whole world, through that world where they were, when living, humbled and martyred, and that their influence with God, for whom they sacrificed every thing, should be testified to us by their works of mercy and of love."

Sefton was silent, and mused on what he had seen and heard all the way back to Naples.

Another expedition, which gave the party great and varied pleasure, consisted in sailing across the bright and sunny Bay to Capri, and its blue grotto, thence visiting the beautiful islands of Procida and Ischia, and returning to Naples by Bæia, Cuma, and Puzzuoli. The days flew like hours in these lovely and classic spots, which recalled to the gentlemen the strains of Virgil, and the lays of Silius, Martial, and Sannazarius, while the lucid softness and glassy smoothness of the sea, with its beautiful bays and inlets, enchanted the whole party.

At Ischia, they all ascended the Epomeus, or Monte San Nicolo, as it is generally called, and their toils were amply rewarded by the extraordinary extent and beauty of the panoramic view around them. The Bishop was very anxious to examine the bathing-house at Casamiccia, a charitable establishment, where the sick and destitute from Naples are brought, if their maladies require the salutary baths of Ischia; these invalids are provided, free of expense, with food and lodging, in an hospital near the bathing-house, for three weeks, and then sent back to Naples at the exoense of the establishment; even Mrs. Boren acknowledged, that nothing but an heroic Christian charity could have founded and supported such an institution. At Puzzuoli, amongst the many profane and sacred relics of antiquity which they were shewn, the exact site of the martyrdom of St. Januarius was pointed out to them, and also that where he was exposed to the fury of the wild beasts; as Sefton seemed much interested on this subject, and asked the guide many questions, the latter insisted on taking him to a convent of Capuchins, not far from Puzzuoli, where the stone on which the saint was decapitated, and which is marked with his blood, is still preserved.

The Bishop and his lady made many objections to going out of their way, especially as it was getting near dinner-time, "merely," as they observed, "to look at a stone, which was most probably after all not genuine, and nothing more curious in it than in any other stone." But Sefton's curiosity had been roused, and he was determined at all events to see what there was to be seen. Monsignore Guidi said he would willingly accompany him, and the rest of the party drove on to Naples, to see about their dinner. Sefton and his friend reached the convent by a steep ascent, and examined at their leisure the slab which they had come to inspect; the Capuchins pointed out a part of it, which is of a red colour, said to have been so stained by the blood of the martyr; and they assured Sefton, that when the blood of St. Januarius liquefied in Naples, this stain became at the same moment of a much deeper and more vivid red. Sefton looked and felt very incredulous; he did not, however, contradict the good religious as he would have done in former days, but contented himself with saying, "that he should return and judge for himself on one of the days that they asserted it would take place." He had learnt from experience, that bold denial does not produce conviction, either in the speaker or the listener; besides, he had determined to examine the whole affair of the miracle with great coolness, and he was determined to keep to his resolution. During their drive back to Naples, Sefton was so silent, that Monsignore Guidi at length took out his office book, and was on the point of beginning his devotions, when Sefton exclaimed, "I had no idea till now that there was any thing known about this Saint Januarius; I think the guide said he was martyred under Dioclesian?"

"Yes," answered Monsignore Guidi; "his martyrdom took place on the 19th of September, in the year 305; he was then only thirty-three years of age; he was decapitated, as you have heard; immediately after his death, his body was carefully buried, and some portion of his blood was put at the same time into two small bottles, which are still preserved, as are also his relics; it is now more than fifteen hundred years since, and the blood is, generally speaking, quite hard from its great age; but whenever it is brought into the presence of the relic of his head, it becomes perfectly liquid, and in that consists the miracle, which you have no doubt heard mentioned. It will take place in a few days, and I trust you will be present at it."

"I shall certainly go and see what there is to be seen," answered Sefton; "but as to its being a miracle, that is quite another thing: you will never get me to believe that, Monsignore; it is all a trick, you may depend upon it, and from what I have heard and read, a very bungling trick too."

"If it is a trick," replied Monsignore Guidi, "it is very odd it should never have been found out during such a long period as fifteen hundred years and more; notwithstanding the numbers of people who have written against it, who have denied it, who have derided it, who have insulted it, there is not one who has been able to prove how the trick is performed."

"Oh! the priests take care of that," said Sefton contemptuously; "it is their interest to keep the people in ignorance, and not to have it properly examined into."

"Then you assert," said Monsignore Guidi, "that all the individuals, clerical as well as secular, who have had this blood in their care for more than fifteen hundred years, have been and are all a set of impostors and rascals, and that in all that time there has not been one honest man amongst them; rather a sweeping assertion, methinks! a greater miracle, truly, than the liquefaction of the blood itself."

"Well, however," said Sefton, looking a little foolish, "I make no doubt if the thing was properly examined into by some clever chemist, it could be all explained and accounted for on natural and philosophical principles."

"It has been so examined by many able chemists and learned men," said Monsignore Guidi, "and especially in modern times by a very celebrated Neapolitan chemist."

"Oh! those were all Catholics; I would not give a fig for such testimony," said Sefton hastily.

"Indeed!" said Monsignore Guidi, somewhat surprised at his friend's warmth; "are they, too, all scoundrels and rascals?"

Sefton bit his lip. "I would much prefer the testimony of some unbiassed English or French chemist," observed he.

"You are not aware, then," said the Prelate, "that it has been examined by a countryman of your own?"

"No; who might that be?"

"Sir Humphrey Davy."

"Sir Humphrey Davy! Really, I was not in the least aware of it; and what said he to it?"

"He said it was impossible to account for it by natural means," answered Monsignore Guidi.

"Really!"

"Yes," continued the Prelate, "that celebrated chemist examined it with the greatest minuteness and rigour. He was particularly struck with the different manner in which the liquefaction takes place at different times, the same natural causes existing around it; he was particularly struck with the liquefaction frequently occurring at periods when the external accidents of time, place, heat, and cold around it, were, chemically and philosophically speaking, in diametrical opposition to its liquefying at all; and its frequently remaining perfectly hard and dry, when, according to natural causes, it was most likely it should liquefy."

"But," said Sefton, "what is the use of its liquefying at all? what is the use of such a miracle taking place at all, supposing it even to be a miracle? I ask that simple question."

"You might as well ask what use there was in Christ's walking on the water, or in raising Lazarus from the dead. Miracles are wrought in confirmation of the true faith. This standing miracle speaks volumes to the learned and to the unlearned, who know full well that the Catholic religion is the only religion in which miracles have ever existed, do now exist, and will, according to the promises of Jesus Christ, exist to the end of the world. St. Januarius shed his blood in confirmation of the true faith, and his blood still liquefies to attest in the most undeniable manner that the Catholic faith is the same faith now as it was when he expired in its defence."

"Then he was put to death because he was a Catholic?" said Sefton thoughtfully.

"Certainly he was."

"But how came Naples to be particularly selected for the performance of this alleged miracle?"

"Because the saint was a citizen of Naples," answered Monsignore Guidi. "He was born there on the 21st of April, in the year 272, under the emperor Aurelian. About two years and a half before his death, he was consecrated Bishop of Benevento, and it was in consequence of his ardent charity in visiting and assisting the persecuted Christians in Puzzuoli that he was imprisoned under the Roman governor, Timotheus, and sent along with others to Nola, which you know we lately visited. There, in consequence of the edicts of Dioclesian, he was condemned to a fiery furnace, which, by a miraculous interposition of God, did not injure him. After various other torments, he, with other Christians, was condemned to accompany on foot the car of Timotheus from Nola to Puzzuoli, a distance of thirty miles. The sufferings of these poor persecuted Christians must have been very great."

"Indeed they must," said Sefton compassionately. "I see now how he came to be martyred at Puzzuoli."

"Yes; the day after his arrival there, he was exposed to the fury of a number of famished bears, but these creatures, forgetting their natural ferocity, laid down at his feet, licking and caressing them; this so enraged the Roman consul, that he ordered St. Januarius and his companions to be beheaded, which order was immediately executed."

"I certainly had not the most distant idea so much was known about him," said Sefton; "it is always interesting to gain a knowledge of facts."

By this time they had reached Naples, and joined the rest of the party.

The first Sunday of May arrived in due time, and Sefton accompanied Monsignore Guidi to the Church of St. Januarius, where the miracle takes place. The Bishop declined going, as he said he was afraid of the heat: the Captain declared he would not miss seeing how it was done on any account; and Mrs. Boren and Lavinia went out of idle curiosity to see a sight. The little chapel, rich in beauty and treasures, in which the head and the blood of St. Januarius are kept, is on the right hand side going up the cathedral, and is called the "Tesoro:" it is officiated by chaplains chosen from the most ancient and respectable Neapolitan families, and the relics of St. Januarius are in their keeping: but not the keys of the depository where they are kept. One of the keys is kept by the Cardinal Archbishop of Naples, and the other by a chosen body of secular nobleman, who each time the depository is opened, depute one of their number to be present. Monsignore Guidi was acquainted with several of the chaplains, and they, with the urbanity which characterizes them, introduced him and his friends within the rails of the sanctuary, and placed Sefton close to the altar, where he could see and examine every thing to his entire satisfaction. Notwithstanding all his efforts to subdue it, he could not help feeling a certain degree of anxiety, and a sensation of awe, which he could not account for. The church was crowded to excess, and this circumstance surprised Sefton very much; but what still more surprised him was the apparent devotion and sincerity of the people. At length the Cardinal Archbishop's chaplain on the part of his Eminence, and the deputy nobleman on the part of his Body, opened the depository where the relics are kept, and the head chaplain of the Tesoro took out the two small glass bottles which are both fixed in a frame, and which contain the blood of the martyr; they examined it very carefully, and then exhibited it to be examined also by the people. Sefton observed it quite near, and saw that one of the bottles was about three parts full of a hard, dark substance, like congealed blood, and though the priest who held it turned the phial upside down several times before his eyes, the blood remained as hard and as firm as if it had been part of the bottle: in the other and smaller phial there seemed to be a small quantity of the dry blood, which stained its sides. The blood in its hard state was then placed on the right side of the altar, and the relic of the head of the saint, which is enclosed in a silver bust, being taken from its depository, was placed on the left side of the same altar. The head chaplain, the deputy nobleman, the assistants, and the people, then recited aloud three times the Apostles' Creed, and the Miserere Psalm: the blood was then examined and found to be perfectly hard; the Creed was then recommenced; Sefton had his eye fixed on the solid blood, when suddenly, in less than a second, he beheld the hard mass dissolve and liquefy like a piece of ice before an intense furnace; he turned deadly pale, and then all his blood seemed to rush to his temples, and he hid his face in his hands. Mrs. Boren stood in mute astonishment for some time, and then exclaimed,

"How very strange!"

"Indeed it is, Mamma!" rejoined Miss Lavinia; "I wonder how it is done."

"By the power of the Almighty," whispered Monsignore Guidi.

The chaplain made a sign, and in a moment the joyful notes of the "Te Deum Laudamus" rushed through the vaulted dome of the sanctuary; the voices of thousands resounded through its roof, proclaiming the miracle; and in tones of the deepest energy and pathos, exclaiming, "All hail to the true and only faith! .... all hail to the Catholic religion! May the true faith live for ever!"*

Sefton pushed his way through the crowd, and left the church. He returned several times during the eight days which the miracle continues to take place, to examine the state of the blood, and to see this occurrence at different times: sometimes he observed the blood was diminished in quantity, and sometimes increased so much that the bottle was entirely full; sometimes it was perfectly liquid, and of a deep and rich red colour; at other times it was hard and dark. One of the days he rode to the convent at Puzzuoli to observe the colour of the stain upon the stone, as he had promised to do, and he commissioned Monsignore Guidi to note the exact time the liquefaction took place that morning in Naples. While he was looking at the stone, he observed the stain of blood become evidently of a deeper red; and on taking Monsignore Guidi's report, he found that the time the liquefaction occurred in Naples corresponded exactly to the moment in which he had seen the change take place in the stone at Puzzuoli; and he spared no pains in examining every circumstance connected with the miracle with the greatest minuteness and attention. About the middle of May, having seen every thing worth seeing in and about Naples, Sefton and Monsignore Guidi returned to Rome, and the Bishop and his family embarked in the steam-vessel for Marseilles on their route back to England.

* "Viva la santa fede! ecco la santa fede! Ecco la fede Catolica! Viva la santa fede!"

CHAPTER XXXVIII.

"Who by repentance is not satisfied,
Is not of heaven, nor earth."

SHAKSPEARE.

WHEN Sefton arrived in Rome, he found a letter laying for him in the post-office from Emma; on opening it, he was surprised to see it dated from Westwood, the seat of General Russell. In it Emma informed him that her uncle having been suddenly seized with a serious and alarming illness, he had sent express for her, and that consequently she had immediately gone to him, and was then at Westwood, employed in nursing him; she begged Edward to give her permission to have the children with her, and entreated him to give her an early and favourable answer. Sefton sighed as he refolded the letter, for it had been some weeks in Rome, and he was sure this involuntary delay in answering it must have given her much anxiety; he was greatly annoyed, too, at the idea of her having had to make the journey from Devonshire to Westwood alone, though he was painfully aware he had no one but himself to blame for it; he immediately wrote to his wife, expressing his approbation at her having gone to the General, but forbidding her to think of moving the children from the cottage in Devonshire, and desiring her to remain with her uncle until she heard from him again. Sefton remained about a fortnight longer in Rome, and then left it with heartfelt regret. Who ever did leave Rome without regret! there is a something in this city of the soul, which imperceptibly intwines itself around the heart and feelings, and no one who has felt its mysterious influence can leave it without sorrow, soothed by a secret hope of again re-visiting its eternal walls. Sefton pursued his travels along the shores of the Adriatic, passing by Venice, on his route to Paris. He remained there a few days, and one of the first things he did was to go to the hospital where he had been so long confined by sickness, to inquire for Sister Angela: but he was informed Sister Angela was no longer to be found in Paris, as she had gone with some other sisters to found a convent of the same order in America. One day, as Sefton was wandering about Paris, he entered a small retired church, and while he was examining the pictures and architecture, he observed a young man closely engaged in a confessional: he had some vague idea that he had formerly seen or known that person, but though he tried to recollect who it might be, he could not at all fix the identity. Whoever he was, Sefton was struck with his demeanour, and he retired behind a pillar to observe him further: he saw him bending lowly down, and beating his breast with unfeigned humility: shortly the penitent rose; a glow of fervour shone on his serene brow, his eyes were humbly cast towards the ground, and the big tear trickled down his emaciated cheek. Sefton instantaneously recognized Le Sage; but, oh! how changed! When Sefton was in Paris before, he had often observed a gloomy melancholy spread over the countenance of this young man, even in the midst of the gayest scenes; he had observed the sudden start and rapid change of features, the knitted brow, the supercilious scowl, the haggard eye, the curled lip, the convulsive quiver of the muscles of his mouth, the rapid motions of his head, the hurried gait, and many other traits, that by fits betrayed a heart ill at ease, and the warring passions of his agitated soul. Now it seemed quite otherwise: Sefton observed in him a placid, though emaciated countenance, a calm brow, a chastened eye, a smile of contentment on his lips, a firm, manly step, and a meek, humble demeanour, that bespoke the joy and peace that then possessed his soul. Le Sage withdrew to a retired altar, and there poured out his soul, in fervent, but silent thanksgiving to his God and Saviour. Sefton looked at him with intense interest for some time, unwilling to interrupt the ardour of his devotions. At length Le Sage rose, and Sefton suddenly presented himself before him. Le Sage started, as if he had seen an inhabitant of the grave rise up before his astonished sight, for he thought Sefton had been slain in the dreadful affray which took place on the Boulevards; but being soon satisfied that his friend was still amongst the living, he clasped his hands together, and in a low, but audible voice, thanked God, who had so mercifully relieved his soul from a most oppressive burden; for he had ever reproached himself as the murderer of his friend, and the chief cause of his eternal perdition. He took Sefton by the arm, and led him out of the church. For a while the friends walked on arm-in-arm, but in perfect silence. Sefton was lost in astonishment, and many subjects were rapidly revolved in those few moments in Le Sage's mind; at length he first broke silence:—"My dear Sefton!" said he, "I know not what you may say or think of me: perhaps you will contemn and despise me, but it matters not. I feel I have an imperious duty to perform, and no false pride, no selfish feeling, shall hinder me from doing it."

"What do you mean, my dear friend?" exclaimed Sefton, still more astonished.

"Listen to me, Sefton," said Le Sage earnestly; "I have deeply injured you, and my conscience tells me that I am bound to repair the injury to the best of my power. Alas! have I not been guilty of the blackest hypocrisy, by boasting of that impiety which the firm conviction of my soul belied? Towards you I have acted as the basest villain, or rather as an envious demon, for I sought, and, alas! perhaps, I too well succeeded in tearing asunder that slender tie, which, till then, had held you to Christianity. I introduced you to the worst of wretches, to the very scum of society; and if I have not succeeded in hurrying your soul into perdition, it is a special mercy of God." Then, letting go Sefton's arm, he paused a moment, and drooping his head in confusion, while deep regret was depicted on his expressive countenance, he continued, "Now, Sefton, reproach me as you please; call me wretch, hypocrite, villain, demon, cast me off, spurn me from you; I have deserved all your contempt—only tell me you forgive me, and I shall then die contented."

Sefton was deeply affected by this unexpected burst of an humbled and contrite heart; but he felt most intensely from the inward reproach of his own conscience; if a passing acquaintance, a stranger almost, could condescend to such humiliation in reparation of crimes, which he felt to be more his own than his, what reparation was not due for the injuries he had inflicted on his innocent wife! At length, summoning courage, he took Le Sage's hand, and in broken accents said, "Let us think no more of the past; you—I—we have both acted foolishly—nay wickedly. We must look to God for pardon. You are, I perceive, a changed man. Perhaps, you have already made your peace with the Almighty. I too think differently on many points to what I did when you last saw me; but will you not now tell me how so wonderful a change in you was brought about?"

"Willingly," replied Le Sage, sighing. By this time they had reached his house. "Will you not enter?" said he. "My father and sister are, alas! now no more, and I am its only inhabitant."

Sefton entered, and when they were seated in the solitary saloon, which he had, within less than one short circling year, seen full of life, and gaiety, and beauty—all, all now gone—Le Sage told him all that had happened to him since they last parted.

"On the last of those dreadful days," said he, "which you, my dear Sefton, have too much reason to remember, I was dangerously wounded, and carried off the Boulevards by my detestable associates. I was very nearly dying, and in those awful moments the fear of death recalled to my mind my early principles of faith, and I remembered the happy and blessed death-bed upon which I had witnessed my excellent mother expire. All her admonitions came then with full force to my remembrance, and were as so many daggers to my heart. I asked to see a priest, but my companions got about me. In vain I called for the succours of religion; for fear a priest should reach me, they, heartlesss wretches, took it in turn, day and night, to watch about me. Yes! they prohibited every one but known infidels from approaching me. My father and sister had fled from Paris, and I soon after was told of his death; then it was I gave way to despair. Oh God! I cannot recal that time, and all the wild desperation of my raging blasphemies and deep despair, without my blood running cold in my veins; but God at length had mercy on me, though I did not deserve aught but chastisement at his hand. An old and faithful servant of my parents at length got by stealth to my bedside. I whispered in his terrified ear, 'Bring me a priest, that he may see a false Christian die in despair.' The old man shuddered. I saw the shudder, and when the priest came, I placed myself like a child in his hands, and in a few minutes I was reconciled to my Creator, and the agonies of despair were succeeded by the sweetness of the most balmy peace. My vile infidel seducers were driven from the house, my poor little orphan sister returned, and I slowly recovered. Alas! a few months after, she went to Heaven, and I am now alone in the world." Le Sage dashed a tear from his eye as he finished his touching narrative. "You see, my dear friend," added he more cheerfully, "the immense importance of sound principles being early instilled into the minds of youth, and the lasting impression they make even amid the greatest temptations and trials of a wicked world; but believe me, Sefton, no religion but the Catholic religion is capable of standing such tests, nor of converting and restoring to the peace and happiness of penitence even the most hardened sinners; there must be a divine foundation for the religion which can accomplish that."

Sefton sighed. "Tell me," said he, "do you know any thing of a Monsieur La Harpe? he was very kind to me, and succoured me when I also was wounded in that detestable affray: he went with me afterwards to Switzerland, and I have in vain inquired for him since my return to Paris."

"He has changed his lodgings," answered Le Sage; "but I will accompany you to his present abode."

They went, and found the excellent old man in the midst of his books, as usual. He was overjoyed to see Sefton again, and the three friends did not separate till Sefton had made them both promise that they should all meet again in England in less than a month from that time.

CHAPTER XXXIX.

"Alas! for those that love, and may not blend in prayer."
HEMANS.

ANXIOUSLY, for many long weeks, did Emma expect an answer to the letter which Sefton had found lying in the Roman Post-office; the delay made her very uneasy. At length the wished-for answer arrived; but when she had read it, all her hopes were dashed from her. The positive refusal to grant her request, to have the children with her, opened her eyes, and she clasped her hands in silent sorrow. From Edward's prolonged absence in Italy, she had almost begun to nourish hopes that he was becoming more reconciled to the Catholic religion, or at least that he would be satisfied to allow her to practise it in peace, and that a reconciliation between them would, by degrees, be brought about; but the tone of the letter she had just received seemed, in common prudence, to forbid her any longer to indulge these fond and flattering hopes. She went to her uncle's room, and put it silently into his hands; but the air of grief and resignation with which she did so went to the General's heart. When he had read it, he returned it to her with a desponding shake of the head.

"I do not like it, indeed, my dear niece," said he; "but put your trust in Providence; God will not forsake you,—'He tempers the wind to the shorn lamb.'"

"My poor children!" exclaimed Emma in a tone of heart-rending sorrow. "Oh! if Edward would but return; if I could but see him once again!......but God's will be done."

"God grant," said the General, "that I may soon be on my legs again, and I'll be off to Italy myself, after this renegade husband of yours; by Jupiter, I will!"

The General was recovering from a pleurisy and inflammation of the lungs, and was still too weak to leave his bed. This last grief of Emma's gave him great annoyance, and he used every effort to keep up her spirits, but in vain; her heart sunk, notwithstanding her efforts to the contrary, with more despondency than ever; she was perfectly resigned to the will of God, but she felt as if all her hopes of happiness in this world were gone for ever. About three weeks after she had received that painful letter, as she was one day listlessly sitting in one of the deep oaken recesses of the spacious saloon, her head leaning on her hand, and grieving at the absence of those she loved, she heard some one near her pronounce her name: she turned, and beheld her husband by her side; in an instant she was in his arms; he held her so long and so tightly to his beating heart that it seemed as though he would, in that embrace, redeem two long years of separation; at length, tears came to his relief, and he exclaimed in impassioned and broken accents, "My own,—my beloved,—my long-lost Emma!"

"Merciful God!" said she, looking up and fixing her eloquent gaze on Edward's eyes as though she would read her fate in them; but all she could gather from their speaking expression was ardent love, mingled with poignant regret. "You love me yet," said she, sinking into a seat, and turning as pale as death.

"I do—most ardently, most tenderly; I have ever loved you, even when you imagined me alienated from you; nay, the very severity which I have shewn towards you sprung from the most sincere affection. In it I sought nothing but your happiness, both for time and for eternity; not a day has passed since we parted that I have not thought of you; prayed for you—flattered myself that my prayer would be heard; that the day was not far distant when we should again be united in one faith and love." He then drew from his bosom his wife's miniature, and continued: "This I have ever worn nearest to my heart, and wept over it daily; twice has it been stolen from me by the hand of violence; twice has it been restored to me by a mysterious dispensation of Providence. I took it as a token that my long-cherished hope would not be frustrated."

"How kind is that in you, Edward! My poor prayers have been daily offered at the Throne of Mercy for the same object; alas! I fear I am unworthy to be heard—I have always hoped, and will still hope, even against hope."

Whilst she was uttering these last words her eye was intensely fixed on the medal of Our Lady, which hung exposed on the breast of her husband; when he drew out of his bosom the miniature, he had incautiously brought out the medal with it.

"Ah," exclaimed Sefton, "you are gazing on that toy; it is nothing but a keepsake given to me by one to whom I am deeply indebted. Sister Angela, who wrote to you, gave it to me when I left Paris, and bade me wear it for her sake. It was very providential that I accepted of it; for, see this deep indenture in it,—it was made by the stiletto of an assassin, who aimed a deadly blow at my heart."

Mrs. Sefton shuddered with horror: "Oh! my love!" said she faintly, "and you never told me of this fearful danger."

"There was no need, dearest, to give you useless pain; I have many other adventures to tell you; but first let me hear from your own lips the sentence which must decide my fate and your own."

All poor Emma's doubts returned, and her heart seemed as though it would burst from her side. At this moment the General, whose room was next to the saloon, hearing the voice of a stranger, called loudly for his niece.

"It is your uncle," said Edward; "poor man! take me to him;" and he followed her to the General's bed-side. The surprise of the General was extreme, and his reproaches to Sefton, loud and just. At length, Edward contrived in some degree to appease him; besides, it is difficult to be angry long, at the moment of the return of those we really love. Sefton remained at Westwood till the evening, and then, telling his wife that business of importance required his presence at home, he left them. Emma was lost in perplexity and doubt: he had told her that he had seen the children well at the cottage in Devonshire, but she did not dare to inquire more; she seemed fearful of losing the little transitory gleam of happiness his presence gave her, by any questions which might dissipate her illusion. It was another fortnight before her uncle was able to leave his bed, and during all that time, no day passed in which he did not spend some hours at Westwood; he seemed much pre-occupied, and he never even mentioned the children, religion, or his future prospects. He had frequent conversations with the General, and Emma observed, that after these conversations, her uncle was more serious and thoughtful than usual; but all she could draw from him were vague hints to her, to be resigned and prepare for the worst. Emma was, consequently, very unhappy; each day she counted the hours which would probably elapse, from the time Sefton left her, till his probable return; each day she hoped he would give her some explanation, and each day she was disappointed. Edward observed, with deep regret, that she was much thinner and paler than when he had abandoned her, and that her vivacity was quite gone; she was as kind and as gentle as ever, but there was a deep shade of melancholy in her soft blue eye, which had not previously existed there: he knew too well it was his own fault.

One day, while they were sitting together on the terrace before the house, Edward said to her abruptly, "Emma, your uncle has been ordered to try change of air, and he has consented to spend a week at Sefton Hall; he will go to-morrow, and you must accompany him; and there," added he with a sigh, "I must hear you finally pronounce upon our future happiness or misery; I must hear you pronounce from your own lips, whether we are to live together in peace and love, or whether we are to be separated for ever."

"Merciful heavens!" exclaimed Emma with the deepest emotion. "Cruel Edward! — why have you returned to awaken anew my love for you; why have you returned to tear open all the deep griefs of my wounded heart?"

Sefton answered her not; casting on her a stern glance, he hurried from her. She burst into an agony of grief; she ardently prayed to God to give her strength to support the worst, and to stand firm in her approaching bitter trial. That day was spent in tears, and grief, and anguish. The following morning, Edward came for them, and accompanied them to Sefton Hall; he seemed a good deal agitated. Emma scarcely dared to think, much less trust herself to speak; every thing at Sefton seemed to her in the same state it was in, when her husband had abandoned her; her sitting-room, and her flowers, seemed as though she had never left them: what sweet and bitter associations did they not recall to her mind; and then the thought that she must, in a few hours, renounce this beautiful, happy home for ever! It was a delicious day in July, and the air all balm; in the evening, Edward led her into the grove where there was a bower, adorned and entwined around with rich clustering lilacs and laburnums; he placed her on a bench by his side: "Now," said he in a voice tremulous with emotion, "I ask you, Emma, for your final decision. Will you return to the Protestant religion, and renounce Catholicity? Take time to answer, for your fate and mine depends upon it."

Emma paused a moment; and then said in a low, but distinct voice, in tones of the most poignant grief, "I cannot, I will not renounce Catholicity: I will live and die in the one, true, and only faith; but I shall not live long," added she faintly, "after my heart is broken." Edward compressed his lips: "And now," said he in a voice choked with emotion, and drawing her to his heart, "my dearest Emma, I must now tell you my irrevocable decision. We will both, with the grace of God, live and die in the same religion, and our children shall be brought up Catholics."

"How so?" said Emma, scarcely breathing.

"Because," answered Edward, "both their father and mother are Catholics."

"You, Edward!" murmured Emma.

"Yes! I have become a Catholic like yourself," answered he.

"Gracious God be praised!" exclaimed Emma; "thou hast at length heard the long, the earnest, the tearful prayer of thy unworthy handmaid: but oh! Edward, my own love, how could you try me so?" said she in a voice scarcely articulate.

He prevented her adding more, by imprinting on her pale lips, a long and fervent kiss; he kept her fragile form in his arms, till her emotions had a little subsided, and their complete reconciliation was soon made. "Now," said Edward, with the greatest tenderness, "you are truly the wife of my bosom, and I will take you to our children, that we may give them our blessing together."

He led, or rather supported, her to the house, and opening a door on the right-hand side of the hall, he whispered to her, "Let us first thank God for his unspeakable mercies to us, and then I will place the children in your arms." He drew aside a curtain, and Emma was surprised to find they were in a beautiful little chapel, richly hung with crimson and gold drapery: the rays of the evening sun played on its marble pavement, tinged with the varied colours of the painted glass window. The Blessed Sacrament was exposed in a rich expository, and Father Oswald, in his vestments, was kneeling at the foot of the altar; while the General and the little children were ranged around. Emma sunk on her knees, and covered her face with her hands: Edward knelt by her side: the feelings of all present were too powerful to be described. Father Oswald intoned the "Te Deum Laudamus," in thanksgiving for the signal benefits conferred upon the family, and in a minute or two, strains of soft music were heard, and young melodious voices swelled its strains and sung also the Litanies of the Blessed Virgin, and the "Tantum ergo Sacramentum;" while Father Oswald, with feelings of the strongest piety and gratitude to God, gave the Benediction of the Blessed Sacrament to the grateful and kneeling group around him.

CHAPTER XL.

"My thoughtless youth was winged with vain desires,
My manhood, long misled by wandering fires,
Followed false lights; and when their glimpse was gone,
My pride struck out new sparkles of her own;
Good life be now my task: my doubts are done."

DRYDEN.

THE next morning, when the emotions of the happy circle at Sefton Hall were somewhat subsided, Edward assembled Emma, Harriet, Father Oswald, and the General, in the library, and gave them a detailed account of his travels and adventures. Harriet, who had witnessed the Benediction the preceding evening, had been delighted with the whole ceremony; but the six handsome candlesticks which adorned the altar particularly struck her fancy. She wished there had been a seventh to make up the exact number of the Apocalypse, when the sudden thought came across her mind, that the absence of the seventh might be a warning token to herself. She easily recognized in the six, Mr. and Mrs. Sefton with their four children: but the seventh, where was it? and she trembled lest her "candlestick had been removed," and resolved to consult Father Oswald on the first occasion about its meaning, and how she might have it replaced; and she now listened with absorbing interest to the account her brother gave them of his whole progress in the search of the true faith, of all his doubts and difficulties, and of his having been at length convinced of its existence in the Catholic religion, by seeing the miracle of the liquefaction of the blood of St. Januarius in

Naples; and of his finally embracing it in Rome, during the fortnight he remained there after his visit to Naples.

"Yes," said Father Oswald; "I had the unspeakable happiness of receiving him into the true Church, and immediately after that, I returned to England. I should have called on you long ago," added he, addressing Mrs. Sefton, "had not your husband wished to convince himself beyond a doubt of the truth of your unbiassed sincerity, and surprise you with the beautiful little chapel which he has so tastefully fitted up for you."

Emma smiled faintly. "It is all past now," said she, casting an affectionate glance at Edward.

"Egad! Sefton," said the General, "you stood a long siege of it! I suppose you would never have surrendered, unless St. Januarius had brought up his artillery, and blown up your citadel."

"Was it really the miracle, Brother, that convinced you at last?" said Harriet somewhat timidly.

"Yes," answered Sefton; "God could not work a miracle in confirmation of error, and I clearly saw the finger of God attesting his acceptance of the profound veneration which Catholics pay to the images and relics of his saints. Like to St. Paul, the scales of error and prejudice fell from my eyes; 'I saw—and I believed.'"

"Or, rather," said Father Oswald, smiling, "like to St. Thomas, 'because thou hast seen, thou hast believed. Blessed are they who have not seen and have believed.'"

Harriet sighed, and said half aloud, "I wish I could have seen also."

"What astonishes me most," continued Sefton, "is that all doubts and difficulties have been swept away like a mist from my mind; I submit, with the greatest ease, my understanding to the dictates of faith, and readily believe every dogma of our holy religion. I discover daily, new beauties, new relations, new connections between the several articles, all combining in one harmonious and magnificent whole."

"It is the gift of faith," observed Father Oswald, "which enlightens the understanding to behold truth in its naked simplicity, which inflames the heart with an ardent affection for it, and strengthens the will to make the voluntary homage of our whole soul to his infallible word. But, believe me, this first great gift of God is more easily obtained at His hands by humble prayer, and an entire submission to the guidance of His Holy Spirit, than by a proud reliance on our own intellectual powers in the war of controversy."

"I feel the full justice of your remark," replied Sefton. "As long as I relied on my own resources I never could form a fixed *opinion* on any subject: *faith*, I now find, was out of the question. To-day I was urged to the very threshold of faith; to-morrow I was on the brink of infidelity; but, blessed be God, I am no longer 'tossed to and fro by every wind of doctrine;' I have found the solid rock, on which I can anchor my frail bark in security from every storm."

"Remember, my dear Sir," said Father Oswald, "that as the gift of faith is a grace which God willingly grants to the humble, it is only by humility, prayer, and diffidence in our own strength, that this grace can be preserved. Although I exhort you to study well the grounds of our faith, thereby to confirm you daily more and more, yet never lose sight of that infallible beacon which God has given us for our direction."

"If I forget thee, O Jerusalem, let my right hand be forgotten; let my tongue cleave to my jaws if I do not remember thee!" exclaimed Sefton in a holy burst of fervour. "Indeed, Father Oswald, you cannot conceive with what different sentiments I now read the holy Scriptures; many passages which formerly appeared to me dark, mysterious, irrelevant, and even contradictory, now appear clear, intelligible, and beautifully harmonizing with the dogmas of Catholic faith. But it is not from the Scripture I have received the greatest confirmation of my faith: I have witnessed its effects in a singular manner as I passed through Paris." He then related to them the extraordinary conversion of Le Sage; "This made a great impression on me," added he. "I had seen the miraculous liquefaction of the blood of St. Januarius, and I remained convinced: it was the testimony of God to the truth of the Catholic faith; but had I never seen that, and God had only deigned that I should witness the change I saw in Le Sage, I should have confessed that the hand of the Most High had wrought it. This, indeed, is a miracle of grace, far surpassing the former: the one is the triumph of Omnipotence over the fixed laws of matter, the other is the triumph of mercy over the free, but perverted will of man: the religion which can produce this effect must be divine."

"I must be of your religion also," exclaimed Harriet, bursting into a flood of tears. "I cannot bear to be the only wretched creature in this happy house."

"Be calm, Sister," said Sefton kindly; "every thing shall be done in due time; you shall be instructed. It is not a sufficient motive to become a Catholic because I am one; your faith must be built on a more solid foundation."

"Leave that to me," said the General; "I will drill her so, that in a few days she shall fall into the ranks with the best of us; but I will have no interlopers in the camp, so we will begin by drumming out of the regiment all croaking ravens and impertinent magpies."

Harriet smiled her approbation, and soon dried up her tears.

All were silent, musing in tranquil and grateful happiness on the wonders they had heard.

"May God in his mercy bless you, my children," said Father Oswald, rising to depart, "and give you many long and happy years to love and serve God, with your whole hearts, and souls, and minds, in the one true, holy, Catholic and Apostolic Church, and to love and cherish one another with pure and undivided affections."

And God did bless them; and Edward and Emma were dearer a thousand times to each other than they had ever been before. Emma soon recovered her loveliness and vivacity, in the peace and happiness she now enjoyed. The General spent his declining years in the happy and united family, alternately at Westwood and Sefton Hall. In a good old age he was gathered to his forefathers, leaving his property to Sefton's second son, who took the name of Russell. Edward and Emma lived long to spread the sweet odour of their charity and good works around them, in the blessed hope, that as they lived here together in the profession and practice of the true Faith, so would they be united together for ever in the bosom of God, through an endless eternity of joy and love.

THE END.

J. L. Cox & Sons, Printers, 75, Great Queen Street, Lincoln's-Inn Fields.

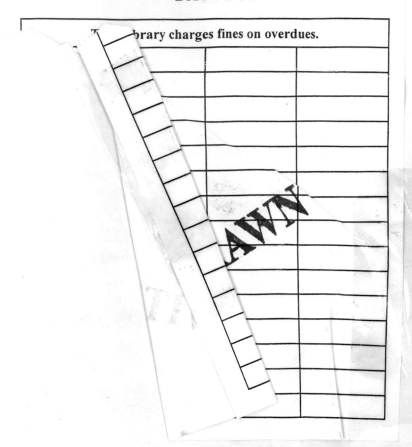